The Stones Corner Series

Darkness

Volume Two

Jane Buckley

Oakleaf Press

WARNING:

This book contains scenes of violence, strong language, and sexual references. It also includes the kind of language used during the 1970s, which some readers may find offensive. While this is a work of fiction, parts of the story are based on real events.

To understand and move on from the Troubles in Northern Ireland, we first need to understand how and why it all happened. We need to recognise the pain and hardship that people lived through, and take time to reflect on what we've learned. *The Stones Corner* series was written with that in mind.

Though it's based on true events and actual history, this novel includes fictional scenes and characters to help bring the story to life.

Cover: Stock Image

www.janebuckleywrites.com

Jacket design: TSL.ie. and Jane Buckley

Thank you, Lynn Curtis and Anne McDonald
I couldn't have done it without you. JB x

In memory of Daddy, Charles, Brian and Frank, sorely missed and much loved and to all the victims of the Troubles.

'By spilling our sweat and not our blood, we will break down the barriers that are based on distrust and prejudice.'

— **John Hume**, Resignation Speech as SDLP Leader, 23 September 2001

Volume 1: Turmoil (First Published2021) ISBN 978-1-9123-2871-0
Revised edition 2025 ISBN 978-1-0687599-0-1
Volume 2: Darkness (First Published 2021) ISBN 978-1-9142-2559-8
Revised edition 2025 ISBN 978-1-0687599-8-7
Volume 3: Light (First Published 2022) ISBN 978-1-9155-0216-2
Revised edition 2025 ISBN 978-1-0687599-2-5
Volume 4: Hope (First Published 2023) ISBN 978-1-3999-7265-9
Revised edition 2025 ISBN 978-1-0687599-9-4

About the Author

Jane Buckley grew up in Derry/Londonderry during the Troubles, and her writing pulls no punches. Her *Stones Corner* series *-Turmoil*, *Darkness*, *Light*, and *Hope* – cuts straight to the heart of one of Northern Ireland's darkest chapters. These are character-driven stories with bite. Brutally honest. Deeply human. The kind of books that stay with you long after the last page.

She doesn't soften the blow or romanticise the past. There's no gloss, no filter, just truth told with grit, empathy, and a sharp eye for the everyday details that shaped people's lives. Her stories are rooted in actual events, voiced in plain language, and built around ordinary men and women trying to survive the extraordinary.

Nor does Jane write to shock. She writes to make sense of it all. To honour those who lived through it. To make sure it's not forgotten.

Having completed the fourth book in the *Stones Corner* series, *Hope*, Jane's next work, written for the US-based Project Children, steps back to the powerful true story behind the initiative featured in the series. Between the seventies and nineties, 23,000 children from both sides of the divide were flown to the United States, welcomed into homes, and given a taste of peace.

It's a story of hope, healing, and the quiet power of kindness. One child. One family. One summer at a time.

My Heart of Tears

My heart was sad that day in Court, though I never shed a tear,
You gave me strength and made me smile and took away my fear.

It hurt me so to say goodbye, I couldn't bear to part,
Yet a smile played upon my lips, and the tears stayed in my heart.

What power lies within your hand? What magic spell's cast o'er me?
How can you make me smile so? When I'm so sad and lonely?

I miss you so and long to cry, though I promised only smiles,
I ache to hold you in my arms, and have you here a while.

But my tears are locked within my heart, and my heart's so far away,
It's with the girl in Armagh, in a land that's still unfree.

My dearest love, you have my tears; you hold them in my heart,
Take gentle care of both, 'til we're no more apart.

Anon.

Chapter One

Derry/Londonderry, 1975

Caitlin McLaughlin sat alone in the kitchen on Blamfield Street, her hands trembling as she picked up a crumpled copy of the *Derry Journal*. The quiet wrapped around her like a damp shroud, heavy and thick, broken only by the low, steady hum of the fridge and the dull tick of the wall clock above the door. It all felt so odd, like the house itself was holding its breath.

Her tears came slowly, falling without drama, slipping from the corners of her swollen eyes. Her shoulders sagged, something inside her had surrendered. She sniffled and dabbed at her face with a piece of toilet paper. The ache in her chest hurt, like it had rooted itself there, and she knew it wouldn't be going away any time soon.

The paper's headline shouted at her from the front page, bold and merciless, dragging her eyes across every sentence. Then she saw it - *Martina Mc Laughlin*. In full, for everyone to see. The sight of it turned her stomach, and for a second, she thought she might have to run to the bathroom and throw up.

'Why, Tina?' she whispered, barely able to speak through the tightness in her throat. She could barely swallow. Then, before she screamed to the high heavens, she slammed the paper across the table, where it slid and dropped onto the floor. She couldn't take in another word. Not yet.

The kitchen was freezing. Not from the cold seeping in through the old windows, but from the kind of chill that sat deep in the walls and settled under your skin. Still trembling in her nightie, she walked to the gas hob, switched on all four rings, and reached for the red tin teapot. The tea was stale, gone bitter from sitting too long, but she poured it anyway, for the comfort of holding something warmish in her hands.

Her gaze to her reflection, she didn't look like herself anymore. Pale skin, blotchy. Eyes puffed up, bruised-looking and empty. Her hair hadn't seen a brush in days, stuck flat on one side, matted on the other. She looked worn-out, finished. Like she'd been pulled inside out and spat back out again.

What the *Journal* printed wasn't shocking. It was brutal. A public shaming dressed up as reporting. Since when was a person guilty until proven innocent? When did people take rumour over truth? Her family was being dragged through the mud. Twisted into something they barely recognised, tied to a nightmare none of them had asked for and could never have imagined.

How hadn't they seen it? How had none of them noticed the change in Tina? It didn't come from nowhere. There must've been signs, things staring them in the face. Things that should've set off alarm bells. Yet they hadn't. Her sister had helped plant a bomb!

Staying in bed would be too easy. Hiding under the covers, pretending the world had nothing left to throw at her. But she couldn't. Not today. Someone had to look after the house, and work. Majella was upstairs, as always, sheltering under the blankets from the big, black world outside that, no matter what, never stopped turning.

Caitlin picked the paper up from the floor, smoothed it out, and forced herself to read it again. She needed to. Wanted to see it with her own eyes again, feel every word, punish herself.

Either way, she read on...

Derry Journal

FRIDAY, 2ND MARCH 1973

TERROR AT CITY HOTEL LEAVES THREE DEAD

SHOOT OUT AND BOMB SCARE AS DERRY'S BISHOP HEGARTY IS FATALLY SHOT

BY WILLIAM J BARTER

What began as a mission of hope involving dignitaries, business leaders, and representatives from across County Derry ended in carnage at one of the city's largest hotels yesterday.

Factory owner Roger Henderson and his nephew James were hosting a high-level bid for funding to protect thousands of jobs at Rocola, one of Derry's major employers. Many of its workers are women from Creggan and the Bogside.

According to witnesses, a lone gunman, Kieran Kelly, 19, from the Bogside, disguised himself as a waiter and planted a bomb in the hotel before becoming embroiled in a gunfight. An unidentified man fatally shot Bishop Hegarty. Kelly returned fire, killing the bishop's assassin, but died soon after from his injuries.

The identity of the bishop's killer remains unknown, though police are investigating possible links to a loyalist gang led by a local figure known only as 'Mr Big'.

Martina McLaughlin, 17, from Blamfield Street, Creggan, was arrested at the scene. Police believe she smuggled the device into the hotel and may be connected to a string of violent attacks, including the murder of a British soldier. She is described by police as a honeytrap, used to lure victims before attacks were carried out.

RUC Chief Constable George Shalham oversaw the evacuation, and within minutes the building was cleared. Armed officers secured the area while bomb disposal teams searched for additional threats.

Several guests were treated for shock and minor injuries, but no further explosives were found.

Chapter Two

Dark Days

Months later, it felt like the world was ending as Caitlin lay stiff in bed, eyes wide, listening to the wind batter the windows and rain hammer the roof like fists. The clock showed just after five, far too early, but her mind was already racing, tearing ahead as if it had somewhere urgent to be.

The hotel bomb scare, the gunfire, the chaos – that had been bad enough. But it wasn't what haunted her in the small hours. What cut deepest was the sight of Tina being taken away. That memory stayed with her, way more than any headline. She'd never forget it.

At first, Tommy had run ragged to the Strand Road barracks, begging for news, pleading to see her, pacing the house like a caged animal. Every time, the same stone wall: no visits, no updates.

If it hadn't been for Brendan Doherty, their solicitor, relentless as ever, Tina would still be stuck in that hellhole. Not long after, she'd gone clean doolally, out of her mind. Once Brendan saw the state she was in, he went for it, fought with the powers that be, and after days of pushing finally had her moved to Gransha, the local psychiatric hospital.

It wasn't perfect, not by any stretch, but it was a damn sight better than being locked in a peeler's cell on her own, staring at bare walls while the world went on without her. At least in Gransha, they treated her like a human being. The nurses didn't look at her like she were some sort of freak. She wasn't just another suspect or a headline in the paper. There, she might have a chance to recover, even if it was slim. They said she'd be assessed before trial, though Brendan had made it clear she wasn't fit for anything, never mind facing a judge. That brought Caitlin and Majella some peace, not much, but enough to cling to when everything else felt like it was slipping through their fingers.

Meanwhile, Martin stayed in Long Kesh, showing no sign of getting out. Caitlin had only forced herself to visit once, and feeling the way she was, she wouldn't have gone at all if her mother hadn't begged her. The moment she sat across from him in that grim grey room, she knew it was a mistake. He looked dreadful — filthy, withdrawn, clothes hanging off him like he no longer cared. His hair was falling out in patches, his skin dull and pulled too tight over his face, and his eyes told her everything. He wasn't angry anymore. He was hardened. Beyond reach.

When he found out what Kieran Kelly had done, he'd erupted. The moment he heard Tina's name mentioned and how she'd got involved, Caitlin watched the rage build in him like a kettle boiling over. The way Kelly had used her, the way he'd groomed her, led her on, pushed her to play a part in something she didn't fully understand, made Martin physically sick. He slammed his fist down so hard on the table that the prisoner officer came over to check what was going on.

Protective didn't even begin to describe him. Martin ranted until he was hoarse, cursed Kelly up and down, and spat that it was as well the bastard was in the ground. He had a feeling about him, that the guy wasn't all there, weird. Sneaky to the core. Never liked the fucker, always thinking he was untouchable. Well, now he was six feet under, Martin wouldn't lose sleep over it. One less snake in the grass.

With only Majella and Caitlin left on Blamfield Street, the Brits still hadn't let it go. Number thirty remained on their radar, and it didn't take much to set them off. They were always looking for a reason to knock the door in, to barge their way through the hall and tear the place apart like they were hunting for some great secret. Week after week, they came, often without warning, always in pairs or more, boots stamping through every room like they owned it. Never found anything, but that wasn't the point. The family knew it was payback. Their own had been tortured or killed, and someone had to feel the heat.

It didn't matter that Caitlin and Majella had nothing to do with Kelly's twisted campaign, or that they were trying to survive what was left of their lives. They got the brunt of it. Cushions slashed, drawers yanked out and emptied across the floor, wardrobes gutted, beds stripped down to the bare frames. They even sliced open Martin's old mattress, which still lay sagging and torn in the corner of his room, untouched since.

Caitlin often wished her daddy were still alive. She missed him more than she could put into words, missed his voice, his laugh, even the way he'd clatter about first thing in the morning, letting everyone know he was up and wanted company.

In the early hours, when sleep wouldn't come and the house sat in that dead stillness, her thoughts turned dark. She'd lie there, staring into the black, wondering what had become of him beneath the soil. Had he rotted away: his skin, his fingernails? Had the cuff links he wore disappeared into the earth? It was a horrible thing to think about, but she couldn't help herself. Her head took her there.

Blamfield wasn't home anymore. The house was more like a tomb than anything else, and the longer she stayed there, the more she felt like one of the ghosts inside it. Her days blurred together. She went through the motions, doing what needed done, cleaning, cooking, showing up at work when she could, without feeling much at all. Everything had gone numb. The only thing that still lived in her properly was fear. Fear of what might come next. Fear of that knock at the front door. Fear that it wasn't over.

Her mother had once been vibrant and strong, before Martin's arrest, her daddy's illness, then his arrest, and Tina's. She couldn't be herself anymore. The woman who'd stormed through the house in her apron, giving out and keeping everything in order, had disappeared. The tablets the doctor prescribed were too strong now, made her woozy, and left her staring at the same corner of the wall for hours on end. Grief had taken her from them, pulled her under and kept her there. She barely got dressed these days and barely spoke. Lay in bed like she was waiting to join Patrick.

Still, the rumours circled. Some of them so far-fetched you'd think no one would believe them, but they were repeated anyway, whispered in kitchens and muttered outside shops like gospel truth. A few disloyal neighbours, ones Majella had lent the odd cup of sugar to, or invited in for a cuppa tea, had plenty to say. They claimed Tina had brought it all on herself, that she'd led Kieran Kelly on, enjoyed the attention. As if any of them had the faintest idea what went on. People were still furious about the bishop's murder. Everyone had loved Bishop Hegarty, and now, because of who Tina had been caught with, a few of the worst gossips had the barefaced audacity to say she was part of that too. As if she'd had a say in any of it. As if she wasn't already broken enough. But once the poison had been planted, it didn't matter what the truth was. The damage was done.

What tore Caitlin apart more than any whisper, more than the constant raids or the looks on the street, was the way James Henderson had looked at her in the hotel, the exact moment when she told him it was Tina who was crumpled in her arms, crying her heart out over Kieran Kelly. James's face, the disgust in his eyes, it had hit harder than anything. Straightaway, he'd blamed her. Blamed the whole lot of them. As if it had all been some elaborate setup. He'd even suggested, without a thought, that Martin had put the two sisters up to it, that the whole thing had been part of some ridiculous Provo plot to ruin Rocola. The words he'd thrown at her, his complete rejection, still hurt. Even now, months later, she struggled to believe he'd actually said them, let alone believed them.

One dark evening, curled up on the sofa in the front room, the fire barely catching, she found herself thinking back to their first kiss. Right here in this very room. It'd been such a shock to see him standing at her front door after the Shipquay Street bombing, where Anne had lost the lower half of her leg. He hadn't come because of words or out of pity. He'd come to see her, to see if she was okay. Somehow, without planning it, they'd ended up sitting close, talking in hushed voices about life, loss, and all the shit in between. Then, out of nowhere, he'd kissed her. She could still feel the surprise of it, how her body had instinctively melted into his arms.

She scoffed. He was such a good kisser too. All soft and lovely.

Looking back, she was sure that was the moment she fell for him. Fell hard. Hook, line and sinker. She remembered his scent, the feel of his fingertips brushing her wrist, the way his mouth found hers like it had always known the way. She would've given anything to go back there, to hold him a little longer, to soak up the safety and warmth of his arms, before the world got in the way.

Her lips curved into a tired smile as another memory surfaced. That weekend in Donegal, the two of them, with no plan other than to discover each other, to escape the noise and be in their own little world. The food had been unreal, rich and comforting, the kind you couldn't help but moan over, and the bath, steaming hot and overflowing with bubbles, had nearly flooded the place. Jesus, how they'd laughed. Later, after they'd made love, he'd wrapped her in his arms and held her close until she drifted off. It had been tender, not rushed, the kind of night that left her feeling weightless in the best possible way, craving more. Craving him.

He'd been so kind back then. So patient. After her daddy died, when the house felt like it was falling in, James had been the one who helped her through. He'd given her hope, kept her busy, made her feel like there was life beyond grief and the Troubles. For those short months, she'd been happy. Alive, not because of his kisses, his reassurances or even the weekend away. It was because of him. The way he saw her. The way he listened.

She could still see the look in his eyes the morning of the meeting at the City Hotel. Excited, hopeful, bursting with ambition. Those vivid green eyes, filled with plans and belief that he could fix Rocola. But it hadn't lasted. Reality barged in wearing the face of Kieran Kelly and some unknown gunman, and in one day, one single day, everything they worked so hard for came crashing in around them.

Once more, hurt and humiliation engulfed her as she replayed the last time she'd seen James – the words he'd used, the hatred on his face, his sheer selfishness in not giving her a chance to defend herself. The injustice of it all made her physically squirm. This grief differed from the grief of losing Daddy. That was a pain she could mourn, in time, she'd it would rest. But James's rejection? That pain stayed. Lived inside her, ate her up and drained her dry.

What he'd done after everything her family had been through made her sick to the heart. Her daddy, dying in police custody. Her mammy, drowning in drink and pills. Martin, locked up for God knows how long. And Tina? Jesus Christ. How the heck did her sister end up warped by some trigger-free Provo? None of it made sense.

Despite living in the same city, James might as well have been on another continent. He'd never called, never wrote, never made the slightest effort to explain himself. Caitlin hadn't planned on going back to Rocola anyway, but the decision was taken out of her hands soon enough. A few days later, a brown envelope had landed on the doormat. Inside was a terse letter from Roger Henderson stating that 'her services were no longer required'. No explanation, only a cheque for forty quid.

She'd stared at it for a second, a rage building inside her. She could almost picture Mrs Parkes, smug as ever, banging it out on her typewriter. In one quick burst, Caitlin had torn the cheque and the letter to shreds, scattering the pieces across the kitchen floor like confetti. She regretted it later. Forty pounds was forty pounds they could've been doing with. Thankfully, she never told anyone.

She found another job quickly, this time at a photographer's studio in the city centre. Tommy had pulled a few strings with the owner, Raymond Burns, who, at first glance, came off as a right little weasel. His fingers were always grubby, yellowed with chemicals, and far too curious for her liking. But Caitlin wasn't having it. One quiet word, one look that reminded him exactly who her brother was, and he'd changed his tune. That was all it took. From then on, Mr Burns kept a polite distance.

Chapter Three

Poor Tommy

Later in her bedroom, wearing her father's worn Aran jumper, Caitlin sifted through photographs of happier days. One in particular caught her eye. It was a Christmas Day. She can't remember who took it years back with Tina's Christmas present, a Kodak camera. Caitlin remembered the shock on her face when she went to pay for processing it. Well expensive it was and Tina hadn't used it since.

Still, the photo had captured them all – smiling and carefree, with their silly, festive paper hats perched on their heads along with a rather impressive turkey spread on the kitchen table. No matter how broke they were, somehow her parents always came up with the goods at Christmas. The McLaughlins, including Tommy and Kathy, together, caught in a carefree moment of fun, but now a distant memory. Granny O'Reilly, dutifully invited, had never turned up.

At around seven o'clock the following morning, someone started hammering at the front door.

'Not again!' Caitlin muttered, her heart thudding as she stood up too quickly. She thought for sure it was the Brits back for another sweep. The banging got louder, more frantic now, rattling through the house like it meant trouble. She cursed under her breath, not sure if it was fear or fury boiling in her chest, but either way, she was ready to kill. Out on the landing, she peered down and spotted Tommy through the top half of the glass door, pacing back and forth.

'All right, all right, hold your horses,' she shouted, relieved that it was him and not the Brits. Fumbling with the lock and barely opening the door, Tommy surprised her by bursting into the hallway.

'Jesus, Caitlin, you took your time!' He looked half frozen and made his way into the kitchen, calling over his shoulder, 'Is your ma up?'

Caitlin doubted it. 'What do you think? Why, what's wrong?'

'They've brought Tina's trial forward. Bastards. Say she's fit for court. Can you fuckin' believe it? Usin' her as a scapegoat.'

Tommy wore his usual khaki parka, the fur-trimmed hood crushed from wear and tear, and a tired pair of jeans that looked like they'd been through the wringer. Time hadn't been kind to him since Tina's arrest and her father's death. The spark he once carried, that easy humour and warmth, had all but vanished. His shoulders drooped with the quiet weight of daily battles, like the world had slowly chipped away at him. His long red hair was gone now, and without it, the spidery veins on his face were more noticeable than ever. She noticed his glasses too, thick black frames barely held together with a crumpled bit of Sellotape, the kind of quick fix that told her everything she needed to know.

All in all, he looked utterly drained, like a man at the end of his rope, his face buried in his hands as he muttered, 'I swear. This'll kill her if nothin' will.'

Caitlin didn't have the heart to argue, because deep down, she feared he was right. Still, she forced a gentler tone, tried to lift him a little.

'Don't be thinking like that, Tommy. She'll be okay. Brendan's on it, you know what he's like. Come on now, I'll stick the kettle on, a bite to eat.'

But Tommy shook his head, barely lifting his gaze. 'Just tea, love, no food.'

He sounded so friggin' sad, as though he was trying to work out how they'd ended up here in the first place and wondering what in God's name they were supposed to do next.

Tommy couldn't eat these days. Any appetite he had had long gone. At one time, he'd have been well chuffed to see the weight dropping off him, but not now. Food was the last thing on his mind. Too much was happening. Too much had already happened. The violence was spiralling – bombings, murders, massacres. Each day dragged on. His time as a Sinn Féin community worker was behind him now. What his family didn't know was that recent events had forced him down a path he'd never thought he'd take.

Brendan Doherty was a rare breed. Sharp as a tack and stubborn with it, he'd already managed to win two extensions to keep Tina in Gransha. But now after this latest blow, they were skating on thin ice. With the trial looming, Tommy feared the worst. He wouldn't be surprised if they moved her to Armagh Gaol now. The thought of her, barely holding on as it was, ending up in a prison cell. He couldn't bear thinking about it. Tina was nowhere near right in the head, and the idea of her being banged up so young and bat crazy was enough to make his blood run cold.

Their solicitor had warned them. Murder, endangering life, and suspected Provo membership were among the charges laid at Tina's door. It was a savage list for anyone, never mind a traumatised seventeen-year-old who'd barely had the chance to grow up. Still, he hadn't given up. He was hellbent on proving to the court that Kieran Kelly had targeted Tina, groomed her, then battered her down with threats until she couldn't say no. He would make it known, without question, that Kelly had even threatened to wipe out her family if she stepped out of line. That changed everything.

Despite the severity of the charges, he'd also told Tommy that the judge might not go in too hard. She was a child, medically unfit, and there was legal precedent for compassion. Again, that gave them all a snippet of hope to hold on to, anything to keep them going. But even with the solicitor's reassurances, the timing couldn't have been worse. Tina had already spent five months in Gransha. The trial was set for the 24th of July, only weeks away. Her eighteenth birthday was four days after that. If the system waited even a few more days, she'd no longer be underage and they all knew what that meant.

As for Armagh Gaol. The tales that came out of there were common knowledge. Girls barely older than Tina locked up for life, some not even charged, some giving up hope. Caitlin had heard enough to fill her nightmares. The idea of her little sister, who could barely string a sentence together now, ending up in a place like that – God help her. God help them all.

She waited for Tommy to say more after she set down his mug of tea.

'Sorry, love, I was gone there,' he said as he raised his eyes to the ceiling and asked about his sister, Majella. 'How's Jella?'

A shake of Caitlin's head gave him her answer. 'Away with it still. No better.'

Can't really blame her, Tommy thought. He'd pleaded with his ma to come back to help, but the miserly old bitch point-blank refused. Ranting on and labelling them an embarrassment. It appeared she'd disowned them.

'I wanted to tell Jella the new court date meself... to warn her. I can imagine what the *Journal* will say. It'll be plastered across the front feckin' page again,' Tommy added, between slurping his tea.

'Course it will. Take your tea, and I'll go wake Mammy. She might come down for you,' Caitlin replied.

Tommy gave a nod and smile. 'You always make a good cuppa. By the way, how's that job of yours goin'?'

'Fine, Tommy. It's fine,' Cailtin lied.

Tommy read her and realised she looked as fucked off as he was. 'Ye sure?' he asked, holding her back with his hand.

Half-smiling, she looked at him. 'It's fine, Tommy, it's a job. I think we've got bigger things to worry about now, don't you? I'll go see if Mammy's awake.'

Tommy gently squeezed her hand. 'You know I'm here for you, love, each and every one of ye. Ye can tell me anythin', anythin' at all.'

'I know that, Tommy. I know. Thanks.' This time, Caitlin squeezed his hand.

Upstairs, she paused outside her parents' bedroom, her fingers hovering above the handle. The narrow landing seemed to close in around her, the air heavy with the scent of old washing powder and unopened windows. Her heart thumped with a sick rhythm, louder now in the dead air. Then came a faint cough from inside the room, rough and phlegmy, snapping her back into the moment. Caitlin closed her eyes, placed a hand on the wood to prepare herself, then pushed the door open and stepped inside.

She noticed the smell before anything else. A nauseating stench of unwashed clothes and stale sweat filled the room. Swallowing hard, Caitlin walked to the window, drew back the light floral curtains, and opened the catch to let some fresh air in. Sunlight flooded the room as she turned to the curled-up figure in the bed.

'Mammy, Tommy's downstairs. Wants to talk to you.'

Under the covers, Majella muttered something unintelligible before tugging the candlewick spread over her greying hair. Caitlin pulled it back, noting how worn out she looked, her face ghostly white and drained.

Still, Majella managed a faint smile as Caitlin sat on the edge of the bed and said gently, 'Say that again, I can't hear you.'

With a tug at the bedclothes, Caitlin urged her to get up. 'Are you comin' down Mammy? Tommy's got news.'

Majella gave a small nod and pushed herself upright. Her frail, blue-veined legs emerged from beneath the covers – thin and wasted.

'What time is it?' she asked, her voice barely above a whisper.

'After seven,' Caitlin replied.

'Will ye take me to the hospital later, love, to see Tina?' she implored, her hand on Caitlin's. 'I can't manage on me own.'

'Can't, Mammy. I have to work.' Caitlin replied. Her boss had warned her enough not to take any more time off without plenty of notice.

She stood up and took away her hand. Although she loved Majella, the room's foul smell and her never-ending grief made her want to run. Seeing her so crushed and broken was soul-destroying.

Majella yawned. 'Tommy'll take me? Maggie brought in a load of Wagon Wheels for Tina. She loves them.'

'That's good of her. Want any help downstairs?' Caitlin offered.

With a limp wave, Majella told her to go. 'Don't worry 'bout me. Go get ready for work.'

'You sure?' Caitlin offered again.

'Nah, I'll be fine,' Majella said, though she was nowhere near 'fine' – truth was she felt like she'd been scraped off the pavement.

Relieved, Caitlin left without saying a word about the new trial date. She hadn't the nerve. Tommy could do it.

After picking out what to wear from her meagre wardrobe but still not getting dressed, Caitlin passed her mum on the landing. As usual, Majella was wrapped in Patrick's oversized navy bathrobe, her crumpled nightdress poking out underneath.

Despite the offensive smell of body odour, she'd tried to look better. Her face was freshly wiped, and she'd scraped her hair into a tiny ponytail. It was a start, Caitlin supposed.

As Majella shuffled off downstairs to the kitchen, Caitlin headed for the bathroom and turned on the hot tap, half-expecting the usual freezing water. To her surprise, hot water came gushing out and holding her breath, she stared at the flow, praying it'd last. When the bath was half full, she climbed in. A shiver rippled across her skin as she sank into the heat.

Her thoughts moved away from the bathroom and drifted back again to Donegal Town, to that weekend with James. The two of them, deep in a bath of hot water and bubbles, their laughter, their tangled legs, skin against skin. She hung on to that happy memory, desperate for anything that wasn't pain or shame or fear.

In her mind, the steam rose again, curling up around them, the bubbles softening the world, dulling everything outside, the warmth of his body pressed against hers. Her eyes fluttered shut, her limbs loose and heavy. As the memory swept through her, she released a low, broken moan, unsure whether it came from aching love or sheer exhaustion.

Then came the scream. It tore through the quiet of the house like a blade, sharp and painful.

Majella. Downstairs. Howling like a banshee.

Poor Tommy.

Chapter Four

The Prosecution

Tina McLaughlin stood in the dock, not a sign of life in her eyes, just a wide, vacant stare. Her hair, once full of fire and bounce, now hung limp and greasy, a tangled mess that clung to her blotchy skin. Her eczema had come back worse than ever, spreading across her cheeks and neck in angry patches, cracked and weeping where she'd scratched it so hard. Even her freckles, once scattered like specks of sunshine, appeared faded, barely seen under the pallor of her face.

Caitlin watched her sister from across the courtroom. Because of her medication, Tina's mouth looked sticky, a faint line of white foam gathering at the corners. The tablets had stripped everything from her, leaving her dry, slow, and bleak. Not once had anyone offered her so much as a sip of water. Caitlin noticed the way one of the guards stared as Tina's head wobbled, tilted forward, then rolled to the side like she couldn't hold it up. Her tongue kept catching against her teeth, desperate for moisture. But the guard simply turned his back, his face blank, his eyes fixed forward like his prisoner wasn't there. Helping her would've taken effort, and to him, Martina McLaughlin wasn't worth the bother. She was another head case, beyond saving.

In the gallery, there were two types of spectators. The ones who couldn't wait for it all to kick off, leaning forward like they were front row at a play. The others, dead quiet, barely moving, watched Tina like they were waiting for her to crumble. The first group wanted drama. The second saw the inevitable and worried.

That morning, Caitlin had helped Tina get dressed. Her clothes drowned her now, hanging loose over a frame that had wasted away with all the weight she'd lost.

Her eyes turned to her mammy, Caitlin, and Tommy, sitting at the very front of the crowd. Disappointed not to see Martin, she gave them a quick, childish wave.

Back on her ward in Gransha, she'd met a woman who never stopped talking about her five-year-old daughter, Rosaleen.

Rosaleen was dead, but the woman spoke about her with such tenderness and quiet love that Tina couldn't help but listen. There was something oddly soothing in the way she talked, soft and sincere, as if the child were only sleeping in the next room. She'd sit there, rocking a rolled-up baby blanket in her arms, worn thin with age, the pink elephant print barely visible anymore. Cradling it as if it were Rosaleen herself, warm and alive, she'd whisper lullabies under her breath, as if the child might stir and blink up at her.

'It's well sad,' Tina had mumbled to Tommy during one of his better visits. 'There was a bomb in some teashop and she's convinced she's holding her wee girl, but she's dead, isn't she?'

Majella and Tommy were hanging on by a thread, each day looking more worn out than the last. They clung to whatever hope they could find, doing everything they could to pull Tina back from the brink. Pleading with her to listen, to take it all in, to take Brendan Doherty seriously. Everyone was saying the same thing, trying to get through to her, but nothing seemed to work.

But Tina wasn't stupid. She understood far more than they realised. It wasn't about the court or what might be said. It was about fear. Genuine fear. Not theirs, but hers too. She knew it. They were scared stiff, not only about the trial, but after. *God love them.*

Back in the courtroom, one of the guards stepped forward, took hold of Tina's shoulders, and pushed her down into a wooden chair set in the middle of the thick oak dock. Around her, the noise swelled as voices rang out across the chamber, some shouting over each other, others whispering in huddles. It felt like every man and his dog had an opinion.

There'd be no jury. No chance for twelve strangers to weigh the facts and decide for themselves. With the introduction of juryless trials, so-called Diplock Courts, the verdict would come down to a single judge. One decision. One sentence.

A few faces in the gallery were seen by Tina, but most were a blur.

Up at the top, the crowd hurled insults down at those seated below. With their fists curled and shaking in fury, they cried. 'This isn't a trial. It's a bloody witch hunt! She's sick. Look at her!'

The shouting grew deafening; the fury in the gallery on the brink of spilling over. On the far side, oversized Union Jacks swayed back and forth as men roared *God Save the Queen* and other Loyalist songs. Nothing to be said other than pandemonium.

A dark-suited, austere individual shouted from the bench, cutting through the din. 'Silence in court. The Honourable Justice Matthew Dodds presiding.'

The chamber quickly simmered down and fell quiet. All eyes turned to the figure seated high above the courtroom, the Honourable Mr Justice Dodds. Settled on the bench in his white wig, he scanned the room: lawyers, clerks, security. With his beady eyes, grey moustache, long pointed nose and jug ears, it was no wonder people called him 'Dumbo.' But despite his near-comical appearance, Dodds had a fearsome reputation for his hardline judgements. When Brendan found out he was presiding, he nearly had a heart attack.

So it began with endless arguments and debates. The young defendant shrank back into her dazed state. Hour after hour, RUC officers, army personnel, forensic and medical experts, and a host of other witnesses gave their evidence. The prosecution sought to establish beyond reasonable doubt their case proving that Martina McLaughlin's involvement in the alleged atrocities was equal to that of the deceased Provo bomber and murderer, the late Kieran Kelly.

Throughout the proceedings, seated quietly in the courtroom, were the parents of Val Holmes, the young British soldier Kelly had murdered in a barn on the hillside above the city. Despite her grief, Susan Holmes held her head high. She was proud, striking even, her dyed blonde hair perfectly styled, her coal-black suit sombre and suited to the occasion. Beside her, her husband sat still, saying nothing. Neither of them showed emotion. They didn't need to. Their wordlessness said it all.

As the long court days dragged on, the moment came for Tina to take the witness box. Like always, she caught her mammy and Tommy's eye and gave a small smile. Caitlin looked so sad.

Tina, in the dock, was ordered to stand. She was still away with the fairies, but there was a flicker of light behind her eyes now, a faint trace of awareness. The tablets, once her soft escape that made everything light and floaty, had lost their grip. Her chest tightened, the way it always did when panic crept in, her heart banging against her ribs as the fear rose up and the tears pressed behind her eyes.

Half-aware of the surrounding courtroom, she noticed the solemn faces, the serious atmosphere, and the worry in her family's eyes.

Then she blinked. Kieran. It was him. Right there, standing at the back of the courtroom. Like she remembered! Smart as ever in his favourite corduroy jacket, white shirt clean and crisp, jeans all neat and pressed. His fringe fell over his eyes the way it always did, soft and familiar. Her breath caught in her throat. For a second, she swore he smiled. She could almost hear his voice, low and calm, like it was when they'd first met. '*Don't worry, Honey. I'm here.*'

Her eyes brimmed over as she watched him, refusing to close her eyes, terrified he'd disappear if she so much as looked away. The tears came fast now, spilling down her raw cheeks, stinging the patches where her skin had broken. She made no effort to wipe them. Kieran was here, telling her everything would be okay.

She didn't even notice the short, stocky man in the black gown and white wig stepping closer, not at first.

Geoff Wilkinson, Queen's Counsel, cleared his throat and stood before her, but Tina didn't move an inch. Her gaze stayed fixed on the back of the courtroom, on the only man she wanted to see.

Before speaking, the QC paused for effect, glancing up at the spectators in the gallery, letting the tension build. Then, in his polished English accent, he turned to face the accused, his voice carrying through the courtroom.

'Miss McLaughlin... or is it Tina. May I use Tina?' He waited for her agreement, but she barely noticed, somewhat distracted by whatever was going on in the back of the courtroom.

A brief pause preceded the QC's almost whispered, 'Perhaps not.'

He hesitated, milking the moment, then fired his first shot.

'Before we begin, Miss McLaughlin. I have a question, a question for the court, and Valentine Holmes's family, who've had to sit here day after day listening to such distressing evidence. Do you wish to say anything to them?'

He gestured to Susan and Tony Homes, whose heads were bowed. His voice swelled, his tone purposely taunting.

'Would the accused care to address the parents who lost their only son – their one and only child – to a night of torture, beatings, and finally, a bullet? Courtesy of Kieran Kelly and you that night in the barn.'

He let his words hang, twisting the knife in. Such a harsh and direct opening surprised the gallery watchers, making them gasp. Judge Dodds demanded order.

After a moment of respite, the QC fixed Tina with a cold, steady stare, not a trace of warmth behind it. Kieran had gone. Vanished, like he'd never been there at all. Her lips trembled as her gaze darted around the room, wide and frantic. One hand crept to her cheek, where she found a bit of dry, peeling skin and started picking at it without thinking. She couldn't stop. The itch, the sting, the nerves, it was all too much. Her eyes flicked back to the QC, unsure what was coming, only knowing it wasn't going to be kind.

She searched for her mother, desperate for some kind of reassurance. Wilkinson followed her gaze. He noticed the mother didn't look up. Neither did the sister. Both sat with their heads down, eyes fixed on the floor, hands clenched in their laps, shoulders huddled. Signs of withdrawal. Possibly shame. Or fear. Only the uncle met the girl's eyes with a faint consoling smile. His hand hovered over the witness box for a second before slamming it down. The crack rang out across the courtroom.

Tina, startled, gave a small cry. In the same instant, her hand jerked back, clipping the prison guard's arm by accident. His reaction was immediate – a rough thrust that nearly knocked her off her feet. She looked to Wilkinson for help. But he ignored her and went on.

'Miss McLaughlin, do I have to repeat my question?'

All Tina could do was nod.

'Is there anything you'd like to say to Valentine Holmes' parents?'

Wilkinson's voice rose, cold and slicing. 'You and Kieran Kelly tortured and murdered Valentine Holmes, didn't you?!' Each word landed hard, the accusation ringing through the courtroom.

Timothy Swalding, QC for the defence, shot to his feet like he'd been burnt. 'M'lord, objection!' he barked. He reminded the judge that his client was still on trial and a verdict hadn't been reached.

'Overruled,' Judge Dodds said, without looking up.

The crowd stirred. Dodds raised a hand to subdue them, then leaned in slightly, his voice pitched low for Wilkinson alone. 'A verdict that remains to be seen, eh? Mr Wilkinson...?'

Wilkinson gave a slow nod, the corner of his mouth lifting enough to show he knew precisely what the judge meant.

'Thank you, m'lord.'

He turned to Tina. 'So, Miss McLaughlin. What do you have to say? Is there nothing at all?'

A single word escaped Tina's lips. 'Sorry.'

As the spectators murmured, Wilkinson allowed Tina's reply to take effect and scoffed. 'That's it? A simple *sorry*?' He shook his head, making his disapproval apparent to the audience, and muttered under his breath, 'Pathetic.'

Stepping back from the witness box, Wilkinson caught Susan Holmes's eye. A twisted idea struck him as he turned back to the defendant.

'Miss McLaughlin,' he drawled, his voice laced with mockery, 'would you be so kind as to inform the court of how you came about Mr Kelly?'

Tina's mood lifted as she thought back to meeting Kieran for the first time. How he'd bowed, taken her hand, and kissed it. The memory sent a strange flutter through her tummy.

'Met him in town,' she said, a small smile creeping in. 'He kissed me hand like a real prince. Asked me to meet him for a cuppa tea.'

The QC barely glanced up from his handheld notes. 'I see,' he murmured.

Tina, eager to carry on, got swept up in the carefree memories of those early months with the man she believed was the love of her life.

'He bought me loads of lovely clothes,' she said, smirking.

Then she giggled without warning. 'He even did me make-up. Was good at it too. Bought me a wig after that. With blonde hair. Real hair an' all. Told me I was beautiful. No one's ever said that before. Not to me. I loved him.' Remembering it all gave her the strength and courage to continue.

'Taught me all sorts of stuff. Irish history and the like. He was sound, and so good-lookin'. Made me feel special.'

Her smile faltered, shrinking at the corners. Had she said too much? She glanced over at Wilkinson, hoping he might've softened, but he wasn't giving her anything. Standing there, still as stone, pen hovering, watching her with a funny look on his face. Her voice dried up.

The hush in the courtroom crushed her, long and uncomfortable. Kieran slipped back into the shadows of her mind, and what was left in his place was reality: a watching courtroom, a waiting cold fish of a man, and a question she'd never really answered. With her reverie finished, the prosecuting counsel zeroed in on one particular point.

'You say Mr Kelly bought a... what was it again?' He paused as if struggling to remember. Then, with deliberate emphasis, 'Ah, yes, a wig. A wig with blonde hair. Real hair.'

His voice hardened. 'Tell me, Miss McLaughlin, was this wig the same one you wore to seduce Private Holmes? The one you used to gain his trust, to *flaunt* yourself at him – only to lead the poor boy straight into a death trap?'

The barrage didn't stop.

'Forensic evidence will prove that you and Kieran Kelly drugged Private Holmes, kidnapped him, tortured him, and finally shot him. After, as if that wasn't enough, you dumped his broken, scorched body in the middle of the road, left him there to be crushed under the wheels of a heavy goods vehicle, his remains desecrated beyond recognition.'

Susan Holmes, forced to listen as her son's murder was laid out in blunt, unforgiving detail, suddenly rose from her seat. A collective intake rippled through the courtroom as she lurched forward, arm trembling, a finger pointed straight at Tina in the witness box.

'Murderer! You murdered my baby! How could you do such a thing?!'

Tony Holmes sprang up beside her, wrapping both arms around his wife as she collapsed into him, sobbing uncontrollably. Her grief poured out, jagged and unfiltered, spreading through the courtroom like smoke from a fire no one could put out. Dodds allowed them some time. Not out of patience, but to let the court settle down.

Turning back to Tina, QC Wilkinson's voice remained cold and steady as he suggested. 'Miss McLaughlin, let's move on, shall we?'

Taking his time, he added. 'It is my belief that you willingly carried that school bag into the City Hotel and that you were entirely aware of its contents? A bomb, no less. Is that not so?'

Tina shook her head. 'No! I didn't know. I swear to God!' The QC's tone turned sly. He took his time, dragging out the pause before speaking.

'Then Miss McLaughlin. Perhaps you can help me here. If I could ask?' He looked around the court and raised his hands.

'Why on earth would Mr Kelly want you dressed like a sweet little schoolgirl? Braids, schoolbag, the lot, then hand him a bag with a bomb in it? All the same, not once. Not once did it occur to you to ask what you were carrying? You knew what Kieran Kelly was. You knew exactly what he was capable of, didn't you?'

He tilted his head, his voice full of sarcasm now, followed by a sardonic smile.

'Of course you did!' he cried.

'No, no... I didn't! I'm tellin' ye!' Tina yelled.

Wilkinson's eyes narrowed. 'Poppycock. Don't tell me you had no idea. That's absurd.'

A scornful laugh rippled through the gallery.

The QC's voice was laced with mockery. 'Are you seriously telling this court it never crossed your mind, not once, to ask Kieran Kelly why he wanted you dressed like that?' The courtroom held its breath as he went in for the kill. Tina shook her head as Wilkinson answered for her.

'Of course!' he sneered. 'Of course. I'm sorry. Makes perfect sense now. Who in their right mind would ever suspect a schoolgirl of carrying a bomb into a packed hotel?'

He let the words hang, eyes fixed on her.

'In fact, Miss McLaughlin, it wouldn't surprise me one bit if you helped Kelly build the thing yourselves.'

'No! No, I told you. I didn't know what was in it. He told me not to look. Kieran scared me to death. Said if I didn't do as he said, he'd kill me family!' Tina screamed, looking around the court for someone to take her side.

Wilkinson raged on. 'I dispute that, Miss McLaughlin! You knew what was in that bag! Let's not pretend, ladies and gentlemen.' He swayed across the room, his voice rising. 'We know. I know. You loved Kieran Kelly, Miss McLaughlin. Didn't you? You were right there with him, playing along in whatever sick games the pair of you cooked up!'

His voice dripped with contempt. 'How cunning you were. One night, a blonde bombshell, flirting with young men, trapping them, only to turn around and help Kelly beat, abuse, and murder them. Then the next night? You're a pigtailed schoolgirl, carrying a lethal weapon into a public place, endangering God knows how many innocent lives!'

His words hit her like bullets, sharp, cold, and meant to harm.

QC Geoff Wilkinson paused, delighted with his performance so far. His role in this trial was no small one, and he knew it. He took another moment for effect, then took a step closer to Tina, jabbing a finger at her.

'You, Miss McLaughlin. All along, you *knew* about Mr Kelly's scheme. The whole sorry time, didn't you?'

He didn't need her to answer. The question was for the gallery. As he scanned the faces, he saw it plain as day. He'd hit the mark. Spot on. The plan was working. Him and the judge had played it right.

After what felt like hours of relentless questioning, the prosecution finally rested its case. The curtain fell, and Wilkinson delivered his performance to perfection. He'd painted

Tina McLaughlin as a *manipulative, dangerous* woman, capable of bending not just naïve young soldiers to her will, but possibly even Kieran Kelly himself!

No one could argue otherwise. Kelly was dead and it was left for Tina to take the fall. Wasn't *she* the one who trapped Arnie Waters, the poor, clueless soldier who ended up beaten so badly he'd spent months in hospital? He lived, but his career was over, discharged from the army, and too weak to stand as a key witness.

Hadn't *she* drugged Val Holmes in the restaurant, gotten him into the car, taken him to the barn, stood by and watched as Kelly tied the poor soldier up and tortured him? Her fingerprints were *everywhere*, on Holmes's belongings, on the black bags that held his bloodied, naked corpse. A bottle of whiskey bore even more damning evidence. She was there. With Kelly. The attempted hotel bombing? Witness after witness swore blind they'd seen her. A schoolgirl with a satchel, in the hotel. The prosecution had done its job. Martina McLaughlin was cornered.

Brendan Doherty sat there, horrified. The trial was running away from them, and fast. They were getting hammered. Their QC hadn't bothered raising half the objections he should have. If he didn't pull a miracle out of the bag soon, they were screwed.

Chapter Five

The Defence

Then came the defence. Timothy Swalding, QC, got to his feet. Short and stout, with wide-set eyes and wild eyebrows, he almost looked a bit lost, as if he'd wandered into the wrong courtroom. His gown didn't help either, creased and grubby, like it hadn't seen a hanger in years. He made his way towards the girl in the box.

Tina sat slumped, one elbow resting against the side of the box to stop herself keeling over. She was shattered, far away, past caring. Nothing left in the tank. All these men ever did was fire questions at her, one after the other, and all she wanted was for it to end.

Swalding's voice was soft as he touched her arm. 'Tina, it's evident to this court that you are unwell. Would you like some water?'

It was the first shred of kindness anyone had shown her. 'Aye, sorry, yes, please,' she whispered. A guard fetched a glass of water, and she sipped from it.

'Better?'

She nodded. 'Aye. Thanks.'

Swalding wasted no time. 'Tina, we already know from my learned friend where and when you met Kieran Kelly. We've heard about your relationship. If I may, I'd like to ask a few further questions.'

Tina hesitated. She didn't want to talk anymore. She searched for Tommy's face, desperate for reassurance. His blue eyes met hers. *It'll be all right*, they told her.

'Okay,' she said at last.

'Good. I'll keep it short. You fell profoundly in love with Mr Kelly, didn't you?'

Tina wasn't all that sure what '*profoundly*' meant, but she got the gist. 'Oh, aye, he was my world at one time.'

'You'd have gone to any lengths for him? Anything at all?'

Wilkinson leapt up. 'Objection, your honour! Leading the witness!'

'Sustained,' Dodds said, firm as ever.

Swalding raised his hands in mock surrender.

'Your Lordship.' He had a strong suspicion the judge was part of some kind of ploy – that the prosecutor and Dodds were in on it together.

'Were you frightened of Mr Kelly?' he asked, turning back to Tina.

Her body tensed. 'I was. He was fun and lovely to start with, but in the end... He was horrible. Aye. I was... I was frightened. Big time.'

'And *when* exactly did he start to scare you? When he threatened you?'

Tina swallowed. 'Yeah. When I went out with Val. Val was lovely. Dead funny and kind. Called me 'Flower' and I think Kieran was jealous. He was ragin' that night. In awful form.'

'The night Private Holmes died?' Swalding verified.

'Aye.'

'Why not tell us what happened that night, Tina? Please. Take your time.'

She moved her head from side to side. 'I can't. I don't wanna!' The memories rushed back. Blood, the stink of piss and burned flesh, whiskey, Val's naked body, Kieran's anger, the black bags...

'I can't!' Her fingers clenched so tight around her glass that it shattered in her hand, water spilling across her lap, bits of glass flying. A sting ran through her palm, but she barely felt it. Not until she saw blood on the floor.

Swalding turned to the judge. 'M'lord, If you'll allow. We need to take a break.'

Dodds hesitated but conceded. 'If we must.'

Thirty minutes later, Tina sat with her bandaged hand in her lap, trying to remember everything Swalding had told her downstairs in the cell. *You need to help me here, Tina. You have to concentrate, make sure you stress how much you adored Kieran, that everything was his fault. He made you do it. He threatened you!'*

Swalding approached her again with a don't-forget-what-I-said smile.

'Tina, I believe you loved Mr Kelly. Based on what we've heard, it's obvious. Considering your father's death at the hands of the security services, your brother Martin's internment, and the pressures of growing up during these dark times, there is no doubt in my mind that Kieran Kelly *preyed* on your vulnerability—'

'Objection!' Wilkinson roared.

Dodds paused long enough to give the illusion of thought, but played along anyway. 'Over-ruled.'

With little choice, Swalding carried on. 'He chose you because you were easy to manipulate. He groomed you, Tina, didn't he? Spoiled you rotten, took you shopping. He even did your make-up, brainwashed you—'

'Objection!' Wilkinson was on his feet again. 'This is absurd!'

'Overruled.'

Swalding kept going, afraid of losing momentum. 'Mr Kelly made you feel special, didn't he? Like you were the only girl in the world. You loved him, didn't you, Tina?'

Tina nodded, her voice barely a whisper. 'I did. I do. I still love him.' Then she saw him again. Kieran. In the exact same place, his chocolate-brown eyes twinkling under the harsh lights, and smiling at her.

'Tell them, Kieran!' she cried. 'Tell them I didn't hurt anyone!' A stunned stillness enveloped the courtroom.

Swalding ran a hand down his face and fell into his seat, muttering, 'Christ on earth.'

Chapter Six

The Verdict

Judge Dodds, cold and composed, listed off the charges against Tina one by one – murder, membership of an illegal organisation, terrorism, and so on. Then came the verdict.

Guilty.

'Martina McLaughlin of 30 Blamfield Street, Londonderry, I have no hesitation in sentencing you to life behind bars. Life meaning life, to be served in Armagh Women's Gaol. Take her down!'

Majella howled, clawing to reach her daughter as the guards forced Tina towards the underground cells. Tommy, struck dumb with shock, rushed forward and seized his sister, pulling her into a fierce embrace before lifting his eyes to Caitlin.

'Life, Tommy?!' Caitlin gasped. 'Life? He can't do that! She's seventeen and not right in the head, Jesus Christ, Tommy!'

Tommy moaned. 'I know, love. I know.'

As they left the courtroom, Caitlin couldn't shake the feeling she'd let Tina down. She should've seen it, asked more, cared more. But she hadn't. She'd been too wrapped up in James Henderson. The charm, the promise, the idea of him. The Protestant golden boy from a world that had only locked her sister up.

It wasn't really his fault; she told herself. He hadn't created the world he'd been born into, nor had he asked for the system that had polished him so carefully and kept him sheltered from harm. All of it had simply been handed to him, laid out as if on a silver plate, and it had made the man he was now, whether or not he liked it. Majella had been right all along. Now Caitlin saw him for what he was.

No more dreaming. No more trying to be someone she wasn't. Time to grow up. Her family needed her now. The way things were going, she needed them as much.

Honestly, could things get any worse?

Chapter Seven

Boodles

Charles Jones smiled and patted Judge Dodds on the back. Job done. The two men were meeting for lunch in Jones's private members' club, Boodles, in Mayfair, London.

Previously, Dodds had only been to the club for Law Society black-tie events, and, by God, he loved the place. He loved its history, ambience, cuisine, and proximity to the nightlife of London Town, especially Soho after Mrs D (as he affectionately called his wife) had gone to bed. The visit was even sweeter because they were Charles Jones, Esq's honoured guests, and the bloody fool was paying for everything.

Dodds had been chasing membership for years, and getting Jones's backing was the stuff of dreams. But it came with a catch. He had to keep official eyes off Jones's old henchman, William Morris. Create a diversion, throw them off the scent of the ex-squaddie turned agent provocateur, the same man who'd shot the bishop at the City Hotel, before Kieran Kelly took him out in revenge. If Jones had known the whole thing was a Provo setup, he'd have held back and kept Morris, a dependable asset, in his pocket.

Still, it worked out in the end. With Kelly dead, they had a perfect scapegoat. Martina McLaughlin.

Dodds' instructions were simple: use the near-adult girl as an example. Send her down for life, and to Armagh Gaol. Thus, stir up outrage. Make a statement and rile the Republicans no end. Did the job. The trial was messy and controversial enough to keep the local media occupied, steering them away from any potential link between the bishop's mysterious shooter and Charles Jones. The judge wasn't sure whether Jones had been involved. He didn't care. He didn't ask. He badly wanted that Boodle's membership, he and Mrs D longed for it.

Mrs D especially enjoyed the club's proximity to Bond Street and Oxford Street and Dodds couldn't even begin to imagine the damage she'd do to their bank account and credit cards once their membership was approved. But he loved her, and she deserved it.

Living daily with the fear of a bomb under their car or an assassin's shot coming from out of nowhere wasn't easy.

As soon as they were sitting comfortably, Jones ordered drinks and the pair made small talk until they arrived. With relief, Jones took a sip of his chilled Sauvignon.

'Delicious,' he murmured. Then, after a quick glance around for eavesdroppers, he leaned in and whispered, 'Bravo, Dodds. Bravo. I couldn't have asked for more.'

The judge, pleased as punch at such an accolade, and from Charles Jones, no less, leaned in with a sly smile.

'Wasn't that difficult, Charles, old boy. Closed case. Anyway, I'd already made up my mind. As for that rascal Kelly, the man was insane. And the girl... stupid. Plain downright stupid. Shame I couldn't give her the rope. Now that would've caused a stir!' He sniggered, half-joking.

Jones laughed, and a small, cruel smile crossed his face. 'One less Taig to bring the place down, eh?'

Dodds raised his glass in salute. 'Absolutely,' he said.

Jones fell back into his chair and lit a Cuban cigar. He'd promised himself that today he'd relax, enjoy the wine, the food, and the company. He neither liked nor disliked the judge. But the man had proved himself very useful, and Jones knew it would be wise to keep him sweet, especially if his forthcoming plans bore fruit. Who knows, he might need him again in the future?

Later that afternoon, after the judge had gone to meet his wife, Jones sat smoking in Boodles, green-panelled library reading his *Telegraph*. He glanced at his IWC watch and noted that James Henderson Snr was twenty minutes late. Jones hated tardiness; it showed a lack of respect.

Tutting, he folded the paper in preparation to leave. Charles Jones didn't wait for anyone.

The next moment, however, a voice bellowed across the stillness of the library. 'Sorry, Charles. Bloody Victoria Line. Some selfish bastard threw themselves in front of a train. My apologies!'

His guest's raised voice drew immediate scowls and muttering from the other members.

Jones heard someone whisper, 'Bloody fool. Bad behaviour.'

At once, he shot James Henderson Snr a warning look and hissed, 'Keep your voice down, for Christ's sake James. Sit!'

James Snr reddened at his host's tone, as if he were being scolded like a naughty five-year-old. Quietly, he sank into the red leather reading chair beside Jones's.

Soon enough, a red-coated waiter appeared, and Jones ordered drinks. He and James Snr sat talking, quietly working through what was happening and how James might get involved. The older man nodded along, eager to please, desperate to keep up appearances, though Jones could see the strain behind his eyes.

It didn't matter. He wasn't here for friendship.

To Jones, Henderson Snr was another pawn in the game, dangling on the hook of his own debts. Easy to reel in, easier still to control. Once the Henderson name had served its purpose, he'd cut the line without a second thought.

Earlier that morning, James Snr had spoken to Roger, his brother in Londonderry, by phone. Ever since the hotel fiasco, he'd been unwell. The entire incident had consumed him. His voice was weak, and he'd sounded tired during the short call. Roger had told him there was nothing he could do to help. He was grateful, at least, that James Jnr had managed the fallout from the episode so well.

Still, people were talking. Everyone had an opinion about Martina McLaughlin's verdict. But it wouldn't last. Sooner or later, the daily horrors unfolding across the province would throw up fresh for the headlines. More fodder for the growing pack of national and international journalists holed up in Ulster's hotels, like scavengers feeding off the chaos.

With his friend George Shalham's unstinting support, Roger had secured a loan from the Northern Ireland Office, enabling the factory to remain open. They'd also been able to pay back the enormous debt owed to Charles Jones – who, upon receiving it, had appeared more annoyed than pleased. He'd reluctantly taken the money and even offered to change the conditions of the loan if they wanted to extend it, but Roger had declined.

Roger had made his position explicit. He wanted nothing more to do with Charles Jones. Said any friendship was long gone. Water under the bridge.

James Snr said he understood. All the same, he didn't mention meeting Jones that afternoon. He couldn't.

His back was against the wall. He needed the man's help. His debts were mounting again, and Jones had the money and the power to make life so much better.

As for his son, ever since the City Hotel, he'd thrown himself into work at the factory. Neither he nor Roger ever understood what happened with the McLaughlin girl. He refused to talk about her, and in the end, the brothers agreed James would only talk when, and if, he was ready.

James Jnr knew nothing about the letter Roger had written to the girl, or the cheque inside. His father was no use to anyone at the factory with little or no experience in shirt manufacturing. His life had been the British Army, who'd pensioned him off years ago. Now, broke as ever, James Snr felt nothing but relief when Jones offered to involve him in his business dealings. A few contacts had already brought in some decent money, and, by Christ, he needed it.

He'd married well and joined the British Army as an officer, thinking it'd be his golden ticket into the upper classes. For a while, it was, until he couldn't keep pace with the expense and, to his downfall, gambled far more than he could afford.

Only the night before, he'd sat hunched over a poker table, a thin sheen of sweat beading across his brow, his trembling fingers clutching at the cards as though the next hand would liberate him. The more he lost, the more he convinced himself the winning streak was coming, that fate had to turn in his favour if only he held on. He'd been thinking the same thing for months, but the cards had turned cruel, and he was still on a losing run. The pressure was mounting, every shuffle and deal tightening a noose he couldn't see a way out of. Dangerous men wanted paid. Soon. He'd do whatever it took to keep his head above water. Whatever it took to stay alive. For the moment, he could offer Jones some valuable military contacts and, if things went well, even introduce him to a few aristocratic pals.

Still, he'd need to tread carefully.

After tagging along to a few of the Belfast man's Loyalist sermons, he'd come to a firm conclusion. He wasn't particularly fond of the arrogant little man with his Hitler tendencies, though, to be fair, he did agree with some of what he preached about the Papists.

Whether he liked Jones wasn't important, he'd come across worse lowlifes in the army. He'd stick with him, deliver what was expected, and take the reward. A win-win, but one he had to keep secret from his family.

Chapter Eight

Marleen Returns

Back at Melrose, James Jnr sat on the edge of his uncle's king-size bed. His voice was concerned as he asked, 'How you feeling? Better for eating?'

Roger shrugged and answered half-heartedly, 'Better, but please don't fuss.'

James rubbed the back of his uncle's hand, noticing how tissue-thin the skin was nowadays. 'I want to fuss. We need to get you better. You're missed at the factory.'

Roger hadn't been on site in months. The factory's atmosphere was full of dread. They knew how close it came to closing, braced for the worst. It wasn't said openly, but if Rocola failed. It'd sink them. All of them.

Mrs Parkes asked after Roger daily. With Caitlin now out of the picture, to his surprise, James Jnr had come to rely on the woman's experience, tenacity, and loyalty. He remembered returning to Rocola the day after the failed meeting, only to find Mrs Parkes, as usual, waiting patiently by the lift. She nearly keeled over when she saw his condition. He looked more like a man of fifty.

'Ock, Mr Henderson, how are you? And your poor uncle? Horrible. Never slept a wink last night.'

She prattled on about how delighted she was to have him back in the office anyway. Everyone would be pleased to see him.

All the same, from what he'd said about the McLaughlin girl being involved, she still wasn't sure. She didn't quite believe him. But then she thought about that mad family of hers and told her young boss word on the street was the mother had gone all loopy, taken straight to her bed with '*the nerves.*' James stared at her. The old girl had warned him. He hadn't listened, and now he felt downright stupid. Exposed. All the while hoping she'd let it go.

Mrs Parkes continued to prove herself, and to her credit, never mentioned Caitlin again. Sometimes he'd come across hand-written notes by Caitlin, and his hands would ball into fists. He despised her, yet he missed everything about her.

As he felt his hand being patted and squeezed, James looked at Roger and asked gently, 'How are you, son? You okay?'

'I'm okay. Lots to do. Getting there.'

To cheer them both up, he asked, 'Told you Marleen was coming for the weekend, didn't I? I can't believe we haven't seen her in well over a year. Funny, but somehow, she and I always pick up where we left off. It'll be nice to see her again.'

'Indeed it will,' Roger replied, remembering their last dinner party when he-who-must-not-be-named, Charles Jones, had ranted and raved so much he'd spilt red wine all over Marleen's white silk dress.

'It'll be good to see her. Been a long time,' he said, thinking of the lovely young woman. The one he'd once hoped James would marry. A different class altogether from that silly secretary, who he suspected had hurt his nephew more than he ever let on. At times, he could lose it with the boy. Hadn't he warned him not to get involved? For all that, he obviously had.

Melrose had been morgue-like lately, with barely a visitor since the hotel catastrophe. However, Marleen's arrival would lift the gloom and doom. She'd cheer James up. Cheer them all up. Marleen was good at that.

Although Roger knew he'd have to pull himself together and dust himself down physically, he wasn't ready. He felt so darn tired. Doctor Harris, the family GP, had left his practice under a cloud after another malpractice case and moved on to God knows where.

To Roger's disdain, his replacement, Alec Quinn, was a mighty poor successor. The man was a clown.

'Spoke to your father today,' Roger said, as his nephew stood to look out the bay window at the rose garden below.

Pulling back the immaculate voiles, James replied, 'Oh, aye? How's he? Haven't spoken to him in an age. I should, but I can't bear the thought of him mixing with that bully boy.' Referring to, but not saying, Charles Jones.

'Hmm. That new friendship... one of life's surprises,' Roger replied, nodding. 'Interesting, too, that he hasn't asked me for money. I suspect he's on you-know-who's payroll.'

James laughed without any humour. 'Shame on him, really. I'm glad that crook is out of the equation. Never liked the man. By the way, he's rattled George Shalham. When I saw him last, he confided that our friend is now on the RUC's radar. Seems he's got ties to the Ulster Volunteer Force, funnelling serious money into arms and propaganda. They've been bombing Catholic businesses across Belfast and are about to be banned.'

He turned from the window and sat again on the edge of his uncle's bed. 'George tells me he thinks Jones has formed some kind of gang, Loyalist militants. Says they've been behind a string of sectarian attacks. Even murder. Bet this too, reckons Jones knew the brute who killed the bishop.' Roger scoffed. James went on, his voice icy with hatred.

'The snake always finds a way to stay afloat, never a mark on him. George can't find a shred of evidence. Thinks he's got someone in the force on his payroll too, someone up there, protecting him. But again, nothing solid. Poor man's beside himself. As for Father... well, I doubt he'd care, so long as there's money in it.'

When it came to his brother, James had hit the nail on the head. Roger couldn't argue. The two brothers were as different as poteen and porter, yet they looked alike. While Roger had worked hard from the ground up, cared nothing for religion, and built Rocola into a solid success, James Snr was a dyed-in-the-wool snob and bigot. He'd a chip on his shoulder about not having the money to match the lifestyle he believed he deserved.

Roger had only ever felt jealous of his brother once — when fate decided Jocelyn, his dead wife, could never carry children. Whereas Catherine, his sister-in-law, was young, beautiful, fit, and healthy, and had given birth to James.

Over the years, Catherine, James's mother, sought a new life in South Africa, meaning the boy spent more and more time at Melrose, Jocelyn began to see him as the next best thing to a son of her own.

Roger thought of his surprise at receiving a strongly worded letter from Catherine recently, posted from Cape Town, asking to see her son. It was the first time she'd suggested coming to Melrose since she'd left. Although the woman had written many times over the years, Roger always made a point of destroying her letters and ignoring her telephone calls.

Catherine would have to wait. He wasn't ready to think about her. She belonged to the past and could stay there. His gut told him now wasn't the time to mention her letter to anyone. James stood up to leave.

'We'll soon know, though, won't we?' he asked.

'Know what?' Roger replied, confused. He'd forgotten what they were talking about.

James smiled. 'Father being on you-know-who's payroll. No doubt he'll update us on the odious creep when we see him next.'

'I expect he will. Not that I'm interested.'

James grabbed his blue and red Donegal tweed jacket and folded it over his arm. He took a deep breath and looked down at his uncle.

Noticing his stare, Roger's strained expression gave way to a genuine smile as he playfully tossed a book at him.

'What are you looking at? Off with you now and give my head peace!'

James laughed. Good to see his uncle with a bit of spark again, a bit of banter. Long overdue. He loved the man. Hands raised in surrender, he grinned.

'Right. I'm away. I'll come up and have some dinner with you later.'

'Grand. Now get outta here,' Roger barked.

James closed the double bedroom doors behind him and stood still. He looked at the winding staircase, noticing its beauty and the beauty of the rest of the house.

It had been almost two years since he'd landed in Londonderry, after his father's gambling lost them their beautiful home in Ayrshire. Cringing at the memory, he thought about how naïve and absurdly arrogant he'd been when he first arrived. Since then, he'd grown to love the city and, given everything that had happened, he'd wised up. Big time.

George Shalham had taken him under his wing and got him out of a few scrapes. Sadly, after the security breach at the hotel, a breach they'd believed impenetrable, Shalham took the brunt of it all. Given no choice, he'd stepped down as RUC Chief Constable.

It seemed that George blamed himself for the bishop's death, even though no one had seen Kelly as a threat. The man was a lone wolf, an outsider, operating under the radar of the security services. What worried most was were there any more Kellys about.

The moment George's desk was cleared, Henry Bonner was at it. Shalham had no say, and most knew the two men couldn't be more different. From experience, Shalham reckoned Bonner was a disaster waiting to happen. A full-blown Loyalist hardliner who hated Catholics, and with sectarian tensions already at boiling point, things weren't about to get better.

Chapter Nine

Armagh Gaol

'Take them off!' Tina heard a woman's voice shriek in anger. 'Fuckin' quick now, ye Fenian bitch!'

Confused, Tina McLaughlin did as she was told, removing her cardigan slowly, one sleeve first, then awkwardly fighting with the second, whilst another miserable-looking guard joined her colleague.

Watching her with contempt and irate at her sluggishness, the first gaoler, Prison Officer (PO) Smyth, repeated her command. 'Quick now! I said, or I'll fuckin' do it meself!'

Tina's thin arm was suddenly and painfully jerked back, and soon her cardigan, blouse, trousers, bra and knickers were maliciously pulled off and thrown aside until she stood frightened, shaking, naked and cold. Next, she was pushed against the wall where her arms were splayed apart; her legs forced open, and her back pressed down as a signal for her to bend over. A gloved hand groped around the inside and outside of her fanny.

Humiliation – it was her time of the month – flooded her as she watched the trickle of light crimson blood flow down the inside of her leg to form a misshapen pool on the wet ground. She was told to open her mouth, and the same gloved hand fished inside, deliberately rubbing her tongue, teeth, and gums. She shuddered as she spat out the bitter taste, then twitched as fingers pulled and hunted through her unwashed red hair in search of lice. Her keepers continued to examine her shivering body, noting any distinguishing marks or tattoos. In the process, they took the piss out of the blotchy, oozing eczema sores that now covered most of the young girl's face, legs, and torso.

Once finished, she was forced to turn and face her guards, one of whom chuckled as she pushed a heavy bar of used, strong-smelling carbolic soap into Tina's hand. This was followed by a vicious thrust towards an old-fashioned and stained enamel bath.

The same voice said, 'Wash yourself, dirty bitch. You fuckin' stink!'

Tina couldn't figure out where she was, but one thing she knew for certain, this place wasn't anything like the hospital she'd been in before. That place had felt safe. Nice and clean. All white and warm, with kind nurses, the woman and her ghost child for company. She missed the endless lullabies, sung so softly and lovely, it had felt like someone was wrapping her up in a song. But this place, this place reeked. It was dirty and freezing, all shadows and strange noises, and it scared the bejesus out of her. Tina hated it. Hated it from the minute she stepped in.

Then, for some unknown reason, some angry fat woman, dressed in black from top to toe, kept hitting and shouting at her. She wished the woman would stop giving off and leave her alone. Sitting in rose-coloured, tepid bathwater that barely reached her waist, Tina slowly washed her arms and body, finishing with her feet. She wondered if she really did smell and washed herself a little harder – just in case.

The voice returned, screaming spittle-filled words. 'Outta there now!'

A threadbare towel was thrown at her to catch, but fell onto the wet floor. Bending down to pick it up, she suddenly jumped in fright at a grating cry coming from the other side of the wet room. To keep some form of modesty, Tina quickly wrapped her cold, emaciated body in the damp towel, grabbed her discarded clothes, and looked back over her shoulder.

She saw a young pregnant girl with wheat-blonde hair being pushed by the other guard towards the now-vacant bath. Tina noticed patches of reddish-brown dried blood on the girl's hairline and at the sides of her white, contorted face. She could barely make out her words between sobs as the girl pointed to the bath, 'I'm not taking me clothes off. Not in front of you lot! Look, there's blood in that there bath. I'm not gettin' in de' that!'

The two screws chuckled, and the short, cruel-eyed one shouted, 'You'll do as you're told. You duffed-up heifer!' Her partner found the insult amusing, silently watching with glee.

But the mother-to-be wasn't having it. She wasn't taking her clothes off for anyone. She wiped her mouth with the back of her hand and stood rigid, refusing to budge an inch. Shivering with cold, Tina quickly put on her bra and knickers, re-fixing the used Dr White's sanitary towel within.

Another uniformed woman appeared and gently steered her, half-dressed, towards an open door that gave access to a long black-and-white tiled corridor. Her custodian closed the door after them and walked on, her tapping heels echoing in the quiet. They came to a heavy green steel-barred gate at the end of the hallway, and the prison officer nodded for

Tina to stand aside. She watched as a large key was extracted from the uniformed woman's pocket and used to open the gate. They passed through, and the screw turned to lock the gate again.

Tina at last had opportunity to study her. The PO wore a long-sleeved pale blue shirt with breast pockets and numbered epaulettes on her shoulders. A chain hung from the waist of her black trousers, and the keys were kept tucked away in one of their deep pockets. Tina noticed that her shoes were well polished, but black, flat, and ugly. What an old man would wear.

Tina tried her hardest to keep calm. She looked around and whispered, 'Where am I, missus?'

Surprisingly kind blue eyes looked back. 'You'll see, love,' the woman replied. 'Come now, get dressed.'

In the changing room area, a trembling Tina finished putting on her only pair of jeans. Before moving from Gransha, her sister Caitlin had given her their daddy's Aran to keep her warm and cheer her up – she swore she could still smell him on it as she put it on over a grey-white T-shirt. In the distance, she could hear the ongoing maniacal cries of the pregnant girl and looked at her warden with worry.

The warden understood and assured her. 'Listen, love. You've passed through admissions in Armagh Gaol. It'll be okay if you do as you're told and follow your OC's orders. You're lucky to have Maureen Molony watching over you.'

An OC? What the heck was an OC then? Tina wondered.

'My name is Quirk,' said the officer as Tina finished dressing. 'I'm gonna take you to A-Wing, where you can get yourself settled down.'

Tina could only nod with a half-smile. Her head felt fuzzy as she tried to grasp what was happening. This wasn't good. She shouldn't be in this place.

Quietly, they continued their journey through another series of corridors with interlocking gates until they finally reached the wing.

As she stepped down into a cell through a small dark green door within a grey-painted frame, Tina found herself in a stone-built room with walls painted half yellow, half cream. It was a tiny space but somehow contained two wrought-iron beds, two white plastic chairs, the smallest wardrobe Tina had ever seen, and a couple of black plastic chamber pots.

There was a small, scratched table and a single battered-looking bedside locker. On top of an empty bed lay two neatly folded coarse brown blankets, a pillow, a pillowcase, and a pair of greyish sheets.

She held herself straight as she was introduced to a young woman who sat with one leg half on and half off the other bed. Although she looked dog-tired, she was extremely pretty, with curly black, shoulder-length hair and a heavy fringe over a pair of pale blue eyes. Her creamy skin was clear and perfect, her lips full. She wore a faded red Beatles T-shirt over a pair of flared black-and-white floral trousers. Tina felt a tinge of envy. The woman's skin was nothing like hers, it was surreal. What she'd give for skin like that.

The girl looked up as soon as she saw Tina, threw her book to one side and smiled warmly as she patted her bed, inviting Tina to join her.

'Sit down, love, and let's see what we've got here,' she said.

Quirk nodded and, whispering to the OC, tapped the side of her head, 'She's fragile that one, delicate like. Not sure she's all there – best keep an eye.'

'Will do,' Maureen Molony answered, watching as the heavy cell door was semi-closed by the seasoned guard who had a reputation for being firm but fair.

Quirk, a married woman in her late fifties, had long served as a prison officer in Armagh. Many long-term inmates felt she was unhappy with the recent prison changes, betting she'd be for the off soon with full benefits.

Tina took in her surroundings, shook her head in confusion and said in a low voice, 'I don't understand. I shouldn't be here. Why am I here?'

Maureen Molony sighed. These girls seemed to get younger and younger. Earlier in the year, they'd had a couple of youngsters of no more than fourteen or fifteen incarcerated inside this fucking shithole. It was madness.

Maureen had been in Armagh Gaol for eighteen months so far, initially interned without trial. The worst part was not knowing what the charge was, why she'd been taken, or when she might get home. Every day, she'd lived with the hope of release until the day she found out she'd been framed by a supergrass who claimed she'd bombed a teashop in Derry. After that, she was sentenced to fifteen years. The maddening part was, it was one act of war she hadn't committed.

Maureen felt old, way beyond her twenty-eight years. Some nights, she wondered how long she could keep herself right, keep the order in here. But she had to. She'd no choice, and she wasn't for giving up now. Hadn't the Provo leadership made her Officer in Command (OC) over the prisoners? These women, her comrades, needed her to look out for them, especially the older ones. Some of the poor critters were grannies, for God's sake! She sure as hell wasn't going to let this so-called prison establishment break them. Not if she had anything to do with it.

Some time ago, they were treated as political prisoners; they could wear their own clothes and move freely between cells and wings. In addition, they were allowed educational privileges, but no Irish classes – only Spanish and French. A lot of them spoke Irish already and Maureen supposed it was just as well. The chances of one of them jetting off to Saint Tropez or Madrid any time soon? About as likely as the Pope popping in for a pint!

She grabbed a blanket and wrapped it around the new girl, who was cadaver-thin with dark-circled eyes and who looked more child-like than woman in the huge, man-sized Aran she wore. Her legs barely filled her jeans. Her red corkscrew hair appeared knotted and unwashed. It was the skin that concerned Maureen the most. It was red-raw and bleeding a little in places. She noticed how the girl scratched herself using the sleeve of the Aran, with what looked like faded bloodstains on it. Dr Harris would have to see her. To Maureen, it looked like raging eczema, red, raw, and angry, like her skin was ready to split.

Other than the state of her skin, Tina reminded Maureen of her younger sister, the one she missed like mad. As gently as she could, she rubbed a blanket up and down the girl's bony shoulders, trying to warm her. With a quiet sigh, she looked up to the heavens and sent up a quick prayer. Then, speaking softly, she shared some vital advice with her new cellmate.

'The first two things to remember about this place, love. Never talk about why you're here, and don't say much about yourself unless you trust them. For now, stick close to me. You can trust me, all right? Tell me anythin'. What's your name?'

'Tina. Tina McLaughlin.'

Ah, shit! Maureen knew straight away who the girl was and her alleged crimes. She also knew her brother, Martin. By Christ. That Derry lark was some fuck-up!

She'd heard how the wee girl had been groomed by that wanker, Kieran Kelly. Without orders, he'd tortured and killed a Brit. If that wasn't enough, the eejit tried to blow up the fuckin' City Hotel in Derry. Didn't go off. Served the bastard right. Got himself shot first, then the poor bishop. Dickhead thought he was untouchable.

What followed was horrific. Night after night, the streets of Derry were on fire, constant rioting, and more than a few innocents shot dead by the Brits and RUC. The poor bishop, loved by all republicans, would be turning in his grave. He'd have hated the bloodshed, the loss of innocent life. *God rest him*. Everyone knew it would've been catastrophic for the Cause if that bomb had gone off, there were plenty of much-needed people in that room, people who could get things done.

Maureen found herself lost for words. They sat in the stillness until a frantic pounding rattled the cell door. She rose and opened it to find a small, dumpy, grey-haired woman calling out, 'Maureen! Quick, you're needed!'

The OC closed her eyes and took a slow breath. 'What is it this time?' she said, weary.

The dumpy woman, well wound up, explained, 'It's that one again. The new girl. She's fightin' with Florence. You'd better get up there!'

Adding a dramatic undertone, she whispered. 'I think Florence is gonna kill her. I really do!'

Fuck it! Maureen swore before grabbing Tina's hand and leading her through the arched door to a cell at the very end of A-wing, near the chapel and opposite the toilets. She daren't leave the mite alone – at least not yet.

Chapter Ten

This Has to Stop!

Armagh Gaol had been built in 1783 on top of an old military barracks. Two main wings ran out from the reception area, called 'the circle': A-Wing, two storeys high, and B-Wing, three. Each held 140 cells. The year before, over 130 male political prisoners had been moved there from the overcrowded Crumlin Road, though they were long gone now, most likely to the damp, makeshift men's prison at the Kesh.

The Kesh had been hacked together out of a disused RAF station outside Lisburn. At first, internees were split into their paramilitary groups and crammed into Nissen huts once used by the air force. The place was never fit for purpose. Thin walls froze them in winter and roasted them in summer. The toilets stank, the food was slop, and if you fell sick, you were lucky to see a doctor. Packed into cages under guards who thrived on cruelty, the men swung between despair and fury, and it was no surprise unrest was always bubbling near the surface.

A year ago, Armagh Gaol had held two women only, but today it housed around eighty, some of whom were pregnant. Seventy of the eighty inmates were sentenced, remanded, or interned political prisoners. The remaining ten were seen as '*normal criminals.*'

Sadly, one woman who'd recently given birth had been forced to hand her tiny baby over to social services only the day before. She remained quiet, unapproachable, and lonely in her cell downstairs, staring into an empty cot. The screws didn't even have the sensitivity to take it away, just left it there.

Following the funeral of Provo volunteer Jim Saunders, the dumpy woman, Florence Shields, got herself arrested after getting caught up in rioting. There'd been no defence to the charge of 'conduct likely to lead to a breach of the peace', and she'd been handed a mandatory six-month sentence. Florence had accepted her fate, but she was struggling with a new arrival who now shared her cell. Katherine 'Katie' Davis, like many girls before her, couldn't cope with being locked up.

The OC understood Katie's fears. She had five children ranging from two to ten years of age, all of whom had been taken from their home and were now being looked after by their elderly grandparents on both sides of the family. Like many of the women's spouses, Katie's husband, John, was in the Kesh, serving twenty years for planting a bomb in Belfast's City Centre.

Week by week, the screws warned the women not to complain about the conditions in the gaol. If they did, they were threatened by the PO's, who told them there was every chance their kids would be taken into care - a nightmare for any mother and Katie was terrified. Word had reached her that both sets of grandparents were finding it hard to cope, and that Social Services were looking at other options.

The agitated woman had started picking on her comrades for no particular reason, and by now, she was getting on everyone's nerves. Tempers were wearing thin, and Maureen, as the OC, knew she'd have to have a quiet but firm word with Katie and get her to pipe down and fall in with the rest of them. As it was, everyone was struggling.

As Maureen was about to step into the cell where the two women were yelling their heads off, a screw blocked her path. It was PO Smyth, using her stocky frame to hold the doorway, baton held firm across the entrance.

Smyth had no idea that she'd been aptly nicknamed the 'Black Widow' by the inmates. She did, however, know that she was disliked not only by the women, but by most of her fellow POs. Was she bothered? Not a diddy bit.

She loved this job. It gave her unfettered access to the Papists she so vehemently hated. Beating the fuck out of them, humiliating them when they first arrived, was what she lived for. She was short, thickset and mannish-looking, with unkempt bushy brows and shoulder-length black greasy hair slicked away from her face and tied into a lifeless ponytail.

It was funny how it was always the small things you noticed, Maureen thought as she stared into Smyth's eyes, noting they were yellowed, runny and bloodshot. Point to note: the cow was a drinker.

'Let me through, Smyth,' Maureen said, gazing stonily at the screw. By now, their faces were almost touching and Maureen's senses were spot on – Smyth reeked.

Fury simmered in her chest as she repeated her request, each word slow and deliberate, leaving no doubt she meant every syllable.

'Let the two of them sort it out,' Smyth replied with amusement. 'See what happens.'

With a glacial stare, Maureen warned her.

'I don't think so, Smyth. I swear on the Archangel Gabriel himself, if you don't let me through, I'll go straight to Father McGuire. It's Tuesday tomorrow and he'll be here. I only have to say the word.'

The old priest was well popular among the Republican prisoners for fighting their corner, which he did with vigour and at every opportunity. He'd go between the men's prison and the women's, hounding the governors. It seemed he never stopped nagging Armagh's governor, driving him crazy about the women's pitiful sanitary facilities, the inedible food, denied requests for family visits, and the many other plights the poor girls faced.

Armagh's governor, in turn, took out his frustration on the POs, who then passed it down to the women. A vicious circle. The gaolers were always looking for a way to get one over on the inmates. Still, depending on the tension outside, they weren't stupid. They had to tread carefully.

Father McGuire didn't know it, but most of the women panicked like feck when they saw him walk into their wing and head for a cell on any other day than a Tuesday. He was always, always the bearer of bad news: either a family illness or, worse, a death.

PO Smyth knew fine well Father McGuire could cause trouble for her. Stubborn as they come, him swanning about dressed all in black. It was pure pride that stopped her giving in.

'I don't give a shit if the Queen of England herself is comin',' she whispered menacingly before attempting, one last time, to push Maureen back from the cell door.

Maureen's gaze sharpened. A small group of women, all shapes and ages, were closing in, forming a loose semi-circle behind the PO. Smyth snarled at them to move back, but they didn't budge. Out the corner of her eye, she spotted Quirk edging closer, pretending to watch the women.

Resentment flared in Smyth. There wasn't a chance in hell Quirk would lift a finger to help her if things kicked off. Spineless. A hundred per cent Pope-lover, always trying to play nice.

'Smyth. For the last time, let me through,' Maureen snapped, her irritation growing.

The standoff lasted as long as Smyth could count to fifteen in her head, then, somewhat reluctantly, she stepped aside. In all the commotion, no one noticed that the cell behind them had gone silent. Quiet as a morgue. The two warring inmates stood fixed to the spot, their quarrel forgotten as they focused on the scene outside their cell door.

Maureen reached for Tina, gently nudged her inside and sat her down on a plastic chair. Turning to the two exhausted women, she confronted them, seething with anger.

'Girls, what the fuck is going on here? For pity's sake, this has to stop!'

Chapter Eleven

Peeling Spuds

Anne Heaney sat by the window in the 'good room' of their house, looking at the frosty scene outside. Christmas was coming, and she dreaded it.

Her mother, Liz, had done her best to decorate the place with red and white homemade paper chains, well-used pink tinsel and a green plastic Christmas tree, missing several of its bottom branches. Multi-coloured flashing lights draped between school-made decorations, whilst the tree lights glowed out onto the street.

She glanced around at the room's sparse furnishings. A decrepit, moth-eaten, flower-patterned armchair sat as if on guard in the corner facing the door. She remembered the day the shiny new fake leather three-piece sofa that once stood pride of place was delivered and how excited they'd all been, including her arsehole father. She almost laughed at its condition now. Molly, their cat, had been at it. Its stretched, pliable fabric was riddled with scratches that snaked up and down the top and edges of its worn seats and cushions.

Anne looked out at the street again and groaned. I'm so feckin' bored, she thought, as her finger traced a raindrop flowing down the windowpane. Another spasm shot through what remained of her right leg.

'Jesus. Fucking. Christ!' she hissed.

As suggested by her doctor, she grabbed and squeezed her thigh forcefully. The pain was fierce. She took a breath, held it for a few seconds, then let it out. All the while repeating to herself, 'In, out, in, out, in, out,' until the agony eased a little.

For weeks she'd been making the 150-mile round trip by bus to Musgrave Park Hospital in Belfast, where they were trying to fit her with a prosthetic limb. What she'd been given was a clumsy, one-size-fits-all contraption that would take time to master. Her mother had urged her to accept the hospital's offer when, out of the blue, a letter arrived saying she was entitled to one. Until then, the family hadn't even known she was eligible, and, rather naively, none of them had ever thought to ask.

Since the attack at the City Hotel last year, she'd barely seen Caitlin. These hospital trips were the closest thing she had to a social life now. The longer she stayed at home, the harder it got to leave. She didn't want pity, didn't want people staring, but she missed her friend. Only Caitlin truly understood. She'd been there when the bomb went off. Seen it all. The chaos. The blood. The moment Anne's life changed for good. The one tiny, minuscule consolation, if it could be called that, was the fuss and attention she got from John Ballantyne, aka 'Porkie'.

Porkie worked in a local slaughterhouse and started to call at the house after Anne got out of the hospital, and did his best to get a date out of her. Short and thinning on top, he had stocky arms, thick legs, and a flabby beer middle instead of a waistline. His face was pudgy, greasy, and riddled with yellow-topped acne. To add fuel to the fire, his doorstep-sized teeth were stained with tobacco and no one could deny it, but he was friggin' rotten to look at.

To begin with, she flat-out refused to entertain him, but it soon became embarrassing for whoever answered the door to keep telling him to get lost. In the end, and without asking, her mother, Liz, invited him in for a cuppa. As he sat at the kitchen table, Anne drank her tea in stony quiet, forced to sit through his pointless ramblings. Not that she ever got a word in — the idiot never shut up.

At least ten years older than Anne, he was once pally with her da and, for all that she could remember, he'd had a mad crush on her. As a teenager, she'd found him gross. She still did. Back then, she wouldn't be seen dead talking to him, never mind fancying him, but given his dogged persistence, she was very slowly, painfully slowly, warming to him.

But it wasn't Porkie that bothered Anne most. It was Dickie.

Kevin McDaid, aka 'Dickie,' was a total slimeball. Obese with scrawny legs, hair all tufted up, a snub nose, and dull, fishy grey eyes. But the worst part? It was that creepy grin he'd always give her, plastered across his big football-shaped face. It had to be said, he looked even worse than Porkie, and that was being polite.

His breath? Christ almighty. Dickie was an all-out worm, and the very thought of him made Anne's skin crawl, made everyone's skin crawl. She could imagine it, like one of those cartoon characters, a human slug. Years ago, she and Caitlin used to cry laughing, watching the duo hanging around the park. Like Dick Dastardly and Muttley – only slower, and a hundred times thicker.

Nearly every day, Anne's mammy would go on and on at her. *'It's a miracle you're alive. You should be grateful!'* Or, *'You're better now, deal with it...'*

Anne had to tune her out. Same conversation. Same old story. Ad nauseam. God forgive her, but sometimes she thought if she could make it down to the Foyle, she'd jump straight in. Then all this would be over. The pain, the misery – gone in seconds.

Anne was smart enough to know that such thoughts meant – she knew she was in trouble. Each day, her anxiety grew more and more. The mind-numbing boredom of her daily routine didn't help. During the day, those still living in the house were either at work or school, though, bless their cotton socks, they did their best to cheer her up when they got in. All the same, she felt like she was walking a fine line with them, her constant mood swings growing worse and worse.

Although her mammy nagged her, Liz Heaney was amazing, considering how tired and sad she was after losing her last baby within a few months of the wee thing being born. Anne would never forget the tiny white coffin her eldest brother carried at the sombre funeral. For weeks, the house remained quiet in its grief.

Their da's neglect was yet another cross to bear, especially his habit of vanishing for weeks on end. Each time, they lived with the constant dread of a bang at the door, either the army storming in for a raid or someone turning up with bad news. Bad news was everywhere. No matter where you looked.

'Ah, fuck it!' Anne groaned, heaving herself up from the chair and deciding tea was the answer.

In Derry, if you felt like shite, the first thing anyone did was stick the kettle on. Didn't matter if your leg was hanging off — someone, somewhere, would shout, *'I'll make us a wee cuppa tea with sugar?'* As if sugar made a difference!

The thought made her smile. Her and Caitlin were always saying a cuppa could fix about anything short of death.

She shuffled into the kitchen, feeling every bit as tired as she looked. The tiny kitchen was so different from Caitlin's, with enough space for a table in front of a Belfast kitchen sink, an antiquated stove and, on the wall above the small fridge, the obligatory portrait of the Pope with the customary set of rosary beads barely hanging on. Their washing machine, that broke down when most needed, stood forlornly in the corner. No money to repair it.

'All right, love?' she heard her mother ask from the sink where she was peeling what looked like a ton of potatoes.

'Grand,' Anne answered.

'Mr Ballantyne coming to see you today, is he?'

'Probably. Highlight of my day.' Anne replied.

'Ah, bless him. Sure he's not that bad – if you close your eyes!' she laughed. 'Has he gone in for a snog with ye yet?' Liz asked, a rare glint of mischief in her eye.

Anne screwed up her face, shivering at the very thought of it. 'Are you friggin' serious, Mammy? What's the shape of him? I'd rather hang meself!'

'Och, give him a break, love. At least he's tryin',' Liz insisted, her potato knife paused mid-air. 'I'll tell ye – that wee fella's been good to us. I know he's older an' all that, but he's the only one who can cheer you up. At least a bit. I have to be honest with ye, you're like a bear with a sore head these days.'

'Well, thanks for that,' Anne scoffed. She sighed and gave in. 'Wanna hand with those spuds?'

'Aye, go on then. I'm nearly there.' Liz moved aside to make room by the sink. She held the knife carefully as she watched what had once been her beautiful, vibrant, and incessantly funny daughter hobbling over.

Life had taken a turn for the worse. Liz's baby-bearing days were well and truly over, and the lump of a man she'd married had hardly been in touch since the baby's funeral. If it weren't for the older girls working, they'd be out on the street. *Lousy bastard!*

His excuse? Told her he was a high-ranking Provo on the run, didn't he? Aye right. Some Provo. The same boy would piss himself at the sound of a car backfiring.

Anne? Now, Anne was a whole different kettle of fish. The moods, the tears, the never-ending silence. At times, Liz didn't know what to do with her. She'd even tried getting Caitlin to call in, hoping it might cheer Anne up, but sure the girl had troubles of her own. She didn't blame her for what happened that day on Shipquay Street, but, by Christ, she could have kept in touch more. Liz, as any Mammy would be, was raging.

Chapter Twelve

A Couple of Buns and a Candy-striped Bag

As Liz was about to wash the spuds, there was a loud whack at the front door.

Quickly washing her hands and rubbing them dry with a tea towel, she made her way out of the kitchen, half shouting over her shoulder to Anne: 'That'll be your beau now!'

Anne shook her head in amused despair, placed her knife down, and shuffled to the kitchen door to look down the hallway.

'Jesus, Mammy. Give over, will ye!' she hissed. Liz looked back at her with a cheeky grin before opening the door.

Indeed, it was. Porkie. Standing there, proud as a drenched peacock, water dripping off his ears and nose. She tried her utmost to keep a straight face, her lips twitching as he asked, through the hailstones bouncing off him.

'How you doin', Mrs Heaney? That's someday, eh? Like the feckin' Arctic out there. Freeze the balls off a snowman!'

'It's bad, John. Hurry up and get yourself in before ye' catch your death!' Liz cried, her voice full of amusement.

'Ah, thanks, Mrs Heaney,' Porkie replied, stepping inside and shaking himself down.

Liz took a final, despairing look at him. God, but he was fat, not cuddly fat, but fat, fat! His effort at a shave was a disaster too – all red nicks and milky spots dotted across most of his face.

With little success, Porkie tried to flatten what hair he had left before stepping through. With no proper coat, just a light jacket over a red-and-white chequered shirt and an ugly purple tie, the poor fella was soaked to the bone. His flared trousers, a fraction too long, trailed like a pair of wet curtains, nearly drowning his shoes, which squelched as he stepped inside.

Liz thought he looked more teenager than grown man, him standing there holding a bunch of pathetic-looking carnations soaked in a waterlogged bit of plastic. Probably got them in the wee shop at Stones Corner, or could've easily nicked them from the cemetery. In the other hand, she saw a candy-striped paper bag. *Buns*. What a sight he was, like a drowned rat trying to look cool.

Still fighting the urge to laugh, Liz led him down the hallway towards the kitchen.

When they reached Anne, Porkie swiped more water off his jacket and, with his arm stuck out stiff as a board; held out the soggy flowers.

'All right, Anne?' he said. 'Here. These'll cheer ye up.'

Seriously. Anne thought.

'Your wile good, thanks,' she replied without thought, tossing the half-dead stems into the sink on top of the potato peels.

'Cuppa tea, John?' Liz asked, squeezing between the pair and throwing her daughter a dagger look. A silent warning to behave herself or else.

'That'd be great. Thanks, Mrs Heaney. Listen, and I keep tellin' ye, it's *Porkie*. Everyone calls me *Porkie*.' He laughed, 'Bet you can't say why?'

Neither woman dared to answer, and bewildered by their expressions, Porkie let it go but added cheerfully, 'Sure look, I even brought us a treat.' He searched his jacket and produced a soggy paper bag containing a few squashed iced buns.

Like they were scorching hot, Anne used her index finger and thumb to take the offerings and put them on a side plate.

Wanting to turn up her nose but knowing Liz was watching, she'd no choice but to say, 'Thanks. They're lovely.'

Liz needed to get out of the kitchen before she peed herself laughing, so suggested, 'Give us that jacket, Porkie, I'll hang it by the front door, let it drip.'

She took it with a smile and left the lovebirds to it, giggling as she headed down the hallway. The second she reached the front room, she doubled over, laughing so hard she had to clamp her legs together in case she showed herself up!

Back in the kitchen, Porkie took a chair and watched Anne put the kettle on.

'So... you're all right then?' he asked again, a tad anxious. *Christ, but she was in some mood the night.*

'Said I was, didn't I?!' Anne snapped.

'Aye. You did. Sorry.' One of those mega, awkward moments.

'Heard the news?' he asked.

'Not interested' was Anne's only reply.

He ignored her and said. 'Ye should be. There's a whole lot of them posh ones up in Belfast, Sunningdoyle or Sunnington or somethin'. Tryin' to sort this place out. Them up from the Irish government an' all. Could end all this trouble. Change everythin'.'

Anne didn't give a toss who was where, with who, or doing what. She couldn't even be bothered to answer.

Once the tea was made, she sat down alongside him, noting her mother's wilful absence. The cow was obviously leaving her to it. What seemed like a lifetime passed before Porkie finally stopped talking, got to his feet and announced it was time to go.

Anne knew she'd been sore on him, but today she wasn't up for it, he'd caught her at her worst. Feeling the tiniest twinge of guilt, she faked disappointment and pointed to the plate.

'Ye sure? There's a bun left if you want it?' He'd already hoovered down the others.

Touched by her fake concern and to Anne's horror, he planted himself back into the chair, asked for another cuppa and wolfed down the last iced bun, crumbs flying and all the while cracking jokes so bad they made her want to tear her hair out.

As soon as he'd left, Anne slumped by the TV with her mother and sisters. Two hours. Two bloody hours she'd been trapped in that kitchen with him. Not one of them came to her rescue. She couldn't believe it. Was raging.

Her murderous glare met her mother's, and she was about to speak when Liz, aware she was in big trouble and about to get her head bitten off, burst out laughing and cried.

'I know, love! Left ye for ages. Don't say anythin'! I know!' Playfully, she tossed a cushion at Anne who caught it but refused to crack a smile.

'I can't believe you, Mammy. You knew he'd drive me up the walls!' she snapped, hurling the cushion straight back at her. She wasn't in the mood for jokes. Not one bit. Eyes fixed on the TV, she went into a huff and blanked them.

Liz stopped laughing and turned her eyes up at her other girls, *there she goes, off on one again.*

Anne caught the look, cursed under her breath, and struggled up the narrow stairs. She slammed the door of her box room as if that might shut the whole bloody lot of them out. She'd had enough.

Given she loved everything to do with the 1950s, her bedroom walls were adorned with film posters, including *The Quiet Man* and *High Society*. A single wardrobe was positioned next to the window. It had once held the flamboyant, full swing-petticoat 1950s skirts she'd made herself, but now merely a few plain everyday dresses hung on wire coat hangers. There wasn't a shoe in sight – certainly no sign of her once much-loved stilettos.

There wasn't enough space in the room for a dressing table. Instead, a small rectangular mirror hung on the wall with coloured glass necklaces draped over the edge. Looking out of the place in the corner was an old tea chest, one she hadn't paid attention to in a very long time. Seeing it made her release a huge, painful sigh.

Sitting on her bed, she began to remove the prosthetic leg. Unbuckling the straps one by one, she felt relief as the pressure eased. During Porkie's visit, she'd had a few sore spasms but refused to give in to them or let him see her flinch.

Throwing the cumbersome contraption across the room, she fell onto the carpeted floor and dragged herself across to the metal-rimmed tea chest. She carefully removed the books that lay on top and put them aside before raising the stubborn lid.

Tears hovered in her eyes as she looked down. Her shoes, her beautiful, coloured stilettos that she'd worked and saved up for over the years, now lay covered in dust, destined never to be worn again. Her joy in life was gone. Her existence now consisted of pain, frustration, and loneliness. The dream of meeting a rich, blond, tanned Yank, who would sweep her off her feet, marry her and take her to America, had been ruined the moment that bomb went off.

That fucking bomb had, within a matter of seconds, robbed the Derry girl of all her dreams and ambitions.

Chapter Thirteen

Soul Mates

Father Cathal Connolly was one of six children born in Boston, USA, who, at a very young age, moved to Tipperary with his American mother and Irish father to live and work on his grandparents' farm. Not long after landing, his father, who had led the IRA North Tipperary brigade, was killed in action.

Young Cathal would never forget the pain on his ma's face at the funeral, which was led by a lone piper and attended by most, if not all, of the village and many of his father's comrades. He'd watched her, his heart jagged with pity at her red, swollen, lifeless eyes and her incessant tears that fell onto her one and only threadbare 'good' coat.

His parents had enjoyed one of those rare marriages. Soul mates who lived for and loved each other. Their simple cottage teemed daily with laughter and love. He'd been lucky up to then; all of them had. It had been a very happy home. Sadly, after his father's death, everything went downhill when their mother became a religious fanatic. Week after week, she'd insist all seven of them sit together by the fire and say the rosary 'for your poor da's soul' at least three or four times a day. It didn't take long before the young man sought a way out of the grieving household by joining the Pallottine Order and becoming a priest – both to appease his ma, but more so to gain a better education.

On this particular evening, Cathal stood staring into an open fire, its fierce burning flames casting shadows across his face in the dining room of St Mary's parochial house in Creggan. A tall, thick-set man with curly marmalade-coloured hair, his naturally sad, light brown eyes, were framed by slightly bushy eyebrows. He could be described as handsome in a rugged kind of way. Tonight, though, he looked like a man who'd walked into Hell itself. No overstatement after the day he'd had. He took a deep breath, raised his chin, and closed his eyes for a brief moment before opening them. All had been good up 'til then.

He'd taken the phone call he was expecting from the States to finalise some last-minute details for his forthcoming trip to Boston and noted the American voice had sounded excited and keen.

'So, we're all set. I've got you speaking at each of the dinners, and we've kept the numbers to a minimum. Quality over quantity, eh? We can expect to raise around five thousand dollars per night, if not more.'

He'd responded quietly so as not to disturb his fellow priests upstairs and said gratefully, 'That's good. As long as the dollars keep rolling in.'

At the beginning of the Troubles in 1969, an Irishman in New York started an organisation with the mission of 'Aiding the Unity of Ireland' and supporting the peace process. Cathal had been asked to help NORAID raise funds. He was well respected as a natural orator and also as a staunch Republican from a hero's family. Everything was in hand, and the caller had agreed to keep in touch as the line clicked off, both men satisfied with what was to happen next.

A while later, the time had come for Cathal to visit the sick at the local hospital, Altnagelvin, but as he was about to leave the house, a panicked and shaken Father McGuire, eldest of the three priests who lived at St Mary's, came crashing through the front door, calling out for him.

As soon as he'd spotted him, he grabbed Cathal and cried, 'Ah, you're here. I need you, son. Quick, with me!'

The young priest had barely time to pick up his jacket and hat as he was pulled with surprising strength through the door and down the parochial house steps.

'What's going on? Where we going?' he cried, as he took two steps at a time to keep up with the older man, who suddenly seemed superhuman.

'I'll explain in a sec,' McGuire urged as they reached his red Ford Anglia, where he threw his keys across the bonnet at Cathal and said, 'You drive. I'll tell ye on the way.'

Cathal was relieved to drive, having experienced a few near-misses with his colleague, whose eyesight was deteriorating at a startling rate. The older priest had been warned numerous times by the RUC for his haphazard driving, but had paid no heed.

The car sped off as Father McGuire explained. 'It's Majella McLaughlin. I just met Maggie McFadden, the neighbour. Told me the poor woman has only gone and hung herself. Such a waste. That family's been to hell and back lately. Hurry up, will ye? 30 Blamfield Street!'

Cathal knew from what he'd been told, his mentor still carried a lot of guilt over Tina McLaughlin. She'd turned up at St Mary's in tears not long before the bomb scare, begging for help. But he'd brushed her off, caught up in his own stuff – some even said he was hungover. He'd never forgiven himself. Not for a second. He tried to make up for it ever since, done all he could, but with little luck as to getting her out.

As they pulled up outside the pebble-dashed house, Cathal noticed a small crowd had gathered round number thirty's broken front gate, likely hoping for news or being downright nosey.

The minute the two priests scrambled out of the car, Tommy O'Reilly came running down the path.

His usual khaki parka drowned him now. He'd once been a big man, broad across the shoulders, but lately he'd lost a power of weight. His cheeks were flushed, his blue eyes glassy with tears as he leaned in close to the older priest, resting a trembling hand on his arm.

'She couldn't take it, Father. First Patrick, then Martin, and now our Tina in Armagh. All too much.'

'I know, son,' Father McGuire murmured, his hand rising to the big man's shoulder, strong and steady. 'I know. Where is the poor woman?'

'I took her down off the door, Father. Had to. She was just hangin' there, ye see. A sight I'll take to me grave. She's on her bed now. Worst thing I've ever seen in me life. I just... I wish we'd kept a closer eye on her.'

The men made their way into the house, taking the narrow staircase to the main bedroom. The same room the dead woman's innocent husband, Patrick had been dragged out of, naked and beaten, by the Brits.

Cathal looked in horrified shock at what he saw in the foul-smelling room. He'd seen his fair share of the dead, but this had to be one of the worst. The woman lay on the bed, her eyes bulging from a barely recognisable face, a rope mark on her neck standing out, livid purple against her pale skin. He had to turn away and look elsewhere. A faded flower print covered stool stood beneath a three-drawer dressing table that held a tarnished silver hairbrush set and very few toiletries on its glass-covered top. He glanced at the black-and-white photographs alongside and then saw an unopened envelope with Tommy's name written on it in neat, cursive handwriting.

Tommy and Cathal couldn't bear the sight of Majella lying on the bed, so out of respect, decided to wait outside.

But Father McGuire stayed where he was, a deep sorrowful hurt overwhelming him as he thought back to Majella's wedding day. She'd been radiant then, full of life. He'd recently been ordained, and it was the first wedding he'd ever performed. Majella and Patrick McLaughlin, proud as anything. He remembered the family baptisms, the First Communions, the Confirmations, all the special moments. They'd been wonderful parents, natural. Did everything they could for their young family.

Now this. A tragedy through and through.

After saying a prayer, the old priest stepped out of the bedroom, Cathal noticed his silent tears and, to allow him privacy, turned away and spoke to Tommy,

'The eldest girl, Caitlin... does she know yet?' he asked.

Tommy shook his head. 'Naw, not yet. Maggie from next door, she's gone with her hubby, Charlie, to get her. Should be here any time now. Maggie'll tell her, knows Caitlin a lifetime.'

His words hung in the air until Cathal, hearing the front door open, rushed to Majella's bedroom door to make sure it was shut tight.

All the men stood at the top of the stairs, blocking the landing. Father Connolly had only ever seen Caitlin at Mass a handful of times. She'd always seemed distant, hard to read. All he cared about was that she shouldn't see their mother lying like that. He heard her before he saw her.

'Mammy! Mammy!' Her cry resounded from the hallway as she charged halfway up the stairs, her eyes wide and clutching a scrunched tissue in one hand. She tried to push past the wall of men, frantic with tears. 'Let me through! Tommy, tell them. Tell them to let me through!'

Fortunately, Maggie McFadden trudged up the stairs behind her and, pulling Caitlin back, openly wept and pleaded, 'Come down with me, love. *Please.*'

Caitlin screeched as her eyes sought Tommy's. 'How could she do it, Tommy? She's gone and left me!'

Her voice broke as she crumpled into her uncle's arms. He held her tight, swaying slightly, but saying nothing. There was nothing to say. Maggie stood a few steps behind, her hands wrung tight in front of her. Rarely was she lost for words, but now she stood still as a statue, her mouth literally hanging open. Shock, sorrow, all of it, but behind it, a terrible sense of relief. She shouldn't be feeling relief, though she knew why. No more screaming in the night for you, Majella. No more raids. No more awful news. *You'll find peace now, my lovely friend. With Patrick.* She crossed herself and whispered, 'Sleep now, love and rest in peace.'

Meanwhile, Tommy stared through the landing window at the growing crowd below. He looked at Father McGuire and asked, 'What the heck are they waitin' for?'

'Pay no attention,' the priest answered ruefully, before adding, 'We need to call the doctor, Tommy. And the police.'

'Aye. Right. I'll go next door and do it. I don't want Caitlin anywhere near that room, need to keep her downstairs.' Without hesitation, the priest agreed and bowed his head in silent prayer.

In the kitchen below, Cathal sat with Caitlin and Maggie. He looked at the girl, sobbing quietly as she rocked back and forth. Her neighbour lifted a packet of cigarettes from the windowsill and quickly lit one, her hands still shaking. He watched as she half-opened the back door to let the smoke out. He needed to say something, anything, to fill the void.

'I'm so sorry, Caitlin, Maggie. I know it's been a horrible time for you this past while.'

Caitlin couldn't reply, but nodded her head out of respect.

'We'll wait for Father McGuire and Tommy. Say a few prayers, if that's okay?' he suggested. 'Be prepared, it's likely a doctor and the police will turn up soon.' He paused. 'Given the circumstances.'

Caitlin gasped, then lost it. 'I'm not having any of those bastards in this house! You hear me, Father? Keep them away from Mammy. This is all their fault, them and the bloody Brits!' She jumped up from the table and marched around the kitchen, raving about how much she hated the peelers, the Brits and anyone who had anything to do with them.

After phoning for the doctor, Tommy burst into the kitchen, pale as a sheet, his eyes on Caitlin. 'Sweet Jesus. What's happened? What is it, love?!'

She pointed at the sitting priest and shrieked, 'It's him! He's just told me the peelers are coming. I'm not letting them anywhere near her, Tommy.' Tearing off down the hallway to lock the front door, she cried, 'I'm locking this door now!'

Tommy shot Father Connolly a cautioning look as if to ask what he'd said, then ran after his niece.

In the kitchen, Maggie braced herself. She pulled her shoulders back, lifted her chin, and looked straight at the young priest, almost afraid to ask what was really on her mind.

'So, Father. I suppose the poor woman's bound for hell now she's topped herself? Youse won't be lettin' her get buried next to Patrick. Is that it?'

Cathal had been half expecting this and dropped a quiet sigh. 'No, Maggie. Thankfully, times have changed, and so has the Church's thinking. You've no need to worry. We'll take care of Majella. Get her next to Patrick. God rest her soul.'

Chapter Fourteen

Alice

Nearly a year. A whole bloody year!

That's how long Alice Wallace, once code-named Iowa, had sat behind this lousy old desk, filling in one mind-numbing form after another. She looked at the two tatty wooden trays on the edge of her desk, 'In' and 'Out', both half full, but couldn't be arsed to get enthusiastic about anything in this god-forsaken dump.

Her day had barely started, and, by God, she dreaded it already, like she did every other day spent here. She was bored, bored, bored beyond belief, and it was killing her.

She heard shouts from the courtyard outside and, on her tiptoes, stepped up to look through the high steel-framed window onto the scene below. Squads of newly arrived troops were enthusiastically jumping off the backs of four-ton lorries. They mustered side by side until they filled the substantial space. She squinted to see the bustling men and women better. Not so long ago, in response to the tragic deaths of three off-duty teenage British soldiers, the army had raised the minimum age for service in Northern Ireland to eighteen.

No doubt about it, a few of these young fellas had slipped through the net. She knew they'd come from Ballykinler after training, likely told, same as her, they were here to *'maintain law and order'*. Yeah, right.

Still alone, she groaned as she sat down again, reflecting on how much her life had changed since the cock-up in Londonderry. She supposed that, on one hand, the good news was that the bomb hadn't gone off, and there had been no fatalities or casualties other than the shootings. But on the other hand, her partner, Robert Sallis, aka 'Kentucky', and she had screwed up. Their cover had been well and truly blown and, as a result, their particularly irate handler quickly broke the pair up and sent them off in different directions.

So Alice found herself here in Ballymurphy, or 'Murph', as the lads called it. As for Sallis, he'd simply said goodbye and left her at Fort George barracks. She'd never forget the anger she'd felt when she'd been partnered with him following their covert training. The Provos had murdered Graham, her soldier fiancé, in cold blood, and she'd sworn revenge for his death. Her goal was to get back into action solo and avenge his killing, but after Londonderry, she was left sitting behind this cursed desk.

Feeling the slightest twinge of remorse, she remembered how rude she'd been to Sallis. Pissed at having to work with him, she'd only speak or respond to him when she had to, and distanced herself as much as she could. He'd accused her of being a man-hater, even called her a 'lesbo.' He'd read her so wrong, she just wanted to kill Provos.

After a while at Ballymurphy, she'd heard Sallis had been sent to West Belfast, taken a head injury during some motherfucker of a riot, and got quietly shipped back to Byker. Discharged on health grounds, apparently. Word was he wasn't fit to marry, and not long after, like plenty of other damaged squaddies before him, went off his rocker. Hit the bottle hard too, which wouldn't have helped his paranoia. His fiancée had done a runner with some fella she'd been seeing on the sly, leaving Sallis and his parents holding the baby. Literally. A newborn boy.

She wandered into the kitchenette to make her usual coffee, three sugars, exactly how she liked it. Sad, really. Poor bastard. Wouldn't be the first squaddie to get shafted. Still, thank Christ, she only had one person to worry about these days. Herself.

As the kettle started to boil, she prayed there wasn't another electricity strike that day. Walkouts were happening all over, mostly the Protestant Ulster Workers, kicking off over the idea of sharing power with that lot down south. The Sunningdale Agreement had them foaming. Strikes like these were a pain in the arse, caused mayhem for everyone, and made no difference. Waste of bloody time, if you asked her.

From a distance, she heard footsteps coming her way and turned to see a tall, tired-looking middle-aged man striding towards her from the corridor, with her sergeant by his side. Alice recognised him straight away and was momentarily stunned. It was her handler from Londonderry.

Shit.

Last time she'd seen him, he'd been ranting and raving, and she hoped he wasn't here to kick off again. A cigarette dangled between his fingers as she watched him lean in to whisper in her sergeant's ear. When he reached her, and with no time to waste, he took a drag, pulled it from his lips with those nicotine-stained fingers, and gave her a nod.

'Private Wallace,' he said.

'Sir,' she replied. The tension was palpable as blood pumped in her ears.

'You're needed again. With me.' His tone told her she'd no choice but to follow, so she did, trailing after him as he walked off.

Alice glanced at her boyish, brown-eyed sergeant, who looked back with a small smile. He liked her. Not once had she complained about being stuck behind that desk, though he knew she'd hated it. She wasn't cut out to be an administrator, but had remained professional, and although he didn't know everything that happened in Londonderry, somehow, he felt she deserved a second chance.

Alice smiled in return but soon stopped as her amused sarge prompted her to switch off the semi-boiling kettle.

'Oh, God, yes! Sorry!' Her face reddened.

'Good luck, Wallace,' he said, and was gone.

As she ran to keep up with the Military Intelligence handler, Alice suppressed a smile. Was she back in? Didn't he say she was needed? *God, please get me out of here. I'll do anything. Please get me outta here!*

Alice was led into a small, dark meeting room with blacked-out windows. A single bulb dangled low from a rope-like wire, casting shadows across the walls. The place was grim, and she could well imagine how many Provos had been dragged in here and grilled.

He lit another cigarette from the pack tucked in his inside pocket and, oddly enough, looked the same as the last time she'd clapped eyes on him. Same navy three-piece suit. Same red tie hanging loose round the neck of a near-white shirt. Same knackered face. She remembered every bit.

Fair play to Kentucky, though. He'd come clean straight away, hadn't tried to wriggle out of it, laid it all out. Said they'd been recognised, that he'd followed William Morris to the City Hotel, then stood there and took the full brunt of their handler's fury without flinching. She'd warned him, told him they needed to check in the second their cover was blown, but by then it was already out of control.

After that, everything went to hell. A shooting in broad daylight, two dead, and her finding the bomb not long after, the nail in the coffin, so to speak. She'd been dead set against going after Morris, told Kentucky so more than once, but even she could understand why he did it. In his head, it was all about revenge. Morris knew who'd killed Val Holmes. Kentucky was certain of it. The way he'd said it, the smug look on his face when he said he *knew* who'd done it. That was all it took. Kentucky held onto it like it was fact, and once he got that into his head, there was no stopping him.

The handler took a long, satisfying drag of his smoke and examined it, then looked at the young woman opposite. She wasn't bad-looking, not at all. The uniform helped, he had a thing for women in uniform. Could've done with a bit more meat on her bones for his taste, but she'd do rightly enough for the op. He didn't hold the Londonderry failure entirely against her, knowing well it hadn't been all her fault. That wasn't the reason he'd come. No, he had something else in mind, and he'd have put good money on her not blinking twice at what he was about to propose.

'I understand you want out of here?' he asked, sniffing loudly whilst rubbing his nose with the back of his hand.

'Yes, sir. Absolutely, sir,' Alice replied.

'Thought so. I'm going to give you another chance, Private Wallace. This time you can't fuck up. Otherwise, it could cost you or others their lives. Understand?'

Alice's eyes narrowed with suspicion as she listened. It didn't take long before her body lit up with a rush of emotions – delight, excitement, fear, and pure exasperation – all crashing in at once. Still, she took in his every word, nodding along in understanding. Oh yes, she didn't think twice about it. What he was offering was exactly what she'd been praying for. Finally!

As soon as she agreed, he ordered her to take a few days off before the op began. Mentally get prepared and get a decent rest. Apart from her sarge, she didn't bother saying goodbye to anyone. That chapter of her life, dull and inglorious as it had been, was well and truly behind her. Time to move on, face reality, aim for the one thing that mattered.

Retribution.

It was standard for army personnel to fly home from Antrim's Aldergrove Airport. However, as time was short, Alice decided not to go home to her mother, but to make her way to Bangor – a seaside resort on the other side of Belfast.

The first thing she did was get her long, brown feathered hair chopped off, then coloured. Afterwards, she caught her reflection in shopfronts and car windows, liking what she saw. This new Alice Wallce made her feel good, even her own mother wouldn't recognise her now.

She'd been stuck behind that desk far too long, so she made sure to work out, keep herself strong. Her frame was small but solid, toned and ready for anything. Back at barracks, a few of the so-called 'bean stealers' or 'pads' – married soldiers with wandering hands – had her tortured, always trying it on, slipping the hand when they thought no one was looking. But she'd made it clear where to put it. Every time. Thankfully, she was booked into a tidy Victorian B&B, a townhouse facing Belfast Lough, nothing like the filthy kip in Londonderry she and Sallis had been dumped in during the op.

Over the next few days, she did little else but read. It was the one thing that never failed her. Books had always been her way out, her lifeline, the thing that carried her through, not the loss of Graham, but life itself. They'd helped her stay upright when she felt like falling, especially over the last year, which had been long, miserable and hard to bear. On her last night, Alice was meeting an old pal. Since Graham's death, he had kept in touch, checking in now and then and catching up whenever they could. He'd been well pleased to hear she was staying nearby.

'Ah, it'll be lovely to see ye,' he'd said warmly on the phone that afternoon.

'You too. But it can't be a late one, I've to be back early tomorrow,' she'd told him.

'Course. Six it is then.'

'Six it is,' she'd said, smiling as she set the receiver down.

Chapter Fifteen

Pull Them Down Yerself!

Since early morning, Tina McLaughlin had been on her knees, scrubbing the floor near the women's showers.

The red tiles were cold and blotched with stains, the sharp reek of cheap bleach stinging her eyes and catching her throat with every breath. The wash area sat directly opposite the cells on the second floor of A-Wing, so there was no escape, no quiet corners, but cell doors clanging, women shouting, and the constant drip of water echoing around the place.

Her back screamed, but her hands were worse. When she held them up, they were even more raw and cracked than usual; the skin reddened from hours of scouring with lukewarm water mixed with cleaning product.

The women lived two to a cell on A and B Wings. Sanitation was a disgrace, with a mortifying slop-out system still in place. Overcrowding was made worse because until recently the women had to share facilities, though kept apart, with male prisoners. These included overspill internees and prisoners on remand from Belfast Prison, along with lads from a boys' borstal that had been sited on the premises for donkeys.

Resources were always directed to the men first, which meant the women were left with limited access to sanitation, exercise, and recreation. They had only one muddy patch of yard to exercise in and were regularly subjected to abuse and obscenities from Brits patrolling the perimeters, not to mention the male prisoners. All they had was a cramped rec room with nothing more than a few board games.

Thankfully, now that the men were gone, the women had freedom to move between A and B Wings via a narrow passage running through the back of the chapel. The newly opened C Wing had recently been built on the site of an old breakers' yard, adding thirty more cells.

Tina had been here nearly six months. At the start, she hadn't a clue where she was or why. Her eighteenth birthday had come and gone, uncelebrated and forgotten. Some days she was all right, other days, a complete blur. But slowly, bit by bit, she was becoming more lucid. The women looked out for her, and she liked it. They'd even nicknamed her the 'young'un'.

In the early days, she took her medication, handed out each morning at the top of the stairs by the medical officer. It never seemed to hit her as bad as the serious stuff they'd given her in the hospital. She'd been a zombie back then, but being here, her thoughts and memories started to come back.

At the OC's morning briefing, Maureen always drilled into the women how important it was to stick to a routine. Work was good for them, far better than being locked up all day with nothing but their own thoughts. Keeping the girls busy stopped them from overthinking, from going barmy. She handed out the daily tasks herself. Some would scrub floors in the bathrooms or clean the showers, toilets, or cells. Others were put to work in the laundry or sewing room.

Aside from allocating work, Maureen made sure to check on each woman, take roll call, and read aloud whatever scraps of news she could find in the leftover papers. The 'political bits' were always cut out with scissors, censored before they ever reached the wing. She'd heard that some of the non-political women were stitching prison uniforms for the men. On his last visit, she'd told her brother, hoping he'd pass it on to the Boys. Bits of intel like that always came in handy.

For now, Republican prisoners, men and women alike, could wear their own clothes, as long as they were officially classed as 'political prisoners.' That had been hard won, thanks to Billy McKee's hunger strike. But Maureen had a feeling things were about to change. If they did, if anyone tried to force them into HMPS uniforms, there'd be trouble. They'd rather die first.

Father McGuire always made a point of catching up with Tina whenever he visited the gaol. She'd half listen to the old priest as he ranted and apologised, over and over, for not helping her that morning before the bomb scare. It didn't matter anymore, she'd tell him.

What did matter was that there'd been no sign of her mother. Majella hadn't been to see her in forever. When she asked why, he was always vague, saying only that her mammy wasn't well enough to travel.

There'd been nothing from Martin, her adored brother, either. That hurt too. He'd been locked up himself, so he should've known. Should've understood how horrible it was, stuck in here with those cruel women – the screws – dressed head to toe in black, always shouting and worse.

Sometimes, Tina pictured herself back in the kitchen in Blamfield Street with her mammy and Caitlin. The night the meter ran out and they had to light some candles. She'd been raging with Caitlin for pinching her lemonade bottles. Now, looking back, it felt childish. Pathetic, even. What a waste of energy. She'd give anything to be back there. The three of them, sitting there, talking and eating their lousy stew.

In the early hours, when she couldn't sleep, that was when the flashbacks came.

The barn. Val's murder.

She could still see the soldier's empty eyes as they wrapped him in torn black bin bags. Kieran had been so devious, so cold, and she'd felt like a complete fool when she realised he'd led her up the garden path. To think - she'd carried a bomb in her schoolbag and handed it over to him. The whole thing haunted her. Her body would start shaking, the sweat pouring off her. The mere thought of it. What a complete idiot. Such a stupid, stupid bitch. She could've killed so many people. Her memory of the past few months was still a bit patchy, but there were some things she'd never forget.

No matter what.

She remembered some of the day she arrived in this dump, downstairs where they stripped her and hustled her into that filthy bath. The next morning wasn't much better. There'd been some sort of meeting with the governor, but most of it was a blur. What happened the following week, though, she'd take to her grave. When she went to the make shift medical centre. Now, that *really* freaked her out.

There wasn't a full-time doctor in the gaol. Agency GPs were brought in during evenings and weekends. Daytime cover came from local surgeries. Cheaper, apparently, than hiring a proper prison medic. They had one full-time nursing sister and a few screws trained in what they called basic medical care.

She'd been met by a gaunt, sour-faced man in a stained white coat. Doctor Harris, they'd said his name was. She'd never seen anyone so thin. All this time, she'd thought her skin was bad until she saw the state of his.

At first, she thought he was a regular GP. She tried to tell him how sore her skin was, hoping he might understand, given his looked worse. But he cut her off, told her he didn't have much time, and to strip down to her underwear. Quick as you like.

She shook her head. No chance.

That bath episode was still on her mind, and she was on her feckin' period. Why now, of all days? Maureen had quietly passed her a few Dr Whites earlier, and if this man thought she was stripping for him, he'd another thing coming. Him on his own too!

From the noise he was making and the look on his face, he wasn't used to being challenged. Flustered, muttering under his breath, he fidgeted with papers on the steel desk, pretending to look busy. Without a word, he got up and walked out.

Tina stayed put, didn't move an inch until the door creaked open again. She half expected him to come back with the nurse.

But it wasn't.

It was *her*.

The green-eyed screw. The same one who'd mocked and humiliated Tina the day before. She stepped into the room all businesslike.

In a whining voice, Harris bawled at the guard, 'I've asked this woman to strip to her underwear, but she refuses.'

Tina looked Smyth squarely in the eye, rallying all her strength to keep calm as the guard ordered, 'McLaughlin. Off. Now.'

'Pull them down yerself,' Tina shot back.

A painful silence hung in the air as the baffled man and woman looked at each other. 'Excuse me?' they asked in chorus.

'You do it,' Tina repeated. Her heart raced as she prayed for strength. Hail Mary, full of grace...

'Right then,' Smyth said, giving her a look that said it all. She'd remember this.

Not too kindly, she started stripping Tina, yanking off her clothes one by one and dropping them in a heap on the floor. Tina said nothing, but stood there, rigid and quiet, in her faded grey bra and knickers.

Harris knew he was supposed to note signs of mistreatment – any bruises or injuries on new arrivals. It was procedure.

But with that attitude? Forget it.

He took in the bruises. Back of the legs, ribs, all down one side.

Said nothing. Wrote nothing.

Looked like she'd been walloped a few times. Most likely over at Hastings Street barracks, then here. Everyone knew what went on these days, especially with women.

Her file was thicker than he expected. His predecessor had been generous with the girl's meds, handing out pills like Smarties.

Martina McLaughlin. Seventeen. Unstable. The staff at Gransha hospital witnessed the blackouts, the mumbling, the vacant stares. Called it madness, signed the form, dosed her with Chlorpromazine. Gaol came after that.

Harris didn't ask questions. He didn't like women, didn't like Republicans, and he definitely didn't like Martina McLaughlin. Way over the top, he thought. So he halved it. No warning. No explanation. A neat line through the dose on her chart.

That'd teach her.

Although the Provos had warned him to get out of Ireland after it looked like no charges would be brought over Patrick McLaughlin's death, Harris refused to budge at first.

Eventually, though, Londonderry became impossible. The petrol bombs through his front window torched most of his medical books and his unique magazines. Then they stole Winston, his King Charles spaniel. Never saw the poor thing again. He'd loved that dog.

Leave the city, yes, but leave the country he loved, no chance.

His friends had rallied round, of course. Always did. Quiet favours here and there, little workarounds, no questions asked. That was how he landed on his feet here. A doddle compared to all hours working for the RUC.

He looked at Smyth and nodded for her to get the girl dressed as he finally wrote in bold print on Tina's notes, 'No evidence of trauma. Fit and well.'

Smyth nodded in acknowledgement and turned to her prisoner. 'Get dressed.'

Tina shook her head again and said, 'Naw. You do it.'

Smyth freaked and grabbed for her baton, but Harris pulled her back, whining, 'No!' in a really girly voice. 'Don't... don't touch her! Get her dressed and out of my sight.'

Tina didn't help as Smyth wrestled with her, trying to get her clothes back on, but stood there, limp, her eyes locked on the wall. She'd no idea where that came from. Face twisted in fury, Smyth yanked the jumper down over her head, muttering curses under her breath.

On the way back to her cell, as Tina climbed the mesh-covered stairwell, Smyth leaned in and hissed, 'Your time will come, missy. Just ye wait.'

Tina ignored her, more focused on the rope net strung between the landings, a crude attempt at suicide prevention. For the first time in a long while, she felt proud. She'd stood her ground and hadn't the foggiest where the nerve had come from.

Somehow, Maureen had managed to get Tina recognised with political status, even though she wasn't part of any paramilitary group. It mattered to the OC. It meant the young'un would stay under her watch, billeted with someone strong. Someone who could be trusted to look out for her.

That had happened ages ago, and now, back on the landing, as she tried to rinse the heavy wet clothes in a steel bucket of murky water, a cloth came flying and smacked Tina right in the face. 'Aargh! Bloody hell, that's freezin'!' she screamed.

Laughter rang down the landing as she looked over at her cellmate, Bridget Barry.

Late fifties, with a loose bun holding back a mix of grey and black wisps, Bridget had the kind of intelligent, lively eyes that missed nothing and skin the colour of weak tea. She'd been here since '71, back when there were only two women in the place. Within minutes, she made Tina feel safe. The woman was a hoot, full of punch and mischief.

Best of all, she spoke to Tina like an equal, not like the others who treated her like some daft wee girl. Bridget, with her lovely lazy smile, retrieved her wet cloth and laughed so hard it made Tina smile.

'You looked like you were in one of your secret places there. Come on, we need to get crackin' and finish this. Have to see what's on the telly and vote!'

With only one TV on the wing, the women voted each night on what to watch. There was rarely much disagreement, with only two channels to pick from, but it was still a big deal – the highlight of their evening before lock-up at 8 PM.

Over dinner, Bridget squeezed in beside Tina and a few others. The OC had asked her to keep an eye on the girl, and Bridget, as adjutant, didn't need telling twice. She had a mammy's touch – the kind that fed you, minded you, and made you laugh when you were about to lose it. The girls relied on her. She got them through the worst. A quiet rock, aye, but with a mouth on her and a wicked sense of humour. Her being around could lift a whole landing, and those corny stories of hers? Pure legend. You never knew if she was winding you up or telling the God's honest truth.

'How you doing, young'un?' She asked Tina, who was scoffing down Thursday's regular mashed potato and soup.

'Grand!' Tina came back at her. 'This is really nice!'

Bridget nodded, astonished. The food here was bloody rotten, all watery and mushy. She couldn't get her head around how the young'un liked it so much, watching her gobble it down without stopping. She was doing well now, nothing like she'd been when she first arrived.

'Listen. Do me a favour, will ye. Don't suppose you'd go to the shop for us in the morning? Martha Sweeney will meet you at the circle at seven-thirty. Me and the girls have a few things we need. Before *Goodlife* or whatever shite we're watching tonight, will ye go around and see what they want. We'll sort you out with the money later?'

Tina stared at her cellmate and the others, her forked dinner halfway to her mouth.

'A shop?' She gasped, wide-eyed. 'You want me to go to the shop?'

They nodded solemnly as she dropped her fork in excitement. 'No bother. What do ye need?'

At such an innocent response, Bridget nearly spat out her potato. She turned to the others and winked. A few covered their mouths, and one slapped the table.

'Christ above,' someone whispered, shaking with laughter. 'Hook, line and sinker!'

The young'un wasn't the first, and she sure as hell wouldn't be the last to fall for that one.

Chapter Sixteen

Lonely

Another Saturday night.

The word *lonely* didn't come close to what Caitlin McLaughlin felt, sitting there staring into space in front of the teak-effect TV, switched on but ignored. The cruel voice in her head never let up. Always there, whispering reminders of how badly she'd fucked up. She had no friends left. Anne hadn't even shown her face at her mother's funeral. *Unforgivable*. Even her granny hadn't shown. That one, Caitlin still couldn't get her head around. As for Martin, her brother – well, he'd cleared off somewhere. Vanished without a trace. No surprises there. Tina, poor girl, was stuck in her own personal hell. As much as she hated to admit it, Caitlin had never felt so lonely. So friggin' lonely. This house? Blamfield Street wasn't a home anymore. Bricks and mortar. Empty.

Her only consolation? As ever, Uncle Tommy and Charlie and Maggie McFadden from next door. None of them had the faintest notion what was really going through her head, or how she felt, because she'd hidden it too well. Was God Himself having a laugh at her expense? She wondered.

The living room was a bloody disgrace. She'd let it go. The net curtains, once snow white, hung limp and dusty. The windows were filthy, she could barely see through them. A few stained teacups sat on the grubby coffee table, buried among too many red bills.

Last night, she'd crashed out on the sofa again, and now the blankets were tangled around her legs. She'd been too done in to drag herself up the stairs and hadn't moved from the same spot all day. Sheer laziness. The fire hadn't been lit for a lifetime. Even the photos on the mantel, all those smiling faces at Christmases and First Communions, were thick with dust now. Forgotten days. Happier days. A long time ago now.

Nothing seemed to matter to her anymore. Losing her mammy so soon after Daddy, then the funeral, had broken her. Even with the Catholic Church now allowing suicides to be buried in consecrated ground, there were still stubborn parishioners, the hardliners, who didn't agree. That was why it stung so much when a few so-called neighbours turned their noses up and stayed away. Against her better judgement, she'd hoped James Henderson would appear. Nope. Not a word. Not even a sympathy card.

Selfish bastard, she thought, when a firm knock sounded at the front door.

With no clue who it might be, she pulled back the grimy net curtain and peered through the streaked windowpane. A darkly dressed figure stood on the doorstep. Hood up, head bowed against the rain. No one had come near the house all day, and with it being fairly late, Caitlin felt a flicker of unease. Whoever it was, they weren't for giving up, rattling the letterbox again, only louder this time. Better to be safe than sorry, she grabbed the poker from beside the fireplace and wrapped her fingers tight around the handle.

The knocking had got louder now and more urgent. *What the Hell?!* Heart thudding, she stormed into the hallway. 'Okay! All right, I'm coming!'

She stopped short of the door, her breath caught somewhere between her chest and throat. Switching on the hallway light, she saw the figure better now, a dark shape behind the small, square panes of glass.

'Who is it?!' she called, her voice coming out higher than intended, the poker raised and ready.

A voice answered, low and muffled, but she couldn't make out the words.

'I can't hear you! Who is it?' she cried.

The silhouette bent down, and a hand opened the letterbox. A deep voice announced. 'It's me, Caitlin. It's Seamus. Seamus Donaghy.'

Jesus! What the heck was Seamus Donaghy doing here? She stumbled back from the door; her legs like rubber.

His voice came again through the gap. 'Caitlin,' he cried. 'For Christ's sake, will ye let me in! I'm soaked!'

She fumbled with the lock, and he burst inside, standing in the middle of the long hallway, shaking the rain off his coat, water dripping onto the tiled floor.

His face broke into a wide smile. 'That weather's so much worse than I remember!' he said. 'It's like the end—' He couldn't finish. The words wouldn't come.

Before arriving, he hadn't known what to expect. Not really. But it wasn't this, and certainly not her, standing like he was some kind of threat, holding a poker in the air.

'Caitlin?' he asked, no idea what was going on.

She looked up. He almost passed out as shock registered on his face. He was staring at a stranger. The change in the girl he once loved was surreal.

Time seemed to have dragged her through a war he hadn't been here to fight. She stood against the wall, motionless, in a worn nightie and oversized cardigan. He could see she was thin, not healthy thin, but sickeningly thin, thin. Her cheekbones were sharp against pale white skin. The black hair she'd once taken so much care over hung limp, long and greasy. Even her once enviable tall frame seemed to have shrunk. He couldn't get over the transformation. Fuck it but Caitlin McLaughlin looked like shit. There were hollows beneath her eyes, and her mouth hung in that half-open way people wore when they'd stopped caring. She didn't smile. Pretty much stared right at him. He could barely look back.

Caitlin got it. She knew she looked like death warmed up, but still tried to appear normal. Without a word, he brushed past her and walked into the kitchen, slinging his wet coat over the back of her mammy's chair.

Back in the day, he'd been very fond of Majella, and she of him. Without thinking, Caitlin's fingers toyed with Majella's wedding ring as she remembered her.

This kitchen had once been full of life and laughter. Now it was quiet, depleted. Like the house itself had given up. He looked around, found the kettle, and filled it at the sink. Dishes were piled high, food scraps were turning grey, some even blooming with blue mould. Crumbs and tea bags littered the once immaculate worktops. He lit the gas, still quiet, then nodded towards the table.

'Sit,' he said.

Caitlin sat. It was as if he'd never been away, Caitlin thought, watching him. As if he'd lived here all his life, opening cupboard doors like he knew exactly where everything was. Yet everything about him had changed. He wasn't a Creggan boy anymore. Far from it, he was tanned, broader, definitely more solid. His fair hair was longer now, bleached nearly white by the sun. He exuded a calm confidence she'd never seen before.

His jeans were immaculate, pressed sharply front and back. The navy V-neck he wore looked expensive and sat over a bold floral shirt with long collar points, pointy enough, she thought, to take off! Unlike James Henderson, the smell of his aftershave was woody. She decided Seamus Donaghy had long gone, and this good-looking and capable man had taken his place. From his confidence and the look of him, he must be doing well for himself.

Caitlin was gobsmacked as they drank their tea. He pulled his chair close to hers and fired off question after question, genuinely interested in hearing about her daddy, her mammy, Martin, and of course, Tina. She nodded when she had to, forced the odd smile, and stuck to one-word answers where she could. The idea of talking about it in detail made her feel ill. Tonight, she wasn't for opening old wounds.

Topping up her mug, he pursed his lips in concentration, took a deep breath, and asked, 'And you, Caitlin? What about you? You look like shit.'

Seamus didn't have to ask. He knew. Christ, how he'd loved her. She'd blown a hole in his heart when she'd refused to marry him, and off he went to New York first, then Boston. He couldn't forget how painful it was for him, leaving his family and Derry, but the worst bit was leaving her. To this day, she'd never know how much it hurt him. After her rejection, there was only one thing for him to do. Make a run for it. Get away. It would've killed him if he'd stayed.

In time, he realised Caitlin had been right to turn him down. He'd been an arrogant gobshite from Creggan, all swagger and no sense, with nothing going for him and even less ambition to change it. Could've ended up like half his friends, all interned left, right and centre. His train of thought was broken when she spoke.

'I'm okay. Working. In a photographer's. It's not bad, I suppose. I quite like it... now.'

'Why did something happen?' He asked with concern.

'Nothing I couldn't handle.'

Relieved, he half-smiled before continuing. 'I liked your mammy, you know? Sorry to hear what happened. A lovely woman. Always kind to me.'

Caitlin nodded. Mammy had wanted her to say yes to Seamus's proposal. But he wasn't for her. She understood that. He'd never stirred in her what James Henderson did, the thrill, the pull, the want. All of it. If only she hadn't met him. If only she hadn't taken that job in Rocola. She wondered how things might've turned out. For her. For him. For all of them.

Martin had been right. She was stuck-up. A puke.

Reading her expression, Seamus grasped her hands and squeezed. 'It'll be fine, Caitlin. You'll see. I know it feels like the end of the world now, but it'll be all right.'

Instinctively, he rose and opened his arms. She stood too and fell into them without a word, resting her head on his chest and closing her eyes. She wasn't looking for comfort. She was so bloody tired. Tired of holding it all together. Tired of pretending, she could. So she stayed where she was, still and quiet, letting the weight of everything rest somewhere else. Just for a while.

The hours passed quickly as the couple sat and spoke about everything. Caitlin, feeling weary but relieved, found it easy to talk to him. Seamus listened in disbelief and astonishment until, feeling a little ashamed to have monopolised the conversation, she asked him about his life. He'd been lucky, extremely lucky. After arriving in New York, he quickly decided he didn't like it and moved to Boston instead. There, he found a casual job with a construction company owned by a man from an old and wealthy Irish-American family.

His first job had been clearing out and tearing down derelict buildings, where he soon proved himself a grafter. The money was good and the craic even better. His crew, like him, had left Ireland chasing something new or running from something old, broken hearts, bad memories, or, in a few cases, the Brits. Real charges or trumped-up, it didn't matter much once they were gone. The older fellas took him under their wing, training him as they went, and before long, he was a jack of all trades, laying bricks, fitting pipes, wiring houses. He took to it like a duck to water and soon caught the eye of Mr Michael McMannus, owner of the property firm.

McMannus's son had no time for the business. Wouldn't dream of getting his soft hands dirty. But the owner saw potential in Seamus. In no time, he'd become a trusted hand. He even offered to pay for night school so Seamus could study business and management, a chance to move up in the world. He was a natural with numbers, with people, and while he was keen to pay his boss back, he was hungrier still to learn more, earn more. He'd come home to see the family. But the minute he heard about Majella's death, he knew. He needed to see Caitlin, try to put the past behind them.

Caitlin listened and watched fondly as he spoke. His face lit up with pride as he told her of his success. *What a change.* He'd made her feel so much better, and she was pleased for him, really pleased. 'I'm so chuffed for you, Seamus. You've done amazing things. And your lot at home. I bet they're well pleased you're here.'

He smiled, raised his eyebrows sceptically and laughed. 'More like they enjoy the money I send back.'

Caitlin nodded. She used to hand over most of her wages to her mammy too, and never once begrudged it.

A flicker of a smile touched her lips as a memory returned. Her and Mammy in the kitchen, chatting away as they pinned fabric to a pattern, bickering over hem lengths while Majella tutted, pins between her teeth. They'd made two skirts that night, one navy, one black.

She puffed out her cheeks. For once, the memory of Mammy didn't make her throat tighten and flashed him a broad smile. 'Tell me about you, Mr America?' she asked, half-joking. 'Has some poor girl snared you yet, or are you still breaking hearts from Boston to Derry?'

He cringed at the thought of the last few years. There'd been a couple of girls, but none anything like Caitlin. His eyes twinkled when he replied. 'Ah, Caitlin, sure, I'm still getting over the one that got away. Anyone in your life?' he asked, not sure he wanted to know.

Caitlin looked straight at him and, almost surprised herself, placed a finger on her chest. 'Who, me? Jesus, Seamus, there's no one in my life. I mean, look around! How could there be, with all this shite going on?'

Chapter Seventeen

H-A-T-E

Charles Jones, flushed and glistening with sweat, muttered incoherently as he stalked back and forth across the polished floor of his study, a decadent space inside a Queen Anne gem tucked behind Victoria Street, behind one of Belfast's main thoroughfares.

The room matched the building's grandeur: a high-corniced ceiling, grey-and-white gilded wallpaper, and a solid Victorian mahogany partner desk smothered in papers, a leather desk set, and two telephones. Set between shuttered sash windows, the desk faced a pair of oxblood reading chairs, all resting on a plush grey carpet that muffled his pacing.

Earlier that morning, his secretary handed him another anonymous death threat. Hand-delivered, printed in bold capitals, same as the others. It was the third since the bomb scare and shootings at the City Hotel, over a year ago. The bishop's murder had never been pinned on him, but anyone with half a brain could put two and two together. In the right circles, it was no secret Billy Morris had been his bodyguard, and the one who fired the first shot.

Jones wasn't about to let a Fenian guttersnipe threaten him. Replacing his dead bodyguard had been a priority but was quickly sorted. Luckily he came across Mark Carroll, aka *Lemon,* a Ballymena loyalist, lesser known than Morris but as dependable. They'd met through the Orange Order, where Jones had been a guest of honour.

H-A-T-E was inked across Lemon's fingers. When he first met Jones, he was a B-Special in the UVF, but had left the organisation as soon as Jones offered him the post.

In hindsight, Morris had been a babe-in-arms next to this miscreant. Jones was quietly impressed. Lemon took it upon himself to sit in the public gallery at Belfast courthouse, watching trials, studying the judges and the peelers, learning the ropes so he wouldn't slip up in the future. The man was no fool. He'd turned out to be a smart, unflinching asset, never once questioning an order.

What had Jones seething today was the BBC bulletin crackling from his radio that was always left on. Two pubs. Five dead, four of them soldiers. It hadn't even happened here. The fucking Provos had taken their war to the mainland, murdering normal, everyday people out for a quiet pint in Guildford. If ever there was a moment that confirmed the righteousness of his cause, this was it.

Without knocking, James Henderson Snr stormed into the study, newspaper in hand. He slammed it onto the desk, gripped the edge, and leaned over, his face taut with fury.

'Have you seen this, Charles? This is off the fucking Richter scale!'

Jones gave a solemn nod, keeping his thrill tucked well out of sight. About bloody time. It had taken longer than he'd liked to light a fire under that old establishment stiff, but by the look of things, Henderson was finally in the net.

He let the moment stretch, then said coolly, 'I have, James, and I'm bloody angry. Think about it, man. It proves we're on the right path. Morally. Politically. We will avenge.'

Jones didn't move at first. He bit down hard, and a vein pulsed at his temple. One of his hands closed slowly into a fist, then released. Twice.

James Snr shook his head in despair and agreement, then fell into a chair opposite Jones' desk.

'So, what's next?' he asked, his face set.

Jones gave a measured nod. 'Well, that rather depends on you, doesn't it? I'd like to think that after reading news like that, you're ready to take things up a notch.' He paused, then added almost breezily, 'Let's say... a little more hands-on, shall we?'

James Snr knew exactly what he meant. He'd been sceptical at first, even found Jones a bit of a caricature, always banging on about perfidious Nationalists and the Catholic menace. But over time, after a few blistering sermons and some careful reflection, he began to see the logic. In fact, Jones had made a lot more sense than he'd wanted to admit, especially now, after this latest atrocity. The man's generous financial support wasn't hurting either.

Blood simmering, James Snr held his gaze. 'Of course. What are you thinking?'

Chapter Eighteen

Slowly, Slowly, Catchy Monkey

Roger Henderson, James Jnr and the lovely Marleen Fry were having a quiet informal dinner back at Melrose in Prehen.

Lately, Marleen had grown unexpectedly fond of the city. She found the people here unsophisticated but so friendly – a welcome change from her London circle.

Then there was James – dear handsome, understanding James. Her best man friend ever since they were both knee high. She found herself in a precarious position. As the only child of rich aristocratic parents, she was under an unspoken but ill-disguised request to find a husband and produce an heir to the family's wealth and position. Ultimately, after much deliberation, she set her sights on James. He'd known about her bisexual leanings for years and had never seemed the least bit fazed. Still, he'd likely die if she so much as hinted at marriage. She'd have to tread carefully. Slowly, slowly, catchy monkey.

Marleen watched him sip his wine, and once again marvelled at him, the man was indeed gorgeous. The kind of gorgeous that could father truly beautiful children. Tall, broad-shouldered, and ridiculously well put together. Those green eyes were absurdly intense, framed by lashes she'd commit a small crime for. His face? Pure joy, and lips that practically begged to be kissed. *Okay, woman, calm down.* His auburn hair was thick and cropped just so, the sort that would stubbornly stick around well into his seventies. That accent? She could bottle it and make a fortune. She smiled at the thought of making beautiful babies with him, hypothetically, of course. More importantly, she knew James was a good man. Solid and loyal. A genuine friend. Wasn't friendship the best foundation for any marriage?

Melrose's dining room was, as usual, stunning. All Adam fireplace, classic antiques and delicate, hand-painted Chinese wallpaper. Marleen could see herself running this place, hosting fabulous dinner parties with ease. She'd never been academic, always a bit old-fashioned, and would be quite content stepping into the role of wife and hostess in this gracious old house. She knew James and Roger were in dire straits with the factory, however, if James were to say yes, then there you go! Her trust fund was substantial, ready to be unlocked the moment she married. They could save Rocola, travel wherever they pleased, whenever they pleased. She could still nip back to London to see certain friends, discreetly, of course, but absolutely essential. Marrying James was the obvious move. Made total sense. The best outcome for everyone, including her.

'How was today?' Roger asked, they looked fresh from their walk.

Marleen had loved their trip to the Giant's Causeway. James had driven her there, and as they stood together on the edge of those strange, funny-shaped rocks, it felt like they were the only two people on the planet. So unusually quiet.

'It was deserted, Roger. We walked from the car park right down to the sea. The light was amazing, and James took some great photographs, didn't you?' she asked, looking at James for affirmation. 'Yeah, it was nice. Peaceful,' he remarked apathetically. 'Nice fresh air.'

Roger remained troubled by James's low mood. He rather enjoyed having a woman about the house again, but felt for poor Marleen. James had welcomed her, but soon slipped back into his usual quiet, distant self with that death row look back on his face, the City Hotel fiasco still trailing him like an unwelcome shadow.

Watching Marleen, Roger had to admire the girl's poise. She had a certain *savoir-faire*, and her blonde good looks were undeniable. An absolute beauty - classic, like Grace Kelly, with bobbed white-blonde hair, expressive hazel eyes, and a smile that lit up her entire face. She was the right height too, nearly up to James's shoulder, elegant and well-proportioned. Roger, ever the old rogue, noted her fine figure. James, he thought, was a damn fool not to see what a catch the girl would be.

Following the bomb scare, Roger insisted that politics were never to be discussed at the dinner table. But tonight was different. The news from Guildford had left him and James horrified. Five innocent people killed in an IRA bombing. It came as a shock that the Provos had taken their campaign to England, and with such brutality. Attacks like this would change everything, no question. The Troubles were about to move into an entirely new and dangerous phase.

'I wonder if they'll catch them when they try to get back?' Roger said, referring to the bombers.

'Hope so. I'd imagine the ports and airports will be well covered.' James replied.

'Aye, makes sense,' Roger replied, and with a sigh added, 'There'll be retaliation. That's all I seem to say these days.'

James kept it shut. Roger was right to be concerned, but now, all he wanted was to stay focused on Rocola and steer clear of divisive politics. He hated any talk about the Provos, the UVF, the whomever.

He'd been working day in, day out to make sure the government funding was used according to priority, and now, at last, they were seeing some positive results. Morale at the factory had lifted, and he was spending more time on the floor, listening to the workers, watching how things ran, weighing up their suggestions. They respected him now and, for the first time, James felt like he belonged.

Rocola was home.

Sensing the tension, Marleen decided it was time for some good news. Clapping her hands to catch their attention, she said brightly, in her cut-glass accent, 'Roger, since I'm here, why don't we throw a small dinner party? You're not to worry about anything. I'll sort it. I think after all this horrible news we need a teeny-weeny bit of fun, don't you?' The thought of entertaining made Roger cringe, but perhaps the girl was right. It had been an age since they'd entertained and could do James some good.

'A splendid idea, Marleen. What do you say, James? A select few.'

Marleen was thrilled. She adored arranging dinner parties, and as she looked around the house again, she knew it'd be perfect for entertaining. Her first dinner party at Melrose. She'd have a blast putting it together, but waiting for James's response felt like forever. Her heart sank when he finally did speak, his voice flat and downright miserable. 'I'm not sure. I'm not brilliant company these days.'

His uncle, goaded by his tone, moved closer and tapped his arm. 'Ah, c'mon, son. It'll cheer you up, cheer us all up. I mean, look at that face!' He chuckled, gesturing at Marleen, 'How on God's earth can you say no to that?!'

James looked at his long-time friend with her pleading, sparkling eyes. He realised he'd been a nuisance and should try both for her and his uncle. He loved Marleen, and she'd done her best to cheer them all up. He narrowed his eyes at the two of them and wagged a finger, making his one and only proviso.

'Under no circumstances is you-know-who allowed anywhere near here. Ye hear me? Not a hope in hell!'

'Absolutely not!' cried Marleen and Roger in unison, and for the first time in months, the splendid dining room crackled with carefree laughter.

So, that was that. Charles Jones was officially barred from Melrose. Good riddance to the gobshite.

Chapter Nineteen

A Plain Loaf and Pint of Milk

Emmett McFadden strolled out of the newsagents by Stones Corner, having finished his paper round and carrying a plain loaf and a pint of milk that he brought home religiously every morning for his ma.

As he turned the corner, groceries in hand, he was grabbed from behind and dragged across the footpath. He fought back on instinct, twisting and kicking to shake whoever it was off. The bottle of milk smashed on the pavement, the loaf burst open as it hit the ground. Seconds later, they had him shoved into a piss-reeking RUC Land Rover. To escape, his right knee slammed against the closing door. Pain exploded through his leg, and he crumpled to the floor, darkness momentarily closing in.

Squealing, he clutched his knee as the vehicle took off, rolling, bouncing, screeching around corners like a getaway car. *What the fuck!*

He swayed violently, scrabbling for anything to hold on to, and finally grabbed a seat, clutching it like his life depended on it, his heart hammering in his chest. What in the name of God was going on? Why would the peelers lift him? Terrified and bewildered, Emmett tried not to think the worst. They lifted poor Patrick McLaughlin and look what happened to him.

Emmett was always slight for his age, but to everyone's surprise, he'd filled out over the past year. The cherubic face was gone. Almost overnight, he'd shot up, as tall and broad as his da, Charlie McFadden – minus the beer belly. He took pride in keeping his mind sharp and his body fit. He loved sport, spent hours in the gym lifting weights, and had his heart set on playing rugby. But the local team, mostly Prods, wouldn't give him a look in, him being a Catholic an' all. He decided to play a more challenging sport instead. Gaelic football.

Joe, his eldest brother, was a big lad too, a natural on the Gaelic pitch, though Emmett couldn't remember the last time he'd seen him play. Joe had been in Long Kesh for ages now, much to their mother's torment. She lived day to day on her nerves ever since losing her job at the City Hotel after it came out that she'd unknowingly hired that murdering prick, Kieran Kelly. Mortified, she barely left the house now, except to go to Mass.

As he'd hoped, Emmett had done well in his exams, and his teacher, Mr McGinley, was pushing hard to get him to the next level. Maybe, just maybe, he'd make it to university. He used to dream about that, about going to uni, then whisking his mother and the first girl he ever loved, Tina McLaughlin, faraway from this place.

No chance of that now. Tina was done for, locked up God knows for how long. It'd knocked him sideways when he'd found out. He'd always thought she was sound, too smart to fall for a dickhead like Kieran bloody Kelly. Of all people... *Kelly*. When Emmett thought about how often he'd passed him in the street. If only he'd known, he'd have punched his lights out there and then.

No point crying over spilt milk. Perhaps it was over for him now, depending on who'd taken him. If it was the Brits, he was in for a hiding. If it was the RUC, it'd be that and more. '*Accidents*' happened all the time these days to fellas in custody. Everyone knew that.

His imagination ran wild. What if it was the Prods, the UVF, or worse! He shuddered, blessed himself and dropped his head into his hands, hot tears spilling down his cheeks as he whispered his prayers. *Oh my God, I am very sorry...*

Out of the blue, a pair of hands landed on his shoulders, solid but firm, and someone dropped down beside him. A quiet voice followed, gentle but sure. 'You're all right, son. Get yourself sorted. Take a deep breath. You're okay.'

They'd been travelling for what felt like hours when, in the back of the darkened jeep, Emmett and its only other occupant, Mickey Boyle, who muttered, 'Thought they'd be takin' us to Strand Road, but we're way past there now. Wherever it is, they're takin' us, son, keep your head down and say nothin'. They're lifting every Tom, Dick and Harry since those bombings in England. Be ready, it'll get physical, they'll give ye a hidin' before they throw us in the Kesh.'

Emmett's voice cracked. 'They can't. I'm not even sixteen!'

'Won't matter a damn. They don't give a flyin' fuck. You any ID on ye son? Any at all?' Mickey asked.

Emmett shook his head. 'Nothin'. I was only finishin' me paper round, not going on me fuckin' holidays!'

Mickey laughed as the jeep jolted violently to a halt, flinging them from their seats. The doors burst open. Dazzling light flooded in, forcing them to squint and shield their eyes.

'Out!' barked a red-faced, stick-thin RUC man, waving a black baton overhead like a conductor in an orchestra.

'Aye, right. Give us a minute, we canny see a thing,' Mickey cried, shielding his eyes with a hand and leaping down from the van. A baton cracked across the back of his legs, and next thing Mickey buckled, dropping hard on the tarmac.

'Stop it!' Emmett cried, still on the edge of the van, his face twisted with fury. 'He hasn't done anythin'!'

'Fuck off. Your turn. Out!' the RUC man yelled.

Emmett clutched his hurt knee, bracing himself as he dropped out into the blinding light.

Mickey was still doubled over. When he eventually looked up, he saw Emmett for real, standing there in his schoolboy trainers and thin windcheater. He shook his head. 'There's no way on God's green earth they're gonna believe a young bull like you is only fifteen,' he murmured. 'By Christ, you're in for it, fella.' He lowered his gaze to the asphalt, brought his crucifix to his lips, and kissed it gently. 'We're both in for it.'

They were marched into a red-brick, bulletproof building. Mickey was limping, one hand pressed to his lower back. Emmett took a quick look at him, he who wore the usual get-up of most young Derry men. Blue jeans, a two-tone donkey jacket over a black polo neck, and a scuffed pair of Doc Martens. His gold crucifix caught the light. He wasn't a big man, but wiry and tight-strung. His scalp was smooth as an egg, face clean-shaven, eyes wary. Looking around, he whispered. 'Where the heck are we?'

The RUC barracks looked more like a fortress than a police station. Thick grey walls, sandbags piled high, and a tangle of wire fencing stretched above the roof. A lookout post loomed overhead, floodlights fixed on the street like watchful eyes. The place reeked of tension, even from the outside. There'd be no welcome mat here, only concrete, metal, and fear.

Mickey moved in closer, his voice clear and low. 'Fucking Castlereagh. We're in fuckin' Castlereagh.'

His words hit Emmett like a hammer.

It was the last place on earth Mickey wanted to be, and the one place he swore he'd never come back to. *So much for that.*

Chapter Twenty

Peg Leg Annie

Anne had been waiting every day for the scrape of the letterbox. With no money left, she'd applied for a loan. A lousy fifty quid.

Thank God, the postman arrived. She heard the soft slap of the envelope hit the mat and moved fast, as fast as the prosthetic would allow, gripping the wall for balance as she plodded down the tiled hallway, the socket cutting into what remained of her leg with every step. She snatched the letter and tore it open, heart pounding, hands shaking. This was it.

Dear Miss Heaney,

We write to inform you that your recent loan application for £50 has been unsuccessful...

Fuck. Fuck. Fuck and fuck! She yelled as she crushed the letter and hurled it into the air. She sank on the bottom stair, shaking with disappointment. She'd saved with that friggin' credit union since her first pay cheque, and until now, hadn't asked for a penny. Her savings were long gone, poured into the household kitty since she got hurt. As for now? She'd no idea what she to do. There wasn't a penny left. She thought long and hard about her options and, admitting defeat, realised she'd only one left. To her absolute horror, Porkie had taken the wind out of her sails last night. The eejit had only gone and proposed. To her!

'Anne, I know your leg's missin' an' all, so you're not the best-lookin' chick in the hen house. Sure, I'm no spring chicken meself, but I wanna marry ye,' he said, puffing his chest out like a proud pigeon.

'What the...?' she'd exclaimed. 'You're not serious?'

He was. Deadly serious. He'd shuffled forward, knees cracking, one hand gripping the radiator, the other digging about in his pocket. Wobbling like a drunk flamingo, he dropped halfway down to the floor with a grunt. Not quite on one knee, but the best he could do. *Sweet mother of fuck, he means it!*

With a face as innocent as a lamb, he retorted. 'Course I'm serious. I reckon we'd have a good chance at a nice house. You know, one of them council ones in Shantallow. Ye gotta see them. They're lovely. Half a' Creggan's movin' down that way.'

She'd heard about the recent development outside the city, all lush countryside at the base of Scalp Mountain. It sounded lovely. The idea of getting out of Creggan had its appeal. But still. The two of them. Having sex. Imagine—'cos that's what it would be. Sex. Shaggin'. Nookie. Humpin'. *Jesus, Mary and Joseph, save me now*, Anne begged silently. She'd imagined fireworks on her wedding night. Passion. Instead, she'd likely get sweat in her eye, another dead leg, and Porkie wheezing like an asthmatic bulldog.

This was her life now. So young and about to get married, she'd soon be slowly flattened by a man who likely thought foreplay was taking his socks off. What happened to her dreams? Of first love. Of making love. Of her big tanned Yank and a life filled with sun, sand and stilettos. Her life was heading the wrong way, and there was fuck-all she could do about it.

She looked up to see her mother standing at the kitchen door, watching her. Liz smiled softly, her eyes full of love for her daughter as she asked tenderly, 'Where were you, love? Away off in a world of your own again?'

'Just thinkin', Mammy,' Anne whispered.

Liz Heaney knew exactly what she was thinking. Porkie, who'd been quietly slipping her the odd fiver or tenner for ages. He'd already asked her permission a week or so ago to pop the question. He wasn't a bad sort, not really. His wee contributions made a difference, especially now Anne wasn't working, and likely couldn't work again.

Fair play to her, the wee cripple had really given it a lash. Sent off form after form, applied for every job going. She'd even done a typing course, for God's sake. But no one wanted to take on an amputee. Said all the right things, mind you, all smiles and sympathy, but you could see it in their faces, hear it in their rejection letters. She made them uncomfortable. Like they were scared because she'd half a leg missing, she'd half a brain missing as well.

The pain was still bloody awful. Anne could barely stand it, lying in the living room with that stump throbbing like a bastard. She never said much, simply got on with it. But for weeks now, a deep sadness had crept in. Quiet, like mould. It took over Anne before any of them even noticed. Liz would've preferred her in bad form, like she was before. This gloominess wasn't like her happy-go-lucky daughter at all. Still, bless her, Anne tried. Sometimes she'd slap on a bit of lippy, brush her hair, try her best to look like someone who hadn't been chewed up and spat out by life. But then there were days when she couldn't even be arsed to get dressed. She'd sit there, staring out the window, one leg tucked beneath her, the other long gone.

Liz understood why her daughter was hesitant. Porkie wasn't exactly Mr Universe, not in a million years, but he seemed to have a kind heart and cared for her. She began to tidy up and waited for the inevitable. It didn't take long; she knew Porkie had done the deed.

Taking her hand, Anne led her to the table. Liz sat. *Here it comes.*

Anne's eyes searched her face. She wasn't sure how her mammy would react to the news. 'You'll never guess what?' she asked.

'What's that, love?' Liz feigned curiosity.

Tears slipped down Anne's cheeks. 'It's Porkie. He's only gone asked me to marry him. I suppose... that's it. Who else is gonna take me on with this thing? She gazed at her bulky prosthetic as she lifted it. 'I mean, look at this thing Mammy. It's impossible. I can't go anywhere without people starin'. It hurts. Feckin' hurts. All the time. I'll never be able to work again and God, I've tried. You know I have. Let's be honest, I'm not fit. For anyone.'

Liz's heart broke as she watched that old cloak of misery settle over her daughter again. The cruel part was Anne wasn't wrong. Who else would have her? Not with the moods, the constant pain, that useless, phony leg. Only Porkie. God love her but she was trapped. Liz knew she didn't have the money or the strength to keep caring for her girl forever, and the truth of it was written all over her face.

Anne saw it. 'No choice have I, eh?'

Liz gave a slow nod and a small smile. Nothing to be said.

Porkie wasn't surprised when Anne said yes. He had her in a corner, who else was going to take her on with that gammy leg? He'd played the long game. Kept the mother sweet with the odd fiver or tenner. He had Anne in his wallet. Came at a price, but then, everything did these days. The girl had no idea he'd been circling her like a vulture ever since her da did a runner. Word was, he was still shacked up with some woman from Dublin.

Back when Anne still had her legs and some fire in her, she would've pissed on him. Her and that McLaughlin one, thick as thieves, whisperin' and sniggerin', lookin' right through him and Dickie like they was dog muck on their shoes. A pair of cheeky, stuck-up bitches they were. He'd never forgotten that. Their faces. Now look at him, he was gonna marry one of them. Two legs – who gives a shite about two legs? All he needed was what was in between! He scoffed. What about those swanky red high heels she used to strut about in too? Sluts' shoes, he called them. They'd be the first to go on the fire soon as she was his.

'Peg Leg Annie,' he called her now. Before long, she'd belong to him, and she'd bloody well do as she was told. No backchat. No miserable moods. No say. Took a while, but it worked out okay in the end.

Sweet.

Chapter Twenty-One

Graham

It was the anniversary of Alice's fiancé, Graham – the young gunner murdered during the Troubles. Not 'til the day she died would Alice forget the moment she'd been taken aside and told he was gone, shot clean through the head. He'd removed his helmet whilst on patrol, though no one knew why, when it was so against the rules.

They'd been going out since she was fifteen, but even before that, she knew him from her first year at grammar school in North London. Unbeknownst to her, or so he claimed, he used to follow her home from school until one day he came straight out with it and asked her out.

After that, he never missed a single day walking her home, no matter the weather, no matter what else was going on. They were mad about each other, inseparable really, and over the years, what started as teenage infatuation grew into something special. When the time came, he proposed in a way that could've been pulled straight out of a film, lining the path to their favourite park bench with little glass jars, each one lit from within, and then kneeling down in the middle of it all with that cheeky smile she knew so well. It had taken her breath away. She'd said yes before he even got the words out. Remembering it, the loss caught in her chest like a cramp. She still loved him, and missed him every single day with an ache that never eased, not even for a second.

Today was her last day at Camp Two. Six months of special duties training, over and done with. Camp One had turned out to be the same training centre where she'd first met Kentucky, right next to what she was told was Bessbrook, a full-blown military base, choppers coming and going day and night.

The fitness regime had been gruelling, but it felt like a holiday camp compared to the training she'd finished. There'd been another round of brutal selection, but she didn't care. She was glad to be back and flew through the tests and exercises. She liked the hard graft. The tougher it got, the better. It kept her mind off Graham, gave her something else to zero in on. Getting mega-fit. Leaving all the Londonderry crap exactly where it belonged. Behind her.

Alice was now part of the Intelligence and Security Group, 14 Intelligence Company, better known as 'The Det,' a covert surveillance unit born from the remains of the Military Reaction Force, the MRF, which had been shut down after violating the rules and colluding with the RUC around a string of sectarian killings. This new group had been pulled together quietly, made up of hardened enforcers and bruisers with a taste for undercover work, and Alice, tough as they came, was the only woman in the lot. They carried out overnight observation drills in some of the worst conditions imaginable, along with relentless memory exercises to hammer in every last detail. Faces, locations, car registrations, snippets of conversation, they had to hold it all. On top of that came the refresher courses, and Alice took to them like a woman on a mission. Map-reading, advanced driving, unarmed combat, weapons handling, she didn't just complete them; she nailed them.

The training never stopped. Each day brought fresh demands, new tests, harder challenges, and she met every one of them head-on. No excuses, no half-measures. Six months passed in a blur of bruises, drills and quiet determination. Then, pretty much, it was done. She signed the Official Secrets Act without so much as a second thought, no hesitation. She was back where she belonged. Stronger than ever, solo, fully focused, with her tidy Walther PPK resting neatly beneath her coat and ready for whatever came next.

As she sat in the canteen, picking at some bland lunch, her mind drifted back to her last night in Bangor, dinner with her old friend Ian Dillon. He was to be their best man. Born in Craigavon, Ian had moved to North London with his parents when he was still a youngster and ended up living next door to Graham and his family. Years later, on a holiday in Scarborough of all places, he met a girl from Newtownards, married her and brought her back to Northern Ireland. They settled in Bangor, had some kids, and Ian split his time now between working as an electrician and serving part-time in the UDR. He loved it, couldn't stop talking about it, and willingly shared some of the crazy antics he and his colleagues got up to.

'You'd never believe it, Alice. The lads are grand craic, love nothin' more than hammerin' the Fenians when the riots kick off. Wee shites at the start, throwin' their bricks and bottles like hard men, but now and then, you catch one, pin 'im, give 'im a proper pastin', and suddenly he's bawlin' for his mammy like it's primary school again. Honestly, it's a laugh.'

She remembered Graham's funeral, when Ian got drunk and ranted and raved about how he'd get the Fenians back for killing his friend. He'd been told fairly quickly to sit down and keep his mouth shut, and his friends soon took him home. But she knew in her heart of hearts that he was the only person besides herself who truly wanted to get back at the Provos for Graham's murder.

The meal in the tiny Bangor restaurant had been simple, but good. Alice and Ian were practically on their own, sitting at the far end of a badly painted red and green-walled room, well hidden from the other patrons. She'd chosen the fisherman's pie, which was lovely, and ate it like it was her last meal on earth. It was amazing compared with army food or *Connor*, as they called it back at barracks. Ian had done most of the talking in between drinking a bottle of Italian red. She'd listened with great interest as the evening wore on and his tongue loosened, sharing more and more indiscreet stories.

That's when Alice came up with a plan.

Placing a cigarette in his mouth, Ian lit it up, breathed in but not for long, looked up and carefully blew out the smoke. While trying to keep his voice low, he shared another rousing antic.

'Get this, Alice. A few of the lads were out on the town a couple of Fridays ago, stag do. Four of us in the car, drivin' through Springfield Road, off the Falls, on our way to the stag. So, there's these two fellas walkin' along, mindin' their own business, when one of our lads swears they're Provos, says he's seen them about or somethin'. Anyway, he's convinced they're Taigs. Jesus, Alice, before I knew it, he'd only gone and stuck a fuckin' SMG out the window and – wham-bam, they're both down! Fuck me, we took off in that car like a dog in heat!'

He smirked as he spoke, as if he were recalling a cracking night out, not a double shooting. The pub noise behind them faded to a low hum. Alice kept her face blank. Ian looked straight at her, waiting for a reaction, but all she gave was a small nod and another sip of her drink. He laughed again, dragged on his cigarette, and let the smoke curl from his nose.

'Best part?' he muttered, lowering his voice. 'Was the way they dropped. Like sacks of meat. One of them tried to crawl away, but his legs were gone. The other just lay there, twitching. Blood everywhere. Drove on, didn't we, with the windys down, music right up. Fodder, the two of 'em.'

In his excitement, his already ruddy face reddened further, accentuating his squinty eyes and jumbled teeth. He wasn't a looker, though the eejit thought he was, but Alice trusted him with her life, as had poor Graham.

A pretty, smiling waitress arrived to pick up their plates and offer dessert. Ian barely looked at the menu but made small talk with the waitress, his obvious flirting making her blush as she took their order.

As soon as she was far enough away, a small smile crossed Ian's face as he gazed at Alice. 'So tell me. Are you thinkin' what I'm thinkin'?' he asked.

She thought before answering, 'Might be.' Her mind turned over. Looking at the expression on his beaming face, Ian was well up for whatever it was, too. 'Can't talk right here. Get dessert, then we'll go somewhere quieter,' she suggested.

He'd nodded enthusiastically.

Walking arm in arm along Bangor's high street, they'd come across a relic of a pub that was practically empty. Inside, Alice was first to the bar and waved Ian off to find a seat while she ordered a pint of Guinness for Ian and an orange juice for her. She'd an early start in the morning, but more importantly, she needed to keep a clear head for what she'd been mulling over.

The barman was inhospitable and grumpy as he handed Alice her change. 'You have a good evening too,' she replied sarcastically as she walked to Ian, who sat on a snug leather chair next to a blazing coal fire.

He took his pint, saying, 'Cheers.'

'Cheers,' Alice replied.

They sat, silent and relaxed, watching the fire.

It was Ian who broke the comfortable silence after taking a quick peep around. Good to talk. 'So, you wanna approach it differently next time, do ye?' he asked.

Alice understood his meaning. 'I do,' she replied, her eyes never leaving his. 'Timing isn't ideal. I'm out of sync for the next six months.' She paused, thinking through other possibilities.

'Six months, eh? That's quite a stint,' Ian admitted, a tad disappointed.

Although the advanced training had been priceless, Alice didn't argue. 'I know, Ian, but we need to think this through. Every step planned. It's fine doing one or two, even three, but we can't keep blasting people in the middle of the street like that. The RUC'll be forced to act, make a show of cracking down. On everyone except the Loyalists, of course. That lot's so far up their arses, they'll swallow whatever lie they're fed and look the other way.'

Ian hadn't considered that angle. But now she'd said it, she was right.

Alice, impatient and jumpy, stared into the fire, her leg bouncing until she suddenly stopped, sat up straighter and turned to him. 'Tell me about the others. What else have you done, Ian? Those fellas in the car, the one who pulled the trigger. Tell me about him.'

Ian Dillon smirked, his eyes gleaming. He didn't need asking twice.

Chapter Twenty-Two

NORAID

The noise from the incessant music and conversation was overwhelming as Father Connolly prepared himself mentally for his speech. He'd rehearsed it numerous times and had given it a great deal of thought. He knew it was good: it was factual, wasn't it? Wasn't that what these people wanted to hear? Nothing more, only the truth.

He'd seen it all himself during his time with the parish. He'd witnessed the fallout from the continual RUC and British Army Gestapo-style raids and beatings. The young rioters, even children as young as ten, getting shot indiscriminately with rubber bullets; the women who worked themselves to the bone in local factories for starvation wages; and worse, much worse, the women and men who simply disappeared and then weren't heard of for days or more – interned. Well, he'd seen enough, and he was frustrated. Things had to change.

Tonight's NORAID event was being held in the vast ballroom of a hotel in Yonkers, New York State. The room overflowed with white, round, plastic-covered tables. In chairs around them, an everyday looking crowd sat drinking and talking whilst others moved from table to table, shaking hands and greeting each other enthusiastically.

The County Cork Pipe Band, Hudson River branch, proudly played old Irish rebel songs from the centre of the wooden dance floor. They looked splendid in their plaid green tartan kilts, long green socks, black tailored jackets embroidered with white shamrocks on one sleeve, and bonnet-like hats topped with green plumes. They played their pipe music loud and bold. Their audience wasn't paying much attention, but the band didn't mind; they were in their element.

Six huge glowing crystal chandeliers hung low from the ceiling and glowed against the mirrored walls – tiny diamonds of reflected light danced around the room.

All night, enthusiastic Irish-Americans shook Cathal's hand, introducing themselves and thanking him for being there. Neither he nor NORAID's publicity director,

Cormack Hughes, could believe they'd sold so many tickets for one night and were likely to surpass their target figure for donations. So far, they'd raised $7000. It was incredible; tonight would be one of their best. Ever.

The music eventually stopped. Right in the middle of Cathal's conversation with the owner of a well-known Otis elevator factory, a high-pitched squeal came from a microphone. It was the city council president, Thomas O'Callaghan, attempting to talk. The band moved aside as he took centre stage.

'Apologies! Apologies for that, ladies and gentlemen.' A little frustrated, he yanked the microphone's long black cable closer and tried again.

'Right. Okay. Is that any better?' he asked, looking around the vast room. Several heads nodded. It was good.

'Grand. Grand,' he said, then paused and broke into a laid-back New York drawl.

'Ladies an' gentlemen, what can I tell ya? This is terrific, ain't it? Really is. Wonderful to see all you fine folks out here tonight. Hey, let's give it up for our good friends, the one and only County Cork Pipe Band.'

He clapped his hands, raising them towards the band leader, who gave a bow as the crowd erupted in cheers.

A calm hush gradually fell as the audience's attention was drawn back to their host. O'Callaghan spoke again, this time in a much more serious tone.

'Tonight, ladies an' gents, we got with us a young man who's come all the way from the heart o' the Troubles, straight outta Derry City. Now he's one of our own, born right here in this great country of ours, before headin' back to Ireland. His father, God rest him, was killed in action. Gave his life for his country. For Ireland. A true Republican hero. So tonight, we've asked Father Cathal Connolly to speak with us. Let's hear it from the man himself, what's really goin' on back home, what's happenin' to our beautiful Mother Ireland.'

There was a buzz of excitement from the diners as Cathal stepped forward. O'Callaghan hugged the priest warmly and whispered a thank you in his ear, offering over the microphone.

Left alone on the stage, Cathal surveyed the room, and then solemnly addressed his waiting audience.

'Good evening, everyone. There is indeed British law and order in the North of Ireland today, but what is the nature of that law, that so-called order? Mr Harold Wilson, the

British prime minister, didn't elaborate on that recently when he spoke out against NORAID and your mission to aid the Irish people under British occupation, but I will.

British law in the North of Ireland has for over five hundred years contradicted and violated the laws of every civil rights charter in the world. It is a law that makes a mockery of the Magna Carta. It is a law that violates the United Nations Declaration of Human Rights and the European Convention on Human Rights. British law in the North of Ireland is the only law in Western Europe since Hitler that allows men, women and children to be imprisoned without charge or trial.

I myself have witnessed the carnage and suffering during and after Bloody Sunday. Our friends, fathers, mothers and our sons – most of whom were shot in the back on that fateful day – were innocents! I've looked into the eyes of family members left behind, who will never, ever forgive or forget their loss. That day started out so full of hope and ended in tragedy beyond our wildest dreams. It will live on in our hearts and minds for the rest of our lives.'

He took a second. You could have heard a pin drop in the room as he added. 'The soul of our beautiful city has been extinguished and will take years to recover – if ever. And remember, we must never forget the Ballymurphy massacre of innocents, five months before Bloody Sunday, and by the very same First Battalion, Parachute Regiment.' The crowd shouted and roared with his every declaration.

'Amongst all the murder and mayhem, young schoolchildren today, ladies and gentlemen, are still being shot and killed simply for being in the wrong place at the wrong time. Their heartbroken mothers will never get them ready for school again, will never see them make their first Holy Communion, will never see them make their Confirmation, or experience their wedding day or celebrate the births of grandchildren. All those wonderful times have been stolen, for always and ever. These men and women and their families live with a pain that none of us in this room could bear to imagine. So many innocent lives lost, so many lives ruined, so many lives changed forever. But you can make a difference here tonight...' He carried on, swept away with passion.

When he was finished, he thanked everyone and watched chairs topple as guests leapt up, applauding and cheering. Some even whistled loudly as Mr O'Callaghan slapped him on the back. He congratulated Father Connolly and whispered enthusiastically, 'Perfect, Father, exactly what they needed to hear.'

He made his way back to his table, greeted with well-wishes, handshakes, and even the odd kiss. At last, he sat down and took stock of his performance. He'd been nervous.

Overdid it. He wasn't sure the new Bishop of Derry, Bishop Carlin, would agree with everything he'd said. The young priest knew getting involved in Derry politics was wrong, but he couldn't stop himself. The city needed NORAID's money. Creggan needed it. It could ease the pressure on mothers working all hours to cover the bills.

It could bring hope to families whose children had been orphaned or murdered, and to victims left broken by the conflict. Their lives would never return to what they'd been. Inevitably some of the money would end up supporting the Provos.

Cathal gulped down the glass of white wine that had stood untouched by his plate all evening. He looked around and smiled. This was what he lived for: to help support and encourage change in the lives of those unfortunate souls in Derry. If it meant he'd have to keep coming back to the US, then he'd do it. Whatever it took.

He watched as a group of around twenty men pushed their way through the grid of tables to reach him. Their leader was a redheaded, red-moustached bruiser of a man with heavy sideburns, a freckled complexion and a crooked grin. He grabbed Father Connolly's hand and shook it eagerly.

'Ah, Father, that was just somethin', y'know?' His Yonkers accent rang clear, fast, full of muscle.

'Me an' the fellas 'ere, we're sittin' back there goin', Jeez, this guy's the real deal.'

He jerked a thumb at the hard-looking crew behind him.

'We were sayin' that a couple of us are thinkin' of comin' over to Derry. For a week or two. Give a dig out, like. Don't know at what exactly, we'll figure it out.'

The lads behind him chuckled, one flicking his cigarette, the rest nodding along.

'See, Father, thing is. We can do anything. We all built our own houses, poured the concrete, wired the electrics. There's gotta be somethin' we can do for the guys back home. What d'ya say?'

The group waited eagerly for Cathal's response. He thought of the many houses around the Bogside and Creggan that could do with improvements. A lot of improvements. More importantly, it would lift morale on the estate, give them a good-news story for a change. To his bewilderment, these guys were New York cops. They'd laughed and jeered, joking they'd hold their own against the RUC if they had to.

Throughout the conversation, Cathal's eyes drifted to a young man sitting at a far table. He'd been watching him all evening, listening intently to his speech and every conversation since. Military type perhaps, with that number one haircut, smooth shave, and perfectly pressed clothes. He wore a light taupe suit with a dark brown shirt and a mustard-coloured tie, dressed to impress. Possibly a peeler too, possibly not; but he'd a niggling, annoying feeling about him.

Eye contact was made. The stranger stood up, smiled, and moved to the next table to chat with a tall, honey-haired woman who looked utterly smitten.

As the night wore on and the time slipped into the early hours, there was no sign of the party ending. A local country band was now on stage, and the dance floor shook in response to the boisterous and somewhat inebriated dancers. The place was awash with noise and buzzing with excitement.

Cathal and his NORAID host agreed they'd had enough and made their way to the lobby for – at Hughes's suggestion – an Irish coffee. Cathal hadn't touched an Irish coffee in years. He smiled sadly at the memory of the last one at home the night before he left for the seminary. Only him and his ma, sitting quietly by the peat fire. He'd made the drinks, sneaking an extra dollop of Jameson into hers, hoping it would help her relax. It worked. He'd laughed as it hit her hard.

After that, she'd spent the evening recalling happy memories of life with his father, and he'd listened eagerly, loving the way she slipped back into her old self. But since then, her health had declined, and he'd found the slow unravelling painful to watch.

The two men sank heavily into the soft settees scattered around the hotel lobby. As soon as their drinks were taken by a youthful, green-jacketed waiter, they relaxed and grinned at each other.

Hughes was ecstatic. 'You're a gold mine, Father. What a find – a maestro! That ballroom was in awe. People practically holdin' their breath. You're a natural. Those rousin' stories, the passion... Christ, you almost had *me* join the Provos!'

He gave a laugh, waving the idea away. 'Mad, I know. But more importantly, speeches like that? They reel people in...' He rubbed his fingers together, as though the money was already in his hand.

Later, as they sat talking through the next event, their coffee arrived. The waiter had barely turned away when the young man who'd been watching Cathal earlier sauntered over.

Without invitation, he dropped into the velvet chair beside them. He smiled, first at Hughes, then at Cathal, and offered his hand.

They exchanged a quick glance, amused, before shaking it. Then came the accent. Derry through and through.

'Father, that was one hell of a speech. Pardon the language, but it was bloody brilliant! I'm well impressed. Martin McLaughlin. Great to meet ye.'

Chapter Twenty-Three

A New Look

Lemon sat outside Charles Jones's office, grinning to himself like the cat that got the cream. He was still riding high from the last op, clean, efficient, no loose ends, and couldn't wait to lay out every gory detail. Jones would appreciate that. He always did. The man was cold as stone, a pitiless bastard who hated Fenians with a depth Lemon respected. No pretence, no apologies. But absolute loyalty to the Union. That's why Lemon followed him without question.

A clean hit it was. Over in seconds. Lemon had spotted the two men laughing as they left the Catholic church, aimed, fired, and bang bang! What stayed with him was the look on their faces. Hadn't a clue what hit them. Two fewer Taigs to worry about.

Jones had made his order plain and simple: he didn't give a hoot who got taken out or where, so long as it was clean, quick, and left no witnesses. Now that it was done, Lemon knew the boss would be pleased. To celebrate, he thought he'd chance his arm again with Jones's snooty secretary, but she shot him a look that could curdle milk. Then, in that prim, schoolmistress tone of hers, she pointed to the chair outside the office and said, 'Sit. Be quiet. Wait.' He half expected her to tell him to stick his fingers on his lips. Bossy bitch, he thought. Someone needs to teach her a lesson, give her a good seein' to. Could do her the world of good.

Jones walked in, dapper in his usual dark suit, white shirt, and a glaring over the top orange tie. Lemon sprang to his feet as Jones looked him up and down, shaking his head in disbelief. What the hell was that supposed to be? He wondered.

Unlike Morris, who always looked razor sharp, his military discipline drilled into every part of him, Lemon was a total sight. The idiot wore a blinding orange polyester bomber jacket with red topstitching, loud enough on its own to draw a crowd. Paired with tight, creased jeans that looked like they'd been dragged through a hedge and black hobnailed boots better suited to delivering coal, he stood out like a spare prick at a wedding.

Jones gave him a brief nod as he walked to his desk, unpacked his briefcase, and sat down. Then, in a voice cold enough to freeze peas, he said, 'Lemon. Don't you think it's time you smartened yourself up?' He threw a wad of £10 notes across the desk. 'Get yourself a decent suit, will ye? Some shirts and a tie. I can't have you hanging around looking like a Provo mural from the Falls.'

Lemon's face drained of colour. No one ever spoke to him like that and got away with it. *No one.*

Jones saw and pulled back, but only just. 'Look, I'm only saying you work for me now. I expect a certain standard, that's all. Calm down and let's not make a big deal of it.'

Then he leaned in, his eyes lighting up with something close to hunger. 'Go on then, tell me, what did it feel like?' He didn't mean the op. He meant the moment the two Cradle Catholics hit the ground.

Lemon gave a haughty grin. 'Soooo wicked. As we planned, the UVF'll take the credit.' Any resentment he'd felt towards the boss vanished the second he started reeling off his report. Every word was delivered with exacting detail, like he was proud of it.

Once Lemon had left to go shopping, Jones leaned back in his chair and picked up the phone. He spoke to Judge Dodds, reassuring him that his Boodles Club membership had been approved. Yes, the IRA had bombed the place, though to little effect. A botched effort: another crude device, tossed into an empty dining room. No, it wouldn't be closed for long. Eventually, he assured him that the club still welcomed *'the right kind of Irish.'*

'Judge, it's fine. 'They'll fix it up quickly,' Jones said while Dodds kept complaining.

'That's all very well, Charles, but the place is an obvious target. Bad enough having strife here, but to bring it to Central London... Barbaric.'

Over the past month, IRA bombings had surged across London and Manchester after the collapse of a ceasefire. They'd gone on a rampage: hitting a military outfitter on Old Bond Street, a couple of four-star hotels, a chemical plant, a gasworks, even a waterworks in North London. The result had been a bloodbath. Civilians dead, dozens more injured, and millions of pounds in damage.

'Couldn't agree more. Now, my apologies, Judge, but I have to run. I'll be in touch soon,' replied Jones. The judge didn't get another word in before Jones replaced the receiver in its cradle.

From the corner of his eye, through the open door, he caught sight of a figure storming towards the office, face like thunder. Jones swallowed. He'd never seen the man look so angry and couldn't help but wonder what the hell had happened.

James Henderson Snr burst into the room and slammed the door behind him. The frame rattled.

'I've just heard!' James bellowed, his face burning with anger.

Jones balked.

'Heard what? What are you on about?' He said it calmly, but his stomach was churning with fear.

'You bastard,' James spat. 'It was you all along, behind that thug who shot the bishop. You've wrecked everything for my family, Charles. Everything!'

Henderson Snr had been quietly pulled aside by an old army pal, a loyal one, who warned him about Jones and his underhand antics with the late William Morris. Word on the street was that the Belfast businessman had been behind the bishop's murder and the almighty cock-up that followed at the City Hotel.

Jones stood and made a move for the door, but Henderson was too quick for him. He met him halfway and gave the small, pug-like man a shove that sent him flopping back into his seat.

'You've made a complete fool of me, Charles. A fucking fool! All this time I've listened to your harangues about the Queen, the Union, and Ulster, and for what? I trusted you. Believed in you. Do you have any idea what you've done? You've nearly killed my brother and devastated my son. They tried, they worked so hard, to make that conference a success, to save the factory, save all those jobs. I admit it now, I was never that interested in Rocola, but this is my blood you're screwing with, my family and, like them, I'm sickened by what happened at that hotel!'

Jones started to get up again, but growled from his seat, 'Oh, James, don't be such a bloody hypocrite. Save those jobs? That's the last thing I wanted. I planned for those Fenian bitches to lose their jobs. Every single one of them. I practically owned that factory! You and your brother have borrowed up to the hilt from me. As for you, you knew exactly what my plans were, and what I needed you for. Took my money though, didn't you?'

Jones lurched to his feet, face twisted with rage, and jabbed a finger an inch from Henderson's nose. 'Everyone's got a price, James, even pompous arseholes like you. So spare me the righteous act. You've been in my pocket for months, whether or not you like it. Now you want to come in here, waving your bloody morals around? You make me sick.

Now get out of my office before I have you thrown out like the pathetic, gutless English bastard you are.'

James Snr shook his head slowly, eyes looking at him with cold disgust. 'You've no idea how much I know already, Charles. What you've been doing, who you've been doing it with, and exactly why. Worse than that, I know what you're planning next. I'll tell you this much, I know where I'm going next and what I'm going to do. So help me God.'

He stepped towards the door and looked back for the last time. 'You'd be surprised, Charles. I still have contacts in prominent places.' He threw open the office door and stormed out, not sparing a word or glance for Jones's secretary, who sat gobsmacked at her desk, too stunned to speak.

Chapter Twenty-Four

A Desperate Phone Call

James Henderson Jnr stepped into the lift at Rocola, heading back up to his office, fresh from yet another productive meeting held at the back of the cutting room. He'd spent the morning with several of the shop stewards, the most experienced among them being Ernie Taggart, a man James respected. Taggart had backbone, wasn't afraid to speak his mind, but, crucially, he listened. He understood the value of give and take, and wasn't the type to dig in his heels for the sake of it.

Alfie McScott, Rocola's accountant, had finally received the last six-month government instalment, and early feedback suggested the Secretary of State's office was broadly satisfied with how the funds had been used. It was a rare bit of good news.

But James had other concerns. The daily riots around the factory had grown worse, always sparked at Stones Corner. It felt like someone was dying every day now, shot or blown up. What disturbed him most was how people were accepting it, growing numb to the grisly sights on the streets and the nightly news. The abnormal was becoming normal.

Opening the glazed office door that now had his name etched on it, James took his seat. Mrs Parkes saw him arrive and promptly followed him inside. Her voice, with its broad East Belfast accent, sounded decidedly worried as she said, 'Mr Henderson, your father's been calling. Tried Melrose too. Anyway, seems he's on his way back from Belfast and will be home in time for dinner. Told me he needs to talk to you urgently. I have to say he sounds worried, upset like.'

James was oblivious as to what it could be about since he'd last spoken to his father ages ago. He wondered what could be so urgent that it justified him driving the entire way from Belfast, where he now spent practically all his time. Feeling a little unnerved, he thanked Mrs Parkes and told her he'd kill for a coffee. She rushed to the kitchenette.

Staring at the empty desk outside his office, James caught himself thinking about Caitlin again. He shook the thought away. Mrs Parkes still ruled her corner office at the far end of the corridor, parked between her two junior assistants like a general flanked by her lieutenants. James had already asked her to find him a new secretary, but she was probably stalling, plainly reluctant to hand over the reins. He knew she liked being in the loop, enjoyed knowing everything that went on at Rocola, and she wasn't about to give that up without a fight.

He was feeling better these days, all down to Marleen. She'd been a blessing and came across to Melrose more often now, all bright colours and boundless energy, making even his uncle laugh. She'd even brought Roger a pup. A scruffy wee terrier, claiming it'd be good for him. To everyone's surprise, Roger adored the mutt. Personally, James detested it and wondered why Marleen even got it, but he kept it shut. Wasn't worth stirring the pot when things were finally getting better.

The office door opened, and Mrs Parkes returned with a cup of piping hot coffee and a chocolate digestive. He smiled. 'Spoiling me again, Mrs Parkes. Thank you.'

She returned the smile and, unlike when he'd first started, she knew this time he meant it. Without a word, she turned and quietly left the office.

As he sipped his coffee, he skimmed through the post, most of it with little thought. It was the usual crap, business correspondence, invoices, memos from suppliers, until one envelope caught his eye. Airmail. Handwritten. A blue South African postmark that stood out against the rest. He turned it over, recognising the elegant cursive writing. His gut tightened. Her again. His mother.

Earlier that day, Marleen had answered the phone in Melrose's hallway to hear James's father speaking earnestly down the line. 'It's me, James. Is my son there?'

Clicking her tongue at the lack of a warm greeting, she replied, 'No, I'm afraid not.' She listened as he ranted on, insisting he needed to speak to James as soon as possible. Then, with no thank you and not so much as a goodbye, the line died. How utterly rude, Marleen thought, turning and heading for the warmth of the basement kitchen.

Mrs McGinty, the housekeeper, had always liked Marleen. Since she'd been coming back and forth, the two of them had struck up an easy rhythm in the kitchen, where Mrs McGinty reigned supreme. She'd begun showing Marleen all sorts of cookery tricks, and the girl soaked it all up like a sponge. Marleen especially loved baking Irish soda bread, but what really got her going was learning how to make herb sausages from scratch, beaming like she'd won the pools every time she got it right.

It was close to tea time and upstairs in the study, Roger was trying to relax, though it wasn't going terribly well. Every few minutes, he was pulled from his thoughts by sharp little nips at his ankles. The culprit, of course, was Ned, his pup and who had already wriggled his way into Roger's heart. He liked it best when the wee fella got too tired and curled up at his feet, his soft head resting on his slippers like that was where he'd always belonged.

The phone rang from across the room. With a long, low grumble, Roger heaved himself up from his seat, stretching out his stiff back and letting out a theatrical yawn. Ned, not one to be outdone, yawned too, a perfect mimic, which made Roger chuckle as he bent down and gave him a gentle pat on the head.

He shuffled across the room, the phone's shrill ring rising in urgency, and muttered, 'Give me a sec, I'm coming!' as he reached for the receiver. 'Henderson,' he snapped, sharper than he meant to, but the moment he heard his nephew's voice, low and unmistakably tense, the mood shifted.

'Hi, it's me. Can you talk?' James asked.

'I can. What is it? You don't sound right.'

James hesitated. 'I'm not sure yet. Only Father's been trying to reach us, and now he's on his way to Melrose. Said he wants us both there when he arrives.'

Roger straightened, the cord of the phone suddenly too tight in his hand. 'Did he say why?'

'I didn't speak to him, but Mrs Parkes says he sounded worried. Not right.'

Roger felt a slow churn of unease settle in his gut.

'Right,' he said quietly. 'Then we'd best be ready for whatever it is. Don't worry, you know what your father's like.' He looked down at the pup and added, ' Your Father will be fine. Ned's here keeping me company, Marleen's buried in the kitchen with Mrs McGinty, busy with... whatever women do down there.'

James couldn't quite picture Marleen cooking, but the thought brought a smile to his face. Before long, he and Roger were chatting about Ernie Taggart and how well the meeting with the shop stewards had gone earlier that day. It was a small win, but one he'd take.

Dinner had been and gone, the plates cleared away hours earlier, eaten more out of duty than anything else. Neither of them had said much. James Snr hadn't turned up, and both Roger and James had done their best not to panic, each one stealing glances at the clock, pretending James Snr's absence was nothing. But it wasn't nothing. Not by a long shot. He'd something he wanted them to hear.

The stillness of the house had grown blacker with every tick of the clock, the kind that made your thoughts run away with you. It was late now, far too late, and neither of them needed to say what was going round in their heads. Like the house itself, they were too quiet, too still, as if bracing for bad news.

Then, at last, a pair of headlights swept across the living room wall, and a car pulled slowly into the gravelled courtyard of Melrose. James was on his feet in an instant. *He'll kill him when he gets his hands on him!* Without waiting, he ran for the front door and yanked it open, expecting to see him standing there, contrite and apologetic.

Instead, standing in the porch light, was George Shalham, his face ghostly pale. He wore a long black coat, heavy wool draped over striped pyjamas, oblivious to the cold night air. James felt a sudden chill run down his spine and the hairs on his arms rose. 'George... what is it? Please. Come in.'

But Shalham didn't move, he simply looked at him and gave the smallest shake of his head.

'It's your father, James. I am so sorry.'

Chapter Twenty-Five

Diplock Courts

The man's heavy boot slammed between his legs, and Emmett McFadden doubled over, the pain beyond excruciating. He and Mickey had been split up the moment they entered the underground corridors of Castlereagh holding station in East Belfast, lined with numbered interview rooms.

He'd lost all sense of time. They'd torn out chunks of his hair and kept hammering the same side of his face, which now felt twice the size of the other. Another boot slammed into his side, catching him beneath the ribs, and Emmett screamed like a girl. His body twisted on the cold floor, arms wrapped tight around his torso, trying to protect himself from the next blow. Above him loomed a dark-headed peeler, his face twisted with rage, spitting every word as he roared down at him.

'We know you did it, Emmett! We've got witnesses!'

Emmett tried to lift his head but dropped it back again with a low groan. His whole body pulsed with pain. He barely heard the next threat.

'Now, before I kick your fuckin' balls off, you gonna sign on the dotted line or what?!'

The room swam in and out of focus, and the pounding in his ears had all but drowned out the man's voice. He wasn't sure how much more of it he could take, but he wasn't daft either. He knew if he signed a single sheet of paper, even scrawled his name at the bottom, they'd have him. Owned and ruined for life. Everything hurt as he yelled, 'I'm signin' nothin'. I don't know what you're on about, me doin' somethin'!' He looked up at his assailant, his eyes wide and pleading. 'Please... Will ye stop, mister, for God's sake, just stop!'

Detective Black had no intention of stopping. He wasn't nearly finished with this one. He laughed, slowly tugged down his white shirtsleeves, then folded them back up again. One neat turn at a time.

Well known for getting results, Black liked that people saw him as a hard man. He'd earned the reputation, and it suited him fine. There was no official handbook for this sort of questioning, no real guidelines either - not that he'd follow them if there were. He didn't need training. He was a natural, and he relished the challenge. Breaking stubborn Republican bastards gave him a kick like no other.

The Diplock courts had changed everything. No juries anymore, only a judge and his signature. A confession, whether beaten out or cleverly coaxed, was all they needed to put you away. Throw in a halfway decent witness statement, and that was that. Done and dusted. The numbers were going up too, as the chief constable ordered. Conviction rates were through the roof, another grand week for law and order. As for the Loyalists? Hardly any had been touched under the new system. Weren't seen as urgent, and not worth the bother.

Everyone was happy. Chief Constable Bonner was happy. The press was happy. Jonathan Black was happy.

He scoffed to himself, thinking about the four fellas brought in earlier, all charged with the same offence. One of them would talk - eventually. Always did.

He'd spent the better part of the day moving from room to room like a butcher pacing a meat locker, taking his time, working on each one methodically. The older Taig who'd come in with the McFadden lad was proving a tougher nut to crack, stubborn and quiet, but he wasn't troubled. It was still early in the game, and there was plenty of time left to wear him down.

Black turned back to the teenager slumped in the chair, his Umbro tracksuit bottoms tangled round his ankles like a discarded rag, and bare from the waist down. McFadden was a big youngster for his age, solid across the shoulders. Not that Black gave a toss what age he was. He shook his head slowly, sneering to himself.

'Let's see what you're made of then, boyo. I'll explain it one more time. We've got two witnesses who say they saw you with a piece. The same piece that shot a colleague of mine dead in Londonderry. First day on the job, him a new dad an' all. Poor sod.'

He stepped in closer as if to whisper, 'So, here's the deal. You're fucked. Completely and wholly. You're going down. Unless...'

He got up, opened his arms wide and looked about. 'If you want all this to stop, it's easy: will ye sign the dotted fuckin' line.' Then, with a lazy wave of his hand, he added. 'We'll get you a nice hot dinner and a cuppa tea after. How does that sound?'

Emmett could barely lift his head. 'Naw,' he whispered. 'I'm not goin' to no gaol. No fuckin' way.'

Black gave a huge sigh and sat back. He knew about Emmett's Provo brother, Joe, currently enjoying the fine hospitality of Her Majesty in Long Kesh.

Leaning over the table in a voice mellowed with fake concern, he asked, 'How many brothers did you say you had, son?'

Emmett blinked, thrown by the change in the peeler's voice. 'Brothers?' he asked.

'Aye, brothers. How many?'

Black had used this trick before. Rarely did it let him down.

Emmett stayed quiet, again unsure what the bastard was on about.

'Come on, son, how many?' Black pressed. Less patient now.

Emmett looked at him, but couldn't see right, his face felt battered, swollen, wet and burning like fuck from all the slapping.

Black's gaze stayed steady as he took in the damage. Blood had leaked from the boy's ear, now dried into a rough line that flaked down his jaw like old paintwork. A few patches of hair were missing too, ripped clean out where Black had gripped a handful and yanked back hard, not once but over and over, until the lad learned to keep his head up when spoken to.

Groaning, Emmett muttered, 'One.'

Black snorted. 'One, eh? Well, not anymore. Your Joe tried to run. He's a goner.'

'No way!' Emmett screamed. He surged upwards, chair and all, and lunged at Black like a rabid dog.

Black leapt back, laughing, retreating to the far corner of the room and holding up his hands in mock surrender. 'Okay, okay. Easy boy. Tell you what, you chew on that bit of news. I'll be back.' He slipped out the door and closed it gently behind him. Outside in the corridor, he clenched a fist and raised it in quiet triumph. Not long now. The lad was so close to losing it and signing. One down, one to go.

Emmett remained hunched in the same awkward position, his hands now tied behind the metal-framed chair. Despite the thumping headache, he couldn't stop from drifting off, and this time when he came to, he realised he'd peed himself. Shame burned right through him.

No one had come in for what felt like hours. Jesus, he was dying for the bog, needed a shite so bad it hurt. A daft, desperate part of him even wished the detective would show his face again, so he could ask, but the second he thought it, he regretted it. If that bastard came back, it would all kick off again. More questions, more digging, more pain. Toilet or not, he wasn't ready for another hiding. Then there was Joe. The thought of him being dead was crawling all over his insides. Please God, don't let it be true. *Please.*

He shifted about again, his wrists rubbed raw from the rope biting in every time he moved. His tracksuit bottoms clung around his ankles, bunched like shackles, and the cold in the room had worked its way under his skin, a creeping damp that settled deep in his bones. He bit down hard on the inside of his cheek to stop the tears. Every creak or rattle from the corridor made him sick. But no one came. Not yet. Only the flickering overhead strip light, buzzing like a wasp in a jar, the stink of stale sweat, dried blood and piss. That slow, crawling dread. This was far from over.

The door creaked, and in stepped Black. He took his time. Stopped by the door, letting his eyes adjust before they narrowed on the Derry man. He stepped closer, boots tapping on the concrete, and noticed the dark puddle on the floor beneath Emmett. A slow, crooked smile crept across his face. 'Trouble keeping it in, is it?' he said, voice lazy with mock concern. 'Bit old for that carry-on.'

Emmett looked up at him, his jaw tightening, refusing to drop his gaze. 'I needed the toilet,' he said, voice low but constant.

'Aye, you said that already,' Black replied, circling him like a dog sniffing at its prey. 'Thing is, Emmett, you don't get to decide when you piss. That's my call.'

'I need the bog,' Emmett said again, louder this time. He was trying to sound firm, but his voice cracked on the last word.

Black stood still, considering him for a moment, then gave a slow, exaggerated nod. He didn't like the stink either, and it was starting to rise. No windows, no air, basically misery floating around like fog. Without looking back at the boy, he opened the door and barked into the corridor, 'Help needed here!'

His voice wasn't raised, but it didn't need to be. It was the kind of voice that made people move. Eventually, a young constable with fair hair came running, flustered, already dreading what fresh mess he was about to be handed. Black jerked a thumb at the boy. 'Get him cleaned up. He needs the toilet. Take off the cuffs. He'll behave.'

The constable wrinkled his nose at the sight of Emmett, half-naked, bruised and bleeding. He looked like hell. *Typical*. Black did the damage, and someone else had to mop up. But as he stepped closer, Emmett straightened himself up. He was still cuffed, still hurting, yet in that moment he'd become a man. Behind the bruises there was a resolve, faint but undeniable, and it wasn’t fear, not exactly. It was harder, a quiet fury, a look that told the peeler — you'll never break me.

Chapter Twenty-Six

A Special Offer

A few rooms along the corridor, CID Detective Adrian Walsh was having far less success than his colleague. He sat across from Mickey Boyle, staring into a pair of bloodshot eyes. The man hadn't cracked. Not even close. Tough bastard, Walsh thought. Didn't flinch. Didn't waver. But stared back like he'd already made peace with whatever was coming.

Walsh had never grown used to the brutality of Castlereagh, not like some of the others who seemed to take it in their stride, even enjoy it. It wasn't about the fists, though that was bad enough. It was the endless hours, the slow, grinding tactics, the deliberate mental battering they dished out, piece by piece. The way they played with people's heads, stripped them of dignity, turned the smallest weakness into a weapon. Men and women kept for days on end, no peace, no rest, interrogated until they didn't know what was real anymore. The whole thing shamed him, and no amount of justifying it could ever make it sit right.

Every Monday morning, the CID held a telephone call with the chief constable to run through the week's arrest and conviction figures. Only numbers to them, it was all about the numbers, reminding him of a production line. Bodies in, bodies out. It wasn't why he'd joined the force. Not even close. As a Christian, he wanted to make change, to do good.

He'd watched DC Black come and go from that room more times than he cared to count, and every time, it was the same routine, only worse. Each visit brought a fresh level of cruelty, as if the man got a thrill from dreaming up new ways to break someone. Boyle had already taken his fair share, fists to the ribs, boots to the thighs, and then, when Black felt like raising the stakes, he pulled out a lighter, flicked it on, and pressed the flame to the man's cheek, holding it there long enough to blister. Then, as if that wasn't enough, he went for the poor fella's balls. In an instant. Like it was part of the job, part of the entertainment.

Walsh had learned the hard way to keep his mouth shut. What else was he meant to do? Speak up and that was you finished. Everyone in the place knew it. You'd be out on your ear, labelled a traitor, not only by his boss upstairs, but by the ones who'd made the rules from day one. So he'd done what the others did. Turned away. Kept his head down. Let that sick bastard get on with it, even when every instinct in him screamed to stop it.

Prisoner Boyle hadn't exactly helped himself. From the second he was dragged into Castlereagh, he acted like he was checking into a bloody hotel. Head up, chest out, the big man, full of swagger. At the custody desk, he came face to face with a tall, bald sergeant who had the charm of a wet cement wall and a face to match.

Boyle, handcuffed and standing stiff beside a scowling guard gripping his baton like it was part of him, looked straight ahead.

'Name?' the sergeant barked, not even glancing up, pen already scratching.

'Michael Sean Boyle.'

'Address?'

'Twenty-nine Roscommons Gardens, Creggan, Derry.'

'Date of birth?'

'Under thirty-five.'

That made the sergeant stop. He stared. His date of birth was right there on the licence they'd recovered during his search.

He sighed and moved on. 'Occupation?'

'Freelancer.'

The sergeant narrowed his eyes. 'Freelance what?'

Boyle didn't miss a beat. 'Undertaker.'

The sarge's pen stopped mid-word.

'You're a smartarse, Boyle.'

'I try. Oh, and by the way, we're runnin' a *special* deal at the minute. For you fellas. Two-for-one. If you or any of your esteemed colleagues need me services anytime soon, I can give ye me number now. Forgot me business cards, ye see. Sorry.' He winked. One second later, a baton came down on the back of his neck so fast it was a wonder the smartarse didn't see stars shaped like coffins.

Mickey Boyle watched Black retreat from the room, his heavy boots echoing down the corridor. He'd been at the bastard's mercy for hours now, battered with the same questions over and over about some peeler shot dead in Derry. Even when Black started in on threats, dragging Mickey's family and friends into it, Mickey knew the man had nothing. Not a shred of evidence. Most volunteers had been warned about Black, been told what to expect and to trust no one.

Not that it mattered. The fucker could easily dig up one of his touts, pay them off or scare them stiff, then get them to swear blind Mickey had confessed. That was how it worked. Worked, far too often. But not this time, Mickey Boyle wasn't for signing or confessing to anything.

He was twenty-five and no stranger to a good hiding, though this one had taken the biscuit. They'd strung him up, and now his feet burned with agony, a dull throb from where a baton had struck him again and again. He'd seen the glint in Black's eyes, that twisted pleasure as he and the other animal set it up. They loved it. But Mickey's hatred ran deep, the kind that stuck in your gut and made you feel brave when you had no right to be. It gave him a lifeline to hold on to, something dependable. They'd have to break their hands on him before they got a signature.

Then, down the corridor, Black's voice rang out, loud and clear, calling for help. It wasn't panicked, but barked out like an order, but it still made Mickey's heart crash like a dropped brick. *Jesus.* What had he done now? If that bastard was calling for help, then whatever occurred in the next room was bad. He closed his eyes and breathed deeply, picturing the big Derry fella. A youngster, probably trembling, sick with fear, thinking only of getting home. Mickey said a quiet prayer the poor bugger hadn't given them anything, signed anything.

Along the corridor, Emmett savoured the brief relief the bathroom gave him, even if it was only for a minute. The cold water stung like hell as he rinsed his hands and splashed his face, the raw skin burning with every touch. He glanced at the cracked mirror above the sink, then looked away just as fast. That swollen mess staring back wasn't him. Didn't feel like him either. Turning from the reflection, he shuffled toward the waiting peeler, hands out, silent and ready to be cuffed again.

Black was back in the room. He'd dragged the small desk dead centre, papers lined up neatly on top. Emmett's chair had been placed right in front of it, with Black's directly opposite. It all looked oddly civilised.

Without a word, Black gestured for him to sit, then slid a single sheet of paper across the desk and set a pen beside it. A curt nod to his colleague told him Emmett's cuffs were to be removed. Then, without so much as a glance, he added, 'You can go now.' He delivered a long, theatrical sigh, the kind that filled the room with trepidation, then scraped his chair forward and leaned in, elbows planted on the desk, face too close for comfort. His voice dropped to a near whisper, low and cold, the sort of tone that made your blood run thin. His eyes, unblinking, drilled straight through Emmett.

'Let me share this with ye, son. I've got all the time in the world for hard men. Respect like for *hard* men. They bleed, they spit, they stand tall, and then they break, same as the rest. But what I can't abide, what boils my piss more than anything, is a dickhead who thinks he's clever. Right now, Mr McFadden, that's exactly what you are. A cocky, clueless mother fucker of a dickhead. So here's what's going to happen. You're going to pick up that pen, you're going to sign that fuckin' document, and you're going to do it quick. Because if I lose my patience, son, you'll wish it was only bruises ye walked out of here with. If ye walk out at all.'

Chapter Twenty-Seven

The Offy

Alice Wallace still wasn't sure how they'd pulled it off, but the powers that be had landed her a job in a West Belfast off-licence, the sort of place she'd never have stepped foot in back home. It all came with an Irish passport, bulletproof documentation, and just enough backstory to keep the nosy neighbours quiet.

According to them, her parents were Irish. Killed along with her little sister in a car crash in Hertfordshire. She'd supposedly moved from London, where she was born, to be near the only family she had left in Belfast. People always went quiet if you mentioned a tragedy like that, the little sister, her being an orphan. Fingers crossed, it worked a treat. Nobody asked too many questions, and if they did, she'd tell them the worst of it, look away, and murmur, 'It's hard to talk about.' That usually shut them up.

She kept her head down, smiled when she needed to, and minded her business behind the counter. She wasn't overly fond of the place, the smell of stale beer, fags, and God knows what else, but it was perfect for what they needed. The best bit? No one suspected a thing. Not the fat fella who ran the shop, not the drinkers who came in red-faced and hung over, not even the kids nicking chocolate when they thought she wasn't looking. She was Alice. That quiet English girl with her sad eyes and dead family. Tragic.

She'd given herself a full revamp. These days, it was short skirts, black stilettos, low-cut jumpers that clung in all the right places, the tighter the better. Her hair was now chopped into a sharp Pixie cut and dyed a deep, burnished auburn, and, surprisingly, she liked it. It suited her. It was more than a makeover. It was a reset, a deliberate shedding of her old self. Brona Doyle had been born.

Her little bedsit above the off-licence wasn't much, but it was easy to keep tidy and warm enough most days, and that did for her. Cosy, manageable, like her cover. People trusted her without thinking. That was the clever bit. Hardly anyone would suspect a woman like her worked for Det, not with those outfits and not with the way she had of locking eyes with you and holding it long enough to make your insides twist.

If all went according to plan, she'd be under for a year or so. Nearly four months in now, and she was finding her rhythm, recognising the faces, picking up the pace of the slang, tuning her ear to the accent and the daily chat. She kept in touch with Ian Dillon, and the two of them had quietly put together a scheme so dark and dangerous it could change everything. For now, it stayed between them, but when the time came, he'd pull in a few of his UDR mates and the real work would begin. It would take time, but she was patient. When the moment came, they'd hit hard, hit the Republicans where it hurt, with no chance of them seeing it coming.

It was a grim, wet Friday night, and unusually quiet. Alice stood behind the offy's glass-topped counter, filing her scarlet nails, when the door burst open. Still holding her steel nail file, she watched as a figure stepped inside. Someone she didn't know.

The man was tall. Broad. Strong build. Mid-thirties, or so. Those eyes – sad as anything. Deep lines carved into his brow and cheekbones, like he hadn't slept in a month. Clean-shaven and, yeah, handsome in a way, with long, curling dark hair, he had thick, neatly trimmed sideburns.

'Hi,' he breathed.

'Hi. Can I help you?' she replied.

'Bottle of Smirnoff please,' he said, studying the shelves laden with alcohol behind her, 'and two bottles of Coke.'

'No bother,' Alice replied. 'Haven't seen you round here before.'

'Nah, just visiting. Up at a wake,' he replied.

'Sorry for your loss. Anyone I know?' she asked, faking sympathy.

'A pal. Shot by the Brits,' the man said, his voice flat, casual as you like.

'Bastards,' Alice replied, carefully placing the three bottles in a large brown paper bag.

'Aye, I know.' He sighed as he took the bag and paid.

Waiting a few moments, he stopped and stared as if trying to place her. 'You're not from 'round here either, are ye, with that accent?'

'No, my mum and dad were, though. Died along with my sister in England. Car accident, so it was. Had to come home,' she answered, encouraging her eyes to well up.

'Ah, Jesus, sorry,' he replied, taken aback.

Alice smiled and thanked the genius who'd thought that one up. Assuming a broken voice, she added, 'A while ago now, not to worry. It's the pain. Hard to talk about it.'

The man smiled and whispered, 'Aye. Can imagine.' He looked like he was about to say more, but thought better of it. Gave a small wave instead, then was out the door before she could blink.

Whoever he was, he'd left a mark, not in words or gestures, but in that quiet, lingering sadness she recognised instantly, the kind that slipped in unnoticed and settled deep. It stayed with her for a few minutes, or more, but the moment passed quickly enough, as the door had barely clicked shut behind him when the next customer belled in, and before long, amid the noise and bustle, Alice had forgotten all about him.

The following week, though, he came back as she was about to close and looking more relaxed this time. Same order as before.

'Another wake?' Alice asked.

'Nah. Not this week. Had to stay up a bit, that's all. Got a bit of a job on.'

'That's good. What do you do?' Alice asked, as if interested.

'Joiner,' he blurted.

'Always work for a carpenter these days.' She flirted and put out a hand to introduce herself.

'Brona Doyle.'

He smiled warmly and took it. 'Patrick Gillispie, mostly Paddy.'

'Nice to meet you, Patrick Gillispie,' she said invitingly.

He didn't get a chance to say another word before the shop bell went like the clackers. She'd locked the door behind him, thinking he'd be the last customer of the night. Tutting, she peered through the barred glass of the door.

Two lads stood outside. Sixteen'ish. Appearing edgy and agitated. Pacing back and forth, muttering over the shop front. One was a rake, tall and twitchy. The other couldn't have been more than five foot one. Both had skin like sandpaper, angry red spots breaking through greasy stubble, and looked like they hadn't washed in days. Their jackets were too big, their jeans hanging off them. Pair of vagabonds.

She paused, uncertain, chewing the inside of her cheek as she weighed it up. Then, with a half-hearted sigh and a muttered, 'Ah, go on then,' she opened the door and stepped back to let them in. She couldn't rightly slam it in their faces, not with Paddy waiting, arms folded, watching the whole thing unfold like it was none of his business, but not quite managing to hide his curiosity.

'Right, fellas, make it quick, I'm closing.' she said.

They shuffled past her without a word, heads low, hands in their filthy pockets. Paddy, she noticed, had stepped into the shadows. Circling the small shop and almost bumping into each other, the duo hadn't seen Paddy, who watched as the tallest of them suddenly pulled out a small pistol and pointed it right at Alice. 'Empty that fuckin' till now!' he snarled, attempting to frighten the life out of her.

Alice smiled, folded her arms, and looked at him like he was asking her to run stark naked around the place. 'Nope,' she said.

He probably hadn't expected that, so tried again, louder this time. 'I said, empty the fuckin' till, bitch! Before I shoot. I'm tellin' ye, I will an' all! The cash. I want the cash. Now!' He waved the gun as if it might do the talking for him.

All the while, his partner in crime stood nearby, grinning like mad, and watching everything. He started sussing the place out, his eyes flicking over the shelves and counter until they landed on Paddy. In an instant, the colour drained from his spotty face, slow and sudden all at once, like water down a sink. He gave his friend's arm a sharp tug, the grin gone, replaced by sheer panic.

'Max!' he whispered urgently.

Pissed off at his interruption, Max tore his arm away and cocked the gun again.

Paddy crept up behind the youngster, walloped him a right one, hard across the back of the head and like a pro, grabbed the handgun.

The boy spun around, spotted Paddy, turned sheet white, and locked eyes with his buddy. In mere seconds, the pair of them took off like scalded cats, both gone in a flash. Alice threw back her head and roared laughing. What a pair of absolute wankers! She hadn't had such a good laugh in a long time. Paddy's stern face broke into a genuine smile.

She went quiet as she watched the way he handled the gun, how he checked it with expertise. He glanced at her, offered a reassuring smile, and said, 'Empty.'

'Small miracles. What are we going to do with it?' she asked.

'I'll sort it,' he replied. 'Them two eejits as well. I know them.'

Jackpot.

She'd clocked it straight away, the way the two hoods froze when they saw him, the way their cocky act crumbled like day-old bread. They knew him, no doubt about it, and by the look on their faces, they were bricking it. Her gut told her he wasn't some face from around the way. No, this fella had clout. Had to be a Provo. High up at that. Ideal. The sort Det had been desperate to get on side. If she was right, she'd got him. Game on.

'Well, I, for one, am glad you were here,' she said, watching him tuck the handgun into one of his deep coat pockets.

'Me too,' he replied. 'By the way, why'd you say no when he asked for the cash?'

Alice shrugged and smiled, 'Because I could.'

Paddy stepped out of the offy, feeling quietly pleased. He'd liked the woman from the moment he'd set eyes on her. She hadn't moved an inch when that wanker shoved that pistol in her face. Stood there like she was made of steel. There was only one woman he'd ever known like that, and that was his twin, Dolores. Brona Doyle wasn't his usual type, not in the slightest, but there was a way about her that didn't sit right. That pixie haircut, for one. It wasn't enough to go digging, not yet, but it was enough to keep her on his radar. He'd look into her soon, check if that story of hers held water - parents and wee sister wiped out in some freak car crash. A bit too neat, he reckoned.

Things were heating up these days, and likely to get worse. Everyone needed to keep their wits about them. You couldn't trust your own shadow. Better to keep people at arm's length, whether or not you knew them. Touts were a scourge. Everywhere you looked, someone was grassing on someone. Command decided it was time for an overhaul. Too many leaks. Too many bodies. First move was to cut cell numbers and isolate every single one. No cross-talk. No crossover. They'd already lost too many good volunteers to grasses. He hadn't planned on staying this long in Belfast, but he was here now, and with the going ons, he couldn't see a way out. Not yet.

The past week had been hell. First burying a comrade, then reading that British propaganda crap in the papers and TV. Poor bastard, him innocently standing on a street corner, minding his own business when the Brits shot him down, there and then. Afterwards, they told the press he'd opened fire on an army patrol, so they fired back. *Bollocks*. The guy was unarmed. If there were an inquest, it'd be the usual farce. Lies and shite.

Christ, but he was tired, but not tired enough to see Brona Doyle again. If she were up for it, he might try it on. It'd been ages since he'd, well, it'd been a while.

By the end of the next week, they sat across from each other in a chippy off St James's Crescent, in the Falls district of Belfast. Paddy had popped into the off-licence to ask her out and she'd jumped at the chance. There wasn't much in the way of decent food nearby, so they'd settled on fish and chips. Alice watched her date. He'd dressed to impress with a pair of Grey flared cords, a white shirt under a patterned jumper and freshly polished black Chelsea boots. She noticed his hands were red and calloused. She'd been right about him. Det were delighted and confirmed Patrick Gillispie was a big old Provo, and not just *any* big old Provo. He was high up, well, high up in the Leadership. One of their most wanted.

She'd struck gold, but they needed solid evidence, and it was up to her to get it. Gillispie spent most of his time in Monaghan; they said. A quiet border town, close enough to watch, plan, and slip over the border when the opportunity called for it. Most of the time, the Provo worked solo. There'd been ructions between the Provos and what was left of the old IRA. Det reckoned big changes were on the way, and Gillispie was bang in the middle of it. Pushing for it. He was smart and well respected amongst his own. They'd been watching him forever and now she had her orders. Stay close, take her time and reel the bastard in.

Over dinner, their conversation flowed. Paddy asked about her childhood, her parents. She knew her cover inside out, so the story came out smoothly, no stumbles. It helped that some of it was true. Memories she'd picked apart and stuck back together to suit. He watched her as she spoke, quiet but alert, throwing in the odd question, never giving much away himself. She was fair craic, and tonight she looked the part. Black V-neck jumper, short leather skirt, white boots up to the knees. Confident with it too. Sexy and he liked it.

The hair was mad, cropped short and blazing red. He hated it. But the way the girl laughed, the fire in her when she argued her point, that stirred him. He liked a woman with a bita' spark, and right now he was wondering what she'd be like in the sack.

All the same, as usual, he kept his thoughts to himself. No sense in scaring her off or giving too much away. He'd play it cool.

For now.

Chapter Twenty-Eight

Friends Again

'Bye, now. See you Monday,' Caitlin shouted as she opened the photographer's shop door, the bell above it jingling.

'Bye, Caitlin. Thanks and be careful on the way home. Friday night, you know what it's like,' Raymond Burns called from his office at the back.

Fair play to him, she thought. He'd been unusually supportive and kind after her mother's death, and she still couldn't believe he'd paid her a little extra to help with the funeral costs.

Her ex Seamus had returned to the US a few weeks before. As they said their goodbyes, he'd made her promise to sort herself out, take better care, and try to get some form of normality back into her life. It was a big ask, but she'd promised she'd try.

Strangely enough, his turning up was a bit of a blessing. The very next day, he'd insisted on paying for her to get her hair done. She hadn't been near a hairdresser in months, and the fresh cut and blow-dry gave her a right lift. Afterwards, they had a nice lunch, then some shopping where he spoiled her, urging her to pick out a new dress and even splashing out on a bottle of perfume. As they strolled through town, Caitlin noticed how people greeted him, old friends stopping for a catch up or shaking his hand. She felt proud at being seen with him.

They even rounded off the evening at the Stardust, the local disco, for a bit of craic. She'd taken her time getting ready, put on some makeup, and tried to enjoy the night. Part of her did. She laughed, danced, made the most of it. But inside, the ache hadn't gone anywhere. James still haunted her. Every love song reminded her of him. Still, she kept smiling, kept going, because what else could she do?

For a long time, she'd thought she'd never be capable of enjoying herself again. The very idea of music, of moving her body freely in front of others, had felt impossible. But at the Stardust, he'd softened her. Not completely, not all the way, but enough to let her dance, let her laugh, let her enjoy herself, even for a while.

On the way home, Seamus didn't go near her, but walked beside her talking about their day. No hassle, no pressure. She didn't think he expected anything more. There was a gentleness about him, respectful in a way that surprised her. It stayed like that for the rest of his trip. So many cuppas, so many stories about New York and Boston, and the occasional quiet, comfortable moment between them. It'd been nice.

When he finally left for the airport, he kissed her lightly on the cheek before climbing aboard the bus to Dublin.

'I'll be back soon,' he'd said, hand on the rail, eyes searching hers.

She gave him a wave and a half-smile, not sure if she believed him, but too tired to dwell on it.

The evening was moonless, bitter and crisp as she made her way home from work, heading along Strand Road towards her bus stop, hoping the service was still running. She was well wrapped up, her scarf snug and hands buried deep in her coat pockets, but she didn't mind the cold. In fact, she welcomed it. The sting of the wintry air on her face made her feel alive, more present. Normally, she loved this time of year, that stretch from Halloween to Christmas, but this year, the thought of Christmas was already too much.

A couple of days ago, a wedding invitation had landed on the mat and shaken her to the core. It was from Anne. She was marrying Porkie! Caitlin had nearly keeled over when she saw it. Jesus Christ, Porkie? That sleazy, greasy creep, and him so old. She couldn't get her head around it.

So, first chance she got, Caitlin headed straight to Anne's. She didn't care how late it was; she needed to see her, ask her why on earth? She banged hard on the door and waited, nerves going half a dozen in her chest. It was Anne's mum, Liz, who answered, eyeing her from head to toe like she'd crawled out of a toilet.

What's that look for? Caitlin asked herself. Liz Heaney had always been so nice.

'Aye, and what do you want?' Liz snapped, eyes sharp as glass.

'Mrs Heaney... is Anne in, please?' Caitlin asked, her voice small.

Liz scoffed, sounding bitter.

'Ah, Anne. You remember our Anne now, do ye? Well, she's not up in Brooke Park playing tennis or out doin' a half marathon now. Is she Caitlin McLaughlin? She's been here in this house for weeks, suffering from a stinking infection in her leg. *Alone*.'

Caitlin gasped. No answer to that one.

Liz folded her arms, her fury evident. 'Not so full of talk now, are ye? There's you vanishin' for ages, not a word, not a card, nothin'. She missed your ma's funeral, cos her leg was so bad, and you didn't as much lift the phone or call over to see why not. Not a sign of ye.'

Caitlin was lost for words. Guilt sat on her chest like a block of stone she couldn't shift. Why hadn't she called over to Anne's sooner? Because she'd been too thick and too stubborn, that's why. Jumping to conclusions. After everything, assuming the worst in people.

Mrs Heaney leaned on the doorframe and said. 'We tried to ring that neighbour of yours to say she couldn't go. No answer. Even wrote a bloody letter. Still, not an iota from ye, nothin'.'

Before Anne posted Caitlin's wedding invitation, mother and daughter had fought. Liz didn't want Caitlin there at all, and now, there the girl was, standing on the doorstep, bold as brass.

She huffed, wondering whether to let Caitlin in. If she didn't, Anne would go off on another one of her rants. Nothing was worth that. So, rather reluctantly, and with a tight smile, Liz opened the door wide.

'You'd better go on in then, hadn't ye. Now that you've graced us with your presence.'

'Thanks Mrs Heaney. Thanks and I'm sorry.' Caitlin said as she warily stepped up into the hallway.

'Who is it, Mammy?' Caitlin heard Anne call from the kitchen.

Liz gave a sharp bob of her head, motioning Caitlin to follow her.

In the kitchen, Anne was sitting at the table, halfway through her dinner. She looked up, surprised to see Caitlin standing there all timid by the door, like a rabbit caught in headlights, then smiled, as if nothing was wrong between them.

'Hello, stranger,' she said, setting down her knife and fork and pushing her half-finished dinner plate aside.

'Hello, you,' Caitlin replied quietly. 'Sorry it's been so long.'

Before anything else could be said, Liz snatched Anne's plate and flung it into the sink with a clatter.

'I'll leave youse to it then,' she muttered, marching out.

As Liz vanished down the hallway, Caitlin exhaled a shaky sigh of relief she hadn't realised she'd been holding onto.

Anne giggled. 'Don't pay heed to me Ma. Sit yourself down and stick the kettle on. By the time I get up and make it, it'll be Sunday week!'

She raised her stump in the air like a trophy. The infection had raged on, and Anne couldn't use her prosthetic leg at all now. The damn thing hurt like hell every time she tried to put it on.

'Always the joker,' Caitlin said with a soft smile, pulling out a chair beside Anne and not bothered about tea. She was '*tead*' out!

'Aye, that's me, a right comedian!' Anne said, making a face.

'Mind you, there's not been much laughin' done in this house of late. You've seen Mammy. Not the happiest bunny rabbit, or hadn't you noticed?'

Caitlin gave a guilty shrug.

'I noticed. I'm sorry for not being in touch. It's just… it's been rotten with everything… well, since Mammy.'

Anne reached for Caitlin, squeezing her hands tight, her voice quieter now.

'I'm sorry, Caitlin. Really. Must've been awful for all of ye. I wanted to be there, but I got a bastard of an infection. We tried the McFaddens. Ended up sending a bloody letter. Did Mammy not tell ye?'

Caitlin pictured their untidy coffee table at home, cluttered with un-opened letters and bills. *Must've missed it.*

'I've not opened the post in donkeys. It's probably lying at the bottom of a pile somewhere. Screwed that one up, didn't I?'

She was all over the place these days, and Liz's outburst hadn't helped. Nevertheless, the look in Anne's eyes said what she needed to hear. Anne was here for her, no matter what. She released the disappointment she'd been dragging around for weeks. She wasn't on her own. Wasn't forgotten. Just a stupid eejit who hadn't opened her post. She broke down. Her tears came fast as she clung to her friend. *God, but she'd missed her.*

Anne said nothing at first, but stroked her hair and let her friend cry. Then she whispered, soft and low, 'You've been missed, ye know. Life's shite at the mo', Caitlin. But we'll be grand, so long as we've got each other. Us two have to stick together, keep each other sane, am I right?'

Caitlin smiled properly for the first time in weeks. They were back. Together.

'Don't be worrying about me Mammy either, that woman's bark is worse than her bite. Deep down, she's as pleased to see ye as I am,' Anne added.

Returning to the kitchen, Liz spotted the two girls wrapped in a tight hug. She paused in the doorway, pretending to tidy up, though she was only being nosy. Watching, listening. Then, with a small, quiet smile, she slipped away.

Thank God for that. With Caitlin back and, with a load of luck, Anne's erratic moods might finally be on their way out.

Caitlin sat and listened, really listened, as Anne talked about Porkie. How he called in, helped them with money, and why she felt she had no choice but to marry him. But Caitlin couldn't bear it. Every time Anne tried to explain, she cut in, her voice rising with frustration. 'But Anne, Jesus, you wanted to go to America. Your dreams, remember?'

Anne rolled her eyes and waved a hand towards the remains of her leg. 'Are you fuckin' serious, Caitlin? I mean, look at me. Who the hell in their right mind would want that?!'

Caitlin opened her mouth but nothing came. She had no answer. Basically sat there, stunned. Again.

Anne shifted in her seat, she'd had enough talking about Porkie. 'Right, enough about me and the wedding shite. What I wanna know is... what happened to your man? The Adonis. I've been dyin' to know for ages. Go on. Spill. All of it.'

Caitlin's chest tightened like a vice. She stared at the table, then said quietly, 'There's not much. It's like I never existed. You were right, you and Mammy. Got what he wanted, then after what happened at the hotel, our Tina going all doo-lally over Kieran Kelly and him planting that bomb, James lost it with me, blamed me.'

She looked up, voice louder now. 'Said we were all in on it. Said our Martin had roped us into blowing the place up. Me and Tina. Imagine that.'

Anne scoffed and kept listening. *Wanker.*

'After that, he lost it with me and disappeared. Wouldn't give us a chance to say I knew fuck-all about what Tina'd been up to. Gone, like that.' She clicked her fingers. 'Not a word, only a letter from his uncle. Cold as ice. Firing me.' No need to mention the cheque she'd regrettably torn up.

Caitlin could still hear James's voice, intense, arrogant and so decisive, like a door slamming somewhere deep inside her. The shame of it all was still suffocating and even now, it upset her, left her shaking, like she might crumble from the inside out.

Anne had always known the relationship was a dead end. But sitting here now, watching her sad, broken friend, the last thing she was going to say was *told you so*. Caitlin wasn't stupid. She knew she'd been used. The whole thing felt surreal when Anne thought about it. How their lives had skewed so far out of shape. She cast her mind back to those mornings that now felt like they belonged to someone else, when they'd stroll to the factory arm in arm like daisy chains, full of gossip, full of hope. Laughing, telling stories, dreaming about the future. They'd been happy then, or as near to. All of them.

Today? Today was like trying to stitch yourself back together with broken thread.

She'd lost part of her leg, her job, and was marrying a man like Porkie because, well, what choice did she have? Caitlin, poor Caitlin, heartbroken by that wanker Henderson, parents both gone, and her brother Martin... Since Caitlin didn't go into detail about him, maybe she didn't know he'd been let out, then gone AWOL. Anne wasn't about to dump that on her tonight. Tina, *Christ*, off her trolley and locked away for life. What a fuckin' mess the whole lot of it was.

Caitlin felt a billion times better being here with Anne. Porkie's name came up again, and yeah, there'd been a few fiery exchanges, voices raised and hands flying, but they'd agreed to disagree. Progress, at least. What mattered most was that they were talking again. No keeping a distance, or being stubborn and thick, the two of them, back where they'd always been. It might take time to mend all the cracks, but this, this was a start. Friends again.

Chapter Twenty-Nine

A Toy Gun

Caitlin had been to Stewart's supermarket in town for a few bits, and by the time she reached her bus stop, a middle-aged man came trudging up, two bulging *Wellworths* bags swinging from his hands. With a grunt, he let them drop to the ground and announced to the queue already waiting, 'Heard the Brits've closed Blighs Lane. Bomb scare. Couple of buses hijacked already. Black cabs can't get up the hill either. We'll have to walk up.'

'Not again,' Caitlin moaned. She couldn't remember the last time life felt ordinary, when people could come and go without hassle, without searches, without riots or bomb scares. No one else in the queue said a word. It was just another day. They quietly disappeared, each heading off on their own long walk home.

She weighed up her options and decided to cut past the cathedral, then climb up to Creggan from there. The fresh air would do her good, she'd been sat on her backside all day, anyway.

But as she headed towards Great James Street, a loud commotion cut through the air. Banging, shouting, screaming. It had to be another riot, most likely near William Street by the Rossville flats, the site of the Bloody Sunday shootings. She picked up her pace. She should've gone the other way.

With the cathedral to her left, she rounded a corner when something shot past her face, so close it swept a few strands of hair across her cheek. Thinking it was some giant insect, she swatted the air. Then she knew. Silly cow had walked straight into a full-blown riot. Masked men with white handkerchiefs over their faces surged past her, shouting, chased by armed soldiers.

Terrified, Caitlin spun around, searching for anywhere to hide. Out of the blue, a hand grabbed her arm and tugged her into the dark doorway of a terraced town house. 'For the love of God, wee girl, that was close!' a man shouted in her ear. 'Get in here now! Quick as you can!'

Caitlin stepped inside and watched as an old man frantically locked his front door. He directed her into a small living room that faced onto the street.

She looked around. A two-seater, floral-covered sofa with fine white crocheted arm covers stood against the wall to the right. A black-and-white TV was positioned in the opposite corner, with a V-shaped wire aerial on top next to an old photograph of a smiling couple on their wedding day. A well-worn chair stood by a simmering coal fire, round gold-framed reading glasses resting atop a copy of the *Derry Journal*.

Facing her rescuer, she saw he was a well-built, white-haired man, dressed in high-waisted tweed trousers held up by a belt and a pair of red braces, into which he'd tucked a tea-stained grandfather shirt. On his feet were half-eaten tartan house slippers, courtesy of the whimpering terrier cowering beside him.

Shaking his head, he looked at her in disbelief. 'Never seen anythin' like that, love! Didn't you feel it? A rubber bullet. Woman, it was that close to your head!' He pinched his thumb and forefinger together to show just how close. 'If you'd moved an inch to the side, you'd have been a goner!'

A bullet? A rubber bullet? she thought. *No way!*

The man briefly left her to switch off some house lights before returning to the living room. He waved her over to the window to look outside at the chaos unfolding.

The smell of tear gas was almost as shocking as the scene beyond: the street had become a battlefield. The night was lit by flames from petrol bombs hurled at the security forces. Army flares turned the dark sky into false daylight, then floated back to earth, while red tracer fire streaked across the sky in crisscrossed bursts. Glass bottles smashed, spilling fire across the pavements. Stones, sticks, anything the rioters could get their hands on, flew through the air.

In the smoke-filled street, heavily armed soldiers and police crouched behind clear plastic shields, faces hidden by hankies and domed, open-faced helmets. Blue lights flashed from the steel-grey armoured vans.

Caitlin watched as a soldier knelt, took aim, and fired rubber bullet after rubber bullet into the pack of rioters. They stampeded like wild animals, scattering and regrouping. Two men drove a small Ford up onto the path, jumped out and left the driver's door swinging open. A lone masked man ran forward, hurled a petrol bomb into the car, and seconds later, a deafening explosion ripped through the night. Behind the safety of the living room window, she screamed.

An eleven- or twelve-year-old boy was standing by the burning car. With his bowl haircut, white shirt under a plaid tank top, and short black pants, he was standing close, like far too close, to the flames that were devouring the car.

'He's going to get burned!' Caitlin cried, about to run for the door.

The old man stepped in front of her, firm but gentle, one hand on her shoulder, and cried. 'You can't go out there, love. Are ye askin' to get yourself killed?'

'But look!' she pleaded, pointing a finger towards the glass, her voice breaking with panic.

Out in the street, the boy raised a chunk of misshapen wood, the poor child's effort of a rifle. They watched in horror as he playfully took aim at something ahead. The crack of the shot was lost in the noise, but suddenly the boy crumpled, sinking to his knees. His head hit the ground sideways, flopping and lifeless.

'Oh my God! Oh my God!' Caitlin sobbed, her voice high and thin. 'They've shot him, mister! They've shot him!'

The aged man's eyes met hers, his breath ragged and his heart about to burst. 'Aye love. They have. They got the critter.'

She clapped her hand over her mouth, about to be sick. She could taste the rising bile. As quickly as he could, the stranger showed her the upstairs toilet and left her to it.

Downstairs, fury radiated from the pensioner like heat. The poor child, he'd been holding a wooden gun. Another time, another place, it would've been just a toy. But not here. Not now. It got him killed. Jesus, Mary and Joseph. A toy. One he probably made himself. That's what the Derry kids did these days. Played pretend.

He'd watched them from the bus. Bored boys and girls acting out what they saw every day, stopping each other, spreading arms and legs, mimicking the Brits. Play-acting soldiers, play-acting shootings, play-acting raids.

Why hadn't the Brit seen it? The toy, why hadn't he seen it?

Caitlin's rescuer's tired heart swelled with sorrow.

It was a day he'd never forget.

Chapter Thirty

Cells with no Doors

'Sorry, pet, we didn't want to tell you until we felt you were ready,' Tommy said as he looked across at his niece in the visitors' room of Armagh Women's Gaol.

Tina's fragile mind was working overtime, trying to comprehend that her mother was gone. For good. Like real life, gone. Dead and buried next to Daddy. She must've been really sick to die like that. To fall asleep and never wake up, Tina mused, as the wrenching ache of loss tore through her.

'It's okay,' she replied, her voice faint, 'at least she's with Daddy now.'

'I know, love, I know. She's with your da now.' Tommy repeated with a heavy sigh.

Caitlin and Tommy had decided not to tell Tina about her mother's passing until they felt she could cope with such news. They certainly weren't prepared to share with the poor soul the gory details of how her mother had died. Looking around the visiting room, he noticed half a dozen POs lined up against the walls, their eyes fixed on every move. Visitors first, then the prisoners. With contraband slipping through so easily, they needed eyes in the back of their heads. The place was a damp, stinky mess; it smelled like mildew and damp clothes.

Tommy had thirty minutes. 'You'll be okay? Won't you?' he asked, studying Tina with a mixture of pity and concern.

'Aye. The women in here are nice. They're taking care of me, especially Bridget. I don't like it here. I'd rather be home, but...'

Nodding toward the screws, Tina told him, 'But those women over there, most of them, they're horrible, Tommy.'

'How do ye mean? Want me to have a word?' Tommy asked. He'd do anything to help.

Her eyes met his for a second, but then, remembering, she clammed up. 'It's nothin'. Forget it. I'll be grand.'

How could she explain it? How do you tell a man that sort of thing, the strip searching, and all the other stuff? Tommy'd end up being as broke as she was.

He shook his head, frustrated. 'Ye sure? If you're not tellin me somethin', I swear to Jesus, I'll sort it. Say the word.'

Tina's deadpan expression was answer enough. Subject closed. Tommy didn't push her. She didn't look great, pale as ever, dark circles under her eyes, but she was more with it than the last time they'd crossed paths. Christ, but he'd never forget the state she'd been in by the end of the court case, barely able to string a sentence together. They'd all thought she'd lost the plot entirely, gone completely la-la. Rock bottom.

Seeing her now, sitting upright, speaking in full sentences, it was a step up. This place, grim as it was, was helping her. God knows how, considering it looked and felt like a proper shithole. But stranger things had happened. Tina could see his concern and, to cheer him up, told him, 'We were jiving last night, Tommy. The craic was great.' She smiled. 'Some of the other girls were useless, but I did all right. I even gave them lessons.'

'Is that right?' he answered, slightly surprised. *Jiving*! How on God's earth could they be jiving in this place?

'It was a genuine laugh, and they did a joke on me too. Made me look like a right eejit. They only asked me to go to the shop. There's me ready to take all their orders, get up mega early like a stupo, and ask the screw to let me out. There's me with me list in me hand!'

The big man hadn't heard her talk so much in ages and was chuffed. He understood that larking about and joking was one way the poor critters in this hellhole coped.

'You were caught there, 'suppose,' he said, chuckling.

Tina half-smiled at the memory.

'Tommy,' she whispered, 'how's Caitlin? Is she speakin' to me?'

He groaned. By keeping the truth from Tina about Majella's death, he'd left her to stew, thinking her sister didn't care enough to visit. But the truth was worse than that. Caitlin had been shattered by her mother's suicide, down to the bone, and then, as if that wasn't enough, she'd watched a wee fella get gunned down by the Brits in front of her.

'Of course, she's speaking to you, she's not the best. She'll come and see you next time. Would you like that?'

'Aye. I miss her and, well, I feel bad about... you know. Everything.'

Tommy gave her a warm, understanding smile. He wasn't about to rake up what'd happened at the hotel. No point in dragging that mess back up. Instead, he launched into all the usual carry-on, chatting away about who was up to what, who'd fallen out, and who was seeing who. Easy talk, nothing serious, like they were sitting in her kitchen, like the old days.

Before they knew it, the visit was over. As Tommy rose to leave, he opened his arms wide for a hug.

Before the screws had a chance to give him a bollocking to back off, Tina stepped forward and threw her arms around him. She held on tight, not wanting to let go, holding on until the bollocking came. Then she stepped back and looked up at him, her eyes brimming.

'Thanks, Tommy. Thanks for coming. For everything.'

He smiled softly and wistfully. 'Love you, darlin'. Take care, and I'll see ye before ye know it. Bye, love.'

Then he turned and walked away.

Tina glanced back, hoping to catch his eye one last time, and gave a small, child-like wave.

Back in their cell, Bridget lay reading one of the many books the inmates shared. When the youngin' turned up, Bridget knew from her face. Bad news.

'What's up, hen?' she asked, sitting upright.

Tina's bottled-up tears finally let go, streaming down her face as she sank onto the bed. Her shoulders shook as she tried to gulp it back, tried to keep it together, but it was no use. The older woman was at her side in seconds, taking her in her arms, holding her close like her mammy used to.

'Ah, love. What is it? Tell us.'

'It's Mammy, Bridget. Fell asleep and didn't wake up. Dead.' she cried into the woman's large, warm and lavender-scented bosom.

'Och no. I'm so sorry,' she said, sharing the girl's pain. She'd never really got over losing her mammy either, all those years back. That was the cruellest thing about being inside - missing everything that mattered. Birthdays, weddings, funerals, all the little family gatherings that kept people together. Her own memories stirred as she spoke, and her eyes clouded over before she could stop them.

Bridget was proud that, under her wing, the young'un had come on leaps and bounds, but was now desperately worried Tina would zone herself out and retreat into her own world again. She'd seen it happen before, that dead-eyed stare, the long silences, the way some girls faded into themselves and never quite came back. She couldn't let that happen to Tina, not after everything.

She hugged the girl hard, holding her close for a moment, then gently let her go. Taking Tina's tear-streaked face in her hands, she looked her square in the eye.

'Listen to me now, you'll be alright. Do ye hear? You'll hurt like hell at first, but we've got you. Remember that. All of us, we'll get you through this.'

Tina nodded slowly, eyes red and raw, but there was a flicker telling Bridget she'd heard her.

Nodding, Tina backhanded away her tears and whispered. 'I know, Bridget, I know. It's well sad after me daddy and me. Thank God Mammy wasn't in pain or anything. Tommy said she went in her sleep.'

Some consolation, at least, Bridget supposed. She pulled Tina back into the refuge of her arms. Although she tried her best to be as upbeat as she could, sometimes Bridget Barry felt she was living her life in nothing but a rotten pit of pain.

The following morning, everyone got up. Tina and Bridget made toast using a Kosangas fire and waited for their post under the arched windows at the end of their wing. They'd finished their chores and were feeling too lazy to exercise in the yard. Together, they sat quietly as they attempted to get their toast just right.

In time, the atmosphere began to change as the wing buzzed with muffled whispers. *Long Kesh was on fire!*

The men were living in brutal conditions, not far off a World War II prison camp, with sometimes eighty or ninety packed into each ramshackle hut. For months now, the internees had been protesting. Refusing meals, accepting only bread, tossing their bed linen onto the perimeter cage wire, and refusing to cooperate with the screws or prison authorities. There was no proper hospital, virtually a filthy, cramped treatment shed that barely qualified as medical. Like Armagh Gaol, there wasn't even a resident doctor.

One young fella had been crying out with shocking pain for a week. No one listened. They left him to suffer, and in the end, he died in agony from some virus he'd picked up. All for the sake of a bit of care. Now the cages were in flames. The lads had set fire to the place themselves, knowing full well what was coming. There'd be savage beatings by the Brits, maybe worse. A lot of the women inside Armagh had husbands, brothers, fathers locked up over there. Maureen, the OC, had heard a few of them had been taken to hospital. Nobody from the Kesh got taken to hospital unless they were in a bad way.

The OC had decided. Enough was enough. It was time the men in the Kesh knew their women were standing with them. What to do? She called a staff meeting, and the women from each wing met, prepared to handle the situation with determination. Ideas flew around the room, but one stood out. They'd wait for the governor's usual morning round at eleven o'clock. When he showed up, they'd grab him, his chief officer, and any other screws on the wing and take them as hostages. Each OC Wing was given her role, and the plan began to take shape.

Prior to kick-off, Maureen had a conversation with the UDA's OC. She didn't know if their men had been involved in the Kesh fires, but they agreed to help all the same. The other Loyalist women, the Ulster Volunteer Force (UVF) refused. Too worried about losing their remissions.

The strongest and tallest among them were picked for the takedown. When Governor Johnston turned up, it went off without a hitch. He and the others were grabbed and crammed into a cell in B-Wing. Job done. From there on, the real work began. They knew the screws would try to lock them down, so each cell door was ripped clean off, tough going, but they managed it. It gave them control fast.

Then the destruction started. Some officers managed to slip out of A-Wing and hit the alarm. A piercing wail filled the air, but it didn't stop the women. Beds were broken to bits. Sheets torn into strips. Bolts were pulled from the frames and laid out in piles to be used as makeshift ammo. Slingshots were fashioned from bra straps and elastic, anything they could get their hands on. They threw metal at the army checkpoint outside, at the gaol walls, the windows, anything that might keep the PO's back.

Water leaked from cracked pipes, spreading across the floors. The women kept going, dashing through it barefoot, laughing nervously, their adrenaline spiking. They barricaded stairwells with whatever they could find; tables, lockers, broken furniture. In the bathrooms, toilets were smashed, sinks cracked open. In the end, the place was unrecognisable.

It was reckless. It was bold. But exactly what they needed.

Governor Johnston and his staff, along with a prisoner who'd taken a knock during the chaos, stayed calm and composed inside the locked cell. They had only a plastic po' between them for a toilet, and no one was in a rush to use it first. Maureen kept in regular contact with Father McGuire, who'd legged it from Derry the moment word of the protest reached him.

Rumours began to swirl that the British Army was gearing up outside, planning to come through the roof if they had to. Through their windows, the women observed a flurry of activity below: flashing blue lights, officers trying to control dogs, and Brits scurrying about. News crews had turned up too, vans everywhere, cameras rolling to catch whatever they could.

Wasting no time, the women scrawled giant messages across their bedsheets - *Prison wrecked, End internment* - and flung them from the windows for the world to see. Someone came up with the idea of killing the lights, give the Brits as little visibility inside as possible. The screws retaliated by shutting off the heating, and within hours, the place turned freezing cold.

Bridget, drained and desperate for five minutes' peace, wandered down the catwalk until she spotted Tina curled up on a torn mattress, trembling and pale. Across from her were Roisin and Eileen Murray, two interned sisters deep in whispered conversation. Bridget lowered herself beside Tina, who barely acknowledged her, and inched a little closer, enough to catch a few snatches of what the other two were saying.

Roisin was on a roll. 'Sure, I nearly died! There he was, this big lump of a fella with a spanner in his hand, and me, for Jesus' sake. We looked like *Little and Large*, we did - remember them wallies off the telly? So I gave him a belt on the knee with a bar, and down he went, flat on his face. Him still clutchin' the spanner like he was about to fix the bog! I wasn't hangin' about. Took off like you've no idea. Ran like fuck.'

She realised that she'd Bridget's full attention and, eager to impress, sat up straighter and spoke louder.

'Felt bad after, like. Turns out they were a couple of chippies from the outside, in doing a day's work. Next thing they know, they're locked in with the governor!'

A brief laugh escaped her, then caught herself on and quickly shut up as her OC came striding over with a face like thunder. Maureen didn't say a word, but cocked her head at Bridget in that no-nonsense way of hers. Asking Bridget to follow her.

Bridget gave the sisters a quick smile, then carefully stepped away from Tina, who'd curled into a foetal ball, fast asleep. The poor girl was wiped. Without a word, she followed Maureen down to the far end of the wing, into a cell with no door and barely any light.

The day had clearly taken its toll on Maureen, leaving her looking beaten down with red, swollen eyes.

'Bridget, we need to stop now,' she said quietly. 'Father McGuire's been in touch. Says the fellas in the Kesh know what we've done, and they're grateful. But it's time to stand down. Spread the word, will ye? Let's get everyone back into their cells, whether or not the doors are still on. I'll see to the governor and the rest.'

Chapter Thirty-One

The Claudette

If you'd paid Martin McLaughlin, he'd never have imagined, not in a million years, that he could feel this sick.

The small, well-travelled freighter he was on pitched and rolled, fighting to climb the Atlantic swell. He almost laughed, thinking back to his misplaced confidence when they'd left Port Gloucester in calm seas, heading out from northeast Boston on the 3,000-mile journey to County Kerry.

As soon as they'd passed the breakwater, all hell broke loose, and at first, he thought he wouldn't survive it. It had taken them a couple of hours to load the ship. Seven tons of munitions: rifles, light and heavy sub-machine guns, grenades, and badly needed ammo. The plan was to meet an Irish dragger off the coast of Kerry and transfer the precious cargo.

It had been a decent year, all things considered. He'd been shocked to get out of the Kesh so suddenly, but didn't hang about to ask questions. Once he crossed the border to Malin Head in the boot of a car, his next surprise came fast. Tommy, bold as brass, showed up out of the blue in Farren's Bar, a place filled with history for the pair of them. Their talk was short, sharp and straight to the point. No niceties. Tommy had grabbed him by the arm, dragged him out of the main bar and into the snug, the one with the old stove that never worked properly, then let rip without holding back.

'We've got to get you outta here, son. You're killin' yourself. For Christ's sake, look at the state of ye. Our Jella would turn in her grave. Don't fuckin' ask how, but I've called in a few favours. You're goin' to New York. I've a contact there, an old pal. One condition, mind. You're to pack in the drinkin'. It stops. No more.'

Before saying goodbye, Tommy walked him back to the cottage Martin had been renting across from the bar. As they stepped inside, he added, 'If anyone can get you back on track, this fella will. He's AA.' Martin hit the roof and kicked off straightaway. Said there was no chance on earth he was an alcoholic. Sure, he liked a drink, didn't everyone?

Said it was harmless fun. Nothing wrong with blowing off a bit of steam now and then. Then came the usual: swore blind he'd never touch the stuff again. Honest to God. Cross his heart and hope to die.

But Tommy wasn't having it. The big man glanced around the mess of the cottage and hissed, 'Listen to me. Now our Jella's gone, and your da too. Neither me, Caitlin, nor God love her, your Tina can take any more death in this family. You're on the road to self-destruction, Martin. If you keep going the way you're goin', you'll be with your ma and da soon enough. So, whether you like it or not, you're off to America. End of.'

After all his faffing about, Martin couldn't say no. A hunch told him he'd be okay. The decision had been made for him, though the real battle would be coming off the sauce. He was right. It wasn't easy. The shakes, the sweats, the fucking DTs. If he was lucky, they'd pass in a week or so. He'd been there before. But this time, he'd no choice but to stick with it.

The fear on Tommy's face and the tone of his voice had gone deep with Martin. For once in his life, he wasn't about to let the big man down. This was his chance. A clean break. A chance to sort himself out. Martin felt a sensation he hadn't experienced in a while after the travel date was agreed. Hope. Not the silly, wide-eyed kind, but a genuine feeling, giving him enough belief that this could be it. A fresh start. Clean slate. Chance to walk away from all the shit that had piled up behind him and, fingers crossed, make a success out of what was left of his life. Before he knew it, Martin McLaughlin from Creggan landed in the Big Apple. Pale as a ghost, sweltering like a pig, and stinking of nerves, though Immigration nearly finished him. His hands were shaking, sweat pouring off him, his shirt stuck to his back. Withdrawal from the old alcohol was well and truly kicking in, he knew the signs. As if his skin didn't fit right.

Still, he did his best to hold it together, clutching the passport like it might go off in his hands. The officer who waved him forward looked no more than thirty, with a mop of red hair, freckles splattered across his pale face, and a smile way too fake. *Jesus,* Martin thought, he looked like a young Tommy. He gave his passport a quick once-over, raised an eyebrow, then looked up at Martin with a smile.

'First time Stateside?'

Martin managed a nod.

'Long trip, huh?' the officer said, tapping the passport closed before sliding it back across the hub. 'Well, welcome to New York, Mister McLaughlin. Make sure you stay outta trouble.' He laughed.

That was it. No questions about the bags, no search, no funny business. Martin did a double take, barely able to believe it. Was it the name? The face? The accent? Or did the fella know he was one of their own. Either way, he wasn't for hanging about to find out. He was in.

Tommy's contact turned out to be the number one Provo man in America, Brian Meenan. On the way from JFK airport, Meenan had been as blunt as Tommy and warned Martin he wouldn't take any shite. No alcohol. Martin should remember his host knew all the tricks in the book and would watch him closely. The man was in his mid-sixties, never married, lived with his sister, and existed for one thing only. The Cause.

Internment had near destroyed Martin. Missing both his ma and da's funerals, then disappearing without a word to Caitlin or Tina, had almost finished him. But somehow, with a bit of fight still left in him and the quiet support of Brian Meenan and his sister Sinead, he'd managed to drag himself back together.

In the beginning, he stayed with them. Sinead was a cracking cook, and he'd eaten some of the best grub of his life under that roof. She took a soft spot for him early on, helped him clean himself up, got him new clothes, cut his hair, made sure he looked half-decent when he stepped outside. He'd never forget the way they looked after him. Not ever. They'd even sorted him a job pulling pints in the *Galtee*, a rough-and-ready Irish bar down the road. Meenan said throwing him in the deep end would test his mettle. See if he was serious. It worked. Martin hadn't touched a drop since.

Father Connolly, the priest he'd met at the NORAID dance in Yonkers, turned out to be a real help. Mad coincidence that he was one of the three priests back home at St Mary's. He'd given him the rundown on Caitlin and Tina. Martin had listened quietly, nodding along, but by the end of it, there was a knot in his gut that wouldn't go away. The more he heard, the heavier the guilt ate him up as he discovered what had happened and what was going on.

'Caitlin took your mother's death bad. She's upset Martin that she never heard a word from you. Tina found out only a while back. Tommy was worried about how she'd take it, whether she could cope. They didn't tell her all, simply said Majella fell asleep and didn't wake up. Kept it simple.' He shook his head sadly, 'She was upset, of course, but the good news is she's doing way better now, under the protection of the Armagh women, would you believe.'

Martin felt depressed. He still hadn't been in touch with them. There was no excuse for it, not one. It was just... time. Time was slipping by, the days disappearing fast. He'd started helping Brian Meenan with a few small jobs for the Boys, nothing major at first. But bit by bit, the op got bigger, the risks greater. Before blinking, he was back in. Deep. The Provos hadn't gone anywhere, and neither, it seemed, had he.

Back on board and sitting opposite Martin on the lower deck of the ship was a new volunteer: Seamus Donaghy. He and his construction boss had been at a few of the black-tie dos in Boston. The ones where Father Connolly gave those fiery speeches that got the crowd all wound up and their hands into their wallets.

Not long after getting back to the States, Seamus had run into Brian Meenan and Martin, and before he knew it, he'd signed up as a volunteer. A few weeks back home had been more than enough. The headlines, the destruction the city was in, what'd happened to Caitlin's da – it all got to him. It stirred inside him and made him realise he couldn't sit across the ocean watching it all unfold as if it wasn't his problem. At that point, it had to give. The conflict had to end, and if that meant getting his hands dirty, that's okay. So, here he was, shoulder to shoulder with Martin McLaughlin, of all people, on an Atlantic arms run. Life had a funny way of throwing things at you.

Martin had barely recognised him at first. The fella had changed. He'd grown up. 'Seamus Donaghy? The same one that went out with our Caitlin?' Martin had asked, eyebrows raised.

Seamus had laughed sore when he realised who Martin was. 'Aye, that's me. Saw her not long ago, funny enough. She's doing okay. Wasn't great at the start, but took her out a few times and had a word. She's promised to keep herself right.'

Martin smiled as another wave of guilt ran through him. 'Ah, that's good. Mind yourself with her now. Same one's got a temper on her. A right hothead at times!'

'Tell me about it,' He gave a smouldering smile and laughed. 'I've seen it!'

Talking about Caitlin made Martin's heart thump. He missed her more than he cared to admit. Things had always been a bit funny between the two of them, but fair play to her, at least she was trying. Fingers crossed, this run, this mad, dangerous op, might bring change. For the better. Getting the gear back to Ireland was no small thing. It was on him now. The risk, the dangerous journey, the fear of getting caught. All of it. But if it helped bring things forward, if it meant one step closer to ending the bloodshed, to finally uniting the country, then it'd be worth its weight in gold.

Chapter Thirty-Two

Republican to the Bone

Father Connolly had been back and forth to the States more times than he could count, fast becoming a celebrity over there. Ever since his first big speech at a NORAID do, the same night he'd met Martin McLaughlin, the New Yorkers and Bostonians couldn't get enough of him.

His absence, though, had left Father McGuire far from happy. What infuriated him the most was that Bishop Carlin, swayed by a glowing write-up of Connolly's New York speech, had given the young priest his blessing to go again! And off he went, gallivanting around the States while the rest of them were left to carry the workload.

With the two of them holding the parish together, it was no joke. 'I can't get my head around it, Father Connolly. How can you be away again? We've a mountain of work here, and that's before the Yankee cops land next month. How on earth are we supposed to manage?' McGuire's voice rose as he spoke, his face flushed with frustration. 'It's not fair on me, and it's definitely not fair on Father Drury.'

Cathal Connolly, calm as ever, said it was all in hand, the itinerary sorted and signed off by Father Drury himself, nothing to worry about. But McGuire wasn't having it. He stood his ground, fists balled tight, refusing to let it go. 'I know what you're up to over there, son. Fundraising for prisoners' wives and families, my arse! That's not who that money's for. It's for the Provos, we both know it. Haven't we seen enough suffering in this city, too many innocents dead, too many businesses blown to shreds. So don't tell me this is helping the needy. There's gotta be another way.' Republican to the bone, Father McGuire was growing sick of the whole bloody mess. Sick of the funerals, the makeshift prisons, the waste of life. He still believed in the Cause, course he did, but prayed daily for the killing to stop.

Cathal said nothing. If the old man only knew half of it. That night in Yonkers had changed everything. First meeting Martin McLaughlin, then later crossing paths with Brian Meenan, things had moved fast. No more passing around envelopes or clapping along to speeches. This was big time. Serious plans were coming together. Action, not talk. Weapons, routes, people willing to take risks. A way to hit back and do actual damage, not noise. A Republican all his life too, Cathal knew it was those speeches in New York that had lit his soul up. The roar from the crowd, the pride, the raw belief in a united Ireland. The British hadn't ruled his country for centuries, they'd humiliated her. It was time to take something back.

Brian Meenan had only gone and secured a cache of weapons from Libya. Flew over there himself and met Colonel Gaddafi face to face. Afterwards, the Libyan leader promised he'd help them wipe out British imperialism and its lapdogs. Promised to send the weapons to do it. And he did. Somehow, Meenan then chartered a stripped-back DC3 cargo plane out of the States, loaded it to the hilt with rockets, rifles and thousands of rounds, and off it went. When it landed safely at Shannon, and its contents were distributed among the volunteers, they were ecstatic. At last, they were ready for actual battle.

Back on board the *Claudette*, Seamus and Martin sat in the galley playing cards, each hoping the game might take the edge off the sway. Neither had managed to eat. They knew exactly where it'd end up. On their shoes. Outside, the wind howled and the rain battered the portholes like it wanted in. Trying to keep his cool in front of Martin, Seamus shifted in his seat, pale as milk, then asked hopefully, 'How long now, Martin? We've gotta be close.'

Martin pulled a smoke from his mouth. 'Not long, mucker.' He looked at his watch, 'Few more hours, that's all.'

Seamus sighed and watched him study his card hand. He wasn't anything like the brother Caitlin had described. She'd always said he was a drunk, a nasty piece of work and scruff bag. He didn't look like a scruff bag to him, but that America had done him good. Even stuck on this floating tin, Martin was immaculate. Not a thread out of place on his brushed brown coat, a mustard-cream scarf tucked neatly under the lapels. His hair was cropped short – military tight.

'Can I ask you somethin'?' Seamus asked carefully.

Martin gave a nod.

'Why didn't you go home after you got out?'

Martin placed his cards face down and looked straight at him. His brows lifted, eyes narrowing, like a memory had come back to haunt him. He stayed like that a good bit and long enough for Seamus to wish he'd kept his gob shut.

'Couldn't,' Martin said. 'So I legged it. Took the coward's road, holed up in Kate Farren's and drank meself stupid. Don't remember half of it. I got offered a way out, a ticket to the States, and grabbed it with both hands. All down to me, Uncle Tommy. Good old Tommy. Came up there one day, gave me a right bollocking, said I was drinkin' meself into the ground, called me a selfish bastard.' Martin sneered, 'I was ragin' at him, all broke like. But he was right. The truth's like that. Hard to hear and hurts like fuck. Haven't touched a drop since.'

Seamus hesitated, then asked, 'What was it like?'

'What was *what* like. The drinkin'?' Martin laughed, though it wasn't funny.

'Gaol.'

Again Martin hesitated. 'The Kesh's a fuckin' nightmare. But before that, the cop shops were worse. Way worse. They'd hood you, stand you with your legs wide, arms out, hands open. Move a finger and they'd hammer you. They went at the soles of me feet till they were twice the size. Screamin' in your ear, over and over. No wonder fellas crack and sign whatever's shoved in front of them.'

With a scoff he added, 'I was stuck in there nine fuckin' days. Still, I didn't say a word and signed nothin'.' Finishing with a deep sigh, he added, 'Still put me away though, didn't they?'

'Jesus,' Seamus muttered. Convinced he'd never have lasted that long.

Martin's eyes turned glassy. 'When I finally made it to the Kesh, a guard asked where I'd been. Couldn't tell him. No idea. I'd been hooded that long, and saw nothin'. Told him all I knew, like. First show of kindness I'd seen in days when all he answered me, "You're grand now, lad. You're among men." I'll never forget that.'

Chapter Thirty-Three

Puppet on a String

Cathal Connolly sat in the Rainbow, a well-known meeting spot in Derry, across from the Strand Road RUC barracks. After it was bombed a while back, they'd rejigged it into a classic American-style diner. Shiny metal stools were bolted to a long counter that ran from the door to the back wall. On the other side were high-backed booths in red vinyl, each with a steel-edged table. Black-and-white prints of New York landmarks dotted the red walls.

A Bible lay open next to his pot of tea and a small jotter filled with scribbles. To anyone watching, it would've looked like he was preparing a sermon, quietly working away. Only he knew he was jotting down car registrations, checking each one against a list tucked into the hollowed-out pages of a Bible. Several recent sectarian killings had been linked to specific vehicles, and Connolly had been asked to help confirm the plates. They knew some covert police and army cars were disguised as family vehicles. All fitted with hidden radios, mics, cameras, even Kevlar panels with narrow firing gaps, ready to roll when needed.

This was his fourth Friday sitting in the same spot, and by now the staff barely noticed him. He always ordered the same. Coffee, two sugars, and a toasted sandwich, and no one batted an eyelid, aside from the odd parishioner who gave a polite nod of recognition on their way in.

He looked up as a white Rover pulled in and parked directly outside the barracks. A man and woman sat inside. After a few exchanged words, the man climbed out and made his way briskly to the entrance. The woman held on, rummaging through her handbag before taking out a compact mirror, dabbing her lips with quiet precision, then stepping out after him.

Connolly recognised the man from the *Derry Journal*, surprised to see him dressed so casually. Then, he turned to see the woman heading straight for the coffee shop. She had a pleasant face. There was a warmth to her, though he couldn't say why. He smiled faintly and decided it was time to make a move.

As he packed up, she approached. 'Excuse me, Father. Are you going? Would you mind if I take your seat?'

'All yours,' he replied, polite and mild.

'Lovely, thank you. It's a nightmare getting a table on a Friday,' she said with a smile. 'Should cheer my husband up.'

He gave her a warm smile. A lovely woman and with a final 'God bless,' Cathal paid his bill and stepped outside.

Across the road, inside the barracks, former Chief Constable George Shalham wandered the corridors, looking for someone worth speaking to. He'd hoped to catch one or two trusted colleagues, but no one was to be seen. Slightly browned off, with nothing better to do, he left to meet his wife, Hilda, for their usual Friday treat.

Retirement was everything he hoped for. His golf handicap was miraculously improving, his lump-sum pension had been more generous than expected, and he'd even treated himself to a new Rover - pure luxury, smooth as silk, an absolute dream to drive.

Remembering he needed to pick up a little something for Hilda from Fallers, the jeweller's up the street, he smiled and looked across at the Rainbow. There she was, seated by the window, waving with that beautiful smile, like she always did. Pleased she'd found a spot.

He cast a quick look along the road and stepped out, but a saloon came tearing round the corner, engine roaring, tyres screeching as it straightened and drove towards him. The rear window slid down, and the first bullet caught him mid-step, slamming through him and sending his body jerking, arms flailing like a puppet on strings. He twisted helplessly in the air before crashing to the tarmac with a sickening thud, the continual gunfire and the stench of burning rubber everywhere.

Yet the sun carried on shining, and in the distance people moved through their day, the steady hum of the city oblivious to what had happened. As if nothing at all had changed. But for George Shalham, everything was slipping from him. His world was unravelling, slowing to a crawl. The noise around him, the shouts and screams, seemed to peel away, thinning into something faint and muffled, like he was sinking under water. He tried to listen, to catch hold of it, but the sounds broke up. Was that the screech of tyres, or the bark of a dog somewhere close by, high-pitched and panicked? Even that was fading, further and further into the distance. Above him, the clouds drifted by in their own time, nonchalant as though they'd all the time in the world. He let his eyes close then, for a mere second, as an icy cold crept deeper into his bones and the last of the light began to leave him.

This was it. They'd done it. They'd got him. *Ah, Hilda, my love. I'm sorry.*

He opened his eyes once more to see a face breaking the light. A young Catholic priest, the colour of chalk, stumbled through a prayer, the words tumbling too fast, too desperate. George lifted a hand weakly, trying to grip the priest's fingers, his chest rising in short bursts as he fought to get the words out, words he'd meant to say before, but only to the right person.

'J... J... Jo... Jo...'

Chapter Thirty-Four

A Honeymoon to Forget

She closed her eyes tight and held her breath, taking herself far away to America. Diners and burgers. Boys in football shirts. Girls in cardigans. Rock 'n' roll. Anything to block out what he was doing to her.

Anne Ballantyne, newly wed to John 'Porkie' Ballantyne, had once dreamed the American dream. But tonight she lay flat on her back in a cheap, sweaty bed, the weight of a man twice her size huffing and grinding on top of her like some mongrel in heat. He whimpered, then rolled off, his sagging belly jiggling as he flopped onto his side. The sharp stink of whiskey drifted across the pillow and caught in her throat. She coughed. It was done, at least. Over in minutes. She stared at the stained ceiling and thought, *What the fuck have I done?!*

She'd joked with Caitlin before the wedding, full of giggles and bravado, trying to convince herself it'd be grand. But she'd known. Deep down, even then, she'd bloody known. Here she was. Stuck in Buncrana. A one-night honeymoon in a grotty B&B. Vodka and Coke hadn't dulled the dread. The second they'd checked in, he was on her. Groping, slobbering, tugging at the wedding dress she'd sewn up herself. Now it lay in a heap on the fag-burned carpet, torn and ruined. She didn't even know if he'd come. She certainly hadn't. All she felt was the weight, the breath, the stink. Nothing else. Nothing but disgust.

The wedding at St Mary's had been quiet. No fuss. Few flowers. Just the loud clack of her shoes against the church's stone floor and everyone watching as she walked, stiff and slow, on her eldest brother's arm. She saw Father McGuire watching as she came in. No smile, like he was saying a quiet sorry without words. The reception was upstairs in the Telstar bar. It stank of stale whiskey and beer. Someone'd strung up a few paper streamers, but they sagged in the heat, curling in on themselves like they couldn't be arsed either. She sat through it like she was watching someone else's day. People eating, drinking, laughing. *As if this were something to celebrate.*

Then Dickie stood up for his speech, swaying already, a daft grin plastered across his ugly face. He raised his pint like he was about to knight someone and slopped Guinness all over the tablecloth. Anne didn't even blink, but stared at the slice of ham curling on her plate, the redcurrant jelly sweating beside it. Porkie leaned in, breathing through his mouth, told her she looked 'a wee ride' and winked. She wanted to throw up, but gave him a weak smile instead. The kind you give when there's nothing else left.

'Here's to the lucky bastard,' Dickie said, nodding at the groom with a slow, sleazy wink. Anne could seriously have gagged, there and then. Every laugh in the room hurt worse than a Chinese burn. They weren't laughing with him; they were laughing at her, weren't they? Wondering why she'd married such an arsehole. Jesus wept, but he kept going, drunk and loud, his words getting nastier, more personal.

She stared at the tablecloth, counted the stains and tried not to cry.

'I swear to Jesus, I never thought he had it in him! What a catch. I mean Anne Heaney, eh? Same woman wouldn't even look at him years back, never mind marry him! Let's be honest. She's not the full 100% these days, is she? It's what's left of the girl he's marryin'. Her missin' 'alf a leg an' all... more like 50%!'

The groom and his best man howled. Course they did. Dickie was on fine form. This was his thing. Get a load of pints in him, then he'll cut someone straight down the middle, all while smiling too wide, like one of those creepy clowns.

All the while, there she was. Porkie's bride, centre stage. One-legged. Humiliated. A punchline. Anne didn't look at him. Hardly breathed. She stared at the ring on her finger like it wasn't hers, like it had got there by mistake. She thought about disappearing, sliding under the table to hide. But she couldn't. Not easily. Not with her leg. Not with everyone watching.

So she sat there, bolt upright. One arm on the white tablecloth, the other curled in her lap. Her cheeks burned, but she didn't cry. Wouldn't give him that pleasure. Beyond the two eejits, the rest of the room had gone quiet as a church. Four tables of stunned faces, frozen forks, half-raised glasses. No one laughed. No one defended her either. Not a single word.

Caitlin groaned, as if someone had beat the breath out of her. She met Anne's eye across the room. Same embarrassment. Same shame. For one long second, they held it between them - a silent understanding. *What have we done?*

Beside her, Liz sat rigid, her mouth a tight line of fury. The same silent fury Anne knew all too well from childhood. The kind that didn't shout, didn't swear, but went for the kill.

Porkie kept laughing, head back, shoulders bouncing. He couldn't speak for laughing so hard and waved Dickie on like it was one big joke. Like he hadn't caught on that his new wife had been publicly shredded. Dickie, half-cut and all proud of himself, took the quiet as permission to keep going.

'He's had his fair share of women, has our Porkie. You wouldn't believe half of it! Never, ever underestimate a Ballantyne.' To prove his point, he gestured towards Porkie's father, who sat, pissed as a fart, at the far end of the table. The lazy bastard hadn't even tried to dress up. A crumpled black shirt, no tie, and a pair of dark green trousers hanging low with a plastic belt. His face was flushed, slick with drink, eyes feverish. His beard, long and wild, was speckled with bits of food.

'Sure, we all know Mr B over there's had his fair share of tits, pussy and arse too!'

The groom's father squinted, lips twitching into a slow, sloppy grin. He laughed like he was still twenty, though his midriff sagged over his belt and the shine had long gone from his eyes. He'd once been a charmer, but now he was another pisshead with a past. Next to him, his wife sat glassy-eyed and still, drifting in her little pill-cloud, expression blank as a snow-covered field.

Anne barely heard a thing anymore. Dickie's voice had turned to slurry, words slipping from his mouth without shape or meaning. Porkie's laugh grated behind him, thick with phlegm and nastiness. The reek of booze, whether spilled or swallowed, seemed to hang in the air, soak into the carpet, and cling to her clothes like shame. The whole scene muddled together in her head, thick and sticky like treacle, weighing her down. Everything felt distant now, as though she were floating above it all, with no control, no dignity, but heat in her cheeks and a pit in her core. She was mortified.

From across the room, Liz caught sight of her daughter's face and that was enough. She stood up, knocking her chair back, and let rip.

'Right, fuckhead, shut the fuck up! Away off with ye, ye... ye wanker! See you? You're nothin' but a dirty, foul-mouthed piece of shite!' Her voice, clear as a bell, cut through the noise, drink, and shame. Her words went through the room like a snapped cable. As if the place agreed, it erupted. Cheers, boos, a few claps. Someone even whistled.

Dickie stumbled back, arms wide, bowing low like he'd wrapped up a standing ovation at the Royal Opera House. Still grinning like a right eejit, he swayed on his feet, soaking up the attention, completely oblivious to the disgust crawling across the room.

Porkie got to his feet, arms flapping like he was herding sheep, drunk as a skunk, but trying his utmost to act sober – it wasn't working.

'Okay, okay, everyone! Sure, he's only jokin', only takin' the piss. Ye all know what Dickie's like!'

By now, Anne's hands were clammy, her face drained. She glanced at Caitlin, her eyes wide with a silent plea. *Get me outta here, Caitlin. Please do something.*

Porkie turned back to the room, swaying slightly. 'He's an eejit, we know that, for fuck's sake. Means no harm.' As if that made it all fine. The room hushed, though the insults still hung in the air.

'Anyway,' he bellowed, 'thanks for comin' the day.' Belching and clueless, he looked down at his bride and asked. 'Isn't she a picture? I couldn't be happier.' There were a few soft nods of agreement, the kind people give when they have to be polite. But Porkie wasn't finished. 'As most of youse know, we're movin' into our new house. So thanks very much for the presents. They'll come in right handy.' Then, as if noticing the mood for the first time, he caught Caitlin's eye and added, 'By the way, thanks to Caitlin over there, for bein' a bridesmaid and a good pal to me wife.'

He gave a dopey laugh. 'You look lovely too.'

Caitlin felt like a right wally. Her bridesmaid's dress was second hand, and the colour of watered-down peach schnapps. She and Anne had tried to fix it up. Took in the seams, added a bit of lace, but it was still a horror show. Made of cheap satin, it clung to all the wrong places. But Anne couldn't afford better, and Caitlin wasn't about to moan about a lousy dress. Not when her best friend had married *that* man. She glanced at Anne's face. That wasn't a bride up there. That was her best friend walking the plank.

Thankfully, the groom finally wrapped up his speech and the room gave a polite round of applause. What a palaver they all thought as the smoke-thick air filled with murmurs and whispers.

'Did you see the bride's face?' one whispered.

'Poor critter. Looked right miserable. Never been to a weddin' like it,' muttered another.

'Certainly not your usual happy smilin' bride, was she?! That best man's speech - disgrace, it was. Awful. Friggin' awful.'

To everyone's relief, the music started. Porkie grabbed Anne's hand and led her to the empty dance floor to the sound of clapping and half-hearted cheer. Their engagement had been so rushed they hadn't even picked a song. Porkie had decided *The Town I Love So Well* would do. He held her tight, pressing in close. His mouth found her ear. 'Wait 'til I get you after,' he growled. 'I'm going to fuck the life out of ye.'

Anne looked at him in horror. 'Sweet Jesus,' she muttered. The song dragged on. She listened to the words, stared past his shoulder and wished the floor would open up and swallow them both.

Salvation at last, the DJ switched to the Bee Gees, and the room lit up with bodies swaying and arses shaking.

Anne made a dive for it and headed straight back to the top table, where she beat back another vodka in one go, then made for the Ladies. Dickie, ever the flirt, lunged for Caitlin, grabbing her by the wrist and dragging her towards the dance floor. She yanked her arm back.

'Get your hands off me, you twat,' she snapped. He didn't take the hint. Face souring, he grabbed her again, only rougher this time, his fingers digging into her skin, until Seamus Donaghy, her plus-one, stepped in and bumped him off. Dickie swung. His fist cracked straight into Seamus's face - the noise sickening, sharp. Blood sprayed as his nose split wide open. Seamus stumbled, then launched himself at Dickie.

The two of them went at it. Fists flying, bodies crashing into tables, chairs screeching. People shouted. Someone screamed. It took four blokes to haul Dickie off. Seamus was a mess. Caitlin didn't wait. She grabbed his arm and half-dragged him down the narrow stairs to the bar below. It was almost empty. The blonde barmaid with the beehive clocked the shape of them, ran a cloth under the tap and hurried over.

'My God, Seamus! Are you okay?' Caitlin asked, breathless.

Her heart was thumping in her chest. He looked like he'd gone the ten rounds with Rocky Marciano. Her own cheek throbbed. She'd caught a fist somewhere in the madness, though she hadn't a clue whose.

Seamus pulled away gently. 'I'm grand, Caitlin. Give us a minute.'

His head was spinning. Bugger. He'd genuinely thought the bastard was going to finish him. Dickie had come at him like a wild dog, biting, yanking his hair, landing punch after punch. The lowlife had even gone for his balls. *Who did that?*

Seamus wasn't a fighter. Never had been. He was lucky to get away with his face still attached. His whole body shook. He'd never been in anything like it before, not a fight like that, and if he hadn't downed those last few Irish whiskeys, which never sat right with him, he wouldn't have gone for the hairy critter in the first place!

But Caitlin looked so worried. At least that was something. Worth it for that. He took her hand, raised it to his lips, and kissed it. First time he'd touched her like that, soft and careful. No bravado, no words, but a small, quiet gesture. She squeezed his fingers back and smiled, a little, while she kept dabbing at the blood on his face with the damp cloth.

Coming back from the loo, oblivious to the fight, Anne went searching for Caitlin. Liz spotted her from across the dance floor and hurried over. She leaned in close enough to shout over the music. 'Who ye lookin' for?'

Anne shouted back. 'Caitlin, have ye seen her?'

Liz's eyes swept the crowd, dizzy with strobe lights and the pulsing beat. She pulled Anne aside and spoke low. 'There'd been a bit of a fight, but nothing to worry about.' She'd seen Caitlin take Seamus down the stairs to the bar.

Anne turned to head for the stairs, but before she could move, she slammed right into Porkie and Dickie, arms around each other, drunk and reeking of whiskey. Porkie's new white shirt was ruined, streaked with blood from Dickie's swollen face. They staggered together as if they were still in school, whiskey bottles clenched in their hands.

'There she is!' Porkie bellowed. 'Me wee wummin! Where've ye bin?' Anne didn't answer, but ducked past them and, as quick as her leg would allow, made her way out.

Behind her, Porkie's voice bellowed across the dance floor, slurred and booming over the music. 'Anne, me love, where'd ye go?' He squinted into the crowd, wobbling on his feet as if the room itself had done a disappearing act. Perplexed, he grabbed at his best man's arm and blurted, 'Dickie, did ye see her? She was there a second ago. Where'd she go?'

She didn't turn. Didn't look back. Didn't want to.

The downstairs bar was dim and hushed, like a different world altogether, hushed from the noise and madness above. At the bottom of the steps, Anne spotted Caitlin crouched beside Seamus, carefully wiping blood from his face with a towel. Her hands moved slowly, gently, like she'd done it a hundred times before.

Anne stopped in the shadows, and something tightened inside her chest. It wasn't jealousy, not in the least, and it wasn't quite sadness either. It was more like a quiet ache, a tenderness that pressed deep in her breast and refused to move. It softened, though, when she saw Seamus take Caitlin's hand and lift it to his lips with such grace. Caitlin's smile answered him straight away, easy and full of warmth. Anne felt her own mouth curve in response, a small smile she couldn't hold back, touched with something honest. Whatever was happening in her life, at least one of them had landed on their feet. She turned back and climbed the stairs, each step heavier than the last. Her leg ached, her heart worse. Porkie was waiting. Dickie was waiting. The rest of the bloody night lay ahead.

Sweet Mother of God, get me through this night!

In the bar below, Caitlin kept dabbing gently at Seamus's face. The blood kept coming, fast and stubborn, even with another cold towel the kind barmaid shared.

'You'll need A&E,' she murmured. 'It's not stopping.'

But Seamus shook his head and fell back a little. He wasn't going anywhere. Not yet. Not while Caitlin was this close, this worried.

'I'm fine. Give us another minute, we'll head back up. It's still early yet.'

Caitlin sighed with relief. She'd been dreading having to walk out and leave Anne to the wolves. She looked at Seamus and smiled again, a tender smile. He was different now. All that cocky nonsense from years back had melted away. He seemed... solid. Steady. An all-round decent fella.

The music above dropped to a slower beat. Seamus caught her eye and moved in. 'Fancy a dance?'

Suddenly, it felt right. She nodded, smile widening, and they made their way up the narrow stairs together, into the noise and the lights and whatever the night still had left to offer.

Chapter Thirty-Five

Keeping Promises

For weeks after, Caitlin kept her promise to Seamus. She'd said she'd get better, and she had. Work had picked up, and to her surprise she was even asked to do a bit of photographic modelling. At first she felt like a right fool, standing in front of the camera pretending to be someone else, trying not to laugh. But she got the hang of it, and to her own surprise, started to like it. A couple of catalogue jobs came next, then pieces in local magazines. The extra money gave her breathing space, took the pressure off for a while.

She and the old man, the one who'd pulled her into his house when the wee fella with a wooden gun had been shot dead, both gave full statements to Brendan Doherty, the solicitor. She could still see the boy fall, clear as a bell. But the statement went nowhere. Brendan said the security services came back blunt, saying their eyewitness accounts wouldn't be accepted at face value.

Night after night, it returned. The crack of the shot. The boy's head snapping back. His blood on the ground. Her own scream tearing out of her. She told Brendan everything she remembered, every tiny detail, but did it make any difference? Did it hell. Case shut down. At the inquest, the official story was that the boy had been '*one of many dangerous rioters posing a serious threat to life and property*'. As if that puny wee thing had ever been a danger to anyone. No surprise when the civil servant coroner sided with the police.

Later, Caitlin and Tommy went to visit Tina. It hurt to see her - grey-skinned, thinner than ever, worn down by the siege at the gaol. The moment she spotted Caitlin, though, her face lit up.

'Ah, Caitlin, I'm glad to see ye. I've gotta say sorry... I'm so, so sorry for everything. Everything I did. I swear to God.'

Then she broke down. Caitlin rose to hug her, but one screw, a hard-faced woman with slicked-back hair and a look that could cut glass, snapped at her to sit down. Caitlin didn't listen, not straightaway, just long enough to catch Tina's trembling hands and squeeze them tight, as if willing her strength across in that one grip.

'Look at me, Tina. And listen. None of this is your fault, you hear? We all know that man took advantage of you. I should've seen it, but I didn't. We all should've. There was me drooling over James feckin' Henderson. It's me who's let *you* down.'

Tina blinked, taken aback by Caitlin's apology and what she'd said about James Henderson. Tommy looked the same, stunned into silence. Fresh tears spilled as she gasped, 'I've wrecked that for you too, with him... haven't I? God, I'm so sorry!'

Caitlin tried to reassure her. 'It doesn't matter, love. None of that matters now. What matters is getting you out of this place. Soon as.'

Tommy cleared his throat and gave a firm nod. 'Couldn't agree more.' Then he filled Tina in on where things stood with her appeal and what their solicitor had said at their last meeting.

People had said Martin was in America, but Caitlin couldn't bring herself to believe it. No way would he have gone that far without telling Tommy first. So she'd asked Tommy straight out, expecting something, anything, but he'd brushed her off, cold as you like, barely even looking at her. Said he hadn't a clue. She didn't buy it. If anything, she figured he was fuming with Martin as well.

Her best guess was her brother was hiding somewhere over the border, likely in Malin. He'd always loved it there. The quiet, the coastline, Farren's Bar tucked out of the way and hidden. He'd once called it the only place he could breathe. If he had run, that's where he'd be. Waiting. Thinking and likely licking his wounds.

Having Seamus back in Ireland had been a stroke of luck. His boss in Boston had sent him over on some job or other, and somehow, they'd ended up spending more time together. It had come easy between them, almost too easy, like nothing had changed, like the years away hadn't touched them at all.

That said, there were moments that made her think. Every now and then, he'd disappear for a day or two, no warning, no explanation, and when he did eventually reappear, he'd act cagey, all quiet and guarded. He never told her where he'd been or who he'd been with. She tried not to push him on it – she knew too well how badly that could go – but it gnawed away at her all the same. She hoped he wasn't getting himself caught up in anything political. Plenty of young fellas were, these days, full of fire and fury, desperate to do their bit for the Cause. But Seamus? With his soft Boston lilt creeping in around the edges, she couldn't see it. Not with the life he had back in the States.

Asking him to the wedding had been harder than she'd expected. She'd gone back and forth on it for weeks, convinced he'd take it the wrong way, that he might read too much into it. But she hadn't wanted to go alone, and in the end, she'd taken the leap. To his credit, he didn't flinch. He smiled and said yes, like it was the most natural thing in the world. Nevertheless, she kept her guard up. Every time she felt herself getting close, she withdrew and knew why. She'd seen James Henderson's Jaguar around town, once outside the bank, another time parked near the Diamond, and it still set her off. The first time, she was sure he'd seen her too, maybe even slowed down to speak, but then, staring straight ahead, kept driving.

The hold he had on her hadn't gone anywhere, and she could pretend it had forever, painting on a brave face, even telling herself the memories were dulling, but they weren't. Sometimes, out of nowhere, they came flooding back, full pelt, like being winded.

Even now.

Chapter Thirty-Six

Blessed Darkness

Bridget Barry, in her favourite flowered nightie, sat cross-legged on her bed, a crochet hook in hand and a baby blanket almost finished on her lap. She wanted it done by morning so she could add it to the pile of arts and crafts the women sold to the outside world.

Unlike the men, the Armagh women weren't allowed to use wood or leather for craft-making. So they embroidered, crocheted, and stitched, not only to raise money for the prisoners' defence fund, but to top up their own meagre spending money and add to the pitiful food parcels they received.

Bridget laughed quietly, watching the young'un dancing in the cramped space between the beds. She was doing so well, better than anyone, even the OC, had expected. The shock of the siege was finally fading. She wasn't the same broken girl who'd first arrived, no longer drugged to the gills, barely speaking. Now she was glowing. Happy. Funny.

The women on the wing adored her. They'd watched her go from lost to found. Most nights they played their imaginary games: who they'd invite to dinner. Hollywood actors, famous singers, made-up menus, glittering clothes, ridiculous chat. They loved it. So did she. Watching the young'un improve day by day had given them all a rare gift in this place. A feeling of being needed. Of making a difference.

Tina had opened up to Bridget about Kieran Kelly. She knew now it wasn't her fault. He'd groomed her, used her, threatened her even. Still, the guilt of what she'd done hadn't gone. She'd made a terrible mistake. People could have died. She'd accepted that. But life in Armagh, amongst this strange, fierce sisterhood, gave her a strength she didn't know she had. These women gave her the will to live. She didn't need the tablets anymore. Sometimes, when it was quiet, she liked to think her mammy and daddy were watching over her.

She missed them. Missed Caitlin, too. God, she hoped her sister had forgiven her. If she ever got out, she'd make it up. Somehow.

Before lights out, PO Smyth appeared at the cell door with another screw neither Bridget nor Tina had seen before. They'd been laughing, still singing their clumsy version of 'American Pie', when Smyth turned the key in the lock.

'McLaughlin, you're movin'!' barked the PO, eyes lit with glee. Splitting up these two devoted women? She'd been waiting for this ever since the little bitch had stood her ground with the doctor. This was payback, and she was going to enjoy it. Tina's face drained of colour. Her eyes widened, her mouth dropped, but she didn't move an inch.

The PO started chucking Tina's few belongings into a small brown cardboard box, tossing each item in as if it didn't matter. Her new sidekick and now girlfriend, Gladys Drake, stood grinning like a dog on a short leash. Desperate to prove herself, she was itching to cause trouble, eager to show she could be as nasty, even nastier than Smyth. Therefore, with a wink in her direction, Drake yanked the mattress off Tina's bed and dumped her blanket on top. Then she spotted the half-filled po' in the corner and snorted loudly before taking a step back. Lining it up like a striker, she booted it with the tip of her boot. The pot smashed against the wall and sprayed its contents across the posters and photographs like muck on a mural. She raised her arms like she'd scored at Windsor Park and yelled, 'Goal!'

Bridget, in fury, flung her crocheting aside and stood up, face blazing, her voice shaking with anger. Tina crouched slightly behind her as Bridget cried, 'What the fuck are ye doin', Smyth? That girl's not goin' anywhere. Ye can't move her!'

Smyth didn't flinch, but stood calm, smug, and began to lie through her teeth. 'The Governor wants all non-political prisoners together in one wing. Orders are orders.'

Bridget scowled. 'That girl's a Republican. Ye know damn well she can't be in with that lot. Look at her. She's not right in the head. For Christ's sake, leave her.'

Tina played the fool with ease, letting her eyes go blank, her mouth hang open, and her head give a lazy shake, slipping into the part of a nutter like it was second nature, like she'd done it a hundred times before. But Smyth shrugged and folded her arms. She didn't believe a word of it. 'There's fuck all wrong with her,' she said. 'She's fakin' it. Come on now, she's outta here.'

When the governor had first been ordered to take Tina under his wing after her transfer from Gransha Psychiatric Hospital, he'd been beyond livid. He didn't need any nut-jobs or more psychos in his prison. He'd enough on his plate already and although he'd challenged the order, he'd lost. Given no choice, the moment McLaughlin arrived, he placed her under the care of A-Wing OC's Maureen Molony. The sensitive girl would be safe there. The Republican women would look out for her. Took the pressure off his already overstretched staff.

In Armagh, all the women needed the approval of their political group to be granted political status. For Tina, being Martin McLaughlin's sister, helped. Although she'd been charged with Provo membership, they were satisfied she hadn't collaborated with the security forces or broken any orders, so let it lie. Molony ran a tight, orderly wing. The Provo leadership had told her, and others like her, not to cooperate with or recognise the British commission or its prison procedures. The Brits saw the commission as a route to freedom for internees. Those who played ball and recognised it were usually released quickly.

The vast majority of Republican women refused to take part. They followed their own rules instead, disciplined and organised, proud of their command both inside and out. They believed they had a reputation to protect, and that mattered. While Governor Johnston often found the Republican OC difficult and unbending, he had to admit, privately; he respected her. She was a natural leader. Most of the Republican women would never dream of defying the OC's orders. They believed they should never have been jailed to begin with. Even if acknowledging the commission meant a quicker release, they wouldn't do it. Not out of pride, but principle.

The gaol was filling up fast. A new wing had been built, and pressure to cut costs was growing. Johnston did his best to be fair, especially after the siege. He'd never say it aloud, but he knew the difference between decent people and troublemakers. Most of these women, he reckoned, had no business being locked up. But the system had him pinned.

Then came more bad news. He'd been told about the government's planned change to the definition of political prisoners, and the stripping away of their rights. He didn't need a crystal ball to see where it was headed. It would blow up in their faces. His included.

In her cell, Bridget Barry didn't even have time to shout. One minute she was standing by the bed, the next she was slammed against the wall, her cheek crushed against the freezing concrete. The new screw was built like a brick shithouse, cruel in the eyes. Bridget should've known from the way she'd stood earlier, eyeing Smyth with that smug, dead look.

Rough hands tore at her nightie, the soft cotton with its wee pink flowers wrenched up past her waist, her knickers yanked down in one violent pull. Then came the baton. No pause, no warning, no shred of hesitation — only cold, merciless force. It rammed into her, brutal and unyielding, so deep it seemed to rip the air from her lungs. Her moan was a strangled cry, fuelled by both rage and agony. Her body jolted, twisting on instinct, but the screw had her pinned. The pain tore through her, burning and raw, rising up from her belly into her chest, then higher, until it clawed at her throat.

Tina screamed. PO Smyth had her crammed against the opposite wall, a baton pressed hard beneath her chin. She kicked, scratched, tried to get free, desperate to reach Bridget, but Bridget had already stopped fighting. Her head was slumped as shame curled through her, hot and dizzying.

Drake pulled back eventually, her arm growing heavy with the effort, and stepped aside with a half-laugh.

With no time to waste, Smyth dragged Tina into the corridor, her cries rattling the metal and concrete all the way down the landing.

Bridget was left behind in the cell, alone and quietly sobbing. Drake toyed with her baton, spinning it in her hand like it was nothing more than a bit of plastic. She waited a second, enough to watch Smyth's back disappear and to let Bridget think it might all be over. Then, slowly, she stepped back into the cell.

The bloodied nightie was dragged up again, but this time, the baton forced its way in from behind. Bridget's head slumped forward, her body folding in on itself. Then it came - a sound so raw and guttural it barely seemed human, ripped straight from her belly like a dying animal's last cry. Drake backed off, her arm aching now. This way was way slower, clumsier and not half as good.

Out in the corridor, the noise kept building. Cell doors slammed. Women shouted over each other. Bridget's name deflected off the walls. Somewhere, Tina was still screaming. Drake glanced at her watch. Nearly time to clock off, she'd better hurry. It was her turn to cook tonight.

Bridget groaned. Not a cry, not words, but a low, broken sound from somewhere deep inside. Her knees gave way beneath her, and her body crumpled. Then, without a word, the baton slammed into the back of her head.

Blessed Darkness.

Drake stood, brushed herself down, and adjusted her belt.

Yanked by the hair, Tina was pulled and kicked down the catwalk by Smyth. She yowled and squealed in fury, dragged on all fours, her knees scraped raw on the concrete floor. Smyth grinned, hauling her like a rag doll. She was having a ball, well impressed by Drake's shenanigans.

Tina gasped and whimpered, twisted up in pain. Every pull of her scalp sent white flashes across her eyes.

Smyth stopped, yanked her upright and yelled. 'On your feet and walk.'

Tina stumbled, legs trembling, shoulders burning. The sound of the prisoners' yells and pounding on their cell doors echoed through the block, wild and rhythmic, answering her and Bridget's cries. It roared through the walls, through the iron bars, through her bones. She turned her head and shrieked, her voice ragged and breaking: 'It's Bridget! That woman's doin' awful things to Bridget!'

The women were still yelling, but their cries grew quiet as Tina was pushed through an exit. Then silence. A thick, choking silence. Tina blinked in the fluorescent glare. The corridor was way colder here. Her breath rattled in her chest. Every part of her was trembling. Until... she heard something. A voice. Somewhere deep in one of the cells below, a woman was singing. Slow, eerie. Beautiful. It floated up and through the corridor like mist. Tina stood still. For a second she thought she was imagining it, but no. Another voice joined in, then another. She knew that song. *Daddy*.

The internees below were singing. *Four Green Fields*. Their voices grew louder, richer. The chorus swelled high and defiant, ricocheting off the stone walls. Everywhere. It sounded like resistance. Like determination. Like rage wrapped in harmony.

Tina sank to the floor, her back against the wall, her legs curled in. She couldn't breathe properly as her whole body continued to tremble. *Bridget? Lovely Bridget was getting hurt.* Like before, she disappeared back into her marshmallow world. Her safe place. Back to Blamfield Street, sitting by the fire, singing with Mammy and Daddy. The room was warm, full of light, the air easy and clean. Their voices rose together, proud and in perfect time. Daddy watched her, his eyes shining, full of love, as she joined in *Four Green Fields*.

PO Smyth cursed and dragged Tina's limp body toward a cell door. Thrusting her against the wall to keep her upright, she fumbled with the keys, trying to unlock the door with one hand.

Eventually, the door opened and she hauled Tina down the step into the cell, where two young women sat upright on a bed, playing cards, clearly annoyed by the intrusion. They looked to be in their early twenties, both dressed in identical Black Sabbath T-shirts and black trousers. One had a small black crucifix tattooed on her right cheek, the other, a red one on her left. Both had long, straight black hair and delicate features, their skin so pale it looked almost see-through. They were strange creatures. Clearly unhinged, Smyth thought.

The one with the black crucifix scowled. 'What the fuck's goin' on?'

'You've got a new cellmate, love,' Smyth muttered, tone thick with disdain. She was done for the night. Drake was cooking and she didn't fancy being late. She thrust Tina towards the empty bed. She landed on it, barely.

'But we've no room!' one girl shrieked, gesturing to the cramped cell. There was hardly enough space for two, never mind three.

'Then make room!' Smyth snapped, slamming the door shut and locking it with a sharp click. The sound was satisfying.

She turned and headed back toward Bridget Barry's cell. Not wanting to miss whatever was happening. Drake had been in her element, and Smyth had caught that look in her eyes - something feral. Her stomach fluttered, though she wasn't sure if it was nerves or excitement. It felt new. Risky. Perhaps it was something she could get used to. Luckily, it was a bank holiday and, with only a skeleton crew in, no one would be checking what they'd been up to.

She was nearly back at Bridget Barry's cell when Drake shouted, 'Oi, Olive. Come see this. Quick!

Smyth picked up speed and, reaching the doorway, looked in. Bridget was face down on the floor, out cold. Her nightie was torn, twisted around her waist. Her bare, wrinkly backside was on show, streaked with a slow line of blood. 'Look at the state of that, will ye?'

Drake's laugh rang out, harsh and mocking, as though the pitiful sight existed purely for her amusement.

Chapter Thirty-Seven

Accidental Death

The coroner called it accidental death.

James Henderson Snr had been tearing through the Sperrins when he lost control of his Austin Allegro. The car left the road, rolled down an embankment, and went up in flames. Out cold, he'd been trapped inside as the fire took hold. Neither Roger nor James ever found out what he'd been so desperate to tell them. Whatever it was, it must have mattered. But now it was gone. Lost for good.

That morning, Roger's pup was doing their head in. Full of beans, yapping away, not a minute's peace. By now, the screechy bark was driving them both up the wall. The dog had picked up on the mood in the house, a cold, grey sort of unhappiness, and was trying everything to break it. Fed up of being ignored, he nipped James on the ankle. James let a shriek, scooped him up in one arm and headed for the back door.

'I'm sorry,' he muttered over his shoulder to Roger, who sat in the study. 'Don't have it in me today. I'm putting the little bugger out.'

Roger nodded, secretly relieved. He hadn't the patience either.

James was in bits. His father's death floored him. After Caitlin, then this, he backed right off, holed himself up, replaying all the ways he should've done more. Tried harder to understand the man. Get close. Poor Marleen, bless her, took the brunt — his moods, snappy replies, icy calm. Every look, every harsh word, when she was only trying to help. She didn't deserve it, but grief's never tidy. It's messy, mean, and though James knew he was being unreasonable, he couldn't stop.

Days after George Shalham's funeral, Roger spotted another of Catherine's letters on his desk. Recognising her handwriting, he threw it straight in the fire. With everything else, Catherine was the last thing they needed.

Out in the garden, James set the moaning pup down and looked at him. His heart sank as the mutt stared back with soft brown doll-like eyes, as if to say, *What did I do?*

'I'll be back for you in a bit, Ned. Play around the garden for now,' he muttered, as if the dog understood. He shut the door on the whining pup and headed back to the study. Roger was in his usual spot behind his old, scarred desk, hunched over a mess of papers.

After tea and homemade shortbread, they read peacefully until the phone rang, loud and shrill. Both men jumped and then laughed at themselves. Roger reached for the receiver, hand trembling slightly, and answered with his usual clipped, no-nonsense greeting. 'Henderson.'

James caught a rush of words - urgent, high-pitched. His eyes went to Roger, watching the colour drain from his face, grey to ghost-white in seconds. Serenely, his uncle removed his glasses and set them on the desk. James leaned in, brow furrowed. *What is it?* he mouthed.

Roger said nothing except raise a hand, eyes still looking ahead. *Wait.* His face gave nothing away, but James felt it, a shift in the room, like any peacefulness had been stolen away. He didn't move, staring at Roger's hand clutching the receiver, his skin stretched tight across the knuckles. Then Roger spoke, lower now, as if holding himself together. 'And where is Mrs Shalham now?' he asked.

More high-speed chatter followed. James couldn't catch a word of it, but the handset shook harder in Roger's grip. That, more than anything, made James worry more.

'I see. No witnesses, you say?'

The way he said it, too calm, too precise, made James's heart sink. Whatever was going on, it was serious. A long minute passed. The room was dead quiet, save for the voice on the line and the steady tick of the mantel clock. Moving closer to the desk, James tried to get Roger's attention. He needed to know what was going on, but watching Roger now, stiff and silent, he started to wonder if he should take the phone off him.

But Roger set the receiver down gently, letting his hand rest on it for a moment. His head dropped forward onto the desk, and when he finally looked up at his nephew, his eyes were full. His tears came, slow and quiet, but he didn't wipe them away. He simply sat there, an old man mourning his much-loved old friend.

Charles Jones had arrived back in Belfast when the newsflash came through. Former RUC Chief Constable George Shalham had been gunned down in a Londonderry street. He sat back and listened for more details, then gave a slow nod. 'Ding-dong,' he muttered. Jones never had time for the ex-chief constable. The man was too soft. Always eager to make peace with the Fenians, bending backwards to appease them and trying to play both sides. A joke.

If Jones had got his way, Shalham would've been out the door long before now. There was no space for sympathy in that kind of role, no room for softness or second chances. You didn't manage a job like that; you ruled it, and the only things that kept order were fear, control, and constant pressure, all timed to perfection. He imagined Shalham's grave and spat at the floor. 'Wouldn't waste my piss on it.'

Shalham's replacement, Henry Bonner, was a different breed altogether. He took no crap from anyone and had spent years in the same Orange Lodge as Jones before his transfer to Londonderry. A big fella for his age, with a loud voice, he had no time for hand-wringing or talk of compromise and Jones admired that about him.

Their relationship was shaping up nicely. Bonner understood the rules of the game and played it well, he knew who the real enemies were, and more importantly, knew when to look the other way. It was pure coincidence, but perfect timing, that they were due to have dinner later that week. Jones had booked a table in one of those quiet, out-of-the-way places with no nosy bastards hanging about. He was looking forward to it after that incident with Shalham. They'd have plenty to talk about. CC Bonner was exactly the kind of man Londonderry needed, and exactly the kind of man Jones liked to work with.

A tap at the door got Jones's attention, and he looked up to see Lemon step in. He'd done exactly what he was told, gone shopping. He stood in the doorway, dressed head to toe in black, he looked like a ridiculous cut-price undertaker. The C&A label was still swinging from the sleeve of the suit. White shirt, red tie, polished shoes. Jones couldn't complain. It was a big step up from Lemon's usual get-up, and with a wave of his hand, he motioned him in.

Lemon smiled, nodded toward Jones's radio, and asked enthusiastically, 'S'pose you've heard the news, boss?'

'I have, Lemon. Yes, indeedy.' Jones smirked.

'Happy?' Lemon asked matter-of-factly.

'I am.' Jones replied with a sneer.

Jones mulled over his success at getting rid of not just James Henderson Snr, but George Shalham too. To the outside world, Henderson's death was a tragic car crash, and Shalham's murder would most likely be pinned on the Provos.

Henderson's killing had been necessary. He'd made the mistake of threatening Jones, and things were only ever going to go one way after that. Shalham was different. A lone witness had come to him directly, claiming they could identify the car that ran Henderson off the road up at Glenshane Pass. Brave, maybe, but foolish. Shalham decided to play detective, poking his nose in like some second-rate private eye. Started asking questions, and his stubborn push to get justice for his friend's brother ended up costing him his life.

Lemon, as usual, had done what needed doing. No mess, no fuss. Still, there was a witness out there somewhere, and Jones was keen to find them before they blabbed. He'd been explicit in his order: find whoever it was and deal with it.

For now, Jones poured them both a drink and told Lemon to sit. They had other matters to talk about, including the quickest, safest route to the Orange Hall at Newtownhamilton, where Jones was expected to speak later that evening.

Chapter Thirty-Eight

A Potato Sprayer

Back at Rocola a few days later, Ernie Taggart stood quietly, watching his boss with a growing sense of unease. Worry lined his face as he took in the state of him. James didn't look right, slumped over the desk, staring into space, skin washed out, eyes flat and far-off, as if he wasn't really in the room at all.

'James, are you okay?' Taggart asked, giving his arm a light tap.

No response.

He tried again, softer this time. 'James.'

That did it. James jolted upright, startled, then sagged back in the chair, running his hands through his hair.

'Shit. I was away there, sorry Ernie,' he muttered, rubbing at his face.

Following George Shalham's horrific murder, Roger had taken to his bedroom and hadn't come out. James tried coaxing him a few times, knocking gently and speaking through the door, but nothing. So he'd rung Marleen, who was in Paris with a friend, but when he told her what had happened, her voice changed straight away. The shock hit her hard too. George Shalham had been a true gent and she liked him. A lot. She'd promised to get the first flight back and return to Melrose as soon as possible. James had told her they needed her, told her to hurry, and for the first time in weeks, it felt wonderful to be wanted. Not just needed, but needed by him, and that meant more than anything.

Back at work and barely functioning himself, James apologised. 'Sorry, Ernie. Roger's sick, and I've been so worried, I'm not sleeping. After what happened to George Shalham, he can't seem to cope.'

Ernie nodded. Everyone knew Roger was close to the chief constable, and he told James he understood, said he wouldn't wish it on anyone. 'Tell you what. Why don't you call it a day, go home, get some sleep, and we'll pick this up tomorrow. There's nothing here that can't wait,' he said gently.

The idea was music to James's ears. He thanked Ernie for his kindness and, in record time, had wrapped things up, sorted a few issues with Mrs Parkes, then driven across the Craigavon Bridge to Melrose and bed.

Charles Jones was furious beyond measure. He sat rigid in the back seat of his car, eyeing a squat yellow-brick building in front of him, while a limp Union Jack above its chipped red door flapped half-heartedly in the breeze. This wasn't Newtownhamilton town. This was Tullyvallen, a back-end dump, a forgotten corner of Ulster.

This meeting reeked of sloppiness. It smacked of someone cutting corners, not thinking things through. Jones hadn't travelled all this way to be insulted. Whoever arranged it hadn't grasped the most basic rule when dealing with a man of his stature. A proper venue showed respect, carried weight, set the tone. Instead, he was stuck out here, surrounded by farmland and quiet, not a soul in sight, no shelter, no cover. It was the sort of place you found by taking a wrong turn, not one you arranged a sermon in. He'd expected a Loyalist stronghold. Not a glorified cattle shed and felt insulted, belittled and thoroughly fucked off.

He conducted sermons only in buildings of significance, locations that unmistakably showed his stature and influence. The First Derry Presbyterian Church, for instance, now that was a building with personality. Stone steps worn smooth by generations, vaulted ceilings that made every word heard. A place with force. Unlike this lot he was parked in front of. His jaw tightened as he kept his eyes fixed ahead, refusing to budge. Whoever had arranged this apparently had no idea what message they were sending. The wrong one. Who the hell did they think they were, asking him to speak in a place like this?

'Turn back!' he shouted angrily at Lemon. 'Take me home. I'm not going anywhere near that dump!'

Lemon was baffled. He'd assumed Jones knew everything about the Tullyvallen Orange Lodge. *Who didn't?* They were legendary within the Orange Order. Fierce Loyalist men, stubborn to the bone, known for never giving an inch. He felt a flicker of admiration at the thought, remembering with pride their claim to fame.

In 1920, during the War of Independence, around two hundred IRA men had surrounded the Royal Irish Constabulary barracks in Newtownhamilton. A full-scale attack. Guns blazing, they kept it up for two solid hours before finally blowing a hole through the outer wall with explosives. You'd think that might have been the end of it, but not a chance. The men holed up inside, all proud card-carrying members of the Tullyvallen Orange Lodge, refused to surrender. They held on until the whole place eventually went up in flames as petrol was sprayed straight through the windows using a converted potato-spraying machine, of all things. A bloody potato-sprayer. You couldn't make it up!

Thinking about it made Lemon chuckle. 'Genius.'

'What the fuck are you laughing at?' Jones snapped.

'Boss, this is one of the most devoted and loyal lodges in the land. Look.'

He pointed towards the red door, now swinging open and one by one, the men filed out, all done up in matching dark trousers and flawless black jackets, white gloves pulled tight, and thick orange sashes weighed down with badges and symbols. Each wore a black bowler hat, making them look like they were headed to some old-fashioned bank on Fleet Street. They chatted as they crossed the gravel, voices rising with energy, full of themselves, keen to make an impression as they made their way over to greet Charles Jones.

'They've been dying for this,' Lemon said, eyes gleaming. 'Been looking forward to you comin' for weeks.'

Jones had already lost interest. He stayed put, face like thunder, making no effort to hide his displeasure. This wasn't what he'd come for. He'd expected reverence, not a bloody welcoming committee.

'Fuck,' he thought. He'd no choice now and glanced at his watch. Eight thirty. Perhaps if he got this over with, he'd be in bed by eleven thirty at the latest.

Chapter Thirty-Nine

Goodbye George

George Shalham's funeral took place the day after Marleen arrived back at Melrose. It was a suitably solemn affair, steeped in formality, as expected. But what caught people off guard was the quiet crowd that had gathered outside the Protestant church, a small group of nationalists, heads bowed, standing respectfully on the opposite pavement. The turnout said it all. Shalham, for all his ties to the RUC, had managed what few could: a level of trust, even from the other side. Perhaps they sensed his decency, or it was simply that he'd tried. Whatever the reason, it was more unity than his replacement, Chief Constable Henry Bonner, would ever inspire. He and the like were the kind who divided first and talked later, if at all.

Afterwards, James stood in the slow-moving line of mourners, with Marleen at his side and Roger not far behind. He was proud to have known a man like Shalham, someone who'd worn the uniform without arrogance. Proud, too, of Hilda, the grieving widow who'd managed to stand with grace despite everything. She looked heartbreakingly small as they approached her, her black gloves trembling ever so slightly. Her eyes were red, the skin beneath them swollen and raw, but she met them with a soft nod of gratitude.

James stepped closer and took her gloved hand in both of his. 'He was a good man, Hilda. We'll not see his like again.' Her eyes filled again and she gave him a sad smile.

'Hilda, our deepest condolences,' Roger added, his voice a mere whisper.

'Thank you, Roger, James,' she answered quietly, nodding to Marleen. She touched Roger's arm. 'If you'll wait for me a while, There's a thing I want you to see.'

For almost an hour, Hilda Shalham was surrounded by well-wishers, shaking hands, nodding, offering thanks through a veil of grief. Then, quietly, she slipped away and rejoined the Hendersons. For some reason, her eyes kept darting, subtle but alert, a quick scan over each shoulder. Then, steadying herself with a small breath, she reached into her handbag and drew out a brown A5 envelope.

She didn't speak at first, but pressed it gently into Roger's hand, her gloved fingers lingering for a moment. 'Keep this safe,' she whispered, almost too low to hear. Then she looked away as if the exchange had never happened and spoke.

'I wanted to give you this,' she murmured. 'George had a feeling about your brother's accident and wrote some things down after he met someone. I don't know who, but whoever it was saw James's car hit sideways, down the embankment. That's why George went to the station. He wanted to tell someone what he'd discovered. Someone he trusted.'

She scoffed and shook her head. 'Can you believe it? No one more loyal to the RUC, but still they cut him loose, blamed him for that bomb scare. He never told me anything, said it was safer that way, but I thought you should see this. Means nothing to me.'

James felt his heart sink. He glanced at Roger, who was already looking back at him, both of them confused but saying nothing. Hilda Shalham was waning now, her grief and emotion taking their toll. On leaving, she looked at Roger and warned, 'Be careful, Roger. Whatever George found out cost him his life.'

James, Roger and Marleen didn't speak of the envelope again until they were safely inside the Jaguar.

Marleen was the first to speak.

'Well, that was all a bit cloak and dagger, don't you think?' Marleen offered, letting out a half-laugh in the hope of lightening the mood. Neither man so much as stirred, their minds elsewhere. She gave a delicate little cough, her cheeks warming with embarrassment. *Well, that one landed beautifully,* she thought drily. About as welcome as a lead balloon.

By the time they reached Melrose, Roger looked pale and drawn. He excused himself almost immediately and headed up to his room. Before disappearing, he and James agreed to go through Shalham's envelope together before dinner. Once he'd gone, Marleen poured James a stiff drink and took him through to the library. The old room was quiet, dimly lit, the familiar smell of leather and polish hanging in the air. It should have been comforting, but James couldn't settle. He sat stiffly, foot tapping, fingers knotted tight in his lap. Every few minutes, his eyes drifted back to the clock, as if willing the hands to move faster. Marleen knew why. He wanted to open the envelope.

'I think we should wait,' she said gently, as this time James stood up and began to pace around the room.

'He was Roger's friend. That's what he wanted,' she added.

But James was halfway out of the library. She followed him into the hallway, where he retrieved the envelope from the inside pocket of Roger's coat.

'I really think you should wait for Roger, James,' Marleen said again. 'He'll be furious.'

James didn't answer. The envelope trembled slightly in his hands as he prised it open, careful but eager. The paper inside was creased, the handwriting rushed. George had scribbled it down in a hurry. Whatever it was, it had been meant for Roger, but James couldn't help himself. His throat was dry, his heart hammering. If his father had been murdered, he needed to know.

He read it without a word. Marleen watched from the bottom of the staircase in the hall, waiting to see what it would say, but instead, James folded the notes back into the envelope, pressed the flap down with care and looked over at her, his face giving nothing away. From the soft glow of the hallway chandelier and dressed in black, Marleen, with her hair swept into a neat chignon, looked elegant. Quietly beautiful and it struck him all over again how lucky he was to have her as a friend.

Interrupting his thoughts, she got up, walked over to him and tugged him gently on the arm. 'What, James? What does it say?'

Even though they were safe in their own house, James lowered his voice, like the walls might be listening. 'Someone saw everything that happened the night Father died. There's a witness. They didn't report it because they recognised the car. They saw my father's car driven off the road. He was murdered.'

Marleen couldn't believe what she was hearing. She stared at him. 'You can't be serious. Who is this witness?'

'Doesn't say. George only wrote their initials. MG. The notes are dated about a month ago. That's all there is.'

She moved closer and slid her arms around him, resting her cheek softly against his shoulder.

Her hair smelled of sandalwood, and after a moment he said, 'Thanks for being here today. Means a lot. To Roger and me.' She'd have preferred it if he'd said, It meant a lot to *me,* not *us.* Even pulled her in and given her a romantic kiss. But she kept schtum, not the right time.

'Try to keep me away,' she replied softly. 'I'll have to pop back to London now and again, and see my parents, but while Roger's like this, I'm happy to stay as long as you need me.' James kissed the top of her head almost absently and Marleen closed her eyes.

When he woke, Roger, too tired to stir up an argument, accepted James's apology for jumping the gun and reading Shalham's notes without him.

Over the coming weeks, the Hendersons thought long and hard about what to do next, until Roger came up with an idea. It wasn't without risk, but they were running out of options. He'd never met the man face to face, only heard of him by reputation, but word was he was fair and extremely well connected, with friends on both sides of the divide. If anyone could dig up the truth about what happened to his brother, Roger said, it was Tommy O'Reilly. James got the feeling Roger hadn't a clue that Tommy was Caitlin's uncle, and he had no intention of filling him in. They needed help, and if that meant turning to O'Reilly, then so be it. James would have dealt with the Devil himself if it got him an answer, as long as he didn't have to face Caitlin.

Roger had asked Ernie Taggart at Rocola to reach out to O'Reilly and arrange a quiet meeting at the factory. Simple enough, or so they'd thought. But tracking Tommy down proved trickier than expected. He wasn't answering calls, wasn't getting back to anyone, and the days kept slipping past, which only added to Roger's growing frustration.

When Ernie turned up one afternoon with an update that told them next to nothing, Roger was gutted. He moaned, more to himself than anyone else. 'Well, it's not to be wondered at, I suppose,' meaning the troubles of Protestant businessmen were hardly top of O'Reilly's to-do list.

'Guess so,' Ernie said, sighing. 'He's taken his sister's death awful hard. That niece of his, the one up in Armagh... I heard she's gone mad, completely lost it. Maybe it's a mercy, considering she'll be in for years.'

Roger didn't say a word, but for a brief moment, he felt a flicker of shame. He hadn't once stopped to consider O'Reilly's own grief. Like half the city, the man had been dealt his share of sorrow.

'I'll keep at it, sir,' Ernie said quietly.

Roger gave a nod, though with little hope. A little before Ernie left, Roger asked about Rocola's order book. The reply wasn't what he wanted to hear. Competition from the Far East was still biting hard, but Ernie added that he and James had been looking into a few new export possibilities.

That evening, over dinner, Roger caught his nephew off guard by floating the idea of bringing in an assistant manager to take charge of overseas expansion. James gave a sigh, said he hadn't the time to draft adverts or sit through interviews, but Roger brushed him off with a shake of his hand.

'Forget the classifieds. It's time Ernie Taggart came off the shop floor and up to the fifth. The man's got a good head on his shoulders. Let's see what he can do with it.'

Chapter Forty

Tá Fáilte Romhat

Still in Castlereagh, Detective Black was still getting nowhere with the two Derry men. It didn't matter what he threw at them, what he did to them, neither of the Fenian buggers would sign a thing. Nothing. You couldn't have forced an X out of them on a piece of bog roll, never mind a confession.

Three days in, Black gave up, he was wasting his time and finally let the Londonderry scum go, dropping them off without a word from the back of a Land Rover somewhere between Bangor and Belfast. Much to Emmett's surprise, Mickey Boyle knew exactly where to go, leading him to a tiny West Belfast corner bar with grilled windows, a heavy steel-reinforced front door, and security gate. The Shamrock. You couldn't say the place was particularly inviting as Mickey hit the buzzer, then looked up at a narrow peephole tucked above the bell. Someone inside had to be watching as, within seconds, the gate was released, and they walked in.

There were very few patrons inside. A well-built, middle-aged barman, fit for his age in blue jeans and a red and white Arsenal shirt, watched them approach. He nodded at Mickey, giving him the go-ahead to walk on through to a back room. Quiet as a mouse, Emmett followed, knowing he had to call his ma. She'd be out of her mind with worry. They entered a lounge area where, sitting at a small table, were two men: Brian Monaghan and Patrick, *Paddy*, Gillispie.

Monaghan, Patrick's winger, was the kind of man you underestimated at your own risk. Tall and immaculately dressed, he could have passed for a civil servant or a solicitor. Every word was chosen with care, every pause left to hang for effect. Behind the calm eyes and tidy haircut was a mind sharp enough to finish *The Times* crossword in minutes. He was a Mensa man, though he never said so, and he didn't need to raise his voice to command a room. He had presence - the quiet kind that came with danger. Beneath the polish, he was a killer.

Paddy trusted him completely, not because he was clever, but because Brian knew when to stay in the background and never let ego trip up an operation. Where Paddy came in with fire, Brian held the line with steel. Quiet, cold and unbending. Paddy gave Mickey a half-smile, told the lads to sit, then began questioning them in his harsh West Belfast accent.

'All the way from Derry, Mickey Boyle. So what happened to you two then?'

Mickey coughed, looked at Emmett and said. 'Castlereagh. Three days. That fucker Black got to us.'

Monaghan shook his head in commiseration. *Black again.*

'Take it you didn't sign anythin'?' he asked.

'Nah. That wee man there didn't either.' Mickey replied, his voice holding an element of pride.

Monaghan looked at Emmett and joked, 'There's nothin' "*wee*" about that fella. He's Derry's answer to The Hulk!'

Taking another look, Gillispie joined in, 'Nah, sure the lad's got the face of an angel. Black put you through it too, son, eh? What age are ye?'

Before answering, Emmett glanced at Mickey and got a small nod. 'Fifteen. Almost sixteen,' Emmett replied.

The men fell silent for a second, then Paddy gave a slow whistle through his teeth. 'Jesus Christ...' he muttered. 'Fifteen. You've no business lookin' like that, son.'

'Still a bit young for us,' Monaghan said, not unkindly, 'but you did well. Fair play to ye.'

'You from Derry too?' Paddy asked Emmett.

'Aye,' Emmett replied. 'But listen, I need to get to a phone, mister. Me mammy'll be goin' off her head, and I need to find out about me brother, Joe. Black told us he's been shot trying to escape from the Kesh.'

'He's a lying cunt. No one's been shot,' Paddy assured him, his voice cold and abrupt. *He's a fucker that Black, him and his mind games.*

Relief flooded Emmett, washing away the fear he'd been holding in for days. He sat quietly, staring at his feet. A single tear ran down his stinging cheek and dropped onto his chest. None of the men spoke. They simply waited, giving him some time, letting him find his bearings. Emmett was embarrassed, but he couldn't help it. The feeling of relief was too great, not purely for himself, but for Joe and his ma - she couldn't have taken much more.

Monaghan felt for the lad. He dug into his pocket for some change and told Emmett there was a phone further out the back, near the toilets. After that, he said, they could go upstairs, have a wash and grab a bite to eat. Emmett didn't hesitate. He took the coins, mumbling his thanks, and hurried through the door in search of the payphone.

Once he was out of earshot, Mickey leaned in. 'You both know rightly, it was me who took care of that peeler in Derry, not him or the rest. But that bastard Black didn't give a rat's arse. Wanted it stuck on someone, anyone, so long as he got a signature.'

Gillispie and Monaghan exchanged a look. Neither said a word, both knew exactly who did what to whom and when.

Mickey took a breath, lit a fag, and spoke his mind.

'See that fella there... aye, he's green as grass, but hard as nails. Held his tongue, never buckled. Fifteen, for fuck's sake. If he's up for it, I'd like to keep him close. He's got something. Something I reckon we could use.'

Maggie McFadden crowed with delight to hear Emmett's voice.

'Ah, Jesus, Emmett, I'd no idea where you were! All I heard was that someone saw you lifted. I've them tortured down at the Strand barracks, but no one'll tell me a thing! Where are you, love?' she cried.

'Somewhere in Belfast, Mammy. Mickey, the fella with me, says we'll get home soon. I'm okay. Don't worry. I'll be back before you know it.' Mother and son continued to reassure each other until the coins ran out and Emmett made his way back to the waiting men.

Emmett and Mickey made it back to Derry eventually, and from that day on, their friendship was sealed. They'd been through hell together.

Mickey had been lifted a few more times since, but it was mostly the usual Strand Road Barracks carry-on. Thanks to Brendan Doherty, who half of Derry seemed to rely on, he was out soon enough each time. He never talked about it or Castlereagh, but kept his head down and got on with the job.

He'd taken it slow with Emmett, given him peace, but when the time felt right, he made his way across the border to Greencastle to find him. He'd heard his mother talking in The Rainbow one afternoon, telling someone how terrified she'd been after her lad had been lifted, how she'd packed him off to her sister's down in Greencastle, over the border.

The change in the young fella was remarkable. Mickey had heard Emmett was a bit of a soft touch. Well, not anymore. This version of him had toughened, wrapped himself in armour you couldn't see but you could feel.

Black's face was seared into Emmett's mind, along with memory of stinking pish running down his legs, the fists hammering at him, and that crazed, frenzied rage that had come with it. But the part that cut deepest wasn't Castlereagh. No, it was Joe rotting away in the Kesh, and Tina locked up in Armagh and, by the sound of it, losing her mind. The pair of them holed up inside while he was out here, drifting with no sense of direction and no notion what to do with himself. His ma worked every hour God gave her, while his da spent most of his days slouched on his fat arse watching the horses.

Emmett still asked after Tina now and then. Tommy O'Reilly always said the same thing, told him she was doing grand. Emmett had written her a couple of letters, handed them to Tommy to pass on, but nothing ever came back. Probably didn't want to know, and he couldn't blame her. Either way, he hadn't seen her in yonks, and the innocent teenage crush he'd once had on her had faded soon enough.

The idea of going to university had gone out the window. There was no room for dreaming when the family could barely make ends meet on a normal day. He'd walked out of school and straight into a job at a garage. The work was fine, nothing special, but it kept the lights on and that was enough. The one bit of good news was that he'd applied for his provisional driver's licence and had his eye on a banger of a car – if his few scraps of savings could stretch that far.

After leaving his aunt's house with Mickey, Emmett stopped, looked at him and said gratefully. 'You were sound, you know, when we landed in Castlereagh and after. I'll never forget it. If you hadn't been there...' He shook his head. 'That place can do things to ye. Can't it? Mess your head up.'

Mickey gave a short laugh. 'Aye. Always, in a fucked-up kinda way.'

Emmett managed a smile. Faint, but it was there. 'I'm glad you came. It's good to see ye,' he said quietly, and meant it. They walked on, passing the old Anglo-Norman fort, the one used for the City's crest. 'I love it here,' he added after a moment. 'Peaceful, like. Helps clear the head.'

The fort stood on the edge of the sunny blue Lough Foyle. Across the water, a mere few kilometres away, lay Magilligan, once a British Army barracks and, not long ago, an internment camp. Mickey looked around, took a deep breath of clean sea air. It was a beautiful evening, still bright despite the hour. The water glittered, and the red sky kept shifting, deepening with the slow setting of the sun. 'You're right, it is lovely here,' he said.

They walked on for a bit until Mickey stopped this time and touched Emmett's sleeve.

'I need to ask you a question, and I want you to listen carefully.'

Emmett knew what was coming as Mickey looked at him hard. 'You know I'm a Provo, right?' he asked.

Emmett nodded.

'I want ye to think about becoming a volunteer, joinin' us. You'd be fully committed to the Cause. Willin' to do whatever we ask.' Mickey let the offer hang.

Not long ago, Emmett wouldn't have dreamt of it. But lately, seeing his hometown shredded to bits, bombs going off in streets he'd walked since he was a boy, families shattered, lives wrecked, it'd changed him. His family, his friends, even himself. Things were only getting worse. He was tempted. Really tempted. But he knew himself. He couldn't hurt anyone. Not like that. Go out and shoot someone? Plant a bomb? He didn't have it in him.

'Mickey, I... I don't know,' he stammered. 'I don't think I could hurt or, worse, kill someone.'

'We don't want ye to hurt anyone, Emmett. Listen. We want you for a special unit very few individuals know about. No questions asked, no messin' about, no disobeyin' orders. You'll be picked for specific ops. Not often. But when asked, you do it by the book. That's it. No hurting anyone. Things like fetchin' and carryin' volunteers. You'll need that driver's licence of yours, though. Soon as.'

Emmett listened. He felt excited. Mickey wasn't asking him to be something he wasn't. He wouldn't have to hurt anyone. He could help, though. Make a difference and end this nightmarish war. With Mickey watching his back, he knew he'd be safe.

Within weeks, Emmett McFadden was sworn in as a Provo volunteer in a secret ceremony held inside an old barn near Sherriff's Mountain. Someone muttered it was the same spot where a Brit had once been tortured by Kieran Kelly, the rogue headcase who'd nearly taken out the City Hotel. After the ceremony, Mickey winked and clapped him on the shoulder. 'Fáilte, Emmett. Tá fáilte romhat.'

Emmett filled his lungs and held it there, the pressure rising in his chest. This was the moment. The line had been crossed, and whether or not he was ready, there was no reversing it. He was in now, bound by words he could never take back, claimed as one of their own. A Provo, not only in name but in action, folded into a tight-knit Republican unit that operated quietly, covertly, without fanfare or fuss.

'The Unknowns.'

Chapter Forty-One

Typical Woman!

Kevin McDaid, better known as *Dickie*, opened the brown envelope and peeked inside. Nice. A few invented names were all he'd given his handler, and in return, a down payment on that car at Desmond Motors. Sliding the envelope into his jacket, careful not to crease it, he headed up the path to Porkie's new pad in Shantallow. The bus from the city centre had dragged on, another reason he couldn't wait for his own set of wheels.

He knocked on Porkie's door, giving the street a quick once-over. New-builds, neat as pins, clean windows, tidy gardens. He had to admit it, there was a flicker of jealousy. Not for the house, not really, but for Anne Heaney, gammy leg or not. Before the wedding, he'd had a go at her once or twice, a quick grope when he thought he'd get away with it, but she'd turned on him, eyes blazing, and told him to get away to fuck. Since then, she wouldn't even look at him, always leaving the room if he was there – which only made him want her more. Typical woman, playing games. He was sure she fancied him, was just stringing him along.

Porkie, on the other hand, was a waste of space. Out of work since the slaughterhouse folded, never even tried to find another job. Always on the scrounge. Now, with Dickie's pot of gold, the odd pound here and there kept him sweet. With the new car coming, Dickie reckoned he might finally get Anne to come around to his way of thinking.

A light rain began as he hammered the door, harder this time. Porkie was intown signing on - Dickie had checked first - so with him out of the way, he'd have the cold bitch to himself. He knocked again. No answer. Then, from the corner of the window, the twitch of a curtain. She was in.

He bent down and bellowed through the letterbox, breath steaming the flap. 'For Jesus' sake, Anne, will ye let me in! I know you're in there!'

Anne stood in the kitchen at the back, her body tight with disgust. Every part of her screamed to stay still, to keep quiet, to focus only on her breathing. She hated Dickie.

Hated his voice, the sour stink of his breath, that greasy smile he wore whenever Porkie wasn't looking. He'd tried it on too many times - pudgy wee hands grabbing, whispers that made her skin crawl. She'd told him to get lost, told him to go away to fuck, but he never listened.

Now he was turning up unannounced. Out of the blue. It wasn't just unwanted anymore. It was scary. The letterbox clattered again 'Anne! Ye better let me in or—!'

She rushed into the living room, snatched the poker from the fireplace, and backed from the window, heart pounding, insides racing like a train. *Not today*, she told herself. Over her dead body would that creep set foot in her house.

Chapter Forty-Two

Bang Bang!

The woman calling herself Brona Doyle kept up appearances behind the counter at the West Belfast offy, always nice as pie, her eyes continually watching and taking every detail in. On her rare days off, she met on the quiet shores near Bangor with Ian Dillon, her only ally in what was fast becoming a dangerous game. Together, they honed their plan, piece by piece, knowing a simple mistake could ruin everything.

Her routine was harsh and her cover solid. The regulars seemed to like her. She'd helped with the prisoners' defence fund, going from bar to bar with a collection box, pushing it under people's noses. It was perfect. Gave her access. Every couple of days, she passed on what she picked up to Det – new and old faces, car registrations, fellas' habits, their regular haunts. All of it noted to the finest detail. She never hung around too long, never asked too much. Enough to be remembered as that friendly, funny-looking girl from the shop, the one who helped with the defence fund, on her nights off an' all. *God love her.*

Course she didn't give a shite about the prisoners' fund. Alice was about results and survival and she'd do whatever it took. Every detail she handed over was a step closer to the endgame or a step closer to getting caught. It all came down to staying one step ahead.

Paddy Gillispie came and went as he pleased. Sometimes he'd vanish for weeks at a time, and she never asked where he'd been or what he'd been doing. She reckoned keeping quiet might win his trust quicker, that holding back could work more than asking questions.

They'd been out a few times now – a dance here, a disco there, even the odd show band brave enough to head up north. She'd met his twin sister, Dolores, once. That had been enough. Four minutes younger, Dolores made up for it in attitude. Razor-sharp, quick with her words, and openly hostile from the start. She didn't bother hiding her suspicion, made it clear Alice wasn't welcome. Fiercely protective of her brother, she was a threat, no doubt about it. But Alice knew exactly how to handle a threat. Keep it close. Smile when needed, nod when you had to, agree with everything, and keep your eyes wide open.

Tonight, she and Paddy were holed up in The Shamrock - his local, and a dive by any measure. The place was thick with smoke, the carpet sticky underfoot, music bouncing off its low, nicotine-stained ceiling. It was loud, cramped and packed with hard men and louder mouths. Didn't matter, it had its uses.

Alice took slow sips from her glass, letting her eyes wander around the room. Laughter, shouting, music, all of it blending into the usual racket. But she wasn't here for the atmosphere, or the craic, or whatever else pulled them in. She was here to study. To observe.

At the bar, three of them stood out straightaway. No question about it - active Provos. She'd picked them the moment she stepped through the door. Loud and cocky, full of themselves, roaring about the latest Gaelic result like they'd been the ones who'd scored. Full of drink, full of bravado, and too careless in their talking for men in their position.

She caught their names easily enough, tucked them away. Then it was on to the rest – mannerisms, eye contact, pecking order. What they were saying? Who didn't like it when they were challenged? The weak link. Who scanned the door every two minutes like he was expecting trouble? It all added up. That was the job. Spot the cracks. Remember the faces. Log the patterns. She made it look effortless, but this was training, instinct and experience, all rolled into one. Not to brag, she bloody loved it.

Paddy took her hand and gave it a squeeze. 'You okay, love?'

She squeezed back. 'Fine. Bit hungry, that's all.'

He nodded towards the last inch of his Guinness. 'I'll finish this and then we'll go. Need a quick piss first.'

Her eyes followed him as he made his way through the crowd, as confident as ever in his dark green duffel coat and flat Donegal tweed cap. He nodded at the barman in passing, then veered off, not towards the toilets but in the opposite direction. *Where was he going?*

Alice shifted in her seat, ready to get up and follow, but as she began to rise, a hand clamped down on her shoulder. Dolores.

Paddy's twin was slim and mid-height, younger-looking than her brother, with long straight brown hair, sculptured cheekbones, and brown eyes that gave little away. 'Where d'you think you're off to?' she snapped.

Alice yanked her arm free. 'Toilet.'

Dolores smirked and flicked her head towards the back of the bar. 'Loo's that way.' She slid into the seat opposite and leaned in close, her voice low and pointed.

'I've a feelin' about ye, Brona Doyle. That's not right. Off like. I swear to Jesus, I–will–find–out!'

Alice raised her eyebrows and leaned back in the seat, cool as anything. She made sure her tone was calm, measured and asked. 'What the fuck are you on about, Dolores?'

Dolores didn't answer, but curled her mouth into a tight sneer, raised her hand, and pressed two fingers to the side of Alice's head, as if she held a gun.

'Bang. Bang,' she whispered, her voice flat, almost bored.

Then she smiled — not friendly, not smug, an empty smile. Her eyes stayed locked on Alice's with a poker face that gave nothing away. Neither woman stirred until a young drunk lurched into them, bellowing rebel tunes at full tilt before pleading with Dolores to dance. Grinning, he hauled her to her feet, and the pair staggered off towards the back of the bar.

Alice sat there fixed to the spot, her back literally glued to the seat. She could hear the music, the laughter, the clink of glasses, but all she could focus on was the thud of her pulse. Her eyes darted across the crowd. *Did Dolores know? Did any of them know she was a Brit?*

So caught up in her thoughts, she didn't even see Paddy return. He stood over her, frowning.

'Jesus, Brona, ye look like you've seen a ghost. Everything alright?'

Dragging herself back to the moment, Alice nodded. 'Yeah. Yeah, fine. Hungry, like I say. Let's get out of here.'

Out on the street, the rain came lashing down, hard and fast, with no warning. Cold needles drove into Alice's thin leopard-print coat, soaking her right through within minutes. The material clung to her arms and back, useless, like she was walking around in a soggy rag.

She shivered, clenched her teeth, but stayed quiet, lost in her own thoughts. Her hands were trembling ever so slightly, but she jammed them into her pockets and kept going. She wasn't giving in. Not to the weather, and certainly not to that witch, Dolores. No chance. Even so, a thought had taken root. If things were ever to go tits up, it wouldn't be any other Provo who'd finish her off. It'd be Dolores. Paddy linked her arm and pulled her along. With heads bowed, they moved fast through the downpour until they reached their favourite chippy.

'Sit down and warm up,' he told her, looking at a table by the window. 'I'll get us the usual, okay?'

Too cold to speak, Alice sank into a chair and wrapped her arms around herself, shivering. Her coat clung damply to her, no warmth at all, while the draught from the door sliced straight through her. She fixed her gaze on the rain-slicked street beyond the window, willing her body not to shake.

Chapter Forty-Three

Massacre

Ian Dillon and his four UDR accomplices stood silently by the roadside, every man stiff as timber, eyes fixed on the darkness ahead. Silent. It was after one in the morning, and their fabricated checkpoint was parked exactly where it needed to be, hugging the border road, not far from the main road to Dublin. Remote, perfect and quiet. He and Alice had combed over every detail. Their target, a Gaelic football team. Creatures of habit, always took the same route back from their Dublin games.

So far, the UDR men had waved a few cars through with polite nods and fake smiles. Mostly locals, no need for alarm bells. Suddenly, Ian lifted his head slightly and listened. He checked his watch. There it was. Bang on time. An engine, distant but drawing near.

'Think this might be us, gents,' he muttered, almost to himself. His voice was quiet but certain. The men caught his words as they gathered in a circle, reading the look on his face, and then moved without hesitation to their positions, hearts pounding beneath the weight of their stolen, ill-fitting RUC uniforms. He allowed himself a flicker of satisfaction. Alice would've loved this part. He could see her now, that sly smile and the glint in her eye when the game was getting good. But she had her own part to play tonight, somewhere else, doing what she did best.

Headlights crept into view and the low hum of an engine was soon joined by loud, off-key singing, the kind fuelled by pints and victory, voices sailing through the still night like a bad choir. Ian stepped out, raised his torch, and flagged the minibus down. It rolled to a stop, then driver leaned lazily across and cranked the window down. Ian lifted the beam to his face. Pale blue eyes, cocky grin, a pretentious Fenian. Probably thought the charm of a few drunken youngsters would be enough to breeze right through. He thought wrong.

'Mornin',' the driver chirped.

'Morning, sir,' Ian replied coolly. 'Can I ask you and your passengers to step out of the bus, please?'

Dermot, part-time minibus driver, full-time coach, gave a long-suffering sigh. A fella in the back grumbled and swore but was quickly hushed by the rest of them and pulled back into his seat. 'C'mon now, Frankie, do as they say. The sooner we get outta here, the sooner we're home.' Frankie sighed and watched as, one by one, the team slowly spilled out of the bus, stretching their legs and yawning. Ian gestured calmly to the top of a grassy embankment and told them to wait. They obeyed with lazy good humour, half-laughing as they walked over to it. Another fella, Ronan Mallon, well worse for the drink, turned back and cheered.

'Why don't you tell them, Dermot, tell them, we've won the Cup!' He broke into song and his teammates joined in, letting out whistles and cheers into the night air.

Ian ordered a couple of his men onto the bus. They clambered inside, boots clattering on the metal steps, the air heavy with the stale reek of sweat from grass-stained Gaelic shirts and shorts rammed into kit bags. Hurley sticks and balls were scattered across the floor, a couple of discarded Lucozade bottles lying under the seats. One of the men decided it was a perfect spot to tuck the device. Another nodded and gave a low, nervous laugh as he jabbed at a sports bag with the tip of his rifle.

Watching from outside, Ian allowed himself the smallest of smiles. Then came the explosion. It ripped through the minibus, a deafening detonation that seemed to split the night in two. The blast lit the country road like a flare, any sound shattered in a single, brutal second. Fire surged from the wreckage, swallowing metal, glass, limbs. The heat was so fierce it blistered the tarmac.

Screams followed - high, panicked, animalistic. Halfway down the embankment, Frankie landed with a dull thud after being flung, drunk and limp as a rag doll. The flames chased after him, curling and snapping as if they wanted more to eat. Then the gunfire started. White tracer rounds tore across the hilltop, cutting the youngsters down mid-run, mid-scream. Their bodies jerked as dum-dum rounds punched through them, their blood painting the grass crimson, their last breaths drowned in bursts of gunfire. A few tried to flee. Others whimpered, some begged. Their journey was cut short.

Dermot, bleeding and half-blind, dragged himself up the embankment, his nails tearing through the grass as he clawed for higher ground, desperate to reach his boys. His chest heaved, lungs on fire, the taste of dirt and blood thick in his mouth. Bullets sliced through the air around him, one so close he felt it split the air beside his head, a hot gust brushing his cheek like a warning.

Then it stopped. The noise, the screaming, the gunfire.

Gone.

What happened next was even more awful. A hollow, unnatural quiet settled over the place, broken only by the hiss of burning rubber and the ragged, stuttering sobs of the dying. Dermot waited halfway up the bank, too afraid to move, his heart thudding against cracked ribs, an indescribable fear rising in him, swallowing him whole.

He had to get to his boys.

Determined to do just that, he crawled toward the edge of the embankment and peered over, in time to see one of his best players, Ronan Mallon, on his knees – the same fella who'd been singing only minutes earlier. His hands were raised, soaked red and shaking. In front of him stood an RUC man, arm outstretched, a handgun aimed between Ronan's eyes. The sight stopped Dermot cold. It was brutal, casual, and sickening. The kind of thing he'd seen in BBC documentaries, the way the German SS used to gun down Jews without warning, without reason.

'Please, please, don't shoot!' Ronan squealed.

The shot rang out, ruthless and final. Dermot's head fell as he pressed his face into the grass, his chest heaving with silent sobs. Only metres away, Dillon stood near him, his expression unreadable, annoyed more than anything that he'd lost a couple of men in the blast. He turned to one of the others and asked, in a voice as calm as ever, 'Sure we've got all the bastards?'

The following morning, the newspapers and TV channels were saturated with images and interviews about the bloodbath. Six of the team, all seventeen or under, murdered. Shot to bits. A handful of others had somehow crawled clear, bloodied and broken, taken away on stretchers with faces ghost-white and eyes staring blankly at nothing. No one had yet claimed responsibility. It hadn't gone exactly as planned. The bomb had gone off too soon, catching two of their own in the blast. A stupid mistake, avoidable too, but even with that, Ian Dillon still counted it as a success. They'd made their point. Loud, brutal, and impossible to ignore. The flames, the bodies, the half-dead teenagers who'd lived through it - it was all there, splashed across every front page, as intended.

Fear. That was the aim. Uncertainty. Let the Provos sing all they liked about their so-called victories. Next time, there'd be no slip-ups. The lads would be better prepared, timings gone over twice, exits memorised, the whole thing tightened from start to finish. Mistakes had been made, but the message had landed, and lessons had been learned.

Back in Belfast, Alice leaned on the kitchen counter in her so-called flat, flicking through *The Belfast Telegraph. Not bad, Ian. Not bad at al*l, she thought, the trace of a smile forming. She set the paper aside and switched on her black-and-white television. They'd agreed not to make contact for a few weeks, and after Dolores Gillispie's antics the other evening, Det had warned her to lie low and reach out only if she truly believed her life was in danger.

Paddy had gone off again, promising he'd be back for the weekend, and hinted he had a surprise for her. Intriguing, she thought, though with him, that could mean anything. So she kept her eyes on the screen, refusing to look away, forcing herself to watch every second. Every stutter. Every shake.

'I heard them! I'm telling ye, I heard one of them askin' if the boys were all dead. You shoulda' heard them screamin' and Ronan, begging for that polisman not to shoot! Awful. Bloody awful.'

Alice felt nothing but cold satisfaction. Mission accomplished. Though next time, they'd need to be smarter with the mop-up. Should've left no witnesses. Should've got the coach too. She made herself a cup of tea and opened the paper again, ready to enjoy every word.

Hours later, the shop buzzer went. Alice glanced over and, to her surprise, spotted Dolores Gillispie standing outside. Here goes, she thought reluctantly, pressing the button to let her in.

'How you doing, Dolores?' Alice asked, not that she gave a flying fuck. Dolores didn't answer but looked agitated. 'Is our Patrick here?'

Alice pursed her lips and shook her head. 'Nope. You mean, for once, you don't know where *your* Paddy is?' Dolores always knew where he was.

'Patrick, not *Paddy*,' Dolores retorted, rolling her eyes to the heavens.

Alice stiffened, every one of her muscles tensed. She'd give anything to deck the Provo bitch right there, right now, but not yet. Not after all those months spent worming her way into Paddy's trust. To come this far, then throw it all away on some twisted freak with a grudge and a God complex, would be sinful.

Dolores leaned over the counter and mouthed, 'Why don't you fuck off, *Brona*.' Then, she was gone.

Alice didn't so much as twitch until the door clicked shut. Even then, she stayed rooted to the spot. Dolores Gillispie, standing on the offy doorstep, that had never happened before. Turning up like that, bold as brass and uninvited, had unnerved her. It wasn't strange; it was bloody terrifying. Not knowing where Paddy was? That was worse again. Every part of it rang wrong. She felt it in her water. Brona Doyle, otherwise known as Alice Wallace, meant to find out exactly what lay behind it.

Chapter Forty-Four

Staying off the Juice

'Forgive me, Father, for I have sinned. It's been a *very*, *very* long time since my last confession,' Martin McLaughlin said, sneering as he settled into the dark confessional in St Mary's Church, Creggan. On the other side of the grille, Father Connolly didn't return the smile. 'I'm not laughing, Martin, and for goodness' sake, put that smoke out, will you?' he snapped.

Martin blinked, he'd forgotten he had a fag dangling from his lip. 'Sorry, Padre. Sure, I'm only jokin' with ye.' He stubbed the fag end out on the inside of the seat and gave a sheepish chuckle, knowing he'd overstepped.

The priest didn't respond, and Martin took the lull for what it was. The Padre wasn't in the humour for jokes, so he dropped the smile and carried on, voice low, serious.

'The boat was stopped by the Irish Navy off Waterford. Every last one of the lads lifted, Brian Meenan included. They were all carted off to Dublin. So that's it for now. Looks like we won't see another run anytime soon.' He let that settle for a second, then added, 'Still, at least the fellas on the QE11 got those three loads through. Thank Christ for that. There was even a couple of RPG7s in the mix. Lethal things. Truth be told, we haven't had anything half-decent for ages.'

Cathal Connolly exhaled slowly. He wasn't surprised by the news, not really, but he couldn't help feeling a stab of irritation. Running arms out of the States came with risks, he knew that well enough, but it didn't make the setback any easier to swallow.

'Shame,' he muttered under his breath. 'You're right. Suggest you lie low for now. I'm flying to Boston week after next, see what they want to do next.' He hesitated. 'By the way, don't suppose we found out who took out that chief constable?'

Ever since Cathal had witnessed Shalham's murder, he'd been keeping quiet tabs on the investigation. Word came in from all directions, and what struck him most was how, despite the man's uniform, there was a quiet, almost grudging respect for Chief Constable George Shalham, even among the Nationalist crowd. It was unspoken, but it was there.

Even the Provos, it seemed, were keen to find out who was behind the killing. Shalham had done what he could for the city. It was him who had warned the British not to send the Parachute Regiment anywhere near Derry that January. And look what happened.

Bloody Sunday.

Not long after that, he was made the fall guy for the City Hotel scare and quietly pushed into retirement. But those who paid attention, the ones who really knew what was going on, understood the truth. It had been Shalham's idea to push for government funding to keep Rocola open, a move that saved hundreds, even thousands, of Catholic jobs. Cathal returned to Shalham's murder in his dreams. The man's shattered body, the blood streaked across his face as he prayed over him, and the way Shalham had tried, and failed, to speak in his last moments. He'd listened as hard as he could, but couldn't make sense of it, but told Shalham's wife what he heard. It was meaningless to her as well, she'd never heard of a Joe.

'Nothin' to do with us,' Martin said. 'He wasn't on our radar, Padre.' Then Cathal heard him whisper, 'Not that day anyway.'

They spoke for a while longer, until the young Father Drury's voice rang out across the church, calling for Cathal. He stepped out of the confessional without a word, leaving Martin to slip away unnoticed.

Martin still hadn't been back to Blamfield Street since the arms run. Not once. He kept his head down instead, moving between safe houses, some in the city, others over the border. With NORAID money in his pocket, he stayed clean, well-fed, and lying low, which suited him just fine. He'd kept his word about the drink too. Staying off the juice. Hadn't touched a drop since swearing to Brian Meenan's sister, Sinead, whom he fancied like mad, that he'd keep well clear. This time he meant it. Drink wasn't his friend. It scrambled his head, made him reckless. Right now, he couldn't afford reckless. Not after the op they'd just pulled, and with more coming down the line.

Always at a distance, always tucked out of sight, he'd been keeping watch on his sister, Caitlin, following her through the rhythm of her day. The first time he saw her step out of the photographer's shop, he'd done a proper double take. The tall, gangly girl he used to torment was gone. In her place stood a woman who drew attention without even trying. There was a striking air about her. Class.

It wasn't only how she looked, though. It was the way people looked at her as she moved through the city centre, blanking the jeers from gobshite workmen and brushing off the smutty digs thrown at her from lads on corners. She walked like someone who'd been through hell and come out the other side, with no time or interest left for anything or anyone that didn't matter.

The guilt churned in his gut, steady and sickening. He hadn't been there for any of it. Not when Caitlin needed someone to stand beside her. Not when Majella did what she did. Not when Tina was sent down. He'd let her carry it all on her own. There was no undoing the past, but he meant to make things right now. He didn't have a plan, not yet, but he'd figure it out. One way or another, he'd find a way to help her, to be the brother she deserved. He would win her back. No matter what it took. On the boat to Kerry, Seamus Donaghy had told him he was hopeful about getting back with Caitlin, but was taking it slow. She was fragile, still hurting, and he didn't want to rush her. Martin appreciated that. Seamus was a decent fella.

Earlier that day, Martin had stood at the city cemetery, staring down at his parents' headstone. The grass was damp, and the sky carried that dull, silvery grey that always seemed to hang over Derry, like a mood it couldn't lift. He let his eyes move slowly over the carved names, trying to make sense of it, still reluctant to believe they were both gone. The anchors of his childhood, his entire world back then, now reduced to a patch of sod and a tangle of bones deep in the boggy soil. It didn't feel real. It didn't feel right. Then there was their Tina.

A volunteer he trusted, a woman with a safe house and who'd only got out of Armagh herself, told him Tina was doing better. Still struggling, in her own way, but the girls inside were keeping an eye on her. Said she'd arrived in bits, a bit sick in the head, after Kieran Kelly and the way their so-called legal system had thrown the poor girl to the wolves.

Martin agreed with her, though the words caught in his throat like splinters. His hatred for Kelly burned even deeper now. Tina had always looked up to him, laughed at his shite jokes, followed him around like a loyal pup. She'd never seen the danger in him being a Provo, only the pride. He'd fed that pride, fed her with swagger and all his talk of republicanism, not to teach her anything, but to impress her, to make himself feel like a big man. He'd send her out in the pissing rain for smokes, for messages, treating her like a lackey, and she'd never once complained. Not once. Now she was locked up for life. What a waste. He rubbed a hand over his face, his guilt rising in his throat like bile. He'd let her down. His ma and da too. The courts might've passed the sentence, but that fucker Kelly had laid the groundwork. Christ, why hadn't he seen it?

Seamus Donaghy had been dropping hints for weeks that Martin should call up to the house and see Caitlin. Kept saying he'd be there too, for moral support. Eventually, Martin gave in. Played it cool. Acted like it was no big deal, like he was doing Seamus a favour, and agreed. But underneath it all, the thought of turning up out of the blue made him queasy. He couldn't quite put his finger on why. Shame, mostly. A bit of fear too, that Caitlin might look him straight in the eye and tell him to fuck off. Whatever it was, it wasn't pleasant, still, he couldn't leave it much longer.

The night he and Seamus agreed on, he turned up early and found himself standing on the doorstep of 30 Blamfield Street, the house he'd grown up in, holding a box of Caitlin's favourite Quality Street, like some half-hearted gesture, a feeble attempt at peace. He stared at the door for a moment, remembering every scrape on the paintwork, every shout from the hallway, then finally knocked, heart thumping like it had no right to.

A second later, it opened. Caitlin answered.

'Alright,' Martin said, managing a sheepish half-smile. He might as well have been a ten-year-old caught with his hand in the biscuit tin. She didn't move, but stood there, silent, like she hadn't quite registered the sight of him. Then Seamus appeared, peering over her shoulder. When he saw Martin, his face lit up.

'Ah, Martin, there you are!' he said, easing past Caitlin and stretching out his hand. 'Good to see ye, it's been a while.' Seamus threw him a cheeky wink, his grin hidden from Caitlin, who stood there like a statue. 'Jesus, love, ye plannin' on keeping your brother parked out there all night? He'll freeze to death!'

Her heart was hammering. Like Seamus, Martin had changed beyond recognition. Flawless. Well-groomed. Standing there like a ninny, holding out a pathetic box of Quality Street as if it were a peace offering. First time for that. She'd heard the rumours, of course. Whispers he was back, but, seeing him now... Dazed, she stepped aside, opened the door wider and said. 'You'd better come in then.'

Martin sighed with relief, gave a loud sniff, and dug a bleached-white handkerchief from his pocket to wipe his nose. 'Sorry... thanks.'

He made his way down the hall, the hush of the place wrapping around him. The wallpaper hadn't changed, nor had the faint smell of damp. In the kitchen, everything sat as he remembered. That old round table, ring-marked and battered, surrounded by the same padded chairs that had seen more Sunday dinners than he could count.

On the shelf above the cooker, two red Liverpool mugs stood like relics, the paint faded, handles worn. And there, it was, the Pope's portrait, ever solemn, ever watching, still lopsided and forgotten. Everything was in its place, but even then nothing was. It felt hollow, so fuckin' empty. Like the life had drained out of it. He waited to hear his da call down from upstairs or Majella clatter through the back door with a bag of groceries. But no one came. The realism of it all hit him. The finality. Sweet Jesus, he thought. What a selfish bastard. Leaving her to face all that on her own. Leaving Caitlin to live in this bloody mausoleum. Alone. He sat in his old seat while she filled the kettle and Seamus helped with the tea things.

All three of them sat at the kitchen table, the atmosphere so thick you could've cut it with a knife, Seamus thought. A painful silence continued until Martin piped up. 'I'm sorry you had to deal with Mammy, the funeral, all of it. I should've been here, I know. I'm sorry for not being in touch since—' He broke off, the words catching in his throat.

'So where were you, Martin?' Caitlin cried. 'Where were you?!'

'America. I couldn't stay here. The peelers, the Brits. Ye know. They had it in for me. I had to get away. Otherwise, they've had me locked up in no time.'

'What they've no post or phones in America?' she shot back.

Seamus stepped in quickly, determined to keep a lid on things. 'Look, Caitlin, the most important thing is... Martin's here now. That's what matters. Isn't it?'

She looked at Seamus and wondered. Why was he so friendly with Martin all of a sudden? Had he seen him before tonight? America, eh? They'd both been in America... Caitlin sized up her options. She could tell him to fuck off and mean it, *or* she could let it go. Let it be. She sat there a moment longer, torn. So much had passed between them. Nevertheless... here he was. Looking better than she'd ever seen him. Clean. Presentable. Other than Tina, he was all the family she had left. Eventually, after a long I-so-don't-want-to-be-here pause, she gave a quiet nod. She stood, stepped towards him and opened her arms. Martin didn't hesitate and stood up too. Eyes glassy, he wrapped his arms around her and held her like he'd never held her before.

Seamus watched the scene unfold with relief and satisfaction. He'd been shitting himself all day, dreading how on earth he was going to break it to Caitlin that her brother was going to turn up on the doorstep. Thank fuck, she hadn't thrown him out.

The tea was soon poured, and Seamus did his usual fussing, passing out mugs and plates like he was hosting a wedding breakfast. Martin, though, barely glanced at his. Instead, he never took his eyes off Caitlin. Question after question came: how she'd been keeping, how work was, how she was managing with money, how they paid for Majella's funeral. You name it; he asked it.

When she'd finished answering, he reached across the table and gently took her hand and gave it a firm squeeze. His eyes, a silent promise telling her that her big brother was here now, and over his dead body would anyone lay a finger or hurt her again.

Chapter Forty-Five

£3.22

The two men sat in Porkie's kitchen, finishing a large bottle of Jameson. Anne, pregnant and miserable upstairs, had left them to it hours before. She could hear Dickie's voice rise higher and higher as the night wore on, followed by her husband's sycophantic laughter.

Over the months, Porkie had gone from bad to worse. At first his demands in bed were beyond belief until she gave in just to get it over with and prayed he'd fall asleep. Now he couldn't find work, and they were living on the breadline. She'd tried telling him about creepy Dickie, him banging on the door when she was on her own, but Porkie wouldn't have it. Said his pal was harmless, that she was a woman, full of drama. Over re-acting.

At first, she'd loved her new house, but now it felt like a birdcage. Cotton curtains hung limp against the cold, the second-hand carpet already worn through in places, and the furniture looked like it'd lived a dozen lives before ending up there. Even the bedclothes, no matter how much bleach she soaked them in, still carried old stains. Nothing felt *really* clean. Nothing felt right. Shantallow was meant to be a fresh start, but all it spelled was poverty.

That morning she'd been refused credit at the mobile shop. Every Friday she cleared the last week's bill with Porkie's giro, then depended on credit to get her through the next week. A vicious circle. The shopkeeper scribbled everything down in her red exercise book, then cashed up on a Friday.

But today, after Anne had settled up, Mrs Divine snapped the book shut. No explanation, no sympathy, just a shake of the head in front of the whole queue. 'Not this week, Anne. No more credit.' Broke to the bone, Anne walked out, catching the muttering gossip behind her — *that one's always late payin'*.

Left with £3.22, she had a week to face: meters to top up, the Pru man, food. The embarrassment followed her all the way home. It was fuckin' dire.

At first she'd been afraid to tell Porkie she was up the spout. Money was so tight she thought he'd go mad. To her surprise, he'd been thrilled and left her to it. Old-fashioned about '*women's stuff*', he'd moved into the box room as soon as she got big, claimed he didn't want to harm the baby. Any demands dropped off, and the relief was incredible. Two months left to go. Two months of Porkie not bothering her. Two months of breathing space.

By now, the racket downstairs was out of order. The neighbours, once friendly, had started blanking her. Dickie's late-night shouting, his filthy language - they'd had enough, same as her. Anne crept down, step by step, keeping as quiet as she could. But instead of barging in, she stopped dead outside the kitchen. Something held her back. Instinct, maybe. Or plain nosiness.

Porkie's voice came first, and he sounded... upset. 'I can't, Dickie. Have you any idea, any idea at all, what they'd do to ye if they found out?'

Anne didn't move. *What in God's name were they up to now?*

'But it's easy money, man, money you could do with a wain on the way. Think about it. Watch and listen, then tell them what ye see and hear. No one'll find out. Easy peasy. Think of the cash.'

Porkie chewed it over in silence. Dickie saw the fear, but also temptation. The poor bastard was skint, with a baby on the way, and he needed a result. Sure here he was, his best pal, offering him the chance of a lifetime.

Picking up his glass, Porkie kicked back the last of his whiskey, then wiped his mouth on his sleeve. His eyes were glazed but his head was overflowing with all sorts.

'It's so fuckin' risky, ye know that, don't ye?' he muttered urgently. 'They catch us grassin', it'll be our knees caps that'll go first. Maybe worse!'

Dickie moved in closer, scowling. 'Don't be such a pussy. No-one's gonna get caught. I've been at this for months. I'm tellin' ye, its easy money. So easy. Like that big Green Cross Code fella on the TV. Ye watch, look and listen. And there you go, a wee brown envelope every Friday. Easy as fuck.'

Porkie's hands trembled as he poured another shot and downed it. This was serious stuff. Everyone knew what happened to touts, but they were broke - so broke -and he hadn't worked in ages. He had his pride, didn't he? A wain on the way too. What choice did he have?

'Give it to me again,' he mumbled, his voice devoid of energy.

Dickie knew there and then. He'd done it. Reeled his friend in like a fat trout. Bonus time. He'd been promised extra for every recruit, but Porkie was the only eejit he'd ask. Safer that way. He trusted him.

'All ye gotta do is sit in the Telstra, keep your ears open. Watch who's talkin', to who, and what about. You and me know who the big fellas are – all you gotta do is confirm it, like. I keep sayin'. Easy money, Porkie. Here's the best bit, you don't even have to speak to the Brits. I'll do it. Feed it to me, and I'll do the rest. That's it.' He paused, letting his words sink in. Adding the icing on the cake, Dickie continued. 'Better than killin' pigs, eh? I swear to Jesus, Porkie, I've made a wee fortune already. Look outside, for fuck's sake. That car there didn't buy itself!'

When asked, he'd told everyone he'd had a stroke of luck on the football pools. No big deal. People believed him, some even said they were happy for him. Why wouldn't they be? Never in a million years would they suspect he was a grass. He was one of them. Came from the same streets, same schools, kicked ball on the same walls. A Creggan man through and through. He gave Porkie a friendly nudge, voice low and coaxing. 'Come on, mucker. You could've a car like that one sittin' out there. Think about it. You'd be mad not to.'

Outside in the hallway, Anne wavered, her hand poised over the kitchen door handle. Should she burst in and confront the two thickos, tell them she'd heard every stinking word? Or leave them to it? One thing was for sure. It would never include her. Ratting out to the Brits was the vilest, most degrading action imaginable. She'd sooner die than sink to such a level.

She crept back upstairs and sat on the edge of the bed, heart pounding, thoughts racing. Then another thought broke through. If she stayed quiet and they got caught, that'd be it. Two birds, one stone. Gone, both of them. She'd finally get some peace. No more shouting. No more Dickie hammering at the door like he was Lord Muck. No more crawling into bed, praying Porkie would leave her be.

But the risk. *Jesus*. If word got out she'd known and kept schtum, she'd be tarred with the same brush. Didn't matter that she'd had nothing to do with it. People talked. Derry didn't forgive a tout, or anyone that lived with one. That sort of stink never washed off. People had been put out for less. Others had been taken out altogether. She rubbed her belly, staring at the ceiling. Caught in the middle, she prayed fora way out.

Downstairs, another hefty splash of Jameson hit Porkie's glass. Dickie edged his chair closer, eyes glinting. Porkie tensed, his head spinning with booze and doubt. He didn't know what the hell to do, but he needed money, and plenty. Surely Anne'd be okay? He'd tell her in the morning, soften her first. She'd be grand. He was the man of the house, wasn't he? Did he even need to tell her? Feck it, he couldn't think straight.

Dickie was already watching, that greedy look fixed on him. Porkie gave a small shrug, barely noticeable, but enough. 'Okay. I'll try it one time first, see how it goes,' he muttered.

Dickie's face lit up like a Christmas tree. He raised his glass within seconds.

'Sláinte,' he said, all slick and charm. Their glasses tapped and the deal was done.

In her bedroom, Anne shifted on the lumpy bed, one hand resting on her belly where the baby kicked hard, as if sensing her worries. She kept staring up at the ceiling, the voices below now little more than a hum. She didn't need to hear them; she knew exactly what was going on down there. *Wankers.*

Like a bolt of lightning, her prayers were answered and a plan began to form. Fine. Let them get on with it. She knew where she'd go. The same boy would protect her, no question. Anne wasn't stupid. If word got out that she'd known she was living with a grass and kept quiet, the Provos would... well, she knew exactly what they'd do. She'd be tainted by association, dragged through the dirt, forced to live under a cloud, always looking over her shoulder. Or worse still, driven out of Derry. No way was she gonna be part of this. The only thing to do, the smart move, was to tip them off. Give the boys a heads-up. It'd be her 'Get Out of Jail Free' card. Enough to show she wasn't part of it. Enough to keep her safe. Not with the baby coming. No bloody way. Better to play it quiet, let the two wankers downstairs think they were running the show.

Chapter Forty-Six

Off the Record

The following morning, a couple of empty bottles of Jameson stood slap-bang in the middle of the kitchen table. Two smeared glasses beside them, almost mocking Porkie as his head throbbed and his cramped belly turned over. He gave his tender skull a slow shake and muttered to no one but himself, 'Jesus... why?'

His wife failed to answer, but sat down opposite him, her arms folded and staring right at him. He stared back, thinking, *not now Anne, please.*

'What! What's that filthy look for?' Slouching back in his chair, he shut his eyes, praying she wasn't about to start. But he heard her chair scrape forward, closer. Then her voice, cool and deliberate: 'Porkie, what were you and Dickie on about last night?'

His eyes snapped open. For a second, he blinked at her, clueless, then he remembered. A flash of memory, him and Dickie talkin' cars and then... *Fuck*. Anne didn't push him. She waited. It was his call, his chance to tell her everything, and then she'd tell him to wise up. Or say nothing, and he could dig his own grave. There was no way on this earth he was going to tell her, so he lied through his teeth. 'Nothin', Anne, honest. The usual rubbish.' She shook her head slowly, disappointment settling in, then rose and carried the glasses to the sink. *That was it then,* she thought.

It was too late to change his mind, he'd decided. Dickie would kill him. Surprisingly, he grabbed Anne's hand, pulling her onto his lap. His palm rested against her belly, and to her astonishment, he kissed it. Soft and kind, hoping it would make everything right again.

A couple of days later, Anne visited her mum. Liz was over the moon about Anne's pregnancy, even though she couldn't hide her worry about how unhappy her daughter appeared. A baby, she thought, would distract Anne. It'd be good for her. The Heaneys' house had grown quiet over the years, as the older kids moved away, most of them to find work. A few of the youngest were still about, tearing round the streets outside where the girls swung from ropes tied to lamp posts till their backsides got too painful and sore. They skipped or played hopscotch, while the boys charged down hills on homemade go-carts or pointed sticks like rifles, playing *'Brits.'* On her way back to Shantallow, Anne passed St Mary's and thought back to her wedding day. Mother of God, it already felt like a lifetime ago.

It was nearly 5.00 PM, and out of nowhere, she decided. What if she did it today? Dealt with it now. Told the priest what she'd overheard last night? Maybe then she'd be rid of this awful dread. A fear that was already burrowing into her soul and eating her alive. Aye, Porkie had been sweet this morning, but that didn't change the facts. Dickie had turned him, she could tell by looking at him. That hangdog face, the way he avoided her eyes. He'd lied through his teeth. No denying that. Well, she wasn't about to sit on her hands and let the pair of them grass. Associating with traitors, working for the Brits, putting her and the baby in danger. No chance.

She perched on a bench outside the church for a moment, her hands resting on her bump, her heart going like the clappers. The priest would listen, he'd advise her. Caitlin told her he was way more modern than old Father McGuire, and that he'd been so open and helpful after Majella's death. Feeling more confident now, she made her way inside and joined the queue for confession. For obvious reasons, she couldn't kneel, so she sat, bowing her head in prayer. She prayed to Saint Bernadette, as always, to help her find the right words.

Inside the confessional, Father Connolly was finishing with the last parishioner. Same old nonsense: nicking milk off someone's front step, hiding the drink and swearing they hadn't touched a drop since, or kids dobbing off school. Nothing new. Nothing worth worrying about. But it'd been a rough week all the same. There was a tout on the loose, feeding the Brits. Because of that bastard, the boys had already lost a few good men. Volunteers. That kind of treachery didn't sit in the gut — it burned.

He stepped out of the box and spotted a heavily pregnant woman nearby, deep in prayer. With a smile, he began to turn back to the confessional, not wanting to disturb her, but she looked up and caught his eye. As she got up awkwardly, he watched her limp towards him. His eyes dropped to the artificial limb, then back to her face. He offered her a small smile, like before.

'Hello there,' he said.

Anne noticed how his eyes dropped to her leg. That glance. She knew it well, the quick calculation, the sympathy most people didn't know how to hide. But she didn't care anymore. What she noticed, what mattered, was what she saw when he looked back up at her. Trusting decent eyes. The kind that didn't dart away. The kind that listened. Relief broke across her being like a wave. She'd made the right decision. This man wouldn't judge her, wouldn't overreact or talk down to her. Most important of all, she'd found her confessor. Someone she could trust. With a small nod, she joked. 'D'you mind if I don't kneel, Father, but have a quick word with ye?'

'Of course,' he laughed, gesturing towards a quiet corner at the far side of the church. 'Over here. We can talk over here.'

Anne followed him to the side, her steps uneven but controlled. She eased herself down, folded her hands gently over her bump, then drew in a breath and held it, searching for the right place to start. Her heart thudded beneath her ribs, not quite from fear, more from the scale of what she was about to share, and how to make him understand. She bit her lip. When she caught the warmth in his smile, for the first time in forever, she didn't feel so alone.

Chapter Forty-Seven

Two Paracetamol

Following the brutal attack on Bridget Barry, Tina McLaughlin's life changed yet again. Her two new cellmates proved resentful and continually found fault with her for impinging on their precious space. They thought it ridiculous the way they'd been forced to put another bed in the tiny cell. It was a blessing Tina had so few possessions. No one could say they were political prisoners. Just two sisters doing a life stretch. The Republican women, because of segregation, hadn't a clue what the sisters were really in for, only that they weren't under the protection of any OC, or answering to one either.

The morning after Bridget's assault, Dr Harris didn't even look up when OC Maureen Molony appeared at the infirmary door with Bridget by her side, pale and unsteady, her face blotched and cheekbones sunken. He already knew what had happened, of course. Everyone did. In a place like Armagh, word travelled fast, even faster when it was something brutal, something ugly, something no one would speak of out loud but all carried in their eyes. Molony had gone straight to the governor, demanding answers, but Harris knew full well that nothing would come of it, not here. This place buried its truths, but they always found a way back up to the surface.

Without saying a word, Harris pulled on his gloves slowly and clinically, then nodded towards the exam table with barely a glance at either woman. Bridget moved like a marionette with frayed strings, stiff and hesitant, her face expressionless, but he caught the set of her jaw, the way it locked tight like she was bracing for another blow. Molony didn't budge from her post, arms folded across her chest, her calmness louder than any accusation, her eyes never leaving him. She didn't trust him. Not for a second. She made damn sure he knew it.

He kept it professional, or at least what passed for professional in a place like this. Detached, expressionless, going through the motions as if it were another part of the job. No emotion, no opinion. Facts. Clinical facts. He considered her, not once meeting her eyes. It didn't take long to see the damage. The internal tearing ran deep. The bruising was ugly. Abrasions, raw and telling. Whatever had been used on her obviously hadn't been a man, or even a fist. It was foreign. Cold and chosen with intent. Still, he said nothing. Asked nothing. Only reached for his pad and scribbled down what he saw, like he was noting the weather or filling in a form. His face didn't move. Not even a flicker.

He paused, then wrote his diagnosis down in the kind of language that hid the truth.

Lacerations and tearing observed, consistent with possible internal penetration by an instrument or similar object. Bruising, bleeding, and trauma to the genital region noted. Aetiology unclear. Possibility of self-inflicted injury cannot be ruled out. No referral indicated.

Neat, professional, the sort of phrasing that looked normal on paper but buried what had really been done to her.

He knew exactly what those last words meant. *No referral indicated.* They shut the door on any inquiry stone dead. No referral, no grounds for escalation. Cover their backs. That was the point. He could have written the truth, but instead he pared it down to avoid suspicion. She'd been brutalised, no doubt about it, yet on record he reduced it to injuries that would heal. In time. Without once meeting her eye, he dropped two paracetamol into her palm like loose change and muttered, 'Take those. You'll be fine in a day or two.' Then he turned away, stripped off his gloves and pulled the next patient's chart as if Bridget amounted to nothing but a tick in a box.

At the back of the room, the OC hadn't moved. She stood with her arms folded, quiet, composed, watching every movement with that same unreadable expression. When the exam was over, she remained impassive, but watchful. Bridget hadn't spoken once. Not a word. She'd only winced when prodded too roughly, lying dead still, her eyes fixed beyond the ceiling, like her body was there but she'd already left the room.

Harris said little either, cold as a morgue slab, barely glancing up from his notes. Everyone knew what the man was – a worm in a white coat, spineless and sly. Still, Maureen held her tongue. There was no use calling him out, not today, not with Bridget lying there like that. The poor woman had been through enough without her piling more tension into the room. She offered a small smile when Bridget looked her way, a feeble effort meant to offer strength, though it barely made it past her own clenched teeth.

Inside, Maureen was crushed. How could this happen? How could a woman, any woman, be capable of such cruelty towards another? It defied everything she understood. But fury wouldn't help now. Bridget didn't need shouting, didn't need fire. She needed peace. So

Maureen stood her ground and helped Bridget sort herself out.

Chapter Forty-Eight

A 'Flexible Friend'

Governor Johnston sat at his desk, fingers steepled, his ulcer gnawing with a familiar burn. The situation with Bridget Barry was positively awful. But to investigate? To drag it out? Face the media? His stomach felt like it was on fire now. A female officer accused of sexual abuse? Of the worst kind. Absolutely not. No way. Couldn't be. Not here. Not in Armagh Gaol. *His gaol*. If word ever got out beyond these walls, it could bring the entire service crashing down on his head. Johnston understood suffering, but his role as Governor demanded stability, not sentiment. So he'd offered Maureen Molony, the Republican OC, what she wanted to hear – platitudes and lots of them.

'I've spoken to Father McGuire and assured him there'll be an exhaustive investigation into these claims,' he said, knowing full well there'd be no such thing. Adding insult to injury, he gave her the line he'd rehearsed. 'Though I've got to warn you, I've been assured by my staff that Mrs Barry was extremely violent and assaulted one of our new officers. I won't have it, Mrs Molony. Fact.'

But the Republican OC wouldn't give up. Of course she wouldn't.

'With respect, I won't have it either, sir. Let me talk to Tina McLaughlin. She was there when it happened. She'll confirm what Bridget said and let's be honest – we both know any investigation wouldn't be an independent one. Leave it to me to look at the facts. Let me deal with this my way, please. I can assure you Bridget doesn't know what the word 'assault' even means. There's not a nasty bone in that woman's body. It's horrendous what's happened to her.' Her voice grew deep and near threatening, 'And it happened under your watch, Governor Johnston. Think about that.'

The governor shivered and checked his watch. She was right, but he'd another meeting in ten minutes and the pressure in his midriff was getting worse. He promptly tried to shut her down.

'That's fine, Molony, but you can't expect me to believe anything McLaughlin says. That girl missed her stop ages ago.'

Maureen continued her relentless pursuit. 'Have you seen Bridget for yourself, Mr Johnston? She's broken. Won't speak, won't eat. She's all but dead – and she was one of the strongest, most incredible women I know here.'

Johnston rubbed his face with both hands, feeling the sweat prick at his temples. He knew Bridget; she was a good woman, but admitting abuse was opening a door he wasn't prepared to walk through.

'Okay, have it your way. You look into it,' he snapped. 'Talk to her. See what she's got to say and report back to me. No one else. Now leave me in peace!'

The OC smiled and, feeling victorious, left before he changed his mind.

Johnston slumped back in his chair completely knackered. He couldn't deal with much more today. His bloody Access bill had landed on his desk that morning, thick as a parish newsletter and twice as depressing. His significant other was up to no good again. No doubt she was off to McAnerney's Drapery, that overpriced shop she always claimed she only went into 'for a wee browse'. Cushions, curtains, some throw she had to have as if her life depended on it. She'd always called her Access card her 'flexible friend'. Aye, right. It might be her friend, but it was fast becoming his worst enemy.

He rubbed his eyes again, muttered on about early retirement, and reached for the pack of *Rennies* in his desk drawer. What a day? Now that Commons bill had been passed, he'd love to walk away and let someone else deal with the lunatics. To tell the women they weren't deemed political prisoners anymore and its implications. *Christ.*

Although the governor had agreed Maureen could speak to Tina, it took another three maddening weeks before she got near the girl. She was told that, like Bridget, Tina wouldn't leave her cell, wouldn't eat, wouldn't speak. Every time Maureen pushed for another word with Governor Johnston, she was turned away with some poor excuse. Then one morning, the Gods were on her side. Tina's cellmates had finally cracked. Sick of her peculiarities, her night time muttering, and the sense of sorrow that hung around her like fog, they'd slung her bedclothes and scabby belongings out onto the landing, shouting for her to clear off. She'd shuffled away without a word, heading for the warmth of the laundry, bits of her life trailing behind her like crumbs.

Maureen had been elbow-deep in laundry when she spotted her. But one look and her heart sank. The young'un looked like she'd been dug up. All the hard work Bridget had put in to make her better had vanished. With thin, trembling arms, the girl, her face grey and dead-eyed, had withdrawn back into a world of her own. The OC moved quickly and caught Tina's arm before pulling her gently into a corner, somewhere private, away from the noise and clatter. She didn't rush her. No point charging in like a bull, not with the girl this fragile. She reached out and tucked a stray strand of hair behind Tina's ear.

'How you feeling, love?' she asked softly.

Tina blinked, slow and tired, like the words were dragging themselves through sludge before landing in her head. The woman talking to her was pretty. Not fancy-pretty like the girls on the TV, but soft-pretty. Gentle face, kind eyes, warm hands. She was holding Tina's hand, not tight but enough to say, *I'm a friend,* and in that second, Tina felt safe. Really safe. Sweat was running down the woman's brow, and without thinking, Tina reached up and wiped it away with her finger. No fuss. Only instinct.

Maureen was moved by the simple gesture. 'Tina,' she said again, her voice still low. 'Are you okay?'

Tina lowered her gaze to the floor. 'I'm okay,' she whispered, her lips barely moving. Maureen realised this would take some time. More than she'd hoped. She kept hold of Tina's hand and moved closer.

'You remember me, Tina, don't ye, love?'

Tina lifted her head, her eyes searching the pretty girl's face like it was a faded photograph she half-recognised. 'Dunno,' she said.

'You're in Armagh Gaol, love. With us. I'm Maureen and the girls, we've been looking after you and Bridget. You remember Bridget, don't you?'

The change was instant. At the mention of Bridget's name, Tina caved in on herself. Her arms wrapped around her middle, body rocking in small, silent waves, as though bracing against an unseen blow. Her eyes had gone wide, staring past the room, locked in a place no one else could see. Maureen recognised it straight away, that flicker of horror, the memory breaking through, creeping back in like damp through stone. She moved in slowly, careful not to crowd her, saying nothing at first but being there. Just close enough.

When the time was right, Molony was ready and said. 'Easy now. Easy. I know it's hard, love, but I need you to tell me what happened to Bridget. Can you do that for me, honey?'

Tina's face twisted, her expression crumbling as silent tears slid down her cheeks. She stared into space, seeing whatever it was that haunted her, a thing no one else in the room could possibly imagine. Her lips parted, but no sound came, only shallow breaths laced with pain. She was somewhere else entirely, dragged back without warning. Maureen, standing nearby, understood at once. There was nothing to say, nothing to do, only wait while Tina came back from wherever she'd been hiding.

On his usual Tuesday visit to the gaol, delayed this week by the bank holiday, Father McGuire was pulled aside by the OC. Her voice was calm, but the significance of what she shared virtually crushed him. As soon she'd finished, he stood and said nothing for a very long time. Then, composing himself with a small cough, he made his way to Bridget Barry's cell. She lay motionless, buried beneath a heap of coarse brown blankets. From where he stood, all he could see was the outline of her body, curled in tight, as if trying to disappear into the mattress.

Two women sat nearby, silent sentries keeping watch. When he nodded, wordlessly asking for privacy, they stood at once. One of them paused, gave the blanket a gentle pat, then followed the other out. The door shut halfway behind them, leaving him alone with the shape of a woman who looked like she no longer wanted to exist. He placed his bag on the floor and lowered himself onto the edge of the iron-framed bed. He didn't open his Bible right away. Instead, he clutched it to his chest, not out of duty, but like a man holding on to the last thing keeping him sane.

'Bridget,' he whispered, his voice barely above a breath. 'It's me. Father McGuire.'

She didn't move, but he didn't expect her to. He lowered his head and shut his eyes, his heart full of sorrow. Not only for her, but for every young girl caught up in this godforsaken mess of a world. From the time they were toddlers, Bridget and her siblings had been taught to respect the clergy. You didn't talk back to a priest. You didn't question one. Especially not a man with silver hair and kind eyes, like this one. So, despite the pain, she forced herself to sit up. Her limbs protested, slow and stiff, and her face creased as a deep, raw ache bloomed low in her body. It took a few seconds to steady herself, to focus, but she managed it. Barely. When she saw the old priest's face, those tear-filled eyes, red-rimmed and searching, a weak smile tugged at the corners of her mouth. Poor man. He had a soft heart, this one. She dropped her gaze and stared down at her hands, unable to meet his eyes. He'd know. She was ashamed.

Her hands shook as she whispered, 'Father.'

'Hello, Bridget. I'm so sorry about what's happened,' he said softly.

Bridget gave a small shrug. 'Nothing to be said, Father. What's done is done.'

He nodded, but not like he believed a word. 'I've seen Governor Johnston. He's told me there'll be an investigation. Under all that bravado, he's a good man.' Bridget didn't have the heart to argue. Let the priest hold on to his faith in the great and good. She knew better. There'd be no independent investigation. No justice. The story would be changed to suit, warped until it landed back on her. They'd say she'd lashed out, resisted orders, that she'd been injured during restraint or the like.

There was no point in replying. Instead, she swallowed the lump in her throat and asked. 'The young'un, Father. Tina... is she okay?'

McGuire hadn't yet laid eyes on Tina, but he didn't need to. He could already see her in his mind - pale, drawn, that hunched, withered way she had when the world got too much and she'd withdraw into her own safe place. The girl had come so far. He'd watched her, little by little, return to herself, and that was down to Bridget Barry and the others who'd cared for her like family. The thought of Tina sliding back into that secret place of hers and the senseless cruelty of it all made him want to yell to the high heavens. His faith was being tested to its limits, and today was one of those days.

A memory surfaced, sudden and vivid. Tina, on her First Communion day, a simple white dress, lace gloves, and that magnificent head of wild red curls that Majella McLaughlin had done her utmost to tame. He could still see her fidgeting in a front row pew, her face glowing with the solemnity of the service. A memory that felt like it belonged to someone else.

He tried to steady himself. 'I haven't seen her. Not yet,' he told Bridget, 'next on my list, I promise you that. Is there anything I can do for you, Bridget, anything at all?'

Bridget looked at her hands, then at him. Her voice, when it came, was barely audible. 'Aye, Father, you can. Get me outta here, will ye? I can't take this place anymore. Not after that.'

He told her he'd do everything he could, promised it even, then bowed his head and offered up a prayer. But Bridget, she stared past him, knowing full well prayers wouldn't help her now. Too late for that.

Back in the laundry room, Maureen was still in conversation with Tina. PO Quirk spotted them huddled in the corner and wandered over. Near enough to hear them, yet distant enough not to intrude. When she saw her, the OC glanced up and gave a small smile. Quirk gave one back. There was nothing to say, not really. She knew what had gone on in that cell. Anyone with half a brain and an ear to the ground did. But what incensed her most wasn't just the act itself, vile as it was. It was the carry-on afterwards. Smyth and Drake, smirking like schoolgirls, turning it into a sick little story for the locker room. Laughing, boasting like they were proud of what they'd done, like it made them big. Quirk had heard enough. She couldn't stand to be around it anymore. Couldn't stand them.

All her working life, Quirk had played it straight. Do the job, don't get involved, keep her opinions to herself, and get home in one piece. She'd always tried to show the women a bit of decency, treat them like human beings, no matter what they were in for. But that wasn't enough now. Not after this. What had been done was beyond cruel. It was calculated. Evil. If she wasn't careful, calling it out could see her name scratched out too. Staff who stepped out of line, who broke ranks, didn't last long. The threats were never written down, but they came all the same. Rota changes, cold shoulders, being left on the landings without back-up. Everyone knew what it meant when they turned on you.

Still, as she watched Tina McLaughlin, hunched over, barely able to sit upright beside Maureen, PO Quirk decided. The girl's eyes were vacant, a walking disaster, and the OC looked as though she might break. A line had been crossed. Not a rule or a policy, but a line no decent person could ignore. Drake and Smyth had gone too far, and Quirk couldn't pretend otherwise.

Not anymore.

Chapter Forty-Nine

A Patchwork Face

Deep in the trees behind the lodge, near Jones's parked car outside the Orange Lodge in Tullyvallen, two armed volunteers and Dolores Gillispie in full camouflage kit crouched low, keeping perfectly still. The sounds of laughter and music carried faintly through the crisp air. They'd watched earlier, concentrating, as Jones and his sidekick were welcomed like royalty, ushered up the shallow steps and through the red door. No guards. No security checks. Not even a lookout. Ten minutes passed. Not a word between them. Only the odd click of a rifle strap being adjusted or the whisper of breath through cloth. The woman in charge of the unit signalled it was time to move out.

One man took off fast, hugging the wall as he darted to the side of the lodge. He dropped to his knees, planted the four-pound bomb, set the timer, then sprinted back across the exposed yard, ducking low, arms pumping, boots crunching against the gravel. Back in the shrubbery, breathless and wired, he gave a thumbs-up. The woman checked her watch and whispered, 'Nice work. Let's give them half an hour to clap their way into eternity.'

Inside, Jones was close to finishing his speech and, for the first time that night, he realised he was enjoying it. The words were flowing, any irritation had gone. Faces watched him, every pause he took rewarded with applause that swelled and rolled back at him like a tide. It was the kind of attention that made a man believe he could go on forever. Then the doors crashed open. Two men came through, masked, rifles tight against their shoulders. For the briefest second, the clapping stuttered but didn't stop; the crowd froze between disbelief and denial. Then the first burst split the air. The sound was deafening, rapid popping that seemed to tear the hall itself apart. Bullets ripped through bodies and walls with a force that seemed to make the hall itself shudder. Glass blew out as a rifle barrel smashed aside a window, shards spinning across the floor before gunfire spat blindly into the crowd.

Smoke spread fast, sharp and acrid, clawing at throats until every breath seared the lungs. Screams rose high and wild, chairs clattered over, bodies slammed into one another in blind panic, people going down under the crush. The stench of gunpowder thickened the air, hot and bitter, clinging to sweat and the raw stink of fear. The noise was fierce - gunfire pounding, voices yelling, feet hammering in every direction. In seconds, the hall was swallowed by terror, a choking haze where no one knew if they'd ever see daylight again.

Lemon grabbed his boss from the stage and shoved him through the curtains, no time to think, just run. Gunfire tore through the hall behind them, loud and relentless, each burst a fresh reminder that this wasn't a warning. Jones had dropped hard, elbows scraping, lungs fighting for air. He heard someone pounding down the aisle, then spotted a figure, pistol out, firing from the hip like it was the Wild West. He hadn't known who it was then, only another lunatic in the madness. Later, he'd learn it was an off-duty RUC man, convinced he'd hit one of the shooters. The idiot had flung himself down beside them, breathing like he'd run a marathon and grinning as if he'd saved the day. He watched the man crouch down, steady himself behind the low partition, take aim again with trembling hands, then fire off another desperate round into the thick, smoky blur ahead, before pulling back and muttering a curse under his breath.

Jones kept his eyes on the room, on the horror happening around him, on the mess that had once been a place of order. His chest thumped with every heartbeat, the sound of it matching the drumbeat of gunfire, which was dying off now. Not gone entirely, not yet, but changing. It was no longer a full-on, frenzied spray of bullets. It came now in stuttering bursts, single shots, random and half-hearted, like whatever storm had torn through here was finally losing strength. The intense stench burned his nose. Beneath it was worse, heavier, raw and metallic - blood, fresh and plenty of it. He forced himself not to gag.

He rose slowly, cautiously, feeling the tight pull on his shoulders, aware of every sound and movement. Lemon was beside him, moving carefully, neither of them speaking, but afraid. Their shoes crunched across the wreckage, splintered wood, shattered glass, torn Union flags, scorched hymn sheets. Bowler hats were scattered across the floor like fallen helmets, some crushed underfoot, others rolled into corners. Chairs had been thrown, benches almost split in two, and scattered amongst it all were shapes, unmoving, limbs splayed at impossible angles, some too still to be alive, others jerking faintly in what looked like pain or panic, or both.

Jones scanned the room, eyes darting through the haze. One man lay face down in a pool of blood, spreading too fast to ignore. Another was slumped over the front pew, head resting at an angle that made his insides turn. A third, younger lad, barely out of school by the look of him, sat slouched against the far wall, blood running down his neck like a broken tap, eyes wide open but seeing nothing. The place was in ruins. Not battered or damaged, but wrecked beyond recognition. A war zone.

That's what did Jones's head in most. The sheer cheek of it. The gall. The Provos hadn't come for bodies. They'd come for the heart of what Loyalists stood for. They'd stormed right in through those doors with their balaclavas and their rifles, torn the place to pieces, opened fire like it was a battlefield and not the hall where loyal Orangemen held remembrance parades, weddings, meetings, christenings — where they'd stood side by side and sung *God Save the Queen* without shame. Blasphemy it was and right here on their own bloody doorstep. He could barely contain the fury rising in his gut. It wasn't panic, not anymore. It was rage, pure and white-hot, bubbling under the surface, held back only by instinct and the need to get the hell out.

Lemon offered him an arm and tried to help, his voice hoarse, urging him to move, but they'd barely taken a step when a blinding white light tore through the air, followed by a sudden, sickening roar. The force of it sent them flying, the ground lifting beneath their feet. A wall of fire ripped through the hall, swallowing chairs, banners, everything in its path. The heat punched through the space, wild and unnatural. Jones felt it strike his chest first, then his hands, then his face, like the sun itself had fallen from the sky and slammed straight into his face. The pain was deep and savage, as though he were being burned from the inside out. Darkness followed.

Days later, barely conscious, he woke to find himself bandaged from head to foot and in agony. Lemon, miraculously, hadn't been as badly hurt. Burns to his arms and legs, but his face, the ugly bastard, had come through fine. Jones's hadn't. A doctor told him it looked like a curtain, or maybe a flag, had caught fire and melted onto his skin. Fused to it. When the bandages were changed for the first time, he caught sight of himself in a small mirror someone had thoughtlessly left nearby. He didn't recognise himself. Not even close. The skin across his cheeks was warped and blistered, patches of it a deep, angry red, others pale and glossy, like new plastic. His hands weren't much better, bandaged in thick gauze. Under the edges he could see pink, blistered flesh, skin stretched unnaturally tight. His fingers curled slightly as if they were learning how to work again. Whoever had done this, whatever scum had dared to storm *their* hall, to spit in the face of everything they stood for, he would find them. When he did, there'd be no speeches, no warnings. *No surrender!*

Today, in his state-of-the-art bathroom in Belfast, he stared at the mirror. What was left of his face was a grotesque patchwork. The first skin grafts had covered the worst, but badly. Raw flesh gleamed under the light, slick and red like butcher's meat. His right eye, bloodshot and half-shut, leaked a steady line down his ruined cheek. The cheekbone beneath had been rebuilt, or so they said, but it jutted too high, too sharp, as if it belonged to someone else. His nose, once straight, had collapsed into a blunt, useless stub.

He wasn't looking at a reflection anymore but a stranger stitched from pain and rage. A mask, not a man. Still, behind it burned the fire that refused to die. He leaned closer. The glass threw back every torn seam, every crooked angle. No grafts, no reconstructive promises could disguise what had been stolen. What stared back wasn't him. Not anymore. Not even close. Sometimes, in the dark hours before dawn, he thought it might have been easier if he'd died with the others — blown apart in the Orange Hall, gone in the blaze. No mirror. No pity. No long crawl back to this.

Afterward, he sat downstairs at his kitchen table with Lemon and three beefy hooligans. They looked like hooligans, because that's what they were. Hooligans. Lemon had sworn blind he'd trust them with his life, but Jones wasn't so sure. He owned them, one way or another, but that didn't mean he trusted them. So, when it came to his proposal, he kept things vague, offering only the bare minimum.

'Remember, gentlemen, you owe me. All of you. I know where you live. I know where your mother and father live. Even better, I know where your grandparents live. If any of you squeal or let me down, you can guarantee my lieutenant here will pay you and your family a visit. And that... you... do... not... want. Understand?'

The three goons nodded fervently, knowing Jones meant every word.

'This supposed truce with the Provos has ended,' he told them in a cynical voice. 'A farce. Nothing more.' He coughed and cowered as a flash of pain ran over his wounded face. He'd have to take more painkillers soon.

'You and Lemon have done a superb job so far. However, I want us to make our mark next time. No more guns, no baseball bats. No more chains or batons. I want knives. Knives gentlemen. I want you to slaughter those Papist bastards like the pigs that they are.'

A hush fell over the kitchen. Even the hooligans were shocked at Jones's ranting. 'I want you to cut those people down. Slice them in half. Butcher them without mercy. Let them know the price for their united Ireland and trying to get rid of me.'

Jones sat back, his eyes moving over their faces. Those big, wide grins. They looked near sick with excitement. *Good*. That's what he wanted. Let them feel important. Let them think they're part of the future. As far as he was concerned, they were tools. Willing ones. He'd use them. Didn't care how far it went. He wanted retribution. The kind that left an unambiguous message.

Chapter Fifty

Run Over

Emmett McFadden had been working in the garage for months, and he loved it. Fortunately, his boss was a good and patient man and Emmett was learning loads.

After passing his driving test first time, they gave him a few small ops with the Unknowns. Nothing major. Pick up a couple of Provos, sneak them over the border, and drop them where some local volunteers would be waiting. No talking, no eye contact, just get in, get out. He was told to keep quiet, and he did. It was better not knowing who they were or why they were running. He didn't care to ask. His job was to drive, hand them over, and get back home in one piece. Grand. At least he was putting his hand in for the Cause, however small.

He hadn't seen Mickey Boyle much since, and when he had, the man looked wrecked. Worn to the bone. The killings were constant now, Catholics and Protestants both, slaughtered one after the other with no end in sight. A Provo bomb wiped out a Catholic family in their drapery shop; not long after, Loyalists retaliated by gunning down two Catholics. Every act answered with more blood. Derry didn't breathe, it bled.

Since the Civil Rights Association ended the rent and rates strike, his mother had been more nervous than ever. Every penny of arrears was clawed back through her benefits, gone before the money even hit the table. His apprentice wages didn't stretch far, but he handed her what he could. She pretended they were fine, wore that forced smile, but he saw through it – every nervous glance at the meter, every lie to make him feel better. His da was a write-off, slumped in his vest and trousers, sweating into the cushions and barking orders like he was still the man of the house. Emmett was angry at him now. Charlie hadn't been anything for a long time. Useless to the last.

Earlier that day, Emmett had spotted Tommy O'Reilly across the street and crossed over, keen for word of Tina. He liked big Tommy - a kind soul, always cheerful, no matter what. But the moment Tina's name came up, the cheer was gone. His face fell in an instant, like a curtain dropping.

'She's not great, son. She was moved to a different wing a while back. Cut off from those lookin' after her.'

Emmett felt for him. 'Ah, shit, Tommy. Sorry to hear that. Why can't you get her to Gransha or take her home?'

Tommy and Caitlin had spent months hounding their local MP, firing off letters to anyone who might listen, anyone who could help get Tina back to Derry. Politicians, journalists, someone even suggested the bloody Pope. All in a bid to highlight her case, her vulnerability, the simple fact she should never have been in that place to begin with. Most never replied. The few that did weren't worth the stamp, only passed them from pillar to post, each one blaming the next.

Tommy had visited Tina again, and it had knocked the stuffing clean out of him. She'd barely looked at him, sat there like a ghost with her empty eyes, her voice so faint he had to move closer to catch the few words she managed, if she spoke at all.

Standing on the street with Emmett, Tommy kept it all to himself. No sense in dumping it on the lad, not when everyone on the estate knew he'd a soft spot for Tina, even if he never came out and said it. Tommy could've told him how awful she'd looked, how the visit had left him gutted, but what good would that do? So instead, they stuck to the football, slagging off who should've been dropped, who'd no right wearing a candy stripe shirt, throwing the usual jabs and having a laugh. Then they shook hands, and that was that.

Nineteen-year-old Darragh lay in an open coffin, while Mickey Boyle could hardly look. They'd done their best, wrapped his head in bandages to keep it together. To make him look his best, for the mourners. But Mickey knew. Knew what lay beneath. Knew his cousin's skull had been shattered. Him a youngster too. Nineteen last week. And now, this was what they had left of him.

His aunt sat beside him, wooden rosary beads knotted in her trembling hands, whispering through her tears, 'They didn't have to run him over, Mickey, like a dog. They didn't have to run him over, or poor Paul.' The small silver cross at her neck rose and fell with her chest, fast and uneven, as if she was holding herself together by sheer will. Barely. For what? For a teenager who hadn't done a thing wrong.

Darragh wasn't a Provo. Never had been. He wasn't running guns or planting bombs. He was a youngster, same as any other, caught up in the madness, throwing the odd stone when the rioting kicked off, laughing with his pals like they were untouchable. That day he and Paul Kennedy were mucking about at the top of the street when the Brit Saracen came out of nowhere, full pelt, no warning, no care. It didn't knock him down. It crushed him.

Paul had rushed to help, only for the Pig to back over them both. Darragh was mangled, and Paul left broken beside him.

Mickey sat ramrod straight, hatred thrumming through him. This wasn't grief anymore. It was darker, a sickness that gripped and wouldn't let go. After a while he'd had enough of the murmurs and half-words. He stood, went to his aunt and hugged her. She clung to him so tight he could hardly breathe, as though letting go might mean she'd collapse right there and then.

Suddenly she grabbed him and whispered in a voice that came low, livid and sure. 'You find that Brit who did this, Mickey Boyle, and sort it. Will ye do that for me?'

Mickey stepped back, then gave her a long, careful look. She didn't bat an eyelid. his aunt knew exactly what she was asking. So did he.

With a quick nod, she got his answer. 'Thank you, love. Thank you.'

Afterward, he stepped outside into the chilly air. His aunt asked him to take care of it, and he would, regardless of how or when.

Chapter Fifty-One

Hypothetically

Martin McLaughlin sat across from Father Connolly in the Rainbow Café, the priest's usual haunt, on a damp Friday morning that matched his mood. It had been a while since they'd last spoken, and when the invite came, passed along by Tommy of all people, Martin had been curious enough to accept. He already knew the Yanks had pulled the plug on the arms shipments, but the talk was Connolly hadn't let go entirely. Still had a hand in NORAID, still pulling the odd string, keeping things ticking over behind the curtain.

Beyond that, they hadn't crossed paths much. All the same, here he was. Cathal Connolly might've been wearing the collar, but he'd never been afraid to get his hands dirty. Martin, for his part, had long since stopped believing in God, had walked away from that long ago, but he hadn't lost respect for a man who stayed true to his convictions, especially when it could cost him everything. Now, across the table, the priest stirred his coffee, distracted, his eyes darting toward the window like someone expecting bad news.

Martin sipped his tea and watched him. Something was eating at him. 'You all right, Father?'

Cathal hesitated. 'Don't really know, Martin. Lots on my mind.'

Martin didn't press him. Leave him be until he was ready. It worked as Cathal leaned over and lowered his voice. 'I've gotta question.'

'Oh aye.' Martin replied. *This should be interesting.*

'You've heard there's a grass out there somewhere and getting worse by the day. Singing like a bird.'

Martin gave a slow nod. Of late, things had gone sideways too many times. The Derry Brigade was on edge, nerves stretched thin, everyone watching their backs. Word going around a few West Belfast fellas were coming, not for support, but to sniff out the rat — or rats.

Cathal kept his voice low. 'Let's say, *hypothetically*, I might know who it... no, know who *they* are. I'd have to tell you, wouldn't I?'

Martin's heart picked up a beat, but his expression didn't change. He loathed touts. They were rot. Sick rot that needed cut out fast and brutal. No excuses, no appeals. Once the damage was done, there was no undoing it, no wiping the board clean. Men ended up in cells or coffins because of loose tongues. That he couldn't forgive. Not ever. He'd seen accomplished volunteers disappear overnight, lives torn apart on the word of some yellow arsed coward who couldn't hack the heat. The tragedy was that it was never the Brits who broke the line. It was always one of their own. Scourge of the Cause they were.

He met the priest's eyes, calm as ever. 'Well then, Father,' he said, voice level, 'if we're talking *hypothetically*, aye. We'd put that kind of information to good use. For the greater good, you might say.' He raised his brows a fraction, letting his expression do the rest. Cathal gave a slow nod.

McLaughlin hadn't changed a bit. Still calm, still methodical, still capable of doing whatever needed done without so much as blinking. A ruthlessness that didn't unsettle him. If anything, it made life simpler. Not cleaner, not by a long stretch, but simpler. He'd never breathe a word of what Anne Ballantyne had told him. She'd come to him in confidence, and he'd given his word he'd be careful. But there were ways to guide without giving too much away, to point in the right direction without saying it outright. As Martin had said himself, it was for the greater good. For the community. For Anne.

To avoid being overheard, Cathal spoke quietly and calmly. 'Right then. For obvious reasons, I can't name names, so don't ask. What I will say is this. Keep them close. Set the pair of them up. Feed them scraps, bits of false intel, purely to tempt them. Then wait. If they bite, you'll have your answer. No guesswork. No maybes. Enough rope to see what they're really up to. If they're doing what I suspect, well... you'll know soon enough.'

Martin was surprised when the priest used the word 'pair' and listened attentively.

'Think about it,' the priest continued. 'Have you seen anyone flashing extra money about lately? Driving a fancy car, bragging about it? One with a bloated friend sprawled in the passenger seat?'

Martin could barely hold it in. He knew who it was. Kevin McDaid aka Dickie and that fuckin' eejit fat arse friend of his, Porkie. Said it all, pair of useless twats. He'd seen Dickie swanning about in his new car, cheeky bastard, even had the nerve to say he'd won a few quid on the pools. *Sure he did.* When he took this back, the order would come straight through. With any luck, they'd make an example of them. Send a message no one would forget. They talked a little more before Connolly stood up, offered his hand, and Martin took it like old comrades. No need for goodbyes. Message received and understood.

Martin stayed where he was, watching the door swing shut. Siobhán appeared, her smile easy, a teapot in hand. 'More tea, love?' she asked.

'Go on then,' he replied.

She poured without rushing, still smiling as if they'd done this dance a hundred times before. Siobhán had always been fond of Martin. He could be a right wally, no doubt, but she liked him all the same. As she walked away, he took another sip and let his eyes drift to the window. Last time he'd been in here, it'd been with Kieran Kelly. He'd replayed that meeting more times than he could count. The warning he'd given... *Christ*. He was sure he'd told Kelly, without spelling it out, that he needed to wise up, knock that gay stuff on the head, and walk away before he landed himself in real bother.

The leadership had been nervous, worried he'd crack under pressure, turn tout if the Brits got hold of it. They could've used it to twist his arm, you didn't shag a priest in Derry. Sooner or later it'd get out. The whole time, that smirking bastard had been stringing their Tina along. Playing the Romeo, acting like some big whoosh, whispering lies in her ear, making her believe he actually gave a toss. Martin stiffened in his seat at the thought of it. Best not to go down that road, not now.

He drank the last of the tea, left a few coins on the saucer, and gave Siobhán a quick wave as he stood to leave. She beamed at him, warm as always.

Outside, the cold air hit his face. He scanned the street, eyes searching for the nearest payphone. They had them. The bastards. Dickie and that slob of a pal. After what the priest said, It all slotted together like a perfect jigsaw. No more guessing.

He'd a call to make. Time to get the word out. Time to act.

Chapter Fifty-Two

Who is Brona Doyle?

Alice Wallace told her boss she needed to head back to England for a bit. Said she was wrecked, needed a holiday. It wasn't true, of course, but one look at her face, and the silly fool knew he'd no choice. The girl was good at the job – no sticky fingers.

At the last minute, she'd been pulled off the Falls Road temporarily. Her instructions were simple. She was to link up, right on the border, with an SAS unit heading south into the Republic. Their target was a senior Provo, possibly one of the three she'd seen that night in The Shamrock, the same night Dolores came at her like a rabid dog. Alice, it turned out, was the only one who could formally identify him.

She hadn't managed to join the team straight away and thank Christ for that. Within a few hours, the whole thing went tits up. The eight-man unit was spotted almost as soon as they'd crossed over, picked up by the Gardaí before they even made it out of the trees. The official story pinned it on a map-reading blunder. Claimed they'd crossed the border 'by accident'. Clever. If she'd gone with them, she'd have been taken too, her cover blown to bits, and she'd be back on her desk.

When Dolores appeared, frantic and angry, looking for Paddy, Alice realised something major was occurring. As if they'd never met, Paddy suddenly became distant, disappearing from her life like smoke escaping her grasp. Not knowing what was going on frustrated her and made her even more suspicious. Still, it hadn't been a complete waste of time. There'd been decent intel and a few clean hits along the way. After that stunt with the young Gaelic team, she and Ian Dillon had gone after several Provo targets, hitting them exactly where it hurt. It shook them, no doubt about it, left them bruised. Yet no one had breathed a word about her or Ian. No charges, no arrests, nothing that traced back. The RUC had snooped around, kicked up a bit of dust, but when nothing stuck, they moved on. Pending further investigation, of course.

Alice played her role flawlessly, sticking to the script. She worked shifts in the shop, turned up on time, collected for the prisoners' fund, made small talk with the regulars, all the while keeping her head down and out of trouble. She said little, listened plenty, and watched everything. Every move, every look was deliberate, all of it aimed at finding out where Paddy had gone and gathering whatever scraps of intel she could.

Around his friends, she kept things light. Took the piss, called him a bastard for clearing off on her, even joked she'd cut his balls off when he showed his face again. A bit of banter. They laughed, told her he was probably off with some bird, living it up. That was Paddy, they said. Always playing the game. But which game? Why hadn't Alice cracked him yet? Was it because of Dolores?

None of his pals were giving anything away, that was for sure, but Alice kept smiling, pretending it was all harmless craic. Inside, her patience was wearing thin. Each day without a solid lead made her itch. Her frustration was constant now and getting right under her skin. Lucky for her, though, she'd become an expert at hiding it.

Dolores Gillispie, on the other hand, was keeping a very close eye on Brona Doyle. She'd found out where Paddy was, but every instinct warned her from trusting this one, this stranger who'd turned up out of nowhere. She'd voiced her concerns to Paddy, only to have him brush her aside, dismissing her suspicions as paranoia. *Again.* He'd tried to placate her, patiently running through Alice Doyle's background one more time, checking every tedious detail for a second time. But the results came back exactly as before. Clean as a whistle. Not even a bloody speeding ticket to her name.

Still, a clean record didn't count. Not to Dolores. Brona Doyle wasn't kosher and Dolores knew it. She couldn't put her finger on it exactly, but it bothered the shite out of her. Could be intuition, or was it because the bitch was English. Dolores hated the English. Always had, always would.

The Englishwoman's smiles weren't enough to overcome centuries of bad blood. That near-posh accent, the short skirts, the daft haircut, spinning her clever little phrases like she thought she was doing them all a favour. She'd soon learn how wrong she was. There wasn't a hope in hell she'd worm her way into their circle, no matter how hard she pushed. Paddy could vouch for her till he was blue in the face, it wouldn't change a thing. Dolores didn't trust her, never would, and there was a stink of her she couldn't quite name, but it was there all the same. Just who was this Brona Doyle, then? Dolores wondered, as she watched her, quiet and calculating, convinced that sooner or later, she'd fuck up.

One day, knowing Doyle was away, Dolores seized her chance and walked into the offy under the pretext of asking for her. The bespectacled owner told her Brona was on holiday and asked if he could help. Spinning a blatant lie, Dolores said she'd lent Brona a book that she needed back, and if she could pop up the stairs to grab it. 'Won't take me a minute,' she said, flashing him a cheesy smile. He nodded and told her it wasn't a bother, well aware of who Dolores Gillispie was and that she wasn't there to collect a book. He was wise enough to know what might follow if he said no, so he handed over the flat keys without question.

Once inside Alice's flat, Dolores drew a steady breath and set about having a good old nosey. The first thing that struck her was that the place was immaculate. Books were everywhere, resting in neat stacks – Dickens, Austen, Orwell and countless others – not one out of place and doubtless in alphabetical order. She moved slowly through cupboards, drawers, shelves, even the bathroom cabinet, yet found no bills, no letters, no family photographs and not a single clue to a life lived now or before. The absence of anything personal unsettled her. This wasn't natural and far from normal. Dolores was right; the woman had a secret.

Empty-handed, she went back downstairs and handed the key back to the owner, who let it fall into the till as casually as spare change without saying a word.

'When will she be back?' Dolores asked, her tone polite but firm.

'Monday,' the owner said, squirming as if arranging a beer can display. Dolores held her gaze on him just long enough to deepen his fear, then gave a slow smile. 'Right then. Thanks.' She turned and walked out.

Paddy Gillispie wondered how Brona Doyle was doing. Most likely, he'd burned his bridges there, he thought, with a twinge of regret. He quite liked her, but had no choice when ordered to go deep into the republic. His absence had been taken up with planning several ops so secret that he couldn't even tell his twin. Dolores would be livid that she hadn't been involved, especially after leading that memorable attack on the Orange Hall in Newtownhamilton.

Tonight, he sat by a blazing peat fire in a small, quiet pub in Clonakilty, miles from Belfast. With a heavy poker in hand, he stirred the flames, sending sparks spiralling upwards like tiny red stars swept up in a whirlwind. His thoughts were cut short when his trusted comrade, Brian Monaghan, walked in carrying two pints of Guinness and two packs of Tayto crisps clamped between his teeth. He handed Paddy his pint, let the crisps drop onto the table, then took a long pull from his own pint before sitting down.

Paddy looked at him with a small smile and pointed at Monaghan's upper lip, now crowned with the cream of the Guinness. Wiping it off, his eyes twinkled as he ran the back of his Aran sleeve across his mouth.

'That's some night out there,' he said, looking out a window made up of six tiny squares of glass set in the bar's thick, whitewashed wall. The rain was hitting it so hard it seemed bent on battling inside to soak them.

'It is that. Glad we're in here,' Paddy replied, taking a gulp of his Guinness. *Nectar*.

It'd been a tough day training on Dunmore Beach with the biting wind and dunes. By the time the sun dipped, Paddy was sure he couldn't feel his hands or feet, convinced his body heat had left him for good. To make matters worse, they were starving and when they arrived; they ordered and devoured two enormous bowls of chowder.

They sat in the dimming evening, utterly shattered, knowing the next operation was up to them. The rest of the volunteers had cleared off days ago, and with only Paddy and Monaghan left, they'd grown closer, drawn together by the enormity of what was ahead. Now that the final details had been ironed out, they sat in comfortable silence as the fire crackled softly in front of them, its flames dancing in the hearth, casting long shadows across the quiet bar. Like a tonic, the timeless smell of turf hung in the air, comforting and familiar.

Following the failed SAS mission in the Republic, Alice didn't go anywhere near England. Instead, she contacted Ian Dillon. He'd invited her to Bangor, and she didn't need much convincing. Bangor might as well have been on the moon, it felt so far removed from the Falls Road. Quiet, clean, and safe. No one knew her there, and there wasn't a chance in hell she'd be recognised. Fuck it, she'd earned a break. A breather from all the lies and shadows of West Belfast. She needed to be herself again, even if for a few nights - Alice Wallace, not Brona Doyle or Iowa. Besides, she liked Ian. Unlike most men, he was dependable, did exactly what was asked, no questions, no complaints.

Once more, they found themselves in the same bar by the water's edge, sitting at the same table, drinking the same drinks and catching up.

Ian was jittery after the mission, hoping Alice had a new strategy. Something fresh he could get sink his teeth into. He wondered what she had up her sleeve next.

'Well. How've you been?' he asked.

'Jesus, Ian, I'm beat. Being Brona Doyle is killing me. Now it's as quiet as a morgue. That guy Gillispie I told you about? He's only gone and done a runner, and no one's telling me a thing. There's me, tearing round half of West Belfast, collecting money for the Republican prisoners' defence fund!'

Ian nodded, grimacing at the irony of it all. She was more than capable of handling herself; she needed to hang in there, he said, and he admired her for it. He couldn't do what she did. Covert? No chance! As for collecting for the Republican prisoners, his father would turn in his grave if Ian were to collect a penny for them!

Alice huddled across the table, her voice low. 'Listen, I've been thinking. Why don't we hit The Shamrock next? I'm near certain that back room of theirs is a Provo HQ. Every time I've tried to get near it, there's some eejit glued to the door like it's 10 Downing Street. Think about it, the place is sealed tighter than a duck's arse. Outer and inner doors, made of reinforced steel.'

Ian slapped his hand on the table in delight. 'Nice one, Alice! What are we talkin', bullets or a motherfucker of a blast?'

The idea occurred to her during her trip to Bangor. A total wipeout. She'd wipe out Dolores. Blow her and the other Provos to smithereens. It was certainly one way to drag Paddy Gillispie back from whatever dark little hole he was hiding in.

'When? How?' Ian said, nudging his pint aside. He sat back, scratching his chin. 'We can't go in all guns blazin', can we? They'll have some bastards carryin' and mindin' the front and rear doors. We'd no sooner get outta the cars than we'd be on our arses.' Counting off the possible scenarios on his fingers, he piped, 'I'll help make it, you plant it. Explosives. That lot would spot me a mile off. A blow-in like me, walking in there on me own? Might as well wear a sign around my neck. Sorry. This one's on you.'

Alice knew he was right. It'd have to be her. Alone. The thought of where to plant the device whirled through her mind. The Ladies? Too tiny. The storeroom, maybe? Didn't feel right. Too far back. No, it had to be close enough to guarantee the kill.

'Can you get me the right gear?' she asked, 'any contacts?'

Without thinking - and regretting it within seconds - he nodded. 'Aye, I know a fella in Belfast. *Lemon*. I'll see if he can sort us out.'

'Good. Let's do it. Soon as.'

The weight of it hit Ian then. If she was caught, it wouldn't just be her. She'd poured everything into planning that last op these past months; to stop now would destroy her. Revenge for Graham was only part of it. Still, if they did do it and she got caught, she wouldn't be the only one facing ruin. He and his pals could be traced for the other ops, swept up, locked away for good. If she did get caught - would she talk, say his name? *Christ*.

He offered to get another round, more for breathing space than thirst. When he came back with the drinks, it was as if she'd read his mind.

'I know you're scared I'll get caught,' Alice said flatly. 'Don't be. If I do, I'll never mention your name. I'll say nothing. But I'm not backing out, Ian. I'm going to level The Shamrock. Blow it to Mars. After this, we're done. It'll be the last op, I promise, then I'm gone. You're a quartermaster, so I'll take you up on that offer to call whatever his name in Belfast. Help me with the gear. After that, for your sake and mine, we don't talk again. We don't see each other. End off.'

Chapter Fifty-Three

The Yanks Have Landed!

Father Connolly had just performed a baptism. His conscience had been screaming all weekend after that meeting with Martin McLaughlin. The young woman, Anne Ballantyne, had trusted him when she had come looking for advice in his church all those weeks ago.

He was caught between his priestly obligations and loyalty to the Cause. In the end, he'd made his choice. The men he'd quietly pointed towards were living on borrowed time. Their blood, when it came, would be on his hands. Sooner or later, he'd have to live with that.

Today, the New York police officers were due to arrive for their two-week stint. A lot of effort had gone into planning and re-planning the visit. At first, Cathal thought they were bluffing, not really serious about their commitment to travelling over. But not long after he got back from America, the phone rang. They wanted to set a date, draft an itinerary, map out a work schedule. Fifteen of them were expected that afternoon, likely jet-lagged, so he'd arranged an early dinner and a good night's rest to start them off. He looked forward to it, the distraction would do him good. So far, he'd raised over £50,000 from his visits and speeches in the US, which delighted him. The Yankee cops had chipped in too, raising a solid sum for timber, paint and decorating supplies for the houses they planned to fix up. To keep things fair, anyone wanting work done had to buy a fifty-pence raffle ticket. Twenty winners would get the renovations. Unfortunately, the homes most in need hadn't made the list. Luck of the draw.

Meanwhile, Cathal drank lukewarm tea with John Deeney, a 75-year-old man who'd been diagnosed with prostate cancer. He'd ignored the signs for ages, too embarrassed to visit the doctor. It was too late now and time was running short. Cathal was fond of the old fella. A WW2 veteran who'd served in the British Army and who'd been captured early on. John always told the same story about being the one and only POW to gain weight in captivity. His mother had been Italian-American, his father, Irish. His wife and baby had died in childbirth years ago, and he'd never remarried.

Everyone liked Deeney. Alongside Tommy O'Reilly, he'd fought hard to make sure Catholics got the support they deserved, especially when it came to housing. Up to then, most new tenants were single, Protestant and hand-picked, primarily to vote for the Unionist council. Gerrymandering had to stop, and John had made sure everyone knew it.

The priest would be sad without him. John's humour, his challenging conversation. They'd hit it off straight away, unlike Father McGuire, who had no time for the man and vice versa. Years ago, something unpleasant happened between the priest and the parishioner after John's wife died. Cathal had never found out what. Thinking of Father McGuire, the old fella seemed to wake up grumpier and grumpier these days.

He leaned forward and asked gently if there was anything John needed.

'You could have a word with that fella up above,' John replied, his eyes lifting towards the ceiling. 'See if he can rush me through those pearly gates. To Olive, the wife.'

Cathal smiled. 'I'll see what I can do. Seriously though, you wanna talk about the inevitable?'

John closed his eyes, sighed and shook his head. 'Father, we both know there's nothing to be said or done. I feel so sad. All those years wasted in that bloody camp, and then losing my Olive and the babe. I can't help thinking I should've done more with me life.'

Cathal waved a hand dismissively. 'Don't you dare say that, John. What happened in wartime wasn't your fault. Olive dying, well, that was cruel, but not down to you either. For all the work you and Tommy have done for Derry over the years, you should be getting the Nobel Peace Prize!'

That made John laugh. 'I'm not sure about the Nobel Peace Prize,' he said, grinning, 'but I'll admit I've enjoyed working with big Tommy. He's a good man.'

Cathal nodded in agreement and asked. 'How's Mrs Kennedy next door? Any news?'

It was John's neighbour's youngest son, Paul, who'd been run down by the British Saracen and was still in a critical state.

John shook his head. 'Haven't seen her, Father. Not these last few days. I think she's at the hospital full-time, sitting by the lad's bedside. Awful. It'd break your heart, wouldn't it?'

They both knew it'd be a cruel and sad way for any young man to leave this world.

That evening, waiting under the dry porch of the City Hotel and watching his American guests climbing down from their mini-bus, Cathal couldn't help but laugh at their obvious enthusiasm. They were waving and calling out his name the moment they spotted him, like a load of kids returning from a school trip.

Next to him was an American journalist who had moved to Derry and loved it. Bill Barter had become a bit of a local celebrity after winning several prestigious awards for his honest, balanced reporting on the Troubles. Both sides respected him – a rare thing these days.

When he'd heard about the revamp project and the arrival of his fellow countrymen, he'd offered to cover it himself. Said it'd be nice to report news that didn't involve funerals, bombs, or yet another grieving family.

Now, watching the motley crew tumble off the van like oversized youths, all elbows and excitement, the journalist bit back a grin. He leaned in slightly to Cathal, muttering in his slow Midwestern drawl, 'Jeez, Father... would you get a load of that? You sure this was a good idea?'

Cathal was having second thoughts. The off-duty cops looked like they'd arrived in Butlin's. Most of them were wearing loud plaid shirts tucked into three-quarter-length shorts, with socks up to their calves and sandals. Meanwhile, Derry had been lashed by rain since lunchtime, and the car park looked more like Lough Neagh than a welcome party.

Still, the weather didn't seem to bother them. Spirits high, they laughed and slapped each other's backs, pointing out their soggy feet like it was all part of the adventure. The poor minibus driver, who'd likely spent the entire journey enduring their booming talking and endless banter, couldn't get shot of them fast enough. He yanked open the side hatch and started unloading suitcases like he was lobbing sandbags during a flood warning.

One of the Yanks broke away from the rest and marched straight over to Cathal and Barter, hand outstretched, wearing the kind of grin that could sell second-hand cars.

'Father! Good to see you again!' he boomed, before turning to the reporter.

'Officer James Halloran, New York Police Department. At your service.'

'William Barter, Boston Globe. Likewise.' Barter laughed.

Halloran whooped and spun back around to face his companions. 'Hey fellas! We got ourselves a real-life journo from the Boston Globe!'

The party whistled and catcalled, hauling their luggage as they went into the hotel. One of them stopped to tip an imaginary cap at the receptionist, who looked like she'd seen it all before and wasn't the least bit impressed. Another tried to flirt, elbow-deep in a soggy holdall, shouting something about needing a room with a view and a bit of company to go with it. Cathal trailed behind them, shaking his head. *Mother of God.* They were here to help, not on a stag night. At this rate, he'd be lucky if the hotel still had windows by the end of the week.

When everyone was finally checked in and away getting changed for dinner, Cathal, Barter and Officer Halloran sat in three tired-looking armchairs in the reception area holding a few beers. Barter had warmed to Halloran straight away. There was no front with the man, no big talk. A quiet curiosity and a decent way about him. He asked questions, legitimate ones, about the Troubles, its history, the people. Said his grandfather had sailed from Derry Quay with his new bride many moons ago, chasing the American dream. After a bit of digging through family records, he'd found a handful of distant cousins likely living nearby. He'd even arranged for his wife to come join him after the work wrapped up.

'I'm due to retire soon, guys, and I thought, why not?' Halloran said, lifting his bottle. 'Why not bring Colette over and make a proper holiday of it? She's a bit nervous, mind, with the Troubles an' all, but what the heck. Life's for livin', ain't it?

Cathal nodded slowly, the kind of nod to reassure. Halloran might have been one of the smaller men in the group, but he was solid through and through. His brown eyes glistened when he spoke, full of hope and talk of the work ahead.

'Halloran, stop worrying. I've had a word with the Boys. You and Colette'll be grand, we'll look after you,' Cathal said, tossing the burly officer an exaggerated wink. Halloran burst out laughing, and Barter joined in, though the sound stuck in his throat. Doubt was creeping in again. It wouldn't have surprised him in the least if the priest had whispered something to the Provos about the Yanks being here, asked them to keep an eye out. Connolly was tied up with NORAID, for sure. Problem was Barter hadn't pinned down the proof. Yet.

Chapter Fifty-Four

Screwed Up Bad

'Wow, Anne, what a handsome boy! You'd never think Porkie had it in him to create something so perfect. It's a miracle!' Caitlin grinned as she leaned in for a better look at the baby Sean.

Anne couldn't argue. Caitlin was right. Sean was perfect. Her freshly hatched, perfect wee boy. Not a blemish on him. Just velvet-soft skin, a button nose, and eyes that were already wide and knowing, like he'd been here before. She was overcome with emotion as she saw him wiggle in his blanket. Not panic, not fear, but a soft, loving feeling she didn't quite have a name for yet. He was hers. Actually hers. Though the world outside the hospital ward was a disaster, none of it mattered anymore. Not with Sean sleeping in her arms, and her heart beating in time with his.

The moment she first held him, gazing into his eyes, it was like he was saying, 'Don't worry, I'm here now, Mammy. I'll look after ye.' A much-needed miracle.

One grey, rain-slicked April afternoon, the two girls sat in Anne's kitchen. Porkie had barely looked at Caitlin when she arrived with a few bits and pieces for the baby. He'd grunted, opened the door, and walked off down the hallway, leaving it swinging behind him. The man was a shadow of who he'd been. He'd dropped a load of weight, and the skin on his jowls now hung loose, giving him the look of someone twice his age. Even his voice had gone thin. When he'd turned to mutter that Anne was in the kitchen, it sounded hollow, drained of anything genuine. The look of someone who'd thrown in the towel. Caitlin had watched him shuffle away and couldn't help but wonder what was going on behind those lost eyes. It was plain as day. The man was ill.

She'd been there when Anne gave birth, right at her side from start to finish. Porkie hadn't bothered his arse. He'd done a disappearing act and hadn't shown his face until the following afternoon, reeking of stale fags, drink and a black mood. Anne had asked where he'd been, her voice surprisingly calm, almost like she already knew the answer.

When he hadn't replied, Caitlin noticed, with some surprise, that Anne didn't push him. Normally she'd go ballistic.

'He is gorgeous, isn't he?' Caitlin said.

Anne smiled warmly, her eyes soft as she looked down at her son. 'I want you to be godmother, Caitlin. You and Seamus. Godmother and godfather.'

Caitlin lit up, thrilled and touched in equal measure. She pulled her friend into a hug, holding on really tight for a moment. Then, of course, she went scarlet to the roots, the memory of her last seeing Seamus flashing through her mind. Anne picked up on it straight away. Always did.

'What's goin' on? What was that redner for?' she asked, grinning.

'Nothing,' Caitlin said, trying and failing to sound innocent.

Anne's jaw dropped. 'You haven't, have ye? You and Seamus – you've only gone and done *it*, haven't ye?!'

One look at Caitlin's face told her everything. Anne clapped her hands like a child at the fair.

'Oh my God, thank Christ! It's about bloody time too! Sure, I thought you'd never get over that Adonis wanker.' She paused, then made the sign of the cross in thanks.

It hurt hearing James talked about like that, but Caitlin knew Anne didn't mean any harm. Not really. She was just being her protective self.

Seamus had made the first move the night Sean was born, when everyone had raised a glass to welcome the new arrival. Later, back at Blamfield Street, the two of them curled up together on the sofa, the glow of the television washing over them as they watched his favourite sitcom, *Porridge*. Somewhere between the laughter and the quiet, he began to trace slow circles along the inside of her palm with his finger. The touch tickled, and she looked over at him, giggling, caught between embarrassment and curiosity. Instead of pulling away, she stayed close, and that was all the encouragement he needed to lean in and kiss her.

It had started slow, almost unsure, but deepened pretty quickly. Their tongues tangled in a way that felt less like a first kiss and more like something long overdue. He pulled away, breathless, and confessed, 'Jesus, Caitlin, I've wanted to do that for so long. You've no idea.'

She hadn't expected her own response to be so eager. Standing up, she crossed the room to draw the curtains, shutting out the rest of the world. When she turned back, he was still watching her.

'Wanna do it again?' she asked, half-laughing. He grinned, he didn't need asking twice, and switched off the TV. The room fell quiet. Moving closer, he spoke in a low voice. 'Are ye sure? I don't want to mess things up.'

'I'm sure,' she said, almost whispering.

They were both lonely, and the moment had taken on a life of its own. Their kisses turned urgent, and they fumbled at buttons and belts, catching their breath, their hands clumsy. She tugged at Seamus's waistband, but the belt got stuck, and he had to undo it himself. Caitlin placed her hand on the front of his trousers. No need to ask. The man was more than ready. They stood face to face, tugging off the last of their clothes, until there was nothing between them at all.

She was everything he'd hoped for. More, even. Her small breasts were perfect, her dark brown nipples proud against her pale skin. Her waist was neat, her belly soft, and a fine line of conker coloured hair trailed down between her legs. He smiled when he saw the birthmark on her hip, a smudge, almost like a thumbprint. She'd never mentioned it before. He couldn't believe it. Couldn't believe she was here, like this, with him. Still, he hesitated. Christ, but she'd said yes, hadn't she? She wanted him, he could see it, feel it, but despite all that, the memory of her turning him down before shot through his mind. He didn't want to mess this or her up. Didn't want to rush or ruin what had started again. This wasn't about sex. He cared about Caitlin, really cared. Loved her, and if he tried to go too far too soon, well... He swallowed and bit the inside of his lip to steady himself. She was right there. Naked, beautiful, open. His heart thudded. He wanted her more than anything, but not at the cost of losing her.

Caitlin caught the doubt in his eyes and touched his face gently, trying to reassure him. She reached for him, stroked him lightly, and pressed herself close, letting him know it was okay. He seemed to get the message as his mouth met hers again, deeper this time, full of need, and he eased her down onto the sofa. His hands moved slowly, exploring her breasts, her belly, until they found the warmth between her legs. She gasped.

He knew exactly what he was doing. As his fingers moved over her, she lost all sense of the room around them. Every part of her focused on that rising feeling, the one that pushed all the heartache to the ends of her mind. Her breath caught in her throat, faster now, her body shaking with pleasure. She didn't want it to end, not yet, but it surged through her like a wave she couldn't stop. Then it happened. Quick and fierce, shooting through her, and with it the name that burst from her lips before she could hold it back.

'Ah, *James*!' Seamus sprang off her like he'd been electrocuted. Caitlin, naked and suddenly more exposed than she'd ever felt, gasped and reached for his hand. But like James Henderson before him, he yanked away, his face tense with fury.

'Bloody hell, Caitlin. I don't fuckin' believe this. Who the fuck is *James* when he's at home?!'

She opened her mouth to speak, but nothing came. Seamus was already grabbing his clothes, stumbling into the hallway. Even his bare feet were loud on the tiled floor. She heard the zip of his trousers and the rustle of fabric as he dressed in silence.

Caitlin scrambled to find her clothes in the half-dark. She called after him, but the front door slammed shut so hard it rattled the frame. She sank onto the sofa with a groan. Christ Almighty, what had she done? Would she ever be free of James bloody Henderson? After that, Seamus had cut her off. She hadn't seen or heard from him since and missed him desperately.

Still smiling and joshing in the kitchen, Caitlin answered Anne, 'We didn't go the full way. Not exactly.' Rolling her eyes to the ceiling, she sighed, 'Fuck it, Anne, I've screwed up. Bad.'

Anne's expression turned serious. 'Why? What happened?'

Caitlin spelt it out. With a puff of her cheeks and a weary headshake, she said, 'You're not going to believe this one... I called him James.'

'Ah, Jesus, Caitlin. Not in the middle of *it*?'

Caitlin nodded.

'Poor bastard. That's bad. That's *really* bad,' Anne murmured. *Definitely a sore one.*

'I know, Anne. I know. I don't think he'll ever forgive me,' Caitlin sighed.

Anne didn't reply. She didn't know what to say. Only she couldn't imagine Seamus letting that one go, not after Caitlin hurting him before. The guy was crazy about her, but he was a proud fella, too and that sort of slip-up would've killed him. Knowing him, he probably thought Caitlin was pure as snow while was away, oblivious to the Adonis. Bugger it, but when Caitlin McLaughlin lands herself in bother, she doesn't do it by halves! Thank Christ for Porkie, who wandered into the kitchen right on cue, for once.

Anne was quietly relieved. It didn't happen often, but she hadn't a clue what advice to give Caitlin. Sometimes it was better to say nothing.

Sensing the awkward atmosphere, Porkie's eyes moved between the two women. 'What's up?' Without waiting for an answer, he crossed the floor and gently lifted Sean, hoisting the baby onto his shoulder like he'd been doing it for years. One hand rubbed the infant's back in steady, practised circles.

Anne and Caitlin exchanged a look, he made it look so natural.

'Not telling me, then?' he asked, glancing over his shoulder.

Anne stepped in, her tone light. 'Girlie stuff, love. Ye don't wanna know. Fancy a cuppa tea?'

Porkie didn't look convinced, but gave a small nod. 'Aye, I'll take a cup.'

Caitlin watched him for a moment, her smile fading slightly. He was much thinner than he'd been last time she saw him. The weight was falling off him, and not in a good way.

'You keeping good, Porkie? You've lost a ton of weight. Hardly recognise you.'

But Porkie wasn't keeping good. Not even close. Porkie was shitting his pants. Every time someone came to the front door, his guts twisted and bile burned in his throat. Was this it? Had they come for him? He knew they would. Sooner or later. He'd tried pulling back from Dickie, made excuses, ducked out of meeting him, but the bastard was like a bloodhound. Always knocking the front door. Always there.

Porkie had overheard a few bits and pieces down his local. Nothing big. Only bitty scraps of intel, but enough to pass on. He hadn't meant to make a habit of it. It just... happened. A nod here, a whisper there. Nothing that would change the course of history, he told himself. Dickie had paid well, and now with the baby, it helped keep them afloat. All the same, deep down, he knew. Sooner or later, they'd find out and land on the doorstep.

Anne had asked where the money came from. He'd told her he'd had a streak of luck on the dogs, he'd backed three winners. She hadn't gone on about it but he was sure she hadn't bought it either. Still, the nappies, the milk, the baby food got paid for.

'I'm all right, Caitlin. Few things on my mind, that's all,' he said, avoiding her eyes. Holding the baby close, he left the kitchen before she could ask him anything more.

One look at Sean's face the day he was born, and Porkie knew he couldn't keep doing it. Dickie had kept him away that day, dragged him out drinking in Mailey's and poured the pints down him until the day and night disappeared. But seeing that tiny face the next morning, seeing himself in it, he changed. Everything changed. He loved the wee critter more than life itself. Anne, too, though God knows she'd every right to hate him. He'd done nothing but let her down from the start. Here he was. Skinnier, twitchier, can't-sleep kind of scared, all because of a few sly bits of intel and a fistful of dirty cash. Enough to keep the lights on, aye, but at what cost?

He held Sean tighter and kissed the top of his head, still carrying that smell of talc and warm milk. Pure. Untouched. Like the world hadn't ruined him yet. Jesus, but what the hell was he doing? Porkie thought. Such a mistake getting involved with Dickie, but he'd gone too far already.

The women watched him leave. Caitlin turned to Anne and questioned, 'Is he really okay? Looks like shit. What's up?'

'I can't tell ye, Caitlin, I can't,' Anne answered with a sigh and a shake of the head.

But Caitlin wasn't taking it and gave it another go. 'You've got to tell me. It's gotta be bad if you're not saying. Come on, Anne, we tell each other everything, don't we?'

Anne looked at her friend for a few seconds, then stood to put the kettle on. Nothing to be said. At least not yet.

In their quiet living room, Porkie cooed at his son and wondered if he'd even be around to see him grow up. He'd warned Dickie more than once. People were asking questions. The new car, the flashy clothes, the rolls of notes in the Stardust. It was only a matter of time before someone put two and two together. If Dickie got found out, it wouldn't take long for him to start finger-pointing.

'Jesus Christ, what have I got myself into, son?' he muttered, eyes fixed on the baby's face, as if searching for an answer. Anne brought him in a cup of tea and caught the tail end of him talking to the baby. She knew rightly what he was at. Talking to wee Sean like that, trying to talk sense into himself. Wasn't going to fix anything now, though, was it? Too late for all that. Still, God love him, he'd turned out to be a brilliant daddy.

These days, he was soft as butter with the wee one, and kind to Anne too, like he was trying to patch over the past with nice words and nappy changes. And the money? Jesus, what was she supposed to do, hand it back? They were skint. Could barely keep the lights on. They needed a pram, nappies, milk. It didn't grow on trees, did it?

She hated what he was into. Hated herself for needing it, but what choice did she have? Since the baby's birth, she'd started seeing Porkie differently. He wasn't bad to the bone, not deep down, only thick and easily led. Like always, especially around that creepy fuck, Dickie. Father Connolly had listened when she told him what she'd overheard in the kitchen. He didn't judge, but gave her that calm look of his on top of a warning.

'You breathe a word of this and those two are dead men walking.'

She believed him. He couldn't say to anyone, not even if he wanted to. *Could he? Would he?* Some said he was a bit of a rebel, even a Provo! All the same, she couldn't forget what Porkie used to be like. The way he'd spoken to her, treated her. He'd been a shit, no doubt about it. Knowing her luck, he'd swing right back to it the minute she let her guard down. If he thought they'd be shagging again anytime soon, he'd be waiting a hell of a long time. In the cold light of day, part of her hoped the priest would inform on the pair of them. Let be done with it. For now, though, she figured she'd leave it to fate. Let the man upstairs decide.

Chapter Fifty-Five

Going Home

'You're outta here this morning.' PO Quirk smiled as she delivered the news to Bridget Barry, who lay tucked tight under her brown blanket in her cell bed. The weary woman didn't react at first, but blinked up at the ceiling, eyes flat and unfocused, like she hadn't quite understood.

After overhearing the exchange between young Tina and the OC, Maureen Molony, Prison Officer Quirk, knew she had to step in. It wasn't often she saw Molony shaken. The woman was usually solid as a rock. Quirk would never say it out loud, and certainly not in this place, but she had a quiet respect for the way the OC handled the Republican women. She gave them structure, kept them occupied. There was always a rota, always a job to be done, always a class of some sort on the go. She pushed education, preached discipline, and somehow managed to keep the worst of them in check. Because if the women were left with nothing but time to think, Quirk knew, same as Molony, that the whole place would suffer for it.

The OC and her Republican comrades still held political prisoner status, which meant free association and access to classes in history, languages and literature. But that morning, Quirk and the rest of the POs at Armagh had received a typed notice. Straight from the top. From now on, special-category privileges would be withdrawn for all new internees. Repercussions were expected. No one said it aloud, but everyone knew what it meant. Political status was on borrowed time, and once it was gone, trouble wouldn't be far behind.

She was quietly relieved she'd only a month left in the job. Then she was done. Out the door and away from it all. She couldn't take much more: the strip searches, the petty abuse, the endless punishments and point-scoring. The place was teetering on a cliff edge, and she knew, as soon as it went over, it would go fast. She didn't want to be anywhere near it when it did.

'What do ye mean, I'm outta here?' Bridget asked, not believing a word.

'I'm saying you're going home. Today. Get your things together,' Quirk answered, still smiling.

'Heard that before, Quirk. I'm not going anywhere. They're trying to get me fuckin' hopes up again.' Bridget tightened the thin blanket around her, pulling it over her head, and muttering she didn't need to hear any more of this shite.

Quirk shook the inmate's shoulder and whispered, 'For Jesus' sake, woman, I'm tellin' ye the truth. Now get up before they *do* change their minds!'

Bridget pulled the blanket half down, reminding Quirk of a child, 'You mean it, don't ye? You're serious?'

Quirk nodded and watched the woman's tired eyes fill up. 'Dead serious, Bridget. Now go on, please. Sort yourself out.'

The PO looked at Bridget's cellmate and asked her to give a hand. She hadn't felt that good in years. Let them get on with it, she thought, as she stepped out of the small cell and made her way along the gangway. She stopped and looked over the iron rail, thinking back to the risks she'd taken. Yet, it started with a simple stroke of luck.

Minding her own business, Quirk was walking past the half-open door of the medical room when she heard PO Smyth and Dr Harris inside, voices raised.

'I can't give you Barry's notes, Smyth. I don't have them!' Harris hissed.

Smyth froze. Her heart started hammering. Fuck, but they were up shit creek now without a paddle. Her, the doctor, Gladys, the lotta them. If Bridget Barry's records got into the hands of Mr Yeaman, their new stand-in governor, they were screwed. Well and truly screwed.

Governor Johnston had thrown in the towel and signed himself off sick for who knows how long. No sign of him coming back anytime soon. Quirk reckoned he couldn't face the riot brewing once word got out they were scrapping the women's political status. It was understandable. Like Johnston, Quirk was getting out for the same reason, before the roof caved in. But for now, she stepped quietly back against the wall and listened hard.

To PO Smyth, the whole squabble with Bridget was already well buried. Swept neatly under the carpet. But PO Quirk had heard whispers. Governor Yeaman had asked for Barry's records within days of arriving. Someone had got to him. Maureen Molony, perhaps or that prick, the Catholic troublemaker, Father McGuire. If they had, she could see Yeaman pushing for an inquiry or would he?

'Where's the notes now, ye fuckin' eejit? What've you done with them?' Smyth barked.

'I don't know. Johnston had them last!' the doctor snapped, his voice growing whiny and edging toward panic. He raised his arms in protest. *How dare she speak to him like that!*

'Shit!' Smyth hissed, pacing around the medical room.

'I... I panicked. I went into his office to change them,' Harris stammered.

'Why? Why on God's earth would you change them?' Smyth asked. She looked at him as if he were a daft pup and shook her head.

When he sat down and re-read Bridget Barry's notes, Harris cringed. What he'd written left no room for doubt – he'd failed to behave professionally during her examination. Worse still, he'd all but implied her injuries were self-inflicted. Christ, what a heel he was. A man in his position should've known better, should've handled it with care, not scribbled words that made him look like a callous bastard. As if anyone with half a brain would believe that the woman could have done that kind of damage to herself. It was beyond ridiculous, and that he'd put it down in black and white only proved how bloody useless he was.

He needed this job. Badly. He couldn't afford to lose it. So when the old governor threw a sickie, he saw an opportunity. Found the file soon enough before the new governor landed. The problem was, Harris had been stotious at the time, and it showed. The handwritten changes he made were a mess. Rushed, careless, full of crossings-out and clumsy attempts at rewording. His tampering was so bloody obvious you'd have to be a thicko not to spot it.

Now he stood facing Prison Officer Smyth, a woman who terrified him more than most men.

'I–I–it's okay, though,' he stammered. 'I p–pushed the file inside another. They won't find it in a hurry.'

'So long as you remember which one,' Smyth said, stepping towards him, her finger pointing right at him.

PO Smyth had to get into that office and find the bloody file. Fast. She didn't know the new governor, Yeaman. Hadn't met the man yet, but for all she knew, he could be one of those do-gooder bastards. The whistle-blowing type, and if he got his hands on that file, it wouldn't only open a can of worms, it'd blow the lid clean off.

'I'm going to get that file, doc,' she growled, narrowing her eyes at him. 'So help me, God. You? You can get off your arse and come with me. We're going to make that fuckin' thing disappear. This time for good.' After hearing all that, PO Quirk knew then she had to speak up and prayed the new governor was a 'do-gooder bastard.'

Back in her cell, Bridget carried on quietly, getting her bits and pieces together. Her heart was thumping as she hugged her comrade and OC tight, burying her face against Maureen's shoulder. She whispered, 'I'll never forget your kindness. You're a credit to A-Company and to every woman in this hole. Mind yourself, and look after them. We'll see each other again. Promise.'

Maureen squeezed her hard. 'I'll miss you. I'm glad you're getting outta here.'

Bridget handed over a few things she wouldn't be needing, the homemade radio, a couple of books, then took one last glance around the cell that had been her home for so long. It was hard to think of leaving. The women in here weren't comrades. They were her sisters. They'd fought together, cried together, and loved each other like family. Ties like that didn't come easy, and they don't fade quickly either. But she'd done her bit. Under the circumstances, she'd given them everything she could. This was her time now. Time to be a mother again. A granny. Time to figure out who she was outside these walls. Time, for once, to put herself first. To make it up to her family. To claw back some of what had been wasted. The funerals, engagements, weddings, birthdays, you name it. All those lost days, weeks and years.

PO Quirk stepped into the cell. Bridget was ready, bags packed, coat on, nerves obvious but keeping herself together. She gave a slight nod. Words weren't needed.

Outside on the landing, the Armagh women had heard the good news and stood shoulder to shoulder, lining the walls along the gangway. Silent and waiting.

For years, Quirk had walked this landing in uniform, keys jangling, her shoulders squared and determined. A professional, but this past while, she'd seen women dragged off in cuffs, seen blood on the floor, bruises on faces, hers included. She'd trained herself not to let it in. Not really. But today, something shifted.

The OC was the first to clap. One slow beat at a time. Steady. Like a heartbeat. Then another woman joined in. Then another. Soon, the sound and vibration filled the landing. Applause thudded off the damp stone walls, rising high into the rafters. This old Victorian gaol wasn't built for joy. It didn't know what to do with it.

The officer stood still, her back straight, but her throat tightened. These women were inmates. Republicans. Some of them dangerous. All of them stubborn. But today, in that moment, they weren't prisoners. They were women. Saying goodbye to one of their own.

Quirk, who had spent her whole career keeping the line between them and her crystal clear, felt it start to dissolve. She looked down the wing, arms stiff at her sides, and thought. Today was a good day. It was a good day when a long-termer got out. Maybe the best kind of day they ever got in a place like this.

Not too far away, Tina McLaughlin could hear clapping, and it made her happy. So she joined in, letting her mop fall with a quiet clatter as she did. She stood in the circle downstairs, outside the governor's office, where she'd been washing the floor. Up above, things were happening. Good things, she could feel it in the air. What was it? She wondered, but the feeling didn't last long. It floated away, light as dust, gone before it could stick.

She looked across the circle and saw a dark-haired woman walking towards her. Familiar, aye. Tina was sure she knew the face, but couldn't think of where from, or why her heart ached all of a sudden, or why everything suddenly felt so strange.

All the same, she smiled as the woman approached. It was the woman's eyes. Not bright exactly, but warm. Kind. They held hers as she got closer, didn't look away for a second. Then, out of nowhere, she stepped in and wrapped her arms around her, pulling her into a mega hug, squeezing her so tight, she was squeezing the air out of her.

Confused. Tina didn't move at first, but the woman smelled of a familiar lavender, soft and clean, and somehow it helped. It was calming.

'Ah, young'un, it's so lovely to see you.' Bridget said, her voice choking. The voice melted everything for Tina; she didn't know why, but she didn't want this stranger to let her go.

Bridget Barry hadn't taken in Tina's appearance at first. She'd been too caught up in the moment, too full of urgency, desperate to find her before she left. But when she stepped back and held Tina at arm's length, the shock hit her hard. Like a smack across the face. There was hardly anything left of the young girl she remembered. Her body had wasted away, now all skin and bone. Her face had caved in, grey and hollow, with wide, unfocused eyes. Her red hair had thinned even more to patchy strands, dull and broken, with whole clumps missing altogether.

Sweet Jesus, Bridget thought. Sweet Mother of Jesus, what've they done to you, wee girl? There was no bringing the girl back. She was already lost. Bridget pulled Tina close again, held her as tight as she dared, and whispered, 'I'll miss ye, pet. Never forget that.' Then she turned and walked away fast before her legs gave out. She didn't look back. If she did, she might not be able to leave at all.

Tina felt a tug in her chest as the sweet-smelling woman released her and walked away. Her voice was soft, familiar in a way Tina couldn't explain. She tried to place her, to recall a name or a memory, but it was gone before it arrived. Why had she said she loved her?

The clapping had stopped. Whatever it had been for, it was done now. Tina picked up her mop and hummed, a low, tuneless sound that comforted her more than words. The floor still wasn't done. She looked it over and realised she'd missed a bit. Letting out a grunt, she grabbed the mop and bucket again and got back to it.

Quirk watched the scene with immense sadness. She escorted Bridget Barry to the spiked security gates, where the two women shook hands before Bridget walked off towards the bus stop. Watching her go, Quirk thought back to that crucial moment days before, when, in fury, she'd knocked hard on Governor Yeaman's door.

'Come!' she'd heard him call through the thick wood. She'd only seen the man from a distance and was surprised when he turned around from searching a filing cabinet. He was young. Mid-thirties, medium height, white-faced and clean-shaven. He wore a dark blue suit, white shirt, but no tie. He looked flustered, rummaging through the drawers for a file.

'Yes. What is it?' he asked in a northern English accent, then snapped over his shoulder to the secretary outside: 'Pot of tea. Now!'

Quirk was taken aback. Not expecting an Englishman. 'Sir. My name is Prison Officer Quirk. I'd like to talk to you—'

Before she could continue, he stood up and looked her over and interrupted, 'Ah, yes. I've heard good things about you, Officer Quirk.'

'Thank you, sir,' she said, unsure what else to say, a bit thrown by his comments.

'In his absence, Governor Johnston kindly left me notes on his team. I'm sorry to see you've decided to leave us. May I ask why?'

This was her chance. At last, she'd nothing to lose. So she told him everything. The degrading strip searches, the abuse, the random cell tosses. But most importantly, she laid out Smyth and Drake's involvement in the brutal assault on Bridget Barry. She told him what she'd overheard between Doctor Harris and PO Smyth in the medical room, and how Barry's notes had been tampered with. Then Smyth's bragging in the locker room. Her sickening laughter. All of it. He listened, asking clipped, but fair, questions. Then waited as the tea arrived.

When the door shut, his tone changed as he sat down. His voice stayed neutral, but his eyes gave him away, he was far from happy.

'That's a coincidence, I've been looking for Barry's medical notes. Why not leave it with me Quirk and when I do find that blasted file, I'll recommend Mrs Barry be sent home. Given her age and how long she's been with us, it's fair to say she'll be released on medical grounds.'

Quirk could hardly believe it, completely gobsmacked.

The young governor stood and leaned over the desk, fed up to the back teeth with the state of Governor Johnston's office. It was a bloody mess. Nothing made sense, and half of what he needed wasn't even there. He looked Quirk square in the face. His voice was serious, edging on threatening, but not quite.

'Off the record, Quirk. I've got reporters crawling all over this town thanks to this criminalisation circus. The last thing I need is this incident blowing up in my face. I've no time for external agencies sniffing around, or some inquest poking into what happened to Mrs Barry. It stops here. Now. Got me?'

Quirk nodded.

He stared at the PO and decided it was the right call to release Barry. One less headache to deal with. But the McLaughlin girl, the old priest, had asked to be released, not a hope in hell. From what he saw this morning, humming to herself and scrubbing the floor like she hadn't a care in the world, she wouldn't have noticed if she was in the Europa Hotel, no matter Armagh Gaol. The girl seemed happy enough cleaning, and if she stayed where she was, it'd save a few quid on his cleaning budget. No-brainer.

'Right then,' he said, already reaching for his next file. 'Away with you, Quirk. Good luck with whatever comes next. Thank you.'

He didn't even look up as Quirk left, but took a sip of tea, spat it straight into the bin and yelled. 'Christ Almighty! Can't I get a decent brew around here?'

Good news at last. Quirk smiled with quiet satisfaction as the door clicked shut behind her, practically dancing her way back upstairs. What a result.

With a sigh, the governor leaned back and stared at the heap of files on his desk. This wasn't the tidy little posting he'd been promised. Six months, they'd said. Keep it ticking over. Instead, it was bloody chaos. Morale scraping the floor. Prisoners on the verge of mutiny and now paperwork vanishing.

He'd walked into a shitstorm.

Chapter Fifty-Six

The Secret's Out

Roger Henderson sat bolt upright in bed, every breath a struggle. The pain in his chest was sharp now, constant. He wasn't naïve. This wasn't a persistent lung infection. He was on his way out. What hurt more than this pain and illness was that he still hadn't found out who'd murdered his brother. That burden, that unfinished business, was killing him faster than any bloody virus. His bones ached, his skin felt like paper, regardless, he kept it to himself. No sense moaning about what can't be fixed. The young ones had enough to worry about.

All the same, he was glad Marleen had come back to Melrose. At least she tried, laughed, talked away, sitting herself on the edge of his bed like she belonged there. She always smelled lovely too, not perfume but more poignant, of life, of want, of excitement. Things he hadn't felt in years. The girl was a tonic. Now that she was back, Roger knew what must come next. His nephew had to marry her. Make an honest woman of her. At last. No more dithering. The clock was ticking, and Roger meant to see them settled before he breathed his last. Until James was settled, Roger wasn't going anywhere.

James had left Rocola and was making his way through the city towards Melrose. He was finally going home with some good news for his uncle, and oddly enough, he was looking forward to seeing Marleen too. Was it guilt after last night, or did he want to clear the air? Either way, he had a sense he needed to sort whatever '*it*' was. Whatever had happened.

Earlier that day, James had an unexpected visitor at the factory. Tommy O'Reilly. Apparently, he'd walked straight through the front door and up the stairs like he'd worked in the place all his life. No phone call ahead, no knock on the door. Just appeared.

Mrs Parkes's face had been a picture when she watched the big man in the donkey jacket stomping into the office and demanding to see James. She looked as if she'd been asked to serve tea to the devil. Which, in fairness, wasn't far off how she probably saw Tommy O'Reilly. It wasn't the first time Caitlin's uncle had dropped in with an update, or more often, a lack of one, on the hunt for the witness to his father's murder. Nevertheless, James liked him. Tommy didn't waste words or time. You knew where you stood.

Mrs Parkes, having been thoroughly offended by the visitor's three-sugar tea request, stormed off, muttering under her breath.

Watching her go, Tommy gave James a sly grin and said, 'Not much of a looker for a secretary, eh? Bit of a comedown after our Caitlin, I'd say.'

James rolled his eyes and muttered, 'Don't start, Tommy. Don't go there. Please.'

It was the first time either of them had openly acknowledged Caitlin by name, and for a moment, the room seemed to hold its breath.

'Fair enough, James. Just sayin', that's all,' Tommy replied, lowering his bulk into the visitor's chair. It groaned under the weight. James leaned across his desk. He could tell this visit wasn't another dead end and asked. 'So. What do we have?'

Tommy nodded slowly. 'Nothin' major, but there's somethin'.'

James said nothing. He waited.

'Now, what I'm going to say is between us, okay? I mean it. I have to stay neutral in all'a this.'

James knew that already. Rocola's shop steward, Ernie Taggart, had once said that Tommy O'Reilly had a talent for slipping between the cracks. He worked with everyone, spoke to everyone, and yet somehow belonged to no one. It was obvious the man knew a hell of a lot more about what went on in this city than he ever let on.

'I understand,' James said. 'I get it.'

Mrs Parkes reappeared with the tea tray and all but slammed it on the desk.

James gave her a look and said. 'I'll pour.' She grunted and left the room, slamming the door for good measure.

Tommy snorted. 'Christ, but she's a piece of work. What's her problem?'

James chuckled. 'She's angry at the world, Tommy. Everyone in it. Like you say, not exactly Caitlin.' Again, Caitlin's name hung in the air. James sat back, staring down at the tea tray. He didn't say it out loud, but the anger he'd felt toward Caitlin had worn thin long ago. He'd turned it over in his mind too many times. The hotel meeting, her sister's involvement, the chaos after. None of it added up. Not to the Caitlin he knew. He'd judged her too quickly and harshly, acted like a fool, and now the damage was done. When he thought of how he'd behaved, what he'd said. It killed him. He knew where she worked. The camera shop down on the Strand Road. More than once, without even realising it, he'd driven by it. Sometimes he told himself it was coincidence. Other times, he didn't even bother with excuses. He missed her.

All the same, too much time had passed. The damage was irreversible, and what they'd had, whatever it was, had been crushed. A wreck. Caitlin deserved better than him. So much better than the weak and angry man he'd been. He'd judged too quickly, yelled at her without thinking, let pride and anger steer him when he should've stopped, listened, shown trust. Instead, he'd stormed off and left her to carry it all. He'd let her down. Thinking of her with that look of pride she got when she was hurting but wouldn't show it, the shame felt bone deep. He hadn't only made a massive mistake. He'd failed her and wasn't sure if he'd ever forgive himself.

Tommy coughed. 'Well, young fella. I'm convinced we know who your witness is. Not only that, I know where she is.'

James stared at him, thrown. '*She*?' he asked.

'*She*,' Tommy replied.

Tommy had been surprised himself when he first heard their witness was a woman. It was no small thing, standing up against a murderer like Jones, knowing full well it could cost you your life. Took some nerve. Still, this one had steel in her. The girl had a way about her – quiet, focused, unyielding. He didn't pretend to understand women, never had. Not really, but saying that, more and more were bravely stepping into the heart of this conflict.

Funny, the way things turned. The old IRA used to roll their eyes at the idea of women getting involved. Claimed they were more hassle than help. Said they should be home minding the wains, making the dinner, not out there playing soldier. Times were changing, though, and changing fast.

He took a sip of tea and went on, steady and measured. 'Aye, a woman. I've spoken to her.'

James sat up. 'But how? How did you find her?'

Tommy wasn't about to hand over the details. No point. The Provos had done the legwork, and not out of charity, either. He knew for a fact they monitored Rocola. Mightn't say so, but they respected the Hendersons. Knew the Hendersons had fought to keep the Derry women (most of them family) in work during tough times and that counted. It'd earned them a sort of quiet protection. Call it a favour repaid.

'I've me ways, James,' he said, waving the question off. 'Doesn't matter now. What matters is this. The man who drove your da off the road is on Charles Jones's payroll.' He watched James closely and waited for his news to sink in.

James loathed Charles Jones with every fibre of his being. The man was a foul-mouthed, swaggering bigot, a bulldog of a brute with a face you wanted to hit and a tongue that never stopped spewing bile. No charm, no polish, pure venom. The kind of man who laughed at his own sick jokes and expected everyone else to laugh along. Of course, it was him! That rotten bastard had been behind his father's murder the whole time. Why? What was it for? A message? A warning? Or sheer bloody hatred? For Christ's sake! His father had been working for the man. *Shit.* That was why!

He sat back, staring at the wall. It made sense now, his father must've been trying to warn them. That would explain the sudden call, the urgency in his messages to the office and to Melrose, the way he'd driven all the way from Belfast that night. He never did that. Him so desperate to talk. It had to be. Importantly, whatever it was, Charles Jones hadn't wanted it getting out. He suddenly felt cold.

'So... Jones. Again.' he said, barely above a whisper.

'Ye know him, then?' Tommy asked, already halfway through drinking his tea. He grabbed a Mikado off the plate and shoved it in his mouth without blinking.

'I do, Tommy. He's... once a supposed friend of my uncle's. And my father. We haven't seen him since the City Hotel thing.'

Talk of the City Hotel event cast a pall over everything. Both men knew it wasn't about who was there that day – it was about who wasn't supposed to be. Kieran Kelly.

Tommy chewed his Mikado, swallowed it and reached for another. 'I remember talk at the time. Jones was there when Bishop Hegarty got shot, wasn't he? The shooter – Morris – seems like he was in Jones's pocket or somethin' too?'

James gave a slow nod. It was all coming together now. The gap was closing. Like a jigsaw, everything was falling into place – and he found it totally revolting. Charles Jones, like a bad penny that always pops up in the end.

Later, back at Melrose, James and Marleen sat at the table set for dinner beside the fire in Roger's bedroom. Roger had been bathed by a local nurse they'd hired and now sat in his robe, fresh but rather quiet.

'I can't believe it,' he said after a long pause. 'Charles Jones. The bastard. But why?' It was rare for him to swear, and almost unheard of, in front of a guest.

James replied gently, 'O'Reilly reckons there's a link to what happened at the City Hotel.'

'But that was a bomb scare, James,' Roger said, frowning. 'Some rogue Provo behind it, and that young girl. The one who ended up in prison.'

'Ah, but no, Uncle. Seems Jones had nothing to do with the bomb. It was the bishop's shooting he'd planned. The gunman who shot Hegarty was one of Jones's men. Kieran Kelly took him out, so the RUC focused all their attention on the bomber. O'Reilly thinks Chief Constable Bonner helped cover up Morris's connection to Jones, and Shalham was digging deep into why. You and I both know Bonner's in Jones's pocket too.' He paused, his voice low.

'I think that's what Father found out. He knew Jones had set out to wreck the conference, and us with it. We owed him money he knew we couldn't pay back. The man never planned on investing in Rocola. He wanted it shut down, wanted to hurt us, and all because the workers are Catholic. In a nutshell. Bishop Hegarty was the cherry on top. We all know the Jones despises Catholics. Father must've realised what was going and was on his way back to warn us… and that bawbag Jones made sure he couldn't. I know it.'

James shook his head in despair. He couldn't go on. Marleen topped up his glass and nudged it towards him.

'I feel a bloody fool,' Roger muttered. 'When I think I had that cretin at my table, pouring him wine, listening to his rants. All the while, he used my brother, my brother, God Bless him. Him on his way to warn us.' Tears rolled down Roger's cheeks, silent and unrelenting.

James rushed to his side and crouched down beside him. Marleen joined them, wrapping her arms around them both. She passed Roger a handkerchief and poured him a glass of water.

A gentle knock came at the door, and Mrs McGinty stepped inside. 'Have you finished with your dinner, sirs? Miss?'

Without a word, they watched her pick up the plates and glasses, placing them carefully on the tray. 'Tea or coffee, anyone?'

Roger gave a weak smile and looked at James. 'Bring another bottle of Burgundy instead, will you, Mrs McGinty?'

She tutted under her breath, but there was a look of satisfaction on her face as she left the room. Roger Henderson, being upset, hurt her. It was nice to see them all together and relaxed. Within five minutes, she was back up the stairs with the Burgundy.

Once they were alone again, Roger looked over at the young couple beside him. They could have stepped straight from the pages of one of those glossy magazines he used to flick through in airport lounges. The ones filled with impossibly handsome couples posed in country houses, wine glasses in hand, firelight soft on their skin.

Marleen stood barefoot on the rug, her daisy-yellow silk dress catching the glow from the hearth, the faintest scattering of blue flowers printed through the fabric. Her blonde hair fell loose around her shoulders, and her crimson-polished toenails flashed each time she moved, catching the light as if on purpose.

James? He looked every inch the heir he was. Wore that Donegal tweed suit that he loved, the navy and brown one, with the matching waistcoat and an open-necked white shirt. Relaxed, composed, timeless, almost. Roger studied his face, the cut of his jaw, the way his hands moved when he spoke, and wondered where the time had gone. Seemed like he was only a boy yesterday. They both should have settled down by now. A man like James, a woman like Marleen. Cheeks flushed with wine, Roger asked jokingly, 'So, tell me, what've you two been up to all day?'

'I've been working, as you well know,' James said with mock indignation.

'I've been taking more cooking lessons from Mrs McGinty,' Marleen smirked.

Roger chuckled. 'So why don't you two lovebirds bugger off outta here? Have some fun, go find somewhere romantic and take what's left of that Burgundy before you go. I need to think about what to do next with Jones. No arguments. Go on now. Enjoy yourselves.' It wasn't a suggestion, and they knew it.

They rose together. James picked up the burgundy, Marleen kissed Roger goodnight, and they made their way downstairs, their steps light and measured, softened by the worn carpet runner.

Marleen was quietly elated. At long last, everything was beginning to fall into place. Roger was firmly on her side now, and her patience was starting to pay off. The smiles, the long, careful conversations, the subtle tilts of her head at the right moment. All of it had been leading to this. She could feel the momentum building. That calm, consistent shift in direction that happened when one played the long game perfectly. With the burgundy, she would ease James into a softer mood, then suggest they take a taxi to the Beechill Hotel. After that, she would simply see where the night led, though she had a strong feeling it would turn out exactly as she hoped.

The following morning, James opened his groggy eyes and stared up at an unfamiliar ceiling. He wasn't in his own bed. Worse still, he wasn't alone. He turned his head and saw Marleen lying on her front, one bare shoulder poking out from under a white cotton sheet. He glanced down, then lifted the covers slightly. Naked. Jesus Christ. Her too!

'Oh, no,' he groaned, flopping back against the pillows, both hands scrubbing through his cropped hair. *What the hell?*

After finishing the bottle of Burgundy, he and Marleen had gone out for a nightcap at a hotel close to Melrose, where they'd drunk far more than they should, that much he remembered. He could still hear the two of them giggling in Melrose's library afterwards, steamin' and talking shite, dredging up old party stories and laughing like teenagers. The last thing he properly remembered was opening a bottle of Dom Pérignon – his uncle's favourite, from the stock he kept tucked away for special occasions. Another deep groan escaped him as he recognised the empty bottle on the bedside table. Of course. He didn't remember coming upstairs, never mind crawling into bed beside Marleen. He shut his eyes and sighed. What had he done? Or worse, what had he said? He slid out of bed as quietly as he could, flinching as the floor creaked. Scooping up his clothes from the carpet one by one, he tiptoed out of the guest room, heart hammering, head thumping, already dreading what was to come.

Marleen knew full well she'd taken shameless advantage of James last night. Not in the way he thought, but that hardly mattered now. That morning she'd kept her eyes closed, breathing slow and steady, feigning sleep. She didn't need to look to know the truth — she heard the pause in his breath, felt the bed shift as he turned, sensed the dread that rolled off him. When she opened her eyes, she saw it. The drop of his face when he saw her there. Panic. The sheer horror of it. Not once did it cross her mind to tell him the truth. Nothing had happened. They'd only shared a bed in the most innocent sense. Why would she ruin it? Everything was going to plan. Slower than she would like, but it was moving. This trip, she was on a mission after the phone call with her pa to get her life in line, get married and have that family he wants so much. There wasn't a chance in hell, she was flying back to London empty-handed.

James Henderson was going to propose. One way or another.

Chapter Fifty-Seven

Put Him on the List

Charles Jones sat slumped in a cracked leather armchair in the Europa foyer, fingers twitching from taking too many painkillers. The place stank of press sweat and aftershave, crawling with hacks chasing headlines they didn't appreciate. Ghosts in flak jackets. Parasites. He'd watched the most bombed hotel in the World, The Europa, take blast after blast, twenty times since 1971, and still it stood – a bit like himself.

He nudged Lemon with a boot. 'See that Yank? Over there at the desk?' Lemon followed his gaze.

A tall American in a creased blazer stood at the desk, cheerfully chatting to the receptionist. He had that easy drawl and polished smile about him that suggested he could talk to anyone or work anywhere, even in a war zone.

'Put him on the list,' Jones muttered.

Lemon tilted his head, waiting.

'That's William Barter. Boston Globe. A Republican apologist. I want him wiped.' Jones didn't raise his voice, but the tone of his words carried weight.

Jones's face ached as he clenched it, pain shooting down the scar that stretched from his ear to his collarbone. He scratched it absentmindedly. The painkillers weren't working fast enough. He'd upped the dose again, and whatever the warnings said, he hadn't bothered reading them in weeks. The chemist had tried giving him a lecture once. That same boy didn't work there anymore.

As for Lemon, he already knew the Yank. That smug, slick bastard standing at the desk with his oversized perfect teeth and that arrogant look all the Yanks wore. Like they were privileged to be here, gave them something to brag about when they got back home. If Jones didn't like him, that was good enough for Lemon. Not once in all the jobs he'd done, had Lemon ever asked why. Why should these ones disappear? Didn't matter. He got the who, the what, the when, and the where. The 'how' he made up himself.

He loved the freedom this job gave him. Loved the risk, the rush, the satisfaction. His mind drifted back to the last one. Some Fenian they'd dragged into the alley behind The Shamrock Bar, off the Falls Road. The one who pissed himself before they'd even raised the axe. It had been well risky, no doubt, but worth every second. Joy.

Jones had told them to use knives, but Lemon thought better. Took axes instead. He liked axes. Solid. Heavier. More personal. You didn't just kill a man with an axe. You erased him. When Jones found out what they'd used, he'd gone off on one. Ranting and raging about the heat it brought, but Lemon knew the wee man got off on it as much as he did and soon it was forgotten. He glanced over at Jones now and saw that the wee man looked like death warmed up. His pale eyes, yellowing at the corners, were twitching like a spider's. Looked like the pain was eating him alive. His tablets weren't cutting it anymore. These days, he was chewing them like Tic Tacs and still snarling at the walls.

People stared at the boss all the time. Lemon had seen them look, part pity, part horror, when they caught sight of the scars carved down his face like melted wax. Seemed like Jones didn't care, though. Never bothered him. The only thing he gave a shite about was control and killing Catholics. Still, when the pills ran out, control went with them, and God help anyone nearby.

'You got that?' Jones asked, voice like gravel and vinegar, still staring at the Yank from afar like he was trying to set him alight with his eyes. 'Don't do it here in Belfast. Wait 'til he's back in Londonderry. I'll follow you in a couple of days.'

'Right, Boss,' Lemon replied, rubbing his hands together. 'Consider it done.'

Chapter Fifty-Eight

Tour de France

Emmett McFadden wasn't best pleased that his mother wanted to get involved with the Women for Peace campaign. In fact, he was rightly pissed off, but daredn't tell her that. She'd have laid into him if she'd known.

The movement had begun after three children were killed walking to school, run over by a wounded IRA man trying to escape the Brits. He'd been shot and lost control of the car, ploughing into the poor souls. Their aunt had organised peace rallies across the North, protesting against violence from all sides. Most Republicans thought it was a waste of time. Another stunt, pro-British at its core. A glossy distraction. But 25,000 protesters had turned out in Belfast all the same. From both communities, side by side, walking from the Shankill to Woodvale Park.

Derry was planning one too. So when his ma said she was going, he'd begged her not to. Women from Derry who'd joined the Belfast march had come back injured and were still getting hassle, but Maggie wasn't for listening. She was going, and that was that.

In the end, over 2,500 people turned up. Marchers of all ages, coats zipped up and scarves tight, defiantly upheld faces walking through the rain. It was happening now, properly happening. More rallies were cropping up across Ireland, north and south. A few even in England. People were paying attention. The media, the public, all of them had started to take notice. It didn't matter whether or not Emmett and the others liked it. Change was coming, and there was no stopping it.

As for his own duty with the Unknowns, Emmett was still ferrying people back and forth across the border. His new partner was a girl called Ashling McKenna, or Ash, as she liked to be called, and, aye, he'd a crush on her too. She wasn't classically stunning, not in the usual sense. A bit of an edge about her, quick as they come, and smart too, like really smart. She wore her blonde hair straight and neat, had pale grey eyes, a delicate face, and full lips. But it wasn't her looks that got him. It was her sense of humour. The way she could lift the mood in a room without even meaning to. She was a catch, all right, but one, he figured, that was well out of his league.

For a while, he'd felt a bit guilty thinking that way about Ash, especially when he used to be so mad about his neighbour, Tina McLaughlin. That had been a schoolboy crush, plain and simple. Tina had never paid him much attention. In fact, now that he was older and a bit more clued in, he was fairly sure he'd got on her tits. One hundred per cent. Not that it mattered now. She was gone. Gone in every way. He wasn't some snotty-nosed kid anymore. He was a man. A man with his own wants. A man with his own needs. He wasn't the least bit ashamed of it.

One Saturday morning, he and Ashling were sent with a package to a cottage out at Malin Head, the most northerly tip of Ireland, up in Donegal. Like most of his family, Emmett loved Malin. Wild waves, sharp Atlantic wind, the kind of skies that went on forever, rain or no rain. Ireland, original and rough. The package was buried deep inside the panelling of Emmett's brown Austin Maxi tucked in so well he was worried he'd never get it out again.

They were easing towards Coshquin, not far outside Derry, when they came to the British Army checkpoint. A soldier stepped forward, rifle in hand, palm raised, signalling for them to stop. Emmett's middle flipped with nerves so much that he stalled the car.

Please God, not now.

The soldier didn't rush towards them but walked slowly, impassive, looking the car over from top to bottom. Emmett glanced at Ash. She didn't say a word, but her lips had pursed. He reached for the window crank, fingers fumbling, the stiff old handle sticking halfway as he tried to wind it down.

He cleared his throat and forced a smile at the Brit. 'Mornin'.'

The soldier leaned in, his eyes scanning the car as if it had already confessed. Emmett knew if they got searched, they were finished.

'Morning, sir, license, please,' he said, smiling.

'Here ye go,' Emmett replied quietly, handing over his newly issued licence. He didn't look at the Brit, but stared ahead out the window.

'Where're you off to today?' the private asked, still friendly as he glanced at the photo, then bent slightly to take in the girl in the passenger seat. Emmett's heart was hammering and he prayed he didn't have 'guilty' written across his forehead.

'Out for a run in me new wheels. Only got her. Thinkin' of headin' to Kate Farren's in Malin,' he told him.

The soldier frowned slightly. He didn't know who or what Kate Farren's was, but stepped back and took a good look at the Austin. He loved cars. All types of cars.

'I'm not about to ask what you forked out for her,' he chuckled, grin stretched ear to ear. 'But whatever it was, lad, you've been done!' He handed back Emmett's licence with a smirk. 'Go on then, enjoy the drive. If she lasts!'

Emmett managed a dutiful smile, rolled the window up, and, with hands somewhat shaking, turned the engine over and drove off. The pair of them kept quiet for a few hundred metres until Ashling roared. 'Sweet Mother of Christ! Me heart's about to burst!'

'Me too!' Emmett gasped. 'Thought I was going to shit me pants there!' They broke down and laughed their way north to Malin.

Mickey Boyle had sworn to avenge his nephew Darragh's death. He was, belly-down on the damp grass of an old embankment at one of the unapproved, rarely used border crossings high on Sherriff's Mountain, on the very edge of Derry. Not alone. Lying beside him was a new fella, Seamus Donaghy. Mickey knew Donaghy. Heard about the work he'd done, running arms from the States. Word was, he was solid. Quiet type, but ruthless when needed. A true comrade.

Seamus was due back in the States soon, and ever since the whole disaster with Caitlin, he'd kept well out of the way. Before everything went to hell, he'd been travelling the length of the country, trying to drum up business with the bigger building suppliers. His boss back in Boston had even hinted at helping him open a franchise over here if he fancied the idea. For a while, things had looked promising, like he might actually be able to build something solid for himself and Caitlin.

But that was before *it* happened, and he'd soon binned the idea of staying altogether. The truth was, the only feckin' reason he'd come back in the first place was for Caitlin. Now that the two of them were well and truly fucked - sadly not in the way he'd hoped – there was nothing keeping him here anymore. Apart from his aging family, not a single thing.

He glanced at Mickey and whispered, 'Any minute now.' They were waiting on a British Army patrol to show. Most days, they turned up at different times, keeping the routine unpredictable, hoping to catch the fellas running back and forth across the border.

Mickey was still fuming. After all this time, he hadn't got the names of the soldiers in the Saracen that ploughed into his nephew and left his pal half-dead. The Brits had buried the finer details, ie, names. All that had been released was a short, snide statement saying the soldiers had been charged with 'reckless driving'. No police follow-up, no military gaol, but a quiet disciplinary, and in no time, they were back on duty. For the time being, blasting this patrol would have to do. It wasn't justice, not even close, but it'd hurt. Enough to ease the itch.

The army had spent years trying to seal off the border. Two hundred and eighty roads, including cow paths or gravel tracks, wound their way between the Republic and the North. There were too many to control properly. Most didn't have permanent checkpoints, and when they couldn't guard them, the Brits either blew up bridges or blocked the crossings with cement cubes, welded steel barriers and rolls of razor barbed wire. But shutting down a three-hundred-and-sixty-mile stretch from Derry to Newry was easier said than done. Patrols came and went round the clock, on foot or in Pigs and Land Rovers, sometimes with helicopters sweeping low over the hedges, trying to flush out so-called bandits.

Mickey and Seamus had planted a couple of landmines earlier, buried neatly and quietly in the gravelled dip beyond the hedgerow. Now they were well dug in, lying low about eight hundred yards back, to be sure nothing wandered too close like people or livestock. The last thing they needed was to maim or kill some poor innocent. They'd already had one close call. A couple of senseless sheep came charging out of nowhere, and without thinking, Seamus had leapt up and chased them off, clapping and hissing like a man possessed. Mickey damn near pissed himself trying not to laugh. You couldn't make it up. Usually, they'd be well away by now, off the hill and over the border before the patrol ever arrived. But today Mickey wasn't for budging. Not yet. He needed to see this happen for himself.

'Hear that?' he whispered as the sound of whirring blades grew louder. Seamus nodded.

Both men pressed deeper into the rise of the embankment, covering themselves with branches and brambles they'd chopped down earlier. Faces inches apart, eyes wide, they lay still, waiting. Ten minutes passed. Nothing. No explosion. Fuck it, Mickey thought, checking his watch. *What'd he do wrong?*

He was for moving, but as he was about to get up and check, a couple of almighty blasts tore through the quiet as the ground shook beneath them. Screams followed. Voices raised in panic. Men shouting and swearing.

Glancing up, the Provos saw the Brits' helicopter drop low and circle the wreckage. Time to get out of there. They had to move. *Fast.*

The heavens opened and the sky turned black; the rain came down on the two Provos in thick, hammering sheets. It bounced off the earth and pelted their backs, but neither of them complained. Rain and darkness made the best kind of cover. You couldn't beat it.

It was all downhill from there. Two shadows in the rain, running like the wind through narrow lanes, hemmed in by thick oaks, the kind that had stood for a hundred years or more, and mile after mile of gorse, wild and overgrown. They moved quickly, legs stiff from lying so long, their boots slipping now and then on the muck as they scrambled down towards the main road.

The two bikes were right where they'd left them, black-framed and dull, stripped of anything that could catch the light. No reflectors, no lamps, nothing to give them away. They'd hidden them deep in the roadside ditch the night before, under nettles and old bracken.

'Quick, Seamus!' Mickey shouted, grabbing a bike and hurling it at him before snatching his own. Soaked already, they could barely see as they rode, the rain streaming into their eyes, stinging like grit. The storm was howling now, the wind slapping their faces raw. All the while, the road churned beneath their tyres, half-mud, half-stone, every bump jarring through their bones.

Behind them, over the ridge, the sky pulsed red and white from the chopper's searchlight, slicing through the dark like a blade. Sirens wailed, distant but rising. Still, Seamus and Mickey hunched low and pedalled like mad, tyres skidding and bouncing, gears grinding. The aged bikes barely stayed together.

One wrong move and they'd be in a ditch or over a wall. But they kept going, teeth clenched, lungs burning, soaked through and half blind. Somewhere between terror and euphoria, Seamus gave an enormous howl. A short, mad, maniacal howl! Mickey barked with laughter, half-crazed, not sure if they were racing for their lives or tearing down a mountain like a pair of maniacs.

By the time they hit the bottom, they were frozen stiff, gasping like old men, battered, bruised, and aching in places they didn't even know they had.

Still, they were alive. Christ knows how. It had been Derry's equivalent to the Tour de France, if the Tour de France let two loonies take part on scrapheap bikes, in sideways rain and thunder, down pitch-black, rocky lanes full of ruts, holes, and bumps that'd shake the fillings out of your head. Who needed the French anyway, when the Provos were breaking land speed records down the hills of Donegal?!

Chapter Fifty-Nine

An Old Tin of Baked Beans

Martin McLaughlin sat hunched over his pint in the Telstar bar, tucked beside Jackson's shop in the heart of the Creggan estate. It wasn't much to look at, a hanging-in-there-for-dear-life bar clinging to the side of the only shopping parade for miles, but it did the job. The place was thick with smoke, the kind that clung to your clothes and followed you home. He scanned the room slowly, taking in the regulars. A few nods, a handful of faint smiles, quiet acknowledgements, and nothing more. No one here was drunk enough to find the energy to chat. Everyone was beat.

It was a Friday evening, and the bar ticked over with the usual mix. A country and western singer stood slouched in one corner, his blue and silver star-spangled get-up shining under the grim strip lighting, belting out old heartbreak songs. Nobody paid any heed really, but one drunken soul, and even then, just. A woman sobbed quietly into her vodka, shoulders trembling as she tried to light a fag with shaky hands. Martin knew her - everyone did. Poor woman had buried her son a while or so back after the Brits shot him dead during a riot. Ten years old. Another case wrapped in red tape and filed away somewhere no one would ever look. Justice again? Don't think so.

Martin rubbed his face with his two hands and sighed. He felt their weariness right through his skin, cumbersome and listless. War didn't kill you outright. It chipped away at you, little by little, until all that was left was a shell, a breath and a pulse, and not much else. He nodded to the barman for another drink, his movement barely noticeable, then turned back as the door creaked open.

In walked his target. Kevin McDaid, better known as 'Dickie', in all his greasy glory. What an absolute twat, Martin thought, watching the fleshy man swagger to the bar and flop onto a stool like he had right to it. Dickie ordered a large Paddy whiskey, peeling a wad of notes from his back pocket as if he were king of the estate. His Celtic shirt strained to cover the hairy flab spilling over the waistband of his too-tight jeans. Pure class. *Not.* Here goes, Martin thought, rising to make his move.

'All right?' he said, sliding onto the stool beside Dickie.

'Aye. Grand,' Dickie muttered, giving him a sideways look, thrown by the fact Martin McLaughlin was not only talking to him but sitting beside him. Martin, for his part, felt the disgust rise. He wouldn't have known the two-faced fucker from Adam until now, and wished he still didn't.

Dickie tossed back his whiskey in one loud gulp, belched and clicked his tongue at the barman for another.

Martin got in first and nodded to the barman. 'Large Bushmills, mucker,' he said, then pointed at Dickie. 'Get him whatever he's drinkin'.'

He watched the barman set the glasses down and lifted his own with a sigh. 'What a day,' he said, before knocking back the so-called Bushmills in one go. He made a show of it hitting him like a blowtorch, choking loud, spluttering as if he'd swallowed fire, his face reddening, eyes streaming, the air catching in his chest. He bent over the counter, gasping for effect, while Dickie sprang to his feet and started thumping at his back, wide-eyed and flapping.

Martin put a hand up to stop him, still wheezing, voice tearing out between coughs. 'Jesus fuckin' Christ,' he croaked. 'For a second there, thought I was done for - and you'd be the last ugly face I'd see.'

Dickie chuckled. 'Me too! By the way, if you thought I'd be givin' ye mouth to mouth, no fuckin' chance!'

Martin laughed and shook his head as Dickie signalled to the barman again, clearly delighted with himself after all the carry-on.

'Another for this wally here,' he said, grinning as he turned to Martin. 'Take it easy this time, mucker, eh?'

Martin grinned back. So far, so good. He had what he needed. Contact was made, and the barman gave him the faintest of winks. He was in on it too. As for Martin's drink, there wasn't a drop of alcohol in it. Flat Coke, same as before.

The music seemed to get louder as the night wore on, or was it the drink? Hard to tell. Either way, Dickie was on a roll now. Pissed, loud, and loving every second of it. He'd never imagined he'd be sitting in the Telstar with Martin McLaughlin, of all people, side by side like they'd known each other all their lives. Not like Porkie, who'd turned into a right moaner these days. McLaughlin wasn't half as bad as people made out. Bit of craic, actually. He laughed his head off at every one of Dickie's jokes, and by the look of things, it was shaping up to be a long night. Not that Dickie minded. He had all the time in the world. The way McLaughlin could hold his drink, matching him shot for shot without blinking, there'd be a serious hangover waiting in the morning.

Ah, fuck it. Who cares. Life's too short. He'd worry about it later.

From the way things were going, Dickie reckoned he'd found himself a new drinking buddy. Or more than that. If he played his cards right, McLaughlin could be well useful. The kind of fella who knew things, the kind who could open doors. Sure, wasn't he a high-up Provo? *Magic.*

Dickie was on a high now. He could almost smell the cash for the kind of intel he'd get if McLaughlin's tongue loosened. It wouldn't take much, a few more jars, a bit more chat and who knows what the Provo might let slip. Happy days, as far as he was concerned. Having a bit of a brag, he shoved his sleeve back and stuck his wrist under McLaughlin's nose.

'See that, Martin?' he slurred, grinning like a wanker. 'Gold Longines. Pools money. Treated meself. Pure Longines, that is. What d'ye think, eh?' Wasn't real at all. Total fake. But he wasn't for letting on, why should he?

Martin leaned in, giving it the right amount of interest. 'Heard that, Dickie. Meant to say, good on ye. The real McCoy is it?'

Dickie bobbed his head like one of those nodding dogs you'd see on a dashboard and threw Martin a sloppy salute. His grin stretched even wider, all teeth and ego, proud as punch with himself.

Martin figured it was time. He'd had more than enough of the wally's jokes and bragging, all louder and more desperate to impress with every drink. Slipping back into character, he took a slow look round the bar, like some clumsy spy from a crap TV sitcom, making a show of checking for nosy bastards. Then he moved closer, a touch, lowering his voice to the kind of tone that made the fool feel important.

'Tell you what, Dickie... I've been meanin' to ask ye. Don't suppose you'd be up for makin' a bit of extra cash? I know you're rollin' in it these days,' he added with a sneer, 'I'm only talkin' about a few wee jobs here and there for the Boys, like. Nothin' major. Shiftin' some goods.' He gave him an over-the-top wink to make sure the penny dropped.

Dickie nodded like a bobblehead on speed. What a bloody night this was turning out to be. If he played this right and got in with McLaughlin and the rest of them, he'd be laughing. Like he'd imagined. Once again, he thought about how much the Brits would cough up. He could already see the pound notes stacking up like a winning slot, could almost hear the sound of them pouring in. Jackpot.

'Anything I can do for the Cause, Martin. Ye say the word. Ask around this place, they'll tell ye. I'm a decent person, so I am. Dead on like,' he slurred, puffing out his chest like a balloon ready to burst and beaming like he'd solved world peace.

Martin gave a slow nod, hiding his satisfaction. 'That's great, Dickie, great. Fair play to ye, I knew we could count on you.' This guy was as thick as two short planks. Then, with an easy smile, he told Dickie exactly what they needed done and, more importantly, how much he'd be paid for doing it. Not that there'd be a penny in it, but Martin knew rightly the greedy bastard worshipped money, so he had to bait the hook.

Dickie woke the following morning fully dressed with a skull like cracked concrete. His head throbbed, belly lurching as he staggered to his tiny, freezing bathroom. He barely made it to the sink before he spewed the insides clean out of himself. Sweat clung to his brow and his hands shook like a pensioner's. *Sweet Jesus.* He couldn't keep doing this. It felt like the lining of his gut had finally given up. His legs wobbled like jelly, and for a second he thought he might collapse right there on the cold tiles. Somehow, hands pressed against the wall, he made it back to bed and flopped under the blankets, groaning, but as soon as he shut his eyes, he felt it - the damp patch.

Fuck. Pissed himself again.

On the way back from the bog, he'd tried to piece together his journey home last night. Not a clue. Not even a whisper of memory. He drew his blankets up, raking through the wreckage of his brain, eyes clenched shut like that might help. Then, like a slow-motion slap, it all came back to him. A flash, but enough. Him, up on the bar, standing right beside the barmaid. That feckin' star-spangled singer on the other side. The three of them, arms draped around each other, singing their heads off like it was bloody Eurovision.

'Come on, ye young rebels, and listen while I sing,
For the love of one's country is a terrible thing...'

After that, nothing. Confusion. Cringing at the thought of what else he might've said or done, he turned his wrist to check the time. 10.30 AM. Noooo!

His head flopped back on the pillow as a fresh wave of regret washed over him. Today was going to be the longest day of his life. His mouth tasted like an ashtray, his damp

Y-fronts were stuck to him, and he was fairly sure there was puke somewhere on his jumper. Every part of him ached. Even his hair hurt.

He was dying. Anxiety eating at him. That creeping, gut-wringing dread that he'd said or done something he shouldn't. To do with Martin McLaughlin, it was nibbling at the back of his brain, but he couldn't quite grab it. Jesus. He'd been all pally with him, hadn't he? Laughing like a bloody eejit, buying rounds like they were long-lost pals. Groaning, he dragged the pillow over his face. Christ almighty, never again.

About a week later, Martin showed up at Dickie's front door. He stood there for a moment, still as anything, giving the street a good look. The Lone Moor Road, deep in the Bogside, was quiet, the sort of quiet that made every footstep sound louder. A line of small terraced houses stretched along, all shut tight, curtains drawn. Midnight and not a soul to be seen. Only the low hum of cars in the distance and the faint whiff of chip fat drifting in the breeze. Martin knocked once, firm but not too loudly, then stepped back, his eyes still flicking up and down the street. Beside him stood Volunteer Mark Bradley, silent as ever. The pair of them waited in the dark, watching the house like hawks. A few minutes passed before a light finally blinked on behind the frosted glass. Then came the sound of footsteps. Slow. Cautious. The door creaked open a crack, enough for a sliver of light to spill out onto the step.

Dickie squinted out at the duo, bleary-eyed and rough-looking, like he'd crawled out of a skip. 'Martin,' he mumbled, voice scratchy. 'I had a feelin' you'd be callin' before now.' He pushed the door open wider, stepping back to let them in. Over the past few days, the worse hangover he'd ever had in his miserable life had faded but the memories hadn't. Every last bit of that mad session had come trickling back, piece by piece. No escaping it now.

'Busy, busy, Dickie boy,' Martin said with a wide smile as he stepped inside.

Dickie was a sight to see. He mooched about in filthy striped pyjama bottoms and a sagging string vest, his hair a wild, matted bird's nest. His face was grey with sleep, stubble, and stale drink, and he smelled rotten too, like a sick dog that had dragged itself in from the street.

'Sorry to get you up,' Martin went on, calm and polite. 'But someone's been grassin' on us and we need your help.'

Dickie's eyes widened. He gave an exaggerated cough and croaked, 'Oh, aye? Bastards.' He put on shock and outrage, but his mouth was dry, and his heart lurched, again and again.

He'd taken full advantage, wasting no time getting word to his handler. They'd met in a quiet bar out in the sticks. The man nearly choked on his pint when Dickie told him. His eyes lit up like a child at Christmas, stunned by the sheer luck of it. But it didn't last. The excitement flickered out as fast as it had come. He leaned in, mouth tight, voice low and all business. No time for backslapping now. There was work to be done.

'Be careful son, how you play it. Don't ask questions straightaway. Play along, and keep in touch, you hear me? Tread carefully. Very carefully.'

After he'd left, Dickie found a thick brown envelope tucked under the cushion of his seat. Inside was more money than he was used to seeing in one go.

Now, standing half-dead in his stinking hallway, alongside McLaughlin and the whiff of last night still clinging to his skin, Dickie wasn't sure about anything anymore.

'Any chance of a cuppa, Dickie?' Martin asked as they made their way into the galley kitchen at the back of the house.

As he and Mark stepped inside, the stench near took the wind out of them. That sickly sweet, rotten reek hit hard, clinging to the back of their throats. Both men stopped in their tracks, eyes meeting with a look that said it all. No woman had set foot in this place for years, and by the looks of it, no man either. The floor was sticky underfoot, the bins overflowing, the Belfast sink piled high with crusted pans, mouldy dishes, and fag ends bobbing in cold, greasy water. Off to the side, an empty tin of Heinz beans lay on the lino, with empty beer cans crushed and flung into the corner like it was some sort of dumping ground. Everything in the place wore a film of filth. Rotten, the place was rotten.

'Jesus wept, but it's a bit of a tip in here, Dickie. Don't you ever clean up?' Martin asked instantly regretting the idea of tea.

'I know, I know. Keep meaning to get round to it, but you know how it is, Martin,' Dickie mumbled, peering round his kitchen as though seeing it for the first time. 'You wanna sit down?' he offered.

The Provos shared another look and together replied, 'Nah, thanks. Ye can forget the tea too.'

Martin couldn't wait to get the hell out. The air inside was full with that sickly sweet stink and God knows what else, so nauseating it near hurt to breathe. He wasn't the same man who'd left for Boston. Brian's sister had seen to that. She'd told him upfront: a man could come from nothing, but he didn't have to live like it forever. Since then, he kept himself and his corner clean, polished his shoes, ironed his shirts. Took pride in the way he carried himself through the world. But this place? This pit made his skin crawl He eyed the grease-smudged table; the broken toaster stuffed with letters, the half-dead fly stuck to the rim of a jam jar. Dickie lived like vermin, and the lazy git didn't see the shame in it. Martin rubbed his hand down his coat sleeve, a reflex, like he might catch whatever was living in the walls.

He turned to Mark and muttered, 'Let's get this done.'

Trying not to stand too close to Dickie, he asked, 'Remember what we talked about? The night you ended up singin' with Debbie and the Star-Spangled Banner?' Martin chuckled. It'd been some sight alright.

'I do, aye,' Dickie replied, suddenly defensive. 'Everyone's been takin' the piss outta me since.'

That wouldn't be hard. It was some sight, Martin thought, 'Wouldn't worry about that. Now, that wee job I mentioned... there's a bit of gear needs moved, but you've to keep it to yourself, Dickie. Swear on it.'

Dickie blessed himself and swore.

'In that case, then, I want ye to—' Martin laid it out plainly, step by step, where, when and how. Straightaway, Martin caught the twitch in Dickie's eyes, like a slot machine rolling to a jackpot. The bastard was probably doing the math, likely the pound signs were stacking up behind those bleary eyes of his.

Chapter Sixty

Set Up

At two in the morning, a couple of nights later, Dickie sat slouched behind the wheel of a hijacked bread van, parked up a narrow side lane near a big barn at the top of Sherriff's Mountain. The engine idled low and steady, barely heard over the wind. His arse had gone completely numb, and he hadn't felt his toes in twenty minutes. His bladder was near bursting, and to top it all off, his bloody lighter had packed in, leaving him without a fag for over an hour. Torture. He leaned forward, pressing his forehead to the steering wheel, and gave a low groan. 'This is shite,' he muttered, jaw tight with cold and nerves. He hadn't the faintest idea what the plan actually was, only that McLaughlin had told him to stay put, keep the engine running, and they'd be back soon. *Aye, right*. Felt like hours ago.

The four lads they'd been ferrying hadn't gone anywhere near the barn. They'd been dropped off well before, somewhere quiet, near a crossroads. What was happening inside now, though, was bedlam. He could hear thuds, scuffling, laughter, someone roaring across the floor like they were moving furniture. He was sure he heard a word or two in Irish. Jesus wept. So much for keeping a low profile. If this was the Provos' idea of a covert op, they were doing a grand job of drawing attention. He half expected disco lights and loud music next.

He was dying to get out for a slash, especially with no one about, the lane pitch black for miles. But McLaughlin had made it crystal clear. Dickie wasn't to move an inch, to stay put. End of. He laughed, remembering the way the Derry man had turned up earlier, dressed like a bloody paramilitary poster boy, head to toe in camo, balaclava, the works, like one of those Provo calendars half of Creggan had pinned to their walls. As he left, he'd tapped the van door and said, 'You know what to do, Dickie. We're relying on ye. We've a bita work to do in the barn first, so sit tight. Won't be long.'

Dickie had nodded, trying not to show how afraid he was, though his hands were already sweating on the wheel. McLaughlin had properly put the wind up him when those two eyes of his locked right on and said, calm as you like, 'Trust me, Dickie. Be back soon.' There'd been a message in that look, in that voice, that told him Martin McLaughlin was the last person on earth he should be trusting. Sitting there in the dark, Dickie didn't have a clue what he was supposed to do next.

'You'd better be,' Dickie had snapped, all mouth. More bravado than bravery.

Nerves in tatters, he sat stewing in the driver's seat, the engine ticking over in low grumbles. He shifted in his seat, stretched one leg, then the other, but there was no getting comfortable. The cold had seeped right into his bones and the stench of old bread and damp plastic was making him gag. He was beginning to sweat too, which made no sense, given the cold. Nerves, maybe. They'd dumped him out here, far from any real action, like a spare prick, and not even had the decency to tell him where the safe house was that they were going to next. That was the bit that really got to him. If he'd known, he could've sold that on. Doubled his money, easy. Maybe more. Could've set himself up for a long time if he'd played it smart. But no, McLaughlin had kept him in the dark.

The longer he sat there, the worse it got. His head wouldn't stop. How long were they going to keep him waiting? They'd said they'd be quick, but it was taking ages. The Brits could land at any second, and the last place Dickie wanted to be was sitting here with the engine running. A bloody sitting duck is what he was. What if it was a test? Or worse, a setup? What if they knew he'd grassed?!

His leg wouldn't stay still, bouncing up and down, his hand gripping the steering wheel tight enough to cramp. He was sweating properly now. What if they knew? What if McLaughlin had worked it out and was waiting inside, counting down the time before he sent someone out to wipe him out? He swallowed, but his throat was bone dry. Christ, he should've listened to himself. You don't cross the Provos. Not ever. Certainly not Martin McLaughlin.

His stomach grumbled, and his thoughts drifted to Anne. What he could do to that woman? In his own way, he loved her, but—*fuck that*, he'd think about her later when he got back to his latest copy of *Penthouse*. As for that husband of hers, Porkie, the useless bastard, he hadn't shown up last night like they'd arranged. Hadn't answered the door today either. Everyone was turning their back on him. Everyone, oddly enough, but Martin McLaughlin. Or was he?

'What the fuck are they doin' in there?' he muttered, more to the wheel than to anyone else. His chest was tight, his breathing quickening. This didn't sound right. They were so fuckin' loud, his ma could probably hear them from the Bogside!

The light in the barn snapped off and the noise died down. Dickie sighed, relief crawling over him like a warm coat. Thank Christ, they were done. He was stiff with cold, teeth chattering, too bloody terrified to step out and check, and far too thick to clock that McLaughlin and the others weren't in the barn at all.

There he sat, gripping the wheel like a child clutching a teddy, thinking maybe if he held on tight enough, they'd magically appear. Not a clue in his head that the lot of them had legged it not long after he'd dumped them near the crossroads. Less than five minutes away was a break in the hedge, practically invisible in the dark unless you knew it was there. Of course they did. They'd shot through it like hares, crossed two fields, and were already tucked up in the safe house, stripping off their gear, scoffing down sausage rolls and roaring with laughter at the wanker they'd left behind. Dickie, bless him, was none the wiser.

As Dickie sat glued to his seat up in Sherriff's mountain, sitting alone in *Jack's*, a male-dominated, but friendly bar off William Street in Derry, Martin McLaughlin chuckled as he pictured the night Tricky Dickie was about to have. The barn up on Sheriff's Mountain had served its purpose. Torture, executions, the odd 'chat' that ended with a body buried out the back. It had seen its fair share, soaked up too much over the years. The place reeked of Kieran Kelly too. The bastard. It wasn't safe anymore, not for what they needed. Too many eyes, too much history clinging to the rafters. Time to be done with it. The right way. Martin didn't just want it done right. He wanted a spectacle and boy, had he planned some entertainment for the Brits. A circus!

They'd paid the farmer, an old Republican who was far keener on tenners than livestock. Told him to sod off for a few days and not look back. Said they were planning to 'improve the place'. He didn't even ask what with. He knew by the size of the wad they handed over. It was way over the odds, more than generous, and that alone told him it wasn't turnips they were planting.

Then came the real magic trick. The performance. Hidden speakers, nicked from the old Stardust disco, had been wired up and fed with a looped reel, recorded in some fella's garage. It wasn't exactly Abbey Road, but it was good enough. Men barking orders, boxes being dragged, metal clanging, the whole works. Even threw in the odd bit of Irish here and there to give it that 'authentic cell' feel. Made it sound like there was a full squad inside shifting crates of RPGs and Semtex by the bloody cartload.

They didn't stop there. The outside was dressed up too. Fresh boot prints stomped into the muck, fag ends left lying about, even a half-eaten sandwich chucked in the corner, crust curling right. The sort of scene that'd have some Brit fella rubbing his hands and scribbling in his little notebook about 'key findings at suspected site of insurgent activity'. Probably add a footnote about the sandwich.

Then, to top it all off, Martin spoon-fed Dickie the perfect bait. Enough to get him excited. Hinted at an arms haul. Said there'd be some high-ranking Provos there an' all, weapons that had landed in from the States, gear that would be on the move. The whole shebang. Enough to get the Brits biting, storming in full tilt, all geared up with faces painted and fingers itching. All of it? Smoke and mirrors. Smoke and mirrors. What they'd find was wires, lots of wires, lots of fire and fuck all else. Should they get wiped out in the blast? Tough. Sure, isn't that the nature of war?

Martin reckoned if they were stupid enough to fall for theatre, they deserved a front-row seat. There'd be no Provo cell to find, no weapons to confiscate, smoke, fire, twisted beams and scorched earth. A low body count from the blast was inconsequential. The point was to send a message. To the Brits, but especially to any greedy bastards out there thinking of grassing.

Don't. *Ever.* He drained his Guinness with a satisfying smile and waited for an update.

Chapter Sixty-One

Listen to Me!

Paddy Gillispie and Brian Monaghan had planned everything with care for weeks. That morning, they hid the 200lb bomb in a drainpipe at the gates of Glencairn House, Dublin.

Now, crouched in the shade across the road, they watched its gates from a safe distance, leaning casually against the black wrought-iron railings outside St Bridget's House Convent School. This target was no ordinary diplomat. The man was a former senior liaison officer, someone who had worked closely with both the British Foreign Office and MI5. Put differently, a spy.

Neither of them spoke. They didn't need to. Instead, they shared a glance and a quiet smile as the school gates opened and small groups of children called out their goodbyes and ran inside, their school bags swinging and their faces lit with excitement. A few of the little ones dragged their feet, reluctant to part with their ma's or da's, until gentle nudges moved them along. One by one, they disappeared into the building. Some mammies hung back, chatting away, swapping stories and gossip in that lazy morning way. The school gates soon closed with the last child gone.

'They'll be okay. Not long now.' Brian said.

They watched as the last of the mothers and nannies drifted off, prams bouncing along the pavement as they chatted among themselves. The two bombers slipped in behind them, calm as you like, blending in without being seen. Not a word passed between them until they reached their battered old Land Rover further down the road. They climbed in and waited. Right on cue, a white Rover P6 edged into view and rolled slowly towards the gates of Glencairn House. Monaghan tracked its approach with practised precision, lips moving as he counted under his breath. 'One, two, three.' He pressed the trigger hard.

The blast was instant. Two hundred pounds of explosive tore the morning apart, a single roaring detonation that flung fire and debris in every direction. Shattered metal, splintered stone, and clumps of earth rained skyward, a storm that ate everything in its path. Screams rose from the bus stop, from women nearby, unhurt but frightened. Flames devoured the car, spilling into the flowerbeds, the shrubs, and across the car roof as if poured from a bucket of paint.

Inside the Land Rover, they both sat still until Monaghan turned to Paddy, the faintest curl at his mouth betraying his satisfaction. Both pleased. He turned the key. The engine coughed, caught, then rumbled into life, and off they went, unhurried, regular as if they'd just left Mass.

'Let's get outta here.' Monaghan said.

When Paddy got back to West Belfast, he headed straight for The Shamrock. The evening news muttered away in the background, but he barely caught a word. He fell into a chair across from his twin sister and watched her go for it, her gob firing on all cylinders. He wasn't really listening, hadn't been since she'd started her ranting. His eyes wandered, then settled on her lips, and for a brief second, caught himself wondering how she managed to talk so much, and so fast. *Impressive.*

Dolores knew he wasn't with her and thumped him hard. 'Are ye fuckin' listenin' to me, Paddy? Have you heard *anythin'* I've just said?'

Nope. Not a word, but nodded anyway. 'Course I have, love.'

She scoffed and folded her arms tight across her chest. She'd been dying to tell her brother what she'd discovered about Brona-so-called-fucking-Doyle.

'You haven't. Have ye? Don't lie. You never listen. I'm tellin' ye, there's somethin' about that woman. There's nothin' in that flat of hers, nothin' personal with her name on it. It's not natural. Not right.' She jabbed the air with her finger, counting off. 'No letters. No bills. No chequebooks. No bank statements. No ID of *any* kind. Books, books and more bloody books. Ye gotta listen to me, Paddy, I think your woman's a Brit. A fuckin' spy!'

Paddy's laughter erupted deeply, as if it had been a long time. *A spy?!* 'Ye think Brona is a spy?' he asked. Dolores' look of annoyance set him off even more.

He grabbed his pint, took a long swig of Guinness and wiped his mouth. 'Jesus, Dee,' he sputtered. 'Are ye feckin' serious? You and your imagination. It'll be the death of ye!'

Dolores was fuming. She'd been waiting half the night to get him on his own, and now that she had, he wasn't even bloody listening. She watched her twin laugh into his pint, wearing that half-arsed, couldn't-give-a-fuck expression he always pulled when he thought she was being dramatic. That was the problem, really. It was like that was all he ever saw when he looked at her – a woman giving off, mouthing off, making noise – never mind that she'd lived through the same horrors and done her bit for the Cause. She'd smuggled weapons under the noses of soldiers, lied to the Brits with a straight face, taken beatings in cells, humiliated, and still made it home in time to put his dinner on the table. But did any of that count for anything? Nah. Not to him. Patrick Gillispie took it all as a given.

'Sometimes you do me head in Paddy.' Dolores whispered.

Despite everything, she loved him. Jesus, but she did. He was her twin, his yin to her bloody yang. She wasn't sure whether he felt the same. Patrick had a streak, a stubborn, pig-headed streak in him, one that most West Belfast men were born with – to be in charge, have the last say, always be right. Drove her barmy. She'd earned her place a dozen times over especially after their success at Tullyvallen, but still, he acted like she only had it because *he* allowed it. Because she was *his* sister.

'I'm not makin' this up, Patrick,' she said through gritted teeth. 'She's not right. I don't trust her. Will ye listen to me, *please*. I mean it.'

She was begging and that got him. He looked at her. His eyes narrowed, and in that lazy grin of his, the one he wore like armour, it dropped. Maybe now he was seeing she wasn't joking. Not about this one. She tilted up her long Grecian nose, set her jaw firm, holding his gaze, daring him to brush her off again. Her big brown eyes, always expressive, were full of quiet warning.

Paddy wiped the Guinness from his mouth with the back of his sleeve, casual as ever, not a bother on him. But he didn't answer right away. Instead, he released a slow *I-so-cannot-be bothered-with-this-crap* sigh; the kind meant to shut her up. Instead, he looked at her face, 'Alright, Dee. I'll go see her. She might not speak to me, but I'll try. Okay?' He reached out and gave her cheek a light fun squeeze. 'You're probably worryin' over nothin'. Let's wait and see, eh?'

It wasn't much, but it was a start. For Dolores, that would do. She leaned back, trying not to look too cocky, but inside she was already picturing his face when he realised she'd been right all along.

Alice Wallace was around The Shamrock, collecting for the Prisoners' Defence Fund, and heard some guys whisper Paddy's name. So, the bastard was back. Had been for a while, by the sound of it. Bloody nerve. After the way he'd blanked her, like she was little else than a quick fuck. Command wasn't happy. Not by a long shot. Her lack of progress had been mentioned more than once, the tone colder with every message. There was even talk of pulling her out altogether, binning the entire operation. She'd begged for more time. One more chance. They'd come around, but barely. One month, they'd said. Thirty days to get results, solid evidence. It gave her enough time to finish what she'd started. Hit The Shamrock. If nothing else, it'd offer her some solace and satisfaction.

The buzzer from the offy snapped her back, and she looked towards the front door. Speak of the bastard. There he was, standing on the doorstep. About to close, she called through the grilled door, her voice bone dry, 'We're closed.' Then she flipped off the outside lights. That'd teach him.

Outside, Paddy shaded his eyes with one hand and peered through the bars. 'I see you in there, Brona. Come on, love, open up.' He thumped harder. After listening to Dee's rants, he wasn't in the mood for games.

Alice stood still, watching him. He was a good-looking man, but tonight he looked angry. The last thing she needed. She was bloody tired of pretending to be someone else, and if she was going to get intel, she needed to be on the ball, ready to take him on. He knocked hard again, and her training kicked in, somehow she had to know what he'd been up to. She sighed, buzzed him in, and stepped back as the door clicked open. Without a word, she turned and walked towards the back of the shop to the storeroom, flicking off the last of the lights as she went. Paddy followed, quiet at first. Then his hand came out and caught her arm. He spun her around to face him, his expression had changed. It was softer now. Almost affectionate.

'Hey, you. Don't be cross. I'd things to do, places to be, that's all. I'm sorry,' he said, running his fingers gently down her cheek. She didn't reply, instead; she folded her arms and pouted like a sulking child.

Before she knew it, he pounced on her, his hands rough and urgent, tearing at her blouse with such force that the buttons shot across the floor like hailstones on a tin roof. Her throat closed as she pushed at his chest, desperate to get him off her, but he was ready for her, too strong, and had already clamped her wrists tight above her head, holding her fast.

His mouth crashed against hers, hot and insistent, like a man starved. She twisted, tried to pull away again, but he didn't let up. His grip was firm, kisses greedy, messy, almost wild. In that moment, without thinking, her body gave him an answer. It moved with its own mind, its own hunger, her brain still trying to catch up. They tugged at each other's clothes, every movement frantic now, driven by heat and want. Her back smacked the wall hard, but she barely noticed. He pinned her there with his weight, his breathing frantic, and she shivered as his hand slid up her thigh, her skirt pushed high in one swift sweep. Without warning, he dropped to his knees. Calm. Steady, in absolute control. He dragged her panties down in one clean motion and flung them aside.

Then his mouth was on her. No hesitation. No fumbling. Only his tongue, confident, knowing and relentless. He worked her like he'd mapped her body in a dream. Each circle, each flick, pulled a jolt from deep inside her. She clutched his hair, her fingers tight, her head tipping back against the wall. Her breathing came in short, sharp bursts. She could feel herself shaking. She heard him moan. Low and guttural.

'Jesus, Brona, but you're delicious.' The words thick with hunger, like he meant every bloody word.

She was speechless. Could barely breathe. Her body was on fire, nerves lit up. She'd never felt anything like it. With Graham, it had been tender, meaningful, close to sacred. Unforgettable in its own way.

But this? This was entirely different. It was raw, primal, a kind of physical madness that made her toes curl and her head swim. There was no thinking now. No guilt. No wondering. Pure sensation. Need. Her body responding without permission. He was killing her. Yet she didn't stop him. Fingers joined tongue, vigorous and confident, like he knew her body better than she did. She was soaked, breathless, unravelled. Her climax hit fast and without warning. Her body seized, knees buckling, hips jerking, the sound of her moan raw and helpless. She couldn't stop it, couldn't hold it back, completely undone by the sheer force of it. Still, he kept on. His fingers moved faster, more demanding, as his mouth trailed back up to her breasts.

'Stop,' she whispered. 'No more. I can't. I can't—'.

She hustled him, her chest heaving, every muscle trembling.

'What the fuck have you done to me?' she gasped.

Her skirt was still bunched around her waist, blouse gaping, hair clinging to the sweat on her neck. Upright, his eyes swept over her slowly, unhurried, full of knowing. He took in every exposed inch of her like he had all the time in the world. Still, he said nothing. Without thinking, her hand cracked across his face. So hard it hurt. She pushed him off with more strength than he expected, then scrambled to gather her clothes.

'You bastard!' she shouted, her eyes fierce. 'You think you can walk in here without a word for weeks and screw me?!'

Paddy blinked, his hand on his cheek, the sting still fresh. Didn't see that one coming. Not the slap, not the fire in her voice. It caught him off guard, and for a second he stood there bewildered. She was ashamed, no question. Disturbed in a way that had little to do with him, and everything to do with her.

He smiled faintly. Aye, he'd touched a nerve alright. She was furious, sure, but he reckoned more at herself. Not him. She was sorry, gutted at how quickly she'd given in. How easily she'd let herself want him. *Typical women.* He took a deep breath, dragging a hand down his face. The hardness had already left him, the mood soured but not lost. He took a step back, watching her with cool detachment as she yanked her knickers back up, her movements jerky and awkward. She dropped her key, cursed under her breath, then snatched it up again.

Mortified at how she'd lost control, Alice shoved the key in the lock and pushed open the door. Without looking back, she stormed up the narrow staircase to her flat above. Paddy followed, slow and steady, a sly smile tugging at the corner of his mouth. Inside, she disappeared into the bathroom and in fury, slammed the door. After all her game-playing, she hadn't put up much of a fight. Maybe she was trying to pull herself together, hoping to scrape back whatever pride she had left. Couldn't care less, he'd enjoyed himself.

He stood in her living room, looking around with his hands buried in his pockets. It was packed with books of all shapes and sizes. Dee hadn't been joking. It really did look like a bloody library. As he mooched around, his thoughts drifted back to what Dee said. As he peeked about, there wasn't a single piece of paper with Brona's name on it. No personal papers. No letters. No trace of her. He'd laughed it off at the time, called it Dee's usual shite. But now, standing here surrounded by books and very little else, could be his twin had a point.

He moved to the bookshelf and pulled a few books free, flicking through them without the faintest idea of what he hoped to find. A photo, a receipt, a bank statement — anything. Nothing. Page after page, and still nothing. He was halfway through another when he sensed it and looked up. She was there, leaning on the bathroom door, arms folded, her face flushed with fury as she watched him.

'Looking for anything in particular?' she asked, striding over and snatching the book clean out of his hands.

Her attitude was irritating him. That voice, so cool, so collected, so typical English — it made her seem above him somehow, like she thought she had him all figured out.

He kept his voice steady. 'No.'

'Well, maybe now that you're finished, you can fuck away off,' she suggested. She didn't shout it. The look was enough.

Catching him rifling through her things threw her off balance, left her sick to the pit of her stomach. He didn't trust her. Was he testing her? She could feel it in the way he just stood there, in his voice. It felt wrong. Whatever *that* was downstairs, she'd lost her sense of reality, he'd made her weak, and she'd dropped her guard. Him poking around her place like a copper on a search, Alice was kicking herself. Furious, not just with him, but with herself for letting *that* happen. *Fuck.*

'I hate you.' she hissed.

Paddy walked toward her, staring at her the whole time. Alice didn't move an inch, he wasn't going to intimidate her, so she stood her ground and stared right back. The way he studied her — it was as if he could see right through her. Not her face, not even Brona Doyle, but the woman beneath. *Alice*. He could see Alice, her fears and everything she'd hidden from him. The shame. The guilt. The mess in her head. He could see past the persona of the last few months, past the rehearsed lines and practised smiles. Suddenly, she knew she was in danger.

'I know ye do.' he replied. He scoffed, not unkindly, and reached up to brush a strand of hair from her face, tucking it behind her ear with a gentleness that surprised even him.

'But Brona,' he said, low and calm, 'what happened down those stairs was class. So why not stop fightin' it. Pour us a drink, and we'll go do it again, but bed this time.'

He caught it right away. A flash in her eyes, barely there, but enough to see a jolt of excitement, the rush at the idea of going to bed. Any resistance crumbling.

'No.' she whispered.

Alice just stood still, her heart banging like mad, wanting to scream. At him. At herself. Scared as she was, she should've kept it shut, turned her back and told him to get the hell out, but mean it. She didn't; she stayed exactly where she was, her arms limp at her sides, caught between resentment and some twisted desire she didn't get or want to feel. She told herself it was all part of the task. A tactic. Let him think he was winning, let him touch her, let him believe she wanted it too. Wasn't that the plan from day one? Get close, but that close? Even she didn't buy that lie, because this wasn't about an op, a task, not anymore. This was about *him*.

'No. I mean it. I really, really despise you. What you did, what you do to me.'

He shrugged, 'Can't be helped, love.'

That was what she hated most. So laid back. The way he got under her skin, how he made her feel as if she had no say, as if her body belonged to him now, not her. Anger rose in her again, shame hot and sickening, yet she stayed still, barely breathing. She didn't refuse him because deep down she wanted him again. So when Paddy pulled her in and kissed her, she didn't fight. She let him. Her body reacted the way it had before, automatic, conditioned, no longer hers. Not because she wanted to, not because the kiss meant anything, but because she didn't know how to stop him. His mouth was warm, hungry, insistent, kissing her as though he owned the air in her lungs and the heat in her blood. All the same, she kissed him back. Not with passion. Not even with desire. Just quiet surrender. She felt herself slipping again, that slow loss of control she'd sworn wouldn't happen twice. But it was happening, and this time it filled her with a cold, furious shame.

She hated him for it. Hated the way he made her forget who she was. What she was. Hated that a part of her, buried somewhere deep, wanted more of him, when all she was meant to be doing was playing a role. Gathering intel. Watching and listening. This wasn't the op anymore. A disaster waiting to happen and she knew it.

Chapter Sixty-Two

Pissed as a Newt

In The Shamrock, a lock-in was in full swing and Dolores was pissed as a newt. Lonely, fed up, and long past the point of caring, she had her eye on a young fella leaning against the bar, giving her the kind of smile that begged for a shag. He had a daft smile, one that might've put her off another night, but not tonight. Tonight she was drunk enough to enjoy the attention. He caught her eye and didn't look away. *Bold wee shite.* A smile that seemed to say, *Come get me.*

So she did. Or at least, she gave it a good go. Dolores made a beeline for him, swaying like a sailor on payday, and gave a daft, guttural laugh as she stumbled halfway across the room, arms flapping like a bird trying to take off. Even she knew she looked a holy show, but for once, she didn't give a shite. Patrick had finally listened to her, was actually sortin' that bitch out. Wait till—

BANG!

A deafening crash tore through the bar, brutal and sudden. The door burst open, splinters flying, and before anyone could blink, a dozen or so Brits and RUC charged in, rifles raised, helmets gleaming under the strip lights. The place went wild. Glasses shattered. Chairs clattered backwards. Screams burst through the air. Then the yelling came, barked from every direction, slicing through the smoke and drink like razors.

Dolores barely had time to turn her head before she was slammed into the bar, her cheek cracking off the wood. Pain fired down her jaw. An RUC man had her pinned, his knee on her back, twisting her arms high behind her. The room around her was bedlam – men dragged up by the scruff of the neck, women propelled against walls, handbags kicked out of the way like rubbish. Even old fellas weren't spared, slapped to the floor with barely a blink. The soldiers didn't move as if they were here for questions. This wasn't a search. This was restitution.

One young lad made a dash for the fire exit and caught a rifle butt to the belly that folded him over. Another man, grey-haired, shouted, 'You've no right!' and got a slap that sent him flying. His false teeth skittered across the carpet like dice. Dolores tried to fight back, but her legs weren't working, and her head was spinning. Hands dragged at her, rough fingers yanking her across the floor like she was nothing but a sack of coal. Her skirt tore as her knees scraped along the sticky floor. She opened her mouth to shout, to tell them she wasn't armed, that she was nobody, but she never got the chance. The peeler above her grabbed her by the hair, yanked her head back and hissed, 'Feelin' brave, are ye, sweetheart?'

She bit down, tasted blood, fury and shame burning through the haze of drink. The whiff of wet coats, old beer and cheap aftershave clung to the air like a fog. Somewhere behind her, someone vomited near the toilets. Somewhere near the jukebox, a radio crackled, still trying to catch a signal that wasn't there. Then the rifle butt came down with a crack to her temple, quick, clean and final.

Out cold.

Chapter Sixty-Three

Cage 11

Tommy O'Reilly had been asked by Father Connolly to accompany him on a visit to Donal Kyle, a young parishioner recently arrested and now incarcerated in the Maze prison, though Republicans, with grim insistence, still called it Long Kesh. Their visit was to H-Block six, one of the newer wings, cold and sterile, built with precision and intent, not to contain but to dismantle, to strip the men down to the bare bone of themselves and remind them, every second of every day, who was in charge. The British had the audacity to boast of it as one of the most secure prisons in Europe, as if that were some mark of civilised achievement, a badge of honour instead of the shame it should have been.

Donal was barely more than a boy, not long out of school. A child, really, now hardened into silence, stone-faced and burning with a fury that had no room for reason, no space for doubt. He wasn't ready for a place like this, not really. Not for H-Blocks and strip searches and dead air broken only by the bark of orders and the clang of metal doors. He might have wanted it, might have even thought he knew what he was walking into, but Tommy knew the truth – this place chewed grown men to bits.

Cathal Connolly, though no fool to the game being played, clung to his faith in reason, in small miracles. He believed decisions could be turned around, that hard-liners could soften, and that the path back from the brink wasn't delusional. That was why he'd brought Tommy along. Not to preach. Not to scold. But to see if anything human could be reached in the boy before Long Kesh destroyed him.

Tommy knew Donal, he'd watched him grow up and knew the family reasonably well. The Kyles were Creggan Heights through and through, steeped in the blood and grit of Ireland's struggle, their history written in the names of the fallen. Salt-of-the-earth people, with fire in their bellies and memory in their bones. Tommy had grown up alongside Donal's father, Andy Kyle, and had seen the man make a name for himself in the Provos, when he took out a British soldier outside Fort George - that mad dash across no-man's-land that every patrol knew well, and feared more.

Afterwards, Andy had vanished into the shadows, skipping between safe house to safe house in Derry, but never staying long enough to be caught. When the time was right, the Unknowns had smuggled him over the border, hidden in the boot of a car. He turned up again in Buncrana, kept his head down, watched the war burn from a safer distance. For a while at least, he was out of reach, but never truly out of the fight.

Then came the word his mother was on her death bed, and, with no choice, Andy crossed back over the border under the cover of darkness, hoping to make it to her dying bedside for a last few quiet minutes, but it turned out that some gobshite had grassed on him. The Brits lifted him before he even stepped over the threshold.

He'd missed his chance, and her soul passed away a few hours later. Now his son was hooked up too, caught in the same trap that was the Troubles, suffering the same punishment and paying the price for the same choices.

Donal Kyle had the misfortune, or depending on who you asked, the honour, of being the first volunteer to be locked up under the British Government's shiny new set of rules. *Criminalisation*, they labelled it. A neat little policy change designed to strip the men of their political status and, with it, any shred of dignity they had left. No more POW recognition, no acknowledgement of the struggle or the war they believed themselves to be part of. Common criminals now, filed under the same heading as junkies, murderers, and wife-beaters. That was the government's plan. Pretend this wasn't political. Pretend these young men weren't giving up their lives, their futures, for something bigger than themselves.

But the prisoners knew better. The families knew better. The Republican movement? Well, they weren't buying the lie either. Not for a second.

Donal told them to fuck off from day one, refused to wear their uniform, refused to abide by their rules, even refused to say 'sir.'

'They'll have to nail it to my back before I wear their rags,' he'd said. So instead, he'd wrapped himself in a single blanket and shut his gob. What was to be the onset of the *Blanket Protest*.

His father had heard about it while still locked up, held in what the Brits liked to hail as the 'cages'. Shell-like prefab huts that stank of piss, damp, and the kind of memories a man spent years trying to forget. His was Cage 11, the one they used for the old hands who still held political status, the seasoned men who remained determined to carry themselves like they had a purpose to hold on to.

For Andy, it didn't last long. All it took was one screw mouthing off and Andy losing his temper, as he was prone to these days. In no time, he was dragged back into court, slapped with a fresh charge, and, in an instant, his political status whipped away.

They threw him into H-Block 6, same block, same cell as his son, Donal, without so much as a word. So began the Blanket Protest. No uniforms, no privileges, no way to fight back that didn't land them in deeper trouble. The mute space, the stench of their own bodies, and a rough, grey wool blanket pulled round their shoulders as if it could shield them from the hell they were living in.

Cathal prayed Tommy's visit might help. Maybe he could get through to them. There was still time to steer them off this path and conform. But in his heart, he already knew the answer.

No chance they'd budge. Not those two.

Father and son didn't mind the half-mile walk from their cell to the visitors' block. Even in the sagging, oversized boiler suits they were made to wear for visits, they looked composed, determined. It wasn't comfort they were after, not in a place like this. The gravel crunched under their feet as they moved in step, handcuffed side by side, cutting a slow, deliberate path across the grey yard. Heads held high, not in arrogance or defiance, but because there was no sense in giving the screws the satisfaction of seeing them beaten down.

No transport had been offered, but even if it had, they wouldn't have taken it. That walk, bleak and exposed as it was, gave them more than any lift ever could. It gave them air in their lungs, a stretch in their legs, and a sliver of time to feel close to normal again. Even if for a few minutes, they were outdoors, under a wide sky, not buried behind bars and concrete walls. The chill clung to their skin and bit at their faces, but compared to the heat and filth they'd come from, it felt like relief. Closer to freedom.

Their voices stayed low, barely more than a murmur, as they passed quiet words back and forth, not because they were afraid, but because they both knew the score. The towers were fully manned; the cameras rolled day and night, and the screws behind them stayed close, listening in on every breath, every pause, every word they dared to share.

Andy would occasionally glance at his son discreetly. Donal walked with purpose. Shoulders back, chin high, eyes locked straight ahead. There was a stillness about him that hadn't been there before. Something anchored. A quiet defiance Andy knew wouldn't bend. That kind of strength didn't come from nowhere. It came from knowing, day after day, what mattered to the Republicans and what didn't, what you held onto, and what you let go of.

The visitors' room in H-Block 6 was no better than the walk there. It was a long, soulless hall, echoey and unforgiving, lined with partitions barely high enough to give the illusion of privacy. The air was close; the walls were painted that drab, institutional beige that dulled everything, and the strip lighting buzzed overhead with a cold, flickering glare. Each cubicle had a table screwed into the floor and four plastic chairs bolted down and too far apart to touch, with a screw watching every move through the small viewing panels cut into the walls. It didn't feel like a place to visit your loved ones. It felt like a place to remind you who held the keys. There was no warmth, no softness, only that dead hush that sat in the corners of the H-Blocks, waiting to catch every word, every look, every breath.

They stood together. When their names were finally called, both men stepped forward as one, scanning the room with a keen eye that never left them, even in here. It didn't take long to spot the priest. He was standing against the far wall, collar stiff, hands folded in front of him like he was at a wake. His unreadable gaze was already fixed on them. And then there was Tommy O'Reilly, standing off to the side, half in shadow, looking awkward in a way that made Andy smile That was unexpected. He hadn't been told Tommy would be there. Didn't matter, he'd always liked the big fella.

Four visits a month, that was the rule, carved in stone and enforced to the letter. If you were appealing, you might get fifteen minutes, but even that came with conditions. It was all about control. One wrong word and they'd cut the visit short or ban them completely.

Today wasn't the usual visit. Today mattered. It'd be the last visit for both of them. It wasn't about a bit of company or catching up. It was a statement. A quiet but calculated line in the sand. From now on, they wouldn't be part of this illegal fiasco. From now on, it'd be Mass only and nothing else.

They weren't thieves or gangsters or scumbags. They were soldiers. Prisoners of war. Under Article 3 of the Geneva Convention, they had the right to be treated with dignity. The right not to be humiliated. The right to resist. That was what this was about. They'd fought a war and they weren't about to beg. From this moment on, every word they spoke, every move they made, would reflect that. They were done playing by British rules.

Donal felt it first. A quick squeeze of his hand. Barely there, but enough. A silent message from his father passed without words. It didn't go unnoticed. A screw was on them right away, his boots hitting the ground hard as he stormed over, spit flying as he shouted, 'No touchin', fuckin' moron, ye hear me?'

The yell cracked beside Andy's ear. He didn't flinch, but gave a small nod, his face set, jaw clamped shut. The screw's breath stank, a foul mix of cheap whiskey and sweat. *Rotten*. Andy knew that smell. Everyone did. It stuck to the place like mould. Most of the screws drank themselves sideways in one of the five staff clubs around the site. Some of them never went home. They lived there, day in, day out, drinking and brooding, too scared to face the world outside and too angry to admit it. They carried the poison back onto the landings and took it out on the men. Morning shifts were always the worst. Heads pounding, tempers short. The hangovers made them nasty.

Inside the H-Blocks, nothing felt human. It was all hard edges and cold light. The walls were painted a strange dead blue, a colour meant to keep you numb. The floors were bare concrete, swept every day if they needed it. Overhead, the strip lights gave off a low hum, bright but somehow never enough to see by. Faces looked grey under it. Sickly. Worn out. Steel doors lined each wing, shut tight with thick panels for watching. The sound carried too. Every step, every cough, every scrape of a boot bounced back louder, like the place was wired to remind you where you were.

Other than those on the blanket, the cells were no better. A narrow bed bolted to the floor, a stainless toilet with no seat, and a shelf barely big enough for a Bible or a book. The air was always damp, sticking to your skin no matter the weather. Windows, if there were any, were tiny slits high up the wall, the glass thick and filthy. They let in light, but little. No view. No warmth. Only a dull patch of grey sky.

You were watched around the clock. This place wasn't made to hold prisoners. It was made to grind them down, day after day, until the few weaklings started to forget who they were, but the Republicans inside hadn't forgotten. Not one of them. They knew why they were there. They knew what they were fighting for. That's what scared the screws more than anything. That's what kept them awake at night.

As Cathal and Tommy approached and reached to shake their hands, the same guard snarled again. 'I said no touchin'!'

'Don't be worryin' about him, Father,' Andy said, brushing it off with a wave and nodding towards the seats. Then, looking at Tommy, he chuckled. 'Didn't expect to see you here, but fair play, it's good to see ye, Tommy. Sit yourselves down and tell us the craic. We hear damn all in this place.'

Cathal and Tommy glanced at one another, unsure where to begin. The sight of the men in front of them had knocked the wind out of them. The boiler suits hung loose on their frames, way too big, sleeves dangling past the wrists, collars sagging. Their growing hair was unwashed, thick with grease and clumped at the sides, and their beards were wild, patchy and rough, Andy's streaked through with grey. The skin on their faces looked drawn, patchy, almost waxy. Even their teeth were yellowed, caked in a grime that spoke of weeks without a toothbrush.

Donal caught the look that passed between them. The way their expressions dipped, for a second, and how quickly they tried to hide it. He gave a small shrug, forced a smirk that didn't quite reach his eyes.

'We've looked better, I know,' he joked, trying to make light of it. 'But what's botherin' me is me da's drivin' me up the walls with his snorin', Father. Any chance of a word before I throttle him in his sleep? Then I'll *really* be in trouble.'

The tension broke. Connolly and Tommy laughed. Andy gave his son a playful clout. 'Oi! Respect your elders, ye cheeky wee bollocks.'

'I said, NO touchin'!' the PO roared again, his voice cutting the air like a whip.

Andy muttered under his breath, 'Fucking wanker.' Then, glancing at Cathal, added sheepishly, 'Sorry, Father.' The priest smiled, but inside, his heart was breaking.

They chatted a little about the usual stuff. News from home. Who was doing what. All under the shadow of the guard, pretending not to listen.

Eventually, Connolly leaned in. 'Tommy... will you tell them what we talked about?'

Tommy hesitated, glanced at the guard, then at the men across the table. He cleared his throat. 'Fellas, please. This blanket protest... it's killin' ye. Would you not wear the uniform? That way, you could go back to the compound together. Get classes. Better meals. A bit of dignity... a chance to breathe again.'

Neither of the prisoners spoke. Donal stared at the floor. Andy looked up at the ceiling. Tommy saw their answer in their eyes. Stone. Quiet, stubborn, final. He softened. 'In that case, is there anything you need for your next visit? Anything at all?' They shook their heads before Donal said it. 'There'll be no more visits, Tommy.' His words landed like a brick. Tommy blinked. 'How do ye mean? No more visits. Jesus, Donal, what are ye saying'?'

Andy answered for his son. 'It's decided. We want no more visitors. We're doin' okay, Tommy.' He looked at his boy, 'Tell him we're doin' okay, son, tell them. We're together and need nothing' else. We won't give up now.'

Donal nodded while Andy's hand twitched, half-reaching out to his son, but stopped himself. *No touching.* What he'd told them shocked Cathal and Tommy to the core and settled across the table like a black cloud. Nobody tried to move it. Their silence didn't feel deep or dramatic, but uncomfortable, like they all knew there was no going back but didn't know what to say about it either. Andy stayed still. Donal didn't blink.

'So... there's nothin' we can do to change your mind?' Tommy asked.

Andy exhaled. There was no point trying to explain. Not to a priest, and not even to Tommy. They hadn't been inside. They hadn't seen the cells. Each one no bigger than a coal shed, concrete walls caked in brown where lately the lads had no choice but to smear their own shit, because the screws refused to let them out to use the toilet. No bed, no mattress, not even a chair. A plastic po dumped in the corner that stank from the minute they got it. It filled up fast too, especially with two men sharing. When it did, they'd slide it under the door, hoping some screw might take pity. But they never did. Most times, they'd no choice but to pour it straight back in, letting it flood the floor. You'd try using the far corner, thinking maybe you could keep the worst of it away. But then they'd sling your blankets into it, or worse, piss through the hatch and laugh while doing it. The floors were never dry. The walls were never clean. Even the air was thick with rot and bleach and damp. The worst bit was knowing it was premeditated. Every single detail was meant to grind you down. With a smile.

It would only get worse, but none of that mattered. Neither one of them, not for anything, would ever wear Her Majesty's uniform.

Chapter Sixty-Four

Guilt

Back in Creggan, Father McGuire zipped up his battered leather bag containing his few worldly possessions, Bible included, the one he used by bedsides and funerals for longer than he cared to admit. It had taken far more time than he'd expected to settle things in the parish, to tie off loose ends, chase up final calls, and reassure the handful of elderly parishioners who still came by unannounced to say goodbye. But now it was done. He was ready, or as ready as he'd ever be. A few weeks with his sister in Mayo, the one he always got on best with, the only one who still made him laugh without trying, then - well, after that, he hadn't a clue. He wasn't going to stress about it. He'd waited long enough for retirement, and if nothing else, he owed himself a bit of peace.

The migraines were coming more often these days, sometimes bad enough to leave him nauseous by nightfall. He needed rest. Some quiet. The sort of quiet you could only find in a small town where nobody knew you. Maybe he'd get a dog. He'd been saying it for years, always half-serious. A wee loyal mutt from the pen, perhaps.

He took one last look around the room. Blue walls, chipped in places, white trim fading to yellow near the windows, and the same heavy oak bed he'd collapsed into night after night, wrecked from visits, from funerals, from trying to hold too many lives together. The old rug beneath his feet was threadbare in spots, worn down by years of pacing during sleepless nights. The crucifix above the dresser sat crooked, like it always did, and he'd long since stopped fixing it.

Ten years he'd lived in this house. Ten long years, and not one of them easy. It had been the hardest stretch of his priesthood, not because of lack of faith, but because of everything else. The violence. The guilt. The void. It had aged him in ways the mirror could never show, from the inside out, until even the sound of his own voice in the pulpit felt weak, less sure.

Lately, his thoughts had been circling the same faces, the same names. The McLaughlins, including wee Tina. The other women locked away in Armagh. The fellas in the Kesh. The ones who came to him broken or angry or holding it all inside, hoping for answers he didn't always have. His congregation. His community. The ones he'd watched walk back out the church doors with nothing but a whispered blessing and a heavy heart, into a world that gave them no space to grieve, no time to mend.

He told himself he'd done what he could and repeated it often enough that it nearly sounded true. But it never felt like enough. Not really. These days, few spoke of Tina McLaughlin. Not in this diocese. Not even in town. She'd faded from the conversation like a secret no one cared to keep. Governor Yeaman, the eager young bastard, practically crossed the road to avoid him these days when he visited Armagh. Seemed he couldn't look him in the eye. At least Governor Johnston, for all his bluster, had listened now and again, depending on his mood.

Poor Tina... she hadn't said a word when he last saw her. Only offered a faint, distant smile, her eyes glazed over. He wasn't even sure she knew who he was.

Earlier that morning, at what would be his last funeral Mass, they'd buried Paul Kennedy. The poor lad left in a coma after a Pig reversed over him and his friend outside the Cathedral. Another name to add to the list. Another young life snatched and soon forgotten.

The boy's mother sat through the service heavily sedated and stone-faced, her hands folded in her lap, eyes fixed on nothing. She didn't even cry at the grave. Didn't flicker an eyelid. It was as if grief had emptied her out, leaving nothing behind but a shell.

He'd hoped the day might get better after that, that maybe one small thing, would go his way. But it didn't. Instead, Bill Barter turned up by the church gate. The bloody reporter with his thick Yankee drawl skulked like he was waiting for permission to enter. Collar turned up against the wind, notepad tucked tight under one arm, he hovered there on the pavement, rocking on his heels.

They spoke a little small talk to start with, but then Barter hit him with a statement that stopped the old priest in his tracks. 'You do realise what Cathal Connolly's really up to, don't you, Father? Those trips to the States, the fundraising, the speeches? They've raised a small fortune. To buy arms. You ever read one of his NORAID statements, Father? Powerful stuff. Man knows how to work a room.'

Father McGuire knew plenty, but he hadn't quite grasped how far in the young priest had gone. Connolly was close to the bishop too, McGuire should've paid more attention. As his mentor, it might've been his place to step in earlier, ask the right questions. But he was tired now, worn out by the years, and whatever hunger he'd once had for church politics had long since drained away. He no longer kept track of who was climbing the ladder, or who was whispering in whose ear. None of it mattered anymore.

'To be honest with you, Mr Barter, I'm outta here. By this afternoon, I'll be gone.' He wanted no fuss, no big send-off. No speeches or plaques or any of that meaningless pageantry. He wanted to go quietly, no big parties. To their credit, most of his parishioners honoured his wishes, but surprisingly, even Barter hadn't heard the priest was retiring, which was unusual.

'What?! Father, c'mon. You can't do this. People round here respect you. You bail now, it sends the wrong message. It ain't right.'

'Shhh. Stop it. Don't fuss.' Father McGuire snapped. His tone came out sharper than intended, tiredness leaking into it without warning.

Barter took the hint, stepped back. 'Sorry. Of course, Father. Your decision.'

He offered a hand and they shook. Then came a pause. The reporter's mind clearly ticking over, refusing to let go of a potential story.

'Would you let me interview you before you go?' he asked, eyes alight, mentally seeing the headline. 'Talk about your years here, how the city's changed, what it meant, what's next. Could be a good send-off. Say goodbye in your own words. All in one go.'

McGuire thought about it. It wasn't a bad idea, not really, though he wasn't sure he wanted it either. Still, he had to admit; the thought wasn't entirely unwelcome. Might help. Maybe it would give him a chance to say a few things that had been niggling him over the years, if he found the right way to say them. If he got the okay with the bishop, well, there was no harm in thinking it over. That was all he'd do, ask, at least for the time being.

He gave a small nod and said. 'Okay, I'll think about it.'

Only *think* about it? Barter wasn't the type to walk away from a story, not when he could smell a headline from a mile off. This one practically wrote itself. Priest retires after a decade in a war zone. The human cost of faith under fire. Hell, it might even land front page back in Boston. He'd call it an exclusive.

He could see it already. There were thousands of readers across the water hungry for stories like this. A priest who'd lived through it, right in the thick of the Troubles, not hiding behind press releases or stitched-up Church statements. An authentic voice. A man who'd buried more young people than he could count, stood with families in their darkest hours, preached from bloodied altars and still somehow turned up next morning with a clean collar and a quiet prayer.

The old bugger didn't know it yet, but he was gold and all Bill needed was thirty minutes and a quiet room. He could picture the lead already.

'Time Out,' says Father McGuire, the quiet man of Creggan...

By hook or by crook, he'd get it.

Chapter Sixty-Five

Taken

Caitlin was still working at the photographer's, most days spent dressing the front window, rearranging props, hanging new portraits, and pretending she hadn't noticed James Henderson's Jaguar easing past on yet another slow lap of the street.

She'd seen him more than once now, always from behind the glass, always when she wasn't ready. The last time, she was almost certain he'd seen her too. The way their eyes locked for a split second while she adjusted a hanger on a rack of baby pictures near the window. He didn't wave. Didn't slow down. Kept driving, staring straight ahead.

What game was he playing? It might nothing. But then, it meant everything. Maybe he wanted her to know he was still knocking about, unable to stay away, but too much of a wimp to call in. What did that make her? Like she'd seen a ghost, standing there in the middle of the window, watching him vanish up the road like they were strangers, as if that weekend between them hadn't meant a bloody thing? It stank. Every part of it. She wished he'd leave her alone.

Seamus. What a bloody mess that turned out to be. He was gone now, really gone, and like James Henderson, he hadn't looked back either. Flew off to wherever, leaving a great big gaping hole in his place.

Martin had made the odd comment over the weeks. Nothing cruel, but a slight teasing in his voice, a tilt of his head, a raised eyebrow that said more than the words did. Things like, 'Haven't seen Seamus about lately,' or, 'Thought you might've had him at the christening.' Eventually, as expected, he grew tired of skirting around it and came straight out with it. When he did, his voice was far gentler than she'd expected.

'What happened to youse two, Caitlin? I mean Seamus. He's a lovely fella.' She told him she didn't want to talk about it, and fair play to him; he let it go.

As for Tina, that last visit to Armagh Gaol had been a shambles from the moment she left the house. She'd taken the bus. Tina's food parcel, including her favourite Wagon

Wheels, safely on her lap. She hadn't spoken a word, hadn't looked at anyone, stared blankly out the window while the fields flew by. The heating on the bus had packed in, and she, along with the rest of the passengers, spent the journey hunched in their coats, teeth chattering, breath misting up the windows as the bus bounced their way through the freezing Irish countryside.

Once inside Armagh Gaol, Caitlin queued up in the usual spot, inside the circle with the other families, her parcel still in hand and holding tight to a bag of craft supplies she'd picked up in *Wellworths*. Then, as they began calling names, a guard stepped forward and told her Tina wasn't well enough for visitors. Even though Caitlin begged, the PO wasn't having it.

That alone would have been hard enough to swallow, but after the long journey, the waiting, the nerves, and the quiet hope of finally seeing Tina, what made it even worse, what really stuck in her throat, was the cocky, self-satisfied look on the prison officer's face. She'd been thrilled at sharing such news to the lanky girl, who looked nothing like Tina McLaughlin.

Prison Officer Smyth, squat and thick-shouldered, stood by the door like a nightclub bouncer, arms folded tight across her chest, her coal-black hair scraped back so severely it looked like it had been painted on. That smug little smile of hers didn't move, the kind that told you straight off she took satisfaction in delivering bad news. She didn't even glance up when Caitlin stepped forward with the food parcel and the few bits she'd brought for Tina. With a lazy shake of the head, she turned and walked away, leaving Caitlin standing there like a buffoon, holding onto the bloody stuff. An older woman next to her, someone who knew the ropes, moved in and said kindly, 'Try not to let her get to you, love. Smyth does that kinda thing all the time. Wants to annoy ye. That's all.'

But it had annoyed her. Of course it had. The frustration of Smyth's attitude went deep with Caitlin, and by the time the bus turned back towards Derry, the feeling of helplessness was taking her down. That ache in her chest, that horrible twist in her gut, like no matter how hard she tried, she couldn't get in to see her own sister. Couldn't even pass over a food parcel. By the time she got back to the house, she was drained, hollowed out, furious and ready to kill. What the friggin' heck was she going to do? This wasn't a life!

These days, the only joy she had came from Anne and the baby, Sean. The christening had gone better than she'd imagined. Anne had looked almost radiant, somehow managing to hold it all together with grace, her face calm, her eyes calm, even though Caitlin knew her nerves were in ribbons. Sean had slept through most of it, unbothered by the fuss, by the crowd, by the handful of people watching him like he was the last good thing left in the world. Somehow, though she still couldn't quite figure out how, Dickie had wormed his way into the role of godfather, standing up front like he was born for it, smug as anything, like he should've been the baby's father. Even Porkie hadn't looked too happy about it, and if he wasn't right, Caitlin knew it could only mean trouble. She'd never taken to Dickie, not from the first second she clapped eyes on him. He gave her the heebie jeebies. That greasy smile of his so fake. Always seemed to look at her a second too long, those darting beady eyes snooping about, sizing people up like he was making a mental list. His so-called jokes had started off bad and only got worse, each one filthier than the last, the kind of muck he thought made him dead funny when really, it made your skin crawl.

A proper sleaze was what he was. Like one of those slimy villains off the TV, the kind that leered through the screen in *Doctor Who* or some late-night Hammer horror, the ones you knew were rotten before they even opened their mouths. She couldn't think of a better way to describe him. Hadn't trusted him then and certainly didn't now.

Oooh. The very sight of him was enough to make her flesh crawl.

Anne, for all her quiet strength, was still on edge most of the time, running on nerves and not much else. It was worse at night, way worse. Every knock or creak had her stiffen, hands gripping the sides of the chair, waiting.

Waiting for them. *The Provos.*

So when the banging started, hard and fast, fists hammering the front door late one evening, Anne nearly jumped clean out of her skin.

'Fuck it, Porkie. If that's Dickie, I swear to Christ, I'll kill him,' she snapped, already on her feet. 'I've only got the baby down!' She didn't wait for a response, didn't even glance at her excuse of a husband, but stormed out of the chair and made straight for the stairs, fists clenched and raging. Let him open it!

Porkie was already on his feet, his heart thudding fast and wild, like a trapped bird slamming itself against the inside of his chest. This was it. After all the warnings, the rumours, the half-whispers in bars and back lanes, the waiting was finally over. Oddly enough, in the middle of all the panic rising up his throat, he felt something else: a strange, unexpected relief.

As he opened the front door, he heard Anne's voice behind him, half-whispering in that way she did when the baby was finally down, and then her footsteps coming down the stairs. She stopped at the bottom, and together, they both saw them. Two men stood on the threshold, wearing dark green army trousers and zipped up jackets, the kind that bristled with purpose. Their faces were covered. Scarves pulled up high, hats down low, sunglasses hiding whatever was left. Each of them held a pistol as if it were nothing more than an everyday habit. The taller fella stepped forward, his voice calm but unmistakably Derry.

'Mrs Ballantyne, you'd better step back now. We need to take your husband for a wee run.'

Anne was petrified. She knew she couldn't scream, couldn't do anything rash, not with the baby lying safely upstairs. She backed away from the hall, forcing herself to stay quiet, while they grabbed Porkie by the scruff of the neck, dragged him out the door, and flung him hard onto the cold pavement.

She couldn't stop herself, but screamed as they laid into him. Vicious kicks to the back, the head, anywhere they could land a boot, and as her voice broke from the effort, a wailing cry came from the small upstairs bedroom. Sean. Torn between whether to leave Porkie or go upstairs to the baby, she stood stock-still. Her wild eyes looked around the street, praying for someone to come out, to help, to speak or step forward, but all she saw were net curtains twitching and faces peering out from behind glass. No one came. Not when it was men like this. A grass. It was common knowledge what a punishment squad looked like, and anyone with a bit of sense avoided them like the plague.

One of the masked men yanked Porkie to his feet, twisting his arms hard behind his back and securing them with a length of thick cable before forcing him forward, nudging him towards a waiting car with its engine already running, exhaust coughing into the quiet street like a warning. The second man, slower and more frightening, turned and began walking back towards her. Anne hadn't moved, but stood rooted to the spot, her arms locked and stiff at her sides, her whole body vibrating with the kind of fear that makes it impossible to run. When he stopped right in front of her, close enough that she could see the edge of his scarf rise and fall as he breathed, she heard it, that rasp in his voice, low and dry, cutting through the wool like a blade.

'Say nothin' to anyone, Mrs Ballantyne. That husband of yours has done enough talkin' already.' Anne nodded as the car pulled away with Porkie in the back, disappearing down the road with no urgency at all. She knew with a cold, sinking certainty that he was a goner.

Chapter Sixty-Six

Die Grass

Porkie never came home.

As soon as it was light, Anne dressed the baby and caught the first bus to Creggan to see Father Connolly. She hadn't slept a wink. Her chest felt jittery, and her hands shook as she clipped the baby's coat closed. She needed to talk to someone about what would happen to her and the baby now. The journey dragged on, slow and torturous, and it wasn't until they were well on their way that she realised she'd forgotten the baby's dummy. Sean, already fretful from a broken night, grew more and more unsettled in her arms, twisting and fussing, picking up on the tension she couldn't hide. He could feel it in her grip, in her breathing, in the way her heart thudded against his tummy. He even refused his bottle, pushing it off with a furious little fist, arching his back and letting out a scream so fierce it felt like his tiny body might tear itself in two.

Anne stared out the window, her eyes fixed on nothing, the tears slipping down her cheeks before she even realised they were there. She didn't wipe them away. Let them fall. Let anyone watching see. She was too tired to care anymore. Too worn down to pretend.

The baby was anxious, his little body tense against her, so she rocked him gently, her hand moving in slow circles on his back the way her mother once had. She even tried humming, soft and low, anything to soothe him, to soothe herself, but nothing worked. His tiny body wriggled and fussed, feeding off her tension. All the while, her thoughts kept racing, looping round and round, loud and unforgiving. Sean caterwauled, wild and inconsolable, his cries fierce, long and unbearable, cutting through her heartstrings. Then came a voice beside her. A woman, older, soft-faced, smelling faintly of violets, eased herself into the seat next to Anne and held out her arms. 'Here, love. Let me have a wee hold.'

The young mother passed the baby over and, to her astonishment, watched the stranger slip a bent thumb between Sean's lips. In seconds he was quiet, sucking away like it was the most natural thing in the world. Her relief was sublime. 'Thank you,' she sniffed, wiping her face, embarrassed now by her tears. She imagined what she looked like. A bad mother, a mother who couldn't cope.

'It's all right, love. Settle yourself there a minute,' the woman whispered. 'Where ye off to?'

'St Mary's. I need to see Father Connolly,' Anne said, reaching for a crumpled tissue from her pocket, her nose running like a train. The woman gave her a look, soft, almost apologetic. 'Ah, pet... sure he's away off to America, I heard meself. This mornin'.'

Anne scoffed. For a second, she didn't quite take it in, and then she remembered. 'Course he was. Of course he fuckin' was. He'd told her he was going! She looked down the aisle to see where the bus might stop next, scanned the signs through the misted windows, and made a snap decision. If she couldn't see the priest, she'd go see her mother. She thanked the woman again, took back her now-snoozing baby, and got off at the next stop nearest to her old house.

Later that day, when Caitlin locked up shop and turned to leave, she was startled to find Anne standing outside with Sean in her arms. The baby was half-asleep, his face blotchy, and Anne didn't look much better with her eyes red and raw, her cheeks streaked from crying, and just about holding herself together like she was trying not to fall apart.

Caitlin ran to her. 'Jesus, Anne, what are you doing out here? Why didn't you come in? It's been dead in there this past hour. I could've finished early. What's happened? It's that fuckin' Porkie again, isn't it?'

Anne didn't answer straightaway. Stood still, looking at nothing in particular, unsure of how much more she could take.

Earlier, as planned, she'd gone to her mother's for help, or comfort, or anything, and it had all gone to hell the moment she's opened her mouth. When she reported what had happened, what Porkie had done, Liz Heaney had flown into a rage, shouting loud enough to shake the windows and demanding why Anne hadn't told her before. She was worse than fuming, not at the danger it put her family in, but by the shame of it, the scandal, the gossip it would cause. She too had taken money from Porkie, willingly, gratefully even, so what the hell would the neighbours think now when they heard?

'Does that make me a grass as well? Is that what your tellin' me? Are we all on their fuckin' list now?' Liz screamed. Her voice soared, higher and higher, as she shrieked out her rage, terrifying poor Sean into another wailing fit and sending Anne's younger brothers and sisters running up the stairs like mice under fire.

Anne had tried to explain what she knew over her mother's constant yelling, tried to reason with her. 'Jesus, Mammy. Listen to me, please! I need help. Can't you see that? Don't you get it?'

But Liz wouldn't hear a word of it, she'd stormed upstairs, and when Anne tried to follow her, she stood at the top of the landing and bellowed down at her, her face and voice shaking with fury and fear. 'Go to hell Anne! All you've ever done is bring trouble to this house! You're a piece of shit! Now fuck away off. Outta me sight!'

So Anne left, humiliated beyond words, full of sadness more than anything. After that, she'd walked aimlessly around the town for a while and ended up in Brooke Park, where she sat alone for hours by the pond, Sean asleep on her shoulder, she watched couples pass by, hand in hand and wondered what it might feel like to live someone else's life. Not to be Anne Heaney. Most of the couples looked so happy. At least they did to her. Who knows?

Eventually, when she couldn't sit any longer and the sky had dimmed, she'd made her way to Caitlin and waited outside the shop, not knowing what else to do.

'It'll be fine, Anne,' Caitlin said, wrapping her arms around both mother and baby. 'Come on. Let's get you home to our house. You can tell me what's happened then.'

When they reached Blamfield Street, Caitlin was straightaway up at the gas meter, rummaging for coins and topping it up. The place was freezing, always was these days. The kitchen was so cold for the baby that she lit and cranked the gas rings up high to warm the place a bit.

Anne was changing Sean on her knee, cooing to him as he kicked and gurgled, completely unaware of the insanity around him. Caitlin busied herself making tea, slicing bread, slathering toast with butter. She watched Anne closely, noting the fatigue behind her eyes, the set of her shoulders. Once the mugs were filled and toast stacked on a plate, she passed it over and said gently, 'Go on, then. Tell me all.'

Anne needed little coaxing. She was starving, hadn't eaten since yesterday, so she gobbled down the toast, talking through mouthfuls. 'Jesus, Caitlin, I've known for ages Porkie and Dickie were grasses! I told Father Connolly about it all when I was in St Mary's, wasn't a full confession like, but near enough. I swear, but he told me to keep me mouth shut. Now the Provos have taken Porkie!'

Caitlin stared at her friend, too thrown to respond straight away. For a split second, the idea sounded so daft it nearly pulled a laugh from her, but there was nothing funny about it. She'd never once believed those two eejits were capable of anything serious, let alone dangerous. Grasses? Christ, the pair of them could barely tie their own laces. Thick as mince always had been. But once the shock settled, her head kicked into gear, and the more she thought about it, the more it started to make a horrible sort of sense. There had been talk, now that she thought of it. Mutters about the young priest. People saying he was connected, even a Provo himself. She hadn't paid it much heed at the time, but now, with this, she wasn't so sure. Maybe those whispers hadn't been so far off after all. Still, could he have really squealed on Porkie?

'He wouldn't have said anything, could he? I mean, he was the one who told you to say nothin, and in the confessional.' Caitlin asked. Anne shook her head. 'Wasn't in the confessional. I couldn't fit in. It was outside. Anyway, who else could it have been?' She hoped it wasn't him, but either way, it didn't matter. It didn't matter who said what. Porkie was gone and it was her fault.

Caitlin sighed, 'Fuck, Anne. You should've told me. No wonder he's lost all that weight. He was disappearing in front of ye. Must've been shitting himself all this time.'

Anne nodded, her eyes wide and brimming, her voice barely together. 'Must've been, God love him. But no matter what I said or asked him, I couldn't get him to say it outright. I heard him and Dickie talkin' one night, whisperin' in the kitchen, but I didn't push it. Kept quiet, and the next day, I went to see Father Connolly. Porkie's been walkin' on ice for ages now. Proper scared and jumpy as hell. Actually, he's been lovely with me and the baby. I don't know! I can't stop thinkin', maybe I shouldn't have said. Left it. Got him to tell me everything. Do ye think I could've stopped him?'

Her words came faster now, tumbling out like the pressure inside her had nowhere else to go. 'I blame that fucker Dickie, I do. He's the one who dragged Porkie into this mess. You know what Porkie's like. He's weak, a dimwit, an eejit, for fuck's sake. Then the same boy, after your Seamus left, insisted Porkie make him godfather. Arrogant wee shite. Can you believe it? The cheek of him! Everything. Everything, Caitlin, it's all Dickie's fault, and it makes me sick to me heart talkin' about it.'

She paused again to catch her breath before the next wave of panic hit. 'I'm shittin' bricks, Caitlin. I swear I am, because I took money from him. For the baby. For nappies and milk and a bloody pram. What if the Provos think that I was a grass? What if they think I'm in on it too? Ah, sweet Jesus.'

She stopped, long enough to slurp her tea, her hands trembling as she held the mug. Still sobbing, she added, 'What am I gonna to do? They'll kill him. I know they will. Both of them. I don't give a fuck about Dickie, but Porkie, he loves Sean.'

She cried on and on, yet her words flowed uninterrupted. 'And Mammy. Jesus, me mammy, lost the plot when I told her. Telling me to fuck off. Screamed at me in front of the wains, like I was filth and threw me out. Said I'd brought nothing but trouble to our house. Like I was a piece of shit stuck under her shoes.' Her voice caught on her last words - *shit* – and the tears streamed down her face, her whole body trembling. Right on cue, Sean began howling, twisting in her arms, his tiny fists clenched, his face scrunched up with her grief and sobs.

Caitlin stood up without saying a word and made her way over to lift the baby gently into her arms. She cradled him close, rocking him with slow, constant movements as she paced the kitchen, the gas rings beginning to give off a sorry bit of warmth. She didn't need to think it over. Anne and the baby were her responsibility now, and that was that. They were all she had left, and no matter how dangerous things got, she wouldn't leave them on their own.

'You'll stay here,' Caitlin said, her voice firm. 'For as long as you want. We'll make up a bed for the baby with the sofa cushions. I'll go speak to Father Connolly. He'll know what to do next.'

Anne shook her head. 'Ah, Caitlin... he left for America this morning.'

Caitlin bit her lower lip, thinking. 'Right well. Then we'll go to Tommy. He'll help us find Porkie, find out what'll happen. It'll have to be Tommy. We've no choice.'

In the end, Anne didn't stay at Caitlin's long. One night. Sean hadn't settled. He needed his cot, his own blankets, his wee routine, even if Anne's life was falling apart. He could probably sense things were off from her fear, her shame, the not knowing of what would come next. Anne was sure he felt it all.

Caitlin had tried to talk her out of leaving, her concern clear. 'You know you can stay as long as you like. Both of you,' she'd said, handing over Anne's bag and brushing the baby's cheek with a finger.

'I know, love. But I need to get him home. He needs his cot, his own corner,' Anne said, her voice low and sad. She pulled Caitlin into a hug, thanked her once more, and started the walk to the bus stop. She wasn't okay. Not even close. But she felt the pull of Shantallow, the need to be back in her own space, to close her front door and bar out the world. Maybe Porkie would come back. Maybe he wouldn't. For now, it was her, the baby, and the long journey home.

That evening, Anne sat on the edge of her sofa, clutching Sean so tightly to her chest he could barely wriggle, her cheek resting on the top of his soft head as tears slid quietly down her face, one after the other. The Brits stormed through the house, tearing it apart like they always did. Drawers were pulled open and emptied onto the floor without a second glance, their contents flung across the room like junk. Cushions were hurled aside, rugs kicked back, cupboard doors slammed with enough force to rattle the windows. Rifles jabbed into corners and behind furniture, poking through shadows, searching for God knows what. None of it made sense, and all of it felt wrong.

Sean whimpered in her arms, his tiny fists curled, the noise and the pressure getting to him. She rocked him, barely breathing and whispering, 'It's alright, sweetheart, shh now, Mammy's got ye.' But her voice shook, and the lie tasted bitter on her tongue. The Brits didn't care that she was there. Didn't care that she was holding a newborn baby.

One soldier, a skinny one, ugly as sin, kicked open the under-stairs door like he was storming a bunker, then turned and grinned when he saw her watching. Her heart dropped like a stone. They wouldn't find anything, but they'd still leave the place upside down. Raiding was a sport to them so she gave up. They could wreck the place for all she cared.

As if sensing her submission, Sean quietened, his crying fading into soft little hiccups that escaped against her chest while she rocked him gently in her arms, whispering shh and shh, over and over again, like some kind of desperate spell she was trying to cast, not only to soothe him but to keep herself right too. The rhythm of it, the closeness, the warmth of his tiny body against hers, it was the only thing stopping her from losing it completely.

The word was out, no doubt about that. Not a single neighbour had come near her, not a knock on the door, not even a face at a window pretending to tidy a curtain. As if she'd disappeared from the street entirely. Everyone knew. Knew not to be seen near the Ballantyne's house. Knew exactly what it meant. If there'd been even the smallest shred of doubt left in her mind, the fresh red spray paint on the front door confirmed it all.

Big block letters, still dripping wet.

DIE GRASS

Chapter Sixty-Seven

We're Dead!

Out of nowhere, the Brits came roaring up the other side of the mountain, a full convoy of Saracens and Land Rovers, headlights glaring through the dark like a warning. Dickie's heart nearly stopped. He ducked low, hand fumbling for the keys, and turned the ignition with fingers that didn't want to work. The van coughed, caught, and roared to life. He jammed it into gear and took off, tyres spitting gravel as he tore down the lane, half-blind, his gut turning like a hamster's wheel.

A couple of hundred yards down, he stopped and watched the mountain light up. A low boom rolled across the valley, then another, louder this time, and then the screaming started. The sky above flared orange, smoke billowing like a nightmare come to life. He didn't have to look to know what had happened. The bastards had done it. They'd only gone and blown the place sky high.

And him? He'd been parked there like a wally, sitting in the middle of it, none the wiser. McLaughlin had known. That look, that voice, all calm and full of shite. He'd known. Likely they'd legged it soon as they left him, gone through the fields or the hedges or God knows where, and left him to take the heat. They'd tricked him, plain and simple. He'd handed over the script like a good little tout and marched straight into their trap. A decoy, no more than that. Just enough intel to sound believable, just enough to make sure the Brits turned up, armed and ready.

Internally, he was screaming. Certainly not audibly, but silently, within his gut, where panic dwells and grows. That barn was bait. Every inch of it. The shouting, the clatter of crates, the noise, even those Irish-speaking voices he'd heard earlier, all of it had seemed so real. He'd told himself it was men shifting gear, getting ready for the next op. But no. All of it, every last bit, was a set-up. A performance. He'd been the mug who bought a ticket. The fuckers. The lying, sneering, two-faced bastards.

If only he'd—

But he didn't finish the thought. The van skidded around a bend, and he kept going, because now he knew. He wasn't running from the Provos now. He was running from the Brits too! He was fucked. He didn't wait, didn't stop to think, just legged it. By the time he hit the first turn into town, he knew he had two choices. Run or die. Simple as that. But even as he made for the safety of his own home, part of him knew it was probably too late. It was time to get out of Derry, fast, before they came to make an example of him. If they weren't already on the move, they soon would be, and once they got their hands on him, he'd be lucky to keep his kneecaps, never mind his life.

He burst through the front door of his house, slammed it behind him and locked it out of habit, as if that flimsy little Yale lock was going to stop what was coming. His heart was hammering so hard it made his head ring, making it impossible to think. But the second he turned into the living room, he came to a stop. Too late. They were already there.

Not sitting, because they couldn't. The sofa was piled high with takeaways, greasy wrappers, empty tins and ash-covered plates. But they stood there, calm as you like, masks over their faces, weapons slung loose like they'd only popped in for a cuppa and were waiting to be offered a seat and a biscuit while the kettle boiled.

Without asking, Dickie's arms shot up. 'Take it easy, all right! Don't shoot!'

It didn't matter what he said, or how he tried to reason it. None of it mattered now. Rough hands were already on him, yanking his arms back, binding his wrists tight with what felt like coarse rope or cable, biting into the skin. Before he could even catch a full breath, they'd yanked a filthy sack down over his head, the stink of oil and mould making him want to gag. He was dragged backwards through the kitchen and out the back door, stumbling over the step, boots scraping the path as he tried to stay upright, but it was hopeless. Somewhere nearby, an engine was running, low and steady, idling like it was in no rush at all, like it had all the time in the world to take him wherever he didn't want to go.

Then came the shove. Hard and fast. He was flung into the back of the van like a sack of spuds, no warning, no hesitation, his body slamming onto the cold metal floor with a sickening thud that knocked the wind clean out of him. He barely had time to move, couldn't even figure out which way was up, before a boot came down with full force, right between his balls, crushing him where it hurt most.

'Jesus fuck!' he howled, writhing in pain, voice bouncing off the metal walls. 'Me balls! Jesus, youse have wrecked me fuckin' balls!' But there was no answer, but the sound of the door slamming shut behind him.

Then, out of the shadows, a voice. 'Dickie...? Is that you, Dickie?'

He howled, teeth clenched, 'Yes, it's me, you jerk! They've crushed me fuckin' nuts!'

Porkie, hooded and bound, followed the sound of Dickie's voice, scrambling his way across the floor of the moving van towards him.

'We're dead, Dickie,' he snivelled. 'We're dead. What the fuck are we gonna do?' This time Dickie didn't answer.

Porkie swallowed hard, his throat thick with fear, and the tears came quickly now, hot and helpless, streaking down his cheeks. They kept coming. Dickie always knew what to do, he'd have a daft line, an excuse, some half-cobbled story that would buy them a bit more time or wriggle them out of the worst sort of trouble, but not this time. Lying there with his chest rising fast, heart thudding so loud it sounded like it was trying to dig its way out of his ribs, Porkie waited, desperate for Dickie to say something, anything, to crack a joke, to pull a miracle out of a hat the way he sometimes did, anything that might make this feel like it wasn't the end. Under his stinking hood, he closed his eyes and pictured his newborn son.

Ashling McKenna looked across at Emmett McFadden, who was hunched in the driver's seat, his mouth twitching as if he'd swallowed a live frog. She'd seen that look before, more than once, usually when things were about to turn serious. Emmett was the type who always seemed half-terrified of his own shadow, yet never said no when asked to show up. It was close to three in the morning and the industrial estate in Pennyburn was silent, apart from the occasional rattle of a loose shutter in the wind and the restless tapping of Emmett's fingers on the steering wheel.

Right on cue, the van appeared from the far end of the yard, a plain white box speeding through the gate with its lights off, cutting through the dark. As it reached them, it gave a quick flash of the headlights, one blink, deliberate, like something lifted straight out of a low-budget spy drama. Two men jumped out, both in dark clothes with balaclavas pulled tight over their faces, and without a word, they yanked open the backdoors. Out came two figures, hooded, staggering, stinking of piss and sheer panic. A fat one made a half-hearted run for it, legs kicking out wildly, but he barely got three paces before one of the masked men brought him down hard with a boot to the back. No shouting, no ceremony, only fast, cold efficiency. Ashling didn't recognise them and didn't want to. She kept her face neutral and waited.

After gags were roughly wound around their mouths, the hostages were bundled into the boot of Emmett's banger like sacks of turf, their muffled noises barely making it through the layers of cloth. Emmett's hand trembled on the key, but he didn't say a word and waited. The two masked men hopped back into their van without a glance back, the driver slamming it into gear so fast the tyres squealed as it tore out of the yard, leaving behind nothing but the faint stink of diesel and nerves.

Ashling gaped at Emmett, who stood stone-faced. 'Jesus, Mary and Joseph. What was that?'

He shook his head and said miserably, 'Get on with it, will ye?' Get it over.'

God love him. Ashling could hear the quiver in his voice and was half-tempted to reach out and give his arm a pat, like you would a frightened child. Instead, she shot him a look. Not unkind, but firm, a clear signal for him to get a grip. Emmett didn't appreciate it. She caught the flash of offence in his face, that quick flare in his eyes, before he turned away in disgust, but she only smiled and reached for the backpack.

Inside, tucked beneath what looked like a couple of towels and a loaded torch, were their written instructions. She pulled them out, unfolded them carefully, and read through each line under the faint orange glow from the car's interior light. Emmett leaned in, squinting, hands still trembling slightly, as if the paper itself might go up.

Chapter Sixty-Eight

Fish Food

Later, when they arrived at the safe house, a sad-looking red-brick bungalow with rotting windowsills and grass growing up through the cracks in the path, Emmett parked up slowly and silently. Together, they hauled the two souls out of the boot and dragged them through the back door. You didn't have to be any sort of genius to tell the smaller one had peed himself. An immediate, sharp, sour smell hit them, followed by soft sobbing that spoke volumes. The fat one was quiet. Too quiet. What was he up to?

To make sure, Ashling yelled, 'On the floor. Now!'

She didn't care who this pair were or what they'd done. Her job was to deliver, nothing more, nothing less. Keep it tidy, follow orders, hand them over in one piece. Truth be told, if Emmett's hands shook any harder, she'd end up doing the whole bloody thing herself.

Dickie and Porkie sat side by side in a stale, freezing living room with the curtains half-drawn, their heads still wrapped in coarse sacks that reeked of whatever had been thrown in them last. The air was close, tainted with the smell of old fags, and Dickie could hear every strained breath Porkie drew, each rasp louder than the one before.

He wriggled, shifting this way and that way in the chair, wrists raw beneath the ropes, trying to find a position that might give him some kind of edge, some bit of slack, some hope, but the cords cut deeper each time. No sound came from outside, no footsteps, no voices, no hint that anyone would come. The realisation hit him hard. They were well and truly fucked. Dumped here to wait. Panic rose in him like bile, sharp and burning, and he lashed out suddenly with both feet, kicking blindly, his boot smacking against Porkie's leg with a dull thud. He didn't care if he hurt him. Maybe the useless wanker would come up with a way to get the hell out.

Porkie groaned and curled into a ball, his whole body shaking. What the hell had he done? The shame of it all, he'd been so stupid to listen to Dickie, and the panic came right after. He wanted to take it all back, undo every second, but it was too late. He'd crossed the line, and now all he could do was lie there, hating himself, terrified of what came next.

Dickie kept going, thrashing and twisting, as if sheer panic alone might set him free, but it was hopeless. Every movement drained more from him until he was left panting and sweating, muscles aching, heart hammering so hard he could barely breathe. In the end, he stopped fighting, closed his eyes and did the only thing he could do. He prayed.

Morning broke grey and bitter, the kind of cold that went right through you. Emmett and Ashling crept back into the front room, neither of them saying much, their movements slow and stiff like they'd both aged ten years overnight. She'd managed a couple of hours stretched awkwardly on the grotty sofa, coat zipped to her chin, boots on, one arm tucked under her head for a pillow.

Emmett hadn't fared as well. He'd spent most of the night hunched over the kitchen table, head buried in his hands, thinking God knows what. When Ashling muttered a quiet 'morning' on her way through, he didn't answer, but gave her a brief nod, eyes down, face drawn, still feeling like shit. If he, their captor, felt this bad, Emmett could only imagine what the two poor bastards tied up in the next room were feeling.

He stood over them now, quiet for a moment, before reaching down and yanking the hoods clean off. The light was brutal. Bright, direct, unkind. With their arms secured behind their backs, there was no shielding from it. The bigger fella didn't move at all, eyes open, dry, fixed on some spot beyond the room. But the smaller one, wiry, dark-haired, jittery, scanned every inch of the place in sharp, jerking movements, chest rising fast, mouth twitching, panic already clawing up his throat as soon as he clocked the figure standing a few feet in front of him.

Dickie tried to scream. Tried to tell them who he was, tried to get them to understand. But the tape across his mouth muffled every word into useless noise. He writhed about, eyes wide and wild, forcing out panicked grunts, willing someone, anyone, to recognise him and stop this from going where it was going.

The young fella in the parka didn't say a word. Just fumbled into his coat, one hand shaking as it disappeared inside. Out it came. A pistol. Small, black, glinting in the harsh light. Dickie's eyes locked on it, horrified. The lad looked holding the thing looked as shit scared as Dickie was in seeing it, his knuckles white where he gripped it too tight, like he wasn't sure if he was meant to shoot it or drop it. But the decision, it seemed, had already been made.

He stepped forward, raised the gun slowly, and pressed the barrel right under Dickie's chin. Dickie sensed the lad's fear and nervousness, he was new to all this. *Advantage, Dickie.*

Dickie tried one more time. He gave a strangled cry behind the tape, loud and desperate, pushing it out with every bit of panic in him, trying to make himself heard, trying to sound human, trying to stop this. But it came out wrong, a cracked, broken sob that filled the room and hung there, useless and pitiful. It wasn't a voice anymore, not really. Noise. Frantic, ugly, full of dread. He was pleading without words, and the worst part was knowing it wouldn't change a thing.

'Stop screamin' will yeah, or I'll do it! I'm taking the tape off so you can drink, ye eejit, but one sound, one move, and I'll shoot ye,' the scared fella cried.

Dickie gave a nod, his heart beating a mile a minute. He turned to Porkie, desperate for some support, a bit of backbone, an exit, but the wally gawked back, as much use as a chocolate teapot in a bonfire.

Ashling and Emmett peeled back the hardened tape from their prisoners' mouths to get water down their gobs. Bitter stuff laced with the necessary. Dickie gulped it, his throat raw. His eyes nearly popped clean out of his head. Jesus Christ almighty, it was Emmett McFadden from McCafferty's garage. The one who'd serviced his old car before he traded it in at Desmonds!

As the man moved back, the gun still shaking in his grip, Dickie took his chance. 'Hey fella. You know me. It's me! Kevin McDaid! Remember? Left me car in with ye, for a service. I was sellin' it?'

The fella didn't move a muscle, but Dickie noticed his eyes moving. The fear of being recognised. Then panic.

Emmett's hand trembled so violently that he almost dropped the gun. He staggered back as if he'd been struck, slid down the wall and crumpled into a heap, his hands covering his face. Dickie stared at him in disbelief. This wasn't some Provo hard man. This was a bloody kid. A scared, shaking one. That's what terrified Dickie more than anything. Because a panicky gunman's finger was well more dangerous than a calm one.

Ashling had been watching Emmett all night. She'd sensed the fear coming off him the moment they'd read their orders in the car. It was a shame. She quite liked him. A decent enough lad, smart in his own way, but he didn't have the nerve for this. She'd have to feed it back. McFadden was a liability now, and this op had quietly become solo. If it was going to be done right, it was down to her now.

Decision made, Ashling yanked the gag back over Dickie's sodden mouth and leaned in close. 'Shut your hole, ye arse head. Hear me? Not another word.' She did the same to Porkie, then slipped the dark hoods back over their heads. Wouldn't be long now. The drug had kicked in.

Porkie seemed ready to sink into it without a fight, but Dickie was wriggling and twitching, resisting whatever was flooding his system. Emmett, poor bastard, was staring at the scene like a man watching his own funeral. Ashling gave him nothing. She couldn't afford sympathy now.

'Time to move on!' she snapped.

Emmett drove the Austin around to the back of the house and popped the boot. Together, they hefted the bigger man first, breathless with the effort, then the second one, easier by comparison. Both men were covered with blankets and stowed away.

At the border checkpoint, a horrendous queue had formed. Army vehicles were everywhere. All on high alert. Ashling caught Emmett's look and moved in, her voice low. 'Time for an Oscar performance,' she murmured, tilting her head towards him.

'Imagine I'm talkin' dirty,' he said with a nervous but convincing chuckle, nodding as his heart pounded, the car moving slowly.

Ashling adjusted her face into a lazy smile, resting a hand lightly on his leg. From the outside, they were an ordinary couple out for a drive. As they neared the front, they saw other cars pulled aside. Seats ripped out, bonnets open, boots emptied onto the road. Christ. They were next. A Brit waved them forward. Emmett wound down the window and fumbled for his licence.

The soldier peered in, then paused, noticing Ashling. At that very moment, Emmett thought he heard a faint knock from the boot. He felt his last bite of breakfast come back up. The Brit spoke, but Emmett didn't catch it.

Ashling elbowed him hard and jumped in with a laugh, leaning over Emmett to flirt. 'Ah Jesus, it's you again?' she said, her eyes twinkling.

'Still slaggin' off me poor fella's car again, are ye?'

The soldier smiled in recognition. 'Aye, that's right! Still surprised the ruddy thing's running.' He said. He remembered this couple well. He remembered the girl well.

Emmett forced a smile.

'We're gettin' married,' Ashling added, flashing a ring that hadn't been there earlier. 'Proposed to me last night. Must be mad. But I thought, why not? Any excuse for a party, know what-a mean? We're off for a wee dirty night away. See if you-know-what works.' She gave him a saucy wink.

The Brit flushed a little and gave Emmett a look that was half amused, half envious. He glanced at the line of cars idling behind them and shook his head. 'Fair play, mate. Off you go then. Don't be doing anything I wouldn't do, eh?'

'Wouldn't dream of it,' she said sweetly, and gave him a wave as they drove on.

Once they were clear, Ashling burst out laughing. 'What a dickhead. Did ye see him flirting away?'

Emmett exhaled for the first time in minutes. 'That ring trick was smart.'

She grinned. 'I've gotta few tricks up my sleeve, love. You-have-no-idea.' Farther on, they passed the Irish customs post with barely a nod.

Behind them, Derry slipped quietly out of reach. By the time the car pulled up at Ned's Point, outside Buncrana, Emmett spotted two men waiting beside a battered green Land Rover. Middle-aged, dressed like well-to-do farmers, both wore long black waxed coats. One had a flat tweed cap pulled low, the other, a woollen hat down to his ears. Neither smiled. Without a word, they moved towards the Austin. The atmosphere was well tense, like an elastic band ready to snap.

Emmett scrambled out first, fumbling at the boot catch, his hands clumsy but fast, more nerves than urgency driving him on. Ashling stayed a step behind, watching, letting him take the lead, knowing he needed that illusion of control to see this through.

The boot creaked open and a stale waft of piss hit them. Together, they grabbed the limp, half-conscious bodies and hauled them out, one at a time. The bigger lad landed with a groan, a soft pathetic sound, his legs kicking feebly out as he hit the mossy ground like a sack of rags. The other one barely moved, drugged to the eyeballs and lost in whatever hell his brain had slipped into.

Their hoods were yanked off, and Emmett flinched at the sight of the two faces staring back, wide-eyed and semi-conscious, barely aware of where they were or what was happening. He eyed Dickie first, couldn't help himself. Everyone knew him, the fella who'd supposedly won the pools, aye right. That's a load of bollocks, that. Him, a grass? He'd have laughed if it weren't so bloody grim. The other one, he recognised the face from somewhere, seen him around the town now and then, but didn't know him from Adam.

Then the kicking started. Steel-toe boots to the core, the head, the groin. No shouting. Only cold, premeditated violence. Emmett watched, rooted to the spot. The two unknown men didn't break stride or blink. He thought of the slaughterhouse workers who came by his garage now and again, mottled in blood up to their eyebrows. Dead-eyed. Efficient. Men who slaughtered and strung up animals as part of their daily routine. These two weren't much different. His head swam.

The man in the woolly hat said in a strong West Belfast accent, 'That'll do. Thanks. We'll manage from here. Away off with ye.'

Emmett nodded, dazed, and climbed back into the car without saying a word. Ashling followed and shut the door with a soft click that somehow made his stomach churn again. She was speaking, trying to keep things light, her tone breezy in that dry, gallows humour kind of way, but none of it landed. Her words floated past him like smoke, faint and meaningless.

A couple of miles up the road, he swung into a lay-by beside a rusted farm gate, flung the door open and stumbled out. His boots slipped on the muck as he crashed into the hedge, doubling over and retching until his throat burned and his ribs ached. His whole body heaved with it, the taste of sick thick in his mouth, the cold air slapping his face. He'd never been so sick in his life. When he finally dragged himself back to the car, head pounding and coat damp with sweat, Ashling was already in the driver's seat, arms folded, watching him. He blinked at her in confusion.

'I didn't know you could drive,' he muttered, still wiping his mouth with a sleeve.

Her grey eyes met his without a flicker of warmth. 'There's a lot you don't know about me, Emmett. Now get in unless you fancy thumbin' it back to Derry. We'll go back through Malin. Different checkpoint. Can't risk running into that Brit again, can we?'

He closed his eyes and nodded again. He hadn't even thought of that. Like he hadn't thought to bring a fake wedding ring or come up with a decent story for why they were together in the first place. Ashling was the one who carried it all. The coy glances, the wink, the pat on the leg. It'd all been a performance, and he'd missed his cue. He knew then that whatever test this was, he'd failed. Miserably. *Thank Christ for that.*

Two days later, he opened the *Derry Journal*, hands trembling slightly as he turned the pages, and there it was in black and white. A man's body had been discovered washed up on the shore at Lough Swilly, near Ned's Point. Some poor soul out walking their dog had seen it drifting close to the rocks. The remains were later confirmed as John Ballantyne, known to most as Porkie, a married man and father of one from Shantallow. Punished by the Provisional Irish Republican Army. Shot point-blank in the back of the head.

They took Kevin McDaid too, a local man from Creggan. He hasn't been seen since. The RUC said that, given how long he's been missing, it's unlikely his body will ever be found.

Fish food.

Chapter Sixty-Nine

Dolores is Back

In Castlereagh, Provo volunteer Dolores Gillispie stared Detective Black down, defiant as ever. She'd been held ninety hours now. No food, little sleep, saying not a word. She held that same bold, resolute stare. By now, the bitch was getting under his skin. Stubborn cow. Black had tried everything. Threats. A few knocks here and there. Even had a quiet whisper in her ear about what might happen if she didn't start talking. Nothing worked. She gave him nothing.

Her twin, Patrick, was the real prize. He'd resurfaced, and Black was sure he'd had a hand in the bombings in England, and the British ambassador's residence in Dublin. For that, they'd raided The Shamrock. Looking for evidence, weapons, anything to nail them with. All they got was Dolores and a few crates of cheap booze. A complete waste of time. Only benefit was they'd stashed the booze in the section house. Might as well keep a load for the next excuse to drink.

Black had taken care of the paperwork. A faxed interim custody order from the Secretary of State, flimsy as tissue and barely legal, had bought him more time. Time to lean on her, to chip away. She'd been tossed into a reeking cell usually used for men, dumped on a mattress that stank of piss and mould, with a blanket that looked like it'd been dragged out of the Lagan and left to rot. Every time she'd nodded off, or started to drift, he was there, rattling the bars or shouting down the corridor to jolt her awake. Reckoned it would wear her down, bit by bit. He didn't.

Afterward, it came to him, clear as day - a stroke of inspiration. Meant he wouldn't have to lift a finger. Not with a couple of staunch Loyalists locked up across the way from her. If he told them they'd a Republican whore, just a few short feet away. Wouldn't take much, would it? Told them he did. Before he knew it, their threats came thick and fast, each one more vicious than the last. *'We'll split her open and send what's left back to the Falls in a shoebox! Let us at her, Blackie. We'll teach the Fenian slut a right lesson! If it's that Gillispie woman, give us five minutes. I'll get her to talk, no bother!'*

They yelled through the bars, banged the steel doors, their voices bouncing down the corridor like a pack of wild dogs, hungry for the kill. Dolores Gillispie heard every word. That was the point. Let the noise carry, let the walls do the talking. Let her know what could be waiting on the other side of that door.

Despite it all, the bitch never balked. Not once. She sat there on that pish-soaked mattress, arms folded, head high, eyes cold as iron. Black had seen grown men shit themselves under half that pressure. Seen them shake, weep, even cry out for their mammies. But this one? This one was carved from stone.

In the end, she gave him nothing. No dates, no names. Sweet fuck all. His only consolation was to charge her with *withholding information*, so he signed the transfer papers and sent her to Armagh Gaol. She didn't look back as they took her out. Her hands were cuffed in front, her head held high, her face unreadable, tough to the core. Each step was deliberate, her knee-high boots striking the floor with purpose. Rubbing it in that she'd kept it shut. Her hair clung in wet tangles, streaked with sweat and whatever muck she'd picked up from the filthy hole he'd thrown her into.

Once she'd gone, Black lit a fag, dragged deep, and stared at the yellowed ceiling of the interview room. The emptiness the bitch left behind bugged the shit out of him. He hated her for it, hated her for her obstinacy. No matter what he'd tried, she didn't break. Because he'd failed. There was nothing he hated more than failure.

Later, a Black Maria took Dolores through the high gates and down the narrow walled lane into Armagh Women's Gaol. Dolores had been a '*resident*' before, more than once, and knew the Republican OC, Maureen Molony, particularly well. There was a strange comfort in returning here. Familiar place, familiar faces. The women, like her, were loyal. Protective and understanding. Funny enough, shithole as it was, this place, these women, made Dolores feel appreciated. Respected even.

The second she walked into the committals hall and the word got around she'd arrived, a shout went up: Dolores is back. She hadn't expected a fuss, but the noise lifted her mood. Big time. That sense of being recognised, remembered. It mattered to her, making everything worthwhile.

What caught her off guard at first was the number of male screws about the joint. First time she'd seen them. Not that it bothered her, after Black and those Loyalist yobbos, she could deal with anything. What disturbed her was that it bothered the newbies, the younger girls coming in. Dolores was beyond all that. No one would break her. Not ever. She was Patrick Gillispie's twin and that carried weight, especially here.

Strip-searches were routine now, another act in the farce they called justice. Within days she'd turned it into a performance, winding the screws up for her own amusement — tits out, arse wagging, like they were punters at a dirty peep show. The rookies stood out a mile. The older ones tried to play it cool, smirking while the young bucks didn't know where to look. Some were red-faced with embarrassment, others lashed out, furious at being caught gawping. Worst were the ones who lingered by the women's showers, pretending to check pipes or tiles, but really watching the girls through the steam, like it was some backstreet picture house. *Dirty bastards!*

After a few days in limbo, they took her to Cell 23 on A-Wing. She hadn't eaten in days, not that the slop deserved to be called food, boiled to mush or scraped from some burnt pot, tasting of metal and steam. The screws tried winding her up as they walked her along the landing, but it didn't work, so they just dumped her inside. Dolores dropped onto the bed, limbs shaky, head spinning, still giving the POs the evil eye until the bulky metal door clanged shut. By now, pretending none of it bothered her was second nature. Truth was, it did bother her. Whether she liked it or not, she was beat, running on fumes. She exhaled, pressed her cheek to the mattress, then turned to look at the adjacent bed.

A girl lay there. Christ Almighty, what a sight. A scrap of a thing, the girl was nothing but bone and tissue-thin skin, seventeen, eighteen at most. Looked like one of those famine kids from Africa — face all fallen in, hair faded and brittle, as if life itself had already gone from her. Nevertheless, the moment she caught Dolores staring, she shot upright like a trap had sprung, stretching what could be called a mouth, into a grim grin. Her gums looked almost bruised, her teeth a dull yellow and clagged with *whatever*, and her skin stretched tight over barbed cheekbones. Pale as chalk, her washed-out tangle of rusty hair that might once have been her glory just hung there, stringy and sad.

'Christ, wee girl, what the fuck happened to you?' Dolores asked, her voice low, barely a whisper. *Tragic.*

The near skeleton laughed - a high, strange laugh. Definitely not right. A sound that didn't belong in this place. Touched in the head. Dolores kept staring. Who was she and what the hell had brought her here? Poor thing should be in the looney bin.

The cell door scraped open again and in came the OC. Maureen's face lit up. She'd a soft spot for Dolores; they'd worked a couple of ops together, and like herself, Dolores was fierce for the Cause. They hugged, a silent embrace that said it all. When Dolores pulled back, her eyes went to the bundle of bones on the bed. She wasn't trying to be cruel, but sweet suffering Christ, the sight of that poor mite — grinning away like some scary doll — definitely off her rocker.

'What in God's name, Maureen? What's the story there?' she whispered.

Maureen stared at the young'un, her jaw tightening, but didn't answer right away. Where should she start?

After Bridget Barry's release, they'd done what they could for Tina McLaughlin. Fed her, washed her, tried coaxing her out of the cell, gentle words at first, then harsher, even begging. Nothing worked. Every time someone so much as stepped near her to take her out, she'd scream the shop down, howling like her skin was being flayed. It wasn't once or twice. It was every single time, like trying to pull someone back who was scared senseless. Too late to care whether she lived or died. She didn't want saving. Didn't even pretend to.

Day after day, Maureen went to see governor, to plead with Father McGuire, to speak to anyone who might listen. She didn't dress it up, told them straight - the girl was sick, dying, fading away in front of their eyes, slowly, bit by bit, right there. It was like watching someone rot from the inside out. But still, nothing changed. No doctor, no concern, no help. Ignored.

'You must've heard of her, Tina McLaughlin? Got tangled up with that wanker, Kieran Kelly. You know, the eejit who tried bombing the City Hotel in Derry. Botched it. Got himself shot, same time as Bishop Hegarty.'

Dolores frowned, then it clicked. 'Jesus, aye. I remember now. But what the hell happened to her?'

Maureen looked back at Tina, still sitting there, grinning away like she was front row at a pantomime. She gave a sad sigh and said. 'Long story. Come on. Food's ready. I'll tell you everythin'.'

As usual, they ate beneath the great barred window; the light fading through the iron struts above, turning the walls a dull orange-grey. Over food, Maureen talked, detailing whole bloody fiasco, poor Bridget Barry, the beatings, the cover-ups, the abuse, the sheer cowardice of it all. Dolores listened, jaw clamped, fury burning under her skin. She wasn't shocked. None of this surprised her. This place broke women. It was built for it. Nothing, no speech or priest or country-wide petition, was ever going to change that.

Between bites, Dolores shared her own news. Things in the H-Blocks were spiralling fast. The blanket protest was growing by the day – shite smeared on walls, screws losing control, fellas dragged out of their cells, battered, then thrown into ice-cold baths. Battle of wills. Maureen knew most of it. Word had ways of travelling back and forth, passed in glances, muttered through doors, smuggled through letters. She'd heard enough to piece it together.

So, by the time they'd sorted their trays, the decision was made. The Armagh women would start their own protest on Monday. No more work. No more cooperation. Everything would stop.

'That new governor, Yeaman - he's a hole,' Maureen said, jabbing her fork. 'Only here to climb the ladder. Stir the pot. If the bastard wants a war, we'll give him one.'

It was Yeaman who'd brought in male screws. Dressed it up as extra security, but everyone knew the truth - more about control, plain and simple. They'd stalk the wings with jangling keys and heavy boots, prowling like hunters, their eyes crawling over the women as if they were theirs to touch, to watch, to claim. Every slammed door carried menace, every smirk or muttered remark chipped away at the women's dignity. Some of the younger girls shrank into themselves, the more experienced ones snapped back in defiance, but either way the men fed off it.

Thinking on it made Maureen's blood boil.

Chapter Seventy

A Declaration of War

A couple of days later, Governor Yeaman stood outside the chief officer's room in the circle, arms folded, his eyes moving slowly across the assembled POs like he was sizing up a row of fresh recruits. He was, in a way; he supposed. Most of the men were new, barely out of training, their uniforms still stiff, boots barely scuffed. A few older hands were tucked among them, standing back a little, quieter but sharper, each one sussing Yeaman's mood. Nobody spoke. Nobody dared. The chief officer began barking out names, assigning wings with her clipped, military rhythm, one after the other like numbers on a sheet. Yeaman said nothing, let it run. Then, as the last name was called and calm returned, he stepped forward, as the chief officer coughed and got ready to speak.

'Ladies and gentlemen,' she announced, squaring up like she was on parade. 'Hold off a minute. Governor Yeaman here wants a word.'

That did it. Every head turned. Spines stiffened, hands clasped tight behind backs. Not a single whisper. He'd their full attention. Exactly how Yeaman liked it. *Good.*

He stepped into the centre of the circle, taking his time, letting his boots echo across the shining floor as his gaze swept over his officers once more. His expression was unreadable, but everyone there could feel it. The man was wound up. He'd had more than enough of the Republican women parading in their black jumpers and black skirts, what he liked to sneer at as martyrs' uniforms, worn bold as brass, like medals pinned to their chests. Provocative, he'd called it. Organised provocation. He wasn't wrong. Every thread was chosen to taunt. But as far as he was concerned, the days of them calling the shots in his prison were over. It was time to reassert control. Time to remind them exactly who ran this place. He did.

'Those assigned to A2, B2, and B3,' he began, voice like cut glass, 'you are to conduct exhaustive searches in every cell. Confiscate the usual contraband. But more importantly, strip out every piece of black clothing. Shirts, trousers, skirts, the lot. I will not have prisoners attempting to dress like soldiers. Not in my prison.'

Some nodded. A few stared straight ahead. But Smyth and Drake? They looked excited. He noticed it, but didn't acknowledge it. He'd questioned the pair after the Barry incident, and noted their answers were slippery as oil, but he'd let it pass. Now that the woman was gone, it wasn't worth the effort to follow it up.

'I want you to move the inmates to the association room,' he went on. 'Keep them there while the searches are carried out. Every cell stripped down. Understood?'

The chorus came back: 'Yes, Gov.' He nodded once, curt, and turned to the chief. 'Full report by the end of the day.'

He made his way back to his office, didn't look round, didn't break stride. As soon as he turned the corner, the line of officers cracked open, voices spilling out straight away, some swearing under their breath, others laughing like they didn't give a toss. All of them braced for another long, shitty shift.

In her wing, Dolores sat in her cell, sorting through the few possessions she'd been allowed, folding each one neatly and handling them with quiet care. From the small pile beside her, she lifted a black-and-white photo and stuck it on the wall at the top of her bed. Her favourite.

It was her and Patrick as children, both smiling, hand in hand. She considered it for a bit. Back then, she'd never thought much of herself. Never a looker, never saw what others might've, but Patrick, now he was different. He always looked the part, walked like he had somewhere important to be, full of himself in the best kind of way. Him in the photo with his long trousers, tidy shirt, a jumper pulled neatly over it, and that hair of his, slicked back with Brylcreem like he was heading to the pictures or a dance. He looked cheeky, full of chat. The way fellas were back then, when they hadn't a clue what was coming.

She smiled without meaning to. She could remember that day clear as anything. The father of a decent foster family in West Belfast took it, them Catholic and kind. Treated the twins like their own. Nearly three years there and they'd had it good. Then Bombay Street got burned out, torched by loyalists. The family was moved into a temporary caravan and the mammy took sick. That was it. No hugs, no tears, a quick ride back to the children's home.

Unusually, her eyes blurred. She blinked and was about to put it away when Tina tugged on her sleeve. She'd seen the photo and was pointing at it now, squinting like she was trying to ask who it was.

'That's me and Patrick. Me twin,' Dolores said, gently.

She stepped closer. Tina's eyes flickered again.

'You gotta brother, love?' Dolores asked.

Tina's eyes shone, her mouth twitching like she had a name ready, but nothing came. Only a garbled sound that stuck in her throat, like the word, couldn't get past her teeth.

Out of nowhere, an almighty roar tore through the wing - metal crashing, feet pounding, voices yelling over each other. Batons smashed against the railings, over and over, like war drums. In no time, the suicide nets below filled with black garments and the place erupted. The PO's barrelled in from every side, bellowing orders no one could hear over the racket. Cell doors crashed open. Women were snatched out by the arms, thrust into line, some still half-dressed, one with a colour still in her hair.

POs Drake and Smyth led the charge, hammering down the corridor as they shot through the wing, heads low, eyes darting like they could sniff out trouble before it even started. They moved fast, all noise and muscle, barking orders, ready to bat someone if it came to it. Clothes were scattered about. Letters were torn. Every black shirt, jumper or item seized, dragged out onto the landing and thrown over the side.

'Out! The lot of ye! Now!' they shouted, cell after cell. Cell doors flung wide as the women were hauled out and shoved into line like cattle on the way to the slaughterhouse. When Smyth reached cell 23, she paused. With her baton raised, her eyes took in Tina McLaughlin, sitting there on the bed, blank as ever, staring straight ahead. Perfect. Another chance to get even.

Smyth stepped inside, but before she got a swing in, Dolores caught the PO's wrist and twisted it so much it hurt like hell.

'You lay a finger on that girl,' she warned, low and deadly, 'and I'll have your name chalked on a wall. You and every last one of your fuckin' brood. You'll be shot before your tea gets cold.'

Smyth froze. Bloody hell. Her heart started thumping, her breath stuck. She didn't doubt this one's threat. Not for a second. Quick as a flash, she dropped her arm and nodded. Turning to Tina first, she then stared back at Dolores. 'Get the fuck out, both of ye,' she hissed.

Dolores stared hard at her before helping Tina to her feet and leading her out onto the landing.

Smyth stayed behind, looked around the cell, and began to turn it over. Suddenly, her eyes caught a lone photo on the wall. The same one Dolores had been showing Tina.

Downstairs, the women were being lined up. Upstairs, Drake and the remaining screws tore through the wing, ransacking every cell they entered. Mattresses were sliced open with blades, insides spilling out like burst guts, posters were ripped from walls, letters shredded, their words and memories lost forever. Sanitary pads were yanked out and torn like confetti, cupboards emptied, toothbrushes snapped in two and binned. Nothing was spared. Nothing was sacred.

Back in cell 23, Tina had few belongings to begin with, but what she did have were soon destroyed. Dolores's stuff went next. As Smyth turned to go, she looked again at the photo taped to the wall. She took it. Turned it over in her hand. A young teenage boy and girl. Must be Gillispie and the brother. Then she picked up a few others lying on the bed and, bit by bit, tore them up into pieces no bigger than a postage stamp. When she was finished, she dropped the scraps and left them where they fell.

The other POs carried on, snapping at the girls downstairs, searching their clothes, turning out their pockets. They found nothing but bits of chocolate, scraps of tobacco, the odd sweet. No homemade weapons. No notes of importance. Just lives, picked apart for the pleasure of it.

Hours later, they were herded back upstairs, starving, and silent with rage. One by one, they returned to their cells to observe the damage. Crying echoed down the wing. Their screams an obvious sign of frustration. Dolores stepped into her cell alongside Tina. Her eyes landed first on the floor. Bits of paper. Torn edges. A nose, a shoe, a piece of Patrick's sleeve. Her precious photos. Gone. Every single one of them, ruined beyond repair. They weren't just photographs. They were all she had left of the days before the Troubles, before the cells, before every bit of her got eaten up and hardened. Black-and-white memories, faded and creased, snapped when they were youngsters. Hand in hand, sitting outside some old church hall, smiling like they hadn't a care in the world. He'd been wearing that teasing smile, really looked the part, while she'd tried to copy her foster mother's smile. It hadn't worked, nor would they've known it wouldn't last. Good times never did. But for a few years, they'd had beds with clean sheets, dinners around a table, and the sound of someone asking if they were all right.

Now their faces were torn to bits, gouged and scratched, her brother's beautiful eyes gone, nothing left but torn paper. Her own smile, that soft little effort she'd painted on, was shredded. A sound she didn't recognise emerged from her, something dragged from the pit of her soul. Part roar, part cry, and it tore through the cell like a warning siren.

Across from her, Tina broke down too, shrieking like the child she still was, a child who'd seen too much and understood even more. She ran the length of the cell, wailing, arms flailing wildly, before crumpling in the corner, sobbing into the crook of her elbow, as if hiding her face could somehow make it all disappear.

Dolores didn't move, but stood still, her fists clenched at her sides, breathing hard, dragging air into her lungs like she was trying not to drown. Her eyes stayed locked on the ripped fragments scattered across the concrete floor.

PO Smyth had meant it as a warning.

Dolores Gillispie took it as a declaration of war.

Chapter Seventy-One

No Way Out

Chief Constable Thomas Bonner stood in his office that looked out over the Strand Road in Londonderry, hands clasped behind his back like he fancied himself a general. But there was nothing impressive about him, not by a long shot. Thinning dark hair, a twitchy nose shaped like a beak, a miserable attempt at a moustache, and sideburns that looked like they'd been drawn on by a four-year-old in a hurry. He was of medium height, round-faced like a football, and so fat it was probable he hadn't turned down a load of Doherty's cream fingers in a lifetime.

But go up a size in uniform? Not a chance. He wouldn't allow it, vain as anything. His green tunic strained across his gut like tarp stretched over a sandbag, the buttons wheezing for mercy, any one of them liable to shoot off across the room if he moved around too quickly. His belt was yanked so tight it dug in deep, making his belly pour over the waistband like a rising loaf, the whole thing held together by stubbornness and denial.

On top of everything else, he was seething. Not only annoyed or put out, but properly wound up. He'd finished filling in Charles Jones on the latest cock-up, a disaster from start to finish. Somehow, and he would bloody well find out how, Roger Henderson had figured out his brother's death hadn't been an accident at all. Worse still, the nosy bastard had started asking questions, sniffing around places he shouldn't, poking into the past like he had a right, and, God forbid, had managed to dig up a witness. A live one. Someone who'd seen enough to crack the whole sorry business open again and expose the truth. If that happened, Jones would be finished, plain and simple, and Bonner too.

Their only saving grace was Mrs Parkes, his nosy little mole over at Rocola, who couldn't keep her beak out of anything. She'd been at it again, hanging about like she had work to do, and this time she'd heard her boss, talking to some Creggan man, Tommy O'Reilly about his father's death and about a girl, a witness who'd seen everything. No names given, mind you. Bonner made a mental note to send the woman a gift, maybe flowers or a Woolworths voucher, nothing flashy, but enough to keep in with her, keep her ears open, and remind her she was appreciated. All he needed was for her to carry on doing what she did best, sticking her nose in where it wasn't wanted and to come back when she'd more to share.

When Bonner told Jones what she'd discovered, he hadn't flinched or looked the slightest bit concerned. He waited, calm as ever, picking at the edge of an old scar on his face. 'What do you suggest you do now?' he asked, like it was no big deal, no reason to panic. Bonner felt his face redden. Jones always had a way of doing this to him, acting like he was in control of everything, and winding him up without even trying.

'Me? What do you mean, what should *I* do?' Bonner snapped, his voice rising before he could stop it. 'This isn't on me, Charles. If this witness, whoever she is, starts talking, your neck deep in it, same as me, so don't pretend otherwise.'

Jones looked at the chief constable with barely disguised contempt. He didn't like the man, didn't need to, but Bonner was a necessity, so he let him rant. If he truly thought Jones was about to mop up after him, he was thicker than he looked. He sank back into his chair, then lifted both hands like he might offer a bit of reassurance. Instead, he stared at Bonner, let the silence go on long enough to make him squirm, then spoke, his voice low, measured, and loaded with threat.

'You wanted him gone, and I delivered. Clean and fast. No mess, no loose ends. You're all twitchy because someone's asking questions. That's not my problem, Chief Constable. That's yours. I've struck the match. You lit the fire.'

He sat back again, calm as ever, not a flicker of doubt on his face. 'So here's what you'll do. You'll go back to your little mole, and you'll tell her to listen harder. I want names, connections, everything and anything she can get. You'll do it with a smile, because if this falls apart, your name's the one in every report, not mine.'

Bonner still said nothing. His throat was dry. The pressure of it all pressed down as if it were written into his skin. Jones laid it out, step by step. There was no wriggling free. *God damn you, Jones.* Everything he said was true. The idea had been his from the start. In hindsight, Bonner had never been able to tolerate George Shalham. The man drifted around the barracks like some medal-draped saint, adored by his officers, praised by the press, and treated like a hero by half the bloody city. It was unbearable. Smug, polished, too clean by half. Bonner's father had worn the same badge, and from the time he could walk, he wanted to follow in his footsteps. He'd waited, year after year, kept his head down, bit his tongue, put the hours in, but with Shalham soaking up every bit of recognition, there was never room for Bonner, or anyone else, to climb the ladder.

Ultimately, after the City Hotel disaster, they reached a compromise. Shalham was out. Bonner was in. When it was done, Jones told him he'd arranged it, told him it was up to him now to keep things quiet, hold the lion's back, and see the whole sorry episode buried for good. Bonner, in his wisdom, had jumped at the chance. At last, he'd follow in his da's footsteps. But at what cost?

Jones owned him now. He'd cleared the way for Bonner to become chief constable, no question about it. Bought him the job, plain and simple. The money? That had its uses too. Jones had been slipping him protection cash for months. No records, no names, but brown envelopes passed hand to hand. Cash was king. It kept Bonner's mistress housed comfortably, tucked away in a tidy little cottage outside the city. Private, quiet, exactly how he liked it. No neighbours sticking their noses in or asking awkward questions. As long as she was happy, well, so was he.

Once again, Jones spoke, his voice smooth but edged with malice. 'So, having said all that. You're the chief constable now, Bonner, so think about it. Once you get hold of this so-called witness, lock her up and throw away the key. You've done it before.'

Bonner gave a disbelieving laugh. 'Are you serious, man? For Christ's sake! Lock a girl up for witnessing a murder? That's madness!'

Jones didn't look up, too busy working at a hangnail on his thumb, leaving his skin red and raw from days of picking at it.

'It's not madness,' he said calmly. 'It's simple. You guys aren't short on options these days, are you? Send the girl off to wherever, nice and tidy.'

Bonner gave another futile laugh and shook his head, Jones was missing the point entirely, so he tried to explain. 'Charles, whoever this witness is, she's smart. She didn't come to us, but straight to Shalham. Obviously, she knows the risks. Even the Hendersons haven't pinned down a name or an address for her yet. Don't you get it, this is serious.'

Jones's patience snapped. He ripped out the painful hangnail, drawing blood this time, and rounded on Bonner. 'Then find out who the fuck she is,' he yelled. 'I don't care if it's Mother bloody Theresa herself. Find her and fix it like I said!'

Chapter Seventy-Two

A Done Deal

James sat beside Marleen on a garden bench at the back of Melrose, the library lights casting a gentle glow behind them. The air was warm and motionless, as if the night itself were listening to him. He spoke quietly about the factory's struggles, the worrying accounts, the uncertain contracts, and the way everything seemed to be smothering him. Marleen simply sat there and listened, truly listened, offering him the kind of attention that made his worries feel less daunting.

She was quiet for a moment. Then, with a half-smile, she said, 'Darling, I need to put an idea to you. May I?'

He didn't hesitate. 'Course you can, what is it?' But as soon as she had his attention, something changed. Her confidence wavered, and he saw it. She was suddenly nervous, which was rare for her.

'What is it?' he asked, taking both her hands, 'You and I, Mar... there's not much we don't know about each other. Come on girl, out with it.'

She took a breath, deep and exaggerated, then squeezed his hands. 'Darling, we've been friends forever. Right? You know me inside out,' she giggled, remembering his face that morning not so long ago, when he woke up naked next to her, 'I mean, you know how I tick.'

He smiled, though he wasn't sure where she was going with this.

'I'll be frank. James. It's like this: Mummy and Daddy are on the warpath. They want me married off and producing an heir. A sprog, as Daddy elegantly put it.'

James raised an eyebrow, trying to follow and she laughed at his puzzled expression.

'What I mean is... I need a husband and a potential father. For my future children. And I thought. Well... well... I thought you might be up for it?' There it was. She'd said it!

James stared at her. Flattered, aye. Shocked, definitely. Somewhere deep down, even amused. Of all the things Marleen might've come out with tonight, this had to be the last thing on earth. He loved her, 'course he did, but not like he'd loved Caitlin. Not even close. In no time, it came back, a tide of memory that caught him off guard. Caitlin. Her laugh, her warmth, the way she'd looked in the sunlight, naked and smiling, that morning in Donegal. God, he missed her. More than he could ever admit.

As his thoughts wandered, Marleen caught them and reeled him back with a quiet nudge. 'Think about it, James,' she said suddenly energised.

'You'd have my money to use as you see fit, but within reason, of course!' She laughed, but there was a flash of sincerity in her eyes. 'You could save Rocola. There's millions in my trust, sitting there. Waiting. You could keep the factory open. Save the jobs you've been fighting so hard for. Help Roger. It all makes perfect sense, don't you see?'

James sat still, the impact of her words sinking in. He hadn't seriously considered how much money she had before. It had never occurred to him, but now... maybe he could see it working. It'd make a hell of a difference. Change everything. She was right. On paper, it may very well work.

Still, as she talked on, her voice climbing higher with excitement, all he could think about was Caitlin. Marrying Marleen; it'd be like marrying his sister. Familiar, easy, safe, maybe, but not actual love, love. Not what he'd want in a wife. He managed a small smile, to keep her talking, while inside, a slow, steady ache gnawed at him.

'We'd work out a business agreement. A partnership. Have a child or two, then live our own lives. Best of both worlds, don't you see. I have my life, you save Rocola. You know I love you to bits, anyway!'

He watched her fondly, even as his thoughts scrambled. They'd known each other forever and, yeah, he did love her. She'd never once brought up that drunken night in the hotel, drinking Roger's expensive champagne afterwards, and waking up the next morning. She'd never tried to twist it into something it wasn't, and he respected her for that. He was near certain nothing had happened. Would've been strange that. Wrong even. Would've spoiled everything. Nevertheless, here she was, offering him a way forward, a lifeline. A way to care for Roger. A way to keep Rocola alive.

He stood up to get his thoughts together, then looked down at her as Caitlin's name flickered through his mind again, quick as a shadow, gone before he could hold on to it. They were over, weren't they? Done. No use crying over spilled milk. He knew that. Still, the thought left a dull ache somewhere in his heart. Maybe in time he could grow to love Marleen in that way. Not in the wild, head-over-heels way it had been with Caitlin. But the normal way. The kind that came with shared holidays and quiet mornings. He wasn't sure, not really, but at this stage, what choice did he have?

So, with a wide smile, he nodded, and Marleen, bright-eyed and breathless, reached for him. 'Oh my darling, James! Is that a yes? Tell me that's a yes!'

He nodded again, faster this time, and kissed her lightly on the cheek. 'Yes, it is, Marleen, it's a yes. But we've a lot to talk about first.'

'Yippee!' she cried, almost bursting with happiness. 'Oh, my darling. At last! Papa will be thrilled!'

Chapter Seventy-Three

Hell's Angels

Somehow, with a bit of charm and a well-timed distraction from the ever-nosy matron, Lemon's bit on the side had sneaked him into the nurses' home at Altnagelvin Hospital after dark. In no time, he was spooned beside her in her narrow single bed. The room was tiny, but it did nicely. Two beds, a shared cupboard, two chests of drawers, and not much more. Lynn's roommate, Mary or Margo or maybe May, he couldn't remember what, was on night duty. He'd never clapped eyes on the girl, but her not being there was doing them both a favour.

Odd thing was, he wasn't in the mood for a shag tonight. Couldn't say why. So instead they lay together, candlelight flickering from the stub on the windowsill, talking about nothing in particular. Lynn was good for him. Decent craic. He liked her more than he thought he would. A far cry from that banshee back home. His wife was always at him, hammering on about bills or the wains or where he'd been, why hadn't he come home. He didn't know how the wee ones stuck her and had long since started dodging the place altogether.

He glanced up at the photos stuck on Lynn's side of the wall and grinned. He was in every one of them. Him and her, side by side, arms around each other, always smiling. The two of them up at the TT on the Causeway Coast, their black leather jackets zipped up tight with their Hell's Angels Belfast T-shirts underneath. God, but they looked the business. Like proper rock stars.

The wee Londonderry girl was mad about him, but then, who could blame her?! It felt good. He trusted her too. Probably told her more than he should. Snippets about what he did for Jones. Not everything, mind, still she never pushed him, never asked what she didn't want to hear. For that, he was grateful.

He was on a roll with wee Charlie Jones for the most part these days. The perks were decent, no denying that. Cash in hand, doors opened, people looked at him differently from before, looking at him with respect. They knew who he was, who he worked for.

But things had turned sour ever since Lemon screwed up over that Yankee reporter, Barter. He'd done exactly what he was told, trailed the bastard all the way from Belfast to Londonderry, never once lost him, but after that, it all went sideways.

Barter stepped out of his flat, knowing full well he was being followed. Had been since Belfast. That meathead in the leather jacket, Lemon, or whatever his name was, hadn't exactly been subtle. He didn't panic, but played it cool. Now, heading down Lawrence Hill, he could hear footsteps behind him. Getting louder. Closer. At the bottom, he stopped dead, turned on his heel, and faced the guy full on.

'Hey, dude,' Barter snapped, his accent cutting through the street, 'If you don't back off, I swear to God, I'll kill ya.'

Lemon blinked, thrown a second at being confronted. The Yank didn't give him time to recover. He stepped in fast, right up close, jabbing a finger hard into Lemon's chest.

'You tell that weasel boss of yours,' he said, low and dangerous, 'I've got photos. Evidence. I know what you guys are into. You, him, and your so-called psycho kids. So don't try anything on me, 'right? Not here. Not *ever*.'

Barter was shitting bricks, no doubt about it, but his voice stayed calm. He met Lemon's stare head-on. Made damn sure the bastard knew he was serious.

Lemon's silence was terrifying. He inched closer, steady and slow, until their noses nearly touched. Barter got a hint of cheap aftershave, the kind that stung more than it smelled. It stuck to the guy. Still, Lemon didn't say a word. Stood stock still, his face like stone, eyes locked on Barter's like he was measuring up a coffin.

Barter held his ground, though his chest thumped hard enough to betray him. A standoff. 'You gonna say somethin'?' he asked, his drawl low and cutting, the words rougher than he meant. 'Or are you just here to breathe on me?'

Again, nothing but that look. Ruthless. Clinical. The kind of look that didn't bluff. Lemon took a few steps back and gave him a sardonic smile.

Barter clenched his fists to keep them from shaking. 'Think I'm scared of you? I've been to Vietnam, pal. I've had rockets skim my roof. You? You're a thug in a jacket two sizes too small.'

Lemon's mouth twitched, but this time it wasn't a smile of any sort. More like he'd tasted something sour.

Barter pressed on, trying to keep the tremble out of his voice. 'Tell Jones I've got copies of everything. Stashed, safe. If I disappear, they don't. It's over.'

It was Barter who stepped forward now, flipping the balance, letting Lemon feel the change. 'If anything, and I mean *anything*, happens to me, you and that lizard you work for? You-are-toast. I'm talkin' headlines, legal, the whole damn shebang. You won't know what hit ya.'

Lemon blinked. But it was there, a brief flicker of doubt. Something else behind it. Fear perhaps? There was a pause. One second. Then another. Long enough to make the Yank wonder if he was about to take a beating or a bullet. With a grunt, Lemon turned on his heel and walked away. Barter remained, his heart still thudding, sweat prickling down his spine, knowing full well this wasn't the end. Not by a long shot. He sighed.

Ned, Roger Henderson's dog, lay curled at the foot of the bed, his head resting gently against Roger's leg. There was something knowing in the way he'd settled tonight, quiet, solemn, watchful. As if he figured out death was in the room. Roger's hand moved slowly, stroking the soft fur along the dog's neck. The warmth of its body comforted him more than anything else could.

As he lay back against the pillows, Roger's eyes half-closed, his body aching with the effort of staying upright for so long. He'd been well pleased when he heard about James and Marleen's engagement. Genuinely delighted for them both. A long time coming. The thought of the pair tying the knot, building a life together, it had given him a buzz. A small bit of light in an otherwise dark stretch of days. They were keen to wed soon, and Roger understood why. They didn't say it out loud, didn't need to. He knew. Deep down, with a slow, dull certainty, he knew that, the way things were going, he might not be around to see it.

Lately, the past had crept in again. Quiet at first, then louder, more insistent. As if the closer he came to the end, the more determined his memories were to have their say. Most mornings, he woke soaked through, heart hammering, dragged from the same bloody dream. Always the same. Those few minutes he couldn't take back. The mistake that had shaped the rest of his life. He'd carried that shame for decades, worn it like a chain no one else could see. He'd carry it to the grave. But James, James must never know.

No matter what, Roger had to protect him from the truth. From him, as he really was. Because if James ever learned the full extent of what he'd done, the cowardice, the selfishness, the cruelty, it would rip everything apart. Everything he'd tried to make up for would turn to dust. And that, that was what he couldn't live with.

Not for a single moment.

Chapter Seventy-Four

Letting Go

In Boston, it was late afternoon on a crisp winter day, the sort Seamus Donaghy used to love back home, when the sky stretched wide and pale and the cold had a bite that woke you right up. The timber yard was in full swing, full of shouts and hammering, the sound of saws and boots and men getting on with it, when a voice rose above the din, calling across the yard.

'Yo! Seamus! You gotta call!'

He pulled off his gloves, tucked them into his hard hat, and made his way across the planks and gravel, his boots crunching steadily until he reached the steps to McMannus's office. The receiver lay off the hook, dangling. He lifted it with care, unsure, cautious, like handling something delicate.

'Hello?'

At first, only the steady hum of the Atlantic answered back. He frowned, about to hang up, when a quiet, fragile voice came through.

'Seamus. Is that you? It's me.'

He shut his eyes.

'Hello, Caitlin.'

'Ah, Seamus... it's so good to hear your voice.'

He could feel the relief in her, like someone taking a proper breath for the first time in days. 'Yours too, Caitlin. How are ye?'

'Awful. I feel awful, Seamus. I tried to ring you over and over. I swear I never meant to hurt you.'

'I know. I know. It's just... I could've done without it. I mean, the timin' an' all.'

He took a breath, tried to keep his voice normal, yet there was something he needed to understand, to ask. 'So go on then. Tell me. Who is he? Who's this James fella?'

She went quiet. Just the low hum of the line, like the ocean itself, had gone quiet.

'Caitlin?'

'I'm here,' she whispered.

'So then. Who is he?'

She told him. Everything. Told him about James Henderson, how they'd met, how it had felt like sunshine breaking through clouds for the first time in ages, how she'd laughed again, really laughed. Then how it had all fallen apart. The bomb scare, the panic, the anger, the chaos she hadn't seen coming. She spoke of James's cruelty, how he'd turned on her, how she couldn't move on, though she'd tried with him and look where that ended up. She hadn't moved on. Not a bit. Not in her heart.

Seamus listened. Every word hit like a slow bruise, but he stayed silent. This wasn't about pride. This was about facing the truth, and finally letting go. By the time the call neared its end, he understood. He wasn't for her. Maybe he never was. Though it hurt like hell, it released him. Like something that had been stuck finally moved on, and he could breathe again. He knew now he had to leave it all behind. Caitlin, the Cause, Derry, everything. Life had drawn a line and it was time to cross over. They wouldn't talk again, he was sure of that, but he still wanted to give her something. A push. A bit of encouragement.

'Caitlin,' he said softly, 'you should talk to him. If you love him, if there's even a bit of what you say still there, you've got to help him see it. Be honest. Tell him what he needs to hear.'

'I doubt James Henderson would believe a word I say after all that,' she said, her voice flat.

'Then convince him,' Seamus replied, calm but certain. 'You're young, you're clever, you're beautiful... you owe yourself a chance at being happy. What've you got to lose? Go talk to him. Do it for you.'

After another moment of quiet, her voice was warmer. 'Okay, Seamus. If you think I should, I'll try.'

'Good girl,' he murmured, trying to keep his own emotions in check.

Outside the office, his name rang out again, his boss calling from the yard. Seamus turned to look. The light had changed, or maybe he had. It wasn't quite as dull anymore, not so grey and heavy.

'I've gotta go, Caitlin. Mind yourself, will ye?'

'You too. Bye, Seamus. Thanks.'

'Bye, Caitlin.' He put the receiver back in place and smiled.

For the first time in ages, he felt good. Like a knot had finally come undone somewhere deep inside him. The world looked different now. A bit cleaner. A bit clearer. As he stepped out into the cold air and made his way back down into the timber yard, a low whistle slipped from his lips, rising faintly above the sounds of the yard. He was ready now. Ready to move on.

Chapter Seventy-Five

Finding Alice

Now Paddy Gillispie had finally got what he'd wanted, having shagged Brona Doyle. Lots. He found himself looking at her through a different lens. Funny how it happened.

Before all Dee's paranoia about Doyle, she'd seemed sexy. Mysterious almost, sharp as a tack, but still that tiny bit out of reach. He saw it now, there was something off about her. Hard to put his finger on it, but it niggled at him all the same. Now with Dee banged up in Armagh after The Shamrock raid, her voice had started to resound in his head. She'd been nagging him for ages, going on and on about Brona being a Brit, a spy, warning him to wise up, saying there were eyes on them, that something had changed and she could feel it. Dee always had a way about her, an instinct like radar. Very rarely wrong. At first, he'd paid no attention to her, told her she was imagining things. Paranoid. But now, he wasn't so sure.

Last time he went over to Brona's, after they'd done it at the back of the shop and headed upstairs, he'd got curious. Waited till she was in the bathroom, then had a good old poke about the place, and just like Dee said, there was nothing that could tell him anything about the girl. More like a library than a home. The place was too perfect, almost staged. No trace of an everyday life. It was like walking into a hotel room. Could've belonged to anyone.

That's when the feeling sank in. Cold and slow. Dee had been right from the first and he didn't like it. Didn't enjoy being made a fool of. He'd told Brian to tail the so-called British spy, while Paddy played his part too, keeping up the pretence of seeing her, all the while knowing it was a likely a trap. For a while it felt like a waste of Brian's time. She stuck to her routine — dull as dishwater. Work, collecting for the defence fund, the odd jar in The Shamrock, a visit to the library, or home on her own, living like a nun. But then something happened that Monaghan didn't like, and he was on the phone to Paddy straight away. They needed to meet.

The next night, tucked away in their usual corner of The Shamrock. Guinness in hand, Paddy gave Brian the nod to tell all.

'Swear to God, Paddy, I nearly didn't recognise her. Saw her heading up to the flat, same as always. Then, half an hour later, she comes back down, hood up, coat pulled tight round her like she's freezin', and the look on her face? It was well weird. Not like her usual self. Not a bit. Different like. I'd a feeling'.' Brian began.

Paddy gave a small wave, urging him on. 'How do ye mean?'

'Give us a minute,' Brian said, tipping back a gulp of his pint before he went on. 'She jumps on the bus into the city, right, and lands at that all-night café beside City Hall. I'm standin' out in the cold looking right at her, freezin' me tits off, when I see this bloke swagger in. I'm tellin' ye, Paddy, looked like he'd stepped out of a Hell's Angel movie - black leather jacket, denim jeans, matching gloves, a battered helmet under his arm. Moved like he owned the feckin' place, the shoulders on him, Paddy, nearly fillin' the doorway, built like a bloody brick shithouse he was. Never seen anythin' like it.'

With a furrowed brow, Paddy moved closer.

'And she, get this, she only pulls her hood down, and it's not your woman anymore! Gotta a blonde wig on, hair right down to her arse. No makeup. No false nails. Nothin' like the woman you've been ridin'. It was like she didn't want this fella knowin' who she really is.'

For fuck's sake. Dee was right. No getting around it now. Fuck but she'd never let this one go. He could see her face, with that bloody '*Told ye, didn't I?*' look. It was Paddy's turn to take a long pull of his Guinness, trying to swallow the picture down.

Brian kept going. 'At first, they're just chattin'. Friendly-like, all normal. But then she starts wavin' her hands around, gettin' all worked up, shoutin' at him across the table. He's tryin' to stay calm, tryin' to talk her down, but she's not for havin' it. Gets louder and louder, her arms flying all over the joint. Then she storms right out and leaves him sittin' there like. Same girl didn't look happy, not a bit.'

It all fell into place for Paddy. After what happened in the storeroom, she hadn't been herself since he came back, restless and on edge, barely sparing him a word. He'd figured it was just woman's stuff or maybe she was still angry because he'd gone quiet on her and their quickie. But now, after hearing about that Hell's Angel stuff, he knew exactly what had been haunting her.

She's scared. But of what and why?

'What else?' Paddy urged, trying to keep the edge out of his voice.

Brian was enjoying himself. It always felt good when he brought solid intel home. He'd never taken to Brona Doyle, if that was even her name, and now he had proof the woman was hiding something. Result. He and Dolores, whom he secretly fancied like fuck, had spent hour after hour slagging the woman off between ops. But now, with this, he reckoned he'd be up there in Dee's good books. Not that he ever dared call her 'Dee' like her twin. He'd tried that once and ended up wearing a pint of Guinness for his trouble.

'So,' he said, sitting back with that look he got when he knew he'd played it smart, 'I gave it a minute, then wandered in. Parked myself near the payphone, figured the big fella might have to make a call. Thank Christ I did.'

Enjoying Paddy's growing interest, Brian went on. 'Your man was pacing about, all riled up and shoutin'. Deadly he was. Whoever was on the other end of that call got an earful, I can tell ye. Cursin' his head off, he was.' Savouring the moment, he took another long drink. Paddy didn't push him, just watched and waited.

'Giving off about her, but kept calling her Alice. That must be her real name, right? Said she was a psycho, a complete nutter. Proper venom in his voice. Then he got quiet, I thought the call was over, but suddenly he's roarin' like a fuckin' bull! Loses it again, tells the person to go fuck themselves and slams the phone down. Almost breaks it.'

Paddy stared down into his pint, suddenly silent. Brian knew. Paddy's thoughts were racing, the kind he'd learned to keep to himself whenever the boss got that look in his eye.

'Ye didn't happen to get the number he called, did ye?' Paddy asked a minute or so later.

Brian grinned. He'd been waiting for that.

'Course I did. Called the operator, said I was a peeler and needed the number that'd just been dialled. Belongs to a fella called Ian Dillon. Works part-time as an electrician. Lives in Bangor.'

For effect, he moved closer and whispered. 'And Paddy... wait for this... he's only a fuckin' part-time UDR man!'

Paddy sat bolt upright. 'Jesus Christ. What the fuck is that woman up to?'

Brian gave a quiet laugh, thinking he could almost slap himself on the back. He'd have made a grand PI, he reckoned. Picture himself in a weather-beaten raincoat and trilby, notebook at the ready, tackling every case that came his way and cracking it every single time.

'There's one more thing,' he added, drawing it out.

Paddy raised an eyebrow. '*More*?'

'Oh, aye. Here's the interesting bit. The big gorilla, right? I asked the wee waitress if she knew him. Told me he's in all the time. Regular, like. Name's something mad... Wait for this. *Lemon*. Can you believe that? Who the fuck calls themselves *Lemon*. He looked more like a fuckin' pumpkin.'

The second Brian said *Lemon*, Paddy stiffened. He knew who that bastard was alright. Lemon and his so-called kids. He'd heard plenty about them. Sadistic animals they were. Tearing through Catholic streets for the fun of it, protected from on high, nobody dared to stop or catch them. Vicious, twisted bastards, they were every one of them. The leadership had their eyes on them, tossing about ways to get back at the ruthless pricks.

So Brona, Alice, whatever the hell the woman was calling herself now, had been hanging round with Lemon, had she? Maybe even working for him. This was good. They'd smoked the Brit out. A bolt of adrenaline surged through him. The night had just taken a turn, and for once, it was going his way.

'Fuck me, Brian,' he said, grinning. 'That's some job, mucker. Bloody genius. Ye could've been a PI, like your man Kojak or the like!' He clapped his comrade's back and stood, already moving towards the bar. 'I'm gettin' us a whiskey to celebrate. Want one?'

Brian couldn't help laughing. He'd done well, got the result he was after, and earned himself a drink. Why not let Paddy buy a round for a change?!

Alice Wallace knew she'd screwed everything up, and badly. There was no one else to blame this time. She was the one who'd let Paddy Gillispie into her bed, knowing full well it broke every rule in the book. It didn't matter how she tried to justify it to herself. The fallout had already begun, creeping in from every side and gaining pace by the hour.

It wasn't just sex, even though he'd done a number on her body that left her head in bits. It was more than that. It was the way he got under her skin, how he made himself part of her world without asking. Ever since he'd turned up at the off-licence after disappearing, she'd been trying her best to get him out of her head. Shut down her emotions, but he kept coming round, telling her what to do, what to wear, shagging the brains out of her. She hated herself for that. Hated how weak he made her feel. But she hadn't been able to stop him.

Now she was running on fumes, and every second counted. Det had ordered her in, but she'd flat out refused. She and Ian were on the brink of hitting The Shamrock. Her handler hadn't a clue what she was really doing, only warned her she was running herself into the ground, that her life was on the line, and to come home. Her only win so far had been getting Dolores out of the way, and Armagh Gaol had done just that. Locking Dolores up had upset Paddy, but by the time Alice and Ian were set, Dolores would be back at The Shamrock again. Bullseye.

She'd caught Paddy and Brian Monaghan in a hushed conversation. Paddy's voice was low, sharp as a blade, 'Thank fuck Dee was spot on about moving that cache. If the Brits got their hands on that lot, I don't know what would've happened.'

With her screwed-up emotions, she'd let a golden chance slip, and it sickened her. How she could've been so incompetent, she didn't know, but she had, and she'd no one to blame but herself.

Tonight she sat alone in her flat and looked around. The place felt bleak, lifeless, stripped of any joy, much like herself. Apart from her books, there was nothing of her in it. No warmth, no softness, nothing that hinted at who Alice Wallace really was. Her thoughts drifted to home. Not this flat, but her *real* home. She saw her mother's gentle touches. Framed family photos, fresh flowers in jam jars, little bits of clutter that gave the place a soul. That soft, familiar messiness that made it feel welcoming and safe. Nothing like here.

A slow ache formed in her chest. She couldn't remember the last time they'd spoken. Months, maybe longer. She'd cut it all out for the job. For Paddy. For the lies. Sitting in this bare flat, all she could feel was the cost of it. Maybe it was time to stop. She was done in. Tired in a way that sleep couldn't save her.

Chapter Seventy-Six

AWOL

Part-time UDR man Ian Dillon was on his way to a last-minute callout. His boss had promised time and a half. Some old dear had been left with no heating and was desperate enough to pay over the odds. He wasn't mad keen on the idea of going, but the extra cash could go towards that holiday his other half kept banging on about. Somewhere warm next year, her and the baby. She'd been on his case for months.

He was still stuck in that slump from the last time he'd seen Alice, the day she'd told him they wouldn't be talking anymore. He'd miss her. She was smart, organised, never passed up a chance, the sort of person you could rely on when things got difficult. Since then he'd tried a few low-risk ops with the fellas but none of them gave him that thrill or sense of satisfaction. Sure, they'd taken out a few Provos but the last one was a shambles, rushed, out of control and twice as dangerous as it needed to be. They'd nearly been caught. After that, he lay low, waiting for The Shamrock.

There was the phone call from Lemon. *Jesus*. His friend Lemon had been incensed. Roared down the line like a lunatic. Ian hadn't heard fury like it in years.

Lemon said Alice had lost it, gone clean off her rocker because he couldn't get her what she wanted. Some rare ammo, specialist stuff. He'd tried to tell her it took time to get that kind of gear. Tried to explain why, but when Lemon asked who the target was, she exploded. Complete meltdown. He'd ended the call by calling Alice every name under the sun. Said she was a headcase and warned Ian never to call him again. Said if either of them so much as breathed in his direction, there'd be murder. Then told him to fuck off.

Pulling up to the pensioner's bungalow, Ian took a minute and looked around. The street was quiet and pleasant and he figured a house here must cost a bundle. He took off his ridiculous baseball cap and stuffed it into the top pocket of the bright overalls he hated. His boss thought that a branded uniform, cap included, made them look more professional. Ian thought it made them look like prize tits.

Toolbox in hand, he made his way up the short path and rapped on the front door. No answer. He knocked again and the door swung open on its own. He paused just long enough to call out, then stepped into the hallway, eager to finish the job and get back home to the baby. Turning left, he moved into the living room.

The bullet hit before he knew a thing. It passed through his right eye, blew out the back of his skull, and dropped him to the carpet. Brain and bone splattered the diamond-patterned wall. The thick pile muffled his last thud.

Brian Monaghan lowered the silencer and stepped back. No panic. He could tick the box on that one. He peeled off his balaclava – had to wear it; you never know – then rolled it tight and slid it into his jeans pocket. Next, he stepped methodically over the UDR man's body and unzipped the extra-large overalls he'd been wearing. No blood marks. Lucky break. Once everything was in order, he pulled the overalls on over his own clothes and gave a faint, ironic smile before wiping down Ian's baseball cap and tugging it low over his head. In the dead fella's pocket, he conveniently found the van keys.

Perfect.

He took a slow look around the room, careful not to stare at what was left of Ian Dillon's face. Brian always believed it best to work at a calm pace with a clear head. He paused at the door and glanced upward. Upstairs, the two old codgers were still bound and gagged in their bedroom, probably scared witless. They'd be fine - someone would turn up – eventually. He closed the door quietly behind him, adjusted the cap, and climbed into the van. Tonight, he'd drive it out to their usual industrial park and set it alight.

Alice Wallace's handler couldn't begin to describe how pissed off he was. He sat opposite her sergeant, face redder than his silk tie, now speckled with ash. He hadn't even finished one cigarette before lighting another, his fingers fluttering. 'I warned you. Told you she'd balls it up. Didn't I tell you?' His voice seething with rage, but Sergeant Dury didn't rise to it.

He'd seen this routine before. Same old. A handler with too much pressure riding on one agent, one op. He felt for the poor bastard, but he wasn't about to be anyone's scapegoat. For the record, no, he hadn't warned him. Not formally, anyway. Still, he wasn't going to waste breath arguing about it now.

'She was to come in,' the handler shouted. 'I ordered her straight back in. What's she done? Vanished. Fucking AWOL!' He slammed his fist on the table, then dragged both hands through his hair, still gripping the cigarette. Ash scattered everywhere.

'We've searched the offy, her digs, the bloody Shamrock. Nothing. Not a trace. They've taken her. The stupid cow. They've fucking taken her. If she were here, I'd kill her myself!' He didn't realise how ludicrous it sounded.

The soldier said nothing, knowing the man didn't mean it. He was incensed because he cared. Losing another agent this soon in the field felt like failure. The handler slumped back into his chair, his face in his hands. 'We've got to find her before it's too fucking late,' he muttered.

Dury picked up his pen but wrote nothing down. He knew what was coming. The handler slammed his fist on the desk, eyes blazing. 'There's nothing else for it,' he spat. 'I don't want him spooked, but we'll stick a fucking tail on Paddy Gillispie and get The Shamrock. Blow the place to smithereens!'

Chapter Seventy-Seven

Bit of a Terrier

Father McGuire had retired, and Father Connolly now carried the weight of St Mary's alone, supported only by the young and earnest Father Drury. The parish numbered around ten and a half thousand souls, all of them relying on two priests for comfort, counsel, and the rites that marked life's hardest moments.

Every morning, Connolly would gather his few essentials and set out on house calls - to parents shattered by loss, to widows who had nothing left but memories, and to children whose questions cut him deeper than he cared to admit. Some days he felt as though the entire parish was draped in mourning, a slow fog that clung to every street and doorway. The anger and fear that people kept tucked away behind their faith, prayers and hymns was beginning to settle into their bones, even into his own. So much violence, so many funerals for boys and girls stolen from life before their time. It was endless. Now, more than ever, he understood why Father McGuire had stepped aside when he did.

That visit to the H-Blocks with Tommy O'Reilly still gnawed at him. He'd gone in full of hope, praying Tommy might reason with Donal Kyle and his father, cajoling them into accepting the new regulations, awful as they were. But it had fallen flat. Donal's refusal to don the prison uniform had ignited a fire. Now hundreds were following his example - locked in their cells day and night, walls smeared with filth, pools of urine gathering on the floor, hair long and matted, beards tangled and wild. They refused to emerge for anything except Sunday Mass.

It was no place for the living.

The priest hadn't been back to Boston in months, and he missed it more than he thought he would. Officer Halloran, now a good friend, had retired to the New York suburbs and started a charity that gave Derry children a chance to get away for a six-week holiday to visit the States. A brief escape from all the horror of the Troubles. Unsurprisingly, it was proving extremely popular.

A few weeks back, Tommy O'Reilly had asked Cathal to speak to Bishop Carlin about his niece, Tina McLaughlin. He'd visited her in Armagh Gaol and come back visibly shaken. Said the poor child was in a shocking state, covered in angry, weeping sores, barely aware of where she was, painfully thin, and undoubtedly neglected by the prison authorities. The Republican women were doing their best, but under the circumstances, things were getting out of control.

Tommy was scared for her. Scared of what might happen if she was left in that place much longer. Cathal had written to the bishop the very next day. Bishop Carlin wanted him to brief his secretary, Father Alex Breslin, in full. If Breslin found merit in the case, he would distil the facts for the bishop and decide how best to intervene. It was only a small step, but it was enough to give them hope.

Father Breslin had been at Bishop Hegarty's side the day he was murdered at the City Hotel. Since then, he had become indispensable to Bishop Carlin, who now led a diocese under pressure from every direction.

When Cathal arrived at the bishop's residence beside St Eugene's Cathedral, Father Breslin welcomed him with open warmth. The two men had grown close. Back when Breslin first landed in Derry, only a few months before the fatal hotel shooting, it had been Cathal who had taken him under his wing. There'd been no grand gestures, no forced pleasantries, only quiet, steady guidance and solid advice whenever it was needed. Even after the rumours began to swirl through the city in the wake of the bomb scare, ugly whispers about Breslin and Kieran Kelly, the kind of talk that stuck whether true or not, Cathal had never wavered. He kept his counsel, stayed loyal, and made it obvious he wasn't interested in petty gossip. Whatever the truth, it was none of his business.

The bishop respected Cathal's fundraising in Boston, where he'd stirred serious support and donations through NORAID. The money kept several local community projects afloat: youth centres, housing schemes, local charities and other supplies of the kind no one ever spoke about openly.

Now came the big question. With Father McGuire retired, there was a sizeable gap in Derry's pastoral leadership. If Cathal were recalled to take the reins, someone else would have to step in on the NORAID work. It was a tall order. Few priests had Cathal's charisma and even fewer could hold a room the way he did. He made people open their wallets without asking outright. Breslin and the bishop had discussed it more than once. There was no easy answer. Cathal was needed in both places but they could have him in only one. Either way, today's meeting was about Tina McLaughlin and, Breslin knew, Cathal wouldn't let it drop. He'd want an answer. Soon.

He looked his friend over. Cathal seemed worn down, hollowed out by sorrow, as though the city's losses had carved themselves into his very frame. But his strength and stubbornness hadn't left him. It was still there, quiet and weathered, the kind that didn't make a fuss. Solid. Reliable. In that rough, raggedy way of his, he was striking and charismatic. He could see why he was such a success in the States, they'd love him.

Since Kieran's death, Alex had felt unmoored, like a man cut adrift, floating with no compass, no anchor, nothing to cling to. Their last conversation still haunted him. He'd gone over it more times than he could count, lying awake most nights, replaying every word. If only he'd said yes. If only he'd agreed to go to Miami, to the sun, to a place where no one cared who they were or where they were from. Maybe things would have turned out differently. Maybe Kieran would still be here. Maybe they both would.

He was perpetually in a state of dread. A haunting fear that the truth might one day leak out. That someone, somewhere, would reveal what had gone on between him and Kieran. Their love. Their nights together. Those stolen hours. Over time, he mastered the art of burying his secret, allowing him to forget and move on. Then Cathal wrote. Asking for help. Not for himself, but for her. Martina McLaughlin.

Her name stopped him cold.

The girl who stood trial for Bishop Hegarty's murder and more, who was blamed for all of it. The one they said helped Kieran, loved him. Some claimed she'd been groomed, was his girlfriend, but Alex had never believed that. He couldn't. Nobody could comprehend what he and Kieran shared. Every time her name came up, he left the room, pretended not to hear, pretended not to care.

But now, Cathal had written a brother priest asking for help. What choice did he have? He had to step up, be professional. Do his duty, say the right words, steady his hands, and keep his voice calm. He'd play the part like it didn't gut him, like it wouldn't cost him emotionally. He'd have to breathe through it.

'Father, please, sit,' he whispered, gesturing Cathal towards a chair. 'Would you like some tea?'

Cathal nodded. Alex poured a splash of milk into the China cups already set out, his hands steady enough, though not without a faint tremble he hoped Cathal didn't notice. He passed a cup across the table and sat down opposite, adjusting his robe out of reflex, pretending this was a meeting between old friends. Nothing to stress about.

'Tough week?' He asked before taking a sip of tea. 'You look wiped out.'

Cathal groaned. 'A nightmare, Father. An absolute nightmare.'

'No need for that after all this time. It's Alex.'

A brief nod. 'Sorry, of course,' Cathal said, resting his cup and saucer on his knee. 'We've had four funerals this week. One for a twenty-year-old, shot by a soldier from a Fort George sanger. Passengers on a bus driving past the barracks. Four rounds fired. Caught one in the neck. No chance. Dead before they got him off the floor. Another fella next to him injured, his insides blown open, and two others, a man and woman. Soldier had a breakdown, apparently. Him a cook too.'

Alex nodded gravely. That he had heard. 'Awful, Cathal. Awful. What else?'

'John Deeney. Parishioner. Prostate cancer. Old bugger held on longer than expected. Sore death, though. Rough. But... thank God he's out of pain now.' He stopped there. Deeney's death had got to him. Maybe it was the sheer drawn-out agony of it. Or maybe it was everything piling up on him. He couldn't help but wonder why God let men with such strong faith suffer like that. 'The other two you'll have heard about. A Provo booby trap blew up early. Meant for the Brits. Took two youngsters instead.'

Alex bowed his head, eyes low, and murmured a quiet prayer to St□Thérèse, the one saint who'd never let him down. His lips barely moved, but the words were there, old and familiar, as always, soothing. He looked up again and spoke gently. 'The bishop and I... we're truly grateful, Cathal. We see what you're doing, and we're here to support you, give you whatever you need. Within reason, of course.' He smiled as he said it, the warmth in his voice softening the point. It was time to go for the kill. Cathal set his tea aside and leaned in, elbows braced on his knees, his gaze fixed. The warmth had gone from his face.

'In that case, Alex... we need to talk about Martina McLaughlin.'

Breslin's heart jumped but he gave a small nod. Then he heard it from the horse's mouth. The grooming. How Kieran manipulated the girl into something she didn't understand until the last minute. Her imprisonment. Her decline. How she was barely functioning now, lost in herself, and how her family were on their knees begging that the bishop would help. He sat still, struggling to absorb it. He'd spent so long keeping her name at arm's length, refusing to follow the case, refusing to read the headlines. Here it was, laid out in front of him, plain as day. God forgive him, but it unnerved him more than he was ready for. She'd been a child, innocent in every way, and hadn't led anyone on. Kieran had played her from the start.

That realisation came slowly, creeping in through the cracks, then rooted itself deep inside him, until it hollowed out his chest. Kieran had lied not only to the wretched girl. He'd lied to him too. Seduced him with that softness, with fire in his voice, conviction in every word, and those chocolate brown eyes that made Alex feel chosen. Trusted. What a fool he'd been. He'd defended him, believed every word, told himself that Kieran was complicated, not cruel. That the wicked rumours were no better than jealousy and bitterness. There had to be another side to him. But there wasn't. Kieran Kelly had used him. Like he'd used that poor child. Alex had to live with it. Every day.

Bill Barter hadn't meant to stay in Derry quite so long. He'd come with nothing but a suitcase and a hangover. On the first day, he'd walked straight into a riot, a bomb scare outside the City Hotel where he was meant to stay, sirens wailing, people shouting, soldiers yelling orders. It felt like a lifetime ago now. In truth, fate had thrust him here. He'd left Boston with little more than a bruised ego and the thinnest sliver of hope that he might still have a future. Jack, his boss at *The Globe*, hadn't minced his words. Gave it to him straight across his cluttered desk, cigar in hand and that no-nonsense Midwest drawl of his that always meant business.

'You go to Ireland, get your head sorted, write me somethin' decent, or you're done, son. I mean it. One more piece of crap and that's it. You'll be outta *The Globe*, outta journalism, and I won't lift a finger to save you. Capiche?'

Barter had nodded, trying not to look as ravaged as he felt. He'd nodded again on the plane, washed down with a couple of whiskies, and once more as the wheels touched down in Belfast. Lo-and-behold, he walked straight into a double shooting and a bloody bomb scare at the very hotel he was meant to stay in. Best run of luck he'd had in decades.

Derry was meant to be his last-chance saloon. Ironically, it ended up saving his life. Still here, he was neck-deep in a city tearing itself apart, among people he'd grown to love, caught up in a story that wouldn't let go. Every day brought another feature to chase, some of them brutal, some impossible to forget. The rush of breaking news still hit him like a drug. Between the telex machine, frantic phone calls, and that temperamental old fax, he'd managed to pull off some cracking exclusives.

The article on old Father McGuire? Bagged him an award. The priest had been a godsend. Shy at first, nervous even, but once he got going, he didn't stop. Spoke in detail about his role in the old IRA in the north in the late Fifties. No holding back. The story wrote itself. It gave *The Globe*'s readers something solid, gave the Provos background and history, context, and gave Barter exactly what he needed. Credibility at last. Confidence too. After that, he couldn't walk into a Republican bar without someone buying him a pint.

Some time back, he'd got a surprise call from an old college buddy, Dale Horn, a longtime CIA agent. They used to be real pals, right up 'til Barter's divorce, when Horn went MIA, likely under orders from his wife, who happened to be best friends with Barter's ex. No hard feelings though, hearing from him again was a pleasant surprise.

Once the small talk was out of the way, Barter reckoned there had to be more to his call, so he cut to the chase. 'You still with the Company, Dale? Chasing spies and stoking coups?'

The CIA man laughed. 'Always had a big mouth, Bill. But yeah, I'm in Belfast. Thought I'd look you up. Been reading your stuff. You've turned into one hell of a journalist.'

Barter snorted. 'Turned into?' He gave a small shake of the head but let it go. 'What the hell are you doin' in Belfast?'

Horn didn't answer straight away. He took a deep breath, as if deciding what to say. Then, cool as ever, he said, 'Let's say I'm followin' up on a few things. Couple of names we're interested in. Yours came up too.'

Barter's eyes narrowed. 'Mine? Don't tell me you've turned me into a person of interest.'

'Nothin' like that,' Horn replied, calm as a breeze. 'But you're close to certain people. You hear things. You write things. We read 'em.'

Barter lit a cigarette, took a drag, squinted through the smoke. 'So what is this, Dale? You wantin' me to pass on gossip? Play spy for Uncle Sam?'

On the other end, Horn smiled. Didn't confirm, didn't deny. 'Let's just meet. See where it goes.'

A few days later, they met for lunch at the Europa. Small talk first. College days. Women trouble. Ex-wives still bein' a pain in the ass. Then Horn leaned in, voice low.

'Wanna know why I'm really here?'

'Not sure,' Barter said, 'but you're gonna tell me, anyway.' He'd a fair idea, of course, but played dumb.

Horn's eyes lit up. 'We're trackin' NORAID. Arms, cash, the lot. You've no idea how many dollars are pourin' outta the States to fund this shit. The Brits are losin' it, throwin' their toys outta the pram, threatenin' trade deals, puttin' the squeeze on us every chance they get.'

Barter looked sceptical. 'Go on.'

'We've got names. We're buildin' profiles. That's where you come in.'

Barter choked on his coffee, coughing into the cup. 'Me? You seriously want me to help the fuckin' CIA? I thought you were jokin'!'

'Keep your damn voice down!' Horn hissed, grabbing his arm. 'We need you, Bill. I need you.'

Barter, in his modesty, shook his head and replied. 'Jesus, Dale. I'm a two-bit reporter, not Jim Phelps.'

Horn laughed. 'Exactly. That's why you're perfect. Keep doin' what you're doin'. You hear somethin', see somethin', you come to us before you print. That's all we're askin'. In return... well, we've got a few stories of our own you might like.'

Next, to Barter's astonishment, he dropped a name: Charles Jones. Barter almost laughed. Couldn't have been better timing. His next piece was already zeroing in on that smug bastard. The speeches, the staged outrage, the not-so-subtle threats. Jones was playing to the crowd like a messiah, but Barter saw through it. He'd been tracking him for months. Everyone knew Jones kept his hands clean, never pulled the trigger himself, but Lemon and the rest of that filthy crew? Different story. They were neck-deep in blood and proud of it.

He thought back to the night Lemon followed him. Big mistake. Barter had stood his ground, looked the thug dead in the eye and told him if anything happened, a certain file would make its way to a certain desk. Names, dates, details. Enough to wreck lives. Truth was, he didn't have a damn thing. Not even a page. But he'd sold the lie with style, and the bastard bought it. Backed off and never came sniffing again.

Now here was Horn, cool as ice. 'Your country would be very grateful,' he said. 'And just so we're on the same wave length, Bill, we're talkin' exclusives. You help us, we help you.'

Barter leaned back, fingers wrapped around his coffee. He didn't need to say a word. He was already halfway there. The stories were his; the headlines were his. If the CIA wanted a middleman with brains, balls and a byline, they'd come to the right guy. He gave a slow grin. Hell yeah, he was in.

Father Breslin relayed to the bishop the details of his meeting with Cathal. The bishop listened closely, his fingers steepled beneath his chin. 'Ah, yeah, poor wee thing. I remember it well. Father McGuire told me about it. The father first, wasn't it? Died in custody, beaten up. Then the mother...' He paused, blessed himself and murmured a prayer when the word 'suicide' ran through his mind.

'What about the brother, what's his name again? Mike? No, Martin, that's it. Back on the scene now, is he?'

'He is,' Breslin replied. 'Along with the eldest sister, Caitlin. She works in a photography shop on the Strand Road. Keeps her head down, Father Connolly tells me. He doesn't know her that well, but says she's a good enough being.'

The bishop sat back and was silent for a moment, eyes fixed on nothing. Then, with a nod of resolve, he said, 'Right. I'll write to Governor Yeaman. A handwritten letter. If he can't be bothered to answer, we'll go to the Secretary of State. After that, if he ignores us, we'll go to the press. Make a statement.' He tapped the arm of his chair with his pen. 'That Yankee reporter, Barter. He's a straight talker, isn't he? We'll talk to him. An exclusive. As for Tommy O'Reilly? That fella's given this city everything. People don't know the half of it. If we can help his family, we'll do it. Soon as.'

Cathal Connolly sat opposite Tommy and Caitlin in the Rainbow. With everything on his plate, it'd been a while since he'd made his usual call-in on a Friday morning, but Siobhan greeted him like no time had passed. The priest had phoned Tommy earlier to say he had news, good news, thank God, and suggested they meet here.

For the first time in weeks, Tommy felt hopeful. Not the kind of hope he forced on himself to keep moving, but the real kind. The kind that came from someplace buried in his gut. He looked at Caitlin. She sat quietly beside him, both hands wrapped round her mug, a soft smile on her face. The tension that had clung to her for days seemed to have eased. Her shoulders were lower, her face relaxed, and her eyes held a flicker of peace. It was as though the priest saying 'good news' had pushed the clouds aside and let a bit of sunshine in at last.

'So you're sayin' the bishop's going to write personally to the prison governor and then, if no luck, the Secretary of State? He's demanding Tina's release on medical grounds?' Tommy asked, almost not daring to believe it.

'If they ignore him, he'll go public, press, TV, the works. That Yankee reporter, Bill what's-his-face. An exclusive. He'll run it too, here and America, no question.' Cathal added.

'That's bloody brilliant, Father. Honestly.' Tommy replied. He couldn't friggin' believe it!

'Thank you, Father,' Caitlin whispered. 'That's the best news we've had in ages.'

Cathal raised a hand to set things straight. 'Don't you two run ahead of yourselves now. It's a start. I won't lie. But you know how these things go. Those civil servants will say anything to keep us quiet, and can drag their feet for months.'

But Tommy couldn't help himself. His smile stretched from ear to ear. 'Aye, I know, but Bishop Carlin's no pushover. Once that man sinks his teeth into somethin', he doesn't let go. He's a bit of a terrier, that one. A man of the people, always has been. If he says he's doin' somethin', he'll do it. I'm tellin' ye now, he'll get our Tina home.'

Chapter Seventy-Eight

Jackie O

For the first morning in an age, Caitlin woke up feeling not only relieved but something closer to hopeful – a rare emotion these days. Now that her sister's fate was finally in safe hands, thanks to Father Connolly and the bishop, she felt she could at last turn her attention back to her own affairs and start acting on Seamus Donaghy's advice.

There was unfinished business with James Henderson, and whether or not she liked it, it was up to her to approach him and set the record straight. Maybe she'd catch him at the factory, or when he was out on one of his runs – she knew his route well enough – or perhaps she'd simply knock on the front door of Melrose and be done with it.

Her morning bus had once again been hijacked, and the remaining service was patchy and late. The usual suspects stood huddled at the bus stop, waiting without complaint. It had been a rough week for the estate, and there was a weariness hanging over the place, heavy and unspoken. More and more funerals, she thought, as her eyes followed yet another coffin being driven past, this one headed for St Mary's, surrounded by the familiar procession of black saloons and sorrowful faces.

By the time she arrived at the photographer's, the city centre was stirring. She unlocked the heavy-duty steel roller door and ducked inside. Her boss, Raymond Burns, had taken the day off. Something about his wedding anniversary, she remembered vaguely.

The shop was bitterly cold, and she crossed straight through to the back office, throwing the keys on the desk with a sigh and rubbing warmth into her arms. She flicked the kettle on. It was going to be a busy one. She was expecting a few couples to collect their wedding portfolios and knew there'd be questions and fussing over missing photos and blurred relatives.

Around eleven o'clock, the bell above the studio door gave a faint jingle, and Caitlin stepped out from the darkroom, rubbing her fingers on a lint-free cloth and bracing for another pensioner wanting a passport photo or a communion print re-touched. She'd barely opened her mouth when she stopped dead.

The woman at the counter looked like she'd wandered in from a film set, all style and swagger, not a hair out of place. Her suit was sharp, mustard yellow with bold lapels, the flared trousers skimming the tops of her gleaming heeled boots and a handbag to match. A silk scarf was knotted neatly at her neck, and her eyes were hidden behind oversized sunglasses, even though the sky outside was its usual grey. Definitely not local. Not with that walk. No cardigan, no pinny, no scent of boiled cabbage. Whoever she was, she wasn't in for family portraits, nor was she from Derry.

'Can I help you?' Caitlin asked, keeping her tone polite but wary.

The woman peeled off her glasses and smiled like they were old friends. 'Ah, good morning, miss. I need your help,' she announced, each word wrapped in ringing English tones. All posh.

Caitlin's instincts kicked in. She disliked this girl on sight, but she held her expression and managed a polite smile. Who in God's name was she? Blonde and blow-dried, with false lashes and frosted pink lipstick. Her outfit was straight off a fashion page. She even had gloves, white kid leather, which she began peeling off, one finger at a time. A right Jackie O.

'Yes, please,' She looked around the studio. 'You see, I'm getting married rather quickly, but not for the usual reason!' Amused by her own humour, she giggled.

'I've been told this man – Burns, is it? Yes, Burns – that he's the best in town. Am I right?'

'You are, Miss,' Caitlin replied, with little warmth in her voice. Sensing something was untoward, Marleen scrutinised the shop assistant. Wow. She was a knockout. Tall, willowy, the kind of girl who could probably eat a whole trifle and still fit into size eight jeans. Not Marleen's type, not that it mattered, but credit where it was due. Her skin was porcelain-smooth, not a blemish or bump to be seen. Her long black hair was tied back, sleek and neat, not a strand out of place. Those eyes – a piercing, pale blue – held a story. Not sadness exactly, more like... life. It was there beneath the surface. Marleen could always tell.

She found herself staring and shook her head lightly, laughing to recover. 'Ah, sorry, off on a tangent there,' she muttered, casting another look around the studio as if to ground herself. 'Yes, right... where was I?'

The woman's affected manner made Caitlin nervous. What on earth was someone like her doing in a place like this?

'You were saying about Mr Burns. Yes, he's the best in the city and very popular. So how can I help?' Caitlin knew she was being rude, but didn't care.

The stranger carefully placed her gloves in a Hermès handbag while she chattered on. 'Well, it's simple, really. I'd like to book him. To do our wedding. If he can.'

'I'll get the diary,' Caitlin replied with a half-hearted smile.

She made her way slowly behind the curtain that concealed the dark room. Reaching Raymond's desk, she picked up the diary; but before she did anything with it, she pulled the curtain back a little to peek at the marvel that stood waiting in the shop.

Marleen was humming to herself and glanced around at the displays. He really was rather good, she thought with surprise. Not ideal, the lighting was a touch unimaginative and the cropping a little boring, but still it was better than expected for someone working in a provincial backwater. Certainly not Vogue, but passable. He'd do.

Roger, bless him, wasn't fit enough to travel, so she and James had agreed on something small and tasteful here in Londonderry. A quiet, intimate ceremony, family and a handful of close friends. Nothing showy. The wedding breakfast would be at Melrose, of course. She loved that house, always had. It felt right. Later though, once things had settled a bit – or more truthfully, once the old bugger had finally popped his clogs – then they'd do it properly. A grand London affair, with all the trimmings. The Savoy, perhaps. Or the Ritz. She adored them both and truly didn't mind which. Either would be exquisite.

She turned as the shop girl, '*Caitlin*', according to her badge, reappeared from the back.

'What date did you have in mind?' she asked, her voice carrying a dry, sceptical lilt.

Marleen beamed. 'Well, believe it or not, we're thinking Christmas Eve. Don't you think that's *sooo* romantic?' She let the word stretch and sparkle a little, one hand fluttering near her chest for effect. 'The lights, the candles, the crisp air, all that festive magic... I mean, really, who could resist a Christmas wedding?'

She scoffed when she caught Caitlin's expression, unreadable at first, though there was a faint trace of amusement in her eyes, the kind that suggested she was humouring her. Marleen paused. Best not to press on. Some people simply didn't recognise glamour when it was laid before them. Either that or they weren't raised to appreciate it.

Caitlin couldn't object, of course she couldn't. A Christmas Eve wedding sounded more than romantic. It sounded amazing. But the thought of one didn't bring her joy, only a fresh feeling of resentment. She disliked this woman even more now. Not only was she stunningly beautiful in that perfect, polished way Caitlin could never abide, but now she was getting married on Christmas bloody Eve – no doubt to some tall, dark, filthy-rich man with a jaw like granite and a heart like gold. *Lucky bitch.* The woman was watching her, waiting. This time Caitlin lost track of the conversation. She flushed when she noticed the raised eyebrow and the faint little cough meant to pull her back to reality.

'I… I'm sorry, I need to check the date, miss. What's your name?'

'Miss Marleen Fry.'

Caitlin practically scratched her name onto the booking form. 'The venue for the wedding, Miss Fry? Where's that then?'

'Ah yes, well, first the ceremony at the Church of Ireland, Prehen. Don't want a huge fuss and hold it at St Columb's – then the wedding breakfast at our house. Silly me, my fiancé's place, that is!'

Caitlin forced a tight smile, her lips drew taut. *Course it is.*

'The address, miss?'

'The address? Oh…' Marleen dipped a hand into her Mulberry-labelled handbag, the sort of sleek, structured thing Caitlin reckoned cost more than her year's wages. From inside, she pulled out a small sheet of snow-white notepaper, thick and posh-looking, with some fancy gold-embossed heading she couldn't quite make out. She held the paper with a hint of theatrical grace and read it out slowly, as if delivering a royal decree. 'Melrose, Albert Park, Prehen, Londonderry, BT47 QR3.' Caitlin tensed like pulled wire. That name again. *Melrose.* For half a second, she was as still as a statue, her pen poised above the paper until she could carry on.

She didn't ask who the groom was. She didn't need to.

Marleen looked at the shopgirl to check she'd got it all down, then paused. She looked dreadful. The poor thing's face had gone whiter than white – almost see-through. For a moment, Marleen thought she might faint, standing so still like a mannequin behind the counter.

Dear, dear me, she thought, is the girl in some kind of trance? Unsure what to do, she raised her hand and waved it in front of her face. 'You poor darling, are you quite alright?'

But Caitlin didn't seem to hear her. Nothing registered except the blood roaring in her ears. The room had narrowed and tilted, and all she could do was grip the counter to keep herself upright. Through sheer force, she forced the words out under her breath, repeating the address and the date like a chant. Like it wasn't real.

Marleen took a step back. This girl's behaviour was odd – quite odd. Something felt off. It made her so uncomfortable she decided to leave. Quick. She'd deal with Mr Burns next time. Herself.

'I have to go now, I'm afraid. Can you tell me if the date works, or do you need to speak to Mr Burns?'

Still pale, Caitlin nodded. The sooner this woman left, the better, 'I'll speak to him.'

'Thank you.' Marleen jotted her number neatly on the order form, her pen gliding across the page with the right amount of flair. She paused, pen still in hand, and cast another look at the sales girl. The poor thing hadn't moved a muscle. Not even blinked, as far as she could tell. Still as a statue and almost as pale. Definitely unwell. Possibly unhinged. Something wasn't quite right, that much was clear. But in this country, under these circumstances, it was probably wiser not to pry. With a gracious smile and a polite nod, Marleen offered a final, 'Thank you and goodbye,' turned on her heel, and swept out without another word.

It took Caitlin a while to pull herself together enough to serve the customers after Marleen Fry. She worked on autopilot, barely noticing faces or names, her head still spinning. She was barely coping when she caught sight of Tommy waving through the shop door, grinning like a schoolboy and gesturing to know if it was alright to come in. She stepped outside, but before she could say a word, he'd already nudged past her into the shop. He turned back to her, face flushed, his sea-blue eyes bright with excitement.

'You'll never believe it, love,' he said, breathless. 'Bishop Carlin's only gone and phoned the Secretary of State himself this mornin', and some big judge in the appeal court too. Gave 'em both a proper rollickin'. He's followed it up with a stinker of a letter, Father Connolly told us. Off the record, there's a good chance it'll do the trick. They're gonna review Tina's case, mistrial or some legal carry on like that. We're gonna get your sister home, Caitlin. We're gonna get her home!'

Caitlin looked at him, really looked at him, and tried to smile. Her lack of excitement must've given her away and he sensed it immediately.

'You alright, love? Jesus, but you look like death warmed up,' he said, gripping her shoulders, concern flooding his face. 'What's happened now?'

Caitlin readied herself. 'I'm fine, Tommy, honest. Surprised. That's all.' She wasn't going to spoil his joy. Not now. Not when he was beaming like a five-year-old who'd got his first bike. She stepped in and hugged him, closing her eyes to keep the tears from spilling. 'I'm happy, Tommy. Really, I am. It'll be wonderful to have her back.'

Tommy pulled back, hands still on her arms, and smiled proudly. 'God love ye, Caitlin,' he murmured, his voice wobbling. 'There's you cryin' 'cos you're happy too, eh?' His own eyes misted as he tilted his head up to the sky. 'Thank you, God. For fuck's sake, give us a break now, will ye please?!' He grabbed another hug from Caitlin, laughing with that familiar deep belly laugh of his, the one that could fill any room.

Despite everything, despite the pain, Tommy's presence was a comfort for Caitlin, a reminder that some things, things like family, would always be there for her.

Chapter Seventy-Nine

Back Home to Derry

Maureen Moloney bent low, her lips close to Tina McLaughlin's ear, and whispered with quiet relief, 'Hear me, love? Time to go home.'

Tina stayed curled up on the narrow bed, facing the wall, tucked beside an old Victorian radiator that hadn't worked in months. The cell was cold, the kind of cold that hurt, and the air stank of damp. The girls had done their best, God love them, bundled extra blankets around her, hot water bottles, whispered kind words, but Tina was done. She hadn't eaten in days. Even the broth they'd got her came back up not long after she ate. Her belly was swollen and sore.

'Tina, love, do ye hear me?' Maureen asked. No response.

Tina was worn out. Friggin' tired. Not the kind of tired a good sleep would fix. Her body had given up. Oddly, she wasn't scared. She was ready. Wouldn't be long. She'd be with Kieran soon. Mammy and daddy. She'd see their faces, hear their voices, hold them. Made it easier somehow. Letting go. Faint as a whisper, her breathing was barely there. Nor was in pain, not really. Just drifting. The way you do when there's nothing left to fight for. She'd welcome death. No fighting it. Peaceful, like slipping into a warm bath, or disappearing into the dark. She wasn't lonely, a feeling she hadn't had in a long time. Her eyes found Maureen's. Sad, but calm. There was no panic in her, just a faint smile, gentle even, like she was seeing something the others couldn't.

The cell faded into view. The stink, the cold, the pain in Tina's belly, all disappeared. What came instead was a soft, warm feeling. And him.

'Kieran.' she whispered, pointing at Maureen who looked around, half expecting to see someone.

There he was, clear as day, sitting at the end of the bed behind Maureen. Elbows on his knees, hands clasped, watching her with that daft, gorgeous look she remembered too well. His eyes told her she was still his girl. The same curls had fallen into his face, just as they always had. His skin glowed golden, just like before. And those eyes – big, brown, glistening with tears, happy just to see her. She longed to tell him she'd missed him, that she'd never stopped loving him, not once, not even when the days were cruel and the nights dragged longer than they had any right to. But she couldn't. Her mouth wouldn't work. She thought he heard her anyway, when he smiled, soft and loving. He reached up, brushed the hair from his face, and spoke, low and sweet, only for her.

'I'm here, Honey. Waiting for ye.'

Tina breathed, long and slow, her body tired beyond words. A hum filled her ears, not loud, not frightening. Peace. The blankets no longer scratched her skin. Her belly didn't hurt and the shivering stopped. She wasn't cold anymore.

'Won't be long,' she replied. She could rest now. She'd heard Maureen. She was going home. Back home to Derry.

Maureen moved closer. 'What was that, love?' she asked, her brow creased with worry, but Tina shook her head, so softly. Her eyelids fluttered and closed, and she drifted off again.

A tear slid down Maureen's cheek as she murmured, 'Jesus, love, what are we gonna do with ye?'

She sat back down. The past few weeks had been savage. After the screws ransacked the gaol, tearing through every last cell, they'd been locked down for two full days. No toilets, no washrooms, no fresh air, nothing. Trapped like animals. When the doors opened, they were thrown scraps. Cold tea, dried-out bread. Might as well have been dogs. The po's were full to bursting. They'd pressed the buzzers, shouted through the flaps, begged to be let out, long enough to empty them. No one came. No one gave a toss.

With no other choice, they poured the lot under the cell doors, some of them crying as they did it, sick with the shame. The screws never flinched. They just swept it back in with a mop like it was nothing. The stench was choking, clinging to the walls, sour and foul. The piss was the worst, sharp enough to make your eyes water. A few tried flinging their waste through the bars, but the screws were quicker, boarding them until no light got in. Only darkness, dampness, filth. A repulsive and debasing darkness. No prison should break people this way. But that was the point, wasn't it? To grind them down, strip every shred of dignity they had left.

Tina was getting worse, and everyone who cared about her knew time was running out. She had to get back to Derry. Soon. The bishop stepped in, and the local MP quickly followed, pushing for the appeal to be fast-tracked and demanding an independent medical review. It caught fire. The early findings only strengthened their case, spelling it out in brutal terms: Martina McLaughlin had been gravely neglected by the medical staff at Armagh Gaol, with one locum, Dr Graham Harris, singled out. His so-called care – or lack of it – was condemned outright. By the time her weight had dropped to five and a half stone, Harris made a half-hearted attempt to force-feed her, more for show than mercy, and abandoned it the moment the order came through. She was to be released to Gransha Hospital and, if she survived, might be home within weeks.

Tommy went straight to Caitlin's studio as soon as he heard. His eyes were dancing, face alive with pure joy, and for once, he couldn't stop smiling. He had news worth shouting about, and he wanted Caitlin to hear it from him first.

'I can't believe it! Isn't it great?' he said, beaming. 'The prison lot and the courts kept draggin' their feet, and didn't your man, the bishop, hit the press, the telly, even radio stations overseas. God bless 'im! That guy Barter too, the paper man, he was brilliant!' Then, breathless, Tommy asked. 'Will you come with me to get her?'

'Wouldn't miss it for the world, Tommy. When?' Caitlin laughed.

'Friday.' She told him she'd be there.

The rest of the week was spent getting Martin's room, now Tina's, ready. Caitlin scrubbed it from top to bottom, warmed the place, dressed the bed with fresh sheets, and hung new curtains she'd made from fabric she'd picked up at the market. The McFaddens handed over a spotless second-hand mattress and a baby-blue fluffy rug for the floor. By Thursday, the place looked warm and welcoming. Tina was coming home, and Caitlin was going to spoil her rotten.

It was over a week till Christmas Eve, and James's wedding to the posh English woman was looming. Between shifts at the studio, sorting Tina's homecoming, working and keeping the house right, time was running out for Caitlin to speak to him. Alone. She was sure she'd seen him recently parked close to the studio, waiting in his car, that unmistakable Jag. Without a second thought, she'd taken off mid-chat with a customer and hurried down the pavement towards him.

Too late. He'd started the car. She waved like a lunatic and called him, but he drove past. Her heart sank, but for a split second, their eyes met. In that one brief glimpse, she saw it. Not anger. Not even bitterness. But sorrow. A raw, aching sorrow she recognised and felt herself.

Could he still care? She wondered as he eyes followed the disappearing car.

Chapter Eighty

Murder Mile

Dolores Gillispie, confined in Armagh Gaol, planned everything in secret with precision. The deed was set for Friday.

She'd been told the two POs would be working that morning. As usual, they'd turn up together in their small red Fiat 125, registration number FRZ 3487. She'd never forgive Smyth. The fat cow had gone too far when she tore through Dolores's cell, ripping up the only photos she had left of her and Paddy. A treasure box of memories. That was when things changed. From then on, Dolores watched the woman like a hawk, and when she could, noted her every move, and waited.

Smyth and her sidekick, Drake, lived in Ballynahone Drive, a stretch of Armagh city locals called 'murder mile', where so many had already been taken out. Fitting, really.

Maureen Moloney folded the letter with care and placed it back inside the envelope, a rare smile tugging at her mouth. Bridget, God love her, sounded more worn out than ever, chasing after those two little grandbabies, but even through the scribbled ink and chaotic descriptions, it was clear she was happy. Content, even. Odd thing was, she admitted, she missed the prison. Not the place itself, obviously, but the women, the routine, the bonds that had formed in the thick of it. She sent her love to the lot of them and promised to visit soon, though Maureen wouldn't be holding her breath. She'd not come back to this place if they paid her.

Still, inside the wing, nothing had improved. The screws hadn't changed, only adapted. Smyth and Drake kept their distance these days, no longer stomping around like they owned the place. They didn't fool anyone. Their cruelty hadn't vanished - it'd gone elsewhere. The girls on remand whispered stories when they could, stories that made Maureen squirm. There were bruises, strip-downs for no reason, comments made loud enough to humiliate but quiet enough to deny. Cowards both of them, hiding behind their uniforms and Yeaman's blessing.

The governor himself, he was worse than ever. Still obsessed with control, still obsessed with punishing the women for the embarrassment they'd caused. He'd brought in a new rule - two strip searches for every court appearance, no exceptions. Before they left the wing, and again as soon as they got back, even if the hearing lasted all of seven minutes. Some solicitors didn't even show up. A bored clerk would ignore the girls while they sat there, silent, handcuffed, wondering what the point of it all was. Back they'd go, dragged through corridors and flung into the same grim ritual, made to strip naked under fluorescent lights while the screws watched on with smirks and clipped commands. It wasn't security. It was domination. A calculated attempt to humiliate.

It worked - especially on the youngsters. The fresh ones. The ones still holding out hope that this was a mistake, temporary, that someone in power might actually care. Never lasted. Hope didn't last long around here. It was hacked away with every snarled order, every unwanted stare, every hand pressed a second too long during a search. It was a slow, deliberate crushing. Maureen saw it. All of it, and she'd be damned if she let it go on.

Prison officers Susan Smyth and Gladys Drake were up early this particular Friday, well-fed after an Ulster fry and in pretty good form as they headed for Armagh gaol. The gov turned out to be exactly their sort, cold, callous and indifferent. A proper bastard and they loved him for it. He'd turned a blind eye over Bridget Barry, believed everything they'd said, and these days, let them get on with their business.

Smyth had been unusually nervous these past few weeks. She'd gone too far that day, tearing up Dolores Gillispie's photographs. Overzealous didn't even cover it. Since then, she'd avoided the Republicans where possible, sticking close to Drake when she could. She told herself it was nothing, that they wouldn't dare touch her. But she'd looking over her shoulder more often. Watching. Waiting. Any bravado drained right out of her.

It started with Dolores Gillispie cornering her outside the chapel a few weeks back, right when there were no other screws around to see it. She'd stood over her and said, calm as you like, 'I got ye, Smyth. Keep looking over that fat, fuckin' shoulder of yours, 'cos I've got ye.'

Smyth hadn't batted an eyeline that day. She'd just given Gillispie a slow curl of the finger, a gesture that spoke louder than any words, daring her to react, before calmly telling her to fuck off as if she hadn't a care in the world. But the act ended the moment she was out of sight. Ever since shredding Gillispie's photos, she'd felt it — eyes on her, waiting. She told herself it was daft. Still, every morning before work, she crouched by the

Fiat, pretending to tie a lace or pick up a coin, scanning underneath for wires or anything deadly. No one ever caught her at it, and she'd sooner die than admit it, but the fear had seeped in, stitched into her routine, impossible to shake.

Republicans don't forgive. Not ever. Smyth knew that well enough. They'd sit back, patient, waiting for their moment. It wasn't only about that lunatic Gillispie anymore. It was all of them – eyes following, marking her, biding their chance. Some days she felt it, a crawl along her spine, the whispers as she passed each cell. She still barked her orders, chin held high, but inside she was shaken. Frightened, and with good reason. She'd brought it on herself. Every bit of it was down to her.

Smyth and Drake were giggling over the night before with a pair of girls off the Lisburn Road. Nothing wild – a few jars, a couple of pirate tapes, and a VHS deck borrowed from a fella Drake knew above a butcher's on the Shankill. He stocked everything from *Jaws* to shady French reels if you gave the nod. For a while it had been a tonic, a night that cut through the stink of the gaol and the chaos wrapped round it. For a few hours, they weren't screws with targets on their backs. They were young women in their twenties again, laughing like the world was a happy, carefree place. Armagh Gaol and its women forgotten.

PO Smyth was up first light, outside, checking under the car like she always did now. *Phew.* No wires. No packages. She didn't tell Drake, but went back inside, lit a cigarette, and started breakfast.

They climbed into the car around seven. Its engine gave its usual groan, coughed twice, then started. Drake gave the dashboard a pat, said something filthy about her car being more reliable than any girl other than Smyth, and with a laugh, they were off. Down Cathedral Road, nice and slowly. The streets were quiet, mist hanging low over the river, and for once, they didn't feel wary. It felt like it was gonna be a good day. Smyth lit up a Woodbine, took a long drag, and soon the car filled up with cigarette smoke.

'Ah, feck, d'you have to do that?' Drake snapped. 'You know rightly I hate it when you smoke in here!'

Smyth giggled and opened the window wide. 'Alright, alright, don't get your knickers in a twist.' She took another long drag, then blew the smoke out through the window, grinning to herself. She loved winding Gladys up. Sometimes she could be a real old biddy, miserable and grumpy. Still, for the briefest moment, Smyth's eyes flicked to the rearview mirror. A peek, no more.

Feeling wound up and annoyed, Gladys swore under her breath and stared straight ahead as they rolled to a stop at a T-junction. The light was red. Course it was. She hated it when Susie teased her like that. Always picked her moment. Always waited until things were calm, almost pleasant, then said or did something nasty enough to ruin it. It knocked Gladys sideways every time. So why didn't she ever listen? Sometimes she really tested her. It made Gladys want to grab her by the collar and—

She bit the thought back, instead watching the red light, impatiently waiting for it to change.

Before they knew it, a lone motorcyclist pulled up on their left and stopped. Dressed head to toe in black. No distinctive markings. No sound but the low rumble of the engine, and in one clean motion, a small, rounded object came sailing through the open window and landed neatly at Smyth's feet. The bike was already pulling away, roaring up the road by the time the light changed.

There were no cries, no panic. Just a second where the world seemed to stop. The object sat there. Squat. Silent. Humming with threat.

Smyth and Drake locked eyes.

Ah, fuck.

Chapter Eighty-One

A Surprise Visitor

To Caitlin's astonishment, the radiant young bride-to-be wasn't her only notable female caller that week. A few days later, when she was about to grab her coat and go for lunch, the studio door opened and in walked an older lady who looked like she'd stepped out of a magazine as well. *What the hell?*

There was something unusual about her, foreign even, but weirdly recognisable. She wore a long black cashmere coat that swayed like it cost a fortune, and her whole look – blonde hair, green eyes, that perfect skin – was the sort of thing you didn't see every day in Derry. Mid-fifties, maybe, but still effortlessly elegant. She was petite and groomed to within an inch, and as she glanced around the studio, Caitlin stood stock still behind the counter.

Then their eyes met. The woman smiled, she knew something Caitlin didn't and walked over with her hand held out. 'Catherine Henderson.' The name stopped Caitlin in her tracks. A wave of dread stirred in her belly. That was it. The eyes. She'd seen them before. *James*. She didn't move until she realised the woman's hand was still outstretched and waiting.

Quickly, she stepped forward and shook it. 'Caitlin McLaughlin.'

'I know who you are, Caitlin.' Her voice had a strange lilt to it. English, but with something harder underneath.

'You do?'

'I knew your mother, Majella. We were good friends once. She was kind to me at a time when I really needed someone I could trust.'

Caitlin was gobsmacked. *Majella knew the Hendersons?!* Before she could ask anything, the doorbell rang and another customer came in, but before she could speak, Catherine quickly stepped in, her voice low. 'Would you mind having a quick coffee with me? Maybe a bite to eat? Given the time, are you due to have lunch?'

'Ah, right, yeah, okay. I need to see to this lady first.'

Caitlin was gobsmacked. Her mother and Catherine Henderson. *Friends*. Who'd have believed it? She wondered if this was why Majella had been so insistent she steer clear of the Hendersons. Did she know something?

While Caitlin served the customer, Catherine wandered around the shop, pretending to read a brochure, but her eyes kept drifting back to the counter. Watching her. Caitlin could feel it. A few minutes later, with her coat now on, Caitlin nodded toward the door.

'There's a place over the road.'

The two women stepped out into the cold, driving rain. Reaching the kerb to cross, a passing bus thundered through a huge puddle, sending dirty water right up over their coats. They both gasped, looked at the damage, and, unbelievably, burst out laughing. Without thinking, Catherine linked her arm through Caitlin's. It felt easy, like it belonged there. It reminded Caitlin of her walks to the factory with Anne, those wet mornings, arms linked, talking absolute rubbish. They rushed towards the Rainbow, hunched against the rain, giggling like schoolgirls. Inside, Siobhan smiled when she saw them, already heading over with menus and once seated, Catherine got straight to it.

'I imagine you're wondering what this is all about?' she asked.

'I am, yeah, tell me and put me out of my misery,' Caitlin said, not hiding her curiosity.

'First of all, I wanted to say how sorry I was to hear about your mother. And your father – Patrick.'

'Thank you,' Caitlin said, her eyes looking down on the table. Siobhan returned with two mugs of tea. Catherine gave her a grateful nod and continued.

'As I said, I knew Majella. She worked for us at Melrose when I was going through an especially bad time. Nursed me, really. We became great friends – I adored her. She had this spark, a bit of lovely madness about her, in the best way. Made me laugh when I hadn't laughed in forever.'

Caitlin swallowed hard, her throat narrowing. It was a version of Majella that she once knew before the Troubles – lively, full of talk, brimming with love for everyone and everything.

'She was so happy back then, madly in love with your father. She'd go on and on about him, and I'd sit there listening. Her stories gave me something I'd lost. Hope, I suppose. That was before my son was born.'

Caitlin waited. *James*. She didn't know what to say. She watched Catherine Henderson's face change, like a bruise rising to the surface. Whatever had gone on back then, it'd done damage. Deep, lasting damage. They drank their tea quietly. Then

Catherine looked up and asked, as if it were nothing, 'I don't suppose you know my son, James, do you?'

Caitlin couldn't breathe. Her pulse rocketed. The mere mention of his name was doing something unimaginable to her. She had to take a minute to answer.

'I… I do. I did, Mrs Henderson. We worked together. For a while. I knew him well,' she said, her voice catching, the words stammered out before she could stop them. Her voice quivered. She coughed, but managed to add, 'There's no one quite like James.' Catherine did a double take. The lines around her mouth trembled.

'You do, you know him?' she whispered. Her eyes, so like his, dulled. 'I haven't seen James since he was tiny. I wrote and wrote… so many letters. Never got so much as a line back. And now – well, that's why I'm here.'

She reached across the table, her hand finding Caitlin's. 'Tell me. Please. What's he like?' Caitlin hesitated. This woman knew her mammy, and Majella had looked after her, seriously looked after her, by the sounds of it. Maybe that meant she could trust her. Then it happened. Like flicking off the latch on a pressure cooker. She told Catherine Henderson. Told her everything.

It came out fast and tangled. First her daddy, then Tina and the bomb scare, the chaos at the hotel, the way James had turned on her, shut her down completely. His cold accusations. Majella, what she'd done, how she'd died. Tina locked away in that place, broken and fading. The words kept coming, pouring out before she could stop them. Messy. Raw. More honest than she'd dared be with anyone in months. My God, the release, saying it out loud, dragging it from the corners where she'd locked it away, left her feeling alive. Something had at last extricated itself from her.

Catherine Henderson kept quiet. She listened, truly fascinated, her fingers wrapped gently around Caitlin's hands, her eyes calm and watchful, not once interrupting, not once looking away. But then came the worst bit. Marleen Fry and the wedding. Caitlin told her about the perfect blonde with the polished manners and her visit. How she'd breezed into the studio and dropped the wedding date on Caitlin. James's wedding. Christmas Eve. By the end, Caitlin felt completely wrung out. Flat as a pancake.

Catherine reached for the teapot and poured them both another cuppa. What a story.

Siobhán, the café owner, kept her distance but kept an eye too. She'd worked behind that counter long enough to know when to butt out, and this was one of those times. The stranger, elegant, groomed, and far too polished to be from round here, was hanging on to Caitlin's every word. Completely taken in. But it was Caitlin Siobhán couldn't stop watching. There was something heartbreaking in her face, a sort of pain that hadn't been there before. Whatever she'd shared had winded her. Big time. You didn't need to hear it to know, the poor girl looked like she'd been dragged up from the deep.

As they talked, Siobhán came over with a fresh pot of tea and a few buns – nothing fancy, something sweet to lift the mood. She didn't say much. Didn't need to. Sometimes it was enough to set things down gently on the table and leave folk to themselves. Everyone knew who Caitlin was. You couldn't grow up here and not. Siobhán didn't know every detail, but she'd heard enough whispers to piece together that Caitlin had been through the wars. She wished her brother Martin was about. She'd have had a word with him. Seeing Caitlin now, shoulders folding in, her face close to breaking, made Siobhán's heart ache in a way she hadn't expected. The poor girl had been through the wringer, no two ways about it.

These days, Siobhán did what little she could for the ones who came through the door. Quiet gestures, small comforts, a free cup of tea where needed, or simply listening without prying. Sometimes that was all there was to give. In times as dark as these, it never felt like enough. Still, she tried. Anything at all to cheer people up, even for a second.

Catherine took Caitlin's hand, her own heart pounding as if trying to carry some of the anguish this girl had kept buried and who was shaking, like someone letting go after holding everything together for so long. Again, she didn't ask or say anything, allowing Caitlin to take her time. Let her cry. Let her get it out. When the time was right, she whispered across the table. 'You've every right to be upset Caitlin. Every bit of it, but listen to me, none of this is your fault. Your father. The hotel. Tina's sentence, not what your mother did. None of it. None of it is your fault.'

Caitlin sat back slightly, wiping her face with a napkin and watched as Catherine gently tucked a strand of her hair behind her ear, the way she used to do with James when he was a toddler.

'I left my son because I thought I had no choice. Not a day's passed that I haven't regretted it,' she told her. 'But I'm here now. I've come all this way. You mustn't give up on him, Caitlin. *Please*. You still have time. It's obvious you love him. I don't know this Marleen Fry girl, but please trust me, don't let silence be the thing that finishes it all. You've got to tell him how you feel. Tell him you had nothing to do with it. So much time has passed now.'

She reached for Caitlin's hand again and squeezed it. 'Please, before he makes a mistake and don't ask me why, but I think he is. Talk to him. Whatever happens, at least you'll know you've tried.'

With a shake of the head, Caitlin explained. 'I'm not sure, Mrs Henderson, he humiliated me. You've no idea, I mean after the trial, then Mammy. I don't know. I heard nothing from him, not even a card.' She wasn't sure whether she should tell her what Seamus had suggested.

'Forget all that for now, Caitlin. What have you got to lose?' Catherine's voice wavered with urgency as she faced her full on. 'Please. Talk to him. Trust me, please.'

Caitlin nodded. 'Okay, I'll try.'

Chapter Eighty-Two

Dread

Charlie McFadden kindly drove Tommy and Caitlin to Armagh Gaol that same Friday morning in his baby, his Zephyr. Everyone was chatting away, reminiscing, having a bit of a laugh. It was shaping up to be a decent drive, surprisingly easy, considering where they were headed.

Caitlin sat up front, giving directions, even though Tommy had done the run plenty of times. They stopped for petrol, which Tommy insisted on paying for. Charlie looked pleased to be of use. Said his Maggie had been on at him nonstop to get off his arse and find work, and even his son Emmett had mouthed off at him. He needed to get out of the house; he said with a shrug and was glad to help. Caitlin's heart was thudding, but it wasn't nerves or fear. It was something good. She actually felt good. An ordinary, run-of-the-mill '*good*'.

She and Catherine Henderson had met up a few times since that day in the Rainbow. They'd talked about everything, but mostly about James. Catherine was dead set on Caitlin contacting him, and Caitlin had agreed, but only once they got Tina home and settled. That came first. The sisters were going to have Christmas together. Sisters. Maybe Tommy too, if Kathy, her cousin, was working. Caitlin would make sure Tina had the best Christmas of her life. She'd be mother, sister, nurse, the works. Things were finally falling into place. For the first time in forever, she felt hopeful. Hopeful with a capital 'H'.

They parked as close to the gaol as they could. After the usual checks, they made their way through the gates and into the circle, then waited outside the governor's office. It was eleven on the dot. For a while, they stood there, watching the time crawl by. Then it dragged a little more. Caitlin glanced at Tommy, then at Charlie, both of them shifting awkwardly, one foot to the other. Tommy gave a small shrug and shook his head, frustration written all over his face. The light-hearted drive, the easy conversation, that brief spell where things had felt almost normal, had all but gone. In its place was something dark.

Dread.

By 11.45 AM, Caitlin had lost count of how many times she'd stepped out to check the corridor. Any minute now, she kept telling herself. Any minute, Tina would appear. Thin, yes, maybe pale and tired. Her feet might shuffle with exhaustion. But she would be there. Smiling. Alive. Ready to come home. Instead, an office door creaked open and out walked a man in a dark suit, who introduced himself as the governor. Governor Yeaman. Beside him stood a priest, tall, balding and stiff as a board. He barely acknowledged them.

Tommy felt it too. That creeping dread. But he leaned over to Caitlin anyway, trying to lift the mood, and joked, 'Must be Father McGuire's replacement. Jesus, look at the bake on him. He'd frighten the Stations of the Cross!' Caitlin wanted to laugh. She really did. It was the sort of daft thing Tommy would come out with, but not now, because this wasn't good.

The governor gestured them to come inside his office. 'Please follow me.'

In that instant, Caitlin knew. *Tina!*

Yeaman stalled before he spoke. He shuffled his papers, shifted in his chair, cleared his throat once, then again. At last, in a flat, official tone, he said, 'Mr O'Reilly, I regret to inform you that prisoner Martina McLaughlin was found dead in her cell this morning.'

Charlie McFadden dropped his head, his hands covering his face. Caitlin didn't move. Couldn't. Her body wouldn't let her. Her chest tightened, her vision blurred, and tears fell without sound or warning.

Tommy shot to his feet so fast, he nearly lost his balance. He grabbed the edge of the desk as if he were about to lift and throw it through the window.

'What?' he yelled. 'How? How did she die?' His voice was stripped bare. 'What happened?'

The governor glanced at the priest beside him, evidently hoping he'd step in and explain, but the man looked straight ahead, expressionless and unmoving, his eyes fixed on a point in the room as if it mattered more than anything being said. He wasn't going to help Yeaman. Not after all he'd witnessed. The mistreatment, the cruelty, the times he'd spoken up and been ignored. Only that morning, he'd written to the Bishop of Armagh, begging for a transfer.

Tommy slammed his fist against the desk. 'I asked, what happened?!' He dropped back into the chair and dragged a hand down his face like he was trying to scrape something off.

It was too much. Caitlin couldn't contain herself. Tina had left her too. Same as Daddy. Same as Mammy, with no warning, no goodbye.

Her sister. Her little sister. Dead.

The sound that came from her didn't feel like her own. It dragged itself out of some ancient part of her, violent and raw, filling the room with guilt, grief, sadness. A long, broken wail that started low and then burst open, like something tearing loose. Let them stare. Let them hear it. Let them squirm. She wanted the bastards to witness her grief.

All of it.

Chapter Eighty-Three

Worthless

William Barter was finishing an interview with James Henderson. Another exclusive in the bag. He'd been impressed, not only by the young man's vision for Rocola, but by how he spoke about the workers, the city, and his quiet love for Derry. All of it delivered in that soft Scottish lilt that gave him a sort of natural authority. They were running late now, still sitting in James's office finishing their coffee.

Outside, it was bitter, and Barter hadn't quite thawed since the site tour. The place had surprised him. Clean, efficient, friendly. The women all smiled or the men cracked jokes when young Henderson passed by, like they might be fond of the guy. That alone spoke volumes. The young boss had even agreed to let Barter chat to a handful of staff. By the end, Barter felt like he had his angle on a great story and couldn't wait to get it down on paper.

A soft knock came at the door. The secretary, a miserable, sour-faced woman with zero charm whatsoever, stuck her head round the glass.

'Mr Henderson, sir. Mr Jones has arrived.' She vanished again before either of them could respond.

James grimaced. 'Sorry, Bill. A last-minute thing. Charles Jones. Wasn't supposed to clash with this, but today's the only time he could do it. Otherwise, I'd have asked you to stay on a bit longer.'

Barter twitched. 'Jones? Wouldn't happen to be *the* Charles Jones? Belfast way, docks, bad press...'

'That's the one,' James said with a sigh. 'Though I wouldn't say I know him well. An old business connection. My uncle, but something we're moving on from, I'm trying to sever any dealings with him, but he insists on meeting.'

Barter, in no hurry to leave, sat back, watching James. His use of words and tone told him the guy didn't like Charles Jones. At all.

'Well, look, James, I've enjoyed today. But before I head off, I'd like to tell you something about our Mr Jones. It's important. I understand you ran that conference at the City Hotel a while back?'

James stood, moving over to the window. He stared down at the factory yard. 'For my sins, aye.'

Adrenaline coursed through Barter. He needed to be careful not to overdo it. Might scare the guy off.

'I've been told by a very reliable source that—' The door burst open. Lemon. The big thug froze like a rabbit caught in headlights when he saw Barter sitting there, coffee cup in hand.

James didn't miss it. The way Barter and Lemon reacted the second they recognised each other. The journalist went pale, like the sight of Lemon caught him off guard. Lemon stood there, rooted to the spot, surprise written all over his face. Before either of them could speak, Jones barged straight past and into the office, oblivious to the elephant in the room.

He started fiddling with his briefcase, papers spilling out as if he worked there all his life. It took him a moment to see James wasn't alone. When he finally looked up and spotted Barter, he paused, then extended his hand with exaggerated ease.

'Mr Barter. Good to meet you at last,' he said, like they were old friends. Barter rose slowly and accepted the handshake with reluctance. His expression gave nothing away, but James could feel the temperature in the room drop.

Without waiting, Jones dropped into the nearest chair, James's, and spread his papers across the desk. Purposely loud, James cleared his throat. It took a while for Jones to pay attention. Realising he was sitting in James's chair, behind James's desk, he chuckled and stood up. 'Silly me,' he muttered, switching chairs.

Barter didn't sit down again, but glanced at James and gave him a tiny tilt of his head, gesturing for James to follow him. Message received and understood. 'Excuse me a moment Charles. I'll show my guest to the door. Won't be long,' James said, already steering Barter towards the exit.

Mrs Parkes, who'd been lurking beyond the glass, perked up as they stepped into the corridor. 'Mrs Parkes, would you mind offering Mr Jones a drink?'

'Of course, Mr Henderson,' she chirped, disappearing into the office with indecent enthusiasm. James and Bill walked a few paces down the corridor towards the lift. Barter moved closer to James, his voice low and urgent. 'We need to talk again, James. You and me. About that guy. I've got something you need to hear.'

James gave a quick nod. 'I'll call you.'

'Good,' Barter said, eyes scanning the hallway. 'Soon, yeah?'

'Sure.' James replied.

As Bill got into the lift and the doors closed, James ran a hand through his hair. Barter looked worried. Whatever it was, it seemed important. James made a mental note to call him as soon as he got rid of the bawbag parked in his office.

Mrs Parkes tottered about, ready to take the drinks order. She wasn't normally this flustered, but today she'd powdered her face twice and freshened her lippy before going in. Not every day she got this close to someone like Charles Jones. Mad about him. Ignoring Lemon, she took Mr Jones's request for coffee. Double shots, black, two sugars. She hesitated at the door, turned on her heel and stood next to her hero.

'Mr Jones,' she whispered, one eye on Lemon who gave her a knowing wink, lounged by the filing cabinet like a bored bouncer, 'I wanted to say... I've been to all your speeches in the Free Derry Church, and I think what your sayin' about you-know-what is spot on. Meself and a few of the WI girls – we're huge fans.'

Her cheeks flushed as Jones thanked her with excessive charm and bravado. She gave him a girlish smile and backed out of the office, her heart skipping the odd beat. Charles Jones actually spoke to her, he thanked her! She left for the kitchen, relishing that she'd some juicy gossip to spill at the next WI meeting.

Jones turned to Lemon, a pompous grin plastered all over his face. 'See that? Got myself a fan club. Silly moo.'

Lemon couldn't hold his laughter as he watched Jones take the mick out of the old boot. The two of them were still chuckling when James walked back in, his expression darkening the moment he saw them. Whatever they were laughing at, it wasn't funny, and you could bet it was at someone else's expense.

Taking back his chair, James fixed his gaze on Jones and waited, saying nothing, giving the man a chance to explain what this meeting was supposed to be about. He had to hold back the instinctive urge to react, to visibly recoil at the sight of him, because truth be told, it was shocking. He hadn't laid eyes on Jones since Newtownhamilton, since the blaze, and Christ, the man had failed. The right side of his face, if it could even be called that anymore, had caved in slightly, the flesh taut and strangely glossy in the light. His right eye refused to stop weeping, trickling down his cheek in a constant stream that no amount of dabbing with his pristine, monogrammed handkerchief could stem. James observed him closely, unmoved. He didn't feel pity, didn't feel anger, only an overwhelming sense of inevitability. Wherever Jones turned up, chaos followed. Fact. There was always a price, always a dilemma, and one that never came cheap.

He'd insisted on meeting, refused to say a word about why on the phone, and now he sat across from him, trying to act like the hard man, but James wasn't buying it. He didn't want to meet, but since Jones had been so cagey, refusing to say what it was about and demanding it was in James's best interests, he'd no choice but to agree.

'How are you, James?' James asked in that deadpan, familiar way of his, like he was speaking through gauze.

James gave a nod. 'Fine, thank you, Charles.' He'd be polite, nothing more, and wasn't for filling the void. This meeting was Jones's doing. He was the one who had something to say.

Chapter Eighty-Four

A Brilliant Con

Charles Jones was excited. He absolutely hated this Scottish gobshite and, after his last defeat, was looking forward to bringing the arrogant gobshite down. 'Sorry I didn't make your father's funeral,' he said, shaking his head feigning sorrow. 'Terrible business.' He watched Henderson's every move, waiting for a flicker of anger, a twitch of his mouth, the slightest tightening around the eyes. But the young buck gave him nothing. Typical. Still full of himself. Didn't matter, wouldn't be for much longer, not after what he had to tell him.

'You must be heartbroken,' Jones went on, leaning back in the chair, getting comfortable. 'I was in London. Flat out, you know, this deal and that deal. I sent flowers.' That was a lie, of course, but who gave a shit? What mattered was how difficult he could make this. Let the lad squirm, keep him guessing. Jones could play polite all day if he had to, but underneath, he was already counting the ways he'd fuck up this egotistical git's world.

Sipping his tea, James watched Jones, his expression inscrutable. The man appeared to be enjoying himself, revelling in his performance. James could have strangled him right there, right then.

Jones leaned over the desk, his fingertips pressed together, and said with mock concern, 'As it stands, young James, I hate to be the bearer of bad news, but I've heard a whisper, well, more than a whisper, to be honest. The grapevine tells me there's a bitta trouble coming your way.' James didn't react. He wasn't going to who, what or why? Exactly what the bastard wanted.

Jones gave a scoff, dismissive and slow, then carried right on, like he hadn't noticed or didn't care how close he was to being tossed out the door. 'Some of your staff, senior staff, I should add, might not be quite as loyal as you think. There's talk going round, the kind that doesn't blow over. I've heard whispers about a walkout, more than one actually, and a contact of mine, quite a good one, mentioned several breaches of contract that could land you in hot water if they decide to go public. Serious stuff, James. Thought you might wanna look into it before it gets out of hand.' He paused there, letting it sink in, then tacked on the last line with a mocking lilt, his words thick with sarcasm. 'Figured I'd tell you myself. Given we're such good friends and all that.'

Jones was lying. James knew it. He was winding him up, but the question was why. James's face gave nothing away as he eyed him, but inside, his mind was racing, already picking apart every meeting, every conversation, scanning through them with surgical precision, looking for the moment things might've turned, for any hint of resentment, a complaint, a disagreement, anything that might explain this. The bastard had to be baiting him. As for James? He didn't believe a word of it. He'd have known. Ernie would have told him.

'Anything specific?' James asked, deciding he'd play along.

Jones smiled lazily. 'Now, that would be telling.'

James placed his cup down. Enough was enough. 'If you've got something to tell me, Charles, please go ahead. Otherwise, let's not waste each other's time.'

The older man's smile didn't falter, but his tone cooled. 'I'm giving you a heads-up. You're not as fireproof as you think.'

James sat back and folded his arms. 'Appreciate the heads-up, if that's what this is,' he said, his tone calm yet assertive. 'Now, if you're done—'

'No. I-am-not-done!' Jones exploded. He was far from finished, and with a flick of the wrist, he lobbed a wad of stock certificates across the desk. Then, he sat back and waited.

James didn't move. He sat perfectly still, eyes fixed on the papers in front of him, the very picture of calm, so composed it only seemed to provoke Jones further. Nothing was said until, sure enough, Jones moved closer, clearly hoping for a flicker of reaction, anything to tell him he'd struck a nerve. Now James understood. This right here was the real reason Jones had wanted to meet.

'Let me tell you something, son,' Jones began, his voice low but loaded with false warmth. 'Your father was a man of his word and very recently, in fact, a few days before he died, he and I came to a financial arrangement.'

He paused, gave a slow, knowing nod, and said. 'He owed me, you see. Those, my young pup,' he said, pointing straight at the shares, 'those belong to me now. Fair and square. Collateral. Shares in Rocola.'

James didn't argue. Instead, he lifted the papers, scanned them quickly, and laid them back down.

His silent insolence annoyed the shit out of Jones even more. 'You think I forged them? Believe me, I'm not playing games. Those bits of paper allow me, Charles Jones, a seat on the board of Rocola. My voice will be heard, with or without your approval, so I suggest you get your lawyer to comb through them if you don't believe me. Won't make a blind bit of difference.'

Ready to leave, he pushed up from his chair with a grunt. 'You'll be hearing from my solicitor.'

It was now James's turn to turn the whole thing around, and Christ, he was going to savour every golden second of it. This right here? This was what he called justice, sweet and long overdue. He reached, unhurried, for the flimsy, gilt-edged papers sitting on the table between them. The memory of Roger, all hushed tones and grim expressions days after his father's funeral, played in his head. He'd told James everything he'd discovered about his brother. Every shady deal his father made behind closed doors, and last but not least, how he'd conned Charles Jones.

'Wait Charles. It's my turn to talk now.' James urged.

When Jones heard the truth, and he was about to, he'd go ballistic. James's father, the late and ever-resourceful James Henderson Snr, former Captain in the British Army, had been a master of deceit. Turns out he was the kind of man who could lie through his teeth while smiling for the cameras, shake your hand with one and rob you blind with the other.

It had all started with a single genuine Rocola share, one perfectly legal and perfectly placed share, used as respectable collateral. From there, somehow he'd spun it into a tidy stack of forged duplicates, each one flawless, right down to the signatures, embossing, and the elegant sheen that made them look official, convincing, and very, very real. Those same shares, the ones Jones believed were his, sat neatly on the table in front of them, crisp and clean, yet utterly useless, worth less than the paper they were printed on. Roger had found more forgeries after the funeral, tucked away among his father's things, hundreds of them - each one as polished as the last, every detail perfect - all of them burned to ash in the fireplace at Melrose, the last trace of a brilliant con.

James sat back, calm and composed, his hands resting lightly on the arms of his chair, watching the man opposite with a quiet satisfaction. It was all there, right in front of him, laid out like a final chess move in a game Jones didn't realise he was playing. The best part? The man hadn't a clue.

Here goes.

James eased back in his chair, calm on the outside, though his heart was thudding hard beneath the surface. He gave nothing away. Nothing. Then, in that same steady tone he'd practised a hundred times in his head, he laid it all out, plain and simple.

'The thing is,' he began, his voice carrying the faintest trace of amusement, 'you've been well and truly played, Charles. Hate to say it, but, by God, superbly. It turns out my father was a con man. A clever bastard when it comes to this sort of thing, I'm told.'

He gestured towards the elegant, gold-edged papers scattered across the desk, pristine, official-looking, and utterly worthless. 'Judging by these, I'd say he was at the very top of his game. Those shares? Forgeries. Every last one of them.'

Charles Jones couldn't believe it. He sat there stiff as stone, right up until he needed to wipe his weeping eye with his handkerchief.

Even Lemon had picked up on it now. He looked from James to Jones, then back again, the change in atmosphere too noticeable to miss. He looked ready to launch himself across the room at James, every muscle coiled for it, but at the last second, Jones raised a hand and held him back.

His eyes stayed on James, cold and unflinching, daring him to finish what he had started.

'I only hope,' James said, not a trace of sympathy in his voice, 'you didn't lend him too much.'

'Seventy-five thousand,' Jones muttered.

James gave a low whistle. 'Seventy-five. Not bad. He did well out of you then.'

It was James's turn to lean across the desk now, his voice smooth, casual, and all the more satisfying for it. 'Here's the thing, Charles. Only my uncle and I knew. Clearly, you didn't. Don't feel too bad though, you're not the only one. After Father died, a whole parade of his hare-brained schemes came crawling out of the woodwork. Honestly, you weren't even close to the top.'

That was a lie. Jones had come off worse than any of them, but James wasn't about to admit it. He stood, gathered the shares, then began to tear them slowly into thin little strips. 'But with Father gone, there's nothing to be done now. No one to chase.' He looked across at Jones, whose colour said it all and added. 'Now, if you'll excuse me, my fiancée's waiting. We've a wedding in a few days. Lots to do.'

Once he stepped into the outer office, James told Mrs Parkes to see his guests out. He didn't bother with a goodbye, but watched their backs disappear down the corridor towards the lift. The moment they were gone, he exhaled hard and dragged a hand down his face. His palms were slick. He'd kept it together. Lied through his teeth. That'd been close. Much too close.

Again, James thanked God he'd never have to see Jones's face again, that the bastard would never set foot in Melrose so long as James had life in him.

Chapter Eighty-Five

A Long Time Ago

Marleen had been travelling to London for dress fittings and a final splash of adventure before the wedding. Penelope had been sulking again, prowling about like a pampered cat, but Marleen knew how to soothe her. A few nights in Mayfair, cocktails at Annabel's, and jazz at Ronnie Scott's always did the trick. They'd danced till dawn, laughed till their ribs ached, and staggered back to Penelope's flat with shoes in hand, giggling at nothing at all. It had been glorious - wild, wicked, exactly what they needed.

She stood in the study at Melrose, finishing her daily call with Penelope. 'I know, wasn't it wonderful!' she said. 'Ah yes, see you soon, Pen. Safe travels.'

Everything was more or less set. The dress was exquisite, the cake done, the guest list polished to perfection, and even the press had taken notice. That morning she and Penelope had giggled over croissants, reading the write-up in mock voices like a pair of dizzy schoolgirls.

James seemed unusually cheerful, smiling as if he were keeping a secret. She suspected it was to do with their honeymoon. She'd first noticed it on a quiet Sunday morning, papers scattered across the kitchen table. He'd been humming, smiling at nothing, stealing glances her way as if fit to burst. Whatever it was, she wasn't about to press. He was hers, and that was enough. Business and practicalities could wait. God, she loved a wedding.

The groom's thoughts weren't on the nuptials. At all. But replaying Jones skulking from the office, head down, pride in tatters. Seventy-five grand gone, and nothing to be done about it. Petty cash for a man like Jones, perhaps, but that wasn't the point. The satisfaction was in the telling. James knew he shouldn't admire his father's scheming – not really - but Heaven help him, he did. It felt, strangely enough, like the only clever move the old man had ever pulled off.

Marleen smiled politely when James told her, then forgot about it. Roger reacted differently. He laughed for a full minute, a proper belly laugh that left him wheezing and clutching his sides. He wasn't well, hadn't been for some time, but the way James had dealt with Jones lifted him more than anything had in weeks. It didn't stop him, unsteady but determined, from joining James and Marleen in the dining room to raise a glass to the day's victory. He looked delighted, grinning across the table, even as his hands trembled around the stem of his glass.

'You should've seen his face, Uncle,' James told him. 'Looked like someone had pulled the floor out from under him. Mrs Parkes practically had to escort him and that goon of his to the lift like lost children. It was magic, pure magic.' He poured Marleen's wine, then Roger's and was reaching for his own glass when Marleen spoke up. She was fed up hearing about Charles Jones, must've heard the story three times already.

'Well, gentlemen,' she began with a bright smile, 'everything's arranged. Caterers, dress, music, photographer. All done and dusted. No hiccups.' She looked at Roger expectantly.

'Well done, Marleen,' Roger said. 'I'm sure it'll be a beautiful day. No hiccups, you say? Good for you.'

'None to speak of. Although the photographer was a bit of a pain. Hard to pin down, all sorted now though.' Marleen replied with a perfect smile.

James was halfway through lifting a forkful of salmon when he froze. 'Photographer?' he asked cautiously, already knowing he wouldn't like the answer.

'Yes, a Mr Burns. The one on the main street, Strand Road, I think?' Marleen gave a small wave of her hand, as if the exact address didn't matter.

'There was a girl there, dreadfully rude. No idea why. Stunning, but strange, in a way.' She paused for a moment, her brow tightening ever so slightly as the memory of the shop girl surfaced, that odd look on her face, as if she might faint or burst into tears, or both. It had been unsettling, if she was honest, though she hadn't said as much at the time. She gave her head a tiny shake, brushing it off.

'She had the oddest name too. I'm not quite sure how one pronounces it... Katlyn? Kate? Something terribly Irishry. Anyway, rehearsal is Thursday evening. Don't forget.'

Caitlin. The name hit James like a blow to the chest, and for a moment, he felt an icy sweep of nausea coil through his stomach. His heart followed with a single, sickening thud, and he had to fight the urge to look away or say something. Jesus Christ. *Nooo!*

Thursday morning came, stormy and wet, James's Jag purring up Melrose's drive on its way to Rocola. His head wasn't right. Not after last night. He kept seeing it - Caitlin realising who Marleen was. He didn't need to be there. He could picture her, the surprise, the way she'd steady herself while Marleen - polished, charming, unruffled - breezed through the wedding talk. He imagined her holding her breath, that flicker in her eyes. She'd never have made a scene, not her way, but inside it would have cut her to pieces. If she still loved him, that is. If she did, no wonder she'd been rude. He felt dreadful.

What the fuck am I going to do now? James wondered.

As he reached the main road, a signed taxi pulled in from the opposite direction and turned into Melrose, easing in beneath the trees. Unusual. As far as he knew, they weren't expecting anyone. He'd ring Melrose when he got to the factory. See who it was. He checked the rearview mirror, watching as the taxi disappeared through the gate, then turned his attention back to the road, gripping the wheel a little harder than necessary, the guilt of Caitlin crawling somewhere behind his ribs.

Catherine Henderson sat in the back of the taxi, her hands resting in her lap, the tiredness behind her eyes sharp and unforgiving. She hadn't slept a wink, but she knew that if she didn't face her demons now, once and for all, she never would. The years of anger, the bitterness that had clung on like a second skin, had gone on long enough.

She found herself wondering why she hadn't heard from Caitlin, and deep down, she felt it. That instinct, cold and certain, that the girl needed rescuing. Maybe, like her mother Majella had once stepped in and pulled her from the brink, she could do the same now. There was a quiet understanding between them, a natural camaraderie, and in a short space of time, they'd already become something close to friends.

After hearing Caitlin speak about James, she changed her mind. She wasn't here to see her son, or even to confront Roger Henderson. She was here now, while she still had the courage to look the woman James planned to marry in the eye and decide for herself whether she was right. Right for him.

From what Caitlin had said, their affair didn't sound like a passing infatuation. Not so long ago, James had loved her. If it had been real, if it had meant something, the way the girl's quiet, aching grief seemed to suggest, then it wouldn't have vanished overnight. Not completely. Catherine's instinct told her the same thing it had told her the moment she first laid eyes on Caitlin. Something here didn't feel right and if it was the last thing she'd do, she'd find out what.

Melrose looked much the same. The rose garden, so carefully designed by Jocelyn, lay bare and colourless in the December cold. Catherine's thoughts drifted to the past, those long, light-filled days when she and Jocelyn would marvel at the hybrid tea roses in crimson, yellow, soft pinks and ivory white. She had loved this place once.

Looking back, Catherine could see it clearly. She and James had married for all the wrong reasons. It had been doomed from the very beginning, no matter how much they tried to pretend otherwise. Jocelyn still came into her thoughts from time to time, never far away. There had been such kindness in her, something delicate and quietly good. The day she found out she couldn't have children had broken something deep inside her. Catherine had tried to console her, had sat with her, held her hand, offered every comfort she could think of, but there were no words strong enough to soften that kind of grief. Nothing could reach it.

The taxi came to a halt at the main entrance. Catherine paid the fare but asked the driver to wait. She stepped out, rapped the lion-headed door knocker, and turned to take in the garden. Even in winter, it was beautiful. As she waited, her heart was thumping. This was a long time coming.

The door opened, and there stood Mrs McGinty in her striped wrap-around apron, shivering in the doorway. 'Jesus wept! Why, it's Mrs Henderson!' she gasped, then hastily crossed herself.

With a wide grin, Catherine stepped up. 'Hello, Mrs Mac.' The housekeeper couldn't believe it, but pulled Catherine into a warm hug, the scent of honeysuckle washing over her like a forgotten song. They held each other so long until Mrs McGinty, misty-eyed, waved the taxi away and ushered Catherine back through the doors of Melrose.

James forgot to call Melrose about the mysterious taxi. It wasn't until lunchtime that it came back to him, a quiet nudge in the back of his mind as he reached for the phone. He dialled the number, half-expecting Mrs McGinty to answer, but the line rang out. She was probably in the kitchen, elbow-deep in flour, and Marleen was off in Belfast with her endless lists and last-minute wedding stuff. Roger would be asleep by now. He needed to think so told Mrs Parkes he had to run an errand, something urgent had come up that he needed to deal with. Personal stuff.

Climbing into the Jag, he decided to go to Lisfannon Beach to think, but took a detour and passed the studio where Caitlin worked. He didn't stop, didn't even slow down, but checked out the building and kept going. Marriage to Marleen meant security for him and Rocola. A future with no surprises. Her father's money would see to that, but as the road stretched out ahead, so did his doubt. He told himself he'd done the right thing, yet it felt like a lie, and deep down, he knew it always would.

In the end, he walked the beach and decided he needed to put an end to this. He made the thirty-minute drive back to the city and found himself once more outside the studio. This time, he didn't drive past or look in the window. This time, he parked the car and stepped inside.

The owner, Raymond Burns, greeted him with a warm smile, recognising James from the City Hotel meeting. 'Hello Mr Henderson! How are ye? You'll be wantin' to talk about the weddin', will ye?'

James shook his head, awkward. 'Actually, I was hoping to speak with your assistant.'

'Why Caitlin? Ah, sorry, no, not here the day. Family stuff. Personal like.'

James backed off. 'Ah, right. Okay. No problem.'

Burns considered him for a minute, intrigued. Why would James Henderson be looking for his Caitlin. 'That's it?' he asked.

'Aye. That's it. Thanks.' James replied. He didn't hang about, but walked right out.

When he got back to Rocola, he phoned Melrose again, but it still rang out. Whoever it was visiting, it could wait. He sighed as he picked up a file and saw Caitlin's handwriting on it.

Caitlin. The memory of was everywhere. Her humour, the way she'd talk about all the places she wanted to see, all the wild, impossible dreams she'd somehow made feel believable. He remembered the way they'd touched, the warmth between them, the way she'd looked at him when they were alone and the outside world didn't matter. Those few days in Donegal. The wedding. Dancing barefoot. Bubble bath, champagne, the soft crackle of the fire, lying together on the fur rug. Her lovemaking. His lovemaking. Her laughter and smile carried on the wind as they walked along Lough Eske. They'd been good together. No. They'd been better than good. They'd been perfect. But...

Then, with a good old dose of common sense and the kind of clarity he should have had months ago, James realised he needed to talk to her. Somehow. There were things he had to say, things that mattered. Even if Caitlin never wanted to see him again, he had to try. He owed her that much.

In the stone-cold light of day, he knew exactly why he'd agreed to marry Marleen. Money. Security. None of it would ever sit right, not while Caitlin haunted him. He'd never settle. Not until he faced what he'd done. The dilemma he'd created. The selfishness. The arrogance. He'd been so caught up in his own anguish after the City Hotel meeting went tits up, so determined to blame someone else, that he hadn't even stopped to think what it would cost. How much he'd hurt her.

Her face. Sweet Jesus, her face the last time he saw her cry, when she'd stood there begging him to take her hand, to listen, to not walk away. He saw it all. Clear as crystal. It made him want to heave.

Chapter Eighty-Six

Right Back to Square One

Maggie McFadden, still in her curlers and pinny, was waiting at the front window of Blamfield Street when she saw Charlie's big, boxy red Ford Zephyr with its wide seats, shiny chrome trim, and long bonnet ease to a halt at the side of the road. Her heart sank.

She'd seen them leave that morning, their spirits high, their hope and excitement practically bouncing off the pavement. What the return journey had been like, she couldn't think to imagine. Charlie had rung earlier from a call box, his voice low and strained, to say that poor Caitlin was coming home without her sister. Here they were back again. Caitlin stepped out of the car like she were made of glass, and the men hovered about, not knowing what to do with themselves.

'Come here, love. Come here!' Maggie sobbed, hurrying down their concrete path. She folded Caitlin into her arms, the poor wee thing all limp and lost. The men exchanged a look.

Charlie, with a heavy sigh, turned to Tommy. 'Come on in, mucker. Gotta couple of beers in the fridge.'

Maggie gave her husband a brisk nod, mouthing at him to go on as she guided Caitlin gently towards number 30. 'Have ye your keys, love?' she asked. Caitlin nodded, searching her bag with unsteady hands. The keys jingled and, as usual, fell to the ground.

Maggie picked them up quietly and pressed them into the lock. 'Let's get you inside,' she whispered. 'I'll make us a nice cuppa. Don't worry about a thing, love. Leave it to me.'

Martin turned up, like Caitlin knew he would. A soft knock at the back door, barely audible, more breath than sound. He'd come through the back way, no doubt, slipping in from the next street over. He wouldn't have risked walking the length of Blamfield Street, not now, not with everything the way it was. Too dangerous. She opened the door, and he pulled her in hard against his chest, his arms locked around her like he wouldn't or couldn't let go. He didn't step inside. Not yet. Said he needed a minute outside. Needed a smoke. By this stage, he knew better than to ask to smoke indoors.

They stood together in the back, the cold damp clinging to them, saying very little for a while. The air between them carried its own sadness, not through words, but through all that wasn't said. Sadness, guilt, even an element of relief. Relief, perhaps, that their sister was finally at peace with their mammy and daddy.

He lit a cigarette with shaking hands, his eyes never quite meeting hers. She let him have his moment.

'They'll kill you one day, you know?' she said eventually, eyeing his half-empty pack.

'Bugger that,' he replied, dragging hard and blowing it out like it proved something. It made her smile, and she was so comforted that he was there.

Martin was edgy, his mind clearly somewhere else, though Caitlin could see he was hurting. That part was obvious, even if he didn't say so. What had happened to the carefree, spotty teenager she used to know, the one who laughed too loud at his own jokes and kicked a ball around the street like nothing in the world could bother him?

She knew of course. Likely he was caught up in something for the Provos. It was in the way he moved, the way his eyes watched the neighbouring houses, checking behind the gate, like he couldn't switch off for a second. It was written all over him. Only a matter of time before he'd be away again.

They'd grown close this last while, not exactly by choice, more by circumstance. Grief had drawn them together, the pair of them hanging onto what little family they had left, trying to make sense of how everything had changed. Whether they liked it or not, they were all they had. No one else. Only the two of them left.

He turned to her, his voice soft and unusually gentle. 'You shouldn't feel bad about Tina, Caitlin. I know you do. But I was the one who filled her head, me and me posters, all that Provo stuff. Made her believe in it. I honestly never thought—' He trailed off, scuffing at the weeds between the slabs with his boot heel.

'It was me. All of it. My fault. I even knew that fucker Kelly. Met him when he was sniffing around her, but I didn't know, did I? If I'd only known. What d'ye think of that, eh?'

Caitlin's heart lurched. 'You knew Kieran Kelly?' She gasped. The hair on her arms lifted.

He looked her straight in the eye, and she caught his tear before it fell. It was the kind of look that spoke louder than words, full of pain and apology and all the things he couldn't bring himself to say. Without thinking, she stepped forward, ready to hold him, to take some of his guilt away. But he stopped her with a hand on her arm. Not in a bad way, a quiet signal to say he didn't deserve her love. Or pity.

'We were watching him. Knew he was dodgy with him being gay an' all. Worried the Brits might try to blackmail him, turn him into a grass, but we missed what he *really* was. Missed the way he used her. He was a fuckin' looney! Sweet Jesus, I should've taken him down when I had the chance!' His voice broke, and suddenly he was on his hunkers, his head in his hands, sobbing like a five-year-old.

Caitlin crouched beside him, one arm around his shoulders, letting him cry. All that guilt, all that pressure, like her, he'd been holding in for so long. She'd done her crying in the governor's office. Hers had dried up. She felt like a husk now. Like an old prune, shrivelled on the inside, too tired to cry anymore. When he finally looked up, his eyes were red and swollen.

'Sorry,' he whispered.

'Don't be. We know you loved her. You were her favourite.' Caitlin said.

He groaned, wiping his face. 'Another bloody waste. I don't even know what this is about anymore.' He flung his arms in the air. 'The killin', everythin'. It keeps goin' on and on. No one thought it'd last this long.'

Caitlin had no answer. He spoke the truth. With a gruff cough, he gave his shoulders a shake, trying to pull himself together, then flicked the last of his smoke away, watching the ember die out on the concrete. He nodded towards the back door, his voice as near to normal, like nothing had happened. 'Saw Anne leavin' earlier.'

She reached for his arm. 'Aye. Speaking of Anne. There's something I've been meaning to ask you. About Anne's Porkie... and Dickie.'

Martin half-smiled and stepped closer to her, 'We know all about it. Tell Anne she's okay. Nothin's going to happen to her and the wain. But listen, it doesn't get mentioned again. Ever. Not by you, not by her. Not by anyone. Understood?'

Caitlin nodded with relief. 'I'll tell her. Thanks, Martin.'

Suddenly, they heard a loud knock that echoed through the house like a warning. Caitlin froze for a second, looked at Martin, then darted down the hallway, her heart pounding. Through the frosted pane of glass, she saw the soft glow of headlights. Had to be the hearse. Tina was back where she belonged. Home.

She turned to Martin, now standing in the kitchen close to the back door, and mouthed, 'Stay there.'

He dipped his head and muttered, 'Fuck me. Here we go again.'

Two days later, Caitlin stood at the edge of a fresh grave, her eyes set on the small, pale wooden coffin as it was lowered into the soaked Derry soil. With two bodies already in the family plot, there hadn't been room. So they'd given Tina a new grave, miles away from Mammy and Daddy. On her own.

The soil was heavy with rain, thick and dark, clinging to the boots of the men as they guided her sister down, their coats damp, their hands careful, almost too careful, as if they were afraid she might break. The coffin was far too light. Five and a half stone, if that. It moved too easily. That was the worst of it. It shouldn't have been so light.

Above them, a blanket of heavy grey clouds drifted, close and threatening. Typical, Caitlin thought. She couldn't remember the last time she'd been to a funeral and the sun had shone.

Martin couldn't be there. He was already on his way to America. She understood the reason. Too risky. Still, he'd promised to write, to call, to stay close. For the first time in years, they were in a good place, and that had to count for something.

Tommy stood beside her, hands in his pockets, shoulders sagging. He swayed a little, pale and drawn, the drink still wearing off. He hadn't said much since the service, but kept close, quiet, like his misery had robbed him of words.

Across the grave, Anne stood holding the baby. She caught Caitlin's eye, raised her chin, and gave the smallest of smiles. That was all. But Caitlin knew what it meant. Word had come through – she and baby Sean were safe. The Provos knew what she'd done. They'd even thanked her.

Later, the house filled with quiet voices, the kind that skimmed over sorrow without ever landing on it. People talked about anything but Tina. None of them really knew her, some still couldn't understand how she got involved with the likes of Kelly, now they knew everything.

Caitlin sat in the corner of the front room, watching the ripples in her teacup as she stirred it. She felt weightless, as if she were floating above them all, watching a life she no longer recognised. Patrick, Majella and Tina dead. Martin gone. Tommy stood in the front garden already stotious and having a smoke.

At least Anne and the baby were safe.

Caitlin was caught in a no-man's-land of her own, stranded somewhere between sorrow and apathy, as if she couldn't quite decide which one to surrender to first. Her gaze drifted to the green mac hanging over the living room door, the one her mother used to wear. It was damp from the funeral, from Caitlin wearing it, and she hadn't the energy to put it under the stairs.

She toyed with the idea of going out. Of ringing James. To hear his voice. To feel less alone. But the thought barely formed before it curled up and faded. Maybe she would. Maybe she wouldn't. She wasn't sure anymore. More than anything, it was what frightened her the most. Like she'd gone right back to square one.

Chapter Eighty-Seven

A South East Girl

Alice Wallace didn't know what else to do, so she slipped into the busiest place she could think of, sat herself down in a corner and tried to disappear. The café near Belfast City Hall wasn't anything special, but it was always full, always humming with chatter and scraped chairs and the sound of heels on cracked tiles. People came and went without looking up. That's what made it perfect. Nobody cared who you were, not unless you gave them reason.

She kept her coat on and pressed her back to the wall, her hands wrapped around a mug of coffee that had long since cooled, untouched since the first sip. The table in front of her was cluttered with sugar sachets and a smudged salt shaker, and someone had carved a name into the edge with a Biro. The air was heavy with chip fat and steam from the milk frother, but it was the radio she kept hearing, even through all the noise. An old battered transistor sat beside the till, pumping out Queen's *Bohemian Rhapsody*, the same song that seemed to follow her everywhere since it hit number one, like the city had chosen it as its theme tune.

A few girls from one of the City Hall offices sat near the window, laughing too loudly over some half-told story while trying not to smudge their lipstick on the rims of their cups. A man in a brown wool coat read a week-old paper, his fingers blackened by ink, turning the pages slow like he didn't want to miss a word. A child wailed for a biscuit and was met with a warning look from a tired mother who didn't have the energy to argue.

Alice kept her head down. There were soldiers outside, probably more tucked out of sight, and she wasn't about to give any of them reason to look her way. She hadn't come here for them to take her in. She'd come to hide. Blend in and let the noise and bustle carry her.

She stared at the copy of the *Belfast Telegraph* someone had left behind, its front page torn, tea-stained, and curling at the edges. The headline stared back at her in thick black print: *Part-Time UDR Man Murdered*. No need to read the rest. She knew already.

Ian Dillon. Lured to a fake job and shot dead without warning. Days after she'd sat in this very café, across from Lemon, his contact, the man who claimed he could get what they needed with no trouble at all. Ian's murder couldn't be down to bad luck and timing. She didn't buy that. Too much of a coincidence.

She'd lost it with Lemon. She remembered it clearly, the very moment. She'd gone in expecting solutions, expecting him to listen, and instead, he sat there like he was running the show. Calm. Smug. Offering only disappointment after disappointment, and still acting like he was doing her a favour. She didn't give him the chance to finish, but cut him off mid-sentence, tore strips off him loud enough for the place to go quiet. She didn't care. It was to be on her terms. What mattered now was that Ian Dillion was dead. Whether or not Lemon had pulled the trigger himself, it didn't make a difference. He had to be part of it. She stared at the door, half-hoping he'd walk through it again, because this time, she wouldn't be ranting and raving. She'd listen. She'd decide what came next.

As far as she was concerned, Alice Wallace had failed. Failed Graham, Ian, Kentucky, everyone including her mum. What to do? Maybe she'd sit here all day, stunned and alone, her head spinning and her hands clasped so tight it felt like she'd fall apart if she let go. Her failure left her emotionally devastated. She was sick of it all. Of everything. Of everyone. There was only one thing that kept her going. The Shamrock.

Plates were cleared with a clatter, not gently, but fast. Cutlery dropped into metal tubs, the sound sharp and annoying. A pan clanged somewhere behind the counter, followed by a roar from the kitchen, abrupt and fed-up. Someone laughed near the front window, too loud for the mood of the place, or maybe just too loud for her.

The floor was slick from the rain, shoes squeaking as people moved across it, coats dripping steadily, the bell above the door giving off the same tired chime every time it swung open. Burnt toast hung in the air, thick and buttery, but nobody noticed.

Alice sat near the back, unseen. Her chair was hard. Her shoulders locked. Hands now hidden beneath the table, fingers twisted tight and fidgeting. She hadn't moved in what felt like hours, afraid that if she did, something inside her might shatter and erupt across the room.

What frightened her most, more than the headline on that crumpled paper, was fear itself - quiet, patient, crawling into her head and settling in.

Because once it got there, it stayed.

Back in Armagh, the OC stood by the door while Dolores packed up the few belongings she had. Everything she needed fit into a plastic bag. She was eager to see Patrick again, to hear what trouble he'd been stirring up. The last time they spoke, he said he'd be waiting outside at 11.00 AM.

'I'll be back before you know it, Maureen,' Dolores said with half a smile. 'You know they'll never leave me be.'

'I know,' the OC replied with a sigh. 'We're all on their radar now, I suppose. It's... try an' keep your head down and stay outta trouble, will ye? I don't wanna see your ugly face again too soon!' she joked.

Dolores laughed and pulled on her coat, her eyes straying to Tina's now empty bed. 'That poor wee girl. Still hard to believe.'

'Don't talk,' Maureen replied, stepping back to let Dolores through.

They walked the catwalk together until they reached the stairs. 'Be seein' ye, Dolores,' Maureen said, giving her friend a good, strong hug.

'Aye, see ye later,' Dolores laughed.

Like Bridget, Dolores would miss this place, but only the women. Their tenacity. Their fierce loyalty. All the same, she was ready to breathe fresh air again.

That RUC man Black hadn't been able to pin a thing on her. No charge, no evidence, not a single soul willing to stand up and say what she was meant to have done. Whatever charge they'd tried to build on her had crumbled fast. Someone had leaned on someone, and before she knew it, she was shown the door. No apology, no warning, only a look that said he wasn't finished. No surprise there. All the same, she was out. For now.

Outside the gate, like he said he would, Paddy waited in the car. He'd missed her, no denying it. All the talk, the warnings, none of it mattered now. What mattered was getting her out, safe, and telling her straight what they'd found out about Brona Doyle. That came first. Then they'd deal with Miss Whatever-the-fuck-her-name-is, once and for all. He peeled the silver off a fresh pack of cigarettes, figuring he had time for one before they hit the road. But as he tapped one loose, he spotted her coming through the main gates. That walk, that look - cool as a cucumber, like she hadn't stepped out of the eye of a storm. He climbed out of the car, fag still unlit between his fingers, and stood waiting, arms loose by his sides, watching her make her way over. Same old Dee, with that insidious smile of hers tugging at her mouth, like she was keeping something from him.

Aye. She was back, all right.

Her eyes landed first on the car, then on Paddy, and without missing a beat, she broke into a run. 'Aha. There you are!'

Paddy caught her in a hug, grabbed her bag, and lobbed it into the back seat. 'Ah Dee, good to see ye. C'mon, it's Baltic out here!'

Dolores slid into the front seat, shivering as much as he was. She threw a glance back at the old Victorian façade of the gaol and gave a quiet smile.

Keep strong, ladies.

On the drive into Belfast, Paddy kept the conversation flowing, throwing her the latest bits from home - who'd said what, who'd landed in bother, the usual carry-on. She listened, but he could see she wasn't that interested.

Sure enough, before long, she brought up Brona Doyle.

Paddy didn't disappoint. He'd come prepared. Said what needed saying, laid it all out clean and steady, no frills, no waffle, full facts, exactly the way he'd rehearsed it in his head. Then he went quiet, eyes on the road, waiting for it. Her reaction. The one he knew was coming.

Didn't take long.

'You're fuckin' jokin' me,' she snapped, twisting round in her seat. 'Tell me you're jokin', Paddy. I was right, wasn't I?'

He smiled, but said nothing.

'You knew this, and you waited till now to tell me? Christ Almighty, I've only walked out of that hole, and you land this on me now? We've been drivin' for ages!'

He kept both hands on the wheel, stayed focused on the traffic ahead and listened to her protests. 'To think I shook that woman's hand. Sat beside her. Talked away like an eejit to her. I told ye, didn't I? I fuckin' told ye!'

Her voice shot up, fierce and rattling, her hands flying in front of her, jabbing the air like she was swatting flies. She looked like she might climb out the window if he didn't stop the car.

'I knew it. Her sittin' there, all that time, bold as brass, collectin' for the Prisoners' fund an' all, her with a face like butter that wouldn't melt. I knew what she was. You believe me now? Bet you're glad you listened.'

He could feel the heat of her, every word bitter with the kind of rage that she'd been building up from the first moment she gave off about the Brit. She wasn't done, but went on and on and on...

'I knew you'd be pleased!' Paddy laughed, with a hand over his ear to get her to stop, 'Has to be said, same girl wasn't a bad fuck for a Brit!'

'Ah, Patrick, that's boggin,' Dolores squealed, thumping him on the arm hard enough to make the car veer slightly.

Dolores, ecstatic now, turned towards the window and drank it all in. Green field after green field rolled past, each one a slightly different shade, soft and wild and endless. It almost made her catch her breath. That old-timer's song had it right, she thought. *Forty Shades of Green.* Every single one of them beautiful.

Whatever way the road twisted, the countryside kept unfurling like a ribbon, and for once, she didn't want to be anywhere else. The news about Brona Doyle - whoever the spy really was - had landed like a win on the lottery. Made her day. Maybe even her year. She leaned her elbow against the glass and let her smile spread. 'Told ye,' she muttered. 'Didn't I bloody tell ye.'

After a quick fifteen-minute snooze, Dolores woke. The first thing she asked Paddy was whether he knew where the Brit was.

Paddy nodded. 'Brian's got someone keepin' tabs. She's holed herself up in some café near City Hall.'

'Are we headin' straight there?'

'Nah. We'll swing by and pick Brian up first. Youse two'll go get her together. She's all yours Dee – but be careful and bring her straight back to The Shamrock. I'll wait there for ye'.'

Dolores couldn't have asked for better. He trusted her with this, which meant she had to do it right. 'Thanks, Patrick. Won't let you down. Swear.' They travelled on, glad to be together again, neither noticing the unmarked car shadowing them from afar.

Chapter Eighty-Eight

Love You Mum. So Much.

Back at The Shamrock, Brian was waiting dutifully outside, looking like a man chuffed to be paired up with Dolores again. He stepped forward as Paddy's car rolled to a stop. 'Good to see you, Dolores. How you doin'?' he asked casually, opening the passenger door.

Dolores looked up at the big married fella and answered. 'Grand, Brian. How's the family?' She knew he had a soft spot for her, so always made a point of mentioning his wife and kids. He was decent fella; she liked him, but she'd been burned badly once by a married man. Never again. Inside the pub, she quickly downed a couple of quick shots in the back room and kissed her brother goodbye. She was itching to get moving, to deal with the Brit and have it done.

'Come on, Brian me boy. We'll go in your car. Let's do this!' she called, already striding for the door.

The city traffic was a nightmare, crawling at a snail's pace through endless junctions and snarl-ups, but eventually they pulled up outside the café. Brian swung the car into a space, turned the engine off, and stepped out for a look. Surprisingly, Donegal Place was relatively quiet.

Across the road, Belfast City Hall loomed, grand and stubborn, its domed roof darkened with rain and grime. The front gates were barricaded with steel barriers and sandbags, flanked by uniformed Brits who looked downright miserable. The fencing was covered in old posters, peeling at the corners, most of them political, some of them already half torn down. Despite that, strung across the railings, someone had hung a few limp garlands, bits of tinsel wrapped round the iron, and a plastic Santa tied to one of the lamp posts, grinning like he didn't know where he was. White bulbs flickered above the main entrance, and a giant Christmas tree stood off to the left, patchy in places, but still lit.

The whole thing looked odd, half celebration, half siege. He scanned the crowd through the café window and nodded. 'She's on the phone at the back.'

Dolores exhaled slowly, steadying herself, then took a peep herself.

'Good luck,' Brian said, quieter this time.

She gave him a smile. 'Won't be long.'

A cold, creeping dread settled over Alice the moment she heard her mother's voice crackle down the line. 'Is that you, Alice?' she asked, uncertain but hopeful, like she wasn't sure if she was speaking to the living or the dead.

'Alice?'

Her name came through again, slow and crackly, the sound stretched thin by static and whatever was sitting between them now. Alice closed her eyes for a moment, gripped the receiver tighter, and swallowed down the rising wave of fear. She'd telephoned because she had to. There was no one left for her. No one left alive, that is.

'Yeah, Mum, it's me,' she whispered. 'How are you?'

'Oooh, Alice, it's so lovely to hear your voice. I've been so worried.'

'I know, Mum. I'm sorry. I can't explain right now, but I've been thinking about you. Lots.'

Even hundreds of miles away, Mrs Wallace knew Alice was in trouble. 'What is it, Alice? What's wrong? I hear it in your voice.'

'Nothing, Mum. Just... missing you. That's all.'

Curled into the corner by the payphone, Alice tried to keep her voice normal. Her mother kept talking, warm and worried. She could tell Alice wasn't right. 'I don't believe you Alice. You don't sound yourself. You've got me worried now.'

'I'm fine. Honest. A bit low, that's all.' Alice reassured her. Instinctively, she turned and scanned the café, barely listening to her mum's concerns. It was then that she came face to face with her worst nightmare.

Dolores Gillispie stormed up the steps and through the front door, her eyes full of rage, her face set with purpose. Alice stopped. The receiver fell from her hand, her mum's voice spilling out the earpiece. She should run, bolt for the back exit, scream, anything, but she couldn't move.

Fumbling, she grabbed the phone again and screamed, 'I have to go! Love you Mum. Love you so much—' The handset was wrenched from her grip. Dolores raised it high and brought it down on the side of Alice's head. The pain of it went off like fireworks.

'With me, bitch!' Dolores snarled into the blood now seeping down Alice's cheek.

Everything blurred as Alice was dragged backwards by the hair, out the café and towards a waiting car. No one got up. No one helped. Turned their faces away. This was no business of theirs.

Back inside the car, Dolores sat stony-faced, content and quiet as a lamb. She and Brian had an idea. Not a word was to be said until they were back at The Shamrock. Let silence do its job. Let the Brit's fear do the work. They'd have plenty to talk about later.

Paddy Gillispie wasn't typically nervous, but he was on edge. Dee had been well wound up earlier, itching to be given the green light, and he'd hoped she'd stuck to the plan. That woman could be so fuckin' impetuous when the mood took her. They'd been gone too long. Over an hour. Should've been back ages ago. He told himself it was traffic. Brits and their checkpoints. That was it. He picked up the *Belfast Telegraph*, his eyes skimming the article about the part-time UDR man shot dead in Bangor. Brian's work. Neat and efficient. Same as ever. Paddy gave a small smile. Brian had never let him down. Quiet, careful, capable. Next on the list was James Carroll, better known to them as Lemon. Brian would take care of that too.

A sound outside pulled his attention. Tyres on gravel. Paddy moved to the back door, tension creeping up his chest with every step.

Thank fuck. There they were. Brian and Dee, dragging *Brona Doyle* across the yard, her arms pinned behind her, head turned to the side. Or rather, Alice Wallace. They'd found out her name. At last. He exhaled, slow and measured, and watched them come in. About bloody time too.

Alice wasn't surprised to see Paddy standing there as Dolores dragged her through the back of the bar. Not shocked. Afraid. Cold and creeping, like frost moving slow through her veins. He didn't speak. Watched every move, his arms folded, his mouth set in a hard line. This kind of quiet unnerved her more than shouting ever could. The car ride had been no better. Not a sound from Dolores or Brian. Only the engine's low growl and the odd clunk of a gear change. Alice hated every second of it. That grim, suffocating quiet told her this wasn't a warning, this was a sentence.

She wasn't going to last the hour.

Pushed again, Alice landed hard on a chair, its legs scraping across the floor beneath her. Dolores still hadn't said a word. The same expression, not quite a grin, more like she was quietly enjoying herself. She reached for a reel of blue nylon rope and began winding it around Alice's wrists, tight and quick, knotting it behind the chair with rigour.

Then finally, she spoke. 'You stayin' for this?' she asked her brother, her voice light, like she was asking if he fancied staying for dinner. Paddy didn't bother answering, but walked straight over to Alice, closed the gap, hawked and spat right into her eyes, and whacked her one. Warm, thick saliva stuck to her eyelids and cheek. She screamed. She screamed then, full force and fury. 'You cowardly bastard!'

She jerked her head, trying to hurl his spit off, but couldn't. Her cheek throbbed, and the sting in her eyes only made it worse.

'They'll find you!' she shrieked. 'All of you. I swear they will!'

Paddy smiled, kissed his twin on the cheek, whispered something in her ear, then muttered, 'All yours. Enjoy,' before heading out to the bar for another well-earned Guinness.

Alice was still squealing when Brian suddenly struck her hard. The back of his hand cracked across her face, his Claddagh ring splitting the skin where the payphone had already cut it, sending pain shooting across her scalp and down her neck.

Dolores tutted, half amused. 'Brian. Manners, please. We don't hit ladies.'

He gave a lopsided grin. 'Oops. Sorry, Dolores.' Then turned to Alice. 'Sorry, miss.'

From a green felt bag, Dolores pulled out a revolver, turned it slowly in her hand, then looked at Alice as she nodded to Brian.

'See this?' she said softly. 'He used this yesterday. On that pal of yours. Ian. Didn't you, Brian?'

He gave a lazy smile.

Dolores weighed the gun in her palm, then stepped forward and pressed the barrel beneath Alice's chin, her touch almost tender, like she might lift her face for a kiss.

'Time to say goodbye, Brona. Or is it *Alice*?'

Alice closed her eyes.

Her fiancé's face came to her, clear and unspoiled. Graham. A day in Brighton, the two of them on a picnic blanket, sea breeze on her skin, sun burning high. She could taste the cheap red wine, remember him fumbling with the ring, the tears and the laughter that followed. The world had felt safe then. She half smiled at the memory - private, perfect, hers alone.

She had never been the military sort. A girl from the southeast England, quiet, bookish, the kind who might have ended up teaching or buried in a library. She'd joined the

Women's Royal Army Corps straight out of university, not for the uniform, not for the pay, but because Graham wanted her to. She'd believed in him, in all his talk about service, about protecting people, about peace being worth the risk. For a while she'd carried that belief like a shield. Even here. Even in Londonderry. Until Graham. Until the day his head was blown apart and with it, all the certainty she had clung to.

Now she sat slumped in the back of a bar in West Belfast, wrists bound, blood warm and sticky as it trickled down her face and neck, her head too heavy to lift. Her eyes were open but dull, staring without focus. No one spoke her name. Beyond the walls the night carried on — voices rising, glasses clinking, laughter spilling into the street. Life carried on, without her. She was finished, drained of everything, too tired even for fear. She knew, with precision sharper than pain, that no one was coming.

Dolores smiled, eyes shining with excitement. She pulled the trigger. The crack tore through the bar like a firework going off in a metal bin. A few punters looked up from their drinks, shrugged, exchanged glances, and for a few seconds went quiet. Only the sound of the racing on the telly. Someone laughed. Then, as if nothing had happened, the talking and drinking continued. Bets were placed. Pints were poured. Another day in West Belfast.

Outside, three plainclothes soldiers sat in a parked Cortina. Too late. The single shot rang out as one of them reached for the car door handle. They sprang out, weapons drawn, sprinting around the corner to the rear entrance of The Shamrock, then stopped suddenly.

The steel door was locked fast. The smoked windows were near black, impossible to see through. No way of knowing what was happening inside, no way of getting in without backup. One man swore, he reached for the radio, his jaw tight. They knew the rules. No support, no entry. Not for anyone. Whatever had happened in there was done. Over. They weren't for going in. They sure as hell weren't dying today. In under a minute, they were gone, back in the car, engine roaring, tyres spitting grit as they disappeared into the dark, leaving what was left of Private Alice Wallace behind, like she'd never mattered to anyone.

Chapter Eighty-Nine

A Breach of Justice

Chief Constable Bonner had no choice but to charge Charles Jones and Lemon with the crimes laid bare in William Barter's exclusive for *The Irish News*, now picked up by what was left of the Irish press and spreading fast across international wires.

The headlines were relentless. Brutal sectarian killings, money laundering, armed robbery, intimidation, anti-Catholic propaganda. All of it laid out in black and white. Jones's face was everywhere, plastered across every front page, filling screens on both Irish and local TV. There was no hiding from it now.

The only way Bonner could still protect his ally was to dismiss Barter's claim that Jones had ordered the fatal shooting of Bishop Hegarty. He maintained in multiple statements that Provo Kieran Kelly had acted alone. An unstable gunman and bomber, far more likely to pull the trigger than someone as 'socially prominent' as Charles Jones. Bonner knew the truth. Jones and Morris were right behind the bishop's murder and many others, but without sufficient evidence, there was no way to pin it on the East Belfast man.

Morris and Kelly made convenient fall guys for the City Hotel debacle. Bonner's public denials were flimsy at best, but somehow, they held. The murder charge was soon dropped. How Barter had uncovered so much solid evidence for the remainder of the charges, Bonner would never know. The man had done a hell of a job. So thorough, even he couldn't sweep it under the rug. Tried everything, but this time, he couldn't save Jones from the inevitable. As promised, Barter had passed everything to his CIA friend first. Dale Horn, thrilled with such intel, returned the favour. What came back was dynamite.

The Honourable Justice Matthew Dodds looked down at Charles Jones, standing beside James Carroll in the dock at Belfast High Court. A handful of Lemon's gang – the so-called 'kids' – flanked their leader, their heads held high, faces impassive. Not one of them, not even Carroll, would say a word against Jones.

They knew better.

Jones had warned them. All it would take was a single word from him, and their nearest and dearest wouldn't be in danger. They'd be gone before anyone had time to look twice.

Dodds studied them a moment longer, then turned his gaze to Jones. Arrogant to the last. There'd always been something about him. A kind of confidence that refused to budge, no matter how close he came to the edge. In truth, Dodds had admired that, in his own quiet way. It hadn't come as a shock when he'd been asked to replace the original judge. Word was, the man had taken ill rather suddenly. Dodds hadn't asked questions. He didn't need to. He knew who pulled the strings, and why. Charles Jones made the call, and Dodds had been happy to oblige.

After all, Boodles had been a gift that kept on giving, and he and Mrs D were still dining out on the story of their evening spent with royalty. The champagne, the cigars, the photo on his desk that said more than words ever could. He'd be getting an OBE or the like soon.

He listened carefully, or at least gave the impression he did, while the Yankee journalist took the stand and laid out reams of damning evidence: interviews, photographs, recordings, and statements. It had all been gathered over months, then passed to a senior RUC man in Newtownabbey. CIA agent Dale Horn assured Barter the officer was fair; this was confirmed. In no time, Jones was arrested and charged.

Dodds found himself almost impressed. William Barter had pulled together more than the police had managed in yonks. That took a certain nerve – and power. But from where? Jones's barristers fought hard, but there was no wriggling free. The Prosecutor had a mountain of evidence. Now came Dodds's rule.

He habitually coughed for effect, bringing the court to heel. Silence fell like a curtain. This was his moment. All eyes forward, the atmosphere of the court tense, every man and woman hanging on his words.

'Charles Anthony Jones,' he began, voice heavy with solemnity. 'This court finds you guilty of the following...'

He'd run through the charge list. Dodds looked over at Jones and allowed his voice to drop an octave. Grave, authoritative. The kind of tone that made headlines. 'I therefore sentence you to three years' imprisonment—' He paused, coughed, this time for real, and dabbed at his nose with a silk handkerchief. '—suspended for two years.' He let his words hit home, then sat back to enjoy the entertainment.

The gallery erupted. Jones's supporters, out in force, clapped and cheered, a wall of Union Jacks waving above their heads like a football crowd. King Billy banners, Orange Lodge standards, even a paper crown or two - it was a carnival in court, a Loyalist knees-up in wigs and robes.

Below the rest of the room turned cold. Gasps, shouts, a woman sobbing. A priest stood up and called it a disgrace. Another man was dragged out after he lunged for the barrier, yelling that justice was dead in this city. Maybe it was.

On the other side of the gallery, the families of the victims sat still and shattered. A few sobbed, others shouted, voices bursting with fury. But most people simply looked at the judge in disbelief. Shellshocked. As if they'd watched justice itself packing its bags and leaving the court. This wasn't a verdict. It was a message. Every Catholic in that courtroom heard it loud and clear. The British Establishment was at play. Still.

As the tension grew worse, Dodds thought it rather distasteful, but not unexpected. He wasn't here to judge them – only the man in the dock. He rapped his gavel loudly and shouted, 'Silence! Silence! Silence in my court!' It was performative, of course, but effective enough.

Jones turned to his supporters high above and raised a clenched fist. 'No surrender!' he roared.

The explosion of cries that answered him was deafening. Beside him, James Carroll stood rigid, almost translucent. He wasn't celebrating. *What the fuck?*

Dodds reached for the next verdict, his eyes on Lemon. Eventually, the gallery hushed. 'James Carroll,' he read, 'you have been found guilty of eleven counts of murder...' Again, the charge list followed, cold, bureaucratic, and by the end of it, Dodds could almost feel Lemon shrinking in the dock.

'I therefore sentence you to life imprisonment. Without the possibility of parole.'

Lemon was near catatonic. His knuckles blanched against the polished wood. He turned to Jones for something, anything, support, a signal, but the Belfast man barely looked at him. Merely raised an eyebrow and shrugged. Cold as a butcher's hook.

Dodds finished up the remaining sentences. Life for the others. No parole. No fanfare. As the dock doors opened and they were led down, a 'kid' bellowed one last defiant cry: 'No surrender!'

Jones looked up at the bench and gave Dodds a slow, knowing smile. Not gratitude. Something darker. More like closer to an understanding. Dodds didn't smile back. But neither did he look away. He simply reached for his gavel again, brought it down and closed the session.

Once the verdict got out, the press had torn into Charles Jones like dogs on a carcass, filling page after page with hostility. They didn't hold back. The headlines screamed their outrage at the fixed verdict, all demanding a retrial.

'Justice for Sale: Jones Walks Free.'

Jones was surprised to find the fallout went deeper than a few bad write-ups. Numerous contracts were pulled overnight, doors that had once been open now stayed shut. The usual hardy handshakes had turned lukewarm, or died out. Well. If they thought that was enough to bring him to his knees, they could go to hell. Bloody fools, the lot of them.

He had to admit, the financial squeeze was starting to bite. Most of his cash had gone where it always did - straight to the UVF. Worth every penny. The boys were efficient, brutal when they needed to be, and loyal to the last. Let the press write whatever they liked. Out there on the ground, the soldiers still took their orders from him.

This wasn't the end. Not even close. He had new ventures waiting, new hands to shake. There were always more people to see, more strings to pull, more fools lining up to play their part.

Let them sneer. Let them write their shite.

Charles Jones wasn't finished. Not by a long shot. They'd started a war they couldn't win.

When the verdict was heard, Bill Barter dropped into his seat, mute with fury, his insides blazing. He couldn't believe what he was hearing. It was a bloody farce. A performance. That judge hadn't only screwed the law - he'd shattered it. Bought. Had to be. There was no other way to explain it.

Three years. Three fucking years. Suspended at that.

Justice? Don't make him laugh.

He stared as Jones descended the dock like a man taking a bow, his lawyers lined up for handshakes, smug and self-congratulatory.

As soon as Jones saw Barter, he swaggered over. 'Well, well, well, Mr Barter. As you see, I'm still here,' he said, his arms outstretched like some crooked messiah.

'So I see,' Barter replied sourly, doing his best to mask the disgust clawing at his very soul.

Jones took a step closer, his voice low, his words like acid. 'Will you give up now, Mr Barter?'

Barter didn't move. Hardly breathed, but said. 'Never.'

Jones laughed. Not kindly. He clapped mockingly, took a few slow steps backwards with that same vile smirk, then turned back to his lawyers like it was all a game.

Later, back at the City Hotel bar, a large gin an absolute must, Barter scribbled out his briefing for Langley. Rage and frustration drove his pen, his writing quick and cutting.

...It is evident that in this case there was an egregious breach of justice, stemming from obvious collusion between the court, Jones, and the cabal, that is, the Ulster Security Service. However, without more proven and documented evidence, any rectification of this situation will not be forthcoming.

Across this province, on a daily basis, disreputable, scandalous and officially sanctioned kangaroo courts are being used to violate and disregard fundamental human rights, thereby, unsurprisingly, adding impetus to the republican terrorists' war against the British government...

He paused, swilled down his gin, then went back to writing. There was more to say. There always was. And he, William Barter, like Charles Jones, was far from done yet.

Chapter Ninety

A Shameful Evening

Two warm, buttered scones and a cup of tea appeared on the table, courtesy of Mrs Mac, as Catherine still fondly called her. The red-and-white striped pot sat between them, steam curling from the spout into the air. The smell of baking hung around the kitchen like a distant memory, but Catherine's throat tightened. She couldn't eat. Couldn't think about food. She searched the kitchen for change, but it was nowhere to be found. The solid oak table still anchored the middle of the flagstone floor. As always, the copper pans over the stove reflected the light. The old black stove, tucked into its arched hearth, gave off a steady heat. Through the sash window above the Belfast sink, she could see the stone steps leading down to the cellar. It was all still here. As it was. Time hadn't dared lay a finger on it.

Across from her, Mrs Mac took her seat, her familiar smile as full of warmth as ever. She poured the tea with her usual care, nodding as if they'd only spoken yesterday. 'And how are you keepin', Mrs Henderson?' she asked.

'I'm good, but nervous, Mrs Mac. Terribly nervous.'

'Och, now, what have ye to be nervous about? This is your home. I'm sorry ye can't see Mr Henderson. He's in bed, love. Not well. Not well at all. Between us I don't think he'll make this wedding.' She reached for Catherine's hand. 'You know about that too, I suppose?'

'I've heard there's to be a wedding, yes,' Catherine murmured. 'That Roger's poorly, too. The thing is, I must speak with him, Mrs Mac. I've written... so many times.'

The housekeeper knew all about the letters. Blue-edged airmail envelopes, dozens of them – mostly ignored, tossed aside, burned, or quietly sent back. She never said a word. Not her place. But she noticed, always noticed, as life carried on. Poor woman. Only now, with Mr Henderson failing fast, did it strike her. Time at last to face the truth, drag out the ghosts, and fix this bloody mess. Mess that it was. She thought back to that summer evening, late in the season, the air thick with midges and cut grass, when she'd helped

Mrs Moore, the housekeeper before her, manage one of the bigger parties. That night had stayed with her. Buried deep, never spoken of, not once, to anyone. A secret she had carried ever since.

Melrose had been at its finest. Lights strung through the garden as always, the house filling with the low hum of talk and the strains of the classical music Mr Henderson loved. She'd spent the day polishing silver and setting out flowers, until every room smelled of roses, beeswax, and expensive cologne. The guests arrived in their finest, tailored suits, silk ties, shoes polished so bright she could see her face in them. They gathered in tight little groups, speaking low, laughing, some of them with a hand tucked in a pocket as if they'd practised the stance in front of a mirror. The women drifted in on clouds of perfume, heels clicking, wrapped in silks and velvets, furs around their shoulders, jewellery catching the light, clutching handbags too small to hold a handkerchief.

It was all very grand, and it must have cost a fortune, but she had to admit it looked beautiful. The candlelight softened every face, the crystal glittered, and for a moment, Melrose seemed less a house than a dream. Lights, music, voices pitched low and posh, as if money had lifted them above the world. Lovely to look at, but not for the likes of her.

Upstairs, Roger endured another of Jocelyn's rants, her bitterness so stale now he could almost mouth the lines for her. He'd had enough. With a tut he rose, leaving her mid-sentence, her voice trailing down the corridor as he headed for the stairs. She'd been at him all day.

At the bottom step, Catherine Henderson stood. At once, the tension eased from his chest. *Thank Christ*. A sight for sore eyes if ever there was one. Alone, she was looking around; composed, half-smiling, cutting through the gloom like light through mist. Everyone knew he was fond of her, and he didn't care who noticed anymore. Catherine was a tonic. She brought warmth into rooms long gone cold, quick-witted and gracious without trying, a quiet charm that made people feel seen. Him most of all.

She looked especially lovely that night – a sky-blue dress hugging her figure, her hair swept back with a coral clasp. Simple, striking. She should never have married his brother, Roger thought, not for the first time. James didn't deserve her.

He reached for her arm and guided her gently into the dining room, where a makeshift bar had been set beside the Adam fireplace. Without a word he ordered two large gins, pausing for breath as if to steady himself. The room buzzed with talk and the clatter of glass, laughter rolling under the glow of polished wood and candlelight. Usually this was his favourite corner of Melrose – oak panelling, soft linens, dusk light spilling through sash windows - a place that carried its own kind of comfort. But not tonight. Not with the nastiness waiting upstairs. Not even Catherine could ease that.

They found two seats and slipped into conversation, easy as ever. Across the room Inspector George Shalham lifted a glass in his direction. Roger raised his own with a quiet smile. Good old George. Always steady, always on his side. Then the dinner bell rang. Roger turned to the long table and spotted Jocelyn at the far end. Their eyes met across linen and candlelight. He tried a smile, tentative, almost hopeful, but her face gave nothing back - cold, lifeless, like the silver laid out before her.

Later, when the last guests had gone and Melrose had settled into silence, Roger lingered in the drawing room. Jocelyn had gone to bed. James too. But Catherine remained. He could talk to her for hours because she listened. Properly listened. She challenged him, teased him, laughed with him. Bright, sharp, full of wit. He could have fallen in love with her. Easily.

Catherine had been watching her brother-in-law all evening, and her heart ached for him. He'd done everything he could, working the room with that effortless charm of his, air-kissing the women, laughing in the right places, even trying more than once to draw Jocelyn in. Useless. His wife barely spoke a word to him. Hardly looked at him. Since the miscarriage, Jocelyn had turned cold. Withdrawn. Bitter. She sat frozen at the end of the table, her silence heavier than words, dominating the room. People noticed. Of course they did.

Now, in the soft hush, Catherine reached across and laid her hand on his arm. 'You okay, Roger?'

He gave a dry laugh, though there was no humour in it, and shook his head. 'That obvious, is it?'

She nodded gently. 'She's not getting any better, is she?'

Roger didn't answer straightaway. He got to his feet, crossed to the fireplace and picked up the poker, jabbing at the glowing embers in the grate. With his back turned and shoulders drawn in, he seemed to be suppressing something or fighting to keep himself from telling her how he felt. About life. Rocola. Jocelyn. Their lost babies. His loneliness.

A few seconds later he returned and sank into the armchair. His face was drawn, his eyes flat. He exhaled, rubbed his hands together, then broke. 'I don't know what to do, Catherine. I don't know what to do. She's impossible. I've told her we can try again.

Losing those babies... so many... it's destroying us. Destroying our love.' His own voice undid him. A torrent of sobs tore out, fresh and loud, as if something inside had split wide open.

Catherine reached for him without thinking. She squeezed his hand, rubbed his back in slow circles, trying to ease the pain, then pulled him close and held him. It wasn't planned. It simply happened. She didn't let go.

He knew he shouldn't. He knew before their lips even met. But her arms were around him, warm and safe, and he wept. The months of silence, Jocelyn's coldness, the crushing loneliness – all of it spilled out. Catherine didn't push him away. She held him the way his wife once had.

So he kissed her.

It was instinct. A last-ditch grasp for something good, something kind, in a world that had turned cruel. Her lips met his, soft and hesitant, and for a fleeting moment he let himself believe it might be okay. But it wasn't. His hands, his mouth, his want - all of it was wrong. She was his brother's wife! The one person he should never touch. Yet here he was, kissing her like a man lost at sea, clinging to the first sign of life he could find. Even as he did it, he knew this could never be undone.

Catherine knew the kiss was too much. Too wanting. It wasn't right, his tongue too deep. It sent a rush of panic through her, sharp and immediate. This was the last thing she wanted. He had looked so broken, so full of sadness, and when he'd cried like that, all she'd wanted was to comfort him. That was all. Not this!

She pressed her hands against his chest, trying to stop him, but he didn't seem to notice. His arms, strong and urgent, only tightened. Before she could stop him, he pulled her down with him onto the rug. His hands were all over her, fast and frantic. His body pressed hard into hers. Her panic gave way to anger. She had to stop him. This was ridiculous, this wasn't the man she knew, the man she respected and cared for.

'Roger, no, stop, stop!' she gasped, still trying to push him off, but he held fast. She tried again, harder this time, but it was like trying to move stone. Roger had vanished, and in his place was someone she didn't recognise, a man with a contorted face, red and sweating, his eyes soulless and unseeing.

His weight pinned her down. She was stuck. *Think, Catherine!* She tried to scream, cry for help, but her voice caught in her throat and came out raspy, useless.

Everything after that became a blur – the raising of silk, the sound of it tearing, her arms flailing, his strength, the power of him, his awful, fixed determination. She fought with everything she had, but it was like screaming into the wind. No matter how she kicked, clawed, or pleaded, she couldn't stop what happened next. Her eyes squeezed shut, bracing against the pain, the shock, the sick disbelief of what he was doing.

When it was over, he turned aside, gasping, his face buried, as if hiding from what he'd done.

Catherine lay perfectly still. Numb. The room around her seemed suspended, yet the fire kept crackling in the hearth, stubbornly alive, casting flickers of light across the panelled walls and the rug beneath her. A room she'd once thought beautiful, now spoiled for life. She tried to move, but couldn't. Shaking, her breathing was shallow, her arms limp at her sides, her legs curled in tight together as if it might make her disappear. She stared at the wall, willing herself to wake up, to find it had all been some twisted dream.

But the sting between her legs told her otherwise.

Christ. Oh, Christ, what have I done?! Roger Henderson's thoughts reeled, his breath catching the back of his throat as shock settled in. He stared at the dishevelled tiny figure beside him, his heart thudding, hands trembling. Shame swept over him like a fever. Catherine wasn't moving. She lay perfectly still; her face turned to the wall. Her cheeks burned red, not from effort, but from humiliation. He could almost hear her unspoken words. *How could you? Why would you do this? After everything. After all the times I've listened, cared, helped you. This is how you repay me? This is what you've done!*

Roger dragged himself backwards, his heart thumping like it wanted out of his chest. He couldn't speak as he fixed his clothing, his hands clumsy, shaking. His eyes flicked over her. Too late. The damage was done, the truth already sinking into his soul. Her face, her beautiful face, was blank and lifeless. That look would follow him for the rest of his days. He'd crossed a line that could never be uncrossed, ravaged the one good person left in his small, pathetic world, the only one who'd shown him any kindness. He didn't know who he was anymore. Only that he despised himself.

'Catherine... I'm so sorry. Dear God, I'm so sorry,' he said, barely able to get the words out. He reached for her hand in some wild hope that she might take it, might somehow forgive him, might say anything to ease the sickness now turning in his gut.

She recoiled like a scared puppy, away from him. She couldn't even look at him, but stood and straightened her dress, quietly and with her characteristic grace. Her shoes lay nearby and he watched as she picked them up one by one, along with her broken hair clasp that must've snapped during the— Almost as an afterthought, she spotted her torn underwear, picked it up and crushed it into her palm without a sound. Keeping her head bowed and avoiding his eyes, she left.

Mrs McGinty had gone to fetch the last of the wine glasses when she caught sight of Catherine coming out of the drawing room. She almost lost her breath. The girl looked all wrong somehow, messy, her usual spark snuffed out, replaced by something broken. *What in God's name?*

Unseen, she stepped back into the shadows beneath the staircase, pressing herself into the dark. As Catherine passed, she saw the wetness on her cheeks, the faraway look in her eyes, the way she moved like she wasn't quite in her own body. Her dress was torn, her shoes clutched in one hand, and a rolled-up piece of fabric in the other. No, no… it looked like a pair of knickers!

Then Mr Henderson appeared at the drawing-room door. He stood there, frozen, pale as chalk, staring up the stairs where his sister-in-law had gone. That was enough. Mrs McGinty knew. Knew in her very heart what occurred.

'Sweet Mary, Mother of God. What have you done, Mr Henderson? What in God's name have you done to that poor, lovely girl?' she whispered.

Now, years later, in the quiet of Melrose's basement kitchen, Mrs Mac placed a fresh pot of tea on the table and looked across at the returned Catherine Henderson. 'What are we going to do with you, Cass, eh?' she asked with a small, knowing smile. Catherine's lips curved. It had been years since anyone had called her Cass. The sound of it melted something inside her.

'Mrs Mac, I need to see James. I have to talk to him, get to know him. I've regretted leaving him every single day,' she said quietly. The housekeeper nodded, though her expression was troubled.

'What about Mr Henderson?' she asked gently. 'Are you going to confront him?' Catherine paused, lifted her cup, but didn't drink. Held it there for a second, then gave a small shrug and shook her head, like she wasn't sure what Mrs Mac meant.

'Confront, Mrs Mac? I'm not sure what you mean.'

But she did. They both did.

Chapter Ninety-One

1950s Ireland

Mrs McGinty had never spoken a word to anyone about what she'd witnessed in the hallway that night. The memory was lodged like a splinter she couldn't pull out. Her heart had broken at the sight of Catherine, dishevelled, desolate, violated.

Despite her better judgement, she felt sorrow for Roger Henderson. Whatever had possessed him that night, he'd looked utterly broken afterwards. So many times, far too many to count, she'd thought about speaking up. Whether she should tell someone what she saw, what she suspected, was the question. Never did. Couldn't. Not that she needed the work, though God knows she did. It was the scandal, the shame it would've brought down on the house. She prayed for him, prayed for that poor girl. Even if she had spoken out, who would've believed her? Against a well-to-do family like the Hendersons?

After that night, Roger Henderson disappeared into his work like a man drowning. He left the house before sunrise, came back well after dark, and barely said two words to anyone. The charm he'd once been known for, that easy laugh and warm presence, vanished overnight. He was half the man he'd been before.

Mrs Henderson, already brittle from grief, began to unravel in a different way. She grew even colder, more withdrawn, often taking to her room for days at a time. She and Roger barely spoke. Whatever marriage they'd once had was now routine and muted, two people locked in their own private miseries, unable to reach each other, or perhaps no longer willing. Melrose, once proud and full of life, seemed to be closing in around them. All of them.

As for Catherine, she wanted nothing more than to leave, to put distance between herself and everything that had happened, but then she found herself pregnant, and the trap quietly closed. 1950s Ireland left her with no options. Abortion was illegal, adoption carried shame, and unmarried mothers were bundled off to institutions where their babies were taken from them, sometimes sold. Catherine was married, so none of that applied.

Instead, she was expected to stay put, keep her head down and get on with it, no matter what. James wouldn't hear of leaving. Over and over he'd say they couldn't afford to move, not now, not with a baby on the way. Besides, he'd argue, where better than Melrose? So comfortable, so respectable. So cheap. She went quiet. What could she say? The thought of being pregnant swirled in her gut like sour milk. The very idea of bringing a child into *that* house, of raising it under *that* roof, simply made her want to die.

In the end, the only person she could bear to have near her was a young girl from Londonderry, Majella O'Reilly, a cheerful sort recommended by Mrs Moore. Majella had a motor mouth and a heart of gold, full of easy chatter and kindness. She never asked questions, not outright, but Catherine sensed she knew something was up. It didn't matter, though. The girl brought a splash of colour into Catherine's grey days, and for now, she was a godsend.

In their upstairs sewing sessions, Majella would rattle on, heart wide open, about her fiancé, Patrick, painting a future that sparkled with plans and promises. She spoke as if nothing in the world could touch them, as if love alone would be enough. Even though her mother was against it from the start.

Catherine would smile, nodding along, threading needles and hemming seams, but inside, her own future felt like a closed door. She was already pregnant. Unlike Majella, there were no plans. No sparkling future. A husband who wouldn't let her leave, and a house she couldn't breathe in...

Majella talked about how Patrick proposed, the tiny house they were saving to rent, the five children they'd agreed on, though they joked about stopping at four if the third was a devil child. Her joy was infectious, her dreams so intact, so unspoiled. It helped cheer Catherine up. Not a lot, but enough to make the hours pass with less uncertainty. In time, Catherine's belly began to swell, undeniable and, to her, shameful. It didn't matter whose baby it was. She didn't want it. Not any part of it. Nor, it seemed, did Roger. She avoided him like the plague.

What followed was half a year of seclusion and false smiles, trapped in Melrose with Jocelyn and Roger, the very walls of the place thick with lies. Until, one brittle March morning, her son came into the world. Nine pounds, two ounces. Healthy. Strong. Perfect. Catherine stared at him in disbelief, as if he belonged to someone else entirely. There was no rush of love, no flood of feeling. A numbness so deep it seemed to become part of her being.

To everyone's surprise, Jocelyn suddenly blossomed. Having a baby in the house seemed to soften her grief, melting the bitterness that had surrounded her for so long, and in its place came a fierce, unexpected love for the bundle. She hovered over James Jnr's cot like a lioness, lifting him up with confident hands, brushing kisses across his warm brow, rocking him until her arms throbbed with the effort. At night, she whispered lullabies under her breath, her voice content. The infant had become her salvation.

Roger too, slowly at first, couldn't help but get drawn in too. At the beginning, he held the child like he might break him, his movements awkward, unsure, his guilt pressed into every look. The pull was stronger than shame. Before long, he was crooning nonsense into the boy's ear with a tenderness no one had seen in him for years. Watching them together, you'd be forgiven for thinking this was how it had always been – the way Roger and Jocelyn clung to the child and, somehow, to each other. As if this tiny, squirming bundle had patched over the ruin of what he'd done.

Then there was Catherine's husband, James Snr. He took one look at the child, nodded politely, and went back to folding his newspaper. Didn't ask to hold him. Didn't comment on whose features the child had. If he had any opinion at all, no one knew or asked. The boy didn't stir anything in him. Not pride. Not suspicion. Not even the bare bones of love. Another Henderson to add to the line.

Catherine did try. She really did. She held the child to her chest, breathed in his scent, and willed herself to feel something, anything, close to maternal love. But it never came. Not the way it should have. Not the way other mothers described it. Jocelyn felt it though. Jocelyn loved him as if he were her own. Catherine made the only decision that felt remotely bearable.

One rainy evening, she sat James Snr down, with her heart racing and voice flat, she told him she was leaving. Their marriage was over. There'd be no drama, no fights. She was going to South Africa, and the baby would stay there with the family who had already claimed him in every way that mattered. She packed and left without saying goodbye to Roger.

Back in Melrose, carefully setting her teacup down, Catherine repeated her question, more quietly this time. 'Why would I confront Mr Henderson, Mrs Mac?'

The housekeeper shrugged and pressed her lips together. She refilled their cups, and adjusted the teapot on the tray. When she finally spoke, her voice was soft but certain as she reached across the table to take Catherine's hand. She gave it a couple of firm squeezes.

Then, eyes steady, confessed, 'I know what happened, my love. I saw you that night... on the stairs. I saw the state you were in.'

Catherine gasped, her body trembling as Mrs Mac's words sank in. For years, she'd carried the fear that no one would ever believe her, that it would always be her word against his. Roger Henderson, the charismatic, well-regarded businessman from Londonderry. Rape? No way! Mrs McGinty knew. She'd been there. She hadn't forgotten.

Too choked to speak, Catherine gave a shaky nod. The truth had lived buried inside her for years, tucked beneath guilt, denial, and a shame so thick it had nearly destroyed her. What haunted her most, what still woke her at night in the loneliest hours, was how she'd turned her back on her baby boy. Not because of him, but because he reminded her of what had been done. She'd blamed him without meaning to. Held him at a distance, convinced herself she couldn't feel, couldn't love, not realising until now that none of it had ever been his fault. For the first time, she saw what it was. She wasn't weak. She hadn't failed. She'd been a victim.

Roger had provided for James. Jocelyn had adored him, maybe even saved him. But Catherine had missed it all. Missed his first words, his first steps, the whole of his childhood, and she'd never get that back.

What she could do, what she had to do now, was tell him the truth. Every hard word of it. He deserved to know she hadn't left because of him. That she loved him. That she was sorry. So sorry. The guilt was like acid in her belly. It had followed her through every country, every year, every single night. The only way to stop it, to breathe again, was to make him understand.

'It's been years, Mrs Mac,' she whispered. 'I can't live with it anymore. I have to see Roger. We need to tell James. All of it.'

Mrs McGinty hesitated. 'I don't know, love. The shock of seeing you, then hearing all that, might kill him. As I say, I'm not sure he'll last till Saturday for the wedding. It'll be a miracle if he does. There's a rehearsal tonight, but no one's expecting him. Young James wants him resting as much as possible.'

'I'm not here to cause a scene, Mrs Mac. Only to talk,' Catherine said softly.

Mrs McGinty was torn. She stood up and crossed the kitchen, only then catching the acrid smell of burning.

'Christ save us, me shortbread!' she exclaimed, yanking open the oven. Smoke billowed out.

She pulled on her mitts and lifted a tray of scorched lumps, clucking her tongue as she dropped them straight into the pedal bin. 'Och, dear. What a shame,' she muttered, tossing the hot tray into the sink.

She stood for a moment at the basement window, staring out and thinking. Catherine didn't move. Neither said a word. Mrs McGinty grunted. The girl was right. Young James deserved the truth. As for Mr Henderson, well, he might not have much time left. Might do him good, owning up to it now. He was close enough to the pearly gates to count.

'I'll go see how he is. If he says okay, then that's fine. Give us a minute.'

Catherine waited.

When Mrs Mac returned, her warm smile was all the go-ahead she needed.

Upstairs, Roger felt his heart pounding beneath the fine bedclothes. He'd imagined this moment for years, dreaded it, hoped for it, and now that it was here, welcomed it. He wasn't long for this world and knew it.

The bedroom door creaked open and Catherine stepped through. He hadn't laid eyes on her in over twenty years, yet the sight of her hit him like a punch in the chest. Older, yes. Thinner too. But it was her. The same long neck, the same graceful way she carried herself, but this time, like she was bracing for something. Her eyes, once so bright, held shadows now. No sparkle, no softness. Quiet.

She looked tired, but still beautiful. She didn't smile. Didn't frown either. But stood, hands clasped in front of her, waiting. As if she'd come prepared for battle but decided not to fight. Christ help him, the shame surged through him all over again.

Mrs McGinty gently ushered Catherine to a red velvet two-seater by the bed. With another warm smile and a reassuring glance, she pulled the double doors closed behind her, leaving them alone at last.

Catherine was stunned by Roger's appearance. The death mask had begun its slow work. His face had hollowed out, his skin sallow, stretched too thin over the bones. He looked old, yes, but more than that, he looked defeated. But to her own frustration, she still saw the man she'd once known. The charm in the brow, the curve of the mouth, the proud set of the shoulders, now softened and slackened. He looked like a man halfway out of this world. To her chagrin, heartbreakingly vulnerable.

His voice, when it came, was barely more than a whisper. 'Hello, Catherine.'

She nodded, wary. Sat back against the settee, folding her hands in her lap to stop them shaking. She hadn't expected this. The man in her head had loomed large, cruel, relentless.

Not this frail figure propped up in a velvet-trimmed bed, clinging to dignity with yellowed fingertips.

'So you came back,' he said, as if he hadn't believed it himself. His lips barely moved.

'Yes,' she said, her voice even. 'I did.'

A pause stretched between them, thick and brittle.

Roger blinked slowly, swallowing with effort. His eyes stayed with her, as if he was afraid she might disappear. 'You look well.'

'Don't,' she said, not unkindly, but with finality. 'Don't start with pleasantries, Roger.'

Another silence. One that rang with everything they weren't saying.

At the foot of the bed, a young dog raised its head, watchful and solemn.

'Not what you imagined, Catherine, eh?' His voice had a faint trace of irony, barely there.

'No,' she admitted quietly.

A coughing fit seized him, deep and violent. He clawed weakly towards a glass of water on the bedside table. Instinctively, she moved to help, lifting the glass and propping up his head. His face scrunched in pain as he drank. When ready, he waved her off; she lowered him back onto the pillows with care she didn't know she possessed.

'I'm so sorry, Catherine,' he rasped. 'I never meant to hurt you. I... I'm so ashamed.'

She said nothing. Not to that. Instead, she straightened, her voice cold and steady. 'We have to tell James.'

He nodded, eyes wet. 'Yes.'

She hadn't expected that either. For a moment, words deserted her. Then another hacking cough overtook him, and after it passed, he looked at her again, frail and pleading.

'Can it wait?' he asked, 'only until the wedding's over? He's so happy, Catherine. I promise I'll tell him. But let him have this first. Please... let him have that.'

The gall of it. The absolute gall. She could kill him for asking and felt her fists curl. He saw her anger and panicked. 'Please, Catherine. Wait. It's only 24 hours.'

Another spasm of coughing hit him, more violent this time, raking his whole body as he gripped the sheets with thin, shaking fingers. His breath came in short, wheezing bursts, and for a moment, Catherine thought he might pass out from the effort.

He looked so insignificant now. Worn down by sickness and, surely, shame. Part of her, the deepest part, the part that had never stopped suffering, hated that he looked like this. Hated that he might die before she ever got the chance to say what needed saying.

So she sat there. Rigid. Silent. Watching the man who had destroyed her from the inside out, and wondering, even now, what the truth could possibly look like.

All the while, Mrs McGinty had been standing outside the bedroom door. At the sound of his groans, she rushed in at once. 'Mr Henderson! You're grand. Slow now, like the doctor said. Nice and easy. Try a sip of water.'

Roger pushed the glass away as his coughing eased.

Mrs McGinty turned to Catherine. 'Best you go, Cass. For a wee while, 'til I get him settled. We'll get this sorted, promise.'

Catherine agreed, got up to leave, but hesitated by the door. She looked behind and saw Mrs Mac settling Roger into bed, tucking the covers up beneath his chin with the kind of care you'd give a child.

The housekeeper caught her eye and, to Catherine's surprise, gave a small signal for her to wait. With Roger now settled and standing quietly by the double doors, both women turned their gaze back to the frail figure on the bed.

'Before you go, love, will ye do me a favour,' Mrs Mac said quietly, 'James's fiancée, Marleen, and that bridesmaid of hers. They're stayin' at the Beech Hill Hotel. You know the one near the hospital?'

Catherine nodded. She'd been there more than once in the early years.

'They're there now. Check out that bridesmaid for me, will ye? There's something not right about her. She's the snooty type, a know-all. But—'

She frowned, hesitating. 'I can't explain it, don't have the words. I mean, don't get me wrong, I like Marleen. Sorta. She's a sweet girl. But that friend of hers... well, she's a funny one. Can't put my finger on it, but it's nigglin' me. Probably nothin'. Still, wouldn't hurt for you to drop in and see them before the rehearsal. That way, you can suss her out and tell me I'm not imaginin' things. Losing me marbles!'

Mrs Mac's remarks worried Catherine. She couldn't shake the feeling that there was more to it. Still, it wasn't a bad idea. In fact, it was a bloody good one. She had nothing else to do, did she, other than sit in an empty hotel room? The thought of sizing up her son's bride and her odd-sounding companion gave her purpose. A taxi was soon ordered, and before long, Catherine was en route to the Beech Hill Hotel to 'suss' them out.

Chapter Ninety-Two

A Stern Faced Doctor

'Mr Henderson! Mr Henderson! You've got to come quickly! I've had to call an ambulance. They're here to take your uncle, Mr Henderson!'

'Calm down, Mrs McGinty. Please tell me again!' James cried into the phone.

Mrs Parkes ran into his office to see what was going on. He held the receiver between his shoulder and ear, struggling to get his coat on. She rushed forward and helped him into it.

'What's happened? Say that again!' James listened as the housekeeper explained. 'I'm on my way, Mrs Mac. I'll go straight to the hospital.'

He slammed the phone back into its cradle and turned to Mrs Parkes, his face pale. 'It's Uncle. He's bad. I have to go.'

'Of course, Mr Henderson, of course. Off you go now. Leave everything here to me.'

On the way to the hospital, James hit the usual army checkpoints. Another round of bomb scares had closed the major routes leading to Craigavon Bridge and the hospital. He tried to keep calm, not to panic, but he was scared. *Please, God. Let him be okay.*

Caitlin wasn't surprised to find herself in Ward Eight of Altnagelvin Hospital, sitting on a hard plastic chair next to her uncle Tommy O'Reilly's bed. Being back wasn't easy. Too many memories drifted through those corridors. She kept thinking about the night she came to see her daddy, how bruised and beaten up he was, how lost. She'd tried to get him talking, but he hadn't said a word. That night had stayed with her ever since.

She'd half-hoped to come across Nurse Gallagher again, the one who'd looked after them back then. The one who'd stood her ground with the two RUC guards outside Patrick's room, not scared in the slightest, yet kind in every way that counted. A calm voice, warm hands, impartial. Sadly, there was no sign of her today. Merely clipped voices, the slap of shoes on polished floors, and faces that gave nothing away.

Caitlin folded her arms across her chest and stared down at the tiles. Hospitals had a way of making people vanish, even when they were sitting alone in plain sight. She'd seen the doctor's face when he caught the stink of whiskey rising off Tommy's breath and skin. That sniff. That look. As if they were wasting his time.

Since Tina's funeral, Tommy had hit the drink hard. She didn't blame him. The months before, it had been nothing but grief and dread. Something had to give. It had. Earlier that morning, right there in her living room. He'd collapsed after another rough night on the sofa. With no one else around, she'd been left to deal with it. The sour smell, the panic, his body like dead weight on the floor, trying to lift him, wake him up. For a moment, she'd genuinely thought he was a goner.

She tore around to the McFaddens' and banged on the door, her heart racing like mad as she asked to use the phone. First the ambulance, then her cousin Kathy, who was on nights and fast asleep. With no other option, Caitlin left a message with one of the medics Kathy shared a flat with, hoping he'd pass it on as soon as she woke.

Now, sitting at his bedside, Caitlin watched the slow rise and fall of Tommy's chest beneath the hospital blanket, each breath a quiet reassurance that he was still with her. He hadn't come round yet, but the colour had returned to his face, and for now, that was enough.

The cold air hit James as he left the Jag in the hospital car park and ran for the A&E entrance beside the grand hall on the ground floor, eyes searching the crowd for his uncle or Mrs McGinty. No sign of either. Inside, the place was roasting. He shrugged off his wool suit jacket, loosened his silk tie, and ran his fingers through his hair, already damp with sweat. There was a queue at reception.

He waited, tense and agitated, his heartbeat pounding like a drum in his ears. When his turn came, the nurse behind the desk barely looked up. 'Yes?' she asked nonchalantly.

'Hello there. I wonder if you can help me? I'm looking for my uncle, Roger Henderson. Brought in earlier by ambulance.'

'Sorry?' Her tone was clipped, mechanical. It had been a long morning, and Liz Blood wasn't in the mood for another lost visitor or some fool asking for directions to X-ray.

'My uncle, Roger Henderson. He's here. I'm his nephew. James Henderson.'

Upon hearing the name '*Henderson*', she stopped and her eyes looked up properly this time. She'd heard of the Henderson family, of course, but had never met one. She noticed James's jacket, the quality of the cloth, and the way he held himself, calm and self-confident. His shirt was perfect white, expensive too. Money, and not new money. Old stock. Breeding. On top of it all, he was a handsome bugger.

'Ah, yes. Mr Henderson's been moved upstairs to Ward Six.' Her voice softened; a Henderson speaking to her was enough to make her nervous. Seeing one here, right in front of her, was something else entirely. She turned on the charm immediately, standing up and pointing. 'Through the double doors ahead, sir, then the lifts on your left. They'll take you straight to the sixth floor.'

He thanked her with a quiet nod, folded his jacket over one arm, and walked away, footsteps firm across the freshly mopped floor.

Liz watched him go, then looked at the queue and barked, 'Next!'

Kathy O'Reilly stepped into the open ward, her eyes scanning the beds with a quick, trained sweep. Last night was full-on. One woman gave birth in the back of the ambulance, a couple of false alarms, and the usual shuffle of minor emergencies. Nothing too out of the ordinary, all things considered. She spotted Caitlin at the far end, standing by the tall window that looked out over the hospital entrance and army checkpoint. Picking up pace, she made her way over, brushing past a trolley left awkwardly near the foot of a bed. When she reached her, Caitlin turned, her voice soft and worn.

'Hello you.'

'Hey. How is he? What did they say?' Kathy asked, a worried look upon her face.

'Don't know yet. They're observing. I think he overdid it last night,' Caitlin whispered.

Kathy knew straightaway what she meant. 'I know, I've been warnin' him to keep off it. He's been takin' on too much. How long have you been here?'

'Doesn't matter,' Caitlin said, gesturing to a chair for Kathy to sit. Her cousin looked knackered.

Kathy sat down and apologised. 'Sorry. I was on nights and only saw your message last minute. That stupid eejit of a flatmate went and left a note, didn't he? Scribbled it on the back of a receipt and dumped it on the kitchen table. Didn't think to wake me before heading out.' She'd been furious at him, stomping around the flat as she got dressed, cursing his name under her breath. Why the hell hadn't the wally wakened her? But now, glancing down at Tommy, her voice relaxed. 'Looks as innocent as a puppy when he's lying there like that, doesn't he? Then again, there are days I could friggin' kill him.'

'I know,' Caitlin said, smiling affectionately at the big man.

Kathy took off her coat. She was due on night shift again later, but more than happy to wait and hear what the doctor had to say.

'You wanna go on home Caitlin? Get a rest?' she offered gently.

'Nah. I'm okay, Kathy. Half-day closing and I've nowhere to be. I'll sit with you a while.'

Mrs McGinty stood in the corridor outside the room where they'd put Roger Henderson, her hands gripping the strap of her handbag. She wasn't even sure she'd turned the oven off before legging it out of Melrose, and her head was still spinning after everything she'd said to Catherine Henderson. Her heart was banging against her chest, nerves all over the place. All she could do now was wait for young James.

Through the half-open door, she spotted her boss tucked in tightly under white and green blankets. He was on oxygen, hooked up to a drip, pale as milk. Poor bugger. A far cry from the man she and Catherine talked about. She sighed slowly.

Suddenly, the door at the far end of the corridor swung open. James, on a mission and heading her way. *Thank God*. She hadn't felt relief like it in donkeys.

'Down here!' she shouted.

James rushed down and grabbed her arm. 'Is he okay, Mrs Mac? Tell me.'

'Not great, sir. Reckon they need to wait, see if he responds to what they've given him,' she said, her voice low and full of sorrow.

James stared through the glass at the still figure lying on the bed. 'He looks so sick,' he murmured.

'We were lucky,' Mrs McGinty said gently. She cared deeply for this family and couldn't stop the worry building in her chest. If anything happened to Roger, then...

James looked at her properly for the first time. She still had her flour-dusted pinny tucked beneath her coat. Her hair was messy, eyes red and puffy. She'd evidently had a fright and looked worn out. Mrs McGinty caught his gaze, gave a tired smile, and squeezed his hand.

'What a day, Mrs McGinty,' James said.

'You've no idea, son. No idea at all,' she replied, shaking her head.

It was already dark by four o'clock on that late December evening when Kathy finally persuaded Caitlin to go home. Tommy remained fast asleep, and Kathy promised she'd do the usual and ring the McFaddens if there was any news.

'Off you go now, please. Sure, look at him. He's out cold. The same boy'll likely sleep straight through till the mornin'!'

Caitlin looked over at Tommy. Kathy was right. The old fella was out cold, sleeping like a baby without a care in the world. Her cousin had been checking his obs since she'd arrived, and everything looked fine.

'Thanks for today, Caitlin. Sorry I didn't make Tina's funeral. I never seem to get a minute off work these days,' Kathy said.

'Don't be silly. Tommy's been unbelievable, but he's hurting, I can see it. There's a lot going on with him, more than any of us know,' Caitlin replied, managing a faint smile. They hugged, Caitlin towering over her. Then she buttoned her coat and headed for the lift, already thinking about the bus stop and praying it wouldn't be one of those nights she'd be left standing in the cold too long.

The housekeeper had left a while back, though only because James had insisted. Roger had stirred a few times since, muttering nonsense, calling out for Catherine, James's mother. He was delirious, certainly, and James hadn't given it much thought.

It was dark outside now. James checked his watch and frowned. The rehearsal. The wedding rehearsal. That was tonight. *Shit.*

As if reading his thoughts, a stern-looking doctor stepped into the room. 'Mr Henderson, the nephew?'

James nodded. 'Yes.'

The doctor's tone sat somewhere between sulky and bored. 'As you know, your uncle's extremely unwell. I'd suggest he stay here for at least the next twenty-four hours. We'll keep him under observation and follow up with a few tests.'

'Do you know exactly what's wrong?'

The man gave what might've been a smirk. 'Not yet. His lungs are well below capacity, but we won't know more until the results come back.'

'So we can't take him home tomorrow?' James asked, though he already knew the answer. He couldn't get married without Roger there.

'I really don't think so, Mr Henderson. As I said, your uncle is a very sick man.'

His pager beeped. 'Excuse me. I have to go. Go home. Try to get some rest. There's nothing more you can do here tonight.' He was out of there in no time. Gone without another word.

James sat still, his eyes fixed on the frail figure in the bed. He couldn't imagine life without the old man. Roger had been his mentor, his teacher, his constant. More of a father than his own had ever been. The tears came quietly. Thinking about his father only made it worse, along with the familiar guilt that followed. Tommy O'Reilly had yet to track down 'MG', the elusive witness to James Snr's murder. It was one dead end after another.

As if sensing James's sorrow, Roger stirred. His eyes opened, and for a moment, he seemed completely present. 'Son... my son', he murmured, his voice thin as paper.

James bowed his head and held Roger's hand, weeping quietly. A faint squeeze made him look up, but Roger had closed his eyes again. Sleep had reclaimed him. Unwilling to leave, James hung about for a while before realising he daredn't miss the rehearsal. Marleen would go apeshit. He bent down, kissed Roger's cheek, and turned to go, his heart heavy as he walked slowly towards the lift.

A few floors above, Caitlin pressed the lift button and waited. The light blinked on. She remembered standing in this exact spot the night she visited her dying father. The smell. Remembered the crimson-headed mop the cleaner had dragged along the bloodied floor after the bombing at that teashop. Every scream still lived in her head. Every stretcher wheeled past, carrying the maimed and dead. Every pale face. The noise. The old woman in black who'd shared the lift with her, that tired smile.

When the lift arrived, it was empty, and Caitlin was glad. She stepped inside, walked to the back corner, and leaned her head against the mirrored wall. A low groan slipped out as she buried both hands deep in her coat pockets. Her eyes closed. She was shattered. Done in. But it wasn't simply the tiredness. It was everything. Christ, but she needed a break. A break of any kind. Would love it if something good happened for a change.

Three floors below, James pressed the lift button and waited, a restless edge building in his chest. He should've been long gone, halfway to the rehearsal by now, but he couldn't have left. Not really. His uncle's ailing health, the wedding, his father's murder, search for the witness. Rocola. *Caitlin*. They all sat like bricks in his stomach.

The lift arrived.

He stepped forward.

She was there.

Alone in the corner, head tilted back, eyes closed, her hair spilled over her shoulders in thick black waves.

She didn't move. Not straight away. But then her eyes opened and found him.

They both froze.

'Hello, Caitlin,' James said, his voice low.

'Hello, James,' she replied.

Time didn't stop, not really. But it felt like it did.

Chapter Ninety-Three

Seriously?!

Catherine Henderson walked into the reception area of the Beech Hill Hotel, keeping an eye out for her son's bride-to-be, Marleen Fry, and the bridesmaid. It was teatime, and going by Mrs McGinty's description, they shouldn't be hard to spot. She wandered through to the bar. It was dressed for Christmas, with garlands strung across the ceiling beams, bowls of pine cones on the windowsills, and soft fairy lights giving everything a golden sheen. Cosy, yes, but the tension was never far off. Especially when the English walked in.

It had to be them.

She watched as two young women entered, their laughter a touch too loud for the time of day. They made their way to a table by the fire, handbags swinging, perfume trailing behind them.

The barman dried glasses with a clean cloth, watching the newcomers with a look of distaste. Catherine didn't blame him. You could spot them a mile off. Glossy, confident, and far too up their own arses.

The blonde wore a cream polo-neck tucked into a high-waisted wool skirt that stopped just below the knee, with tall leather boots polished to a shine. Her makeup was immaculate, the kind that didn't look caked but definitely cost money. The other one, horsey type, loud and rather curvy, had squeezed herself into a black velour dress with puffed sleeves and a wide belt. Her jewellery was flashy, the sort that caught the light and wanted attention. A silk scarf was knotted round her neck like she'd stepped out of a catalogue. She barked her drink order as if it were owed to her.

Catherine watched them from a quiet corner. She hoped the blonde was Marleen. There was poise in her, something a bit softer. The other one, Penelope she guessed, was all show and noise. Not the type to understand this country. Too far above her station. A total snob.

Mrs McGinty had been right. There was something about her that didn't sit well. Catherine folded her hands in her lap and kept watching.

'Mr Barman, over here!' Penelope shouted, giggling.

He stayed at the far end of the bar, ignoring her, wiping down the counter as if she wasn't there. Catherine watched, quietly amused. That sort of behaviour didn't go down well in places like this. Rightly so. But Penelope wasn't having it. She snapped her fingers, sharp and impatient, then called out even louder, her voice carrying across the room like a foghorn.

'I say. You fellow. Two large gin and tonics. Soon as!'

A few heads turned. One man in the corner raised an eyebrow. The barman didn't rush. He walked the length of the bar as slowly as he pleased, placed two coasters down in front of her, and waited without a word.

Penelope smiled, all teeth and no warmth. 'Double Tanqueray, slimline tonic, ice and lemon. In a proper glass, not one of those chunky things. Don't drown it.'

Catherine studied her from across the room. The woman was half-cut already; plain as day. The way she held herself, all flounce and sway, as if the place was lucky to have her. Not a clue that every eye on her was judging. This was who James's fiancée had brought to Londonderry?

Penelope didn't wait for a response. She leaned in and murmured something to Marleen. Whatever it was nearly sent the girl tumbling from her chair. She gave a loud, throaty laugh that turned heads. She was pissed. *Pull yourself together, girl*, she told herself, trying to straighten up. *The rehearsal.* She hiccupped and let out a roar.

Some guests had had enough. They tutted, folded their papers, and left in quiet protest. The barman's eyes narrowed. Catherine recognised that look. Irritated but powerless. The pair had already rubbed a few guests up the wrong way, but he couldn't say a word. Of course he couldn't. The woman was marrying a Henderson, for God's sake.

Catherine edged closer, trying to catch what was being said. There was definitely something off about the pair. Their behaviour had a strangeness to it, something she couldn't quite place. She watched as the blonde leaned in, voice soft and coaxing, like a mother calming a fretful child.

'I told you, Pen, it's fine. It'll work. James and I have an understanding. I need a man, an heir for Daddy, and he desperately needs my money. It's that simple. Trust me, darling. It's all business.'

She drained the rest of her drink and handed the empty glass to the barman with a bright smile.

That was Catherine's cue. She approached them, putting on an exaggerated English accent. 'Excuse me, darlings. Could I have a quick word?' It sounded ridiculous, even to her own ears, but it worked.

'Why, hello!' Penelope declared. 'How frightfully reassuring to meet another Brit in this dreary, godforsaken place!' She flung out an arm, gesturing grandly at the hotel.

Marleen gave her a light slap on the arm and laughed. 'Don't be so rude, Pen. Remember, Londonderry's going to be my home. Behave. You naughty girl.'

Catherine disliked the horsey one on sight. Then, right in front of her, Penelope, with a chuckle, kissed Marleen full on the mouth. It wasn't a peck either. It lingered. Bold, careless, as if no one else in the bar existed.

'I'll get you back later, you're the naughty girl,' she whispered, her voice syrupy, sexual.

Catherine blinked twice in disbelief. *God Almighty, seriously? That's it!*

'I must apologise for my dear friend,' Marleen said, louder now, as though performing for the barman and the handful of guests still watching and trying to sober up.

'Not to worry. May I?' Catherine asked, nodding toward the sofa.

'Yes, of course. Please do,' Marleen said, motioning for her to sit.

The barman appeared beside them. 'Mrs Henderson, can I get you another?'

'Ah no, I'm fine, thank you,' Catherine replied, all sweetness and light. He gave a polite nod and stepped away.

'Mrs Henderson?' Marleen repeated, raising an eyebrow. 'Any relation to the Hendersons of Rocola?'

Catherine kept her tone breezy. 'Actually, yes. Though a very long time ago.'

'Really?' Marleen leaned in. 'How?'

Catherine smiled. 'Ah, now that would be telling. A conversation for another day. I hear you're getting married this weekend?'

'I am, yes.'

'How exciting! I love weddings.' Catherine gasped. Swerving neatly away from the question about her background, she encouraged the bride to talk about her plans. Best keep her cards close for now.

Time passed quickly as Marleen chatted away to the elegant Englishwoman with the peculiar accent. She hadn't expected to enjoy the conversation quite so much. But now her mouth was dry and her head light. She glanced at her Cartier and muttered a curse. 'I'm so sorry, but we've a rehearsal in half an hour. We really must dash! So lovely to meet you.'

'You too,' Catherine said, rising with her. She asked the barman to ring her a taxi and turned to Marleen. 'Bye now, and best of luck.'

'Thank you!' Marleen called after her, already reaching for a glass of water. She downed it in one go, then poured another and did the same. Her head was throbbing.

She turned to Penelope, expecting a smirk or a clever remark, but found her slumped in the chair beside her. Head tipped back, mouth wide open, chin pointed at the ceiling. A long, glassy thread of drool clung to the corner of her lipstick-smeared mouth. Red, flushed, and completely gone. It was a sorry sight.

Marleen winced. *Oh, Pen.* She grunted and jabbed Penelope hard with her elbow.

Penelope woke up startled and looked around. 'What the—?'

'Rehearsal!' Marleen hissed. 'Now. Get up!'

'Oh God... The rehearsal.' Penelope groaned, clutching her forehead. 'I don't think I can bear it.'

Catherine's taxi took fifteen minutes to reach the church, cutting through damp back roads lined with bare trees and half-lit houses, the sort of route she used to know well in a different life, back when everything still made sense, or at least gave the impression it did. She'd driven past the little Church of Ireland building more times than she could count over the early years, usually on the way to some garden party or charity do at Prehen House, yet had never once stepped through its door. It was a quiet structure, set back from the road and framed by winter branches, its stone walls grey and moss-flecked, its arched windows narrow.

Unlike her ex-husband, who had been raised on Sunday sermons and knew his way around every line of Presbyterian scripture, Catherine had never placed much stock in faith. Her own wedding had taken place in Westminster Abbey, of all places, an overwhelming and impersonal ceremony wrapped in grandeur, watched by strangers, padded with formality and pomp, and utterly void of warmth. The scale of it had swallowed her whole, and though she'd smiled and nodded her way through it like a good girl, she'd spent most of the day feeling more like a guest than a bride.

This church, by contrast, was quiet, small and rather lovely, and as she stepped out of the taxi and approached the entrance, she found herself slowing down, to have a good look. The stone path beneath her feet was damp from earlier rain, and the scent of wet leaves mixed with something floral in the air, likely blown from inside. She paused near the doorway, drifting briefly through the small patch of gravestones that flanked the entrance, their inscriptions barely legible in the soft golden wash of the nearby lamps. Some of the names she even recognised. Most she didn't. It struck her that even here, in a quiet corner of Londonderry, the past was always close.

When she heard the crunch of tyres and the faint murmur of car doors behind her, she made her way inside, not wanting to be caught loitering, and chose a seat near the back. The pew creaked under her as she sat, her hands folded neatly in her lap. It was freezing, though she hadn't expected the interior to be quite so beautiful. It was simple, yes, but carefully kept. Pale stone walls met dark wood beams overhead, and the stained-glass window behind the altar gave off a soft wash of colour that touched everything with the gentlest hue. The florists had been in, judging by the smell and arrangement. Cream roses, tight stephanotis blooms, and glossy green leaves filled the air with a thick, heady scent. It was almost too much. She resisted the urge to loosen her scarf.

Chapter Ninety-Four

More Pantomime Than Pageantry

Catherine sat there, silent and composed, watching as light pooled across the polished aisle. It was, if nothing else, a lovely setting for a wedding. Intimate. To think her son would be married here. Her son. The thought pulled at something deep inside. Not sadness exactly, not pride either, but a strange feeling that grew the longer she sat. Although the flowers were in place, the wedding party was on its way, and the whole thing had been organised to within an inch, there was a question that still sat stubbornly in the back of her mind, quiet but insistent. A sense that something about this didn't quite add up. Was it truly happening? Was James really getting married?

Voices broke the quiet as a small group of people filed through the main doors. The first was a young-looking vicar in blue jeans and a grey jumper, his white collar about visible underneath. He looked flustered, slightly out of his depth, his eyes searching the church as though trying to remember what came next. Behind him came a man who didn't seem flustered at all. Handsome, well-dressed, and moving quickly to keep up, he spoke in that easy way some people have, voice smooth, almost too smooth, full of charm. The kind of charm that came naturally, the kind that made everyone comfortable before he even spoke.

'My apologies, vicar. Timothy Armstrong, best man. Call me Tim.' They stood by the entrance as he offered his hand, but the vicar didn't take it.

Timothy had been close with James Henderson since their Oxford days. A decent bloke, James. Quiet in his own way, but reliable. Timothy liked a friend who didn't need constant check-ins, though they hadn't seen much of each other recently. A few years of polite calls, the odd pint when diaries lined up, but it was one of those friendships that didn't ask much and didn't fade either. So when James asked him to be best man, he'd been quietly pleased. No fuss, but nice all the same. He knew Marleen well enough too, mostly through London circles. Sharp as a tack, quick with a line, and never short of attention. She had presence, no doubt about that. Maybe a bit wild for James, but then again, James wasn't the man he was at uni. People change, don't they?

As for Penelope… well. That was complicated. He knew her. Knew her better than he should, if he was honest. This wasn't the time or place for dredging things up. Especially as the vicar looked like he was ready to blow his top. This was James's time. His wedding. Whatever Timothy thought or remembered or might have once said about the horsey-faced girl, it could stay exactly where it belonged.

'I've spoken to James just now. He's running a tad late,' Tim continued, still cheerful and doing his best to keep everyone calm. 'His uncle's been taken into hospital. Poor man. Look, why don't I stand in for him? I'll do my best, promise.'

Reverend Andrew Ward looked less than thrilled. He tugged at his collar, more from habit than discomfort, though the shirt always seemed a touch too tight when he was annoyed. His lips thinned as he regarded the man in front of him.

'I don't suppose I've much choice in the matter, Mr Armstrong,' he said, his tone clipped but polite. 'But I'll be frank. I'm not at all happy about it. Marriage is a sacred commitment, not a performance. To be honest, I'm no longer convinced the younger generation understands that.'

He saw it too often these days. Couples swept up in flowers and music and photographs, but not a single sign they'd thought about what came after the reception. People wanted the ceremony, the spectacle, the applause, but not the vows. Not the quiet work of keeping promises. Faith, in his view, had started to disappear behind a curtain of convenience. Even here in Londonderry, where tradition had once meant something, it was dying. He saw it in the dwindling numbers on Sunday mornings, in the way people mumbled through hymns they no longer knew.

Tim chuckled and gave his arm a friendly pat, guiding him gently down the aisle. 'Ah, don't worry, vicar. James will be along soon, I'm sure. A slight delay. Now, where do you want me?'

'Tim! Tim! Is James here?' Marleen's voice rang out from the church doors, loaded with panic. 'What's happened? Is he okay? Oh my God, what's happened?!'

Tim turned in time to see her hurtling up the aisle, hands flailing like she was bracing for impact. He scoffed. Marleen did nothing quietly.

'He's fine,' he said, stepping in to meet her. 'Honestly. His uncle's had a bit of a scare, that's all. James is at the hospital. He'll be here. If not,' he added, with a faint shrug, 'I'll stand in.'

Penelope stumbled in behind her like the tail end of a pantomime horse. She looked ruined – pale, glassy-eyed, still half-cut. Tim resisted the urge to roll his eyes. This rehearsal was already more pantomime than pageantry. He turned to Marleen with an encouraging smile. 'Let's keep things ticking over, shall we?'

Meanwhile, Catherine didn't make a sound, didn't move, kept her head bowed as though in prayer, though her thoughts were anything but calm. No one noticed her. Tucked away at the very back of the church, hidden in plain sight, she listened to the commotion beginning to stir and felt a flicker of something she hadn't expected. Fear. Roger Henderson in hospital. A scare. She didn't know the details, not yet, but the news alone was enough to upset her. Worse was the quiet, creeping thought she couldn't shake, the one that whispered maybe, maybe, it was all her fault.

She berated herself. She should've come years ago, long before today. Maybe if she had, things might have been different. Maybe James would have listened. Maybe they could have talked properly without a wedding hanging over his head. But she hadn't. Now her son was only minutes away, somewhere nearby, yet it felt like miles.

What now? What was she meant to do? Her eyes lifted slowly to the front of the church, to the altar and the wedding decorations, the carefully placed flowers, the unlit candles, the space where vows were meant to be exchanged. In that moment, with everything sitting quiet and half-finished around her, she saw it for what it was. A dilemma. A quiet, painful mess wrapped in white ribbon. Nothing about this day had gone the way she'd imagined.

Reverend Ward pressed on with the rehearsal, far from happy but determined to see it through despite the groom's glaring absence. By the time they reached the end, James still hadn't appeared.

The wedding party filtered back towards the church doors, their mood none the better. Marleen was seething, her heels striking the stone floor with purpose as she marched ahead without so much as a glance behind. Penelope floated after her, dragging her feet and already looking as though she had one eye on the hotel bar. Their goodbyes were short and stiff.

Reverend Ward remained near the front with the best man, his hands clasped, his expression set. His concerns had nothing to do with logistics. This wasn't about schedules or rehearsals. It was about what was missing. In his experience, when the groom didn't show at the right time, they rarely believed in what they were doing. Not good, not good at all.

'Thank you, vicar,' the best man said, his voice low. 'I'd hoped James could make it, but with his uncle, well, too late now, I suppose.' Feeling he might've overdone it a little, being so sharp and borderline rude, Reverend Ward relaxed. 'Would you join me for a drink in the vicarage, perhaps?' he offered.

Tim smiled, he'd love a drink, needed it, but knew if he went back to the hotel, Penelope would be in the bar and that he couldn't face.

'Love one.'

As they turned to leave, the vicar caught sight of a solitary figure at the back of the church. He raised a hand gently to pause Tim and walked across to Catherine.

'I'm sorry,' he said, almost whispering, 'but I'll need to lock up soon.'

The stranger lifted her head. She was striking, yes, but what caught him more was the fear in her tired eyes. There was something about the way she sat, folded in on herself, that stopped him from asking her to leave, from hurrying her. 'Sorry. You take your time,' he murmured. 'No rush. I'll come back in a little while.'

Catherine gave him a faint, grateful smile. As he turned, he reached out and lightly touched her hand. 'Whatever it is, it'll sort itself out. You're in the right place,' he said, then returned to the best man and headed towards the vicarage.

Chapter Ninety-Five

Walking on Air

Caitlin could hardly believe it. James Henderson stood in front of her, close enough to touch, his handsome face pale and tired but still striking in a way that hurt.

They'd said hello. That was it, barely audible. They gaped at each other, rooted to the spot, as if neither of them knew what came next. The quiet went on forever, full of all the things they wanted to say, but didn't know how. The lift doors began to close. That surprised her. She moved quickly, thumbed the button to hold them open, her breath catching a little as the spell of silence broke and the world came back into focus.

'Going down?' she asked softly.

'Yes. Yes, please. Sorry,' James replied, flustered. 'I... I just... Shit, I can't believe it. You're the last person I expected to see tonight, Caitlin.'

'And you,' she said, her voice edged with something close to excitement.

Still, he didn't move.

She nodded at the panel. 'Guess I'd better press Ground or we'll be stuck here till morning,' she joked.

Flustered, James struggled about what to do next. He had so much to say and no idea where to begin. Only that he had to get it right. This might be his only chance.

But Caitlin, as ever, stepped in. 'You look tired, James. Everything okay? Visiting someone?'

'Roger. Had a turn of some sort. He's not been well. Not since...' He faltered. 'Well, you know.'

She nodded. 'I'd heard,' she said. 'Sorry to hear that.'

The lift reached the ground floor and they stepped out together, James held the door as they walked into A&E. First came the heat; it smelled faintly of disinfectant, old blood, and cheap coffee. Nurse Blood was still there, parked behind her desk. But the energy had changed. It had quietened a little. James glanced around, tense but excited, his hand brushing against Caitlin's for a second too long before he pulled it away.

He was well late for the rehearsal. They stood awkwardly outside in the cold, both shifting from one foot to another. James looked around, his eyes scanning the car park. He didn't want to leave, not now, not after meeting Caitlin, but he knew he had to. Marleen would've had a fit by now.

'Caitlin, I've gotta go. There's something I need to do and I'm already well late,' he said, his voice low but firm. 'But please, can we meet after? I need to talk to you. Properly.'

He paused, uncertain whether to keep going, then added, 'I went to the studio. Did your boss tell you?'

'I haven't been in,' she replied.

'Ah, right. Yeah, he said. Family stuff. He mentioned that.'

'It's more than family stuff, James. Tina, my sister, she's dead.'

James nearly died himself there and then. Buried in work and busy, he'd heard nothing about it.

'Ah, Christ, Caitlin. I'm so sorry. I didn't know.'

'It's a long story,' she said quietly. Then, suddenly, 'I hear you're getting married?' she asked.

'Yeah,' he replied miserably. 'Tomorrow.'

She scoffed and looked him over again. 'You don't look too thrilled. In fact, you look miserable.'

He didn't reply. Instead, he reached for her hands and drew her into a shadowed corner, out of sight, and kissed her without hesitation, like it was the first and only thing that had ever made sense.

She kissed him back with the same fire, her whole body straining toward him, aching with the need to feel him close again. Her skin, every part of her, came alive under his touch, as though she'd been holding herself in for too long. She'd tried to forget him, tried to carry on, but here he was, and she couldn't help herself. She drank him like water after a long thirst, and for the first time in what felt like forever, she didn't care who saw, who guessed, or what came next.

James reached the church. He ran up the path toward the dimly lit building, his chest tight, willing them to have waited a little longer. Breathless, he pushed through the heavy doors, only to find the place completely empty, apart from a woman sitting alone at the back.

'Shit,' he muttered under his breath. He was about to turn and go when he heard her voice.

'James?'

He froze. *Had he imagined it?*

'James, over here.'

He stepped forward, cautious, his eyes adjusting to the light. Then he saw her. She hadn't changed much from the few photographs he'd come across over the years. Same posture, same eyes, same sadness behind the way she looked at him.

Catherine Henderson. His mother. The woman who'd walked out and left him. Who'd disappeared and left his father to carry the burden. He didn't say a word. Merely turned, purposeful and certain, and headed back toward the exit. Not tonight. He wasn't doing this.

Tonight belonged to Caitlin. He'd seen her. Spoken to her. Kissed her. Held her. Nothing, no one, was going to take that time away from her. They were meant to meet later at the Rainbow. It stayed open late on Fridays. That was where he needed to be. Not here. Not with Catherine Henderson.

'James, wait, please. Let me explain,' she called. But he kept walking, fumbling in his coat for the keys to the Jag.

By the entrance, she caught up and grabbed his arm. He shook her off, his anger mounting as his car keys dropped, clattering into the shadows.

'Don't come near me, Mother,' he growled.

She stepped forward again, this time gripping his arm even tighter. 'No, you listen to me, James Henderson,' she exclaimed. 'I have to tell you something. The truth.'

What was she talking about? He already knew the truth. His father had told him. Again and again. How she ran off. Disappeared. Left them with nothing. Not a single word for years. Not until those sad, guilt-soaked letters started turning up. He didn't want them. He didn't want her.

She was crying now.

Cold with fury, he snapped, 'I've nothing to say to you. I don't want to hear anything about any truth.'

'I've met Caitlin,' she said suddenly. 'I know about you two.' He grew still. That name. That name stopped him cold.

'*Caitlin*?'

'Yes,' she said, trembling. 'I know everything. I'll tell you how, James. But first, I need to tell you why I left Ireland. Please. It won't take long. Come back inside. Sit with me.' With a gentle tug on his arm and pleading eyes, she looked at his face. James hesitated. He would hear her out. If she were quick. But his thoughts were already somewhere else. With Caitlin. Only Caitlin.

Back in the church, they sat side by side on a cold wooden pew. Catherine half expected the vicar to reappear and throw them out, but the building remained hushed and undisturbed. There was no sign of him, nor of the best man.

James sat with his arms folded tightly across his chest, his expression blank. He contained himself, but was impatient. Catherine knew she had one shot and that if she didn't get it right, she'd lose him again. For good.

'I didn't leave Ireland because I wanted to,' she began, her voice soft. 'I left because I was desperately unhappy. I felt like I was dying here. I didn't run off with anyone, if that's what you were told. I went on my own. First to Southampton, then I got a ship to Cape Town.'

She turned to look at him, but his face remained blank. 'I don't know exactly what your father told you, James,' she continued, her words slow and careful now, 'but this isn't easy for me. Never has been.' She took a breath, then shut her eyes for a moment before adding. 'Roger is your biological father.'

There. It was said. When she opened her eyes again, she met his stare directly. 'I'm sorry.'

James's face drained of colour. 'What?' he said, barely above a whisper. 'How is that even possible?'

She hesitated, torn between honesty and damage control. There were things she couldn't say, things that would destroy everything between James and Roger.

'Your father and I were deeply unhappy for a long time. I felt like a shadow in my own house. It only happened once, James. Once. You have to believe that.'

His thoughts were already spinning, reaching backwards, pulling at old memories that now took on a different perspective. It explained everything. There had always been something off between him and James Snr, a quiet strain that never quite let up. Not open hostility, but a low, constant friction, the kind that ultimately wore a person down. They were never close, never easy in each other's company, and no matter how hard he'd tried, something always sat between them.

But Roger had been different. Roger had shown up. Listened. Guided him without ever making it feel like a lecture. He'd pushed when it mattered and stood back when it didn't. He believed in him. Saw him. That part had never felt in doubt. All these years thinking he'd been the uncle who stepped in when needed. When in truth he'd been there all along. A father. *Poor Jocelyn.*

'Did Aunt Jocelyn know? James asked, his voice strained.

'No. Never.' Catherine replied.

'She'd no idea who fathered me?' He stood suddenly and began pacing up and down the narrow aisle. 'I don't know what I'm supposed to say. I don't know what you want from me, Catherine. I don't even know what I'm meant to feel!'

She remained seated, watching him with tired eyes. 'How is Roger now?'

'Ill. Very ill. Did you see him today? Upset him?' James exclaimed.

'No. I saw him, but he was fine.' she said quietly. 'I needed to talk to him. He deserved to know I was coming to see you. I owed him that.'

James turned to her, incredulous. 'Why now?' he demanded, throwing his arms wide to gesture at the decorated altar, the flowered pew ends. 'Why the night before my wedding?'

'I've tried to contact you, James,' she replied, calmer now. 'For months. Years, actually. But none of my letters were ever answered.'

He pursed his lips, remembering. A letter, he had it but left it somewhere. Never gave it a second thought. He shifted uncomfortably, embarrassed.

'And Caitlin?' he asked. 'Why were you talking? What's she got to do with any of this?'

'I didn't know you were involved with her when we met. I knew her mother. Years ago.' Catherine told him.

He stared at her, astonished again. 'How do you mean?'

'I knew Majella McLaughlin,' she explained softly. 'She was there for me when I needed help. When I was pregnant with you. Always kind to me, we stayed in touch for a while after I left. I went to see Caitlin only because I heard about Majella's death. I wanted to offer my sympathy.'

He dropped back onto a pew, bewildered. Somehow, in the middle of all this madness, there was a thread that connected them – his mother and Caitlin's. Hadn't seen that coming.

'Do you love her?' Catherine asked out of the blue, her voice distinct and to the point.

He blinked. 'Why? What did she say?'

Her tone was gentle now. She reached for his hand, but he pulled it away. 'She cares deeply for you. Loves you,' she said. 'From where I'm sitting, it's obvious you feel the same.'

James gave no reply. He was angry and confused, desperate to get his head around it all.

'This is a big decision, James,' Catherine went on. 'I've been where you are. Please think about what really matters. Make sure you choose the right girl, because true happiness – when it comes – is rare. Easily lost.' Before he could answer, a familiar voice called out from the entrance. 'Oi James! Bit late, aren't you?' Tim Armstrong's voice bounced up the church. 'Saw your Jag parked outside.'

James rose, looked down once more at his mother, and then Tim stomped in. He slowed when he saw Catherine, his brow furrowing as his eyes moved between them, trying to piece together what was going on. There was a story here, for sure.

Without a chance to explain, James, stammering, introduced his mother. 'Tim, this is—this is Catherine Henderson. My mother.'

Tim squinted, not quite trusting what he was seeing. For a second, he didn't know what to say. In all the years he'd known James Henderson, through college, late-night conversations, messy nights out, not once had he ever heard him mention a mother. A father, yes, but this...

'Mrs Henderson,' he said, recovering quickly and offering his hand. 'So lovely to meet you.'

'You too,' Catherine replied, her gaze still fixed on her son.

The atmosphere was thick with unease and Tim, being Tim, did his best to fill it. 'I hope we'll see you tomorrow, Mrs Henderson?'

'No,' Catherine said plainly. 'I fly back to South Africa tomorrow.'

James looked at her, his eyes full of surprise. 'You are?'

'I have to,' she mumbled, already starting to gather her things.

Tim said no more. He could read a room. Whatever this was, it didn't need him standing in the middle of it. He spotted Reverend Ward coming back in through the main entrance, looking more relaxed, and gave him a vague nod before turning back to the others.

'I'll go check something with the vicar,' he said casually, already moving. Let them finish whatever that was in peace. He didn't need to be part of it.

Left alone, mother and son looked at one another. Catherine, her face drawn with exhaustion, reached for her bag.

'I'm sorry it went like this,' she said quietly. 'I'm sorry Roger's so unwell. I never meant to cause trouble. I just wanted to see you again.' Her voice broke. 'James. Truly. Please forgive me. For everything.'

He didn't speak right away, but she could see the storm had passed from his eyes. He was a little angry, yes, but it had begun to cool. There was a softness now. His eyes, so much like hers, glistened under the church lights. At last, he spoke.

'Stay. For a few more days. We've got the wedding, and we're not going anywhere till Tuesday. We need to finish this.'

Her relief was indescribable. 'Of course I'll stay. If that's what you want.' She got to her feet and, with a quiet sadness, added, 'Again. Please James. Take your time. Think about what I've said. Think about what will make *you* truly happy.' Although he remained silent, Catherine sensed he'd heard her as they walked through the church doors together.

Outside, he offered to drive his mother back to the hotel. He had time before meeting Caitlin and Catherine, walking on air, accepted her son's offer without hesitation.

Chapter Ninety-Six

New Beginnings

Inside the Rainbow Café, by the window, Caitlin sat alone, nursing a lukewarm tea that had gone bitter with time. James was late. Not five or ten minutes late. But late, late. She checked her watch again, then turned to the window, scanning the street outside for what felt like the hundredth time. Almost an hour now, maybe more.

The rain had stopped, but the pavements were still wet, shining under the streetlights. A few people wandered past, heads down, coats pulled tight. Still no sign of him.

She ran a hand over her knee, trying to keep calm, but her mind was already racing. She'd planned what she wanted to say. Not all of it, not like a script, but enough to get through it without stumbling. She wanted to tell him everything. About Tina. About her job. About Tommy and how things had changed. She'd even practised it in her head on the bus over, trying not to sound too desperate. But now, with every minute ticking by, she felt less sure. The words weren't lining up the same way. She sipped the tea out of habit, barely tasting it now.

Still a no-show.

The frosted windows, sprayed with mock snow and lined with cheap flashing Christmas lights, gave the street a soft, wintry glow. It was a crisp night, the sort that bit at your nose and turned every breath to mist. Inside, the café was quiet. Nearly empty.

Then headlights across the street. A car she knew pulled up and parked. She couldn't breathe. *James.*

She watched as he climbed out, moving quickly, his coat unbuttoned, collar up. Straight towards the entrance. Her heart pounded so hard she was convinced Siobhan behind the counter could hear it. He stepped inside, pausing only a second before his eyes found hers.

He smiled. Her insides turned upside down.

'Ah, Caitlin, I'm so sorry. You wouldn't believe the evening I've had,' he said as he hurried over and kissed her on the cheek. His agitated look worried her.

'Sit down and get warm. I'll order you a drink. What'll you have?' she offered.

'Coffee, please. Strong.'

Quick as a flash, Siobhan was on them and promptly took their order. As soon as she'd disappeared, Caitlin asked, 'So what is it, what's happened? Is it Roger?'

'No, he's stable, thank God. But I'm not sure if what I have to tell you is good news or bad.' James said, taking his coat off and laying it on the side.

He leaned across and took her hand. 'It's my mother, Caitlin. She turned up out of the blue.' Caitlin listened quietly, she couldn't get a word in as he went on. 'Told me you two met. Have to admit, I was surprised at that. I never knew she and your mother were friends.'

'Neither did I, James. I'm as surprised as you are,' Caitlin said. 'What else did Catherine say?'

'That Roger Henderson is my real father!' James scoffed and shook his head. Saying it out loud seemed to knock the air clean out of him. He sank back into the seat and groaned. 'Jesus, Caitlin. All this time, and I never knew.'

His grip tightened, as if he didn't want to let go of her hand. 'Adds up now. Really does. I always felt uncomfortable with the man I thought was my father... like strangers forced to pretend. But with Uncle... I don't know, all this time I've cared so much more for him. Trusted him. Looked up to him. He was so much easier than James.' He gave a weak laugh. 'I don't even know what to call him now.'

As soon as the hot drinks arrived, James sipped his coffee.' Do I tell him I know everything or what?'

Caitlin watched him in a daze. 'You've got to remember, Mr Henderson loves you. Everyone knows that. Don't be cross with him. Especially now he's so sick.'

James nodded. 'I know, but it's still a tremendous shock.'

He looked up at her after drinking more coffee. 'Listen, Caitlin. No more secrets. I've had enough. I love you, Caitlin McLaughlin. I really do. I've missed you beyond words. Have you any idea how many times I've driven past that studio, hoping for a glimpse of you?'

His words were like music, soft and tempting, and for a moment she allowed herself to believe him. She let herself feel everything, that this could be it, that at long last they might have a chance.

Then it came, like she knew it would.

Reality. In all its glory.

She braced for the *but*, and sure enough, it followed right on cue.

'*But* I have to marry Marleen. It's the only way to save the factory. She's agreed to fund it, keep Rocola afloat, protect the workforce. I can't turn my back on those women, nor on their families. I can't stand by and watch the place shut down, not after all we've fought for. Roger's relying on me. Honestly, I don't think he's got much time left.'

Nothing he said came as a shock to her. Whilst she believed he was marrying for money, she needed to hear it from him.

'Don't you love her at all?' she asked softly.

'Who, Marleen? Of course I do, but as a friend! Not the way I love you. As a friend. Always. She's a lesbian, bi—whatever, for Christ's sake, even her parents don't know.'

Caitlin was stunned. 'She's a what?!'

James offered a small smile. 'I've known for years. She's tremendous fun, always up for a laugh. But she's from one of the richest, most connected families in England and under serious pressure to marry, produce an heir. It's a business arrangement, Caitlin. That's all.'

He paused, aware of how callous it sounded, then squeezed her hand gently. 'It's only ever been you. No one else.'

'I love you too,' Caitlin whispered. There. It was said. 'I think about you all the time, James. But you need to speak to your uncle. If he's as ill as you say, do it soon. Be kind and make peace. He deserves to know you talked to Catherine. It'll bring him comfort.'

'You're right. Again. Thank you,' James sighed.

Caitlin watched him as the ever-reliable Siobhan topped up his coffee while he went to the bathroom. All smiles and charm. Thinking about it now that he'd gone, Caitlin reckoned she'd been through more than enough. Once again, he hadn't given her a chance to tell her side of the story. Hadn't asked what she knew, or didn't know, about Tina, Kieran Kelly or the bomb scare. No questions about how Tina died, where or when, or the court case, or the time she'd spent in prison. None of it. He'd come charging in, full of his own drama, acting like hers didn't count for anything.

Now he was calling the wedding a business arrangement. A *business arrangement*, as if he were signing papers for a rental flat instead of marrying someone. She groaned loudly enough that Siobhan looked over.

Hearing him say he loved her had meant the world. She'd said it back without thinking, because she meant it. She still meant it. But now what? Was she meant to wait around while he trotted off to tie the knot with someone else? Was that it? Because of money. And she, she was to hang back, pretend she didn't mind, play the role of the tart on the side?

No way in hell.

The anger rose fast, preparing her. She'd her own life to see to now. Everyone else had gone, and Derry, in her mind, was nothing but a ghost town. Tommy would manage, Kathy would see to that. Her heart might be cracking down the middle now, but her mind was clear. She wasn't going to chase after anyone who didn't want her.

This time, she'd put herself first. Things had to change now, whether James Henderson was part of her future or not.

Time to lay it all out. Say it as it is.

Falling back into his seat with a smile, she went for it, right between the eyes.

'I'm leaving tomorrow, James. Belfast first, then London. I can't stay here and watch you get married. Hurts too much. It's been hell already, wondering where you were, how you are, if I'd ever see you again and I can't keep doing that. Why not come with me? A new beginning, just us, far away from this hellhole.'

James couldn't get a word out. His throat was closing. She wasn't asking for the world. Christ, she wasn't even asking for much. Not compared to what he'd put her through. But somehow it still felt like a mountain. Because he did love her. With everything he had. Every bit of him. It hurt. It hurt in a way he hadn't been prepared for.

He couldn't imagine not seeing her again, not hearing that laugh of hers or watching her face change when she got annoyed but tried not to show it. She made him feel like he mattered. Like he wasn't a Henderson clone, fated to repeat the same bloody mistakes.

Nevertheless, here he was. Likely letting her down all over again. What was he asking of her? To be his bit on the side. Probably. Let's face it, it wouldn't work here. Not in a place like Londonderry.

He'd walked off and left her to deal with the fallout from the City Hotel, all of it, her sister and what came after it. He hadn't known the truth, fair enough, but it didn't change what she'd lived through. He'd turned up tonight declaring his love like that was enough to make her forget, make her forgive. He dropped his gaze in shame. He wanted to grab her, beg her not to leave like this. But what right did he have?

'I love you, Caitlin. Only you,' was about all he could muster.

From his voice, she heard what he didn't say and understood. He'd made his choice. All the same, she gave him one last chance.

'My train leaves at three. Waterside Station. Go to your uncle. Tell him you know everything. As I said, if it gives him peace, then good. But I'll be on that train, James. Whether you are or not.'

He couldn't bring himself to say it, couldn't admit that at three o'clock tomorrow, he was supposed to be standing at the altar beside Marleen. After a long silence, he walked across to the payphone and called her a taxi.

By the doorstep, they stood together in the cold, their breath curling into the dark, disappearing as quickly as any words they might have said. Neither of them spoke. What was there to say? The silence between them wasn't angry, but it was full of sorrow, aching for everything they'd had, and everything they couldn't have had. Caitlin stared at the street, wishing Tommy hadn't collapsed, that she'd never gone near the hospital, never stepped into that lift, because this, standing out here on this street and saying goodbye to him, hurt far more than she'd ever have dreamed.

When the taxi appeared at the top of the road, its headlights brushing across the pavement, James moved closer. He pressed his face into the crook of her neck, breathed her in, and moaned. Then came a strange little laugh, he looked up, but his eyes held no laughter.

He raised her chin and kissed her, slow and deep, a kiss that tried to make up for every wrong turn he'd made. A kiss that told her she mattered. That she was loved, truly, even if it was too late.

In that single moment, she let herself believe it could have been different. That if they had met somewhere else, away from all these Troubles, they might have made it. Had a future together. Be happy.

The car pulled up beside them. James opened the door, helped her in, and when their hands touched, his fingers stayed wrapped around hers a few seconds longer, as if holding on could keep her there, could stall time.

She pulled away.

With a deep sigh, he gave the driver her address, stepped back without a word, and stood on the pavement like a man who didn't quite know what to do next. As the car began to roll forward, he raised a hand and blew her a kiss. No smile. The air held a hushed goodbye until she was gone.

Chapter Ninety-Seven

A Wedding

On the morning of the wedding, James managed a mouthful of toast but couldn't take another bite. No appetite.

Outside, the day had arrived crisp and bright, the lawn at Melrose dusted with frost that sparkled like crushed glass in the sunlight.

Inside, the place looked immaculate, almost too perfect. Enormous black and white vases stood like sentries, bursting with white tea roses and hydrangeas. This was where the reception would be held, right after the ceremony. Twists of green foliage and white heather trailed through the banisters, winding from the top of the stairs all the way to the tiled hall below. It was a sight to behold.

James paused before leaving for the hospital. He stood quietly at the top of the staircase, his eyes tracing the curves of the garland. A memory surfaced, sudden and uninvited, one he hadn't summoned in years. As a boy, he used to sit on the landing, there by the banister, and watch two men stride down those very steps in their black ties, all polish and purpose, heading off to yet another evening where they'd be clapped on the back and welcomed like old friends. His father and Roger. Roger and his father. Always a double act.

To his surprise, Roger was sitting up and alert when he arrived at the hospital and stepped into the room.

'Hello, you. Come sit,' he said weakly, patting the bed beside him. 'How are you? I'm so happy for you, you know that? You and Marleen are perfect for each other. I'm only sorry I can't be there.'

Roger looked at his nephew then, silent and searching, and James felt a pressure begin to build deep in his chest, one that made it hard to breathe. He knew he ought to tell all, get straight to it, that he'd seen Catherine, that he knew everything. But once again, the words wouldn't come. They lingered, remaining on the tip of his tongue. He didn't know how to begin, or if he even had it in him to say them. How do you open a conversation like that dressed in a morning suit, about to leave for your wedding?

Instead, he replied. 'Let's be honest, Uncle. It's about Marleen's money and taking care of Rocola.'

Roger felt the blow of James's words, all right. Straight as a hammer to the chest. But he didn't react, not on the outside. What was the point? He spoke the truth. Slowly he took the plastic oxygen mask, pressed it to his face, and pulled the air into his lungs. His eyes closed for a second or two, more to gather himself than anything else, then opened again, glassy with fatigue. He tried to speak, but the words caught in his throat. His lips parted, then pressed together again. It wasn't the pain. It was a consequence of saying what needed said, and knowing it might already be too late.

'That's why I want you to have Rocola. It's yours.'

James, worn out and running on fumes, got up. He didn't meet Roger's eye. 'I'm not sure I want it,' he muttered.

Roger's heart kicked against his ribs, not with anger, but a fierce, helpless sort of frustration. He reached out, caught James's hand, and squeezed it with what little strength he had. 'Don't be silly,' he said, almost weeping. 'It's my bloody wedding gift. That's the end of it. Too late now anyhow.'

But as the words left him, the walls seemed to give a little. He squeezed his eyes shut, trying to shake the blur creeping into the edges of his vision. A wave of dizziness rolled in, worse than before, and the ache in his chest flared sharp and unforgiving. It held on longer this time. He didn't say a word about it, pretending he was okay, and pulled what he could into a smile. It barely made it to his lips, never mind his eyes, but he gave it anyway. He didn't want to leave things cold. Not today of all days.

'You've got to take it, son. It's yours. All I've ever wanted... is for you to have it,' he said, quieter now, but certain. *Son.* He'd said the word aloud and meant it. *Son.* James was his. Always had been.

From the boy's expression, Roger knew Catherine told him, but not everything. She'd left the *how* out, softened the worst of it, protected him and James in a way only a mother could. For that, he felt nothing but thanks. For the first time in hours, even days, things didn't feel quite so frightening. All the same, his body was flagging. Breathing was harder now, each inhale shorter, more laboured than the last. The dragging ache in his chest was still there and was digging in badly. It wasn't easing this time, but there, stubborn and unrelenting. He grabbed his chest and suddenly knew he was in trouble.

James ran to him, knocking the chair leg against the wall. He scrambled for the call bell, then bolted for the corridor, calling out for help.

Roger let his head sink back into the pillow. The pain clawed at him, but he paid it no mind. The oxygen mask had slipped down to his neck, forgotten. None of it mattered now. He'd said what counted. The boy knew. Nevertheless, with James beside him, a wedding on the horizon, and the idea of children running through Melrose, he clung on. He wasn't ready to be put in the ground. Over his dead body.

Tommy O'Reilly had been discharged that morning and was back at home, resting under Kathy's watchful eye. Her cousin had phoned to say he'd be okay, so long as he used his head and looked after himself. Caitlin told them she was going away for a few days over Christmas and promised to check in soon. There was no point dragging everything up. She'd write to him once things had settled.

She arrived at the platform a full hour early, clinging to a small hope that James might turn up. Throughout the night, his voice had followed her. *I love you Caitlin. Only you.* Someone nearby tried to strike up a conversation with her while they waited. She gave a quick, polite smile and moved off towards the far end of the platform. She didn't have the patience for small talk.

Not today.

'I assure you, Mr Henderson, your uncle's condition isn't likely to change anytime soon. He's in very capable hands. Now off you go man, you're gettin' married!' With a warm smile and a playful nudge, Sister Moira Gallagher scolded James again. 'He's told me all about it, and he'd be heartbroken if you're late. Go!'

She turned at the sound of footsteps behind her and a familiar voice called out, 'Sorry to interrupt, MG. Can I have a quick word?'

Moira shook her head gently and called back, 'Give us a minute.'

She turned back to James, stealing a glance at the way he bent over Roger, whispering something and clasping the old man's hand. Her roommate had referred to her as 'MG,' a nickname only a handful ever used, but the groom hadn't flinched. Hadn't even looked up. His mind was elsewhere, caught between concern and duty, too tangled in the moment to notice.

Part of her hoped he had heard. Hoped the name might stir something, make him look up, recognise it. *MG.* The mystery witness no one had managed to track down. The one who'd seen everything that night. She remembered it all with brutal clarity - his father's calculated murder. The way the car veered off the embankment. The noise. The splash. The headlights vanishing beneath the water, like they'd been snuffed out by the hand of God.

Following George Shalham's death, she'd been terrified. She'd thought about coming forward more times than she could count. About writing to the Hendersons, but life had got in the way. Or maybe fear had.

After all this time, here she was, next to him. She couldn't say. Not yet, not today, the poor fella was getting married. It'd be so unfair. She'd have to wait. The right time will come.

'Are you sure it's okay to go?' James asked, lifting his Crombie and folding it over his arm.

'Absolutely sure. It's an adverse reaction to the medication, that's all. Nothing we can't handle. What he needs now is rest. What you need is to get out of here before I march you to the door meself!' Moira laughed.

James released a strained laugh, nodded his thanks, and ran.

Tim Armstrong had begun to worry about the delay and gave a massive sigh of relief when James's sleek Jag finally turned into the drive at Melrose. Already dressed in his morning suit, he rushed outside as James climbed out of the car.

'Christ, James, where've you been? Thought you'd scarpered!'

James smiled. 'Sorry. I had to see Roger. Things took longer than I thought. Everything sorted here?'

Tim studied him for a second. Again, he sensed something was off. It wasn't nerves or the worry of seeing Roger ill. There was a weirdness about his friend, a distance. Something bad had happened. Was it to do with Marleen? Or had Penelope stirred the pot again? Maybe the Mother. He never talked about her. Fine-looking woman too.

Trying to lift his mood, Tim threw him a look. 'You'd better get ready before you get your head torn off. We're really late!'

James took the stairs two at a time. In his room, he stood before the tall walnut mirror, retying the knot on his cravat, watching his reflection. Everything looked okay on the surface. The suit, the hair, the stance. But it wasn't. He turned away and dropped onto the edge of the bed. His thoughts were jumbled. Rocola was his now, the whole sorry lot. The name, the responsibility, the debt, the future. Everything Roger had planned. Everything he'd worked towards. But still, his only thought was Caitlin. Her voice, her laugh, the way she made him feel whole. Complete. He loved her. Needed her. Not for comfort, not for rescue, but because without her, he was half a man.

Back at Waterside Station, Caitlin looked up at the platform clock, its thick black hands creeping closer to the hour. Two fifty-seven. The train sat waiting, humming quietly under the pale sky. All around her, people shuffled bags and suitcases, the air filled with low conversation and diesel fumes. She held onto the handle of her small case, scuffed and worn, everything she hadn't been able to leave behind packed tightly inside. Her few clothes. A couple of photos, even her mother's old green mac. She checked the entrance once more. No sign of him.

A guard passed and yelled, 'Two minutes, Ladies and Gentlemen. Board the train now please!'

Caitlin felt a stinging sensation in her eyes. Her throat was dry as she stepped closer to the open doors. The train gave a soft jolt beneath her feet, like it was growing restless. No James. The only sounds were the train and a faraway signal clanging.

Elsewhere, Marleen Fry was on her way to Prehen Chapel with Penelope, her dress spread clumsily across the back seat of the wedding car. Penelope was half-cut, muttering nonsense under her breath. Marleen was, in a word, a mess. Her parents had missed their flight, and now everything was ruined. She hadn't forgiven James for not showing up for the rehearsal either. His excuses have been constant recently. Too much on. Too busy. Always something.

As they reached the church road, an usher came barrelling into view, his arms waving like a madman. The driver braked hard and watched the man shout something, pointing wildly ahead, then motioning for them to keep moving.

'What's happening?!' Marleen screamed, leaning forward so suddenly she gave Penelope the scare of her life, but no one answered.

Caitlin stepped onto the train, then turned and looked back one last time. The platform was quiet, empty but for a few stragglers. No James. No rush of footsteps. No voice calling her name.

A sigh escaped her lips before she boarded and took her seat.

Alone.

Thank you for reading Darkness.

This volume wasn't easy to write. It's long, raw, unflinching, and like the women at its core, it doesn't apologise. *Darkness* dives into the grimmest years of the Troubles. Still, through it all, there's resilience. Defiance. The quiet fight to hold on to love and dignity. This book wasn't written to cheer. It was written to be remembered. So thank you for reading with an open mind, for not turning away, and for seeing the strength in the stories of ordinary people, especially the women, who endured the worst of it.

If you're heading for *Light*, hold on. There's still more to face, but hope isn't lost. Use the QR code below to buy *Light* direct from me! I get more pennies that way. Those online fellas (you know who I mean) can take up to 70%. *Ouch*.

AND...

I know, I know, there's always an '*and*', but if you liked *Darkness* (even just the cover), please leave a review on goodreads.com. It'll take two secs, and I'll love you forever. Mwah!
JB x

www.ingramcontent.com/pod-product-compliance
Ingram Content Group UK Ltd.
Pitfield, Milton Keynes, MK11 3LW, UK
UKHW042212071125
464792UK00003B/13

9 781068 759987